Colin de Silva was born in Ceylon (now Sri Lanka) in 1920, and was brought up there. During the Second World War he served as a commissioned officer in the British Army. From 1946–56 he worked in the Ceylon Civil Service, and in 1962 he emigrated to Hawaii, where he now lives and works.

He first began researching *The Winds of Sinhala* in 1957. Of the novel's major characters, only the narrator, Prince Rodana, is purely fictional.

COLIN DE SILVA

The Winds of Sinhala

GRANADA
London Toronto Sydney New York

Published in paperback by Granada Publishing Limited in 1982
Special overseas edition

ISBN 0 586 05648 3

First published in Great Britain by
Granada Publishing 1982
Copyright © Colin de Silva 1982

Granada Publishing Limited
Frogmore, St Albans, Herts AL2 2NF
and
36 Golden Square, London W1R 4AH
515 Madison Avenue, New York, NY 10022, USA
117 York Street, Sydney, NSW 2000, Australia
100 Skyway Avenue, Rexdale, Ontario, M9W 3A6, Canada
61 Beach Road, Auckland, New Zealand

Made and printed in Great Britain by
Cox and Wyman Ltd, Reading
Set in Baskerville

Granada ®
Granada Publishing ®

To
My father
John William de Silva
who made it all possible.

Acknowledgement

I received invaluable assistance in preparing and submitting my manuscript from the late Mr Burroughs Mitchell, editor par excellence and gentleman.

Author's Foreword

King Abhaya Gamini, or Dutu Gemunu as he is generally known in Ceylon, lived in the second century B.C. His story is told in ancient historical chronicles, such as the Mahavamsa (I have used the translation by Wilhelm Geiger) and in rock inscriptions. The city of Anu, the Anuradhapura of today, still contains tangible evidence of his reign.

I have woven my novel from the bare threads of facts, introducing fictitious characters, incidents, customs and ceremonial to complete the tapestry. As for the life and government of those early times, I have combined imagination and an assumption of strong Aryan influences stemming from the Indian Emperor Chandra Gupta Moriya, with the sparse records available.

What of the story is history then?

I do not know, any more than I know what of it is fiction, for it could all have happened just as I have written.

COLIN DE SILVA
Honolulu, Hawaii
1981

CEYLON

The island's original name was Lanka, the Resplendent Land. The Ancient Greeks and Romans called it Taprobane, the Arabs of those times Serendib, the Isle of Serendipity. In 1971 the island was renamed Sri-Lanka.

N

Mantota

Thambapanni

LANKA

Anuradhapura

Kahagalla

Girilaka

Vijitapura

Mahaveli River

SERU

Kasotota

SOMA

Ambati River

Gallaka

MALAYA

Ambati

Kimbula
Kasa

Dighavapi

Kelaniya

Kotmale

Wera

Culanaganiya

Kumbuk River

RUHUNA

Menik River

Mahagama

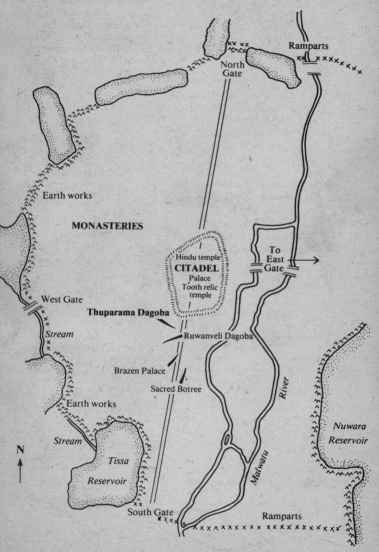

2nd CENTURY B.C.

ANURADHAPURA

Ramparts

North Gate

Earth works

MONASTERIES

West Gate

Stream

Thuparama Dagoba

Hindu temple
CITADEL
Palace
Tooth relic
temple

To East Gate

Ruwanveli Dagoba

Brazen Palace

Sacred Botree

Earth works

Stream

Tissa Reservoir

N

South Gate

Malwatu River

Nuwara Reservoir

Ramparts

THE ROYAL LINE OF SUCCESSION

Sinha m. Suppa Devi
|
Sinha Bahu m. Sinha Seevali
(Brother wed sister)

Vijaya
First King of Lanka
483-445 b.c.
Interregnum 445-444 b.c.
|
Panduvasudeva m. Subhaddakaccana
(Nephew of Vijaya)
444-414 b.c.
|
Abhaya 414-394 b.c.
Interregnum 394-377 b.c.
|
Pandukabhaya 377-307 b.c. m. Pali
Son of Abhaya's youngest sister and a prince
|
Mutasiva 307-247 b.c.
|
Devanam Piya Tissa 247-207 b.c.

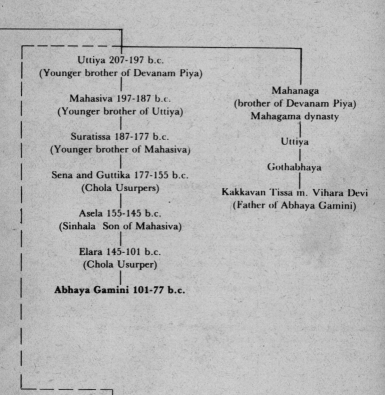

Uttiya 207-197 b.c.
(Younger brother of Devanam Piya)

Mahasiva 197-187 b.c.
(Younger brother of Uttiya)

Suratissa 187-177 b.c.
(Younger brother of Mahasiva)

Sena and Guttika 177-155 b.c.
(Chola Usurpers)

Asela 155-145 b.c.
(Sinhala Son of Mahasiva)

Elara 145-101 b.c.
(Chola Usurper)

Abhaya Gamini 101-77 b.c.

Mahanaga
(brother of Devanam Piya)
Mahagama dynasty

Uttiya

Gothabhaya

Kakkavan Tissa m. Vihara Devi
(Father of Abhaya Gamini)

*Prince Vipula

*Prince Rodana
(Nephew of Prince Vipula
and tutor to Abhaya Gamini)

* *Fictitious characters*

Prologue

The blessed gift of inner sight possesses me and I see a vision of the future.

A strange people, wearing strange garments, living in lands unknown in my time, are reading the substance of my *olas*, but from a different *ola* material, in a different language. The *ola* is white, the ink black, the letters perfectly formed, each one separate from the other. The leaves are not strung together through holes in the *olas* and bound with slim covers of wood, but are held between hard materials.

My name is in the *olas* as I once wrote them. You are therefore reading the story of Abhaya Gamini, King of Lanka, but recounted by a Sinhala of your time, two thousand two hundred years after mine.

I see how it happened. My own *olas*, with their beautiful writing, were destroyed by Chola invaders; but the seed of me, borne by my eternal life-stream, held every word of them as written, through successive rebirths, until the time was right. Then, like underground waters suddenly released, the words burst forth again.

Every experience of ours – each thought, word, deed and feeling – becomes stored in our seed, to issue forth at the right time. The new-born have such information within them to sustain life before they ever learn from it; the mango seed knows to become a mango tree rather than a jasmine bush.

Filled with joy at the knowledge that my writing will not be in vain and that the truth about my king will never be lost, the I of my time, joins the I of your time to send you greetings. Your present life is the effect of the *kharma* we shared in my time; my words are but links in the chain that always bound us. The love I have known is the same love you know in your hearts and lives. It is God.

Wherever we may be, whenever we draw from the God-force, love, we become one. So are you and I one in truth and honour, about which I write – yes, even deceit and betrayal – for these are all a part of the love that makes us cohere through time and space.

As I gaze through these mists of time, I have a stark vision of a desolate hill with three great crosses on it, two hundred years after the events about which I write. Nailed to the centre cross is a naked man wearing a crown of thorns. He is Jesus of Nazareth, King of the Jews – a king born of lowly estate. How may that be?

I have my answer. He looks at his enemies below with love on his anguished countenance, then rolls his eyes to heaven, praying 'Father, forgive them ...' He loves his murderers. Love, being perfect in him, makes him the true son of the one God, the God of love whom I have discovered in my own life, at a time when He is almost unknown in a single form.

This Jesus yet to come will be a king among men. So can we all, the children of God, be kings.

My king! The dying Gamini lies very still on the elevated couch, soon to be his bier.

He was the greatest warrior the Sinhala have known in three hundred and six years of existence. He was a master of military strategy at age twenty-one and of politics at twenty-five. He brought honour to the Sinhala, the Lion people. Yet when the war was ended and his goal accomplished, he stepped back, giving equality to all, ending up as the greatest Buddhist king.

His body, so vital in life, is propped up by creamy silken cushions, his head slumped to one side. Raji, the only woman he loved, whom he never consecrated his queen, and I, his constant companion and devoted subject, take our places on either side of the couch. The men carrying it move forward as if on a single impulse.

We step into the fitful light of the yellow flames of a million clay lamps on the balustrades of the great *thupa*, to begin our long death march around its square, three-tiered base. Only my breathing seems alive – and the strong aroma of incense from thousands of glowing braziers. Even the silvery moonlight, tarnished by the shadows from whence it first emerged and absorbed by endless night stretching across the earth, is dead. The grief of the multitudes lies so heavily on the air that it crushes the spirit, buries itself in the soil and will dwell within our land forever.

The plodding footsteps of the couch bearers break into my senses. I glance more closely at Gamini, anxious at the rocking motion. Save for an occasional fluttering of the eyes, he could be sleeping. His naturally dark complexion is ashen; his face is so gaunt that his wide cheekbones and heavy jaw look like a death mask. His long black hair is streaked with silver. His whole physical presence has shrunk during the past months of his illness. Now the white *khaddar* tunic flops on broad shoulders and narrow hips, the pantaloons lie loose on spindly legs that once could kill a boar with a kick. His feet, slender and beautiful as a woman's, are bare, as is proper in the sacred place. My breath catches at this one familiar sight of him, remembering the first day I saw them and the message they gave me of his sensitivity beneath a strong, watchful exterior. I have looked at his feet every day for thirty-two years and he is forty-four now.

Anguish swells within me. I choke. Tears sting my eyes and I look away. Dear *devas*, give me strength not to break down before all these people. I must look anywhere but at the people, or the air, or an earth so soaked with grief that it will drown me in my own.

My eyes drift upward. A full moon sails through an open blue sea of sky and white eddies of cloud, a silver craft heading with certainty to a night's destiny and an assignation with daybreak. Nothing will change its course, as nothing can change the course of life toward death.

Hear me, you heavens. Pause awhile and hearken to me, fleeing moon.

I am Rodana Sinha, a Sinhala prince, born out of wedlock in the court of Anu. My mother, the princess Seevali, was descended from our great king Devanam Piya. He accepted the Buddhist doctrine into Lanka two hundred years ago from Mahinda, missionary son of King Asoka, true believer in the *Dhamma*. Asoka was the grandson of Chandra Gupta Moriya, the first Gupta, the foremost Moriya, greatest of all Arya, who seized the Indian possessions of the famed Emperor Sikander ten years after he, Alexander, withdrew whence he had come.

King Devanam Piya built the famed city of Anu, where I was born. Through his endeavours, our country became known throughout the world. Persians, Romans and Greeks call it Taprobanus. To Arabi traders, who sail here to barter carpets, silks and horses for our gold and jewels, spices and food, it is Serendib, the Isle of Serendipity, from the peace the Buddha's Doctrine brought to us in King Devanam Piya's time. We know it as Lanka-dwipaya, the island of Ceylon.

My father, I never knew. Rumour had it that he was a labourer of the lowly street-cleaner caste, the Chandala, and that he was murdered for the sacrilege of having lain with a royal princess. My mother was heartbroken. She lived only long enough to give me birth. I was raised by her brother, Prince Vipula, but ended up dedicating my life to Abhaya Gamini. I gave Gamini my whole being, my every purpose, my heart and some part of my *prana*, my life-force. Small wonder, therefore, that when I return to the palace after his funeral rites, I shall be a hollow man, with nothing save memories and a desire to die.

Gamini emits a rasping from his lungs. He opens his black eyes. Seeing me, a faint smile glances off his lips. My breath quickens. His gaze drifts toward the great bell-shaped *thupa*, ghostly white in the moonlight. He is trying to tell me something. I guess what it is before his eyelids droop and close again.

We approach the east side now. The hush of the *bhikkus'* meditation reaches us before we get to them. They are motionless figures in the distance, carved in saffron, eyes downcast, their thoughts a tangible peace force in the moon-silver air, but unable to give me peace. I look for the moon again. It is hidden by the great pinnacle of the *thupa*.

What will they write about Gamini, these monks? My grief refuses to dwell on it. I think instead of our history and my experiences with the Noble Order of Monks.

The earliest known people in India were the Dasa, consisting today of Chola, Pandya and Chera. Dasa origins must go back through time to a period when their land extended continuously to those distant countries where black people dwell. The ocean must have separated this land mass, just as it later destroyed the bridge of Hanuman, between South India and northern Lanka.

Then came the invaders from the Caucasus, calling themselves Arya, the Noble Ones. They made their way through the great mountain passes in northwest India until they reached the fertile Valley of Indhoos, through which a great river flows. Here they could give up their nomadic existence and settle down – but their restless spirits made them drive west and south to conquer more Dasa lands, except those in the extreme west and south of India.

Our island, however, which lies near the southern tip of India, remained an independent kingdom until Prince Vijaya and his seven hundred noblemen arrived. These were Arya banished from their native Sinha Pura, the Lion City, in North India and cast adrift in ships on the ocean.

Shipwrecked on the northwestern coast of the island, they found a fertile land. When two of the men were seized by Kuveni, a royal princess, Prince Vijaya led a punitive raid against Kuveni's abode and captured her. He then discovered that he was in Lanka, the resplendent land, a fertile country inhabited by Yakka and Naga tribes. These tribes were looked down upon by both Arya and Dasa, as being so uncivilized that the *Ramayana*, a great legend of South India, casts a Lankan king in the role of the villain who seizes the chaste and beautiful Princess Sita from her home in India and carries her off in his air-chariot to his palace in Lanka, from which she is finally rescued by her husband, Rama.

The princess Kuveni, a Yakka, fell in love with the handsome Arya, Prince Vijaya. She betrayed her people by leading Prince Vijaya and his men secretly to her capital city, Priti, where they killed the King and all his followers in a single assault. Once the city was captured, Prince Vijaya made Kuveni his consort. Together they took over the entire island and made it their kingdom.

After becoming the ruler, however, Prince Vijaya in turn betrayed Kuveni. He brought in princesses and noblewomen from India for brides, to keep the Arya bloodline pure, and drove Kuveni and their children away from the city. Kuveni was killed by her own people for her act of betrayal. The two children, a girl and a boy, escaped into the jungle, where they bred a primitive tribe.

So Lanka remained a single Arya kingdom, knowing its greatest grandeur when King Devanam Piya embraced the Doctrine of Lord Buddha and expanded the royal city of Anu. The earliest Dasa adventurers were Sena and Guttika, who visited the country to trade horses for Lanka's food and riches. They coveted what they discovered in the land of the Lion that no longer roared because it was tamed by the nonviolent doctrines of Lord Buddha. Returning with a mighty army of mercenaries from South India, they conquered Lanka.

These two Cholas ruled justly for twenty-two years before being overthrown by the royal Sinhala, Asela. Ten years later, another Chola of noble descent, a great warrior named Elara, invaded the country with a magnificent army. He routed Asela and became ruler of Lanka, reigning justly for forty-four years. He was strong and ruthless—cunning, too, as I discovered. The first thirteen years of my life were spent in his court, but I never met him face-to-face until the fateful evening that decided my destiny.

Throughout those many campaigns, no Chola ever conquered the Ruhuna subkingdom in the southeast of Lanka, where Gamini and his father were born, or the southwestern Malaya lands from which Gamini's mother came. Both these territories are protected by great rivers at their borders, by mountains and by dense jungle. Thus they became independent kingdoms in King Elara's time, Ruhuna spawning a host of proud, fiercely independent people, the continuation of the Sinhala.

Unlike most of them, I have had the gift of acceptance, which belongs only to those who know they have the strength to change circumstances they can control. An essential part of strength is purpose. Gamini gave me both during his lifetime. When he dies, purpose will be extinguished like a flame, and my strength with it. That is why my vision of the inner sight puzzles me. How can I write a story when my future is with Gamini, in the chill of tombs where our ashes will lie?

Instinctively, my eyes sweep down to Gamini. Look at me just once before you die, my king, my old comrade.

The flesh slowly comes back to Gamini's body. Suddenly he begins filling out, miraculously assuming his familiar form. He rises from the couch and springs lightly to the ground. His eyes flash as he smiles confidently at me. He is the warrior girded for battle. The moon has vanished before a sun he creates to give himself light in which he can shine. He is breastplated. His long sword, in the royal golden scabbard, swings at his side. He holds a gleaming spear in one hand, a shield in the other. Dark, but not as dark as his father, he is a little over four cubits – six feet – in height. His shiny black hair, falling straight to his shoulders, frames a solid neck on which a broad-chiselled face sits, cast in the Arya mould except for a flaring of the nostrils. His chest is deep, his waist narrow. I cannot see his feet.

Before my eyes, his body begins to fade away in an emerging light of great intensity. I see his *prana*, a white wraith shimmering in this light of his creation. The black, glittering eyes have vanished. Instead, there remains horror pulsing – at his bloodlust, his indifference to causing pain, his ecstasy at the kill. I alone can see these emanations of his *prana*, for even the woman, Raji, never reached the wellsprings of his loneliness, as I did.

The image slowly dissolves. The light dims and fades away. I am left staring stupefied at a dying man, haggard, emaciated, lying on an ebony couch carried through scattered light from the moon and a million little clay lamps. As I realize that my mind is playing tricks, creating past images to escape the weight of my grief, my sense of longing mushrooms to desperation within me.

My own eyes sting and start to blur. I stumble and hold on to a page boy to steady myself. He glances sharply at me and I look away, closing my eyes against the tears.

Although old men cry more easily, I will not weep. Gamini never wept when his heart was breaking, when his wounds ached or when his hopes seemed shattered. He never wept at betrayal, defeat or death. He had no time for men who did. I shall offer him non-tears as part of my tribute.

For what would I weep? For his life, his death? For my own life, or death? It is too late for me to weep for myself, too late for me even to be afraid of death. I have done what I have done, thought what I have thought, felt what I have felt. There is neither time nor any way now by which I can alter my *kharma*. No attribute of mine can measurably change the reflexes of my death-moment, which will automatically eject a final thought to propel me to a new existence – especially because I expect to take my own life after he dies.

What difference does any of it make? We are creatures who can do no more at any time than we do. The effort is what gives us hope. Success is in the striving. When a life's ambition is achieved, what more follows save fresh effort for a new ambition? The only true ambition is the desire to try one's hardest. This was the latent force in Gamini; he should be my example.

But why ambition? Why is it not enough for man to live and enjoy the fruit of the earth and all its glory? Food, clothing and shelter are there to be produced. The bounty of the world awaits discovery. The senses are expectant for sights, sounds, smells, the feel of beauty and the joy of love. Why must man passionately seek for more, especially his own salvation in a *kharmic* cycle, like the old trying to rediscover some spark of life in dying genitals?

As for me, what I had is now going. I have no more effort left in my aging body or my numb mind. Therefore I do not even need to be strong. My lifework done, I no longer have any desire to live. Does this mean that all desire has ceased in me? No, for there is something I still desire fiercely . . . death.

The stump of my right hand starts to throb. Was it not Gamini who with his strength, courage and love made me learn to write with my left hand after the right hand that could produce such beautiful *olas* was chopped off? Suddenly, sharply, swiftly, like a great flash of lightning illuminating a black night, a connection that my selfish sorrowing had blocked is established.

I am the only person able to record who and what Gamini was, so that generations to follow may know his glory and shame, still counting him a man as no other. How better then can I consecrate my love and devotion to him than by writing of his life, so that the *bhikku* historians may not make a mockery of him by depicting him as a god instead of a man?

I have purpose again, briefly.

My *olas* record that King Abhaya Gamini fought thirty-two battles yet built sixty-eight temples. He had one hundred and twenty-eight concubines in his palace, yet he loved only one woman.

Here was a man capable of love and hatred, cruelty and compassion, bloodlust and kindness. Here was a man both gentle and ruthless, brave in war but fearful before his *kharma*.

Who was the real Gamini? Perhaps even I do not know. Does anyone ever know all about someone else? Is there not some inner core of a person that is forever secret, never shared? Perhaps even God wants some parts kept from Him, though He can know everything – and rightly so. All I can do, therefore, is give Gamini rebirth with my words, making this my one remaining life-task. Thus, the vision of the blessed inner sight that I experienced before we began our walk around the *thupa* was no dream. I shall record Gamini's life story and it shall be implanted in the seed of my life-source, to be carried through my other lifetimes to that final one, which I witnessed tonight.

PART ONE

Raja Rata

The Vassal State of Chola Kings

Chapter 1

I kept my eyes on King Kakkavan while he spoke, as was the custom – but I could feel his son's gaze vibrant on me. Its intentness was peculiar to Prince Abhaya Gamini.

I could understand curiosity about me, his new tutor, a twenty-five-year-old bastard prince, but he was going beyond curiosity. There was a unique penetration in his look, a probing, like an ear to a closed door, that was a part of his being. He was only twelve years old and he already had the watchfulness of a jungle cat on the prowl.

Was it my deep feeling for the jungle and its animals, then, that made my heart leap toward him? Or was it that my desire to fulfil the command of my uncle, Prince Vipula, blindly reached for a cause, a reason, some supreme logic of that most illogical, irrational emotion, love?

I knew it was neither. My years in the temple had developed an unusual awareness in me, which told me that I was responding to the magnetism of this boy as a human being, like a drum skin beneath the fingers of a master, a flute on the lips of a practised player. Whether it came from common flesh and blood in past births, or a communion of *prana* in between, or merely the composition of our present beings, I was drawn to Abhaya Gamini as I had never before been to any person.

Morning sunlight streaming in through the high, ornamental windows of King Kakkavan's study, in the Mahagama palace of the Ruhuna kingdom, gave a deep purple sheen to the King's black skin, which was so dark it made the creamy satinwood desk and chair at which he sat seem even lighter. I could see why he was called Kakkavan. Although he was indeed black as a *kakka*, a crow, it was not only his colour, but also his pointed, crow's-beak nose, alert eyes and small, sprightly appearance that gave him the name. The two pieces of furniture, however, went well with the floor of mountain crystal and relieved the gaudy tapestries on the walls, depicting the life of Lord Buddha, as well as the mosaic patterns of green, yellow and red squares on the ceiling.

During the past twelve years, I had frequently seen the King with the Queen, Vihara Devi, and their two sons, Abhaya Gamini and Sadha Tissa, when they came to worship at the great temple at Tissa, where I was *abithaya*, apprentice monk, to the Venerable Sri Rahula. King Kakkavan was held to be a just and kindly ruler, devoted to the Doctrine. The Queen was regarded as a pious, religious lady. Their two children were being brought up in a Buddhist atmosphere. We were all aware of the events that had placed King Kakkavan on the throne of the Ruhuna kingdom.

When the great King Devanam Piya died in Anu, his brother, Mahanaga, should have reigned in his stead. His widow, however, coveted the succession for her son, Uttiya, and plotted to kill Mahanaga, who finally fled the kingdom and sought refuge in the shrine capital, Kataragama. There, the ten *kshastriyas*, holy ruler-priests of the highest caste, not only protected Mahanaga, but created the sub-kingdom of Ruhuna for him, with its capital at Mahagama, the great village. As the years went by, Mahanaga added to his territories, foully murdering his former benefactors, the ten *kshastriyas*, for the purpose. While this impious deed was abhorrent to man and god alike, it created a stronger kingdom, able to withstand the onslaughts of the Cholas, who had meanwhile invaded Lanka from India and seized the capital city of Anu.

Mahanaga attempted to expiate his sin by building temples and following the Doctrine. On his death, his son, Gothabhaya, did likewise, as did Gothabhaya's brother, who succeeded him, and Gothabhaya's son, Kakkavan, when he became king. When Abhaya Gamini was born, he was therefore heir to the throne.

Now, as King Kakkavan began detailing to me the duties of my new office, the reality of my situation burst upon me with the force of sunshine after a long, hopeless night. I was already familiar with the requirements for the training of princes from my reading of the great *olas*, including Kautilya's *Artha Shastra*, written for the great emperor Chandra Gupta Moriya, who took over the Indian possessions of Sikander after the latter's death. Now they would cease to be theory. I was actually to be responsible for the training and education of a prince. I was to be responsible for shaping a life. I was to be responsible for someone at last.

True, I had been trained to detachment, but I was nonetheless human and had frequently thought the monastic life to be dull and monotonous. I enjoyed the wealth of opportunity for study and meditation, but these were all part of the routine of each twenty-four hours, divided into the four night watches and the labours of the daylight hours. I had to perform my duties scrupulously and to live my life by the highest standards. Yet I was also required to remain detached, whether in performing those duties or in my relationships with others. I found this impossible. Detachment is a stagnant pool. It cannot flow toward anything, least of all a happier life. I conceded that these feelings could have been caused by a lack in me. Perhaps my eternal life-stream had not reached a level of development that would enable me to grasp such a rare opportunity when it was placed before me. Perhaps I was deviating from the road to *arahat*-ship and Buddhahood. But I was *me* in this birth. I did not want to become a *bhikku*. It was not enough for me. The Venerable Rahula, in his infinite wisdom, must have perceived all this when he recommended that I be appointed tutor to young Prince Gamini.

Good news seldom reaches us at the moment of its receipt.

That is merely the knocking on a closed door. It takes us time to get to the door, open it and become enraptured at our good fortune. So when the Venerable Rahula informed me of the appointment and sent me on my way to the palace, I only heard that knocking on my door. It took this first vibrant glance from Prince Gamini to make me open that door.

I am about to give of myself at last, I thought. I can breathe again, live again. And I am well fitted for my role. Being of royal birth, I received princely training in the court of Anu, capital of the Kingdom of Lanka, under the supervision of my uncle, Prince Vipula, the most elegant and noble of all men. I then had six months at King Kakkavan's court and twelve years in the temple. What better tutor for this young prince, who was conceived when the holy *samanera*, the sage-monk Gotama, at his death-moment, deliberately cast his *paramanu* – his atom of consciousness – into the previously barren womb of Queen Vihara Devi, at her behest? Had not Gotama once been a great warrior and a prince among men? Did it not mean that Prince Gamini would be a warrior-king dedicated to the Doctrine?

No wonder I listened intently to King Kakkavan, impatient at all distraction. Even the smell of incense from braziers burning before the gold statue of Lord Buddha, on the satinwood pedestal at the far corner of the room, was now a hindrance to concentration.

Besides, there was noise everywhere: a large grey dove outside, irritating me with its 'ko-ka-kroooow,' alternating with an 'ok-wa-kroooow' when I least expected it; the yapping of a puppy and the twitter of myna birds. An occasional laugh or scream in the distance, rising above that undefinable hum of the bustle and activity of a palace by day. My mind conjured sentries at their posts, guards patrolling, nobles sedately strolling the corridors, attendants fussing everywhere and sequestered ladies chattering behind peacock-feather fans.

There is no real silence left anywhere, except in the temples, I thought disgustedly – but I would not return to a temple. I realized then that the problem was mine. Because I had lived twelve years in a secluded environment, my senses had become attuned to concentration the easy way, in the quietude and calm atmosphere of a temple. Now I had to use my willpower to find silence within myself, a much more difficult task. Yet I had the mental training to do it, so I shut out all the sounds, deliberately and coldly separating my being from them. Now I was totally one with the King's words.

'We are a *dharma-dwipaya*, an island dedicated to the Doctrine.' King Kakkavan's voice was deep and reedy, unusually strong for so small a man. 'The first attribute of a prince is princely conduct. In our realm, it has to be based on the Precepts and the Noble Eightfold Path. Our Lord Buddha's teaching is unique in that it has codes of conduct fitted for each person, whose state in this life is based upon his *kharma* from past births. So the Doctrine provides for laymen and *bhikkus*, commoners and princes. And yet there is nothing, save one's own *kharma*, to prevent the transition across these boundaries. Prince Abhaya Gamini shall be trained to observe the highest code of the Arya, the Noble Ones. First to last, honour. This has come to be regarded as a concept that cannot be lived and therefore exists only while frailties remain undiscovered.' His dark eyes glowed at me through their strange metallic glaze and his voice rang out. 'Honour is what each of us lives with, in the most secret recesses of his being. We know when we fail, even if it is a secret never revealed. Therein lies shame. You must inculcate the honour of this prince into his very *prana*, from which it shall also spring.' He paused and looked away. Why?

Suddenly I sensed what he was thinking. He faced his own shame from the past. I wondered fiercely whether he would be man enough to quote the example. I was surprised at the intensity of my feeling, for it had been suppressed so long. Was the release of emotion for Gamini already turning me into a more passionate human being?

'You have been privileged to have the embodiment of honour in our time teach you,' the King declared. His voice was distant and a trifle strained. I could not blame him for it. Yet I respected him for being able to speak of the man against whom he had plotted. 'Prince Vipula.'

A tremor ran through me. I could not identify its source. Perhaps it was at hearing my uncle's name spoken aloud for the first time in years.

I felt Gamini stir. I sensed some feeling in him, too, and knew without looking that it had been for me. Could it be the beginning of response from the boy I had given my heart to in an instant? If so, his nature made it precious and delicate as finely filigreed gold. One firm grasp and it would shatter.

'Closely allied to the ideal of honour is deportment,' the King continued. 'This is as essential in a prince as is the concept of honour, for conduct of all kinds, whether in public or private, toward outsiders or family, must be governed by good manners. You, above all, must know what makes good manners.' His look was a question.

'Awareness every moment, so offence is never given,' I responded. 'Including to oneself, alone with oneself.'

His sparse black eyebrows arched at my unconventional reply. 'How so?' he demanded.

'Sire, I believe that the truly civilized man is the totally aware man. When we are aware, we know what gives offence. We take care not to say or do anything to hurt or annoy, unless it is essential in the interests of honour and good sense. We are then able to regulate our conduct. Good manners are useless merely as a code of social behaviour. If we have the deeper understanding of which I speak, we can alter social codes for a higher purpose, sacrificing blind adherence to them, in our dedication to concern for people – even for animals and inanimate objects.'

The King leaned forward, thinking. I could feel Gamini's heightened interest and knew I had scored a small victory with him as well.

'Hmm . . . you have certainly grown since we last talked,' the King finally conceded. 'And why not? You had the promise . . . and you have the blood.' The hint of admiration in his voice thrilled me. 'You have developed a thinking mind – and yes . . . a certain stature.'

King Kakkavan went on to give me the subjects he wanted Gamini taught and the arduous daily work schedule of a prince, as required in the *Artha Shastra*.

'You will have complete control over the Prince's time and studies,' he concluded. He turned a dark visage to his son. Gamini looked squarely back, without expression in his eyes. Father and son were not communicating. Something lay between them. What could it be? Two remote people? I did not know why, but this seemed the immediate answer. King Kakkavan looked away first and I felt a moment's sadness for them both.

'You were very young when the Prince was born,' King Kakkavan stated, his voice low. 'In case you have been unaware of it, the portents at the time of the Prince's birth were most propitious.' He seemed to be conceding something, not relating glorious facts. 'On that very day, seven ships laden with valuable cargo, including precious gems, were washed ashore on the Devundara coast. They must have been wrecked earlier in a storm on the great ocean. An elephant of the six-tusked race brought her baby close to the Kirinda beach and left it there. We named it Kandula, after the fisherman who found it and bestowed it on the Prince as his royal elephant. Many other omens and prophecies point to a great reign for our son.'

I half turned, as it was now permissible, to look for the first time at Prince Gamini. His black eyes were strange – inscrutable and withdrawn for a young boy. The characteristic Arya features with slightly flaring nostrils were immobile. His teeth showed white between full black-red lips, yet he was not smiling. The lean, muscular body,

31

shoulders wide, hips narrow, gracing a close-fitting white silk tunic and cotton *hulwar*, had a new alertness. You hear your father's words, but do not trust them, I thought and glanced down again. Then I noticed Prince Gamini's feet for the first time. They were curiously beautiful, long and slender, with fine bones. The toes were evenly formed and tapered like the soles of the leather sandals he wore.

'The question that only the future can decide is *where* our son will reign.' A grim note entered the King's voice. 'Conquest ill befits a Buddhist monarch.' He shot a sidelong glance at his son.

Young Gamini's eyes flashed. His look became challenging. He cocked his head to one side and locked his hands decisively behind his back, to speak for the first time. 'A Sinhala king can only reign in Anu, sire! We are one race, one language, one religion.' The words rang out like a battle cry.

It had its answer in my heart. Acolyte, *abithaya*, call me what you will, I heard the sound of trumpets. I saw the flags unfurl as a thousand Sinhala voices roared out that cry. The screams of men rent the air, the clash of metal rang out, streaked by the neighing of horses. A fortress blazed. I was choked by the pungency of its billowing smoke. Winds swept the grey smoke northward, like a great finger pointing toward Anu. I heard our marching song borne on those winds of Sinhala.

My eyes widened. Gamini's gaze locked with mine. He knew what I had seen. His face relaxed.

I understood then that inevitable conflicts lay ahead, not just between father and son, but with the Cholas in years to come.

Were the prophecies to be fulfilled?

The King dismissed us abruptly. As I made obeisance and backed toward the door, I recalled the three *dola-dhook*, the birth cravings of Gamini's mother when she was pregnant with him. Had they been the cause of this unique young man, or had they produced their effect on him?

Remembering one of those cravings, I was suddenly transported back thirteen years to that day in the jungle when I, then only twelve years old, had witnessed the beginnings of this mighty drama that would surely unfold.

Chapter 2

On that warm, dry afternoon, I slipped out of my uncle's lodge and made my way toward the Bintenne jungle, in order to watch the animals that came to the water hole at dusk.

My uncle, Prince Vipula, whose ward I had been since my mother's death shortly after I was born, was bathing with his friends in the lake fronting the hunting lodge. This was located less than a day's journey south of the Anu palace in which the Chola conqueror from India, King Elara, ruled. Mahagama, capital of the southern kingdom, Ruhuna, was a little farther south.

My uncle and his friends would hunt after dinner. One concession made by hunters to decency is that they spare animals at the water holes. These therefore remain havens in which one can observe animals in their natural state.

I love the jungle. It has ghosts that sometimes make me tremble with fear. They emerge from the darkness beneath tall trees – the shining green tops hidden from view, reaching for the skies since the beginning of time. I am often lost in wonder at their agelessness.

Although every animal roams wild and free, the price of life, whether in parkland or shadow, can be sudden death. Yet I have always sensed some inexplicable freedom, even in death, probably because jungle creatures do not kill for pleasure, only for food or self-protection. Insects on the brown soil, grey gulls on the silver lakes, multicoloured butterflies on the wing, they all kill to exist and I comprehend these circles of life. I once saw a leopard spring from the top of a bank and sink bared white fangs into a deer's neck. He snapped the helpless creature's spine with a single jerk, rendering it immobile. Then, snarling and growling, he dragged the body to where he could devour it in peace.

Something of terror, something of joy within me responds to the cough and roar of the leopard, the shrill trumpeting of an elephant, the unearthly screams of peacocks which sound like lost souls at night. I find primeval delight in the dank odour of leaves, the harsh stench of rotting carcasses.

All of it is life in the raw – splendid, beautiful, imbued with wild grandeur. I become part of that life, finding delight in it even when I am alone, for loneliness is but a product of man.

My uncle used his lodge close to the Bintenne forest for regular hunting expeditions and he often took me with him. Poor people, especially the aboriginal Veddahs, customarily hunt for food. Princes and noblemen hunt for sport. It affords them peacetime practice for skill with weapons and trains them for warfare by developing courage, split-second timing and deadly accuracy. It creates the instinct of the hunter, the armour of ruthlessness, joy at the kill. It prepares the *prana* for war, even while exposing a man to the danger of *akusala-kharma*, evil causes. Hunting is therefore considered work for the warrior, the nobleman, the prince.

Even as a young boy I could not reconcile the unnecessary taking of life with the Doctrine of Lord Buddha, or what seemed to be inherent feelings of right and wrong. After seeing tears in the eyes of a mother monkey wantonly shot by a boy with an arrow and hearing the anguished death screams of a stuck pig, too often have I wondered how it feels

34

to receive the shaft, to know that death draws near. Then my heart has overflowed with compassion and I have known myself to be strange, reacting in this manner.

The sun shone brightly. So, dressed as I was in dark pantaloons and a long-sleeved tunic for my all-night vigil on the treetop *massa*, a kind of platform, I was sweating even before I hit the side trail leading from the lodge. Impatient to reach the jungle, I broke into a run, the shoulder bag holding my night meal and a flask of water bumping against my hip.

The trail wound around the lake, along the base of its tall eastern bound, a green slope scattered with dark bushes and topped with the stark grey silhouettes of trees that had lost their leaves during recent storms. The vast spread of landscape and sky filled me with a sense of adventure. Had not my uncle thought me man enough to spend the night by myself on the *massa*?

Being lean and tall for my age and in fine physical condition, I soon left the lake's dam behind and came to the main route between Anu and Mahagama, both many *yojana* away in opposite directions. The broad, sandy highway was riddled with the ruts of wagon wheels, traces of horse and mule hooves and ample quantities of their droppings. It was not a well-travelled road, but when caravans, troops and travellers used it, they did so in large numbers. Before the days of the three kingdoms, Sinhala kings had ruled the entire island. A good horseman from Anu could then cross the rivers on ferryboats, ride through the streams at fords and be in Mahagama, the Ruhuna capital, in two days and a night. Now, foreign troops could stop anyone in Lanka; once the river border between the two kingdoms was reached, outposts and patrols barred the way. Only the jungle had even a semblance of freedom for the Sinhala.

The highway became a mixture of red dust and fine, buff sand sparkling with mica. My rope-soled sandals crunched on it, giving spring to my step, as I ran easily between drying jungle scrub, yellow and red lantana, the green leaves pallid with dust. A covey of swifts broke cover and took flight, brown specks screaming shrilly from a blue sky. Even in their fear they were as orderly as trained cavalry.

Soon I could distinguish the first bright green fringe of jungle trees that ended the scrub land. I reached it and followed the loop of the highway, beneath a rocky cliff, then slowed down to a walk as I passed through a clearing. To my right, at the bottom of a jagged escarpment of black granite, was the water hole, created from natural springs. Jungle animals preferred to drink in its shadow, rather than from the lake. The lake's water was rather salty and some approaches to it were boggy. It was more the cool refuge of elephants and water buffaloes, who wallowed grey-humped in it, than the well from which deer, leopard and bear drank. The animals had not yet arrived at the water hole.

I now entered the gloom of the forest and strode beneath its canopy of tall wood-apple, ebony and *sal* trees, the columns of grey-brown bark rising sharply above a smother of undergrowth.

I was panting lightly, but feeling fine, the blood tingling through my body, my limbs light-sprung as chariot wheels. When I reached the tallest tree at the edge of the clearing, I paused to recover my breath, looking up to see that the tree house was intact. The branches hung low. I climbed with ease, agile as a monkey, and quickly reached the platform. It was open on all sides, except for a wooden rail, with a roof of light coconut thatch. Although it was cooler in its shade, there was not even a breath of wind and I began streaming with sweat. I approached the railing and looked around.

The tree had been well chosen for its commanding view. It was a little less than one *gavuta*, three miles, from the lodge. Although I could not see the lodge or the lake because of the cliff and the dark curve of jungle trees, I had an excellent view of the highway for many *gavuta* through the scrub, as well as the immediate area of jungle, the clearing and the water hole.

36

Having absorbed as much of the afternoon heat as it could hold, the earth's oven was sending it upward in shimmering waves. Above the haze of the open land, a flight of heron, winging to their night stop on the lake, made an orderly pattern against the sky. The sun still shone bright on the leaves, but had begun mellowing to the subtle gold that announces the approach of evening. With about two hours to dusk, it was time for deer to arrive at the water hole. Life and death had settled the times at which different animals would come here. When the first shadows of night began to darken the air, the deer would amble away before the grey ghosts of elephants. After nightfall, bear would move cautiously through the gloom and finally leopard, slinking wraiths between the tree trunks, their wide-apart eyes glowing like twin points of fire.

The thrills of night were yet to come, but now whining eye-flies and mosquitoes began to attack me and my mouth and my nostrils quivered at the sickly smells of raw animal excrement and a rotting carcass. I reached inside my bag and fished out my container of yellow citronella liquid. I drew the cork, sniffed its sweet pungency and began applying the repellent on my face and the exposed parts of my body. The whining continued, but at least the irritation of tiny feet and needle pricks stopped.

As I applied the oil on my face, my eyes turned toward the north. I was not looking for anything when I saw the moving cloud in the distance. Curious, I stopped rubbing, the container in my hand. The cloud drew nearer, winding like a snake, growing larger until it showed as pale red dust. Before my keen eyes, trained to distinguish objects or movements even a *yojana* away, a black form soon became visible and materialized into a horseman, galloping furiously through the scrub.

It is late for a traveller to be on the road to Ruhuna, I thought – and he rides too fast to be on a casual journey.

A rumble reached me quickly, separating into the swift

37

drumming of a horse's hooves, like approaching monsoon rain on rooftops. The sound began to pound in my blood. The horse was a noble Scindi, extended in full gallop, its glossy black skin lathered with foam, its motion a dance to its own drumbeat.

Although it was big, the horse could not dwarf the rider, who was sitting semi-erect, rather than crouched over the neck like normal horsemen in the gallop. The movement of his hands with the head of the horse was regular and swift as a drum tattoo. I watched horse and rider take a slight curve on the highway, entranced by their perfect union. If only I could ride like that!

Now I could distinguish the rider's features. He had a young, strong face, streaked with dust and sweat. Dark hair streamed behind him. His mouth was half open in a smile. Clad in a white *dhoti* with a broad red belt, above which the fair skin of his bare chest shone with sweat, the man was not dark enough to be a Chola. His face was vaguely familiar, but I was unable to place it.

The rider flung a glance backward, trying to see through the dust cloud he was creating. He feared pursuit. Following his gaze, my heart started to beat faster. Less than a half *gavuta* behind, another pale red cloud-form was fast approaching. Breathless with excitement, I leaned forward to watch, torn between a desire to have the first rider reach the safety of the dense jungle and the urge to witness a fight in the naked sunlight. Although he was obviously trying to escape, the first rider appeared strong, capable of defending himself with the long sword he carried at his side. The silver scabbard and winking jewels on its hilt showed he was a warrior.

Then it struck me like a thunderbolt. I *did* know that first rider. He was no warrior, but a groom in King Elara's stables, riding Vaha, King Elara's State horse. No wonder it had seemed a noble creature. What on earth was a Sinhala groom doing on the State horse? Was he a thief? And how dare he carry a Sinhala warrior's sword?

The drumming of hooves was like thunder now, the first set echoed in the distance by the second. My sharp hearing detected each set, though both were almost in unison. As the reverberation quickened my blood, the groom slackened rein, to my surprise. Why? Was he sick, or faltering? Had he decided to give up – or to stop and fight?

Horse and rider swept into the shelter of the first short jungle trees.

My chest and throat hurt. I had been holding my breath. I exhaled silently, not wishing to call attention to myself. Then I realized that I could not have been heard anyway.

As he took the long, looping bend of the highway, the groom slowed down to a canter. Suddenly my eyes nearly popped out of my head and I grabbed the handrail in astonishment. He had risen on his stirrups, giving easily with the movement of his horse, gripping the flanks firmly with strong calves. At the edge of the clearing, he reached for an overhanging branch and swung away from the saddle into the tree. The horse kept going, lengthening its stride at the removal of its load. The groom now crouched, half hidden, in the dim recesses of thick branches. Something gleamed in the darkness. He had drawn his sword.

My eyes turned to the second rider thundering up. His foam-flecked horse was a grey Arabi, at least seventeen hands tall, though Arabi horses are generally smaller. I recognized the man, before he reached the fringe of trees, as Ratne Mahela, King Elara's Chief Warrior. He was a dark Chola, with broad features and black hair tied in a knot on top of his head. Although he was crouched above the horse's neck, his immense size was unmistakable, the bare muscles glowing like ebony against his white pantaloon trousers and silver scabbard. Mahela was a man to be avoided. Any thought of warning him vanished from my mind.

Mahela broke into the jungle, galloping furiously around the bend. He reached the branch on which the groom

crouched and the sword flashed down. A crunching thud
followed and a head rolled across the clearing – a human
head, left behind while the body, upright on the galloping
horse, spilled blood.

Slowly the body began to collapse sideways. It fell, a foot
caught in the stirrup. The horse neighed shrilly and
disappeared in the tall trees. I did not fully believe what had
happened until my eyes returned to that dark head with
sightless eyes now lying still on the side of the trail, as if it
had been broken from a statue.

The groom swung down lithely from his branch with one
hand, grasping his sword in the other, his teeth white in their
half-smile. I shrank back with a gasp. He looked down at the
head, bent and picked it up. He held it by the topknot and
inspected it more closely, holding it away from him to avoid
the blood-drip. He nodded with satisfaction. He laid down
the head again, raised two fingers to his mouth and let out a
piercing whistle. He sheathed his sword without wiping it.

The two horses came trotting back, Vaha leading. The
second still dragged its headless corpse. It was a grisly sight,
devoid of all dignity, that great body dangling and bumping
the trail. Then I noticed the garland of fresh lotus around
Vaha's neck, obscene, flowers on the altar of human
sacrifice.

I did not see more. The reality of what I had witnessed
finally hit me and a shock ran up my spine. Mahela had been
waylaid and foully murdered by an assassin and I had been
helpless to do anything about it. My stomach rolled. I
retched, desperately trying to muffle the sound from the
murderer beneath me. The world began to spin. I lay back
on the *massa* and closed my eyes.

I must have fainted, for when I opened my eyes again and
sat up on an elbow, there was nothing below me save the
headless corpse at the side of the trail. The groom and the
two horses had vanished.

I heard the 'ho-ro-ro-ho-ro-ho-ro' of a monkey in the

distance. It seemed a cry of derision. The stink of that rotting animal carcass, driven by a hot breeze that had sprung up, was evil now. I sat up and searched the jungle, then turned to stare north along the highway. The murderer had indeed vanished.

Dust whipped up by the breeze swirled and settled on the leaves. The sun still filtered through dark branches. Nothing stirred. Shivering with a sudden cold loneliness, I glanced down at the *massa*. A line of red ants was scurrying along its edge and down the tree. I had never been so glad to see evidence of life.

Chapter 3

Lying on that *massa* in the Bintenne jungle, just twelve years old, I first experienced God. I do not know how He came to me. It was like having a dreadful accident alone, then suddenly finding that a man one has never known before is riding to one's rescue and that he is a physician.

This God was neither Brahma, the Creator, supreme among the countless Hindu gods, nor Rama, whom the Jina hold above all other gods. And He was certainly foreign to my Buddhist upbringing, for Lord Buddha declared that belief in gods is unnecessary in this life for the attainment of Enlightenment.

The only source I could recall was an Arabi traveller from the arid desert regions west of India, who spoke of the wandering tribe of which the wise Sul Oman had once been king. They believe in a single God, so powerful that they call Him only by the four letters symbolizing His name. When

41

spoken, it is Jahweh. He was closest to the God of my present consciousness.

I concluded then that my God was my own. He had emerged from within me, reaching back through each birth to my original creation. He is unknown to men who do not dare risk the wrath of the god-multitude they worship by denying its existence. This made me feel very much alone.

God spoke to me then, from within me: You found me in your loneliness and desperation. How can you ever be alone or afraid again?

For a few moments, I set aside my terror. I even felt sorry for those of the Buddha's faith, because they could not turn to any god. Lord Buddha had been born Prince Siddhartha of the royal family in Nepal, north of India. He married and had two children. His early life was confined to the palace and its environs; he was deliberately shielded from the poverty and misery of the world. When he first encountered senility, disease and sorrow, he was shocked. Determined to find their causes and remedies, he slipped away one night to search for truth. He wandered west to the region of ascetics. Through them, he attained every mental state, all fifty-two levels of consciousness of the yogi supreme, but his body had become so thin and emaciated that he could touch his spine by placing a finger on his navel. Still the truth eluded him.

He gave up the life of penance and resumed his wanderings. On a full-moon night, while meditating under a *pipul*, called the *bodhi*-tree, he reached Enlightenment, having discovered the Middle Way.

Enlightenment means reaching Nibbhana, Buddhahood, the final escape from the chain of causation, that cycle of birth, life, death and rebirth from which all suffering emerges.

I was taught in the temple that any man can finally reach Nibbhana. By understanding the Four Noble Truths and following the Noble Eightfold Path, he will automatically have a thought at his final death-moment that will project his atom of consciousness into a better rebirth each time, unto Buddhahood.

I deliberately went over the Buddha's teachings in my mind, seeking help from them in my present predicament.

The first noble truth is that we are all subject to birth, decay, disease and death. The second noble truth is that suffering is caused by craving. The third noble truth is the complete cessation of suffering, which is Nibbhana, bliss supreme. The fourth noble truth is that the Noble Eightfold Path leads to the cessation of suffering.

The Noble Eightfold Path consists of Right Speech, Right Action, Right Livelihood, all called *sila*; Right Effort, Right Mindfulness, Right Concentration, called *samadhi;* Right Understanding and Right Thoughts, called *pañña*.

How could any of this help a frightened boy?

Being too young as yet to comprehend, I turned to God again and found comfort in Him. Fear being more powerful in a child than faith, this comfort lasted but a few seconds. The sharp cry of a parakeet above me brought back terror, which led to panic. As my blood ran cold, I started to shiver, then to shake. God whispered another message to me.

I can only act through you, He said. Even if you have fear within you, do not lie there, fearful. Raise yourself up and leave, fearful. I will save you, if you save yourself.

I suddenly decided that God had sent the line of red ants disappearing over the edge of the *massa* to point my direction. With a final plea to this unfamiliar God, I steeled myself to clamber down from the *massa* and leave the jungle, which had suddenly lost its peacefulness for me. I had been a witness to ambush and murder. The victim was the Chief Warrior of King Elara, whose two best war-horses, almost as important as warriors, had also been stolen.

I peered anxiously into the impenetrable wall of the forest gloom. What if the murderer was still around and saw me? He might kill me too. Panic seized me again, but this time I knew it would not stop me.

I slid down the tree in my haste and hit the ground. My knees, weak with fear, gave way and I ended up in a heap.

Scrambling to my feet, I glanced around. The headless corpse sprawled some distance away. Flies were beginning to swarm around it. Jackals and other flesh-eating creatures would attack it in the night. Where was the head? The murderer had taken it with him. Why?

Pity welled up within me. I should ensure the dead man a decent burial – yet all I wanted to do was to get away fast. To ease my conscience, I rationalized that it would be imprudent for me to stay. I turned toward the trail to run.

A rustle of leaves came from a nearby thicket. My heart thudded to a halt. I froze. The killer had been waiting for me after all. Breathless, I gazed at the thicket, unable to move, awaiting my fate. A bird fluttered out and sped away. I sped back toward the lodge, heedless of my footing, thankful that the Sinhala groom had obviously fled in the opposite direction.

I have no clear recollection of that run, from the time it began until I left the highway and turned to the lodge. I was desperately tired. My chest heaved, my legs ached, my lungs laboured for breath and my blood was pounding. Soon after I hit the side trail, I tripped over a stone and fell, sprawling.

I remained there, eyes closed, inhaling dust with each tortured breath. I wanted desperately to get up and run again, but my lungs were completely pumped out, like the air from a torn drum.

The pause did me good. I saw myself lying in the dust, abjectly quivering with fear, contrary to all I had been taught. I was not acting like a prince. I began to feel shame.

Princes are trained to be different to commoners, to be the embodiment, of courage and honour. This was one of the fundamentals of all I had been taught since I could remember. If princes are cowardly, their people will be cowardly. People may run away, but never a prince. He has to be the example, as well as the precept, to stand up and fight – against all odds, to the death if need be – but as a prince.

Shame is sometimes the springboard of courage. No one else had witnessed my abject behaviour, thank the *devas*, but I was its supreme witness. As deepest shame filled my being, my courage slowly returned.

I rested until my breathing was normal and the resolve to act like a prince became cold and firm within me. Then I heaved myself up with the palms of my hands, dusted myself and walked slowly back to the lodge, determined not to run or look back,

As I walked, still fearful, but with head held high, I realized that I had won a signal battle over myself. The stimulus of fear is ignorance. By refusing to react, I had developed a greater ability not to give way to unidentified terror.

Presently, above a high masonry wall, the two-storey grey granite lodge, capped by its red-tiled roof, came into view. It was framed by a giant green banyan tree and great orange-blossomed flamboyants. The building was set on a knoll, with grassy grounds sloping gently to the silver waters of the lake, now ruffled by a breeze. This was my haven, not the jungle from which I had just fled!

I forced myself to stroll through the entrance gates. The front of the building was deserted, but my uncle, Prince Vipula, and his two friends, having finished their bath, were in the rear, inspecting the horses at the entrance to the stables.

My feelings for my uncle had always been ambivalent. A part of me hated him, because I judged him to be the murderer of both my parents. I kept deliberately withdrawn from him, because I had been told that it was he who had my father murdered for what he deemed an act of sacrilege on the part of a low-caste man – lying with a princess, my uncle's sister. After all, I was the product of that union.

Yet I greatly admired my uncle, too. For one thing, he

was the most handsome, courtly man I had ever seen. He was forty-three at this time, haughty-looking, lean and supple as a sword blade. His finely chiselled features were clean-shaven and golden-skinned. Gleaming black hair streaked lightly with silver at the temples gave him great dignity.

With a start, I realized that it was him I had sought as my refuge, not the lodge. The knowledge spun like a top on the surface of my consciousness. I glimpsed the truth. My uncle had been my refuge all these years. My resentment had kept me withdrawn from this strong, silent man, always there, always looking after me. I now wanted to cry out to him, but the habit of the years held me back.

Prince Vipula looked up at my approach. 'I thought you had already left for your big night out.' His voice was deep, golden like his skin. Noticing my dust-streaked face, his fine black eyes swept down to take in my dishevelled appearance. He gestured toward me. 'You seem to have been grovelling in the dust!' he added good-humouredly.

I realized with shame that I had indeed been grovelling in the dust, though I could never tell my uncle. Then my eyes met his and I was stunned at his changed expression. All the years I had known him, I had never had to go directly to him when I was sick, hurt or wounded at games or military training. There was the day I fell off my imaginary tree horse when the branch I had been riding so gallantly broke. I fell several cubits to the ground, suffering a cracked rib, many bruises and the deeper wounds of embarrassment. There was the time I swung too high on my swing, when it deposited me unceremoniously on a heap of nettles that ravaged my skin. On such occasions, my uncle had come to visit me as I lay on my sickbed after receiving the ministrations of the physicians and my nurse. He made formal, cheerful inquiries, indulged in a few lighthearted remarks and left.

Now, for the first time, he was faced directly with a fearful, confused boy and his response was immediate, instinctive, his expression gentle, almost tender. He had dropped his mask. He laid a hand on my shoulder, gripping it firmly, as if willing his strength to me. I no longer thought of myself, but of what the murder of Mahela might mean for my uncle's fortune.

After he assumed power, King Elara had been wise enough to retain the former King Asela's appointees in nominal control, but with Chola supervisors at every level. The latter ensured honesty, loyalty and Chola bias, so that an accelerated influx of Cholas from their native land under a policy of colonization could occur. The Sinhala officials therefore had responsibility without power. They were, in fact, hostages of the King and had to ensure the subjection, co-operation and dedication of the Sinhala people, if their positions – and indeed, their lives – were to be safe.

Prince Vipula, being a direct descendant of King Devanam Piya and heir to the throne, was the chief hostage, functioning as head of the Sinhala people of Lanka and answerable for all their actions. The recollection smote me dumb.

'Do you know our family motto?' Prince Vipula's voice was quiet, but it penetrated my thoughts.

'Yes, uncle.'

'Repeat it.'

'I'll lay me down and bleed awhile and then I'll rise and fight again.'

'All right. Don't you think you've bled enough?'

I nodded, unable to take my eyes off him, entranced now by our powerful communion.

'Then tell me your story.'

Hari and Vira, the Sinhala noblemen who were my uncle's guests, moved forward to hear me, anxiety on their faces.

One of the horses in the stables blew violently. It seemed the signal for a babble of words to break loose from me. I began to sweat again, this time not from the heat but from

47

blazing demons of fear for my uncle's safety. My uncle gripped both my arms, squeezing firmly to steady me. 'Speak slowly and clearly!' he commanded. His friends drew yet closer, their necks craning forward.

The words came tumbling out, but in orderly array now. They all listened intently while I told them what I had seen.

When I finally concluded, I looked fearfully at my uncle. Save for the acuteness of his attention and the warmth of his hands on me, he gave no indication of his reactions.

'This could be disastrous for us!' Vira exclaimed excitedly. 'The Chola's Chief Warrior slain by a Sinhala – his two best steeds stolen.'

'Since we were here, we might even be accused of the murder,' Hari volunteered. He was more calm than Vira, but his anxiety showed nonetheless.

Only my uncle seemed unmoved. Releasing his grip on me, he turned around and gazed thoughtfully in the direction from which I had come, as if it would in turn give him direction. I suddenly had a feeling, though he had neither said nor done anything to cause it, that he knew or guessed more about the affair than he would say.

'Don't you think we'd better get back to Anu immediately?' Vira suggested anxiously.

My uncle seemed to make up his mind. He swung back to face us. 'No, that would be fatal,' he declared flatly. 'We'll hunt tonight and return to Anu tomorrow, exactly as planned. Otherwise, we will indeed be suspected of complicity.'

He turned to me. 'Have you been seen? Has anyone spoken to you?'

I shook my head.

'You get back to the *massa* and be here early tomorrow, so we can leave at dawn. Hurry away now. Remember, we know nothing of what took place.' His voice became sharp as an axe and he stepped forward to emphasize his words. 'Even if they torture you, Prince Rodana.' His look was one

48

of command now. Gone was the earlier concern.

The thought of returning alone to the *massa* and remaining there a whole night with that corpse beneath it was torture, but it was surpassed by my burning desire to search my uncle's face in order to discover in it the same feelings that he had released in me.

I glimpsed his look of love again before I turned to leave.

Chapter 4

I was terrified at the prospect of spending an entire night on the *massa* in the Bintenne jungle, with the headless corpse of the Chola Chief Warrior beneath me and a lurking murderer perhaps watching me through the gloom, yet I forced myself to do it out of a sense of duty.

The smell from the first putrefaction of the body, accelerated by the day's heat, reached me even before I crossed the little glade. A small herd of deer, frightened by my approach, darted away from the water hole. Their fear attached itself to me and I quickened my pace, glancing apprehensively in all directions. I deliberately avoided looking at the grisly remains of Mahela's body as I hastened by, but I could hear flies buzzing around it. Rather late in the evening for flies, I thought, but where do they go at night?

I shinned up the tree in record time, thinking that there would be greater security on the *massa* than on the ground below. I felt easier when I reached the platform. Mahela's body was barely distinguishable in the gathering gloom. Night falls quickly in the jungle.

This time, I was in no mood to observe animals and the aesthetic delights of the jungle eluded me. All I wanted was daybreak.

Most of the animals who came to the water hole during the night sniffed at the decomposing body and moved along. Fortunately there were no jackals, else it would have been torn to pieces.

I tried vainly to sleep. I was oppressed by the dark and the increasing death smell, fearful of every rustle, pant and grunt from below and overwhelmed by my own fears. My one refuge came from patches of cloudy sky glowing through the branches. I reached there for my new God, finding comfort each time I made a connexion. I suppose I grew up that night.

Prince Vipula and his companions were long back from their hunt by the time I returned to the lodge. They had bagged a deer, a cheetah and a bear, all of which the servants had promptly skinned and dressed. It only required one approving glance from my uncle for all I had endured to be worthwhile.

So that the servants might not suspect anything, we had a leisurely breakfast of *appa*, milk-rice, red fish curry, *sambole*, red-gold *kitul* honey and mangoes. We then set out on horseback for Anu, followed by the wagon containing our supplies, the animal skins and the dressed game.

Soon after we hit the main highway, a troop of Chola cavalrymen galloped furiously past us in the opposite direction.

'Such indecent haste!' Prince Vipula observed dryly. 'And so early in the morning.'

'Could they have lost their chief?' Vira inquired straight-faced.

Only a short time passed before we again heard galloping hooves, this time coming from behind us. We drew up our horses at the side of the road and watched in silence as a pair of grim-faced Cholas pounded past us toward Anu on labouring mounts. Clearly, the news that Mahela's body had been discovered would precede us to the city.

The rest of the journey was uneventful. With a pause for lunch, we reached the environs of Anu by late afternoon. We reined out horses on the crest of a low hill, dismounted and tethered them to trees. They could do with a rest while we waited for the wagon to catch up.

A black-haired boy, his chest bare, clad in a red span-cloth, drove two bulls yoked together toward a rocky track off the main road. Wiping a snotty nose with the back of his hand, he glanced curiously in our direction but kept on his way, guiding the cattle with his stick and clicking his tongue at them in a grown-up manner. The smell of fresh-suckled udder lay faintly on the air from a brown-and-white cow tethered at the edge of a glade, her little calf nuzzling her for more milk.

We strolled to a clearing at the top of the hill and paused in the shade of tall *pini-jambu* trees to look down at the green plain sprawling below.

The city of Anu spread its red rooftops north into the distance, between two great reservoirs sparkling silver in the afternoon sun and the muddy meandering of the broad river on the east. A wide strip of grey granite extending from the river to the reservoirs was its southern rampart, the channel of muddy water at its base the moat. The city was too vast for us to distinguish the northern rampart, but I knew that it, too, joined the river and the reservoir and was protected by a moat. With water on two sides and ramparts served by moats on the other two sides, the great city was impregnable.

'Each time I see Anu, I marvel at the vision of King Devanam Piya, who built it,' my uncle said in a low voice. 'It is indeed a *raja pura*, a royal city. Travellers from abroad say that this is the most splendid city they have ever seen. Asleep or awake, its vibrance reaches all the way up here.'

'Your ancestors' creation, Prince,' Vira reminded him,

' – and your heritage.'

Prince Vipula's smile had a hint of sadness. He continued staring down at the city as if he saw more than his eyes beheld.

One of the horses snorted, seemingly in dissent, but indeed it was difficult for me to imagine a finer city anywhere in the world at any time, especially at this moment when it lay sleeping in the hot afternoon sunlight. Yet it was not entirely asleep, because the wooden drawbridge was alive with figures emerging from the giant teakwood gates that served the southern entrance. These gates were normally kept closed. Even open, I could distinguish their iron ribbing, interspersed with the white wounds from battering rams and dark scars from the impact of flameballs flung by catapults.

Broad avenues, coloured pale rose from the sand, crossed the centre of the city, curving around the citadel. One joined the southern and northern gates. The other, running from east to west, crossed the silver river running through the city and ended at the streaks of great reservoir dams. Both avenues were surprisingly deserted, except for a few moving blotches that would be covered wagons and the smaller, dark blobs of men on horseback.

The city was divided into four sectors, with the citadel in the centre, yet its entirety was a vast mosaic of dark green treetops, open parkland of lighter green, pale brown ribbons of streets and red roofs, relieved by the muddy slash of a tributary of the meandering river. Patches of grey smoke slowly curling upward spoke of life – people would be cooking the evening meal.

My glance instinctively sought the northwest sector, where my father would have lived with the *maha janaya*, the ordinary folk, in the separate area meant for people of the lowest caste. He had walked this city, yet I had never seen him. For the thousandth time a gnawing sense of hopeless loss choked me. I wondered what he looked like, what thoughts and feelings he had, how he came to meet my mother, a princess of most royal blood living in that exclusive domain of the royal family, princes and noblemen, the citadel. Had he been cleaning the royal privies? Had love passed between them at the first glance? How had he dared lift his eyes to hers? Had they loved each other long and hopelessly before co-habiting, or was I the product of a sudden hasty moment of sexual passion? I had always clung fiercely to the belief that my mother and father had loved each other deeply and that my mother had died of grief after my father's murder. It was the only way I could give dignity to my birth and life.

I quickly set aside these thoughts, but not before observing again the difference between the two areas. The roofs of the palace, the audience hall, the secretariat, treasury and granaries were great red patches, like blood-wounds on a lake of green, while the pinpoint clusters of the roofs of the common people were blood-blotched skin. Citadel and sector seemed to merge into each other, but the gap between my mother and father had been greater than life – it had brought them both death.

Just as the city had made me lost in thought, it had the same effect on my companions. Any great city, especially a sacred one, reaches out to those who love it with a mother's embrace. Lovers speak to each other, but a mother and child are silent in each other's arms. Oh well . . . The squeaking of wheels interrupted us.

'That must be our wagon straining up the hill,' Prince Vipula observed. 'Time for us to move on. And we had best keep with the wagon.' He nodded toward the city gates. 'There are dozens more guards around and they seem to be checking everyone with greater care than usual.'

We remounted and awaited the wagon, taking our places at its head once it laboured into view. Sensing that they were close to home, our horses became restive, but we held them back, I with some difficulty, because my grey Arabi was

53

young and eager to scamper downhill to his stables.

We were stopped by grim-looking armed guards with crossed spears at the entrance to the drawbridge. We knew their captain, a dark, grizzled Chola in white uniform who came over to check us out personally. He normally had a cheery greeting for Prince Vipula, but he was silent and aloof today. He saluted us and checked our safe-conduct passes carefully. He even inspected the wagon himself, while we sat our horses in the westerly sun's glare, sweating in the heat.

He finally signalled his troops curtly to allow us to proceed. The line of foot soldiers moved away from the massive gates. We walked our horses under the arched rampart, past the Chola guards in red uniforms. All were heavily armed. These were unsmiling men, most of them dark and bearded. Their eyes, beneath white turbans, were watchful. It was like fording an angry red river, only the river did not splash and roar, but maintained an ominous silence.

Indeed, the entire city was strangely silent today. The courtyard, which was normally a cacophony of voices, had been cleared of the street vendors who set up their carts every morning opposite the guards' quarters to sell food and other wares to soldiers and travellers. Only the after-odours of fish, onions, garlic and rotting vegetables remained.

The horses tossed their heads nervously. My Arabi kept jittering his skin as if to get rid of flies, but there were no flies on his body. I patted his sweat-strewn neck to steady him.

'Word has reached them already,' my uncle observed as we finally trotted down the broad avenue, grateful for the shade of flamboyants, which made a red carpet of flowers under our horses' hooves. 'They obviously fear a rebellion.'

It was still light when we arrived at the drawbridge over the moat surrounding the palace. Sentries on the granite ramparts and at the gates were very much on the alert, tension and watchfulness literally pouring out of them. We clip-clopped over the drawbridge. We were better known here, but our wagon was subjected to an even more rigorous search at the palace gates than before, this time by two giant Cholas of the palace guard, their expressions stern.

'Whatever happened to the king who was always accessible to his subjects?' Vira whispered when we were cleared and began an even trot towards our quarters.

'You cannot blame him for not wanting to suffer the fate of his Chief Warrior!' Hari retorted dryly.

It was only then that I had the feeling that my uncle and his friends read more into the bizarre incident of the previous afternoon than I had. Dissident Sinhala could exist anywhere – in the palace, the temples or the other sectors, and particularly in the northeast sector, which is devoted to trade and commerce. It is a clutter of shops, taverns, inns and the residences of members of the twenty-eight craftsmen's guilds. Being a centre for travellers, this sector teems with life by day and into the night. A rigid system of registration, strictly supervised by the Minister for Security, is maintained against spies and subversionists, but no system is foolproof, or an obstacle to genius.

We rode past the empty flagstoned courtyard of the audience hall at the front of the palace. The hall towered above us on a giant base of granite blocks, with soaring columns of ebony supporting its sloping red-tiled roof. A great half-moon of flat rock, heavily carved with figures of birds and animals, formed the apron of its entrance, from which broad steps led up to the reception hall. Curved balustrades of rock, with bas-reliefs of *bahiraya*, guardian deities, ran on either side of the steps. Silent Chola guards, spears at the rest position, stood on the side of each landing and at the entrances to the hall. On one side of the audience hall was the Secretariat; behind it was the Treasury.

Vira nodded toward the palace as we turned left and rode past it. 'That's where you should be going,' he observed to Prince Vipula. 'Through the audience hall and the pleasure gardens to the King's quarters.' A note of bitterness entered his voice. 'There's a Chola in them now.'

Instead of heading for the King's quarters at the rear of the gardens, we were riding in the direction of the residences formerly used by high Sinhala officials, one of which had been made available by King Elara for my uncle's use.

'Some day!' Hari said with a sigh.

My uncle made no comment.

'But first we'll have to rid the place of the smell of sesame-seed oil,' Vira remarked.

'Ugh!' Hari grimaced.

Cholas use *thala thell* in their cooking and even for bathing. We Sinhala find its smell offensive, preferring to use the oil from the kernel of the coconut.

'You wouldn't wait for any cleansing if you were going in that direction, you stud,' Hari retorted, nodding toward the walled ladies' quarters, which were on one side of the King's chambers, affording the King easy access. Vira was a well-known ladies' man.

My uncle rode on, still without comment. He had very little time for women. It was said that he had vowed not to get married until a Sinhala monarch sat on the three-hundred-year-old Sinhala throne of Lanka. He did not wish to limit his freedom of action with a family, or expose a wife and children to the dangers of his situation. Being a direct descendant of King Devanam Piya and the rightful heir to the Sinhala throne, my uncle's position was always one of special danger. What other reasons he had for his celibacy, no one guessed, but within twenty-four hours I was to discover one of them.

Chola guards were swarming around the palace grounds. My uncle was one of the few Sinhala still left in the precincts of the palace – only because of the position he had been accorded by King Elara. He once described his situation as riding a drunken elephant on a slippery floor. He had demonstrated himself a skilled rider for fourteen years!

Our residence was a two-storey brick mansion, within a shady grove of mango, breadfruit and jak trees. Behind its front boundary wall, running along the street, was a large garden and then the house, which was built around a centre courtyard, as was the custom.

We slowed our horses and walked them through the entrance gates. A sentry, dressed in the blue-and-white uniform of Prince Vipula's small personal guard, sprang to attention and saluted us by raising his long spear. Returning the salute, we rode past a clear pool and the water cascade to the front door, to be greeted by the ever-present groom and attendants.

We were not surprised to find a summons from the King awaiting our arrival. The summons included Vira, Hari and me. It must have been prompted by our absence from the city – or our presence at the hunting lodge – the previous day.

The chief attendant had already caused the servants to prepare our baths downstairs and lay out fresh clothes for us in our upstairs bedrooms. Hari and Vira were to spend a few days as my uncle's guests before leaving for their homes in the country.

I hastened with my toilet, nearly bruising myself once or twice with the scrubbing stone meant to peel only dust and dirt and not the skin off me! Never had I been summoned to the royal presence before. I was just a bastard prince, an orphan, being brought up by a kind uncle. What could the King want with me?

I was first in the entrance foyer of the residence. Impatiently I awaited the others. Yes, it was Prince Vipula who came last, freshly shaved, carefully groomed, immaculately dressed as always. His white silk pantaloons and gold brocade tunic fitted him to perfection. His black-and-silver hair was oiled and carefully brushed. He smelled of sandalwood. From his manner, one would have thought we were going to a palace party.

Chapter 5

It was inevitable that the exchange between King Kakkavan and the twelve-year-old Prince Gamini, during the first conference I had with them, should remind me of these events from my boyhood.

Upon the King's dismissal, Gamini and I went our separate ways. It would have been a mistake for me to attempt any conversation with the Prince immediately.

Gamini had received a message that he was to attend his mother, the Queen, in the midafternoon. Wanting to get it over and done with, he decided to drop in on her quarters, since it was now her bath hour, on the off-chance that she could spare some time. He therefore made his way toward the central courtyard of the ladies' quarters. When he got there, shouts and shrieks of laughter reached his ears. The ladies were obviously at the bathing pool before the noon meal. He pushed through the door and entered the enclosed area. The pool was large and circular, with steps leading down to the water. Its bottom was of blue ceramic, making the water sparkle azure in the sunlight.

The Queen's ladies-in-waiting and female attendants were disporting themselves in and around the pool. Their high-pitched laughter rang like golden bells in his ears. He had been here before, when he was younger and thought nothing of it. Today, the sight of female bodies, flimsy bath-cloths wrapped just above their breasts and reaching only to the knees, excited him. The wet cloths clung to their figures, showing off curves of soft flesh gleaming in the sunlight. The half-sight of their bodies through bathing cloths, weaving into heady scents of sandalwood and citronella, was more arousing than nakedness.

A lissom attendant frisked sideways in a joyous dance, shapely arms outstretched, a goddess-nymph of the woodlands. Her name was Leela Wathie, he knew. She was fourteen and of noble birth – the new, favourite handmaiden of his mother. Her skin was golden and shone as if it had been rubbed with oil. Her wet hair gleamed black in the sunlight. The cleavage between her breasts held drops of water glistening like dew.

Something within Gamini burst into bloom. His eyes roved towards the other half-naked bodies.

Nona, the chief lady-in-waiting, saw him and let out a scream. 'Men are not allowed in this enclosure,' she cried, ' – and you are no longer a boy.'

'Where's my royal mother, the Queen?'

They all herded together, laughing and giggling now. He wanted to plunge naked into their midst, manhood proud and erect.

'The Queen's unwell. She is alone in her chambers,' the old crone shouted back. 'But you, Prince, be off with you. You can't come into this restricted area any longer. As I said, you're a man now.'

'Why don't you check for proof that he's indeed a man?' The mellow voice was that of Padma, a shapely lady-in-waiting who had often cast lustful glances at him.

There was nothing he could do here but look. He turned abruptly and walked away towards his mother's quarters, barely hearing the shrill laughter and ribald comments that followed him.

The verandas and the entrance lobby of the Queen's rooms were deserted. He opened the door and crossed the deserted anteroom, his soft sandals silent on the floors of white mountain crystal. He let himself forget that no one entered the Queen's quarters without being announced.

He raised his hand to knock on the door of the sleeping quarters, but his dark fist remained poised above the brown teakwood as if held in a smith's vice. It was the vice of his

59

own bidding. A man's voice was murmuring inside. It was not his father's – and the Queen was supposed to be alone.

At first he was merely surprised. Who could be there with his mother? A monk perhaps? He should not intrude. Then a hammering began in his brain. He started to sweat. His mind, his raw brain, his body and his *prana* seemed strangely separated and apart from each other.

Dear *devas*, keep this truth from my mind, his *prana* suddenly implored. In the imploring, the battle was lost.

The man inside his mother's bedroom was Velu Sumana – his friend, the King's Chief Warrior, his own tutor in the arts of horsemanship, charioteering, swordsmanship and combat, his comrade-in-arms someday.

He caught the soft spoken words like the last of the tail of a shooting star. 'You are all I have, my only real source of strength . . . the only person I truly love . . .'

The perfidious queen softly replied, 'And I you. We have only each other. No one must discover the truth, else you will be killed and I will be alone.'

'The King . . .'

'What can we expect from the King . . .' The Queen's voice trailed off into a murmur.

Gamini trembled before the sudden stab of vulnerability. Then, as if it were not enough, 'I love Gamini as my son,' the man was saying. 'Why must the King sign such a treaty and condemn him to something foreign to his destiny?'

'Hush! You are more Gamini's father than he. But it is our little Tissa we must safeguard, even from his brother. Let the treaty be executed. It may help the younger child. As for Gamini . . .'

Again the Queen's voice was lost, this time in the black mist that swept over Gamini. Now he knew the dreadful worst. Velu Sumana was not only his mother's lover, he was Tissa's father and possibly his own. That made him a bastard, with no right to the throne.

He watched the closed door, fascinated, like a bird before

60

a cobra. One final spasm of the old weakness seized him. This must be a dream. Dear *devas*, take it away from me, he implored. My bright stare will surely penetrate that door and find nothing, no one there. Then I shall tear out my eardrums and smash them for the foul lies they heard.

But the gods made no response and his hand dropped to his side. His shoulders drooped. He did not care to hear any more. Everything was finished, his life's purpose ended.

Then he straightened himself. His chin jutted out. He became savagely determined. Henceforth, I trust no one. We are born alone. We live alone. We die alone. If I have no right to the throne, I shall seize it, with my bare hands if necessary.

He turned swiftly and strode away. His final cold thought was, No one must know my shame – no one shall ever know my shame.

Gamini's presence in the bath area had reminded Leela Wathie, the Queen's handmaiden, that she should be returning to her mistress. She hastily wiped herself, wrung out her long black hair and wound a cloth around it to make it dry sooner. She tied her wiping cloth around her, slipped off her wet bathing cloth and squeezed it. The wash attendants would pick it up, wash it thoroughly by hammering it on stones and hang it up on the long clothes-lines just outside the palace to dry in the sun. She donned her bodice, jacket and skirt, then clip-clopped swiftly on sandalled feet to the Queen's quarters.

She had been selected as the Queen's handmaiden three years ago, shortly after she had attained maidenhood at eleven. Although it took her away from home, this had to be her lot, her destiny. She accepted it willingly and would live it to the full, as long as the Queen lived or needed her.

Leela knocked on the door of the anteroom and entered. It was a long, sunlit room with floors of white and green mountain crystal on which was spread a magnificent Persian rug. Couches of creamy-gold satinwood, with pale green cushions, lined the walls. At the far end of the room, a statue of Lord Buddha, carved in alabaster, was placed on a white alabaster stand.

The Queen, dressed in a blue sari and bodice, and Velu Sumana, in his uniform of white *dhoti* and red overshirt, were seated on separate couches. Leela made obeisance, thinking, Not a day goes by without my marvelling at my lady's beauty. The long, wavy black hair framed a perfectly proportioned face with skin the colour of *ran-thambili*, revered by Sinhala poets. The tall, shapely figure could not be hidden even when the Queen was seated. Not even that slight hint of fullness at the hip from childbearing could disguise its grace.

The Queen looked up at Leela, her dark eyes crinkling at the sides, teeth white as coconut kernel revealed in her beautiful smile. 'Oh, there you are, Leela.' She pointed delicately at the girl with her peacock-feather fan.

'Madam, you are the most beautiful lady in the world!' Leela exclaimed impulsively.

'No wonder we love you as a daughter,' the Queen responded, shaking her head slowly from side to side.

'You should say "sister", my queen,' Velu Sumana intervened with ponderous gallantry. A half-smile played on his light-skinned, handsome face. 'No one would believe you were Leela's mother.'

The Queen started working her fan. 'You are too kind, sir,' she dimpled. 'Daughter, sister, what does it matter, though? We love the child . . . and trust her.' The last words were softly spoken, the dark eyes suddenly keen on Leela.

The handmaiden dropped to both knees and placed the palms of her hands together. She bowed as in worship. 'I would gladly give my life to prove that trust, madam.' She looked up, her gaze deep and earnest.

The Queen's eyes went moist. 'We know,' she replied huskily. 'And we have need of at least one more trustworthy subject.' Her look at Velu Sumana indicated that he was the other. She sighed. 'And to be loved. Truly loved. We can only trust those whom we know to love us truly.'

You are a queen, the most beautiful woman in the kingdom, so why do you speak thus? Leela wondered.

Suddenly, she heard the sound of a great wind in the distance. It began swirling, wailing and howling as it drew closer. The world grew dark on the instant. Lightning flashed. Thunder crackled, rolled and burst as if to tear the earth asunder.

A new sound arose – the roar and crash of waves. The waters of a mighty ocean now seethed, roared and swelled before her. In the trough of a giant wave was a boat – a frail craft bearing a cowering figure hidden beneath a dark mantle. On the boat's side was an inscription.

Frenzied waters and blinding rain, splattering and foaming, drenched Leela, preventing her from seeing the words. She kept wiping her eyes, staring so hard they hurt, but she still could not read them. She felt a tremendous surge of pity for that desolate figure and then the words became clear: 'I am Vihara Devi, daughter of King Kelani Tissa, consigned to the deep as an offering to the gods.'

Leela stared through the storm, through its darkness and horror, at the pitiful maiden in the boat. Her compassion became boundless, reaching out to that figure, compelling it to turn in response. Beneath cascading waters, Leela saw the white face and terror-stricken eyes of a beautiful girl of fourteen, her own present age.

The storm subsided in that instant. The face remained. Only now it was that of her queen, gazing intently at her. She wiped her face again to rid it of raindrops. She was wiping her tears.

The Queen's eyes widened. The whites became larger, the dark depth receded. You have identified my knowledge, though not my vision, Leela thought with amazement and a filtering of joy. You have discovered the depth of

63

understanding and love created within me. Your father, King Kelani Tissa, did indeed reject you to appease the gods, after they punished his Kelaniya kingdom with unending storms, for his impious act, having a *bhikku*, whom he wrongly suspected of adultery with his wife, boiled in oil. He consigned you to the waves in a frail craft, but the storm would not subside. Only when a giant tidal wave carried off your father himself, as he rode his elephant, inspecting storm damage on the seashore, were the gods satisfied. You, my queen, were then washed ashore on the Ruhuna coast, where King Kakkavan Tissa discovered you and eventually married you.

A knock on the door disturbed the silence. Leela rose to her feet and went to answer it. She opened the door. Prince Tissa stood before her, immaculately dressed in blue. He must know what his mother wears, Leela thought, for he is always dressed in the same colour as my lady.

Whatever the colour, clothes suited Prince Tissa. He was a beautiful boy of ten, the image of the Queen. His complexion was very light, almost pink, his hair black and curly. The eyes were dark and luminous, the bones of the face too delicate for a male. He was of slim, slight build, but looked wiry. She had heard he was manly with weapons and in the wrestling ring.

'May I see my royal mother?' Prince Tissa inquired courteously. His voice had a long way to go before it broke into manhood, but he had such good manners and he always smiled, unlike his remote brother, Gamini.

Leela stepped aside. 'Certainly, Prince.'

Prince Tissa walked into the room and made obeisance. The Queen acknowledged it, then opened her arms to him. He rushed up to her and was enfolded in them, half kneeling, his dark head against the Queen's waist. She rocked him lightly. 'What does my *bada pissa* want?'

'My brother hates me.' Prince Tissa's voice came out muffled.

The Queen exchanged glances with Velu Sumana. 'What has he done now, *putha*?'

Prince Tissa raised his head but continued kneeling at his mother's feet. 'Nothing today,' he replied petulantly, 'but he is forever scolding me.'

'Has he ever struck you?'

'No. But he will, he will. He always takes my things, saying he will be king one day. Older brother is so rough. It is against Lord Buddha's teachings. What will happen to me if he does become king? He might even drive me away from the palace.'

Once again the Queen and Velu Sumana exchanged glances, this time nodding slowly at each other. The Queen's eyes shifted to Leela, as if she were seeking some reassurance.

Leela nodded too, without knowing why.

'You have no reason to fear, son,' the Queen assured Prince Tissa. She seemed to make up her mind. She reached out and took his face in her hands, willing an undefined promise into him.

'But I *am* afraid, Mother.' The Prince's eyes filled with tears. 'Do not ever leave me, for if you are gone, my whole life will be miserable, and everyone will mistreat me.'

'Oh, my son! Do not say such things.' The Queen drew Prince Tissa to her again, leaning down to hold him closer. She placed her fair cheek against his dark head and rocked him, crooning. 'We shall not let any harm befall you. We shall do something about this.'

'I need you, Mother.'

Chapter 6

Although he was only twelve at the time, perhaps Gamini's most gallant moments were those he lived alone after concluding that his mother and Velu Sumana were lovers. Gallantry has many splendours, most of them unsung, some unheard, existing in the secret recesses of hearts and lives.

I knew a wife and mother who was dying of a dreadful incurable disease, the lump that grows within the body and spreads its malignancy, like a parasite creeper, until it destroys that which it feeds on and thus exterminates itself. She finally reached a stage where her skin hung over pitiful bones like the wrinkled peel of a dried fruit. One night she supervised the servants, as usual, when they served dinner to her husband and children, as was her duty, though she herself was too exhausted to eat. When dinner was over, she pleaded that she was sleepy and retired to bed. In less than an hour, she was semi-conscious. Soon she lapsed into unconsciousness, but her face kept wincing and her body twitching with the agonies of the disease. She was not the moaning kind. She never rose from that bed. She never regained consciousness. It took her twenty-one silent hours to die.

Can you imagine the resolve of someone fulfilling that last duty, though weary unto death? Her house never received a banner for her dedication to duty or for the supreme gallantry of her life and death. Women are always the unsung heroes. Yes, heroes, not heroines, which means something different.

Gamini's heroism on the battlefield was known and recognized. His gallantry on this tragic day would only be revealed much later, to me alone. At this time I was not yet his source of comfort. Rather, his hard couch was his only refuge whenever he was badly hurt. He would lie on it, all curled up like an unborn baby, and retire into a world of his own, from which he would emerge strengthened and resolute. Today, when he had evidence that his mother and the Chief Warrior were lovers and he himself might be of bastard birth, he instinctively lay in that same position.

He had replaced a soft mattress and pillows with planks and a mat when he was but six, in order to toughen his body. On this couch, he dreamed of campaigns ahead during which he would frequently have only the earth for a bed. Yes indeed, he would eat and sleep like his troops, who served his cause and risked their lives for him. He would never exercise the privilege of rank, with camp followers carrying beds and tents wherever he went.

This afternoon his head was spinning and his thoughts were confused. How could they blaze so madly through a brain so physically numb? Had he misheard his mother and Velu Sumana? He tried to recall their conversation, but the exact words kept evading him. When he strove to force recall, his brain only became raw with the effort. Each time he seemed to grasp a phrase, it slipped away, like an eel coiling around his hand, visibly there, yet impossible to hold. Other thoughts kept intruding: his pain, terror at the thought of being a bastard, its effect on the succession. The more he dwelt on these, the farther the words he sought to recapture receded.

If he was indeed a bastard, why had he taken naturally to his father in his early years? He remembered being given horseback rides on his father's knee. Mostly, he remembered his father's dedication to creating the means for him to fulfil his destiny. The King had raised a superb army for him, under the Ten Great Warriors, who had been specially selected for their role in the campaign he would direct against the Chola. To support that endeavour, the King had organized the production of weapons, and means of transport, as well as the accumulation of raw materials. He had always regarded his father as a brave man, a fine strategist and a proud Sinhala.

Shortly after his seventh birthday, everything gradually began to change. His father's fixity of purpose started evaporating like water in harsh sunlight. The dream of a Sinhala Lanka slowly gave way before the reality of a Buddhist Ruhuna. He had been more than disappointed. The whole basis of his life started to erode, quicksands beneath unwary feet.

Had he stopped loving his father then? He did not know; it might be that he had never really loved his father. Perhaps it was respect he had felt, not love, and when the cause of that respect was removed, there was nothing. One thing he did know was that he had never been able to break through his father's inner reserve. It was always there, solid as black granite, even when the King was smiling.

Dimly, a question arose in Gamini's mind. Did he himself not have that inner reserve? He knew he did, but he set the question aside as being irrelevant. More to the point, his father's changed attitude had produced disrespect and therefore resentment within him. Thus, unlike other children, he was now remote from his father. It made him acknowledge that he himself was a remote person through and through.

He heard a loud sniff. His eyes jerked towards the door, then he realized it was his own bitter sniff. He half smiled and shook his head at himself.

What of his mother? He had loved her quietly and deeply. He was not the demonstrative kind, though, and in his earliest years some of her coddling had embarrassed him. Yet feeling for her had been there, the need to commune occasionally with eyes that had no veils over them, to touch and be cared for without effusiveness. He, of course, would receive such expressions of love with affectionate tolerance because of his inner reserve, but his mother would know the

68

truth and there would be a secret bond between them. None of this happened. Instead, his mother showered all her affection on his younger brother, Sadha Tissa, and the little monster lapped it up. He was driven to believe that his mother loved Tissa more.

Very early in life, he found his mother siding with Tissa in their little disputes. After all, he is the *bada pissa*, the youngest, the child who swept the womb clear, she would say fondly, as if that excused unfairness. His mother's voice took on a special tenderness even when she admonished Tissa.

He often wondered whether some of his mother's attitude to him could not have been caused by his not being the kind to be petted and coddled, but he drew final conclusions from the proof of his eyes and ears and therefore became increasingly aloof from her. What he learned today had exiled her from his heart and life for all time.

Tissa was a beautiful boy, with moist brown eyes, pale skin and black hair – very unlike him. The ladies of the court, preferring fair children, were forever fussing over Tissa. In spite of all this, he himself would have been closer to Tissa if they could have shared concern about a usurper being on the throne of Lanka and developed a common fixity of purpose to re-establish Sinhala rule throughout the country.

Having little in common with his brother, he generally ignored him. Was he jealous of Tissa? He could not honestly say so, but rather suspected that Tissa resented an older brother who was destined to become the saviour of Lanka.

From as far back as he could remember, he had been hailed as the future king of a united Sinhala Lanka. Every omen, every portent, every hope of people of all classes had been hurled at him. If he had been weaker, he would have been smothered by it all. As it was, it inspired him and became his whole life. Every preparation of his father for war had supported that life. The unspoken understanding was that as soon as his father died or abdicated the throne, he, Gamini, would be free to move against the Chola with a superb fighting machine.

69

Velu Sumana, his teacher and friend, was to help him lead that machine. He had liked and trusted the Chief Warrior, but the man had proved to be more deceitful than a cobra. Chill hatred for Velu Sumana entered his being.

Resentment against his father, exile from his mother and hatred of his teacher. Who else was left?

He had a puppy once, but it had died. He could talk to his elephant, Kandula, but an elephant did not have the soulful eyes of a dog. Besides, it could not frisk around or lie at your feet.

His thoughts flitted to the future. He had a tremendous task ahead of him. He must watch Prince Digha Bahu, who wanted the throne and would plot to get it, perhaps even seek to kill him later on, if he stood in the way. The Chief Minister would help him. There was no affection between him and Kirthi Siri – only a secret, unspoken understanding. They were two of a kind, needing each other. Kirthi Siri kept an eye on everyone and had recently started passing information to him. The old jackal. He knew which side of his *appa* had the honey!

Gamini smiled to himself at the thought. Kirthi Siri at least had confidence in his future. His headache began to abate.

What of his new tutor, Rodana? He had a strange inclination to like the man. Those born under Aquarius were supposed to have intuition, especially in the early hours of the morning, and all his intuitions about Rodana were good. He had begun to feel that here, at last, was a man he could trust – but enough of that. From now on, he would trust no one. Never again.

People always desire things. They follow whoever can fulfil these desires. He must make the people of Ruhuna desire and need him. He did not have to love or be loved by them to get their support. He only had to offer them what they wanted. All he required from them was their help in achieving his destiny: not his ambition, nor his objective,

70

nor his goal, but his destiny. He was convinced of it and inextricably bound to it.

He became pleased at the orderly progression of his thoughts. He was mastering a terrible situation. That was good. He had to cultivate such qualities.

He turned to stretch and lie on his back. He began to see things again. I am glad the wooden ceiling is so high, he thought – else it might stifle me. I do not like the faded colours of the paintings on it.

I must remain detached. I must not let emotion rack me. I must use emotion in a controlled manner. If I do this with myself, I can control others – my commanders and troops someday.

How had he come to know that he was destined to free the entire island of Lanka from Chola rule and re-unify it under a Sinhala king? Was it from his *kharmic* consciousness, the cause of his birth? The cause of his birth . . . He was jolted and paused. Should not that part of his thinking be ruthlessly eliminated? No, he was born neither of Kakkavan Tissa nor Velu Sumana, but of a *samanera*. His parents had had no children for twelve years after their marriage. The story was that his mother had visited the dying *samanera*, who had once been a great warrior and later became a monk. She begged him to project himself into her womb at his final death-moment, so that she could bring forth a baby, from King Kakkavan's seed, who would be the greatest Sinhala warrior ever and a champion of the Doctrine. The *samanera* had refused the Queen twice, but on her third visit, he had agreed. The conception had taken place on his death.

For the first time in his life, Gamini had a flash of doubt as to the truth of this story. Could it not have been that a barren king and an immoral queen . . . ?

Calmly and deliberately, Gamini thrust the thought from his mind. Not because he wanted to be fair by his mother, but in order to support his future with unshakable faith in the security of his birth. Now, more than ever, he needed to separate the physical origins of his birth from the beginning and end of this journey. True, he knew from the conversation he had overheard that, quite distinct from the possibility of his being a bastard, his father also was trying to take away his whole life by a peace treaty with the Chola. A few words on *ola* signed by two old men sought to destroy his birthright and what he had been nurtured on by everyone, including one of those two old men – but none of it would make any difference to him.

He could not help reflecting grimly on people. His mother had destroyed the child in him, the nature of his life. Velu Sumana had destroyed the friend in him, the substance of his life. Now his father, if indeed the King was his father, would probably destroy the prince in him, the purpose of his life.

A lizard appeared on the ceiling, stalking a winged insect. Although he had seen this before, Gamini watched in fascination as the lizard slowly crept toward its prey. It paused a few inches away. The insect remained unaware of the danger. It made a short, swift dart, then flicked out a long tongue. The insect struggled pitifully in the lizard's mouth. Soon it passed into the transparent skin of the lizard's bowels, to become merely a dark mass. It had paid the price for thinking the enemy was far enough away, for its own smug sense of security, for its unconscious belief in its power to survive.

I must never be so trapped or preoccupied, he thought. I must have total awareness. Only thus can I escape the snares of men, including my father's treaties. If the King truly is my father, what a despicable father – a Sinhala king agreeing to a foreign ruler over Sinhala territory!

He began to sweat with the heat. It renewed the smell of dried sweat on his body. He should have bathed before lying down. He looked at the sand in the clock on the table. It was well past noon. Through the window, he saw trees drooping shadowless beneath a hot sun.

Shadowless. He recalled the Brahmins. They would not

eat food on which the shadow of a person from an untouchable caste had fallen. Proud Brahmins and their priests. They brought to his mind a Hindu custom. Women who were barren of child for years went to the temple to live, work and worship there for their cycle of twenty-eight days. Under the tutelage of the priests, when they lay sleeping in their cells at night, they dreamed that Lord Brahma, the creator, visited them, lay and coupled with them. Thus impregnated by the god, they invariably went home and bore a child nine months later.

He had overheard cynics say that the truth of this matter was simple. The women's husbands were invariably impotent. When the women slept in the temple, they were visited by young, virile Brahmin priests – great studs of men, bred for this purpose, but kept hidden from view by day. Most women they visited accepted them as the god of their dreaming. Unless a woman was infertile, it only required nightly ministrations at her most receptive time for her to accept seed.

Had Velu Sumana been the stud that impregnated his mother after she had been barren from the King for years? If so, it still did not affect the truth of his continuing life-force being that of the *samanera*, but Gamini was nauseated by the thought that he might have developed from Velu Sumana's seed.

Who was his real father then? King Kakkavan Tissa? The *samanera*? Or Velu Sumana?

He felt a curious suspension of himself, as if he had no identity, on realizing that he had just thought of the King as his father, while believing that the *samanera* might have projected him and Velu Sumana might have created him. How were the distinctions important? They were not. As his mother had said this morning, his destiny awaited him regardless. He must cling to this belief at all costs. After all, the Emperor Sikander, this Alexander the Great, had been of bastard birth. Far from destroying the Emperor, this knowledge was said to have been the chief spur to his achievements. So it would be within him from now on, in the secret recesses of his own mind. Thoughts about his parentage would be destroyed. He would be his own ancestor. He was the product of the *samanera*'s atom of consciousness.

But what did that atom feel when it realized that it had entered the union of his mother's seed with that of someone other than her husband – when it knew that the supposedly virtuous queen was guilty of adultery? Did it desire to go screaming to some other destiny, when it was too late?

If his mother had indeed turned to the handsome, virile Velu Sumana for fulfilment, the Chief Warrior's muscular buttocks, with the large purple birthmark on the right side, must have . . .

Such thoughts were for the weak. Abruptly, he swung out of bed. He went to the privy, then to the bathing room to wash himself before having a belated noon meal. Everything must appear to be normal.

Chapter 7

Thirteen years earlier, I had been only twelve, too, when I witnessed the murder of King Elara's Chief Warrior, returned to the Anu palace from the Bintenne jungle and found a summons from King Elara. How my uncle, Prince Vipula, dressed up for that occasion!

We entered our gold-tasselled palanquins and were carried swiftly by brown, muscular Sinhala bearers, clad in prince Vipula's blue-and-white uniforms, through silver evening air, now cool, to the audience hall. We alighted at the half-moon-shaped apron to find a tight knot of security guards crowding it. We identified ourselves and were escorted up the broad granite steps, between two rows of Chola guards lining the central aisle of the hall, to the inner audience chamber.

An aide to King Elara rapped with his gold staff on the antechamber door. 'Prince Devanam Piya Tissalage Vipula Singha Raja Singha!' he announced. My uncle walked slowly into the antechamber. We followed him.

The last of the sun was slanting in through the windows. In its fading light, two dozen pairs of hostile eyes were suddenly focused on us. Keeping an even pace, we advanced into the high-ceilinged chamber. The sound of doors being shut and bolts rattling behind us disturbed the silence. I heard these sounds vaguely, because my attention was directed to the central figure on the platform at the far end of the chamber. King Elara was seated on the three-hundred-year-old golden, gem-studded Lion Throne of the Sinhala kings, beneath the gold umbrella of state, tasselled with red rubies, green emeralds, blue sapphires and pearls.

Even seated, the King was majestic. A white cotton tunic and pantaloons closely fitted his long body, revealing no bulge of fat anywhere. The white turban under which his silver hair had been gathered was held together by a great ruby stud. It gave him added height and dignity. Most remarkable, however, was his hawk-like face, clean-shaven, with dark, alert features slashed by a beak of a nose between eyes brown and hard as tourmalines.

Chola courtiers in blue silk tunics stood on either side of the platform, alongside Chola warriors, their broad chests dark and bare. I could not help noticing one of the men, a striking giant, standing head and shoulders above the rest. His eyes were as black as his skin. A pronounced harelip gave his otherwise regular features a scornful twist. I did not spare him a second glance, however, because my attention was drawn to the massive, sinister figure, arms folded, beside the throne. This young man – fair-skinned, unlike the King – was Digha Jantu, the Second Warrior. His enormous muscles rippled with the slightest movement of his body. The flat nose, dipping over a short upper lip and the half-open mouth, gave him a perpetual snarl.

I trembled a little and my stomach felt watery as Prince Vipula gave salutation and we made obeisance to the King. I had never been this close to King Elara. It did not require any imagination for me to realize that both the King and his warrior regarded us with suspicion and mistrust.

When we stood up again, the King appraised my uncle with brooding eyes. Long moments of tension passed before he motioned us to stand aside, not saying a word. My fear vanished as my blood boiled at the affront. This was no treatment for a prince of the royal blood, let alone the true heir to the Sinhala throne. I expected some outburst from Prince Vipula. His face impassive, his bearing courtly, his dignity unimpaired, he walked to the right of the platform. He was correct to act as he did. It was a statement that royalty and dignity can never be assailed from outside.

We followed my uncle and took our places behind him. It was only when I faced back in the direction of the doors that I noted the granite table set in the centre of the chamber. Wondering whether one or all of us would be tortured publicly on it, I began to sweat. Yet the lesson of the previous evening was well ingrained in me and Prince Vipula's example was a shining reminder of it. I would not succumb to fear, blind or otherwise, today – and it would be easier to show courage with people around than when alone.

Attendants, clad in white pantaloons with royal red sashes, entered from the rear of the chamber, carrying lighted tapers, the flickering flames dancing on their bare brown torsos, sweat-filmed from the heat of the chamber.

Setting about their work with the grace of practice, like slow dancers who know their positions on stage, they started lighting the torches set against the walls and columns and the giant, many-tiered brass lamps placed at regular intervals along the walls.

The chamber became full of dancing lights, great shadows, wispy smoke-curls and the hiss of torches, in a ponderous silence heightened by the gloom and tension. I wished that someone would at least clear his throat, but, emulating Prince Vipula, I stared straight ahead of me.

'Make way there, in the name of the King!' The voice outside the chamber reached us faintly.

The attendants paused in their duties and took their places along the walls. They now were dancers posed to the beat of rattling bolts.

The doors swung open again. A cluster of bare-chested warriors entered the chamber, followed by six soldiers, their breastplates gleaming, swords swinging at their sides, carrying a stretcher covered with a white sheet. They trooped solemnly toward the granite table. King Elara rose to his feet.

My breath caught. The body of Mahela had to lie beneath that sheet. A strange mixture of fear, pity and horror gripped me. I had been the last person to see the corpse before those who found it. I had been the last person, other than the murderer, to see Mahela alive. How vital and strong he had looked galloping his grey horse. Whatever his faults, his death was murder, the method of it repugnant.

Tall and regal, his face carved in dark stone, King Elara gazed broodingly at the stretcher. Even after it was placed on the table and the warriors and soldiers began backing away to the far end of the chamber, the King stood immobile, a great eagle-hawk poised above its prey. The silence in the chamber made my ears start to sing. People were still, like characters in a mime-play, while only the soldiers moved, their bare feet softly scraping the cold crystal floor.

Silence is a weapon. There are men who know how to use it with deadly effect. A king is well able to do so, because no one dares speak in his presence unless spoken to. King Elara had the dynamism of a military commander and the experience of a monarch who had ruled people for many years. He was using silence effectively tonight. I did not know whether it was his weapon or the pungent smell of tapers mingled with incense that made me start to feel dizzy.

The warriors and soldiers stopped, assembled in rows and made deep obeisance, palms on the floor, foreheads touching it. Slowly and with dignity, shoes clicking on the floor, King Elara descended the steps of the platform and advanced, a gaunt predator. He reached the stretcher and stood to its left, facing it. He glanced almost casually in our direction. His eyes began to glitter as they sought and held those of Prince Vipula.

Most men would have quailed before that look, but not Prince Vipula. There was a glint of amusement somewhere in the corners of his steady eyes. Standing straight and tall, head erect, but very relaxed, he returned the King's piercing look with the calm hauteur of the aristocrat. The battle was that of two men at either end of the rope in a tug-of-war. Neither contestant would give an inch. The tension, worse than the pull on a rope, vibrated the air.

Suddenly there came a thump, a creak on the platform. All eyes were riveted immediately to its source.

From behind the throne a small figure emerged, a stumpy body clad in a black-and-white clown's costume. The large, rolling head was covered by a yellow cap, the bells on it jingling. The eyes were full of mischief. A sigh of something like relief swept the chamber.

I glanced at King Elara. He was staring at his court jester, the dwarf Junda, puzzled by the interruption. I

78

looked at my uncle. His body was as relaxed as before. His eyes were still on the King. They had never wavered. A thrill of pride shot through me. The love I felt for my uncle surged and throbbed within me, seeking to pour out of my eyes.

King Elara's gaze flickered momentarily back to Prince Vipula. The amused glint in the Prince's eyes had become slightly more obvious. I could feel rather than see King Elara flush. He had been the one to look away during the tug-of-war. I knew then that he had suffered a wound he would not lightly forgive or forget, perhaps for the very reason that it had been self-inflicted through the innate lack in him of something that Prince Vipula possessed. After all, King Elara was only a nobleman by birth, a soldier by profession, a king by conquest. Prince Vipula had the blood of many generations of kings in his veins.

King Elara turned to the dwarf again. 'What means this unseemly interruption?' he demanded harshly.

Again I felt his sudden flush at having unthinkingly broken his own weapon of silence. He had lost twice to Prince Vipula, the first time with a glance, now with words.

'No interruption, sire,' the jester countered in a piping voice. 'I come forward to stand beside my king and pay my respects to a dead friend.'

King Elara waved the jester away with a flick of his wrist, then, in the same motion, swiftly drew back the white sheet. A gasp from those watching rose to the painted ceiling, to be lost in its medley of gaudy figures depicting Chola mythology. The King's eyes were fixed on the corpse.

Suddenly, unexpectedly, he spoke again, his voice quiet, contrasting with his bitter eyes. 'Come forward with your companions, Prince Vipula,' he commanded. His eyes remained riveted to the corpse, as if he could not take them away, while some other part of him spoke the words. It was terrifying to witness and my stomach turned to *cunjee*.

Prince Vipula walked slowly and easily toward King Elara. In comparison, we shuffled behind him. He stopped on the opposite side of the table, still looking at the King. We ranged close to him. I found comfort in his easy grace.

More moments of silence followed again. Prince Vipula did not move his gaze from King Elara.

The King pointed to the corpse on the stretcher. 'What Sinhala did this?' he demanded, his voice emerging from a tight throat.

Prince Vipula looked at the corpse. My eyes followed to the horror of the mutilated neck, with its exposed white bone, blood-dried gristle, raw flesh and frayed skin, all blackened and decaying. Its high, sickly odour was beginning to mingle horribly with the spices used to disguise the stench of death. Seeing the corpse at close quarters was vastly different to what I had witnessed the previous evening. What a massive neck, I thought irrelevantly. What power in that stroke that sliced through it.

'Why a Sinhala, lord, when we do not even know whose body this is?' Prince Vipula questioned steadily. 'As you can see, it has no head.'

A flicker of expression crossed King Elara's face, so brief that few would have noticed it. Seeing it, I knew that my uncle had escaped the trap. I had not even known that it was laid.

King Elara spoke again, his voice more normal. 'We ought to be glad that you do not know of this murder.' Was he serious? 'This is all that remains of our Chief Warrior, the mighty Ratne Mahela. As you see, his great voice, which struck terror into enemy hearts on the battlefield, is stilled forever at its very source. He was foully murdered by a Sinhala named Velu Sumana, who claimed to be a Great Warrior of your cousin, Kakkavan Tissa, the overlord of Ruhuna.'

80

'Are you implying that my cousin, Kakkavan Tissa, Sovereign of Ruhuna, is involved, sire?' Prince Vipula inquired, pointedly giving the Ruhuna king the title King Elara had omitted. 'What reason would he have for such a deed?'

The King's face hardened. 'Listen to the story, in case you do not know it already.' This time there was no mistaking his meaning. 'Your Velu Sumana recently sought work in our palace, as a groom to Rasiah, our Chief Horsekeeper. He was given a job and soon showed himself so expert with horses that Rasiah entrusted him with the care of Vaha, our State horse. Early last morning Velu Sumana took Vaha to the Tissa Wewa to wash him down. Having gathered lotus there and woven a garland of it, Velu Sumana drew his sword, announced his true identity and sent a challenge to our Chief Warrior to meet him in single combat on neutral ground along the Ruhuna trail. He then galloped off. Mahela obtained our approval and gave chase on our second horse, ordering his men not to interfere. He obviously caught up with Velu Sumana at the edge of the Bintenne jungle.'

King Elara paused. He was trying to control his emotion, but his eyes were bright and unwinking on my uncle.

'I presume he lost the duel,' Prince Vipula observed dryly.

'Having lost his head and accepted a challenge, he lost the duel and lost his head,' Junda squeaked. 'In fact, he lost everything.'

'Be quiet!' the King shouted angrily. Mahela had been with him in many battles before the fourteen years of peace. He had cause to love the dead man, or at least to admire him.

The dwarf gave a lopsided grin and lapsed into silence.

'Our investigation of the body and reports we have had of the scene reveal that there could not have been a duel,' the King resumed quietly. He pointed a long, claw-like finger at the remains of the neck, from which the stink of rotting flesh was now more intense. 'We are told that there are no sword wounds on the body. Only the single slash of the executioner's sword that severed the neck – and the ravage of wild beasts and carrion who preyed on the corpse.' His voice shook, but he controlled himself. His glittering eyes returned to my uncle. 'When the Chief Warrior did not return last night, some of his men rode out early this morning to investigate. They found the body and reconstructed the crime. Mahela was waylaid, surprised and executed before he had a chance to defend himself. It had to be a surprise attack – else there would have been a few more dead bodies on the scene. One murder and two stolen horses. None but the Sinhala could be guilty, and we know of only four Sinhala, besides this Velu Sumana, who were at that very spot.' His eyes shot dark fire at each of us in turn.

I must confess that I quailed before his gaze, though I did not show it. My comfort was the knowledge that no one guessed at the facts, which only the four of us Sinhala knew.

'The very spot, my lord?' Prince Vipula's voice was quizzical. 'You mean he was executed at my lodge? Come now, that does no credit even to our intelligence.'

'Near enough, Prince,' King Elara retorted, but softly. 'Near enough. You and your three companions were near enough at the time.'

'You also credit us with too little honour, to suppose that we would take part in any such event, my lord, and too little good sense to return to Anu if we were involved. We are neither murderers nor horse thieves, and well you know it.'

'Are you denying any part in this matter, Prince?' King Elara demanded.

'Certainly, my lord.'

'On your honour as a prince?'

'Honour is honour, my lord, for prince or commoner. My word requires no oath. None of us even knew that Velu Sumana was in Anu. We have heard his name as a skilled

82

horseman and sword fighter, but we would not have recognized him for King Kakkavan Tissa's Chief Warrior, even if we had seen him.' My uncle turned around to look at each of us in turn. We all nodded.

The King seemed relieved. He was silent awhile, contemplating. He knew that my uncle would not lie. Yet I felt apprehension. If intensive interrogation were ordered, I would be the first to be questioned, since I was the youngest and the most likely to blurt out the truth under torture. I could almost feel the rack, the thin lighted tapers under my fingernails and the twisting irons, but I also had a desperate resolve to submit to anything without divulging what I knew. The feeling for my uncle, which had been steadily growing because of his courage and dignity, was now so tangible that I could grasp it and hold it to me for strength.

'Then who else could have been involved?'

The King's question removed most of the tension in the chamber. I could feel the bodies of the spectators relaxing and I too began feeling easier. It made me conscious of the increasing heat in the chamber, from the tapers and the human bodies. Someone even dared to cough. The smell of taper smoke now mingled with the horrible odour from Mahela's corpse.

'Velu Sumana may have had others from Ruhuna to help him,' my uncle responded. 'Yet if your Chief Warrior met his fate in the jungle, it could have been the work of Velu Sumana alone. A Chief Warrior in hot pursuit of a foe, expecting only a duel when he reached that foe, would easily succumb to a surprise attack.'

'But it was from the rear? How from the rear?'

My uncle thought awhile. Then his face brightened as if with inspiration. 'When a man is galloping a horse in the Chola style of riding, his rear is above him, lord.'

King Elara's head came up. He blinked rapidly in thought, then smote a hand against the dark granite table. 'Of course,' he grated. 'That's how it was done. The brave

Velu Sumana was perched on a tree and sliced our warrior's head as he rode beneath. Dear *devas*, what a way for Mahela to die. He could not even take on his enemy face to face, as he has done a hundred times.'

'Perhaps it was better so,' Prince Vipula remarked soberly. 'He never knew what was going to happen, so he will never experience the dishonour a man feels as he draws his last breath from being vanquished in battle. To have lain on the battlefield some day, knowing such shame, would have been a worse fate for a warrior so proud. And as for you, my lord,' – his eyes turned toward Digha Jantu's massive figure on the platform – 'your loss is also your gain, for I see standing there a worthy successor to the mighty Ratne Mahela as your Chief Warrior.'

A pleased look entered Digha Jantu's eyes. His nostrils distended. He bowed stiffly.

King Elara's attention was focused totally on my uncle. He had grasped the soothing words, but he also seemed to be in the grip of some dire feeling. I had a moment of stark intuition then. It filled me with pity. My mind struggled to capture it, but fruitlessly, so I gave up without even comprehending for whom it had been.

'You speak of future battles,' the King said. 'Do you then consider that this event presages war?'

'Only if you decree it, lord. I doubt that the Sinhala in Lanka desire it, since you have been a just ruler. I am unaware of any preparation for war in the Ruhuna or Malaya kingdoms. They are strong enough to defend, but not to attack. And if it were otherwise, you would be better informed of it than I.'

'There is no such evidence. Why then was this foul deed done? Is it some kind of defiance, some challenge?'

'I know why it was done,' Junda, the dwarf, interrupted. He sounded so deadly serious that we were all surprised, for it is the duty of court jesters to jest, not to be serious.

The King turned sharply on Junda. 'Why?' The single

word shot out of him like an arrow.

'I'll tell you, if you promise there will be no reprisals on any Sinhala in Lanka,' the dwarf asserted boldly.

'You shall tell us because otherwise we shall have you beaten and if necessary tortured.'

'But you won't, sire,' Junda retorted, very sure of himself, 'since you are the king of this foolish clown and others of your court, you are the King of Clowns.'

The dwarf's glance was at the courtiers and warriors, though his reference appeared to be to the other official jesters in the court. Catching his true meaning, King Elara could not restrain a slow smile.

'If you tortured one whose sole duty is to make jokes and tell funny stories, merely to discover the truth, people would say you were a foolish king,' Junda continued.

'How so?'

'Because only folly exists in a fool's brain and only a fool would take another fool seriously. A royal fool would become more a laughingstock of his subjects than a common fool like me. You wouldn't want that, would you?' The dwarf rolled his great eyes suggestively and bobbed his large, unwieldy head, the bells jingling once more.

A titter ran through the chamber. I felt a sudden respect for Junda. He was shrewd and he knew his king. Suddenly I realised that everything Junda had done this evening was deliberate, inviting the King's wrath against himself to save us.

'We shall do you the honour of taking you seriously for once and grant your wish with two exceptions.' King Elara looked pointedly at my uncle. 'First, we shall take drastic action if war or rebellion is intended anywhere. Next, we must take adequate measures for the present. But both exceptions depend on what you say being the truth.'

'Agreed. Here, then, is the truth.' The dwarf stood straight, his tiny sandalled feet apart, hands clasped behind his back, suddenly commanding the attention of everyone in the chamber. 'As you know, our Sinhala queen of Ruhuna, Vihara Maha Devi, may the *devas* protect her, became pregnant after many years of sterility. This had to be a gift of the *devas*, so when the Queen had three cravings, her *doladhook*, they also had to be from the *devas*, who must be satisfied regardless of the codes and affairs of men.'

King Elara seemed puzzled. 'What has all this to do with our Chief Warrior's death?' he demanded.

'Have patience, my lord, and hear what the cravings were. The first was that, while making a pillow for her head of a honeycomb one *usabha* long and resting on her left side in a beautiful bed, she should eat the honey remaining from that honeycomb, after she had given twelve hundred *bhikkus* of the true faith to eat of it. Now who would imagine that such a great honeycomb could ever exist?' He looked to the King for an answer.

The King shook his head. 'You tell us.'

'A fisherman miraculously found a canoe, one *usabha* long, filled with honey, lying on the Kirinda beach. It had no owner. A gift of the gods, wouldn't you say? Thus was Queen Devi's first craving satisfied.'

A look of wonderment entered the King's face. Being a Hindu, he believed completely in the power of the deities. He gestured briefly. 'Go on.'

'Queen Devi's second craving was that she should adorn herself with a garland of fresh lotus from the Tissa Wewa in Anu. The third was that she should drink water that had cleansed the sword that had severed the head of your Chief Warrior, with one of her feet placed on that very head!'

A shocked murmur went through the chamber. King Elara stood transfixed, staring at the dwarf, who ignored him and started playing with one of the bells on his cap, its pleasant tinkle incongruous in that sombre atmosphere. 'So you have earned merit by playing your part, sire, even indirectly, in satisfying cravings that could only come from the *devas*,' Junda added almost absently.

Oh! Shrewd, shrewd dwarf, I thought. Your mind is as great as your body is small.

'How do you know all this, fool?' Notwithstanding the question, the King's tone indicated that he believed Junda. I detected some relief in it, too. This did not surprise me, because it must indeed have been a pleasing resolution after all his alarm.

'Because it is the privilege of fools to discover more than the wise, who know all and need discover nothing and therefore end up knowing nothing. Kings are mainly concerned with their daily reports from spies in secret places. Neither spies nor kings listen to common gossip in the marketplace!'

The King's smile was almost cordial now. 'So you think there is no more to it? No plot, no plan for invasion?' The questions were directed to everyone in general.

Receiving no reply, the King proceeded. 'Then it only remains to avenge our Chief Warrior's murder. A life for a life is our law – regardless of whose life is taken. This Velu Sumana is a murderer and we must have his life. We shall demand his return from Ruhuna.'

'A demand that will not be met and can't be extracted is a foolish demand,' Junda countered imprudently, ' – and worthy only of a court jester!'

'Will you answer to the *devas* for this Velu Sumana's life while you believe that his actions were taken to satisfy the *devas*' desires, lord?' My uncle's voice was urbane, but his thrust was cunning.

King Elara's eyes turned hard. They began to glitter again. 'Justice must be meted out,' he stated harshly. 'The Sinhala are barbaric for the *devas* to make such gruesome demands through them.'

Prince Vipula's eyes flashed, but he only permitted himself a scornful smile.

'An example must be made,' the King continued. 'We cannot allow this sort of act in our kingdom, else everyone will satisfy their cravings and blame the *devas*.' A thoughtful note entered his voice and a gleam of malice showed in his eyes. 'Either Velu Sumana must be brought to us for justice, or we shall seek ways of bringing the lady for whom this foul deed was done to our court, so that the seed that prompted her mad craving might be destroyed.'

I was appalled, not merely at the words but at the quietude of their delivery. The hush in the chamber indicated that most of those present shared my horror.

Only Prince Vipula showed no visible sign of reaction. 'Are you saying that you would wage war on a woman and her unborn child, lord?' An edge, almost of contempt, tinged his voice.

'I repeat, our law is a life for a life, regardless,' the King declared grimly. His voice became charged with a deadly intention. 'We shall determine whose life it shall be in due course. Meanwhile, the jester's tale has the ring of truth. We shall investigate it thoroughly. For the present we shall take hostages, to ensure punishment of someone after our inquiries are made.'

His face hardened and the brown eyes took on a malignant expression. He looked pointedly at Prince Vipula. 'What more fitting hostage than a prince of royal blood, first cousin of both the queen who had such mad cravings and her husband, who sowed the seed of them in her. Prince Vipula, you shall be our hostage. You are under house arrest from this moment.'

I blanched, but my uncle merely smiled gravely and bowed. I could not escape the conclusion that he had expected this move and even invited it by his attitude. After all, he was capable of making a judgement as to what King Elara would do, because he knew what he would have done if he had been king. 'One request, my lord, if I am to remain a willing prisoner,' my uncle asserted.

'What is that?'

My uncle half turned to me. He looked at me with

affection such as I had never seen before in his eyes. It made my heart dance and my head sing. Then he faced the King again. 'As you know, Prince Rodana is an orphan and my ward. I have no brothers, sisters or blood relations in this court, Like me, the prince has no one here either. I request a safe-conduct for him to the Ruhuna court, where he can be looked after and spend the rest of his days with his kin.'

A thunderous force swept through me. No, no, I wanted to cry. I will stay with you, my uncle, and suffer any fate that might befall us.

King Elara's brooding eyes were on me. Deliberately, I avoided his gaze, but I knew that he nonetheless sensed my deep, desperate feelings for my uncle. I had given him a weapon. Desperately I thought of something wild I could do that would condemn me to live forever, or die, with my uncle.

My training held. Princes cannot act impulsively. Princes are obedient and disciplined. Such is the Code – but how I hated the Code at this moment!

'He will become a stalwart prince one day,' King Elara observed at last. 'He could rally Sinhala in Lanka to the cause, if the child of Kakkavan is the male for whom great things, including our own throne, have been predicted. We want no threats to our rule and that of Prince Muthiah after us. Besides, we suspect that his loyalty to you, the present Sinhala heir, could exceed good sense!'

Only then did it dawn on me that the King also had aims for his seventeen-year-old son. Prince Muthiah was King Elara's only child. Kings look far into the future – beyond their own life-spans – when they have children. King Elara would stop at nothing to ensure safe succession for his son, which he might desire even more than his own security on the throne.

'We must keep potential enemies either where we can observe them, or where they cannot harm us,' the King went on, his smile enigmatic.

'What does my lord desire, since my request would obviously remove Prince Rodana from your observation?' Prince Vipula inquired.

'Prince Rodana shall have a safe-conduct to the Ruhuna court, on a condition that would ensure his security and that of our succession for the rest of his life.'

'And that condition, my lord?'

'Your nephew shall enter one of the Ruhuna temples as an *abithaya* no later than seven days after the child is born to the Ruhuna queen, if it turns out to be a male child. Provided, of course, that we are unable to destroy the evil seed before it springs to life.' The King's expression was totally malignant now, yet his white teeth were bared in an urbane smile. He raised a dark hand, fingers pointing upward. 'Do you swear this on your sacred word of honour, Prince?'

My uncle turned his head to look expressionlessly at me, except for a quick shaft of compassion in his glance. Then he faced King Elara again. 'You must realize, lord, that I can give you my word today, as I am Prince Rodana's guardian, but I am in no position to ensure that he will qualify to become a fully fledged monk when he is of age, or that he would wish to be ordained, or even that he will remain in a temple thereafter.'

'Your point is well taken. Let us not talk of future situations, then. Do you give us your word that the Prince will enter one of the Ruhuna temples as an *abithaya* and remain there until he comes of age?'

My uncle squared his shoulders. 'I swear it,' he said firmly, with a lift of his head.

'If we are denied the presence of Velu Sumana, or of this lady before the end of this year, the child will reportedly be born early in the month of Citta. We shall arrange, through our channels, for information as to whether Prince Rodana was admitted to a temple accordingly. If he was not, your life shall immediately be forfeit, Prince Vipula, at your own hands?'

Prince Vipula bowed courteously in acquiescence. 'You have my word on it,' he affirmed.

Chapter 8

Prince Vipula was anxious to get me off to Ruhuna the very next morning, fearing that King Elara might change his mind. Being only twelve, I had no choice, though I longed to remain with him.

On our return to the mansion, he directed Vira and Hari to return before daylight with their escorts to their homes in the country. He sent his chief aide to collect my safe-conduct pass from the palace, requesting that it be a permanent one and not merely for the journey to Ruhuna.

'After all, I want you to be free to come back to me someday,' he declared, placing a hand briefly on my shoulder. In spite of his words, I recognized that his life was in jeopardy.

After all the arrangements for my journey were made, the four of us had dinner together. When we had eaten, the servants retired with final salutations and Prince Vipula directed me to accompany him to his study. We excused ourselves from Vira and Hari and I bade them farewell. They would be gone before I was up and about the next morning.

The study was a large, elegant room, decorated in white and gold to set off the black ebony furniture. I looked around it dismally in the light of the tall brass oil lamps.

My earlier visits to this study had been for formal conversations about my lessons, military training or welfare – occasionally for reproof. Tonight was different. I could tell from feelings within me, the atmosphere of the room and the spirit-force emanating from Prince Vipula. He indicated a chair opposite his desk and I sat down.

'It is important that you know something about the politics of our island kingdom,' Prince Vipula said gravely, 'so listen carefully.' He was talking man-to-man.

I nodded, wide-eyed.

Prince Vipula smiled at my obvious pleasure. His dark eyes crinkled at the sides. I smiled back. It was the first genuine smile we had ever exchanged and I felt a sense of intense well-being.

A quick nod indicated Prince Vipula's own acknowledgement of what now existed between us. 'As you know, we have three kingdoms in our beloved island,' he resumed. 'Lanka, Ruhuna, of which Mahagama is the capital city; and Malaya, the capital of which is Kelaniya. King Kakkavan Tissa succeeded to the throne of Ruhuna only because his uncle, Jaya Bahu, died leaving only a son, Digha Bahu, who was but a child at the time and unable to rule. Shortly after King Kakkavan's accession, King Elara used guile and force to establish a subkingdom in Seru, between the southeastern border of Lanka and the northeastern border of Ruhuna. He set up a puppet king in Seru, named Siva, thus creating a buffer for Lanka and a threat to Ruhuna in the event of attack. This is the political setup in which Prince Digha Bahu, who is governor and sub-king of the Dighavapi region, finds himself. Have you heard of him?'

I shook my head. 'I have but heard his name mentioned in passing,' I replied.

'Then it is time you learned something about this young man.' A sober note entered my uncle's voice. 'As soon as the Prince came of age, King Kakkavan scored a diplomatic triumph by giving the Prince his own sister, Kusuma, in marriage. Prince Digha Bahu and the Princess Kusuma now have a three-year-old boy, Prince Panduka. I have a feeling this boy will be just as dangerous as his father when he grows up. Prince Rodana, can you see the forces that are gathering?'

'Prince Digha Bahu will want the succession for himself,' I responded eagerly, 'at least after King Kakkavan dies. He will certainly want it for his son as well.'

My uncle nodded approvingly. 'Good! And?'

The knowledge hit me like a flash. 'Prince Digha Bahu will be mortified at the birth of a male heir to King Kakkavan,' I almost shouted.

'Precisely. But what you do not know is that, being the sort of person he is, the Prince will not be content to let matters rest. He is greedy and ambitious. Of this I must warn you. Although I would normally prefer you to find out such things for yourself, the time is short.' A sombre expression flitted across my uncle's face.

'Thank you for telling me, uncle. I know you do not like to speak ill of others.'

My uncle acknowledged my remark with a graceful wave of his hand. 'You will therefore see that, apart from King Elara, there is another source of danger, within the Ruhuna palace itself, for the baby that is still in its mother's womb. Once he is born, his real problems will develop if Prince Digha Bahu and King Elara join forces.'

'How could that ever happen?' I asked in amazement.

The handsome face before me tightened into grim lines. 'Prince Digha Bahu is ambitious enough to want to rule the entire island kingdom. Such men make the strangest alliances to serve their ends, hoping with each step to tread on those who stand immediately in their way and finally to turn on their allies one by one. Even thieves unite against a common enemy, before they slit each other's throats!'

'But King Elara wants his son, Prince Muthiah, to succeed him,' I persisted. 'He said as much tonight.'

'Certainly, but much can happen between now and King Elara's death. Prince Digha Bahu's first and most direct threat is the new baby. If it is a male, he will do everything in his power to destroy it.'

I was aghast.

My uncle stood up to give his words emphasis and I immediately stood up too, because we are trained not to be seated when our elders are standing. 'He would go to any lengths, because he does not believe in honour. He is typical of those who connive for power.' The conviction in my uncle's voice was reflected in his eyes as he looked down at me. 'The baby on whom we have pinned all our hopes has so much against him. So very much.' His voice dropped almost to a whisper, but his eyes penetrated mine. 'Your purpose in life will be to help this child to your utmost in the achievement of the hopes of all Sinhala patriots.'

'How can I, uncle? I am not equipped for it. Besides, I am now destined for the temple.'

He shook his head. He was gripped by the inner sight at that moment. 'No!' His voice rang clear. 'Even if you enter the temple, you will return to serve the saviour of our country and our pride. You were born to this destiny.'

I stared at him, speechless. He seemed exalted. Suddenly the question hit me in the pit of my stomach and I felt sick with it. I tried three times to speak, but could not, because of the pain and disappointment.

It was only when the look left his face that my clamour found its outlet in words. 'Is this why you are rescuing me and sending me to Ruhuna?' I cried.

He looked at me, his brow knit in bewilderment for a few moments, this man who never displayed his feelings. Then his face cleared. 'No!' he declared steadily. 'You might as well know the real reason, for I had not thought of your future role until after the decision to send you away to safety.' He paused, as if he were on unfamiliar ground and needed to fix his bearings. Finally, he looked at me with great tenderness. 'It is because I love you,' he said quietly. He paused. 'Now go to bed. You have a long day ahead of you.' There was a hush to his voice. He felt the emotion, but did not want to display it.

I left the study without looking back.

I slept only in fits and starts that night. Each time I woke, I seemed to hear the words of the Buddha, 'Desire causes clinging and clinging begets suffering,' against the background of a new and more satisfying sentiment: the desire to hold onto the uncle I loved.

The next morning was cool and grey. I stood on the veranda of the house, ready to leave. The air was so thin that the sweet scent of jasmine lay fine on it, not heady. The dark outlines of trees were white-clothed in mist and dew sparkled at their roots. Cocks began crowing lustily to greet the pale silver of the first dawn streaks.

A crystal-clear clip-clop of hooves announced the arrival of the wagon, drawn by two horses. It emerged from the mists like a ghost vehicle in a bad dream. This was indeed a nightmare to me.

Hari and Vira had departed hastily for their homes some time earlier. On the veranda, I bade farewell to the servants and family retainers who had gathered to offer me salutations, gifts and, unexpectedly, a few tears. I was particularly sad to bid good-bye to old Banda, a lean, tall Sinhala with silver hair and a stern face that could break into a kindly smile. I had been his special care for years. He broke down, sobbing unashamedly, and I was hard put to restrain myself. I turned aside hastily and strode away, for my uncle awaited me in front of the house.

As I stepped from the veranda, he held his arms out to me. I ran to him, stunned but joyful. It was the first time any person had ever held me. He had a clean odour of sandalwood. The feel of him was so firm and strong, it infused me with a sense of security. Its curious comfort made my spirit dissolve into shimmering air, like water in a noonday haze. Unknown, unexpressed needs of a little boy wanting family, without ever realizing it, broke loose from their hidden confines, to mingle with untold fears about my barren future and my uncle's safety. They found their outlet in weeping.

Yes, I wept as my uncle embraced me, his body rigid with self-control, his arms fast around me. I breathed the essence of his *prana* then, strangely mixed with his scent. In so doing, I had knowledge of that part of Prince Vipula's spirit that was empty, lonely, bereft, because he, too, like me, had no one. It was so much more bitter for him because, unlike me, he was an adult; he had known the communion of parents, relatives and women. While I could only guess at my lack, he knew what he did not have. Surely, when you have tasted the fragrant caress of mountain breezes, your longing to return to them from the hot, barren wastes of the salt pans is more intense.

In spite of his obvious feelings, Prince Vipula's concern in those final moments remained for me. His hands moved to my arms. Gripping them gently, he held me back to look at me. 'You need never fear life,' he advised. 'You are well equipped for it. I have only promised King Elara that you will enter the temple, not that you will become a monk or remain one. You are free to leave the temple when you are old enough to make your own decisions. You do not have to remain his hostage, as he intends. And if I die, you are immediately free of the promise.'

He saw that I was about to break down at his words and drew me to him again, to comfort me. I wanted to cry out to him, to beg him not to let me go, but that was not our way, so I merely clung to his embrace until he pushed me gently back once more and looked at my swimming eyes. His own were clear and bright, but his face was drawn.

'I'm going to tell you something that no one else knows,' he declared. 'It is said that I had your father killed. That is not true. My guilt is that I might have prevented his murder – it was no less – but could not intervene in time.'

I stifled my cry.

'Having deprived you of a father, I have not married, to deprive myself of a child. It resulted in my holding back from you. It was only the day before yesterday that I realized I had made you pay for my guilt. So you have paid twice and a hundredfold. And it is tearing at me, especially now that I'm losing you.'

He paused to control himself. 'I told myself in the past that I was doing my best. How pathetic! Doing one's best is never enough. It is the lame excuse of those who fail.' He held me still closer. 'Give your all to this new prince and you will surely develop more to give. I shall miss you deeply. Think of me at times and, when you do, think of me kindly.'

He kissed my cheek and turned me towards the wagon. '*Ayubowan*, my *putha*.' It was the first time he had called me son.

I was too young to realize that my turn for atonement had to lie ahead. I felt as if my heart was breaking. Sobs jerked out of me. My face was streaming with tears. My throat was sore, my chest tight. I looked at the wagon. The blur of my trunk was being lifted into the back – all my future worldly possessions.

My escort of four armed Sinhala retainers rode up, with a clatter of hooves and creaking leather, to take their positions on either side of the wagon. They were all sturdy men with wrinkled faces, long hair tied up beneath white turbans and well-trimmed beards. They had been with our family for years.

One of the horses sneezed violently. Another blew in unison. I felt the pocket of my tunic to ensure that my safe-conduct pass under the King's seal was in it.

Almost as an afterthought, my uncle called to me. I swung around and he came up close. 'When Queen Devi's child is born, I am sure it will be a male child,' he stated quietly. 'For whatever cause, my life may then be sacrificed. Do not take it hard.'

I gazed at him speechlessly and he smiled. 'You have yet

to learn the cruelty and cunning of those who govern and those who would wield power behind thrones. Despite mighty titles, rulers are still human and it is in the nature of humans to be inhuman.' This time his smile was slow and sad. 'Serve the prince to be born. Set his life and its purpose before your own and even before your daily living, until he unifies this entire island kingdom under his rule as a Sinhala king.' Prince Vipula's voice had grown fierce, his whole being vibrant. 'He is our saviour. He will make the winds of Sinhala sweep through our land and unite it under our banner.'

'I promise.'

'Go now. The blessings of the Triple Gem be with you and may the *devas* guard you.'

I turned, walked slowly to the wagon and sat beside the driver. My last glimpse of my uncle was of his slim, elegant figure outlined against the white house, his raised palms together in salute. It was partly farewell, partly benediction, partly an invitation to gallantry lying ahead.

Chapter 9

Following my uncle's orders, we pushed on as hard as the horses would allow and spent the first night at the hunting lodge. I felt miserably alone here, remembering other times.

After yet another sleepless night, I was up before dawn the next day for the resumption of our journey. My eyes stung when the servants and retainers made final salutation to me, but I walked away without breaking down. I would weep no more. So much had always been bottled up within me. Now it seemed too much. It was choking me. I was a tight bubble of misery being squeezed and ready to burst at any time, but I would remain intact, I would be a man. I would be like my uncle.

Having fresh horses, we made good speed and quickly arrived at the place of Mahela's execution. The *massa* was intact. The green glade and the shadowy tree on which Velu Sumana had awaited his quarry were there, but they were unreal to me, as if the events they had enfolded were part of a play.

It is difficult to comprehend that unrelated events can cause such drastic changes. I simply could not ascribe all such events to some *kharmic* cycle. The lives of people are intertwined, as are the lives of all things, including these horses, the trees around me, those rocks, this creaking wagon and even the parts of which they are made. How can there be a destiny based exclusively upon the consequences of one's own actions?

I had learned the Buddhist doctrine at the temple school. *Kharma* is cause, *vipaka* effect. Every cause has an effect, which in turn becomes a cause for another effect, all in an endless cycle. There is no invisible, eternal, infinite score being kept, as in a game of *chuk-goodoo* between two teams. The cause and effect are there. Yet how could I ordain my own life, guide it in its firm direction toward the goal of Enlightenment, by the simple expedient of following the Noble Eightfold Path, when myriad other lives and life forms were having their own causes and effects within me and without me?

Alas, I was too young then to do more than conjecture that I had carried the feel of the one God, the superior creator, in my *prana* for years. Without realizing it, I had already reached Him the only possible way, through an inner consciousness, rather than from thought, reasoning or even feeling.

By the time I ended my contemplation, we had left the dark jungle behind and were jogging through sunlit rice fields. Green paddy leaves bent in waves before flurries of wind. The peasants' cottages were more lowly here, built of wattle and daub, some stained white with lime plaster. They had roofs of grey *cadjan* coconut thatch or faded yellow straw.

Women dressed in bright cloths and jackets, with baskets of vegetables on their heads or clay water-chatties at their hips, swayed gracefully at the sides of the highway. The occasional bullock cart was laden with produce. A driver would jab a toe at his animal's soft posterior, crying '*Chuk-pita-muk!*' to make it sprint. As its head tossed from side to side, the bells around the beast's neck would jingle and rhyme with the sharp clatter of its hooves.

In a large village, a group of bare-bodied beggars sat leaning against the boundary wall of its temple. One of them, an ancient, rose painfully to his feet and came hobbling toward us with the aid of a stick, extending a gnarled brown hand, begging for alms. It was probably his turn in the schedule these beggars set for themselves. I tossed him a coin and was rewarded with the words 'May the gods bless you with more and more.' He was blind.

A young, sunburned man pushed himself along on a board with a pair of wheels at either end. His long hair was well combed; his body glittered with beads of sweat. Both his legs were stumps at the knees.

I stopped reflecting on my own plight in the face of the tragedies in this village.

Farther on, we rode through miles of jungle again, then entered cultivated areas and poor villages, the mud huts mere hovels. We also passed many forts, including the massive Vijitapura, which was manned by Cholas. Over a thousand Sinhala clad only in span-cloths were toiling here in the noonday sun, improving the moat under the watchful eyes of Chola guards. Tired as they were, taut muscles gleaming beneath sweat-soaked skins, they sang to time their efforts. '*Ho-di . . . hellay! Hellay, hellay!*'

'They are prisoners,' the wagoner observed quietly. 'Free

labour for the Cholas.'

We arrived at the border outpost on the north bank of the great river late in the evening. The place teemed with Chola soldiers. The ferryboat awaited us. It did not take us long to get through the formalities needed for my crossing into Ruhuna. The King's safe-conduct, with his seals on it, cleared the way. I scanned it before replacing it in my tunic pocket.

The grey ferryboat, time- and water-worn, pulled slowly away into the dusk-gleam of a river caught up with the deep crimson of the setting sun. I returned the final shouted farewells of my escort and the wagon driver. As they gradually became shadows on the bank, a feeling of utter desolation gripped me. Free at last from the fear that accompanies life in a foreigner's court, I should have been happy, relieved. Instead, I was miserable and lonely. So must a solitary star feel in a clouded night sky.

As the ferryboat creaked across the water, silver-grey in the semi-darkness, the old boatman started a chant: '*Bada gini vela* . . .' It was the tale of a hungry woman, begging for food from her rich son, who is doled out a single *chundoo* of rice by him. 'Did I measure my milk, my son, when I fed you at my breast?'

Transported by the sad, haunting notes of the chant, I heard the river speak to me from its eternal bosom. For the first time, I knew a river's heart, beneath its splash and gurgle. The endless flow of its communion was the kin of unceasing winds in the air, the consistent drumming of the earth and the whispering within the body of a fire. Fire, air, earth, water – the four elements – all have the gift of communion with man, whom they created, from whom they derive and with whom they are joined. I reached in quietude for the abandonment of my personal being, to merge with the river and the life-pulse within its flow.

The river beat became my heartbeat and I knew that we did indeed each come from the other. Out of my innermost being, I gave back my own message of oneness and love. The river heard me and acknowledged it. I felt uplifted. The sigh of the waters turned into a song that melted into the old man's chant again.

A 'hoo-oo-oo!' distracted me and I turned to find the opposite bank suddenly looming before us. Flaming torches lighted up clusters of Sinhala border guards and the shadowy figures of a group of men who were obviously there to meet the boat. Since I was its only occupant, they had to be waiting for me. I felt a glow of security.

The boat glided toward the landing. The ferryman's chanting turned to grunts as he helped his comrade brake the boat. I heard a murmur of voices from the waiting group, one voice dominant.

I was surprised to find that the Ruhuna side looked no different to the Lanka side. The trees fringing the high yellow bank had the same outlines, the bushes cluttering its edge the same shapes. Even the mud smelled the same and the air was just as humid. Now, deep inside me, I suddenly understood the oneness of my country.

In the foreground of the group awaiting me at the Ruhuna side of the ferry was a tall, stoutly built young man with fair skin and a black moustache. He was dressed in red pantaloons and a gold tunic. I could tell from his headgear – a tasselled gold turban – the gold scabbard of his sword, studded with jewels, and his arrogant air that he was of the royal family. He did not come forward to greet me, but leaned on his silver-mounted ebony staff, waiting for me to go to him and make my salutation. Even when he returned it, his smile was belied by pale, inscrutable eyes, which immediately troubled me.

'I am Prince Rodana Singha Devanam Piyalage Sri Wickrema,' I announced formally, as I had been taught.

'You are a second cousin of ours, I understand . . . er . . . sort of . . .' He emphasized the last words. His features were broad, the nose small but fleshy. Even in that uncertain light, I noticed that his eyes were pale brown, like pebbles. A wise monk had once warned me never to trust men with such eyes. His obvious dig at my bastard birth was shocking.

'You are greeting Digha Bahu Devanam Piyalage Kumara Singha,' the Prince continued. 'I am governor and sub-king of this province. As the King's brother-in-law and the heir to the kingdom, I welcome you to Ruhuna. I hope you had a pleasant journey.'

'Yes, thank you. We made speed, but the journey itself was uneventful.'

'Did you take note of the Chola fortresses of Ambati, Vijitapura and Gallaka along the way?'

'No, sir. There was scarcely time for more than a cursory glance when we were stopped at the checkpoints.'

Prince Digha frowned disapprovingly. 'A wasted opportunity,' he remarked.

He turned away, pointing with his staff in the direction of a spread of yellow lights, flickering in the dark between trees and vegetation. 'Our palanquins will take us to the *Kimbul-tota* fort, where you will spend the night. It is one of seven forts I command on our borders. I am commander-in-chief of the entire northern region of Ruhuna.' He looked at my single trunk with scorn. 'Is that all the luggage you have?'

I nodded.

'Do they not teach you how to live in the Chola court, or are you all ascetic like King Elara?' he demanded. 'By the way, I understand that Elara has taken the vow of *brachmachariya*. Tell me, does he never lie with anyone? Can it be that he is homosexual?'

Prince Digha's pale eyes surveyed me with malicious enjoyment, the thin eyebrows arched.

I had been trained to show respect and restraint, especially toward elders, but I suddenly knew that I was going to have to assert myself if I was to survive in this strange new world. From beneath an instinctive longing for my uncle to protect me, something savage, yet cold as hailstones in the high mountains, burst forth within me. Perhaps it was the stronger instinct for survival. 'I am afraid I cannot enlighten you, cousin,' I replied. 'I have been taught that curiosity, especially about the sex lives of others, is the prerogative of pimps and panderers. I am certain you would not seriously expect me to be guilty of such a breach of etiquette. You must surely be testing me!'

While upbraiding him for his poor manners, I had left him an outlet to save face.

Prince Digha scowled. 'Of course,' he responded. 'I'm glad you passed the test. Let us be on our way.'

The fort rose above the river. The jungle around it had been cleared, so its orange *kabook* ramparts and massive wooden gates were stark against the night sky, except where flickering lights from the turrets pricked the dark mass like stars.

I was so tired and seat-weary when we finally reached the fort that I barely noticed my surroundings or ate dinner. The food, served in a great central hall, was quite different from that of the Anu court. They used more spices and salt here, especially chili (which stung my mouth, setting it on fire), gamboge for sourness and sweet anise – a superb blend. There was also an abundance of tasty white fish such as I had never eaten before, called *thora*.

I sat on Prince Digha's right, as an honoured guest, at the teakwood dining table. By the time we were halfway through dinner, Prince Digha was halfway to being drunk on the heady *sura* that he and his commanders were consuming, and his tongue had been loosened. 'You must understand, cousin,' he said, more amiable now, but the eyes still merciless, 'that I am by birth the real heir to this kingdom. I was too young to succeed when my father died.' He leaned closer to me. 'King Kakkavan is but a usurper,' he whispered confidentially. 'Actually, as a matter of fact, he holds the throne in trust for me.' He nodded slowly and deliberately, in the manner of drunks.

I was disgusted and ready to ignore him, but suddenly I remembered my promise to my uncle. If Prince Digha expected to succeed King Kakkavan, what of the prince to be born? What of all the prophecies? What of the united island kingdom? I somehow had to discover more about Prince Digha's intentions while I had the opportunity.

'What of the baby Queen Vihara Maha Devi is expecting?' I ventured.

Prince Digha blew through his lips coarsely. 'Actually, as a matter of fact, it had best be a girl.' He was stuttering. Then his eyes became sharp and his face grew taut. 'If it is a boy, he will have a long way to go before he becomes king. A *long* way.' He drew out the word 'long' with a wealth of meaning to it and I shuddered involuntarily. 'First me as king – not just of Ruhuna, but the entire island after the Chola dies. Then my son, Prince Panduka. King Kakkavan has already agreed. Digha will go down in history as the glorious name of a house in its own right.' His voice grew fierce, the more intense because he was speaking for my ears alone. 'There is no room in this kingdom for any other rulers. Actually, as a matter of fact' – I was to discover that this was his favourite phrase when excited – 'you give me your loyalty and I shall reward you.'

I drew back instinctively. This was almost treason, but there were no witnesses to it. Prince Digha noted my reaction. 'Pah!' he exclaimed. 'Do you deny me?' He glowered at me. 'Remember, I rule here. These forts' – he gestured with his hand – 'this region. They are all vital to the defence of Ruhuna. They are a springboard to any assault on Lanka. I hold the balance of power with twenty thousand trained men.'

'Your words are bright with promises,' I stated, looking him in the eye, 'but I am meant for the temple, so there is no way in which I can serve you.'

Prince Digha appraised me and I returned his look unflinchingly. He seemed to sense something in me that

105

made him look away, then glance quickly back as if to catch me off guard. He could not, because my face was inscrutable. He resumed his conversation with his commanders.

Immediately after dinner, the events of the past three days, including the tensions of the journey and my strange conversation, caught up with me. I excused myself from Prince Digha and went to my bed-chamber, leaving him with his commanders and courtiers to carry on drinking the *sura* they seemed to be enjoying so much.

I quickly dozed off and slept as one who had taken *ganja*.

We left the next morning. After a breakfast of *appa*, milk-rice, assorted curries and fruit, I was glad to find a horse awaiting me, along with a cart for my trunk. Prince Digha was not there to see me off, but sent his excuses. He was perhaps sleeping off the effects of his drinking bout of last night. I could not say I missed him. One of his captains and six cavalrymen formed my escort.

We first rode through forest lands. At noon, we stopped by a crystal-clear stream for a brief meal and to water the horses. It was peaceful here. Wild wood-apple trees, with their thick, dark clusters of leaves, between which sunlight just prickled, tall emerald elephant grass, the gurgle of the stream, the smell of the sweating horses and wet leather brought to mind the jungle lodge. My throat constricted and hurt, my eyes began to smart, but I thrust the grief aside. Oh, indeed I have grown to manhood, I thought. And then, as the river had done last evening, the jungle, with its myriad secret sounds, began speaking to me.

Last evening, water; this noon, earth. I had a feeling that it would be a long time before air and fire gave me their messages.

The countryside slowly changed after we left that jungle nook. It became completely flat, except for the seven hills of the sacred shrine of Kataragama, which the captain showed me with veneration, looming purple in the distance. The air was drier and more invigorating, in spite of the heat.

We rode in silence through vast stretches of bright green rice fields. Brown paddy birds darted off at our approach. Black-and-red flies swarmed around manure heaps. The occasional cottage, with mud or whitewashed walls and roofs of grey coconut thatch, was set in green islands of coconut palm, breadfruit, jak and mango.

It was peaceful until we came to the first village and heard the shrill screams of children playing *marsok*, a team game, in the compound of the village centre. Some of them were about my age, but I had no desire to join in their play.

Soon we began passing bare-bodied peasants returning home from the fields, with mud-stained *mamoties* on their shoulders. Their skins were burned dark by the sun, their faces shaded by white turbans. They grinned at us as we rode by.

Along an open stretch of fields, we heard the cackle of laughter and glanced in its direction. Two rheumy-eyed old hags had set up a small, open straw-roofed shed outside their *cadjan* cottage. Within the shed was a counter laden with fresh vegetables, half-ripe mangoes and blackened clay pots containing buffalo curd. White sacks made of kenaf, filled with *kitul* honey, hung from the support beams of the shed along with bunches of yellow plantains.

'Buy some delicious curd, travellers!' one of the old women called out. 'You won't get it this fresh in Mahagama.'

'Nothing is fresh in Mahagama for the young!' the other hag shouted, her toothless gums bared in a bawdy laugh.

I was amazed at the freedom of these women. Did the people of Ruhuna not observe Sinhala manners?

We made good progress and reached the outskirts of Mahagama by late afternoon. To our right, the giant white pinnacle of the Tissa *dagoba* thrust upward to the skies from a green ridge of trees. It was a remarkable sight, this cathedral of Ruhuna. Having a suspicion that it was where I would be sent as apprentice monk, I wanted very much to see the temple, but we were expected in Mahagama before nightfall and the trail looped away from the temple premises, around the great silver sheet of the Tissa reservoir.

The captain nodded toward the reservoir. 'It not only provides irrigation, flood control and water to the people, but is also one of Mahagama's natural western defences. The eastern defence line is the sea, which turns westward to form our southern barrier as well. Salt pans and marshes to the south of the city add to Nature's ocean defence.'

The bridge on which we began clattering spanned a river that had to be the northern defence line of the city. It had all undoubtedly helped deter King Elara from invading Ruhuna.

When we finally reached Mahagama, I was disappointed to find it to be no more than a collection of scattered townships. I had expected something on the order of a miniature Anu. Instead, we rode over a paved main street, fronted by walls inset by doors leading into small homes with baked-brick walls and white country-tiled roofs. The tradesmen's homes and display rooms would be on back streets, but it was obvious that, unlike Anu, Mahagama did not have separate areas for the twenty-eight craftsmen's guilds. I surmised that a weekly fair, to which farmers and vendors would bring their produce, rather than a regular marketplace, served the day-to-day needs of the townships.

A steady roar in the distance, accompanied by a strange, clammy feel to the air and a distinctive smell, reached us. I cocked an ear and sniffed.

The captain smiled. 'You have never seen the ocean, have you?' he inquired.

'No,' I confessed. 'The Tissa lake in Anu is big as an ocean, but that is all.'

'Wait until you see the noisy *ho-gana-pokuna*,' he remarked. He was a very pleasant middle-aged fellow.

I was stunned at my first glimpse of the sea. I had heard descriptions of it, but still could not believe my eyes and ears.

We dismounted on a white sand beach that seemed to stretch endlessly, fringed by green ground-cover on one side and the sea on the other. I stood spellbound, though the sun was pitiless and the glare hurt my eyes. The unending expanse of dark blue water, scuffed by whitecaps that breezes spurred, with nothing on it save its own movement, has to be seen to be believed. The heaving bosom, the rolling waves, scarred by brown sand, finally splashing and foaming with a seething noise, only to retreat endlessly, held me captive. This is not the work of *devas*, I thought, or of some *kharmic* law. How could it be? It always existed, the body of the Creator, or was created of itself through its own forces.

'This is the Kirinda beach, on which our Queen Vihara Devi was washed ashore in her boat after she was consigned to the ocean, while still a maiden, by her father, the King of Kelaniya.' The captain interrupted my thoughts. 'Our King Kakkavan Tissa found her here and married her.'

He saw that I knew of the event and was pleased.

I had a glimmer of understanding of what the lonely maiden must have endured while a speck at the mercy of the infinite, for if this was the ocean in calm, it had to be awesome in storm.

'It's time we were going,' the captain reminded me.

After an hour of riding, judging from the shadows, we saw the turreted ramparts of the Mahagama palace. It was set on a slight promontory, around which was open grassland burned brown by the sun, dotted with shrub and cactus. Its southern barrier of salt pans shimmered white and pink beyond. A sapphire ocean formed a natural moat to the east and a dark man-made moat encircled the ramparts to the north and west.

We trotted slowly over the north drawbridge and stopped to identify ourselves at the guard posts. Onlookers stared at us curiously. They must have known that we had ridden a long way, because our horses were lathered with sweat and we too were wet and covered with dust.

I was surprised to find that security measures were very lax here. People kept coming and going into the palace premises as if it were a fairground. A young family walked in through the gates without being checked. The broad-shouldered man strutted ahead, while his fat, rosy-cheeked wife and four plump children trailed in single file behind him like a gaggle of ducks.

A group of men, wearing white *dhotis* and bright-coloured *kurthas*, squatted in a circle on the courtyard beyond, chewing betel and arguing loudly. One of them turned sideways to project a stream of red betel juice onto the grey paving stones.

The reedy melody of a snake charmer's flute curled through the air. I could see his green-turbaned head and crouched figure through the screen of spectators around him. I even caught a fleeting glimpse of his cobra in the open wicker basket, hood unbared, swaying to the music. The poor creature must have been defanged long ago and its hiss was less impressive than a threat through empty guns. No wonder the spectators looked bored. They were only killing time, watching the show.

A black racing buggy, drawn by two smart brown-and-white bullocks, rattled through the gates as if emerging from a private mansion. Its owner, a bald man, obviously a newly rich *mudalali* businessman, had a great moon face, supported by a brace of double chins. His head gleamed with sweat, his eyes with pride at having an unquestioned right-of-way to the palace.

We were greeted by attendants who had been awaiting our arrival. I thanked my escort, with a special smile for the captain. They saluted, wheeled their horses around and headed for the barracks outside the fort. They would return on the morrow to their river outpost.

I rode slowly on towards my quarters, the attendants on foot to guide me. We made our way through the jumble of people in the great courtyard, where the King obviously reviewed his troops and people who desired audience with him awaited their turn to be summoned to the great hall. This imposing structure loomed before us, its red gable roof supported by great granite columns. Although the facade was sculptured above the cornices, the entire effect was simple and typical of the Sinhala, so different to the intricate carvings of Chola architecture, which are as elaborate as their music, their pantheistic religion and their hawking and spitting.

We veered right and I saw that the layout of the palace was the same as that of Anu, except for the location of the Treasury. The tall buildings of the Secretariat were on one side of the audience hall, the Treasury and the granaries on the other. The quarters of princes and nobles were to the right, while the ladies' quarters were to the left. The King's quarters would be to the rear, I guessed. The whole would enclose a park, with pleasure gardens and pools. Single-storey guards' barracks ran in an orderly pattern along the ramparts, with a sandy approach road separating them from the palace buildings.

My quarters were with those of the princes. Gold flames spurting from lighted tapers along the walls revealed them to be furnished with some degree of luxury. Even the smell of incense, wafted by grey smoke curling upward from sticks glowing in braziers, however, could not disguise that combination of armpit odour and mildew that betrays a room kept closed too long. Bamboo matting covered the entire floor, with woven rugs scattered here and there. Frescoes of scenes from the Jataka stories, done in vivid hues of red, orange, yellow, brown and black, were painted on the walls and ceiling. The furniture was heavily carved black ebony. My couch was a fine piece, adorned with bright cushions of orange and yellow.

I made for the ornamented bedroom windows to breathe a whiff of fresh air. They opened onto a park-like garden where birds were twittering and chirping good-night calls to each other in the slowly darkening branches. The creak and whistle of mynas was especially dominant. At least there is comfort and peace here, I thought. Yet my throat hurt at remembering eventide at home in Anu. The longing to be back with my uncle rose like a sickness within me. It swelled when the chief attendant announced that I was to have an audience with the King immediately.

As I quickly bathed and changed into formal clothes, I felt resentment at being summoned to the royal presence after such a long and tiring journey, with no opportunity even to rest awhile, merely because of events resulting from a queen's crazy cravings and a king's irresponsibility.

Chapter 10

It was dark by the time I arrived at the audience hall. The air was turning cool because of a northeasterly breeze, but my goose pimples were caused by the memory of the last time I had audience with a king. Had it happened only three nights ago in Anu, to me, a boy of twelve? Or was that in another life, another body?

The audience chamber was located at the far end of the audience hall. My first impression of it was of red drapes behind a platform at the far end of the chamber, on which was placed a throne of blackest ebony, lined with gleaming gold, inlaid with mother-of-pearl and sparkling with gems. The royal umbrella of white silk, gold-tasselled, was poised above the throne, on one side of which was the red silk footstool with a crown and sword, both of gold, upon it. The crown was studded with pearls and flashing red rubies. The scabbard and hilt of the sword were jewelled with the *navaratna* – red rubies, green emeralds, blue sapphires, purple amethyst, brown tourmaline, yellow topaz, pale aquamarine, cat's-eyes and white *diamanthi*.

I took all this in, with one swift glance, before my eyes fell on the man seated on the throne. He was small! Slightly hunched and dressed in white tunic and pantaloons, which made his dark face seem even darker, here sat Kakkavan Tissa, King of Ruhuna. I made obeisance to him and he bade me come forward. His voice was raspy and surprisingly deep. As I slowly approached him, I noticed jet black hair and beard, lightly streaked with silver, framing a small, pointed face with a nose jutting like a crow's beak. The bright, alert eyes were so like those of a crow that I almost expected them to have yellow rims. They had a magnetic quality, compelling, with a glazy sort of shine to them.

One does not look elsewhere when one approaches a king, so it was only when I stopped in front of the platform and the moment was right that I took stock of the other persons in the chamber.

The King presented me to his queen, who sat on a low stool beside the throne. She was the most beautiful woman I had ever seen. Dark hair falling in masses to her waist made her delicate face seem more fair, accented the rosy-gold of her complexion. I was surprised to find her eyes appraising me, but was soon lost in their appeal. They were large, with the longest black lashes. She had the limpid look that glistens from within and I melted before it. Dressed in a long blue skirt and full bodice to hide the slight bulge of the child in her womb, she was obviously tall and slender, but well proportioned. It was no wonder this little crow of a king had adored her from the moment he first set eyes on her, for I was immediately captivated.

I had barely finished my salutation to the Queen when the King presented to me his newly appointed Chief Warrior. A sharp stab ran through me at seeing the handsome, fair-skinned giant with the half-smile that was now wide and full. It was indeed Velu Sumana, the jungle murderer. My stomach began contracting with fear.' In this light and at close quarters he seemed less than twenty-five years of age and absurdly young to have such a high rank. Did he know me? What would he do if he recognized me? I gazed at him wide-eyed, but his disarming, almost ingenuous look told me that he saw me only as an unknown boy. I returned his salutation and turned to face the last of those in the chamber.

Kirthi Siri, the Chief Minister, was a thin, craggy hunchback. He had a cadaverous face and deep-sunk cadaverous eyes, half covered by hoods like a cockatoo's on either side of them, which seemed to open or fold over, depending on his mood. His long, high-bridged nose and great dome of a forehead were capped by stringy hair. All of this made him look woebegone. Only the flash of a moment when he first fixed me directly with piercing eyes, the hoods drawn back, told me that this man was intensely cunning, utterly ruthless and terribly dangerous.

'You are welcome to our court and our kingdom,' the King rasped after the introductions were over. His smile carried into his eyes and I felt myself warming towards him. 'You would have been gladly received anyhow, because you are of our family, but now you are doubly welcome, because you bring us firsthand news about events in Anu, following the . . . er . . . little incident involving our Chief Warrior.' He glanced towards Velu Sumana, who made no comment.

'Our Chief Warrior nobly carried out the dictates of the gods,' the Queen interposed, almost defiant.

'Surely, surely, my dear,' the King replied soothingly. 'He took the law into his own hands. Now we must assess the consequences.'

So Velu Sumana had acted without the King's knowledge, but the Queen was grateful. Had she known what the Chief Warrior had planned? Did anyone know how Mahela had been killed? I was beginning to get scared now, the victim of my own knowledge.

114

'May I suggest, sire, that the prince here tell us from the beginning all that transpired in Anu since word of the . . . uh . . . sad demise of Mahela was received?' Kirthi Siri intervened in a thin, reedy voice that was almost a whine in intonation.

'Good idea!' the King replied. 'Please proceed, Prince. But first, sit down. No, do not stand on formality. You are one of us.' He pointed to the top of the platform. 'Sit here and eat some of these sweetmeats. Our *kalu dodol* jelly is made of real *kitul* honey. Try it.' He indicated a silver tray with sweetmeats of assorted colours on it.

I was touched by his kindliness. I sat on the step and reached for the *kalu dodol*. I had never tasted the Ruhuna variety before. It was delicious, melting in the mouth and leaving behind the flavour of burnt honey.

In simple words, I began telling them my story. They listened in silence. Only the hiss and splutter of flaming tapers, giving forth the pungent odour of burning oil to mingle with the smell of incense, accompanied my voice. Above it all lay a delicate scent of some jasmine-tinted perfume worn by the Queen. Pleased at their attention, I told them almost all I knew. Their taut faces revealed that they were deeply concerned at King Elara's threats. Only Kirthi Siri remained impassive.

'So here I am, your subject and soon to be an apprentice monk,' I concluded somewhat dismally.

'A noble price to pay,' the King briefly observed, but I did not understand his meaning. 'What do you think, Chief Minister?'

I looked at Kirthi. The hoods were over the eyes. They opened slightly. 'The motivations of the Chola king are extremely interesting, even intriguing . . . and, uh . . . thought-provoking.' He turned to me. 'You are sure King Elara implied that his sole remaining aim in life is to ensure the succession for his son?' His eyes opened, sharp and bright upon me.

'I am certain.'

'And if you don't become an apprentice monk seven days after our prince is born, your uncle's life will be forfeit.'

I could only nod this time, because of the lump that suddenly arose in my throat.

'Hmm! Strange. It would appear that King Elara would welcome the event.' Kirthi scratched his chin reflectively. He murmured to himself. 'Hmm . . . hmm . . .' His eyes peeped out. 'Two obstacles with a single shove!'

'What do you mean?' the King demanded.

'It would appear that King Elara's principal ambition now is to secure the throne for his son. This is understandable. After all, we have somewhat similar goals here.' A light smile touched Kirthi's face, revealing yellow teeth and making him look ghoulish, because the eyes had vanished and the sockets became hollow. 'Don't you think that this makes King Elara both predictable and vulnerable, sire, laying open certain courses of action to us?'

'How so, Minister?' It was the Queen who asked the question, her mellow voice sharp with inquiry. I was glad for the opportunity to gaze at her beauty again.

'Well, King Elara is predictable in that we know his unswerving course of action will be to safeguard the succession. Vulnerable, because his ambition for his son seems to be his main goal. He no longer desires conquest for himself, merely a safe kingdom for his seventeen-year-old boy. For this, he would even run the risk of rebellion, by forcing Prince Vipula's suicide. So it seems to me that if the cause of his ambition can somehow be removed, in a manner that would not provoke . . . er . . . retaliation, we will have a king without ambition and this will certainly be an advantage to our unborn prince.' Kirthi's eyes pierced through the hoods for a moment and his lean throat wobbled, probably in appreciation of his own cleverness. 'Then the only claimant to the throne ahead of him will be Prince Vipula, the heir by birth, who will surely give way before . . . shall we say . . . the heir of fate.'

Kirthi's face was inscrutable. The King looked troubled. Remembering my conversation with Prince Digha Bahu, I could understand why. The others obviously did not know or care about King Kakkavan's promises to make Prince Digha his heir.

'You will work on it?' the King inquired of Kirthi.

'Certainly, sire.'

'Good. And how do we protect the Queen?'

'I have already increased our border patrols, guards and reserves against armed attack,' Velu Sumana said. 'The Queen's palace guards will be doubled.'

'We know we can depend on you.' The King's face relaxed somewhat, yet a tightness about the mouth remained. 'It's damnable that King Elara should want to make war on a woman and an unborn child.'

'The King makes war on danger, whatever its source,' Kirthi observed. He began to pace the chamber slowly, his leather sandals clicking on the polished floor. All our eyes swivelled in his direction. 'We must devise measures to protect the Queen at all costs. She must be guarded night and day, even when she visits the temple.'

The Queen's dark head went up with a jerk. 'I shall never permit guards in the sacred precincts of the temple,' she flashed. I felt a throb of pride for her.

'We will arrange for the monks to come to the palace,' the King promised.

'Must I then be a prisoner of this palace, lord? I who am to be the mother of the saviour of our island kingdom?'

'No – not of the palace. You will be the prisoner of the unborn prince,' the King responded.

I would have expected at least a fond look from the Queen at this poetic statement, but her face was inscrutable. She looked at her husband with shutters over her eyes.

'But I also have another plan, to make assurance doubly sure,' Kirthi intervened.

'What is that?' the King demanded.

'I shall unveil it to you in due course,' Kirthi declared solemnly. 'After it has been perfected.' Nose poised beneath his head like a beak, eyes closed, he was a sleeping eagle-hawk. 'All things necessary to safeguard our unborn prince and our queen must be done.' The words filtered through yellow teeth. 'No one, nothing, must stand in the way of his destiny.' He scratched the sparse hairs on his head, then raised the hoods from his eyes. 'Every obstacle to that destiny will be removed.'

Chapter 11

The very next evening, I was summoned again by King Kakkavan, this time to his study.

'We have a few minutes to spare before our nephew, Prince Digha Bahu, attends us,' he explained. 'He obviously comes in irate haste, having learned of certain recent events!' He smiled and shook his head, then abruptly changed the subject. 'You remind us of our royal mother, your cousin-aunt. You have her dark brown eyes and glossy black hair. You also have the family characteristics. The men are tall, slim, with wide shoulders and narrow hips – supple as sword blades.' He sighed.

'Our mother was a lady of high principle, strong character and enormous compassion.' The King seemed to be speaking to himself now. 'These are indeed the legacy of the descendants of our great King, Devanam Piya. Unfortunately, our mother died of food poisoning when we were but twelve, no older than you are today. Do you know, she was very talented musically? She used to make up *kavi* and sing them to us every night. Hmm . . .' He paused, contemplating. 'Our royal father would come in and listen occasionally. He was devoted to the Doctrine. He felt he had to expiate . . .' The King stopped abruptly, as if he had already said too much, and ran a dark hand over his brow. He had slender, long fingers.

Before he could even change the subject, Prince Digha Bahu was announced. The Prince stalked in and made obeisance, obviously outraged. Barely had the King given him leave to state his mission before the words came pouring out. He had learned of Velu Sumana's exploit only that morning, from one of his informers, and had ridden post-haste to Mahagama to discover the truth from the King. Why had the entire incident been kept secret from him? Was he not commander of the border forces?

The King explained that my presence at this interview was indeed to brief him at first hand about the situation in Anu. He nodded to me to commence.

I had risen to my feet at Prince Digha Bahu's entry. I now gave him the news of Mahela's slaying and details of all that had transpired since. Deducing that my presence was a diversionary tactic of the King, I said my piece and retired to stand behind his high-backed black ebony chair, trying to make myself as inconspicuous as possible.

Prince Digha Bahu invariably stuttered when he was angry. 'Am I but a palace servant, lord, to be treated in this manner?' he demanded, his cheeks quivering. He paused, standing foursquare before the seated king, sweaty palms outstretched to emphasize his humiliation. His red-and-silver attire made a striking figure of him in the golden sunlight slanting through the windows. 'One of your warriors sneaks across the border, which it is my duty to guard. He wangles a job as groom to the enemy king. Actually, as a matter of fact, he steals a horse, issues a public challenge to the enemy's Chief Warrior, does not meet him in fair combat but foully murders the man and sneaks back across the border with the enemy king's two finest war-horses . . . and, er . . . the head . . . uh . . . just the head of the warrior . . .'

'Yes, yes! All you say is true,' King Kakkavan began somewhat testily, then restrained himself. 'Are you complaining that he did not bring the warrior's whole body?' His smile was quizzical, but some hoarseness in his normally deep voice and a runny nose indicated that he was starting the sniffles common at this changing season of the year, in the warm month of Assayuja. 'We assure you that no disrespect was meant by anyone toward you.'

Prince Digha Bahu's face went red, almost the colour of his tunic. 'No disrespect meant, lord,' he flared, 'but given – definitely given. No one considered the consequences to me. What will my troops think of me with all this happening behind my back? What will the people think? I have become an object of ridicule.'

'No one need know,' the King responded mildly. 'Immediately Velu Sumana returned, you received orders to increase your guards and border patrols. Since you did so, everyone will suppose that you were aware all along of what was transpiring. You are most welcome to share in the guilt, if you desire!' His cough smothered a laugh. He pointed a dark, slim finger towards a gold-cushioned sofa opposite him. 'Sit down there, nephew. You tire us with your marching up and down as if you were patrolling the border. Relax and have a chew of *sara bulath*.'

The Prince glanced briefly at the brass stand containing green betel leaves, brown areca nut, black tobacco, white chunam and fragrant cardamoms and cloves. He ignored the invitation, but strode to a brass spittoon at the far end of the room, cleared his throat and spat. I was surprised at this breach of etiquette, but gratified that at least the King's spittoon was sacrosanct in Mahagama.

When Prince Digha returned to the King again, his face

120

was still clouded with resentment. 'The decision to acknowledge complicity or not with this murderous deed should have been left to me,' he declared emphatically.

Although the King made a placatory gesture with his palm, a hint of irritation now entered his voice. 'Be reasonable, nephew. No harm has been done to you.'

'No harm? Think what could have happened. The Chola was given provocation to attack our kingdom. It is I and my troops who would have borne the brunt of their first assault and we would not even have known what it was all about. Men would have died without just cause or reason. To add insult to that injury, I have had to ride all the way here like a lackey to discover the truth. And what a truth! The *dola-dhook* of our Queen – which, to say the least, are a trifle unusual, especially in a lady renowned for Buddhist piety. But even if we grant that a lady is not responsible for her desires at such a time, surely the head of the man who risked plunging us into war to satisfy them, with no authority from his king, should be forfeit. It should be sent on a platter to King Elara to make amends for the insult to him. Instead, he has been confirmed, like a hero, in the position of your Chief Warrior. However, all that is beside the point. My grievance that I have been insulted remains. This is no way to treat your heir!'

The King glanced sharply back at me. My interest quickened, though I pretended that Prince Digha Bahu's remark had not registered with me. I remembered my uncle's analysis of the political situation in Ruhuna. What he said was true. I wished so much that I could tell him so. I looked out of the open window, as if I were more interested in the two dark-chested gardeners weeding the multicoloured canna beds bordering the green lawn outside than with these affairs of state.

'Our promise was that you would be our heir, not that you would share our rule,' King Kakkavan retorted, his voice sharp and low, the cutting edge of anger in it. I had wondered how long he would endure the Prince's aggressiveness. It was more than King Elara would have stomached from anyone.

Suddenly King Kakkavan sneezed violently. Placing one finger on each nostril, in turn, he blew his nose expertly into the spittoon, going through the wiping ritual with his napkin slowly, probably to help restrain his anger. 'Excuse me.' He rose and started pacing the room with short, quick steps, his sandals clip-clopping on the polished black floors. Instead of being curbed, his irritation seemed to be mounting. Yet he was a lonely figure and I felt sorry for him.

Prince Digha Bahu observed the King in frustration.

'You must understand the situation as we faced it from day to day, nephew,' the King finally resumed, his speech now clipped. 'There was no conspiracy to exclude you. The sequence of events was . . . very simple. Our Queen had her yearnings. She mentioned them to us. We summoned Velu Sumana and told him about them, more in jest at the time. He took us seriously, but did not express his intentions. He merely asked for eight weeks' leave of absence. We granted it. The next thing we knew, he appeared with Mahela's head. Also the sword with dried blood on it, the garland of lotus and of course two fine steeds. What did you expect us to do? Spread news of the exploit by beat of tom-tom? Have the Queen satisfy her *dola-dhook* in public?' A note of sarcasm had entered his voice. He stopped his pacing to confront Prince Digha Bahu. His small dark figure, with the head tilted to one side, was alert as a crow's. 'Or perhaps you feel that we should have sent the head back to King Elara with our apologies, plus Velu Sumans's head to keep it company. And oh . . . we must not forget the recipe for refixing heads on corpses. Or that other for bringing the whole to life again!' He paused to shake a finger at Prince Digha Bahu. 'Come, nephew, be reasonable. Admit that if it happened again, there is no way it could be any different.'

'You should have informed me immediately once you

122

knew the truth,' Digha Bahu grated harshly, taking advantage of the King's change of mood. His pale eyes were accusing. 'It was your duty . . .'

'Do not dictate our duty to us,' the King warned quietly, the steel finally out. Although he was much smaller than the portly Digha Bahu, he suddenly seemed to dominate the Prince by sheer force of personality. 'That would be presumptuous. You want to be the Heir Presumptive, not the presumptuous heir, do you not?'

Prince Digha Bahu paled visibly. He turned aside. 'I meant no disrespect,' he muttered. Then he noticed me and a look of hatred crossed his plump face. Here he had someone on whom he could vent his anger. He pointed at me. 'But this thief ate at my board, enjoyed my hospitality and did not say a word to me. He at least could have been frank.'

I ignored the pointing finger and looked at King Kakkavan. Sensing his sympathy, I decided to be bold. 'You never asked me, cousin,' I responded, stepping forward from behind the chair. 'How was I to know that one so important as you made yourself out to be that night was unaware of the facts?' I shrugged, then nodded at his finger. 'So please replace that finger where it belongs, with its four companions, and take your hand away from my face, for it is indecorous.'

Prince Digha Bahu was taken aback. His thin eyebrows creased incredulously. Then the black pinpoints of his pale eyes shot fire. I had never seen such a look in a man's eyes before. It reminded me of flame spitting from the dull glow of brown stones in a furnace. He took a step forward, finger thrust toward me. 'Wha – what did you say, *paraballa*, you filthy pi-dog?' Face crimson with rage, hand now upraised, he advanced threateningly toward me. I stood my ground, though shocked by his crude epithet and rude behaviour.

The King's low laugh intruded. He slipped between us, as if making for his chair again. 'The young prince rightly reminds us of deportment!' he exclaimed. He paused, pretending to be struck by a thought, but in reality to remain standing between us, a reminder to Prince Digha Bahu that no one resorts to violence in the presence of the King. 'He also happens to speak the truth. Do not involve him in this affair.' His whole bearing turned to command. He had allowed Prince Digha Bahu his say, but enough was enough. He nodded toward me. 'Prince Rodana showed remarkable discretion by not bleating about what he knew.' He turned around and faced me. 'We commend you, Prince.'

The King resumed his seat. I moved behind it again.

Prince Digha Bahu stood with his feet firmly apart, still glowering at me. 'I find this little bastard quite lacking in respect and discretion when he addresses me,' he ripped out. 'When I become king, he shall pay for it.'

The word 'bastard' no longer held any pain for me. I gave the Prince that amused smile, slightly scornful, such as I had seen my uncle give on occasion, which generally infuriated people. 'When you become king, I shall probably be a monk and safe from your kind attentions,' I asserted. 'Until then, if you address me in a civil manner, you will not find me lacking in respect, cousin. It is something that comes naturally to me, except when I meet intemperance.'

'Enough of that,' the King cut in harshly. 'We will not have you bickering in our presence. Come forward, Prince Rodana.' He beckoned me with his hand, the jewelled rings sparkling.

Ignoring Prince Digha Bahu's vicious glance, I quickly moved to stand before the King.

King Kakkavan fixed me with eyes turned hypnotic, the dark depths covered by that strange sheen. 'Remember that everything you have heard this evening is secret,' he charged me. 'These are affairs of state.'

It was only then that the real significance of the discussion hit me. King Kakkavan had promised the succession to Prince Digha Bahu. He must have done so at the time he despaired of having an heir. He had arranged for his sister to marry the Prince in order to prevent a bid from Digha Bahu for his throne. Now he expected his own heir. If it was a girl, some disposition by marriage, perhaps to Prince Digha Bahu's son, Prince Panduka, could be arranged. But what if it were the boy that everyone seemed to be expecting?

The King interrupted my thoughts. 'You may take your leave now, Prince Rodana,' he directed in a kindly voice.

'Before he leaves, I would like an affirmation of your intentions, lord,' Prince Digha Bahu intervened. 'In his presence as a witness.'

'Are you attempting to sit on our throne before the event?' the King asked sternly.

'There are events we should anticipate to avoid any misunderstanding.'

'You may predecease us.'

'Then my son would be heir. Your promise must still hold good.'

'It must?'

'Yes! All these omens and *dola-dhook* I have heard of can be the breeding ground for even an ordinary prince to grow up imagining himself to be a divine ruler, the saviour of the kingdom. That would run counter to your sacred oath and my right of succession.'

'It could, couldn't it?' The King's voice had grown calm. 'Although our oath was given under other circumstances, you still have it, Prince. Have no fear. We shall honour that oath by proclamation at the appropriate time. It will bind you, too . . . not to harm the child.'

Thirteen years later, having just assumed duties as Gamini's tutor, I had yet to comprehend the full magnitude of the forces confronting the boy prince. I had a feeling, however, that of all people, it was his mother, the Queen, who was to bear watching.

King Kakkavan was in his study when the Queen was ushered in. Leela, her newly favoured handmaiden, had never been directly in the King's presence before. She followed the Queen's lead as she had been instructed and made obeisance to the King. She then stood beside the entrance door, eyes downcast, enjoying the sharp scent of incense emanating from the burners placed before the gold Buddha statue.

The Queen advanced, unhurried, to the ebony desk at which the King sat. He indicated a settle and she sank gracefully onto it, adjusting the folds of her white *saree* around her knees and placing her white bird-of-paradise-feather fan on her lap.

Leela discreetly looked at the King. He was so dark in the flare-light. He had just returned from riding and his skin shone almost a deep purple with sweat. He looked like a large, wet crow.

'Well, madam, you requested this audience,' the King stated formally. 'To what do we owe the pleasure?'

Funny, Leela thought. They have slept together, made love and borne children, but observe the formalities of the court even on such a private occasion.

'We are very concerned about the way our older son is growing up, sire,' the Queen responded, her voice low and controlled.

'What is the problem?'

'You know he is a remote person, lord. No one can reach him.'

The King sighed. 'Would that be the fault of the remote person, or those of us who are unable to reach him?'

'People who are remote pay a price, regardless of who is responsible.'

The King pondered this awhile. He ran white upper teeth over his dark lower lip. He seemed about to say something, glanced at Leela and changed his mind. 'Remoteness is a quality that can be hidden by an approachable surface,' he remarked. 'But we discuss abstruse matters when you obviously have a specific problem.' He smiled with his teeth, a smile of courtesy that did not reach his eyes.

'Prince Gamini has reached a stage where even his younger brother is afraid of him.'

'Does Gamini beat or scold Tissa then?'

'No, but Tissa is really frightened.'

'Ah! The *bada pissa*.' A glint of amusement lit the King's face briefly.

'It is our duty to protect the youngest, lord. Older brothers are not always as concerned as parents – and, with due respect, we will not be around forever.'

'True. True. What would you have us do?'

'Prince Gamini is too sure of his right of succession. At birth, he was hailed as the saviour King of Lanka. All through his early years, he was bred to this belief. It has gone to his head. We beg you to find some method of disabusing his mind of these grand notions, so that he can become a simple little boy.'

'But, madam, he is not a simple little boy. You ask me to turn a panther into a kitten!'

The Queen opened her fan and started working it furiously. 'If I may say so respectfully, lord, since you agree that he is a panther, please clip his talons so he cannot claw his way to his desires.'

127

'You want a raging wildcat? What of his teeth, madam? Do we draw them too?'

'He can rage as much as he likes, as long as he cannot hurt others.'

'You are principally concerned about your other son.'

'We are equally concerned for both our sons, yours and mine, lord. But concern cannot be shown in the same manner to both children.'

The King remained silent awhile, the Queen's troubled eyes upon him. He reached absentmindedly for a white cloth on the ebony desk, wiped the sweat from his face and replaced the cloth. 'Are you suggesting that we withhold from our eldest son his right to succession under the Arya code of our *charlithraya*?'

'Let it be known at least to him for the present, lord, even if it is not publicized, that his right to the succession will depend upon his conduct.'

King Kakkavan's black fingers drummed rapidly on the arm of his chair.

Leela could not help but admire the Queen for her courage. Dimly inside her mind, however, the thought that the Queen was also very clever began to take seed. As it sprouted, she saw that this was how the Queen had survived and established her position in this court, where Ruhuna's Tissa family was held greater than the Kelani Tissa family of the Queen. She could have remained a bystander, a figurehead. Instead, she was in the forefront of the affairs of the kingdom, invariably taking the lead in religious and educational matters.

The King's voice interrupted Leela's reflections. 'We shall think on your submissions,' he stated. 'When decisions are made, they shall be conveyed to you in private.' There was reproof in his emphasis of the last word. 'Meanwhile, let us hope that your choice of Prince Rodana as our son's tutor will prove helpful. With his temple background he should be able to temper some of Prince Gamini's aggressiveness.'

128

A smile crossed the Queen's face for the first time. 'Do you think an *abithaya* can tame a panther, lord?'

'We trust the Doctrine can, madam. And now you have our permission to retire.' The King smiled graciously, but seemed rather tired.

The Queen made obeisance. Leela followed suit. When she rose to her feet, she observed King Kakkavan's eyes on her and immediately dropped her own.

'Your new handmaiden, and already your confidante at an audience with a king.' There was amusement in the King's voice. 'Such a pretty girl.' He busied himself with an *ola* on his desk.

When they returned to the Queen's quarters, Nona, the senior lady-in-waiting, greeted them in the anteroom. She was dressed, as always, in white, with her grey hair tied in a knot at the nape of her neck. The shapely Padma, looking as cheerful as the yellow of her sari, was seated beside her. Both ladies rose and made obeisance as the Queen entered.

'We have a surprise for you, my lady,' Nona announced. Her quavery voice had the strange, unctuous quality of one who has been in the service of royalty for years.

The Queen clapped her hands in delight. 'We adore surprises,' she exclaimed.

'Pray accompany us to your private courtyard then.' Nona led the way through the anteroom. Instead of turning right to the Queen's bed-chamber, she turned left into the small passage leading to a walled courtyard.

Torches flamed golden along the four sides of the courtyard, placing the dark branches of taller trees in gloom, but lighting up bushes and flower beds that lined the walls. At the far end of the courtyard, across the red-brick-paved floor, was a water cascade, in front of which large pots of flowers and ferns had been arranged in a square to create a stage.

The Queen's ladies-in-waiting and attendants were

129

assembled here, sitting on garden seats or on the brick-paved floor. They rose as one and made obeisance, crying 'Greetings, O Queen!' in unison. The effect of more than twenty female voices was melodious, but like a group of schoolchildren reciting a lesson.

The Queen sank onto the pale green cushions of a creamy satinwood couch, placed so as to give the best view of the stage. She indicated a low settle for Leela to sit on. Padma took her place on the right of the stage, facing the audience. Nona moved back to the corridor and clapped her hands.

The tink-tink-tink of *talam-pota* arose in a steady rhythm, like the sound of a cobra at night. A *geta bere* commenced its sharp beat. A nasal voice began the chant of a *vannam*. *Thanna-thumya-thanna-thanna-thumya* . . .

Leela felt prickles of anticipation on her skin as she gazed at the open door. How had Nona found a dancer to do the *shastriya natya*? The man had to be from the Kanda Uda Rata hill country and these dancers rarely visited the low country except for a special festival or by summons from the King. The Queen would be happy. Glancing sideways for her lady's reaction, Leela felt a stab of disappointment. The Queen looked attentive and pleased, but somehow preoccupied as well.

As was customary in the Kanda Uda style, the dancer swaggered through the door, each hip alternately swinging forward, the bells on his anklets tinkling. He was of medium height, with broad features, a wide, sensuous nose and full lips. His tight bone structure was accentuated in the torchlight by a great circular headdress, with large silver earmuffs and a crown of brass and jewels jutting out horizontally from its base. His skin was smooth, like dark brown silk. Not a muscle showed through the bodice of open red-and-white beadwork, or the gold armbands and shoulder guards, so supple was his body, yet it had the power and grace of a leopard. He wore white pantaloons beneath a red-and-white ruffled trouser-skirt. He held himself with pride, even when he made obeisance to the Queen.

'Madam, permit me to present Gunaya, the foremost dancer from the Uda Rata,' Padma announced in a voice as deep gold as the torchlight. It had earned her the role of announcer at these informal gatherings. 'Such is the excellence of his technique that he will dance an hour, a watch, an entire night without ceasing, at Your Majesty's pleasure.'

The Queen straightened up and leaned forward, totally expectant now, for Gunaya was the acknowledged king of the dance in all the island kingdoms.

Cymbal chant and drumbeat stopped abruptly.

Eyes closed, Gunaya placed the palms of his hands together before his chest, raised them to his forehead, greeting his Queen, then placed them on his head, worshipping his god. When he opened his eyes again, they had a strange, magnetic quality to them, the pupils seeming to shine like twin *diamanthi* from dark but living pools. In one smooth motion, he bent at the knees, his arms dropping horizontal to the ground, elbows bent, palms downward, the fingers almost touching, thumbs outstretched. He raised one leg, still bent at the knee. He thrust his hands outward, palms away from him.

The nasal voice began a different chant. Cymbal and drum took up the beat. Gunaya's hands moved to the rhythm, drawing in, thrusting out. He joined in the chant, his voice reedy but strong. He moved forward and back to the music. The bells of his anklets jingled when he stamped. He paused, alert. He leaped. He ran, he bounded. His dancing was virile, but the transition between movements was smooth as a sword blade. He swept into a giddy race, leaping, only to land back on his feet light as night dews.

Leela had never seen Kanda Uda Rata dancing before. It had a rare combination of strength and delicacy, the union of warrior and gentle maiden. The offspring was her entrancement.

When each wild incident was over, Gunaya returned to his dance-swagger, head and body held proud, arms outstretched and half-bent again, anklet bells jingling boastfully. During the hour of his dancing, he was the hare, the hawk, the warrior Gotama and the god Krishna.

Leela watched, completely absorbed. Through the veils of that absorption, a pinpoint of light appeared, sharp as a single star on a black sky. As it grew, she knew it to be something within her that distinguished her from everyone else there, save Gunaya, to whom she was linked by some magic they both possessed – he to express, she to receive. He possessed the gift of perceiving what others experienced, even what was recorded in their *prana*. She could read it as if it were recorded on *ola*. This was how she had relived her Queen's experience on the stormy ocean.

Stunned at first, then fearful and elated, she wondered whether she could also look into the future. At that instant, as if recognizing her knowledge, the pinpoints of fire in Gunaya's eyes linked with the light shining before her.

He knows. Dear *devas*, he knows. How wonderful. Those of us who have this magic recognize each other. So we are never alone.

Gunaya became lost in a flurry of acrobatic dancing, then suddenly everything stopped. Silence fell with a thud upon the courtyard. For long moments, there was only the soundless tribute of those held in thrall. Then murmurs of praise, like gently foaming waters, more profound than shouting and cheers, cascaded around the dancer.

Gunaya made obeisance. His dark eyes shifted briefly to Leela and a thrill of joy coursed through her body. He had included her in his greeting to the Queen – and only he and she knew it. He stood there a few moments, palms together before his heaving chest, greeting the rest of his audience.

The Queen took off her aquamarine necklace and handed it to Padma, who sex-swayed to Gunaya and offered it to him. He received it with both hands, moved forward and

132

knelt before the Queen, who murmured words of praise.

You are a king in the outpouring of your precious gift, Leela thought. It is we who should kneel to you. She was terrified at her own temerity, for a dancer is of low caste.

'You were under Gunaya's spell,' the Queen whispered to Leela as Gunaya backed away. 'You have the power to be spellbound. Can you also cast spells?'

Leela turned a bright gaze, rich with her experience, on the Queen. The Queen's dark eyes, more liquid because of *kohl* on the long, curving lashes, widened with inquiry. 'I think you can,' she whispered. Her glance travelled to Leela's slim, lissom body, the newly formed breasts rounded beneath the tight green bodice.

'A sensitive man will find you irresistible,' the Queen said softly. 'I may call on you to cast a spell on one in the near future.'

Chapter 13

On learning that I had been appointed Gamini's tutor, Prince Digha Bahu shrewdly requested and obtained King Kakkavan's approval for his son, Prince Panduka, to participate in Gamini's religious studies with me. Panduka was thereupon allotted quarters in the palace and began attending Gamini's classes in these subjects.

The antipathy between the two princes became obvious from the start.

Sinhala architecture is different to the Indian, where palaces and temples generally consist of buildings surrounding a great square centre courtyard. The Ruhuna palace was built in traditional Sinhala style, also with a large centre courtyard, but with sets of rooms surrounding it, each with its own centre courtyard.

The palace is surrounded on all four sides by rampart walls with sentry towers and a moat. It has huge wooden entrance gates, ribbed with metal and leading to a great square. Directly beyond this square is the audience hall, with a smaller audience chamber behind it. On one side of the hall is the Treasury; on the other side is the Secretariat. Two corridors lead from the rear of the audience hall – one to the men's, the other to the ladies' quarters. The King's and the Queen's chambers are side by side, at the far end of the palace, with the princes' rooms adjoining the King's and the princesses' adjacent to the Queen's. Each courtyard is walled with yellow-flowering *surya* trees and red-blossomed flamboyants on the borders, fronted by flower beds and cooled by water cascades. Some have paved walks leading through green lawns. All the quarters are linked by roofed verandas, open on the sides. Behind the residences are grassy, tree-shaded lawns and fountains reaching to the road running around the entire palace, on the farther side of which are the granaries and guards' quarters. The rear walls of these are the ramparts.

My own quarters adjoined Gamini's. They consisted of an anteroom, study and bedroom, all side-by-side. The garden at the rear was a pleasant place and I had selected it for Gamini's and Panduka's lessons that midmorning. We sat on a stone bench beside a smooth lawn. Pigeons cooed in green branches above us. Children's voices echoed in the distance, reciting a *kaviya*. A billy goat's 'Um-baa-a' reminded me that one of the young princes had not obtained permission to keep the animal as a pet. Knowing it was there, however, made me feel such a sense of home that I did not even find the smell of its dung, wafted by a breeze, distasteful.

We were discussing the effects of religion on the Ruhuna succession when a dispute ensued. I let the princes debate, in order to allow them some freedom of expression. The debate soon became an argument. They got worked up and sprang to their feet, pacing the brick-paved walkway, arguing heatedly, their voices raised. I continued sitting placid as a *bhikku* on the stone bench.

Prince Panduka finally made his real point. 'You will never be king of Ruhuna!' he shouted. 'My father is the heir to the throne. He will be king when your father dies and I shall rule after him.'

At fifteen, Prince Panduka was much larger than the twelve-year-old Gamini. His voice was just breaking into manhood, though, and it had a croaking quality that made it sound unsure and contrasted with his bravado.

Gamini's fists clenched and blood rushed to his face, making it purple beneath his dark skin. Although he made no reply, the silver morning sunlight glowing on his bare chest showed him lithe and dangerous as a panther.

Responding to Gamini's anger, Prince Panduka squared right up to him. 'I'm bigger than you. Try anything and I'll squash you.' He was half a span taller and about twenty pounds heavier than Gamini.

The pleasing coolness of the palace garden and a lesson in religion were ill-suited to fist fights. The time had come for me to intervene. 'No one's going to beat anyone else,' I said firmly. I placed my staff on the seat and stood up to enforce my authority.

'Who is going to stop me?' The angry derision in Prince Panduka's brown eyes made them shine like river stones. 'You are only an ex-*abithaya*, teaching me part time, though you may be the regular tutor of the *kalu kumaraya* here. Monks have no guts, so you could not even stop your own bowels, let alone me.'

His words stung through the mask of loving kindness I had acquired from twelve years in the temple. Life there had been rigorous. Although much of my time had been spent in meditation and study, my body was fit and I knew I was stronger than both boys. Even so, my inclination was to give Prince Panduka a stern lecture on loving kindness, instead of a buffet.

But before I could begin to speak, I heard Gamini say with deadly quiet, 'Stopping you would indeed be like stopping bowels, because you are what is in them. You have no respect for your elders, your betters, or even the monks. How can you ever rule?' The words were ground out of him as chili from a grinding stone. His eyes were as hot.

Prince Panduka was taken aback. 'What are you talking about?' he demanded. 'I am a prince of the royal blood. Others must respect me. Why should I respect any other than my superiors in rank?'

'I will teach you some respect,' Gamini said. He took up a fighting stance. Clad only in a green *hulwar*, he looked the trained wrestler, arms slightly raised, sturdy black legs bent at the knees, physically relaxed. I could not help but admire him for standing up to a bigger opponent. It was the expression on his face that was frightening.

'Not in my presence, if you do indeed respect your elders and teachers, Prince,' I reminded Gamini in a steely voice, surprised at the thought that I would have loved to see him beat this flabby Panduka.

For a while Gamini held his stance and I expected him to erupt after all. Then he stood erect. He nodded. 'Your point is well taken, *guru*. But I will have the liver of this bogus prince some day.'

I felt a surge of relief, not the least because of my discovery that Gamini could be reached, even when he was furious. It had to be through quiet steel, I now knew, and not through shouted commands, pleas or emotion.

Having expected to be only a tutor, I was not quite prepared to act as peacemaker between two warring princes. Yet I had to, because I knew that the choice of a near-monk as tutor for Gamini was intended as a curb on his aggressive spirit. Although my life in the temple was far removed from the realities of everyday living, I had been enlightened on some political matters by the Venerable Rahula before I left for the palace. I knew that King Kakkavan desired peace, at any price – yet there was no question about his desiring the succession for Gamini. Surely Prince Digha Bahu and his flabby son had to have been apprised of the situation. No wonder Prince Panduka hated Gamini. My mind whirled with fears of intrigues to come as the little tableau unfolded before me.

Gamini turned away. Panduka sneered. 'Yellow fish belly,' he grunted.·

'Pork shit!' Gamini snarled back over his shoulder.

I stared at them in astonishment. 'You call yourselves princes!' I exploded in disgust. 'Where have you learned your manners? In the hovels of Veddah aborigines? Why, even they would be ashamed to use such language. We are a civilized people, remember? – the Sinhala, with a culture that goes back hundreds of years to the Aryans of the Indhoos valley, who even civilized the great Sikander. You will learn to mind your manners always, but especially before me.'

'Ho, ho, ho!' Panduka placed palms on hips bulging beneath a blue *hulwar* and laughed aloud.

In a flash I reached for my staff. One twirl, as I had been taught by my uncle, and anger brought it all back from the distant past as smoothly as water blocked by soil before a digger's tool.

I swung the staff again, this time at Panduka. I missed his face by the mere inch I had intended. He sprang back in alarm.

'Next time, I'll crack your head,' I hissed.

I advanced, leaping, expertly twirling the staff. Panduka retreated, stunned. He had not expected physical violence from me. I stalked him like a leopard. He kept retreating, stumbling, leaping. Gamini followed us, bellowing with laughter. 'Whack him!' he shouted. 'Crack his skull and

137

show he has only mud inside, not brains.'

I stopped when Panduka's breath started labouring. 'Our lesson on religion is over for the day,' I quietly told him. 'Remember I have treated you with loving kindness by not cracking your head. Make no mistake in future about my ability to enforce my rules.' My anger was gone, but I was pleased to have exposed him for a bully.

Gamini came up to me, his face relaxed and friendly for the first time. 'That is one lesson my fat cousin will never forget,' he said. Noting a hint of new respect in him, I felt a thrill of pleasure, but decided to make no comment. This was too precious to risk. I merely nodded, bade them both good day and returned to my quarters. I placed my staff on a stool and sat at the table by the window opening onto the garden, to record the event on *ola*.

I had barely sat down when I heard a soggy thud. I glanced sharply through the window. The two princes were no longer on the walk, but on the lawn, with Gamini sprawled on the green grass. Panduka was standing over him, having knocked him down with a heavy blow.

Springing to my feet, I was about to jump through the window when Gamini propped himself up on one elbow. He wiped his face with the back of his hand. Something about him – the deadly, pent-up hatred and anger as he slowly rose – rooted me to the spot. This was not a boy, but a grown man, moving slowly, inexorably to vengeance, leaving me powerless to intervene.

Panduka danced about Gamini, fists poised, ready to smite again. Now Gamini was on one knee. Panduka took a flying kick at him. Right palm turned down, left palm upward, Gamini gripped Panduka's ankle and twisted viciously. Panduka fell face downward with a grunt. Gamini was already poised. Growling low in his throat like a beast, he sprang. He landed foursquare on Panduka. The fat prince's breath exploded in an agonized gasp.

Then I witnessed one of the most extraordinary sights I

have ever seen. Panduka tried to rise, but Gamini held him down grimly. Like a bull terrier that grips and cannot let go even while the bull dashes him to death, he clung to Panduka, who frantically twisted, turned and tried to push him away. Flung from side to side, Gamini still hung on, flaying Panduka with a clenched fist at each pause, or banging his head on the turf.

Gamini's blows were like axe strokes, timed to perfection. Panduka began weakening. Who could take such a pounding? Suddenly, with a tremendous effort of instinctive timing, he flung off his tormentor and scrambled to his feet.

The two boys faced each other again, on a path now. Panduka's face was a mass of bruises from Gamini's fists. The blood flowed red from his nose. Gamini had only a great bruise on his cheek, from the first and only blow Panduka had landed.

Terror struck me when I saw Gamini's face in the sunlight. It was set like granite, the black eyes glittering, insane. Some foreign god possessed him. He was no longer himself, but completely lost in a blind, insensate rage. As far away as I was, I could see Panduka panic.

A cloud passed over the sun, casting a fleeting shadow on the two opponents. In that instant, so swiftly that I barely saw him, Gamini leaped. A terrific right, hooked up from his waist, caught Panduka on the jaw, exactly at the point. Panduka's head snapped back. Gamini's left ploughed into the stomach. Panduka cried out and doubled forward. Gamini raised both fists together in a single hammer and chopped the exposed neck. A grown man striking such a blow would have killed his opponent.

Panduka groaned, then went down as if he had been poleaxed. He collapsed, lying very still, his face in the brown dust.

For a moment, I thought that Gamini would run wild. He stood poised above Panduka, almost snarling. Moments passed in utter silence. Now I could, but would not interfere.

This was a battle Gamini would have to win by himself.

To my relief, he slowly relaxed. Breathing heavily, he stood looking down at Panduka's inert form. His face slowly cleared. Turning on his heel, he walked away, disappearing behind the green foliage.

My eyes returned to the form of Panduka, now stirring in the dust. With a shock, I realized that I had neither pity nor compassion for him. He was a bully, as I knew his father to be. I was raw with the desire for vengeance, raw as the side of a bull where the brand has seared too deeply.

Dear *devas*, what was happening to me, the *abithaya* of the Compassionate One? Like some dread, insidious disease, the stark moods and naked, bleeding ambition of this court had begun to lay their infection within me. Gone was the white simplicity, the shining honour of my uncle's home. Gone was the seeming peace of the temple with its mantle of goodness. What did the mantle cover? The answer slipped easily into my staring mind. Every rotting desire. At that moment, when my eyes were blinded by the sudden glare of the sun, my mind saw the truth. Lying beneath the sweet scent of every temple was rotting human flesh. Religion, philosophy, the system of government are only as good as the people beneath them. Mostly they cover what lies beneath, as the patch of grass over there, close to where Panduka was lying, covers a heap of dung, stored for manure.

I sped to my privy. The clay pitcher was full of water, still cool as the first dews. Grasping it, I strode to the window, placed the pitcher on the sill and vaulted to the garden.

I carried the pitcher over to Panduka. The water splashed silver on his face. He spluttered and snorted, lifted his face slightly and slid back again to wherever he had been. The water had made a filthy puddle. I had an insane desire to rub the Prince's face in the mud. The goat started bleating again while I poured the cold water in a steady, glistening stream over his face until he sat up, blowing, grunting and half choked.

'What . . . what happened?' he breathed. 'Where am I?'

'Lucky to be alive,' I retorted.

A pigeon cooed from the overhanging branches of a mango tree. I looked up at the sound. A line of red ants was scurrying along one of the branches. My eyes followed it to the green nest of mango leaves incredibly pasted together. These were not the small sharp-stinging *kadiya* ants, nor the red *dhimiya* ants, nor the *ambalaya* brown ants, but the *koombiya* that live on trees.

When I was little, a retainer once told me that the only way to get at mangoes on trees infested by these ants without being attacked by them was to kill a couple of ants, stick them in the folds of mango leaves and climb for the fruit. The other ants would be scared away by the death smell of their kind. I had tried the experiment, boldly climbing a mango tree, a leaf stuffed with dead ants tucked into my waistband. Once was enough. That retainer was lucky not to be around when I climbed down from the tree swollen with ant bites!

That Digha family were united as a nest of ants. What protection would Gamini have against them?

Chapter 14

The trail around the Tissa Wewa reservoir winds mäny *usabha* on three sides, but in Anu runs straight as an arrow along the high, broad dam on the edge of the city. The vast waters of the *wewa* sparkle silver below the western boundary of the dam, the other side of which is a grassy green slope, scattered with occasional shade trees, kumbuk, banyan and red-flowered flamboyant. Once the dam leaves the city precincts, it still heads south, then bends into scrub and jungle land until it is lost in the murky swamps and mud flats that meander around the tributary waters serving the reservoir.

Four weeks after I, a twelve-year-old boy, had my first interview with King Kakkavan in the Ruhuna palace, a group of figures was clustered around horses and chariots in a pale morning mist, at the junction of the dam and the main street, which stretched from the distant city of Anu to the reservoir. The horses stamped their feet and snorted violently to clear their nostrils of the damp air. Grooms, dressed in white *dhotis* and broad red sashes, guards and charioteers in bright blue uniforms were gathered around a young man who was obviously their leader.

About fifty cubits away squatted a Sinhala, his face, head and shoulders muffled in a great grey shawl. He seemed like a casual observer. A middle-aged Sinhala villager, he was indulging in one of the national pastimes, *nikkam*, doing nothing. Only his eyes showed, and they were fixed with interest on the seventeen-year-old leader of the Chola group, Prince Muthiah, son of King Elara. He was heir, by his father's conquest, to the throne of Lanka. The Sinhala watcher must have known that the Prince raced his chariots along this dam unfailingly at the crack of dawn each day.

The Prince stood discoursing in lively fashion in the centre of the group, the strident tone of his voice punctuated by occasional sycophantic laughter from the men around him. His arrogance was obvious, his manner condescending. He was an equally tall but thinner version of his father, with the same long frame, dark complexion, hawk nose and penetrating eyes, but he displayed none of his father's asceticism. He was dressed in blue pantaloons and pale blue tunic with a blue-and-white scarf around his neck, heightening the careless grace of youth. His curly black hair hung, glistening, to his shoulders. He kept tossing a forelock carelessly from his eyes as he spoke.

The Prince broke loose from the crowd with a parting remark that evoked shouts of laughter. He mounted his chariot and picked up the reins. The frail vehicle consisted of a teakwood yoke and wheels, metal shaft, axles and footboard. Two fiery horses, harnessed to the chariot, were perfectly matched Scindi, their glossy black coats gleaming with every muscle ripple.

When the other charioteers had mounted their vehicles and swung them around to face north, the Prince grasped the reins with his left hand, snatched the long whip from its socket and cracked it, flipping the reins at the same time. The horses darted forward, immediately gathering speed. Six chariots, drawn by grey, bay and chestnut horses, followed that of the prince. Only the Prince's horses were black. He sped through the low mist like a *deva* emerging from the clouds. Soon all the charioteers were lost in the spirit of the race.

'*Po! Po! Po-da! Vadi-po!*' they shouted to their horses.

The Prince soon began to outstrip the others, though they were all rattling along the straightaway at breakneck speed. They passed occasional Sinhala peasants minding cattle on the grassy slope, heads huddled in great brown or grey shawls against the cold. The peasants looked up at the racing chariots with seemingly indifferent eyes. At the bend in the dam, where the treeline began, birds took off with squawks and shrill cries before the drumming of hooves and the clatter of wheels. A single peasant squatted here, shrouded in the usual shawl.

The broad trail now became narrower, twisting and turning amid green jungle trees and dark, matted undergrowth. The mist clung thicker here in the shadows. This was one of the real tests of the charioteer, to maintain the speed of the straightaway in the bends and loops. The Prince flashed on without reducing his speed.

The hooded figures of peasants along the route were now like ghosts in the mist. They obligingly leaped aside to make

143

way and the Prince laughed uproariously, his thick hair blown by the wind, his white teeth bared.

Muthiah spun around the bends, sometimes on a single wheel, with no hesitation or slackening of speed. He was well ahead of the others now. To the vigilant Sinhala, it was obvious that on this wondrous morning, the Prince felt strong and powerful, exulting in his skill as a charioteer, certain of the love and pride of his father, the King.

He entered the difficult loop with reckless abandon. Wheels rattling, wood creaking against wood in protest, squeaking metal are all music to those who race chariots. The sweat-smell of galloping horses is more heady than perfume, the snaking whip sheer mastery, the reins control, posture on the footboard delicate poise – everything a man can desire.

Suddenly, the Prince glimpsed the outline of a small object on the trail, white through the white mist. A calf, he realized. If he avoided it, he would lose speed. If he galloped on, the collision would make the horses stumble. The race was all that mattered. He swerved the horses deftly, but very slightly, then thundered on without losing speed. The calf stood there in the manner of its kind, immobilized by the hidden ropes tied to each of its four feet and also bewildered by the approaching vehicle.

The left wheel of the chariot swung out, as the Prince knew it would. Its spoke caught the animal and flung it sideways. The death cry of the calf to its mother cow, 'Umbaa-aa', tore plaintively through the mist, ending abruptly with a thud.

The chariot careened on a single wheel, the other spinning madly in the air. Surely the vehicle would spill over. The shrill neighing of horses mingled with a series of great bumps and the grinding of protesting wheels. With cool skill, the Prince flipped the horses slightly in the opposite direction. The left wheel hit the ground. Scattering soil, the vehicle righted itself. The chariot was under control. The horses snorted and swept forward before the cracking whip. The Prince had barely lost speed.

'Ha!' the Prince shouted in triumph. He cast a quick backward glance. So he had killed a calf – a white calf. Why should he stop? He was the Prince. For nothing would he stop. Dimly he recalled his father's laws. No killing of animals on this day of the week. No killing of white cows, sacred to Hindus from ancient times. A life for a life.

The chariot flashed past two men, looming up on the side of the trail, huddled in their great shawls.

'He does not know his own father,' one of them observed with a knowing smile.

That same day, in the distant Ruhuna court, Velu Sumana did me the honour of asking me to share his secret vigil outside the Queen's chamber. Unknown to anyone, even the King, the Chief Warrior had personally kept guard over the Queen every night since my arrival in the court with news of King Elara's intentions.

Why Velu Sumana invited me, a twelve-year-old boy, to help him, I did not know at the time. All he said was something about an extra pair of eyes, ears and senses, young and sharpened by princely training and jungle-watching.

We dressed in black and dyed our faces and hands the colour of the night with a water-soluble *dhun*-berry mixture. We protected ourselves from mosquito bites with an application of citronella bark.

The Queen's quarters were in the most private portion of those reserved for ladies of the court. Although she normally slept in chambers adjoining those of the King, she now occupied separate chambers as she was in an advanced state of pregnancy. Being unable to satisfy her lord's sexual desires, she thus left him free to take one of the palace concubines if he so desired.

The ladies' quarters were set apart at the western end

145

of the palace grounds, behind extensive lawns, trees and shrubbery. A high wall, fronted by gates, ran right around these quarters, protecting them even from the palace and the great assembly hall. Guards patrolled the outer side of the wall and sentries were posted at the entrance.

The single-storey buildings for the ladies ran around a courtyard – actually, a pleasure garden – with fountains, a walled bathing pool and even a man-made stream. At the entrance was a reception, living and dining area. On the right side were the bed-chambers of the royal ladies and on the left those of the ladies-in-waiting and concubines. At the back were the Queen's private quarters. An inner open corridor ran around the courtyard, serving each side.

We kept our vigil in the courtyard opposite the Queen's quarters, hidden in a space between clumps of *kurundu*.

Velu Sumana seemed uncomfortable. Perhaps he was over-tired. He had kept watch for many nights. Besides, the mosquitoes were trying. The citronella bark prevented them from biting, but not from whining around, to our intense annoyance. Accursed insects!

It was a warm, muggy night. I could not see a single star in the overcast sky. Darkness pressed around us, revealing only vague outlines of shrubs and the building. Squatting endlessly in the same position on such a sultry night made keeping a sharp watch increasingly difficult. By midnight, all my faculties were directed toward fighting off overpowering drowsiness. My eyelids started getting heavier and heavier; I struggled to keep them open.

Suddenly, my hunter's instinct penetrated the drowsiness to warn me of danger. I came alert as if something had snapped in my brain. I gently eased cramped muscles and quietly shifted my position. I glanced at Velu Sumana. He was like a hound at the scent.

What reached us was neither sound nor movement. It was knowledge. We both looked in its direction. I saw nothing. I

146

blinked and a dark, hooded outline materialized at the Queen's door.

I looked at Velu Sumana. His eyes, gleaming in the darkness, were looking in the right direction. He had noticed the figure too. He moved his eyes away, then slowly moved them back. I did the same. The dark blur remained, silent as a tomb in a cemetery.

A thrill of excitement shot through my veins. I grasped my sword. Until now, I had only shared a vigil, my mind closed to any thought of action. Now we faced enemies. I was totally unafraid, only eager.

Velu Sumana relaxed, laying a quiet hand on mine, bidding me remain. His sword at the ready, he slowly started to rise. He rose as if he were part of the night, this giant, obviously an expert hunter. Why not? Had he not often done so with quarry in the scrub land of his native Devundara and the jungles of Ranna?

What was I to do? I suddenly feared the sword in my hand. Never had I killed a man. My heart pounded. My breath ran short. Through clouds of fear I called upon my uncle's image. I would be worthy of him! I was of royal blood and had a task before me. I would kill if necessary. I stopped shaking and steadied my breathing. Resolve began flooding through me. Tonight, I would prove myself.

The intruder must have at least one accomplice. How in the name of the *devas* had they slipped past the sentries and the guards? My heart grew sick at the knowledge that some of our men had already been murdered silently, in cold blood.

Velu Sumana would need me to cover his back. Already he had become a vague figure at the edge of the corridor. I followed, feet flat on the grass, feeling each step before putting my weight on that foot. Silence was vital and I must avoid being revealed against the night. I must move so slowly that I must not seem to move. My heart was beating

147

fast and loudly now. Surely it would betray my presence.

As I stood at the edge of the lawn it seemed an eternity before Velu Sumana reached the corridor wall. The dark figure at the door now had a distinct outline. The black hood made him seem a demon. Velu Sumana paused by the grey wall, then edged along it. I prayed he would not be noticed. My watchful eyes darted here and there, trying to spot other enemies, but met only the darkness and an anxious ache in my head. The intruder still stood by the door. He had made no move to open it. He must be confident that his rear was guarded.

Suddenly, I knew why he merely stood there. He was not going to enter. He was there to let someone out. That meant . . . I had to tell Velu Sumana –

There was no time. One swift leap and Velu Sumana was on the man, sword lunging, aiming for the soft kidney. The sword sank in smooth as a stake into mud. A short, sharp gasp turned to a groan. The man collapsed, in slow motion, almost gracefully. The sword was pulled out before he hit the ground.

Velu Sumana jumped sideways and around. I heard a swish and lunged swiftly at a figure looming towards him. A classic thrust, straight through the rib cage. The dying man's groan added to my fierce joy. I withdrew my sword before the man slowly collapsed. Then my feet found the firm granite of the veranda. With a throb of horror, my mind identified the swish I had heard. The garotte. I should have been sick, but having killed the man who wielded it, I was suddenly caught by the desire to kill and kill again.

I ran toward Velu Sumana. His swinging sword sliced through the neck of yet another attacker with stupendous power and timing. I felt a warm liquid splatter on me as the dead man's head began to topple off its shoulders.

Velu Sumana raised his leg, kicked at the Queen's door with the sole of his foot. The hinges collapsed like matchwood. The frame caved in. The door gave with a crash. It had been unbarred. We were too late. A savage cry escaped Velu Sumana as he sprang inside the chamber. Its oil lamp was still burning. I barely saw the gap of the open window.

Two shadows came at Velu Sumana, knives shining in their hands. How had they got in? How many more of them were there? The questions flashed through me as Velu Sumana jumped sideways, his back to the wall to protect his rear. He went on guard with his sword and began circling. I stood in the doorway, dripping sword in hand, guarding the entrance and waiting for an opportunity to intervene. My blood was pumping through my veins. I was bright and alert. My consciousness was fine-honed as a sharp blade. This was total awareness and the bloodlust was within me.

Voices sounded outside. Feet started to pound. A command rang out. 'Over there! The Queen's chambers!' Help was arriving. I could move in to assist Velu Sumana. Even as I took my first step forward, the Chief Warrior feinted and parried a knife advance from one of the men. His counterthrust was swifter than a cobra's strike – right through the man's stomach. He withdrew his sword in the same motion. In the fitful yellow light, maroon blood gouted from the slit stomach like wine from a spout.

I barely saw the flash of the thrown knife. Velu Sumana swayed to avoid it. Too late. A sickly thud and it was in his chest.

Ignoring the knife, Velu Sumana raised his sword with both hands. One mighty leap and the sword descended on the second man's head. The terrible stroke took the sword through skull and soft brain to the jaw, where it crunched to a shuddering halt. It was so swift and unexpected, the man did not make a sound. He was dead before he knew it.

Velu Sumana let the sword go and staggered to the Queen's bedroom. I recovered and followed in alarm. The tall brass lampstand flickered with its ten dozen wicks. As one, we both looked towards the great canopied bed. It was empty, the crumples of the white sheets forming a dozen mocking mouths.

Velu Sumana began to fall. He tried to steady himself, holding onto the back of a chair. Before I could get to him, he was sprawled on the floor. I bent above him, shouting his name. He was unconscious. A red stain of blood had begun to trickle beneath the knife sticking out of his chest. I was relieved, though, to see that the knife had entered the upper part of the chest, well above the heart. I reached to pull it out, but stayed my hand. A knife thrust should be handled with care. The right *patthu* ointment must be available to staunch the blood that would gush forth the moment the knife was removed. This was business for the physicians.

In desperation, I started to turn around to call for help, but stopped short when my eyes fell on an *ola* placed on the bed. I knew a moment of dread before picking up the *ola* to read:

> We have your queen. Any move to follow or intercept will result in her immediate death. Await our instructions.

Chapter 15

Even as I stared in horror at the message on the *ola* in the Queen's chamber, sleep was eluding King Elara in the Anu palace. His royal bed, placed on a platform served by steps, was a great canopied four-poster of brass, with orange drapes. It had planks and a mat instead of a mattress, pillows, cushions and silken sheets. The canopy was drawn back, but even the movement of the *punkah* manipulated from the adjoining room was of no help on this sweltering night.

It was not the heat, however, but the King's preoccupation that made him lie back, hands clasped behind his head, dark eyes staring at the red, green and white figures of *devas* floating on clouds painted on the high ceiling. If all went well, this was the night on which his agents would abduct the pregnant Vihara Maha Devi to bring her to Anu. He had laid his plans with great care, precision and secrecy, dealing directly with the chief of the gang, the notorious *thuggee*, whom he had imported from India. Now, within sixty days of the infamous death of Mahela, his justice would be administered, his comrade-at-arms avenged.

The *thuggee* would succeed in their mission. They always did. The Ruhuna king was unprepared to wage a major war of retaliation. Why then had he succumbed to his wife's whims? Totally irresponsible. Now he must pay the price by losing the woman. After she had known the ignominy of being produced before her Chola captor, she would be whisked away to a well-guarded hideout. Her baby would be strangled at birth and her person would be offered the Ruhuna king in exchange for Velu Sumana. King Elara smiled grimly. The way Kakkavan, the crow, doted on his sparkling wife, there could be no question about his accepting the ultimatum.

A king who loved too well was vulnerable! Although he had loved his queen, Pushpa, dearly, he had never allowed himself to dote on her even while she was alive. He had taken the vow of *brachmachariya* on the day Pushpa was cremated, not only because he did not wish to lie with any other woman, but also because sex creates effects in the mind that draw people away from God-consciousness. The *rishis* of old had discovered this. King Elara no longer made use of his concubines or yielded to the desires of the flesh, concentrating instead on developing mind and spirit in the Hindu *yogi* tradition.

His present spiritual goals derived from Vedic writings that had emerged from earliest times. These were not the

151

instructions to priests in the Yajur Veda, the ritual formulas of the Sama Veda, or the magic spells of the Atharva Veda, but the hymns of the Rig Veda, over a thousand in number. His greatest delight, however, was in the Upanishad. It stimulated him, opening up, as it did, many possibilites of thought concerning the universe and man's place in it. It started him asking thought-provoking questions which allowed his mind to soar in order to find the answers. All this only reconfirmed his well-learned Hindu beliefs.

As a Dasa, one of the original inhabitants of India, he resented the religion of those who had invaded his country centuries earlier from the Cokkasu, in the northern regions. They had given themselves the name Arya, meaning Noble Ones, but they were originally nomads and therefore barbarians.

King Elara sighed. He did not know why. Perhaps the heat was getting to him, though he was clad only in a white *verti* of light, hand-loom material. Yet he shivered involuntarily. 'Are you awake, dwarf?' he demanded.

'Yes, sire!' The dwarf sat up on the small teakwood couch at the far end of the room. He leaned back against the curving arm of the couch and arranged the sarong to cover his short legs.

Fan in hand, the King propped himself against the bedhead. 'What are your origins? Arya, Chola, or mixed?'

Junda grimaced. 'What an odd question, lord.' He paused, his look quizzical. 'I was abandoned as a baby, adopted first by the *bhikkus* and now by you!' He chuckled to himself. 'Yet, to answer your question, I am most likely a Sinhala by birth.'

'We are sorry about your parents. As for adopting you, whatever the motive of your *bhikkus*, our own was not compassion. We saw your talent as jester and have now grown to trust you.'

Junda was silent awhile. 'Why do you ask about my origins, lord?' he finally inquired.

152

'You and I get on so well together, yet the events of the past few months have convinced me that there are serious differences between us Dasa and you Arya. True, we have learned some good customs from the Arya and from all races who now live side by side in Lanka. But are these other races happy? We would have said yes, a few months ago. Now we are not sure. We have been made to feel like intruders, in spite of our just rule.'

'Men are all intruders upon this earth. They take of it by conquest, as you took Lanka!'

'We have no guilt whatsoever at being King of Lanka by conquest. It is our *dharma*, the duty of our station, bestowed on us through previous births into this reincarnation. Only by rigid adherence to *dharma* can we build *kharma* to give us a better incarnation in our next birth.'

Junda scratched his bald head thoughtfully with the tips of his tiny fingers. 'You Hindus think differently to us Buddhists, lord,' he soon asserted. 'Every creature is indeed the product of his *kharma*, yet we further believe that even animals can be reborn in a better form by following the rules of conduct which are universal to all beings, such as the animals who look after their young without abandoning them.'

The King paused to cock an ear at a quiet 'chink . . . chink . . . chink' that intruded through the window. 'There's a cobra out there,' he remarked, identifying the noise. 'Even a snake must dedicate himself, as best he can, to the duty of his station, which may well be to sting a man!'

'Even a snake can have a better rebirth through right conduct within its sphere.'

'Hindu and Buddhist react in the same way. It is our beliefs that are different. Your Buddha had Hindu beliefs once. While we Hindus kept our doctrine of *dharma* pure, he bastardized it with his *maitriya*, loving kindness, and *ahimsa*, abstinence toward enemies.' A short, derisive laugh escaped the King. 'These observances have helped emasculate the Sinhala Lion!'

153

Junda shrugged. 'At least the *lingam* is not one of our symbols, lord,' he declared boldly. 'We don't need that kind of crotch – er, crutch. Nor gods either, for we are born alone, we live and die alone, after making our own destinies.'

'You are being absurd,' the King retorted with some irritation. 'Gods existed before man and man needs them to strengthen him. It is not weakness, but strength that makes us turn to gods. We draw from their strength to become stronger. How else do you think your king has come thus far in life?'

He paused to reach for the clay water bowl on his bedside table. He took a sip from it. The fragrance of jasmine petals floating on the water caused his dark, strong nostrils to dilate. He replaced the bowl, swizzled the water around his mouth and spat into a tall brass spittoon. His eyes flashed back to the dwarf.

'The truth for one is not the same as for another,' the dwarf boldy persisted. 'Why, even among yourselves, you Hindus do not worship the same gods!'

'Your attitude merely confirms our conviction that Hindus and Buddhists are fundamentally opposed,' the King declared. 'This does not arise from different doctrines alone. It is a schism out of the very *atman* and *prana*, the basic source and the being of each Hindu and Buddhist, born of differing *kharma* to differing thought processes and life patterns.'

Junda relapsed into silence, obviously digesting this startling conclusion. Watching him, King Elara realized that this statement had shut off any further argument from the dwarf. No matter! If he were fair, Junda would finally admit that, in pursuance of *dharma*, his king had dispensed justice and fair play equally to Hindu and Buddhist.

A smile of pride touched King Elara's lips at recalling his dedication to justice. As for strength, what did this dwarf, with his misshapen body and lonely life, know of the strength

154

that comes from pride? Muthiah – a handsome youth, bold and daring – the image of him, true seed of his *atman*. Muthiah would make a great king some day, perhaps conquer the entire island. Elimination of the prince to be born to the Ruhuna queen, paving the way for Muthiah, was his duty as the father-king. It never even occurred to him that the Ruhuna queen might give birth to a girl.

Once his immediate plans were accomplished, only Prince Vipula would remain as the true Sinhala heir to contest the succession. That conniving upstart, Digha Bahu, was no competition.

King Elara's jaw tightened at the thought of Prince Vipula. He hated the man and feared his rights to the throne. Having already created the climate for the baby's demise, King Elara knew how he could remove Prince Vipula, thus killing two royal peacocks with a single arrow!

Two royal peacocks screamed from the palace garden outside the bedchamber, a favourable omen.

Suddenly spurred by a desire to rid the dwarf of his hope for a Sinhala on the throne of Lanka, King Elara began pouring out his most secret plan to Junda, enjoying its elements and finding greater reality in the telling of his ambitions for his son.

Crickets creaked outside and tapers hissed within the chamber. The dwarf listened intently. He never made jokes when his master was confiding in him.

'So you see, the succession is assured for our son,' the King concluded triumphantly.

He looked across the room. Sensing the sadness in Junda, he knew a mixture of pity and savage satisfaction at having trodden on the dwarf's loyalty to the Sinhala people. It surprised him. Both were strange emotions for him. He always tried to be detached and fair. 'We have not wanted this action, dwarf,' he volunteered, his voice more calm. 'We were forced to it by the evil deeds of the Ruhuna royalty and their tool, Velu Sumana.'

'No one can force a king to do anything.'

King Elara was taken aback. 'Not so,' he replied. 'A king governs by cause and effect. Having made the laws, he has to follow them regardless. That is *kharma* administered by him as a deity, the instrument of *kharma*. Our law says, a life for a life. Velu Sumana has taken a life. His masters in Ruhuna, as accessories, are equally guilty of the crime. We but provide the effects of their cause.'

'Regardless of all else?'

'Justice must be blind, if it is to be absolute.'

'Need it be absolute?'

'Otherwise it is not consistent. When there is no consistency, there is no justice. When there is no justice there is no law. Where there is no law, there is no society. Swift and terrible punishment is an essential ingredient of government, the only deterrent we know, the only real remedy.'

'Should you not, as a ruler, consider the causes of criminal behaviour?' Junda's eyebrows lifted.

'Causes can never excuse wrongdoing. Criminals, rebels, secessionists neither need nor deserve rehabilitation, which is a concept of the weak. Its existence would constitute an admission of guilt or liability on the part of the sovereign and would weaken the fabric of his justice. It is advocated by a few on grounds of compassion, or the theory that the criminal is but a product of environment. Such liberal views attack society's very roots. No! No! Dwarf, we are powerless before our own rules and shall see them enforced in the most ruthless manner.'

'Yet on your own admission, much of what you want to do is to ensure the succession for your son.'

'Rightful succession is one of our laws, a dictate of *dharma*.'

Junda moved to the edge of the couch and swung his legs out. Hands on the seat, short legs swinging like a child's, he was silent, while the sweating king watched him curiously,

156

not knowing what to expect from his dwarf.

'I'm glad I'm only the king of clowns and the clown of kings,' Junda finally observed soberly. 'Like any king, I make my own rules and they have their consequences, but my rules are invariably to make jokes and the consequences are funny. The rules of kings contain the substance of tragedy.'

'That is part of the price kings have to pay for their divinity, as the gods must surely pay when they enforce their laws of calamity, pain and death.'

Absolute justice . . . part of the price. The King's eyes shifted to the bronze bell hanging beside the brass post at the foot of the bed. He had set it up shortly after he seized the throne and established himself at Anu. It had a long cord, running from the bedroom through the garden to a column outside the palace gate. Anyone, be it Sinhala or Chola, who wanted justice from the King at any hour of the day or night had but to pull the rope. The King would hear and personally respond, for the bell was one of the symbols of his dedication to *dharma*.

As he watched the bell, it began to shine with a ghostly radiance. This gradually spread into a golden glow, from the centre of which a black, hooded head emerged. The King blanched. Had the cobra he had heard in the garden crept into his chamber? He was about to leap out of bed when the cobra head began growing larger. Its eyes were sightless, its flickering tongue directed toward him.

Mouth dry, powerless to move, he watched the bell's glow expand and the head approach him, the thin, sharp tongue continually flicking. Why, the cobra had no body. As for the golden aura, it was the good he had done.

Whom was the snake god emerging out of good to destroy?

The hood came closer and closer. He raised a hand to ward it off. Spellbound, he saw the black tongue turn into a shaft. Suddenly, it pierced his heart. He felt no pain, only a shooting chill of premonition.

'Clang!

The bell jangled harshly and suddenly, jarring the stillness. One ring, but its swinging motion remained, beating time to ear-singing echoes that finally died in an eerie silence. Then came another jarring jangle and more echoes.

The black tongue was withdrawn from his body. The cobra head began to recede, the golden glow to fade. The dying echoes of the bell took the radiance with them. Finally, only the bell remained – and silence.

'What means this?' the King demanded of himself in a whisper.

The dwarf's puzzled expression brought him back to reality.

'This bell has not rung for more than two years,' he explained. 'The last time was when the old Sinhala woman spread out her rice to dry and the heavens suddenly poured rain out of season. We fasted in penance until the skies frowned no more and rain fell only at night.' Some understanding of his vision entered his mind and fear reached down to clutch at his genitals. He shuddered as with the chill fever, his indrawn breath shaking his great frame and making the dark flesh quiver. The blood slowly drained from his face; his eyes rolled upward to his gods.

The dwarf started from his couch, fearful that the King might be having an attack.

'Dear gods, spare us from whatever it is we feel,' the King muttered. He glanced at Junda. 'We fear this bell tolls evil for us tonight, jester. After so long a silence . . . why?'

'There's only one way to answer that,' the dwarf suggested briskly. He stood firm, hands clasped behind his back. 'Let's go and discover who rang it.'

'Yes, indeed.' The King sprang out of bed and reached for his red robe. He strode to the door, the dwarf trotting at his side.

158

They had almost reached the audience chamber when palace attendants came panting up to them.

'What means the bell?' the King demanded. 'Who rang it?'

'My lord, it was a cow,' the chief attendant, a dark, grey-haired Chola with prominent white teeth, announced. 'Trouble thyself no more. It was only a cow that had seized the rope between its teeth and pulled it.'

Relief swept the King's face. 'A cow?' He laughed, turning to the dwarf. His features relaxed and his eyes twinkled. 'Hear you that, jester? It was a cow. That explains the manner of its ringing. Such foolish imaginings. Let us go back to bed.'

The attendants bowed. The King half turned to leave, then halted in his tracks. 'Wait!' he commanded, standing as if carved in red and black stone, his smile set on his lips. He thought a few moments, then slowly turned an ashen face to the dwarf. He took a deep breath and squared his shoulders. 'Our justice extends to man and beast alike,' he stated. 'Let us discover what justice the cow demands.' He turned to the chief attendant. 'Do you know?'

The man hesitated, blinking nervously, a guilty look on his face.

'Speak up!' the King commanded sharply.

'It is nothing, my lord,' the chief attendant ventured.

'If it is nothing, why did the cow ring the bell and why are you afraid to speak of it?'

'It is n-nothing.' Cheeks twitching, the attendant had suddenly begun stuttering.

Something broke loose within the King. He knew that what he was about to hear boded him no good, but he had to hear it. 'Speak, on pain of death,' he thundered. 'What manner of cow was it?'

'A white cow.'

'Dear *devas*.' The King paused, his stomach churning with dread. 'What justice does the sacred cow demand?'

159

The chief attendant knelt, trembling now, hands clasped together in supplication, while his fellow attendants cowered behind him. 'Forgive me, lord, and may the gods forgive me. This morning, as always, the Prince, your son, raced his chariot along the bound of the Tissa reservoir. He . . . uh . . . ran over the newborn calf of this cow. There can be no connexion . . .' his voice trailed away before the look in the King's eyes.'

'And it was a sacred white calf?' the King questioned, but almost as if he already knew the answer. 'Killed on the forbidden day . . . by our own son?'

'Yes, lord,' the chief attendant whispered.

Posed like figures in a sculpture, everyone looked at the King in silence.

Oh, the bitterness of it. Cattle had not been venerated by the Dasa until the Arya came. These Arya were originally nomadic herdsmen, to whom cattle, especially the cow with its fertility and milk, were of prime importance. The Arya instilled into all the existing peoples of India the value and therefore the sanctity of the cow. Having conquered Indian territories because they used fast-moving chariots while their foes fought ponderously on foot, at first the Arya taught the lesson of the sanctity of cattle through punishment meted out to those who slew these animals. With the passage of time, everyone in the land, including the Dasa, had made the law their own. White being the colour of purity, daylight and security, the white cow was most sacred of all.

King Elara's law had therefore stemmed from the very Arya whose religious views he resented. He had no choice but to promulgate it. Now his son had broken that law. For a second, his shoulders sagged. Then he made up his mind. 'A white cow, sacred to our religion, has been slain,' he stated grimly. 'We shall hold an inquiry three days from now. Meanwhile, let the Prince attend us tomorrow morning at the time of justice in the chamber.'

He drew himself to his full height and started walking back

160

to his quarters with a firm step – yet he could not dislodge from his mind the image of two proud peacocks fearful of a cobra.

The dwarf trotted behind him, the bells of his jester's cap jingling merrily.

Chapter 16

On the night of the Queen's abduction, King Kakkavan Tissa received me in his study immediately upon my requesting an audience. I was surprised to find Kirthi Siri with him at so late an hour.

'You requested immediate audience.' The King drew his yellow night robe more closely around him. 'Why?'

'It is a grave emergency, lord,' I began, trying to steady my stammering and speak like a man. 'I regret to inform you that Her Majesty, your wife, was abducted tonight from her bedchamber.'

To my surprise, my news was met with silence. I therefore plunged into my whole story, ending by proffering the kidnappers' message to the King, left hand to my right elbow, right hand outstretched, as I had been taught.

The King looked at Kirthi and inclined his head toward the *ola*. Kirthi took the *ola*, carried it over to one of the lighted tapers and read it aloud.

Silence followed again, with no action.

'How does all this seem to you, Chief Minister?' the King finally inquired.

The folds above Kirthi's eyes rose sharply, revealing his piercing eyes, with a strangely bleak expression in them. He ran talon-like fingers reflectively down the surface of his long nose, as if trying to draw it out further. 'This is obviously the work of King Elara. The fine precision of the operation shows the Chola must have access to plans of our kingdom, maps of the city, and the layout of the palace . . . even our guard arrangements. This confirms that Elara has spies in our court.' A sardonic, yellow-toothed smile crossed his face. 'Ah . . . and indeed, if I may make bold to say so, all has transpired as I advised you. This message . . .' He held out the *ola* in his long fingers. 'This message is probably intended to give us hope and prevent us from taking action. I respectfully suggest that the best time for bargaining will be *after* the child is born. The mother must be protected at all costs.'

I could have wept with bewilderment. The Queen had been abducted; her life was in danger; the Chief Warrior had been wounded; sentries and *thuggee* were dead – and all this useless old official could do was boast of his own success in predicting it. He looked so smug, I suddenly wanted to shake him physically and propel him into action.

King Kakkavan Tissa nodded gravely. 'We are in a shocking emergency situation. It is not a time for displays of grief or for precipitate action. Some of our hotheads might want to go after the Queen. They must be restrained. It is our decree that we ensure Her Majesty's safety at any price.' He sounded composed and very firm.

I looked at the King, astonished. He spoke before I could. 'We can only wait for word from them to negotiate! They cannot harm the baby. It is destined otherwise.'

Kirthi Siri tittered. 'Indeed! Indeed!' he exclaimed.

'We will, in consultation with our Chief Minister, consider what action to take,' the King continued. 'We had anticipated this abduction. Meanwhile, there is not much more that you can do, Prince Rodana. You may retire. You have acquitted yourself with distinction tonight.'

Having become a celebrity overnight, I had already received a stream of visitors, all eager for my story, when

Prince Digha Bahu visited me in my study late the next evening. He alone reminded me of a jackal on the scent of a leopard's kill.

'So the Queen is in King Elara's hands.' His pale eyes were glowing with satisfaction, his face glistening with sweat. 'He is unlikely to release her unless Velu Sumana is delivered to him. Even if this is done, we cannot be certain that he will fulfil his side of the bargain. Don't you think that he will kill the baby at birth, in order to keep the succession for his son, Prince Muthiah?'

My outrage was growing with his excitement.

'Actually, as a matter of fact,' the Prince now stuttered, 'this event places me in my rightful position.' He began to pace my study, tap-tapping with his ebony staff, while I remained standing by the window. 'With the Queen gone and the baby to be killed at birth as King Elara threatened in your presence, the *devas* have delivered the succession of the kingdom to me and my heirs.'

All I suddenly felt was loathing. My fists clenched and a mist swam before my eyes. I stepped toward him. 'Filthy jackal!' I shouted.

Ashamed at my outburst, I turned away, but not before noticing that Prince Digha Bahu's jaw had dropped. Possibly no one had ever addressed him thus before.

I moved towards the open window and gazed outside at the falling dusk. Trees in the distance looked like dark grey ghosts; crows cawed sadly from their nests.

'Please take your joy away and leave me with my grief,' I said.

I was met by a menacing silence.

'Indeed I shall leave now, but not at your bidding.' The words finally came out, stone-cold and hard, as I knew his eyes had to be. Imagining them, a shiver ran through me. 'Someday you and those dear to you will pay for this insult.'

I heard him turn on his heel and leave, the staff tap-tapping.

The days that followed were melancholy. A palace

responds to good and bad news like the plucked strings of a *veena*. If the minstrel sings a sad song, the sound, the feel of the notes, the mood are different to when his ballad is gay. Sorrow, doubt, uncertainty lay like a pall wherever people were gathered and even in the gardens, corridors and chambers. Among the noblemen and courtiers there was bold and fearless talk of war, but everyone waited for word from the kidnappers.

When the King resumed his regular routine, he was grave and withdrawn. Although I saw him only in passing, the feeling of compassion for him remained within me, because he now looked more lonely than ever.

I was happy to be summoned to the royal presence one week later at the ninth hour, which is set aside by Arya custom for the king's recreation and rest. Could there be some news of the Queen? I wore a white tunic for the occasion and presented myself to the King's study at the appointed time.

'Come and sit beside me,' he invited, pointing to a place for me beside him on the couch.

Noting my hesitancy, he laughed softly. 'We see you are accustomed to nothing but formality in the court,' he observed. He jerked his head sideways and gazed at me quizzically, like a crow. 'Ceremonial is right and proper. We must all know our place in the order of things, but you are our cousin, are you not? So we can be less formal when we are alone.' This time he patted the seat beside him in command.

I sat gingerly on the edge of the couch. He smiled.

'Since you will be spending some time with us, we thought it a splendid opportunity to discover more about life in the Anu court,' the King continued. 'Also, you are reported to be well read, versed in the Doctrine and skilled with the stylus. We have given directions for you to be visited by monks daily, except on *poya* days, so that your princely education may proceed.' He paused, cleared his throat and spat expertly into a brass spittoon beside the couch.

The King wiped his mouth with a red silk handkerchief. 'But the cultivation of the mind is not enough,' he resumed. 'You will also continue with instruction in the use of weapons. Our warriors are as good as those of King Elara, if not better. We have neglected you far too long.' A warmth entered his eyes. 'Meanwhile, we shall summon you frequently for little talks. You have demonstrated an active mind. Frankly, we have no one quite like you in our court.'

'My lord,' I began, 'you are – '

My words were interrupted by an agitated knocking on the door. King Kakkavan looked up impatiently. 'See who it is,' he bade me.

I had barely stood up when the door opened. The King's chief attendant was already in the posture of obeisance at the entrance.

'Rise!' King Kakkavan directed. 'Do not grovel there forever. We told you we were not to be interrupted.'

'F-f-forgive me, sire,' the man stammered, his whole appearance one of fear. 'B-b-but Prince Digha Bahu seeks immediate audience. He claims to have news of great importance, meant only for your ears. I thought perhaps he may have word of our Queen.'

King Kakkavan's face tightened. 'You were right!' he exclaimed. 'Show him in immediately.'

The attendant made obeisance again and backed out. I made to leave, but the King held up a hand. 'No, do not leave,' he commanded. A whimsical expression briefly crossed his face. He lowered his voice conspiratorially. 'You do well with the Prince. You infuriate him.'

Prince Digha Bahu made quick obeisance and bustled in. His face was beaded with sweat and his black tunic and white pantaloons were dusty. He had obviously just ridden from his fortress, as he had the other evening. I looked for an indication of his news. The pale brown eyes beamed with excitement and there was a hint of triumph in them. When he noticed me, an expression of distaste crossed his face, as if he were holding his nose against a bad smell.

'I bring news of the utmost importance.' He was stuttering with excitement, but still pompous.

'Speak!' King Kakkavan directed briefly.

Prince Digha Bahu jerked his head in my direction. 'Before this bastard?' he demanded.

King Kakkavan gripped the edge of the couch so hard that his knuckles showed white. He half rose, then sat back, shaking his head in sad contempt. My own fury was submerged before the King's wrath on my behalf, which touched me. 'You will never learn restraint, or deportment, will you, Prince?' he inquired. 'Prince Rodana is our cousin. You may speak before him.'

Prince Digha Bahu flushed. His angry eyes flickered at me, sharp as a lizard's tongue. He deliberately turned his back to me. 'Actually, as a matter of fact, I will not allow his odious presence to spoil my enjoyment of the news I bring.' He rubbed his hands together, then took a deep breath. 'Last morning, King Elara had his only son, Prince Muthiah, executed,' he declared. 'The youth was strung on the wheel of his own chariot and beheaded.'

I stiffened with disbelief. I stared at the Prince's back, then looked at the King. He leaned casually on the arm of his couch, almost as if this were stale news.

'Well, are you not astonished?' A note of bewilderment had crept into Prince Digha Bahu's voice.

King Kakkavan reached over to finger the platter on the ebony stool beside him. He finally selected a sweetmeat. 'Would you like to sample one of these?' he inquired, his eyes twinkling maliciously.

'I bring you momentous news and you offer me sweetmeats?' Prince Digha Bahu demanded incredulously, making no move to take one. 'Are you not curious as to the whys and wherefores of this strange tale? Or have you had the news already?'

166

'No, we have not had the news,' King Kakkavan responded. He took a bite of the piece of *kalu dodol*. 'Delicious! You really should try one,' he said, munching.

Prince Digha Bahu was now nonplussed.

'If you will not eat, be seated and tell us the whole story,' King Kakkavan invited, indicating the place on the couch that I had just vacated.

Prince Digha Bahu sat down and launched into his tale. The conclusion of it all was that King Elara had decreed justice against his own son in the tradition of the Chola kings that the law must be enforced regardless of rank. A white calf had been wantonly murdered by Prince Muthia on a forbidden day, in flagrant violation of the King's laws. The son's life had to be forfeit in consequence.

'Actually, as a matter of fact, my spies brought me word last night,' Prince Digha Bahu concluded. 'I rode without delay to give you the news myself.'

King Kakkavan and I had listened in silence. 'We are most grateful,' the King commented. His dark eyes, fixed on the Prince, took on that strange metallic glitter. 'But you obviously had other reasons for acting as messenger!'

Prince Digha Bahu's jaw dropped. Thin eyebrows raised, he stared blankly at the King. You could have heard a fly's breath in the silence. The King merely continued looking at the Prince.

Moments passed with the two men posed as in a painting. Finally, the Prince locked his jaw back with an effort. I almost heard the click. He glanced quickly aside, then smiled to himself. 'You are right,' he agreed, complacently now. 'Actually, as a matter of fact, I thought it only right to bring you the news at first hand, since it affects me most.' He deliberately drew a small gem-studded snuffbox from his tunic pocket, took a pinch of brown dried *adathoda* powder into one nostril and sneezed. 'Aaargh! Good stuff,' he commented. 'You should try it sometime.' He was trying to appear urbane. He cleared his throat, then faced the King.

'The devas are obviously trying to ensure my succession, not only to the Ruhuna throne, but also to that of Lanka,' he announced ponderously. 'They made King Elara destroy his own seed.' He paused for effect, then drew a deep breath. 'They will cause him to destroy yours, too, sire.' He sounded more evil than his words.

I shuddered. Unable to comprehend that such a grotesque statement could be made by anyone, least of all by a Prince, my eyes sought the King's face. It was calm as a dark forest pool, without a ripple on it. At that moment, his poise reminded me of Prince Vipula.

'Only one person now remains between me and the throne of the entire island of Lanka,' Prince Digha Bahu added softly. 'Prince Vipula.' He was thoughtful awhile. His voice dwindled to a whisper. 'The devas will destroy him too. Nothing will stand between me and my destiny.'

'Except the present kings of Anu and Malaya,' King Kakkavan reminded him gently. He cleared his throat. 'Not to mention Ruhuna.'

Chapter 17

King Elara paced his bed-chamber, gaunt in his customary white verti-cloth.

'Had he only held his tongue, I might still have saved him,' he cried. He was no longer an awe-inspiring monarch, but a father drained by uncertainty after having relentlessly enforced his law by executing his only son and heir.

Junda, standing by his little couch, searched his master's face in silence.

The few tapers that remained lit cast flickering lights on the King's giant frame. His black shadow stretched before him and he felt he was being engulfed by it. The heat of the room had caused his dark features to glisten with sweat. The overpowering smell of incense and burning oil reminded him of sacrificial altars, of himself as a victim of his gods.

The bull was the Chola symbol. As King Elara restlessly paced up and down in the silence of the night, it seemed to him that he was a great, bewildered Chola bull, with heaving, sweat-streaked flanks, wracked with pain from a goring that had been inevitable.

'To have bred such a son!' He burst forth again. 'How did this happen? Where did we fail?'

'You placed your trust in a human being.'

'But he was the product of our own seed.'

'You should have had faith without trust. Take me, for example. I am incapable of reproducing. Even if I had seed, what soil would accept it? I have no family to trust in, only faith that human beings will behave as such. As for your son, he merely behaved as your seed.'

Jolted by the dwarf's observation, the King pondered it awhile. 'You mean the unconcerned arrogance of our son is one of our own traits?'

'Yes.'

'And my own were the ones of my father,' the King observed to himself.

He saw his tall, dark father, the silver-haired widower – a wealthy nobleman in the hot, barren Chola lands. He had to be tough, even arrogant, in order to hold his lands against marauders and ambitious fellow noblemen. He had to be strong and ruthless with himself to cultivate the sandy soil, shaded by dry palmyra palms and littered with cactus, where vultures awaited corpses.

The inevitability of his tragedy struck him with telling force. 'Tell me, clown, could this be some monstrous joke of the gods?'

Junda lolled his head back to meet the King's eyes. 'Isn't all life a monstrous joke, King?' he inquired soberly. 'Look at me.' He grimaced and pointed at his body with both hands. 'Am I not a monstrous joke?' He gestured pathetically. 'This is a living being you see before you. Who created me? The great Brahma of Hindu and Jina? Your own special Hindu god, Lord Krishna? Jahweh, the one God of that tribe wandering the desert lands of wise King Sul Oman, who sent emissaries to buy jewels from our country for his Queen of Shaybah? Or am I merely one product in a *kharmic* line that is the real me – like a hideous knot on a straight, tall tree? And what of all that is my mind? Who put it there? A creator? Those who scoff at me, merely because I am different? Or I myself, weak before my deformity? Whatever your answer and even if the truth lies beyond our ken, what you see before you is the joke that is life. I am the product of my parents' seed, as your son was the product of yours. So why do you not accept your monstrous joke, as I accept mine?'

The dwarf's words were gently spoken, with no trace of bitterness. They had their impact. The King's breath caught with compassion. His fists clenched. The lids involuntarily closed over his eyes, as if shutting out the sight of the dwarf could exclude his own misery.

The dwarf hitched his green sarong tighter around his waist and looked towards the window.

'Poor Junda!' the King exclaimed, opening his eyes again and deliberately scrutinizing every part of the dwarf's deformity for the first time. 'How right you are. We seldom look deeply into others' misery and we never realize the pain behind the mask, do we?'

Junda's eyes misted. Then pride took over. 'I need no pity, King,' he said shortly.

'Not even compassion?'

'Not even compassion.'

'You are so hard?' There was wonderment in the King's

voice. 'Your fate has made you so hard?'

'I feel no hardness in me – merely acceptance of the truth.'

'Hmm.' The King turned and walked away, pausing to peer through the only open window.

The dwarf ambled up to his master. Holding the windowsill with both hands, he stood on tiptoe to see outside.

King Elara looked up at the dark blue sky, brilliant with festoons of glittering stars that seemed especially large tonight. His gaze dropped to the dark umbrellas of trees spangled by fireflies, an echo of the heavens. A dog barked. It was a lonely sound, until other dogs took it up and rent the stillness as if with firecrackers.

'All those actions we had taken to preserve the kingdom for our son. Useless. Futile.'

The dwarf's eyes jerked sharply toward his master. 'What actions, King?'

'You will witness one of them tonight.'

As if to confirm the King's words, shadows materialized before the bushes outside. The dwarf could barely see them because his head did not reach high enough, but the rustle of garments was unmistakable.

'You have the prize?' the King inquired softly.

'Yes, lord.' The reply was just above a whisper, but crystal clear through the gloom.

'We wish to pay our respects to the lady and assure her of our hospitality,' the King declared, his voice quiet. Noticing Junda craning his neck, he hesitated, then made up his mind. 'You too, dwarf. You shall look upon the famed beauty of your Sinhala queen again. Bring over that footstool, so you can see properly.' He nodded toward the side of the window.

The dwarf pattered quickly to the footstool, grabbed it, set it against the wall and climbed onto it.

'Your Queen Vihara Maha Devi has been kidnapped,' the King explained. 'This single open window was a beacon

171

to guide the kidnappers. The great Chola bull has struck as we promised. Swiftly. Secretly.'

The King could not read what was in the dwarf's mind, because the outsize face was impassive as it peered into the night.

King Elara seized one of the tapers and held it to the window. Its flame broke harshly through the gloom. Four figures were suddenly framed like shadows in the light. Three of them were dressed in close-fitting black clothes. Black masks over their faces, with slits for eyes, made them look like the undead. The fourth figure was obviously that of a woman, her stomach so heavy with child that not even her mantle could hide it. Her head was bowed and her whole being spoke of utter weariness.

Then she lifted her face. Even in the feeble light, her skin glowed and her dark eyes glistened beneath their frame of long black tresses.

A short gasp escaped Junda.

King Elara glanced at the dwarf. 'Well you may gasp at the beauty of this lady,' he conceded. 'And well you may sympathize with her plight.' His eyes moved back to the group. 'Madam, they lied about you,' he said softly. 'They had no words to speak truly of your beauty. Be assured of our hospitality in the secret place to which you will be taken. Should you have any hopes of rescue, please dismiss them. Our men left a message for your husband, King Kakkavan Tissa of Ruhuna, that we will execute you if there is any evidence of efforts to rescue you.'

The lady looked back at him calmly. She straightened her shoulders. Her face was tranquil. She made no reply. The three men closed around her. It was as if she had been enveloped. The group moved away. They were soon lost in the shadows.

Chapter 18

Although the weeks following the Queen's abduction were busy ones for me, there was a lassitude about the Ruhuna palace, as of a fire without flame, sputtering fitfully. I discovered that the presence of both a king and a queen is central to a country's vitality. Remove one or the other without a surrogate and a vacuum results. In the case of Ruhuna, the abduction was as critical as a deathblow dealt by an enemy king. When shame cannot find an outlet in renewed valour, it gradually extinguishes the flame of life.

Velu Sumana visibly suffered most during this period. He had, on his own initiative, precipitated the calamity. From being hailed as a hero who delivered the head of King Elara's Chief Warrior, Ratne Mahela, he was now ridiculed, albeit behind his back.

I could not help respecting the King, however begrudgingly, for his sticking by his decision to appoint Velu Sumana Chief Warrior and his consistency in the face of shifting circumstances. Having promoted Velu Sumana to be Chief Warrior when he brought back Ratne Mahela's head, it would not be honourable to punish him now for the same feat. The King was too remote for me to love, yet I felt respect and a vague sympathy for him in his lonely dedication to consistency.

On the evening of the sixteenth day of the cold month of Citta, King Kakkavan and I happened to be seated on the couch in his study when Prince Digha Bahu requested audience. Not again, I thought with a sinking heart.

My eyes sought those of the King. An amused look crossed his dark face. 'You seem to be fated to greet the Prince each time he rushes to the palace with stale news of extraordinary importance,' he observed sardonically. 'See that you behave yourself today.'

I grinned. 'Perhaps my lord will give me leave to retire?' I inquired.

He sobered in an instant. His dark eyes flickered to mine and away again. I began to feel alarmed. It was never his way to avoid anyone's gaze. 'No,' he directed thoughtfully. 'We summoned you here today with a purpose. You had best see it through.'

Now alarm became fear, which began to churn in my stomach. Whether it was caused by intuition or by the King's words or by his change of attitude, I could not tell. I only knew the fear – and it was very real.

'Show Prince Digha Bahu in!' the King commanded the chief attendant, who had remained at the door.

Once again Prince Digha Bahu strode into the study, dusty and dishevelled, but this time he was vibrating with excitement. There was a triumphant gleam in his pale eyes. His obeisance was rushed and perfunctory. I stood up because he was my elder. He saw me, but took no notice, so caught up was he with his news. He faced the King, legs apart, hands clasped behind him. His eyes were slightly blood-shot from the ride. 'Sire, I have good news and bad!' he exclaimed.

'From your appearance, the good news must outweigh the bad,' King Kakkavan retorted. 'So let us have the good news first.'

'The good news is that our Queen is alive. She will be returned to us as soon as you deliver the Chief Warrior to King Elara.' The Prince fished out a document bearing King Elara's seal from his tunic pocket and held it up for the King to see.

Showing no emotion, the King reached for the document. He held it in his hand awhile, as if weighing it, then placed it on the couch beside him without reading it. 'Now the bad news,' he requested.

Prince Digha Bahu looked chagrined at the King's calm. 'Are you not going to read that document – er . . . sire?'

'Perhaps we should do so after hearing the bad news, in order to lessen its impact.'

As always when he was excited, Prince Digha Bahu came out with his characteristic phrase. 'Actually, as a matter of fact' – he paused a moment, directing a probing look at the King – 'you sired a son, born to our Queen on the eleventh day of this month of Citta,' he declared. He watched the King, certain of a reaction this time.

King Kakkavan remained composed, as if receiving news that he had fathered a son was an everyday occurrence. I could not help admiring his superb self-control. Yet Prince Digha Bahu had obviously not finished, so why should the King react prematurely, I thought.

I watched the Prince. I sensed that he wanted to make the King react, yet he was also bursting with the desire to spill out more information. Unable to hold it back any longer, he finally stammered, 'I regret to inform you that King Elara had your son strangled soon after he was born.'

I heard a gasp and realized it was mine. Dear *devas*, this man is more inhuman than the murdering Chola king!

King Kakkavan said nothing. He picked up the document and began studying it in silence. Pity tearing me, I watched his face closely in the golden light, but saw no reaction there, nor in his body. Long moments passed while the tapers hissed and sputtered.

'This leaves you with a clear line of succession to the throne once I die, does it not?' King Kakkavan's reedy voice was low and uneven. Holding the document in his hand, he looked up at Prince Digha Bahu with inscrutable eyes.

The Prince took no pains to hide his triumph. 'Did I not say the *devas* were on my side in spite of all the portents and predictions?'

'You certainly did!'

Prince Digha Bahu turned to me. With a sinking heart, I

175

sensed that he was about to deliver some bad news to me as well. 'I have some further news of lesser importance.' Although Prince Digha Bahu was looking at the King again, I knew he was addressing his words to me. 'Two nights ago, my troops apprehended a couple of men who had come by boat from the east coast of King Elara's kingdom.' He shot a look of hatred and derision at me. 'They claimed to be Prince Vipula's best friends. They said they had organized a desperate plan to bring news of the baby's birth to Mahagama in time to have this ... er ... prince' – he nodded toward me – 'join a temple and save Prince Vipula from having to comply with the oath to take his life. A likely tale! They were obviously spies sent by King Elara to try and infiltrate our court. I therefore had them executed.'

My stomach dropped as I grasped the truth. 'What names did they give?' I demanded hoarsely.

He saw the desperation in my eyes and savoured moments of delight before he replied. 'Hari and Vira.' His smile was devilish.

A black void overwhelmed me. I shrieked. 'You murderer! Those were Sinhala noblemen – indeed, my uncle's best friends. They spoke the truth.' I turned to the King, tears streaming down my cheeks. 'Do something, sire!' I begged.

'You had two Sinhala noblemen killed?' the King demanded, sitting up straight.

'No! I had two spies executed,' the Prince replied defiantly. 'By virtue of powers vested in me.' He glared back at the King.

King Kakkavan slumped in his seat. He knew the truth. Prince Digha Bahu had deliberately executed the two men to prevent them from contacting me, transporting me to the temple and carrying the news back to Anu temple in time to save my uncle. They could not have believed that King Elara would commit the inhuman act of having a newborn baby killed. Did they not know that to a king who could have had

176

his own son executed as an inevitable consequence of his justice, the slaying of a baby was nothing? Still, theirs had been a gallant effort to help Prince Vipula, whom they held to be their king. I remembered their vitality, their comradeship, their jokes, and the tears stung my eyes. How loyal they had been; how pitiful the end of their last endeavour. Yet I was not going to give Prince Digha Bahu the satisfaction of knowing my feelings any longer.

As I raised my head high, there was a knock at the door. He half turned to look in its direction.

The door opened slowly, without any announcement. The wail of a baby echoed through the study. My first reaction was one of stupefaction at seeing the group of people standing at the entrance. Then my heart leaped with joy.

Leading the group was the Queen herself!

A low cry, as of a wounded animal, escaped Prince Digha Bahu as the Queen entered. She was less slender, more plump of face, but there was no mistaking her. She was carrying a baby wrapped in a blue silken quilt, with a tiny black head showing above it. How was she here? Had she been sent back by King Elara? Who was this baby in her arms, if her own had been strangled?

Contrary to custom, the King rose to greet his queen. His face was wreathed in a welcoming smile, the white teeth showing, the beak nose distended with suppressed emotion.

Prince Digha Bahu stood gawking at the Queen, his whole body slack, his jaw dropped, the mouth flaccid. Then, despite my joy at seeing the Queen, I thought of poor Hari and Vira and remembered the object of their mission. 'Is it a boy, or a girl?' I demanded, regardless of protocol, my voice ringing clear.

'A boy,' the Queen replied. 'A beautiful, strong boy prince.'

Thoughts whirled like mad dervishes within my mind.

King Kakkavan strode to the Queen. He embraced her and the tiny bundle in her arms. Taller than him, she placed her fair cheek against his black-and-silver hair. They stood together thus, briefly. Then the King drew back, as it is not proper for royalty to display emotion in public. He bent to poke a finger at the baby's cheek, clucking to it.

Stupid king, I thought, do you not know my uncle's life is at stake? End your playtime and let me get to the temple!

'My lord, I deliver to you Prince Abhaya Gamini, the future King of Lanka!' the Queen formally announced. She carefully placed the bundle in the King's arms. He received it awkwardly, dead now to all else but the tiny wrinkled face.

'Our saviour is safely delivered.' The whining voice was that of Kirthi Siri, who had entered behind the Queen. His gaunt figure was poised behind her, like a bird of prey. 'Sire, all I planned has been accomplished. I have brought your queen and your son from their sanctuary.'

'Thank you, Chief Minister. Your plan to substitute another lady of like appearance for the Queen was brilliant. It has saved our Queen, our heir and our kingdom. We do thank you.' He glanced down at the baby. 'Do you think the baby will be fair?' he inquired, as if the baby's colour superseded all other considerations.

'Not really, I regret to say, sire,' Kirthi Siri responded softly.

'How can you tell? See how pink his skin is.'

Kirthi Siri folded his arms in the pose of an ancient's wisdom. 'Ah! – but you tell the real colour from the edges of the ears. You will have a black prince for a son, but he is manly already.

As if to prove him right, a series of lusty wails emerged from the baby. The Queen moved forward swiftly, hushing the child. Presently its cries died down. Incredible how a mother's voice can soothe, I thought. Then the impact of the King's words to Kirthi Siri hit me. If the clever Chief Minister had really substituted another pregnant woman for the Queen shortly before the abduction, that woman's child, an innocent baby, had been destroyed by King Elara. A

178

monstrous trick had been played on the man who prided himself on his justice. Now that he had strangled the wrong child, he could not send agents to Ruhuna again without facing a charge of making a campaign against babies. And how would he live with the consequences of his error!

Aghast at it all, I could not even find pleasure in Prince Digha Bahu's stupefaction. He too had been tricked. Dear *devas*, there was no honour anywhere – except with my uncle. He was in grave danger and I could not command King Kakkavan's attention.

Suddenly, I felt sick. I saw the boy's pink little face, so different from my handsome, dashing uncle, to whom I had promised I would serve this little creature for the rest of my days. This birth in exchange for my uncle's possible death.

As if to jeer at me, the King exclaimed, 'He's wet me!'

'An omen of good fortune!' Kirthi Siri whined.

Attendants rushed forward to change the boy's clothes. The heir to the throne of Lanka! The heir to the entire island kingdom? The prince that everyone has awaited, I thought, greeting his patrimony with a burst of wetness!

More knowledge hit me, this time with the force of a tempest, flinging thoughts through my mind like windswept rain. The devilish cunning of King Elara's oath had been that it took effect even if the baby died or was killed after being born. Prince Vipula would take his life, without pleading excuses, whether because of that strangled baby or this living one, unless I entered the temple in time.

Hopelessness seized me. I could certainly fulfil the condition of the oath tonight, but how in all the world could I get the information through to my uncle and King Elara in time? I knew beyond doubt that King Elara had gambled on the baby being a boy and had planned to ensure that news of my entering the temple would not reach Anu in time. Cunning, filthy, accursed king! I hope you suffer the tortures of the damned for having your own son executed.

I recalled the dread foreboding I had experienced in Anu,

on the journey to Ruhuna and at the end of that first conference with King Kakkavan. I recalled fragments of speech and the final awesome truth exploded in my mind with the force of a thunderbolt. Kirthi Siri had planned more than a substitute for the pregnant queen. He had conspired to cause Prince Vipula's death, because Prince Vipula was the only person with a direct claim to the throne of Lanka. His demise would give clear succession to this newborn prince. As for Prince Digha Bahu, no one gave any serious thought to the promises King Kakkavan had extended to him.

Fear for my uncle opened up the knowledge of the inner sight. More words from the past three months came tumbling before me, like a scroll of *ola* being unfolded. The white calf had been deliberately set before King Elara's son, Prince Muthiah, with the knowledge of what he would do and the certainty that it would result in a sentence of death being passed on him by his father. Kirthi and his spies had organized everything, right down to the pulling of that bell rope at the Anu palace gates, making believe that the mother cow had done it to demand justice from the King.

What dreadful people were these – a wife and mother among them. This queen, for whom I had experienced an immediate attraction, had been involved in the plot to have Prince Muthiah and my uncle killed. I looked at her, horror-stricken. For a moment there was uncertainty on her beautiful face. Then the dark eyes gleamed as they had done just once that fateful night in King Kakkavan's audience chamber. Her whole expression changed, as if it had been wiped clean, leaving her face blank, more deadly than any response. She knew that I had deduced the truth: Behind the mask of her dedicated religious life, her compassion toward all, the ambitious mother had taken over, greedy, grasping, determined to suckle her infant with blood even if it meant the death of her *prana*. Now, she would banish me to the temple regardless.

180

The attendants left. The King held his son again. The little face puckered in its sleep, as if the baby were having a bad dream. You have been named Abhaya Gamini, I thought. You will have to be strong indeed if you are to survive. Perhaps you will prove to be a saviour, but only to the extent that you do not pander to the demands of these others.

Suddenly I saw my uncle standing before me. He was so real, he was in this very study. The physical form was his, every feature of the chiselled face distinct; even the scent of his sandalwood was in the air. The dark eyes gazed at me with love. He smiled. Then I saw the golden aura around him and realized that this was his *prana*, not his body.

'First, honour,' he whispered, 'and honour to the end!' He paused, seeming to listen. 'I hear winds, *putha*.' The words were formed only by his lips, hardly with his breath. 'They come from the south, but not to caress.' A triumphant laugh escaped him. 'They are born of the tramp of feet, the songs of warriors, the breath of a nation on the march. I see a great new *thupa* in our sacred Anu, rising to the heavens. The winds sweep around its giant pinnacle. You who create these winds are born of them . . . are one with them . . . for they are the winds of Sinhala.'

Slowly he dissolved. A chill wind blew over me in that closed room. My uncle would die very shortly.

Helplessness, bleak as the grave, descended on me – cold, relentless. I trembled, but I was powerless to cry out. My own *prana* seemed to have ebbed away from my body. I saw a wild-eyed boy. I felt his throat gurgling before an insane desire to scream with wild laughter which would not come.

By the time my *prana* returned, despair had settled over me, but I knew my destiny. I needed no banishment. All I wanted for my corpse of a body was some refuge from these terrible people. I would gladly retreat to a temple to find peace.

PART TWO

Ruhuna Rata

The Free State of the Sinhala

Chapter 19

It was early enough for the morning sunlight to hold dawn-tints in the air. The blue sky was limpid, with gulls making white patterns above green treetops. Gentleness was everywhere except for the harsh cawing of black crows.

White-clad crowds were packed in front of the palace gates. Some of them had waited hours to watch the event, not the least because merit is acquired by waiting for *bhikkus*, especially at the time of Wesak, which commemorates the day of the birth, Enlightenment and death of Lord Buddha. Celebrated on the appropriate full moon day rather than on a specific calendar date, this year it fell at the end of the month of Vesakha.

A gigantic *thorana* archway had been erected over the gates for the occasion. It was built of tall coconut trunks, intertwined with their woven green leaves and decorated with pink king-coconuts and festoons. of bright-coloured flowers. The upper panels contained red-and-yellow paintings of events of the life of Lord Buddha, done on cloth by Mahagama's leading artists. Everyone was dressed in white, including the palace guards, drawn up without weapons in the great courtyard. Princes and noblemen stood, in order of rank, at the foot of the broad granite steps leading up to the audience hall. King Kakkavan, back from Mahaiyangana, was at our head, chatting quietly to Prince Digha Bahu, Velu Sumana and Kirthi Siri. On sacred occasions, enmities are as hushed as prayers! We were all dressed in *dhotis* and loose overshirts. Beside us, on low ebony stools, were golden bowls of clear water sprinkled with sweet-smelling flower petals – *olu*, *nelun* and jasmine, the flowers of religion and lovers, possibly because their heady perfume transports the senses.

Decorative arches of green ferns graced the sculptured bas-reliefs on the four sides of the audience hall. Huge brass pots with creamy coconut flowers in them were placed beneath each arch. Along the floor of the hall thousands of little clay lamps in rows flickered and smoked lightly with each gentle breeze.

Gamini, twelve, and his younger brother, Tissa, stood beside me. Behind us were noblemen and courtiers with towels in their hands to wipe the monks' feet after we had washed them.

Gamini remained still and relaxed, lost in his thoughts. He was well disciplined. Tissa was restless. He kept shifting on his feet, constantly asking me when the monks were due to arrive.

We did not have long to wait before hearing the creak of wagons in the distance.

'Sadhu! Sadhu! Saa-a . . .' The thunderous roar of the devout greeting the monks filled the air.

By the time the cries tapered off to silence, the creaking of the wagons had stopped. A saffron stream of monks began to flow through the entrance gates and into the road leading to the audience hall. My heart contracted when I saw the Venerable Rahula, my Chief Monk, at their head.

Buddhist monks own nothing. Their temples are bestowed on them by monarchs, princes, nobles or the people. Their only possessions are two saffron robes, a shell-shaped umbrella woven from palmyra leaves, an indi-leaf fan, a black begging bowl and a pair of slippers. There are no kitchens in the temples. Monks visit people's abodes daily, eyes downcast, begging bowls in hand, seeking alms. They do not eat fish, meat or eggs. They are allowed only one meal a day, which has to be taken before noon. The rest of the time they only drink water.

I could not help a slight feeling of guilt at seeing the Maha Nayake, the Chief Monk. If I had still been in the temple, I would have walked behind him to look after his needs. When he started *bana* preaching, I would have knelt beside him, so that whenever he made a telling point in his sermon and asked in his soft, dispassionate tones, '*Ahaima ney the?*' ('Is that not so?'), I would have answered '*Ahey, hamuduruwo!*' ('Yes, venerable sir!').

Instead, I was only here to help wash the feet of his fellow monks. I suddenly had the strange feeling that I had torn myself out of the cool peace of the womb for a world of heat, sweat, flies and human failings. Rotting flesh may sometimes appear to disfigure the Doctrine, but can never remove its essential gentleness. There is no physical violence, not even the clash of eyes, in that secluded life. Seeing the Maha Nayake, with his wrinkled face and calm mien, his shaven head symbolizing peace, made me realize how irrevocable was my decision to leave that seclusion.

As was proper, the Venerable Rahula took no notice of me. As was proper, his gnarled feet were washed by the King.

The whole process of foot-washing took about half an hour. We made obeisance to our particular *bhikku*. We splashed water from a golden bowl on his feet. He rubbed each foot on the other to wipe off dust. We poured more water and he moved on to have his feet wiped.

It was an endless procession of feet of all shapes, sizes, colour and appearance: black feet, brown feet, fair feet, slender feet, fat feet, misshapen feet. There were sore feet and feet with bunions, corns and scars, all passing before my eyes until I began to feel somewhat dizzy.

I was glad when the last monk ascended the steps and I could follow the King and the princes into the hall. The monks were already seated on their yellow mats in the hall – endless rows of them in the lotus pose, begging bowls placed before them, shaven heads bowed. It was a solemn scene in a dignified setting. The lofty building was supported by four long lines of ebony columns on each side, with

187

wooden ceilings sloping sharply up beneath the roof to the high centre-line thirty *ratana* above the ground. The cornices were sculptured heavily in the style of pure Sinhala architecture, rather than with the highly intricate patterns of the Chola. Built to catch ocean breezes, the great hall was open on three sides. On the fourth side was a wall painted with frescoes in orange, yellow and red. Double doors in the centre of the wall led into the audience chamber, from which a bell now started clanging. It rang loud and silver through the hall, so insistently that its clangour entered the being and hurt the head. We knelt, foreheads to the ground.

Presently, the clanging stopped. Its clamour evaporated, but slowly. The final silence was an ache.

The Chief Monk began his chant in a high, nasal voice: '*Namo thassa bagavatho . . .* ,' as a prelude to administering Pan-sil, the Five Precepts, by reciting them as stated in Lord Buddha's scriptures. The other monks took up the chant. Soon it was like the sound of a great, steady wind or the roar of the ocean, but more melodious because of the intermingling of many qualities of voice.

It is a Buddhist belief that the words matter – that uttering holy words produces good – but I think that the nature of the sound, including voice quality, is important. It reveals the spirit.

As always, the chanting wafted me away from mortal existence, riding closer on its harmony to God. The holy music enfolded me and entered my whole being, so I was a part of it and it was a part of me. There was no separation, but a single entity rising in God, who accepted its beauty.

Even with my eyes closed, the sound had the warm colour and texture of lamp-glow, so mellow was it, borne on the heady scent of flowers and incense, like a white-clad maiden on a golden chariot. My ears deaf to all other sounds, I exulted in the resonant timbre of the thrumming of the space between me and the stars.

There is no way in which I could accept the Buddhist

doctrines of no God being necessary in this life, or *Anatta*, non-soul, before this experience. Pan-sil and God! Why not?

When the last sacred words of the chant were over, the sound lingered in the air, delicate as the perfume of that maiden after she left the room. Then there was silence in which you could have heard the silk-rustle she also left behind.

I had not eaten the whole day. Such is our custom on these occasions. The smell of cooked milk-rice, the spicy scents of the potato, *dhall*, cabbage, bitter melon and fried herb curries and the pungent odour of grated coconut *sambole*, *seeni-sambole* and chili pickles came from the audience chamber. An endless succession of attendants had brought steaming black cauldrons of food there from the royal kitchen, where princesses and ladies of the court, under the personal supervision of the Queen, ladled the food into bowls. Attendants carried the bowls into the hall, where each of us men began serving the monks in our allotted areas. These mouth-watering odours made my stomach feel emptier than ever. Even so, I could not help but be impressed by the orderliness of the entire operation, organized entirely by the ladies, under the Queen's direction.

When all the monks were finally served, we moved about quietly, watching them eat and looking to their needs. Monks never refuse anything. Whatever is left in their bowls after they finish eating is taken back to the temple in the bowls. If a monk desires another helping, he points to a brother monk's bowl and says, soft-voiced, 'Why do you not serve some cabbage curry to that *bhikku*?' We know to serve him instead. It is a charming, civilized custom – very hypocritical, but then such hypocrisy is one of the essentials of a civilized existence.

The monks ate slowly, stolidly, reflectively. Young white teeth, blackened teeth and toothless gums ground away,

189

punctuated by an occasional belch or a hiccup. A fat middle-aged *bhikku* with shiny, plump cheeks had obviously not overcome the evil of gluttony, he was so repeatedly solicitous of the needs of so many of his companions!

When the monks had finished their rice and curry, the attendants brought in buffalo milk curd, *kitul* honey and fruit of all kinds – mangoes, bananas, mangosteen, papaya, ripe jak and *rambutang*.

Finally, it was over. An attendant called for attention in the name of the King. Other attendants took up the cry, 'Silence, in the name of the King.' The babble of voices ebbed away.

'We request the permission of the *bhikkus* here gathered for a ceremony,' the King announced. His deep voice sounded thin and reedy in that great hall. He looked toward the Chief Monk. The Venerable Rahula nodded assent.

The King clapped his hands. Six white-clad attendants came toward him from the rear of the hall. Each held a golden eating bowl and a spoon in his hand. They placed the bowls at the feet of the Chief Monk.

My eyes were fixed on the King. I wondered what he had in mind.

In the hush, he knelt down and used one of the spoons to serve some milk-rice that the Chief Monk had left on the side of his begging bowl into each of the golden eating bowls.

Still kneeling, the King turned his head to where the two princes, Gamini and Tissa, stood slightly behind him. 'Come forward, Princes, and kneel on either side of us,' he commanded. His face was exalted. A strange fervour pierced through the glaze of his dark eyes.

The two princes stepped forward and knelt beside the King, Gamini on his right, Tissa to his left.

'Now repeat after me,' the King directed firmly. 'We swear that we will never turn away from the *bhikkus*, the guardian spirits of our house.'

The two boys repeated the oath after him in clear tones.

190

'Now eat this milk-rice made sacred by its proof that the Noble Order has been fed, and if your oath be false may the rice be undigested in your bellies.'

Gravely the King held a spoon of milk-rice to the mouths of each of the princes. Gravely they first touched the floor with their heads, then ate.

A sigh of religious satisfaction rippled through the hall, as if the people had not believed the princes would take the oath until they had taken it. These princes have no option but to take the oath, I thought. People witness such events with the sweet credibility of children listening to a story.

The King's voice broke through the hush again. 'Now repeat after me: We swear that we two brothers will forever be without enmity, one toward another.'

Gamini glanced swiftly at his brother. I caught the strange non-look. There was nothing in it, whereas I had expected love, or at least affection. Tissa did not even turn in his brother's direction.

Both brothers slowly repeated the words.

The King proffered the spoon of milk-rice to each of them in turn, saying, 'If your oath be false may this milk-rice be indigestible in your bellies.'

Both brothers touched the floor with their heads, then ate the milk-rice.

I wondered what separated the brothers. There was some invisible barrier that I could not identify.

The King cleared his throat and turned to the third set of bowls.

My thoughts became irreverent. If the brothers were to have indigestion, I wondered how one would ever know for certain whether it was the milk-rice that had caused it.

My reflections were interrupted by the King's voice administering the third and final oath, but my attention was caught only when he paused. At first the words he had spoken did not register. Then they suddenly hit me.

'We swear never to fight the Cholas,' the King had said.

191

His gaze was now intent on Gamini alone.

My jaw tightened. My gaze darted toward Gamini. He looked stricken. My heart went out to him suddenly, like a quick gasp of pity.

'Now repeat this final oath and take it upon eating the sacred milk-rice . . .'

I did not hear the rest of the King's words. My whole attention was on Gamini. It was one of those sickening moments when one realizes something soul-shaking is going to happen and time stands still as one watches, powerless, fascinated.

For a fleeting second, Gamini continued looking stricken. Then his expression turned to shock and disbelief. He was like one who has been struck a mortal blow, but cannot accept its source. Disbelief changed to accusation. Then his eyes flashed in anger. Fixed on the King, those eyes called his father traitor and coward.

The changes were so swift, I felt I was watching a scene illumined by flashes of lightning on a dark night. Every time I blinked, a different aspect lay vivid before me, until only the last scene remained as if the sun had finally broken through clouds and the day had dawned to reveal a holocaust.

My chest ached. I had been holding my breath. I let go. My breathing seemed to be the only sound in the room. Everyone, everything, was poised, pendant, expectant, like the hand of the King holding up the spoon of milk-rice to the Prince. Vaguely, I was conscious of the rapt attention of even the normally imperturbable monks.

Moments passed. My heartbeats seemed to count them. The tension in the hall built up. Still the dark little king, one hand extended like a claw and the dusky kneeling prince, motionless except for the anger blazing in his eyes, held their pose.

Like a striking snake, Gamini's dark hand hit the golden bowl from which his father had taken the rice. It went

192

spinning along the floor, tinkling and scattering a mosaic of food on the mountain crystal.

Gamini rose, so slowly that it did not seem as if he were moving at all. Meanwhile, his blazing gaze never left the dark, glittering eyes of the King.

Now Gamini stood to his full height. Face lifted to his son's, the kneeling king seemed a suppliant. Although he was only a boy, Gamini seemed to tower above his father.

The inner sight burst forth in my mind. Gamini continued towering above the King until his head touched the roof and the King was totally absorbed by him. A golden haze flickered around them both. Gamini's aura was touched by the colours of the rainbow. Then I noted a black shadow within the outer core. Some instinct told me it reflected the evil in his life and I became sorely afraid.

The haze began to dissolve, until finally Gamini was left again in my line of vision, lonely, angry. He made obeisance to the monks, then turned his back on the King and walked steadily away. It was the final insult, for no one turns his back on a king.

Kakkavan Tissa was dumbfounded. He knelt there like a pathetic crow, but few noticed him. They had eyes only for Gamini. He reached the door of the chamber, walking slowly and with great dignity. Once there, his self-control gave. He started to run.

A single sound from the onlookers, like a great groan, resounded through the hall.

The King's hand shook when he replaced the spoon in one of the golden bowls. He made obeisance to the Chief Monk. 'We humbly beg the pardon of the Venerable Chief Monk and all the other venerable *bhikkus* here for the dreadful display of deportment by our son, Prince Gamini,' he said huskily. 'The fault is ours.' A grim note entered his voice. 'But the Prince is old enough to know better. For this, he shall be punished.'

'Punish him not, O King,' the Chief Monk urged. His

gentle, even voice was full of strange authority. 'He but refused to take an oath that offended him. It must have run counter to his *kharma*, which is something no human being, not even kings or chief monks, can oppose. The fault belongs to no one, for each of you acted as your respective *kharmas* dictated.'

'Yet each of us must learn to govern our *kharmic* reactions in a civilized fashion,' the King persisted. 'We are the ruling monarch. Our dictates must be obeyed.'

'An oath taken under dictation is no oath at all,' the Venerable Rahula advised him. 'Blest with the gift of the inner sight and being the member of the Noble Order whose leavings would have sanctified the Prince's oath, I beg you, sire, to remember the invocation of our Great Teacher and practise *maitriya* on this occasion. Forgive the Prince and turn this event to the profit of yourself and the Prince, to the greater glory of the Sinhala people.'

King Kakkavan remained kneeling, a tragic figure, gazing back at the Chief Monk, whose words confirmed what I had always suspected, that for all his detachment, he remained a patriot at heart. He knew that the King had just concluded a secret treaty with the foreign usurper, Elara.

Chapter 20

As soon as the *bhikkus* started to leave, I followed the King and his companions to the base of the audience hall steps. I watched the King closely. He looked sad, but there was also repressed anger and conflict within him. Suddenly, he held his breath. His eyelids drooped, his nostrils dilated. A hand flew to his chest. He broke into a sweat. I started forward, but he controlled his breathing and returned to normal. So brief was the event, I thought he must simply have choked on his own spittle.

We stood outside in the glare of the hot noonday sun. The saffron-robed monks flowed steadily down the steps. Their faces and shaven heads shone with sweat. Most of them were replete from their meal. A few burped loudly. I gave them only perfunctory salutation, because I had begun to wonder about the purpose and effect of this great *dana*. It was obviously to acquire merit. Kings even maintain Books of Meritorious Deeds, like misers keeping a record of everything they own, all that people owe them. *Kharma* thus becomes the debtor of kings!

Surely one has to do more than observe the form of prescribed deeds to attain true merit – perhaps practise kindliness, compassion and giving without a thought for oneself. Lord Buddha could not possibly have intended that this king, who had just given *dana* to a thousand monks almost with a snap of his fingers, would acquire more merit than a poor widow who, perhaps at this very moment, had given part of her scanty meal to a starving child. No, men have altered the Buddha's Doctrine to their own selfish needs.

I was impatient for the last monk to leave. I wanted to go after Gamini. He would be in his room, where his couch was frequently his refuge.

When the last wagon creaked away, we ascended the broad steps again and re-entered the audience hall. Now it was our turn to be fed and I was starved. My body had grown accustomed to the routine of the temple, where the midday meal is eaten before the eleventh hour of the day. Knowing that the Queen, or one of the ladies of the court, would send Gamini's food to his room, I was tempted to eat first and then go to him. My concern for him decided me. I made obeisance to the King and requested his permission to withdraw. He granted it, but looked at me strangely. Did he

195

hold me responsible for his son's conduct, I wondered. Surely not, when I had been there only three weeks?

I hastened toward the chamber door leading to the rear entrance. Someone blocked my way. 'Pray pardon me,' I said and stepped aside.

It was Prince Panduka. He had deliberately stepped before me. His grin was sly. 'You do not teach your pupil good manners, or wisdom,' he said in a low voice. 'When your aggressiveness to me with your staff becomes known to the King, he will deduce the source of his son's violent behaviour.'

'The King will hardly believe you when you tell him the story so belatedly,' I retorted.

'Ah – but he will! After all, it was not told him earlier because I did not want to tattle on you. Today's incident makes it my solemn duty.'

'How noble of you, Prince,' I retorted dryly.

'On the contrary, how despicable of me! There is nothing I will not do to get even with you both. And for your information, even my royal father has no great affection for you. He knows you are a bastard. He thinks you are an upstart.'

My fists clenched and I made for him to strike him down. It was the memory of my uncle that stopped me. I gave Panduka a glance of amused contempt instead. 'You have a spot of curry on your shirt, nephew,' I observed, nodding toward the stain. 'Not very decorous, don't you think?'

He looked confused, then his brown eyes bulged and nearly popped out of his head with anger. I smiled sweetly at him. 'Now if you will please excuse me,' I said.

I walked swiftly through the audience chamber. Set up as a sort of pantry for the *dana*, it was crammed full of cauldrons of varying sizes and crowded with ladies and attendants, also of varying sizes. The Queen was in the centre of the group, giving orders for the serving of food to the men. She seemed strangely cool in a room where everyone was sweating with

196

the heat from warm black cauldrons and the mass of human bodies. She glanced up as I eased by, acknowledging my salutation with a brief nod. I could not tell what she was thinking.

Even the wide, open corridor leading to the residential quarters was crowded with white-clad people bustling to and fro, each person's mission always so important, each thinking of the event merely in terms of his part in it.

Only when I turned toward the quarters of the King and the princes did I find a deserted passageway, except for a group of attendants in earnest conversation. A dark man was holding forth, doubtless an eyewitness giving firsthand information about the shocking incident. They parted, shamefaced, at my approach and gave me salutation. Returning it perfunctorily, I hurried toward Gamini's quarters, wondering how I could help him.

What would Prince Vipula have done? The stark uselessness of what had happened to my uncle struck me again. The years had not healed the wound. My eyes stung. Tears of anger, frustration, sorrow, I know not what, gathered in them. I paused beside a pillar and stared at the bright blue sky, fighting the impulse to weep. All this had to be the will of my God. The passions of men are so conflicting, their affairs so confused, that at times even God must wonder where they stand. I prayed that He might show me how I could best play my part in implementing His will.

As I prayed, my vibrant link with God became manifest. It was like water sparkling in the sunlight, linking two islands. It was crystal, like the sunlit air. I saw the array of facts, not with the inner sight, but with a kind of outward vision. King Kakkavan had made many preparations to launch his son on a successful campaign against the Cholas. He had wanted to go down in history as the father of the man who reunited the Sinhala kingdoms. Why the change of heart?

The answer was simple. Kakkavan Tissa was never a

warlike man. He wanted a peaceful old age. So did King Elara. Neither of the two kings was in a bad situation. Both kingdoms were wisely ruled. Most people were prosperous and satisfied. The kings had therefore become complacent, even lazy.

There had probably never been a real change of heart, merely a change of mind on the part of the Ruhuna king. King Kakkavan had at the beginning been led by his Queen, Chief Minister and Chief Warrior to a course of conduct that was foreign to him. They had exploited his pride and joy at fathering a son. With the years, his true nature and natural good sense had emerged. How had he found the fortitude to follow his own dictates regardless of the silent, overt opposition of those closest to him? My mind reached to grasp the answer. It was there one moment, but slipped away the next.

Then I remembered that momentary spasm of King Kakkavan, when he seemed to hold his breath. I had read in some medical *olas* at the temple that it could be one of the symptoms of an ailing heart. Three such and the heart stops beating. With this truth, everything fell into place. King Kakkavan's change of attitude first started when he began to suspect that he had heart trouble. He was not the sort to tell anyone about it, but his Buddhist mind would automatically turn to thoughts of rebirth. In order to ensure himself a good *kharma*, he must not only avoid war, killing and bloodshed, but must work actively against them. He must pursue *dharma* in all compassionate directions only. He must reorganize his life for his death and time might be short.

A feeling of pity for the sad, lonely monarch overwhelmed me. I leaned my head against the pillar. Conflict inevitably lay ahead for him – for Gamini and for those closest to them, too.

I closed my eyes and prayed with all the fervour of my being that comfort come to the King and Prince Gamini. God's strength began to flow into my being. It surged within me, bringing the peace of determination. I looked outside to the utmost ends of the world. I looked within me and found the reality of the God-link. I knew what I must do. I thanked God for answering my prayers. I sped to Gamini's quarters.

I turned down Gamini's private corridor. The door to his rooms was open. I walked into an empty study. The bedroom door was ajar. I tiptoed through the study and walked soundlessly inside.

Gamini lay on his couch, face to the wall. His body was hunched, the knees drawn up to his chin, arms bent, in the position babies are supposed to have within a mother's womb.

He looked small, vulnerable, somehow helpless. My heart went out to him. I wanted to hold him to me as I had never held a child. It was a totally new feeling for me, perhaps one of God's answers to my prayer.

On the instant, I saw the blackness of Gamini's loneliness. It was an empty nothing, the darkness within the flame I had seen a little while ago. Its vacuum was bubbling within him and had already reached every fibre of his being. Now it spilled over and came toward me, casting a dread chill before it. I shivered as it hid Gamini from my eyes. He would be consumed by it forever unless I could overcome it.

Resolutely, I welcomed the black mass. Strong with the strength of compassion, I absorbed it, drawing it away from him, like sucking the poison from a snakebite. Moments passed. My effort was so intense that my sweat was as cold upon me as that vile black mass. My strength began to fail. The fear of losing made my bowels weak. 'Oh God,' I whispered. He heard me, for suddenly He thrust before me the memory of my own years of bitter childhood loneliness. Those years were the one weapon with which I could fight. As wood battling wood, steel clashing against steel, vapour fighting vapour, I would absorb this chill into my greater chill, for I knew the enemy so well. As I did draw it in, the black aura began miraculously to clear.

Suddenly, I faltered. Was I to lose after all?

A great shudder ran through my body. I prayed this time for strength and God sent it. My uncle stood beside me – straight, elegant, resolute, invincible. The oath I had sworn, to dedicate my whole life and being to this prince, rang inside my brain with the clangour of giant temple bells.

I soaked up the dead mass of that miasma like a sponge. I flung my *prana* into Gamini, so he was not alone.

Suddenly the mass was gone. I was trembling, my body bathed in sweat, but I could see Gamini clearly at last. He was still huddled, but his *prana* and mine were as one. Henceforth, he would never be alone, though he might not know it.

My eyes were wet with tears. An overwhelming new sensation came pouring out of me. I realized with wonder that, for this still, dark figure lying before me, the isolation of my being since birth had been removed. I felt cleansed and reborn. I loved him.

I had barely settled back on a bench by the door when I smelled the curries and heard footsteps. I glanced through the open bedroom door. The Queen entered Gamini's study. She looked around it, noticed where Gamini lay and beckoned to a female attendant, who brought forward a silver tray of food, followed by another attendant with a pitcher of drink which I knew to be melon juice.

The Queen pointed to a table in the study. The attendants placed the tray and the pitcher on the table and backed away as silently as they had entered.

The Queen walked toward the bedroom. I stood up. She seemed surprised to see me. Although she wore neither make-up nor perfume, she looked as beautiful as ever. She returned my salutation and glided toward Gamini's bed. Ironic, I thought. Gamini's loneliness flows out and the mother he has isolated himself from, one of the causes of his loneliness, flows in. Will she be enough?

The Queen stopped short when she saw how Gamini was

lying. Her back was towards me, so I could not see her reaction, but I could tell that she had lost some of her certainty. She had come with the sure knowledge that she could comfort her son, make him have his meal and restore the normalcy of his life. Seeing him lying in this manner, she was obviously nonplussed. How little she knew of the depths of Gamini.

Presently she stepped up to the couch and reached out a hand to touch Gamini's shoulder. He did not move.

'Why, my son?' The Queen's voice was soft, low and caressing. I had heard it in mothers' voices before and each time never failed to wonder what it would have been like to hear my mother speak thus to me. 'Why do you lie all curled up in this heat, when you can lie freely and easily on that bed with your limbs outstretched?'

Gamini made no reply.

'Did you not hear me, my son?' The Queen spoke a little louder, her voice had an even warmer tone, but there was a hint of doubt in it.

Moments passed in silence. 'How can I lie with my limbs outstretched?' Gamini finally demanded. His voice was hollow and seemed to come from outside him. He enunciated the words slowly and clearly, but with intense bitterness. 'To the west of me are the impenetrable mountains, to the south and east the impregnable seas. To the north are the inviolate Cholas. What room is there for me, a Sinhala, to lie with limbs outstretched in this realm?'

The Queen gasped. A hand flew to her mouth. She remained staring at him as if cast in marble, but I could sense the furious working of her mind. 'I understand,' she finally said quietly. 'I have already spoken to your royal father about your conduct this morning. He has agreed that it is not all your fault.' She half turned to me. 'Those responsible will be questioned and, if necessary, punished.'

I knew then that my fears had been realized. I could be in trouble for something that was not of my doing, if I was not sufficiently ingenious. Well, I would face that situation when it arose. Gamini was more important to me at this moment.

'I have brought you some food,' the Queen continued. 'It is on a tray in your study. Why do you not get up and eat? You must be starved. Let me see you started before I return to our guests.'

Gamini did not stir. 'Do you think food would pass down my throat, Mother, when I am being strangled?' he finally inquired, still in that strange, detached voice.

'Strangled by whom, my son, by what?' There was genuine puzzlement in the Queen's voice.

'By those who profess to be concerned about my welfare,' Gamini snapped back. He turned his head slightly. His dark eyes were completely blank. He could have been looking at a piece of wood or a stone, instead of at his mother.

The Queen gasped again, but this time it was almost a sob. I could not see her eyes. Only her tense body betrayed shock at what she saw, or perhaps did not see, in Gamini's eyes.

Mother and son held their pose for moments that seemed like an eternity. I saw the sand slowly slipping in the clock without noticing it. My own thoughts were whirling. Why was Gamini so withdrawn from his mother? There had to be something hidden here, something almost dreadful.

My thoughts were interrupted by the Queen. She turned abruptly, with a sharp rustle of her robe. Her eyes were strangely hard and dry. I had expected her to be near weeping. Strange, I thought, there is an interplay of forces here of which I am unaware. I must discover the truth if I am to help Gamini.

The Queen began to walk out of the bedroom without acknowledging my salutation. I wondered whether I would have to pay some added price for having witnessed this scene.

She paused in her stride, then glided away. Gamini remained curled up on his couch. He had not observed me.

202

Chapter 21

The odour of the curries from the study was delicious, reminding me that I had not yet eaten. My stomach growled its response, but I had no thought of eating now.

I resumed my seat. It was a hot, bright afternoon. This was the warm season of the year. Framed in the open window, green mango leaves were beginning to wilt in the sun. Flies swarmed around an overripe fruit, eaten by birds and hanging like a red scar from its half-dried stem. I heard the whine of gnats and hoped they would not enter the room. They are irritating insects, difficult to accept as a part of God's body – but then, just as we swipe at gnats, breezes must, in turn, find us so irritating when we get in their way that they become tempestuous winds.

Knowing I had a long wait, I tried to relax as I had been taught in the temple. Starting with my toes and fingertips, I slowly untensed my muscles until they felt like air. Then I moved gently inward to my feet and hands and gradually, ever inward, to the arms and legs. Finally, I moved to the torso and upwards into the head, to a mind already soothed by freedom from other thoughts through concentration on my slow ritual. Now I felt as if I had no body, because all the physical me was one with the air. Every object and the air and I were one, and we were all infinite. Indeed, at times I seemed to soar outside my body, seeing it seated on the bench, still and without life. Only the spark of consciousness connected me with it. Into that consciousness, I now injected Gamini. I saw him, I heard his breathing, I sensed him. All the while, I watched over him, a dark head above white clothes on a yellow mat. I was a guardian parent watching a sleeping child.

Time moved on without my noticing it. I continued holding my concentration on Gamini. He remained in that one position, still as my own body. I could not tell whether he was asleep or awake, because he never moved.

Finally, a cat mewed mournfully outside and he stirred. His movement broke the thread of my meditation and I returned to my body. The 'um-baa-a' of that prince's goat intruded to complete the breaking of Gamini's spell. He stretched his legs, pointing the toes to restore circulation. He turned on his back and extended his arms. He was still in the realm of his thoughts and I knew then that he had not slept. At age twelve, he was already an extraordinary human being, capable of the greatest concentration and intensity in whatever he did.

He felt me before he noticed me. With a sideways flicker of the eyes, he saw me. He seemed surprised. 'What time is it?' he inquired.

I studied the sand-clock. 'Over three hours past the beginning of the noon watch.'

He considered that. 'Have you been here long?' His tone was casual. He looked up at the frescoed ceiling.

'Since just before your royal mother entered.'

'I see.' He was thoughtful a moment. Then his eyes flicked sideways again in my direction. 'So you heard what took place?'

'Yes.'

A frown crossed his face. 'I came here because I wanted to be alone.' He sounded decisive, but there was a petulant undertone to his voice.

'You were alone.'

He looked at me in surprise. 'How – ' he began, but stopped abruptly. 'I must think on that,' he added.

'Surely.'

Moments passed in silence. I was in no hurry, sitting there relaxed, gently moving the love-force of my *prana* toward him. I had my reward, for he was soon at greater ease.

'Did you sit there all this time?' he finally inquired.

'Yes.'

'Why?'

'Because I love you and want to share your grief.'

His head jerked in my direction. 'I'm not one of your kind,' he lashed out.

It stung like a whiplash. Indeed, it stung. I could have stumbled out blindly in pain and anger, but my love sustained me. 'I know,' I responded gently. 'I also know that you and everyone else in the palace think, because I spent most of my youth in the temple, that I seek out boys and not young women. But all of you are wrong, Prince. If I were that kind of man, I would not have stayed, because then I would only have wanted you physically.' I added, 'I would have been too proud to give this assurance to anyone else but you. I do so now only because it is vital that there be no lies or deceit between us.'

He sat up with a start, swinging his legs out. The couch creaked with the sudden movement. His dark eyes were bright on me, searching. The purity of my love for him shone in my face and radiated from my whole being. He knew the truth. He had enough soul-force in him to know.

'I am sorry I said those words,' he responded quietly. 'Please forgive me.'

'Of course.'

Now he held my look without fear or shame. There was some subtle imploring within him and my heart reached out, but I did not know what more to say.

Finally he nodded. 'The feel of you is good,' he said quietly, 'but I do not trust anyone. People lie all the time.'

'People often lie because they do not want to cause hurt feelings.' I thought of King Kakkavan's change of heart. 'Sometimes they change and we see a lie or deceit in a necessary or inevitable shift of attitude, point of view or course of action.'

'I do not lie.'

'Of course you do, Prince. And you will.' I noted his angry look and held up a hand. 'You won your fencing match with Prince Jaya yesterday, did you not?'

A puzzled expression crossed his face. 'What has that to do with it?'

'You won by feinting and thrusting?'

'Yes.'

'Your feint was a lie.'

His eyes widened and I drove home my point. 'You will also discover that a great deal of statecraft is lying, or deliberately withholding truth, which is another form of lying.'

He understood immediately. 'But I still do not trust anyone,' he parried defiantly. 'Not even you – for the very reasons you have given.'

'You must have been bitterly hurt to feel that, but I have not asked you to trust me. I merely answered your questions.'

'No one is trustworthy,' he repeated fiercely, trying to justify his thrust at me.

'Are you?'

'Yes,' he began, but stopped, thinking. He tried to be honest, even with himself, I could see.

'We have to be certain that we do not subconsciously make trust a mould into which we seek to cast those whom we love, so that we can shape them to the images of our own desiring.'

He considered my words. 'I must think on it.'

I smiled at the repetition. 'Yes, do that. One of the most important things in life is to remember that people can only be themselves. You expect them to behave in a certain way. When they do not, your reaction – the hurt, the sorrow, the grief – is indeed the final product of their action. But it is still your own reaction. After all, the same behaviour can make one person laugh and another cry. You will never know whether people try as hard to make you happy as you would like them to, or whether they have tried at all, but you must not blame them for being what they are, merely because it is a disappointment to you.'

'If what you say is true, what remains?'

'Love. It is love that enables us to accept people as they are. Love can emerge suddenly, or it can be the product of a relationship. Since its seemingly natural form is with blood ties, such as between parents and children, brothers and sisters, we expect too much from these ties. For any form of true love, the intermingling of the forces of the *prana* must take place.'

'What are those forces?'

'I do not know. I can only recognize them when they exist.'

'So there is something you do not know!'

I laughed then. 'Your point is well taken. The appearance of certainty is a faculty we develop in the temple.'

He placed an elbow on his knee, cupped his chin on his palm and stared into space. His fingers were long and full, sensitive like his feet. Already there was a dusky power to the hands. May you never grasp all that you reach for, I thought, else your hands will wither and your soul will die.

'Compared to most people, however, there are few things I do not know,' I added, wanting to break the tension.

He laughed then, his head thrown back, hands clutching the edge of the couch. It was a wholesome sound. I made a mental note that I should make him laugh as often as possible.

'At times you talk like a grandfather,' he volunteered. 'Were you always like this?'

'I cannot tell. I grew up very much alone.'

'Oh!' He became serious. 'I know,' he said.

'You know?'

'Yes, I made it a point to discover everything I could

about you when I heard you were going to be my tutor.'

'Then you know . . .'

'About your father and mother. That your uncle, Prince Vipula, had your father killed because he was of a low caste and your mother died of grief soon afterwards.'

'I see.' I stared out of the window, not ready as yet to correct him, looking back a great distance in time.

Gamini watched me intently as I gazed out of that window recalling the tragic events of Prince Vipula's death. Although he was only a boy of twelve, he was sensitive enough to allow me my memories in peace.

'You should try not to be sad about the past,' he advised finally, sounding very serious and very grown up. 'Besides, fathers and mothers are not always trustworthy. Knowing pain, you were probably spared more pain.'

I was shocked. He must have experienced some shattering disillusionment to speak in this manner. Neither his father's changed attitude toward his destiny, nor the reported treaty between King Kakkavan and King Elara, nor the events of that morning, could have driven a stake so deeply into his spirit. Other bits of evidence he had given started moving into my mind, but I thrust them aside.

He sensed my reaction. I was beginning to realize that he had an uncanny ability to do so. 'Why did you not kill your uncle?' he demanded, changing the subject almost casually. He sounded as if killing uncles was an everyday occurrence.

'Because by the time I grew old enough to kill him – your age, in fact – I realized that he was the finest man living,' I replied.

His head jerked up in surprise. 'How so?'

'Just that. He had nothing to do with my father's death. He was a worthy heir to the Sinhala throne and a man of great nobility, elegance and dignity.'

'You love elegance and dignity, don't you?'

'They befit every civilized human being, especially kings. No one would have made a better king than my uncle.'

His eyes flashed. 'Not even me?'

'Not even you,' I replied firmly. 'But you could be as good if you tried.'

'I must think on that,' he said thoughtfully. 'I am destined to be a great king.'

'We all know that, but greatness in a king comes from the cultivation of many qualities. Pride is not enough. True pride will make a man humble, causing him to care about his every thought, word and deed and those of others. The result, as I told your father, the King, on the day I first met you, is total awareness, which is the finest product of a civilized human being.'

'That's all very well after one reaches one's goal,' he shot back. 'But it requires other qualities to get there. Ruthlessness, deceit – as you have just said, a total lack of concern about anything else but that goal. Take King Elara. He is supposed to be a good and just king, but how do you think he became one?' His eyes glowed fiercely. 'Only through brute strength of mind and body, cunning, hypocrisy, lies and complete toughness.'

I was stunned, the more because I could see he was deadly serious. My mind searched feverishly until it found the seed of an idea.

'We are concerned with two separate things,' I said slowly. 'First, let us take the qualities you must have to achieve your goal. It is useless my telling you to abandon your goal merely because the qualities you need to reach it are evil. You are already committed to the course of your destiny. So instead, let us consider your *prana*. What will all these attributes do to you as a person? Is that not the problem?'

'Yes,' he responded, somewhat taken aback.

'The only solution is for you to generate the attributes necessary without becoming a person with those qualities.'

209

'How so?' He was puzzled.

'Learn to kill without being a murderer.'

I could see an answering glimmer in Gamini's expression. 'I must think on it.'

'Remember, too, that the goal of reuniting our country is only an objective. Even the living of the rest of your life is an objective. Your object is the development of your atom of consciousness, the putting into it of qualities that will pull it through successive births to God and your final escape from the cycle of birth and rebirth.'

'God? You speak of God?' He sounded almost angry. 'Are you a Hindu or something?'

'No, I am not,' I replied firmly, 'but I happen to believe in the God whom Lord Buddha declared to be unnecessary for us in this life. I search for Him all the time.'

He simmered down. 'Hmm. With me, you can say anything you want, but your search is silly.'

'Why silly?'

'Seeking anything that is unnecessary is silly.'

'But I need to search.'

'Needing something unnecessary is more than silly, it is stupid.'

I pondered that a few moments. 'God does not become unnecessary merely because the Buddha says so,' I finally replied. 'It is like saying that a man cannot get to Mahagama from Anu on foot because the King finds it unnecessary to walk.'

He threw back his head and gave that wholesome laugh. 'You are clever with words,' he granted. 'But there are so many gods, and even some variations of the Supreme God. Tell me about them.' He paused and looked me straight in the eye. 'I warn you, though, that all I need is information. You will never convert me.'

'If your mind is closed to the use of knowledge, it is unnecessary for you. Why do you seek it?'

'I told you. I need the information. Is that not enough?'

'Certainly. But you are then judged by your own conclusions.'

'How so?'

'You said a few moments ago that seeking what is unnecessary is silly and needing it is stupid.'

Gamini's jaw dropped slightly. 'You are a sharp-witted *guru*,' he declared, shaking his head from side to side. 'I am beginning to like you. I shall like you even more if you tell me what is unnecessary!'

Now it was my turn to laugh.

I began pacing the room, gathering my thoughts to answer him. Gamini sat on his bed, dark hands gripping its edge, black eyes following me closely. I stopped by the window a moment, looking out, then swung around to face him.

'Two great religions existed in India before the Jina,' I commenced. 'One had to be the product of the migrant Arya. Their beliefs and practices found expression in the four Vedas, written by Arya priests and accrued during a thousand years. The Vedas are not history, but ritual – the only direct connection the Arya knew between man and the gods. The original religion was no more than worship of entities important in the Arya regions. Agni, god of fire. Indra, god of heroes and war, whose weapon was a thunderbolt. Pipal, god of the trees. Vayu, born of the life-breath, Purusa. Even Soma, god of that plant, the juice of which, obtained by pressing it between stones, is mixed with milk and drunk during ritual to produce hallucinations, including illusions of godlike size and strength.'

'Like our *sura*?'

'Far worse and quite dangerous. The important conclusions are, however, the need of these people to worship gods and the simplicity of their rites, in which they offered the gods the fruit of their endeavour – cooked grain, slaughtered animals, *ghee* and libations of water – at

211

an open altar before the sacred fire.'

'How barbaric! That is why the Buddha's way is best. We have no gods, no altars, no libations.'

'Yet the need of the Buddhist people for gods finds its expression in altars for Lord Buddha and the *devas*.'

'Hmmm. I must think on it.'

I smiled at the now familiar phrase and proceeded. 'We do not know how the second religion, Hinduism, originated. What we do know is that in addition to the worship of deities governing their daily lives, the Hindus conceived more powerful deities connected with their needs for achievement and of the spirit. They thus have a pantheon of over a thousand gods to choose from. Yet, their most interesting concept to me is that of God the Creator. They call him Brahma.'

Gamini nodded. 'Yes, he is depicted in our sacred shrine at Kataragama.'

'The Hindus also crystallized the Arya belief in *kharma* and reincarnation,' I proceeded. 'More significantly, they enhanced the concept of *dharma*, of which you are well aware. As for Brahma, since millions of people believe in him, he must surely emerge from their seed of consciousness.
consciousness.

'It also had to be God-consciousness that inspired the nobleman, Vardhamana, just before Lord Buddha's time, to the twelve years of austere living that led to his goal of the single *thathpara*, the one second during which he perceived the meaning of life and death. People called him Mahavira, the Great Hero, and Jina, the Conqueror. That word defines the religion, for the Jina regard themselves as conquerors.

'Vardhamana redefined *kharma* as a material substance, consisting of impurities that cling to our souls. He believed that everything has a soul, even trees and stones, rivers and mountains. Our life's aim, he said, should be to cleanse the soul, and this can best be done by his code of right conduct. Devout Jina even wear masks lest they breathe in a living

212

creature and cause its death. Only by ridding the body of all impurities will final God-consciousness and union with God be assured at death. So the supreme end for Jina is to starve to death, as the emperor Chandra Gupta Moriya did.'

'Astonishing! No wonder Lord Buddha tried their methods and rejected them.'

'Indeed he did. After his asceticism made him so thin that he could feel his spine by placing his fingers on his stomach, he found the Middle Way to salvation. As for the Jina, viewed objectively, their two great contributions are their code of right conduct – the common element of all religions – and the fact that, of the many people of our world, they come nearest to belief in a single God.'

'Is it the Jina God you believe in, then?'

'Not really. We must go beyond India to the land of the Arabi to get closest to my concept of God.'

'So far to discover something you say is within you?'

I glanced sharply at him. 'You are a sharp-witted pupil!' I retorted. 'I realize that you are not being serious, but the truth is we are discussing religion, not my beliefs.'

'Tell me about this other God.'

'He was conceived by the head of a wandering tribe called Juda, to whose leader He spoke from a burning bush, it is said. The Juda call Him Jahweh, which is the pronunciation of the four letters symbolizing His name. They believe in no other God but Him.'

'How do you know this?'

'An Arabi from those lands came to the court of Anu as head of a group of traders, when I was a boy. He was very interested in religion and visited the Thuparama temple. I heard him in discourse with the *bhikkus*.'

'Did this influence your views?'

'Not as far as I know, though it may have slipped into my mind to emerge later. You see, each of us will find God differently, depending upon our substance. A tree may soar to the sun, which a night creature avoids. Yet both act out

213

their lives. I find everything to be an extension of God, even the many millions of living *paramanu* that the Jina spoke of and the *paramatthas* that Lord Buddha discovered. This belief has the beauty of embodying even deities and *devas* as a part of God, though I, for my part, do not believe in them except as something to use for swearing! Of course, I realize my beliefs are heretical . . .'

'You can have any beliefs you like as far as I'm concerned.'

'What about your battle cry: one race, one language, one religion?'

Rather than answer me, Gamini characteristically shot off in another direction. 'Your uncle's death was manipulated, Prince Rodana, to clear my way to the throne of Lanka. King Elara had planned to kill the baby supposed to be me and not divulge its birth for seven days, so that you would not enter the temple in time and your uncle would have to take his own life. Since I was born in Ruhuna and you were there too, my father and Kirthi Siri could have ensured your entry into the temple as soon as I was born and saved your uncle's life. Did you know that?'

'Yes.'

He seemed surprised, even a little disappointed that he had not been first with the news. He thought awhile, scratching his dark head gently, then rubbing his forehead with the tips of his fingers. 'Did you also know that your uncle left you all his possessions, so you could have independent means?'

I was stunned. 'No!' I almost whispered.

'Of course, King Elara confiscated them.'

'Oh?'

'Your uncle had ample property in Ruhuna.'

'Did he?'

'Yes, but they were taken by my father into his private treasury, in spite of the formal *ola* bequest he received from your uncle. I shall return them to you when I become king.'

214

'So then . . .'

'You should have been looked after regardless, as my father's cousin, and especially because your uncle commended you to my father's care, when he first sent you to Ruhuna.'

I stared at him in disbelief. He was obviously trying to goad me. Why?

'And do you know,' he went on inexorably, his glance almost merciless with the persistence of his intentions, 'that all this was at my mother's dictation? She sent you to the temple for the sole purpose of having you acquire the background and knowledge to become my tutor!'

Some deep wound opened in me and I groaned aloud. I thought I knew about the inhumanity of man, but this . . . this utter callousness, the cold, calculated plots of princes, transcended even brutality. I clung in anguish to the memory of my uncle, that noblest of men.

'You see, for all your talk, you too have been betrayed.'

Gamini must have seen my ravaged face. He gave a short laugh. 'Ha! Enough!' His white teeth showed briefly in an odd smile. 'You are shocked.' He paused. 'Your uncle also told my father of the oath he made you take to serve me. Is that why you are here today?'

My questions vanished. Reason returned. I set aside my pain and faced his look.

'No!' I answered steadily. 'And you know it. Else you would waste neither time nor words on me.' My eyes were as level as my voice and all of me was full of gentleness and love. 'I came to this court because I was bidden. I came to this room out of a sense of duty, but I stayed because I discovered that for the first time in my life I can love a living human being face to face.'

I did not mind the minutes that passed while his dark, haunted eyes probed my spirit, my *prana* almost. My every moment was full of love for him. I had nothing to hide. I had only feelings I could reveal with joy.

215

Finally, he seemed satisfied. He looked down at his feet and wiggled his toes. He wanted to say something, but the words would not come. He tried, but still the words failed him.

Then, apparently having raised his determination to the necessary level, he looked squarely at me, his eyes underlain by a strange vulnerability. 'Will you teach me to be like your uncle, Prince Vipula?' he inquired. 'He must have been a great man to have inspired the ruthless plots of two kings and a queen, as well as the respect of one such as you.'

Chapter 22

I was not surprised to receive a summons to attend King Kakkavan in his private chamber at the hour of the sixth watch, the very day after Gamini so violently refused to take an oath never to fight the Cholas. Although I had been Gamini's tutor for only four weeks, it would be easier to call an apprentice monk to account rather than a twelve-year-old prince.

A king's schedule is necessarily tight, based upon an exhortation of the Artha Sastra: 'For a king, his religious vow is constant activity in the cause of his people; his best religious ceremony is the work of administration.' According to the daily schedule of Arya monarchs, the sixth watch is customarily reserved for the King's bath, meals and the study of religious texts, not for audiences, so I concluded that

216

the King was agitated and in need of immediate answers.

The chamber adjoined King Kakkavan's study and I had not seen it since that fateful night when the Queen had returned from her alleged abduction, thirteen years earlier.

The colours of the chamber were still of red silk with gold trimmings, but time had given the cloth a warmer look and the furniture remained of polished ebony, black and gleaming as a late dusk. King Kakkavan was spending more money on charitable works nowadays and refurbishing of the palace had lost its priority. Today the Queen's sandalwood scent lay like a light veil over the musty odour of a room closed up at night and just opened for the day.

The King, dressed in white, was seated on the familiar carved ebony couch. If he had worn black, he would have looked like an ageing crow perched on those red cushions.

The Queen, dressed in a long blue skirt and bodice, sat on a stool beside him. Kirthi Siri – gaunt, craggy, hunched – stood to one side of the couch. To my surprise, Prince Digha Bahu stood on the other side. He wore a cream silk tunic and pantaloons over his portly figure and a hostile expression on his face. He had grown more stout with the years and had lost much of his hair. His skin shone, from his chubby cheeks to the top of his head. He must have been drinking the previous night, though it was the time of Wesak, because the whites of his hard pebble eyes were red-veined.

I made obeisance to the King and stood before him, awaiting his pleasure.

'You were chosen to be Prince Gamini's tutor because of your training in the peaceful ways of the temple,' King Kakkavan began in his deep, raspy voice. He looked grim, the beak of his nose slightly lifted, his black eyes penetrating. 'We now hear you are practising physical violence instead.'

My glance shifted uncertainly from the King to the Queen. There was a strange look on her face. Was it veiled triumph?

217

My gaze returned squarely to the King. 'May I know the occasions on which I am alleged to have practised violence, sire?'

King Kakkavan was taken aback. 'What do you mean, "occasions"?'

'To "practise" anything implies a regular exercise.'

'You are playing with words,' Prince Digha Bahu snapped. 'His Majesty is inquiring into your inclination to violence.'

I ignored him and addressed the King. 'May I respectfully inquire why Your Majesty feels that I am inclined to violence?'

The King cleared his throat. 'It has been reported to us, for instance, that you took a staff to young Prince Panduka on a certain occasion recently.'

'I did not take a staff to the Prince, sire. Nor did I do him any violence. I twirled my staff – expertly, as I had been taught – close enough to him for him to take notice. I did not strike him at all, else he would have had a cracked crown.'

'Violence is not merely an act, but an attitude,' the Queen interposed, her voice smooth and gentle, more pained than angry. 'We had you released from the temple to inspire our son with feeling for the Doctrine. The great future so many predict for him could go to his head and make him act rashly. Only the Noble Eightfold Path offers him a good destiny.' She revealed white teeth in a sparkling smile. 'You are in daily contact with the Prince. You alone can guide him in the ways of righteousness and restraint. We would rather he became a *bhikku* than a warrior king.'

A remarkable transition, my lady, I thought. You drank bloody water while your son was in your womb and now you want the blood separated from the water. Why?

'Well put, cousin!' Prince Digha Bahu remarked before I could reply. He raised a finger for emphasis, glancing his approval at the Queen.

'If a person gives a threatening look or makes an angry gesture, it is still violence,' Kirthi Siri whined.

I could not tell why the Queen was taking this attitude, but it suddenly struck me that, with the exception of the King, the other players were going through a rehearsed script. My one hope, therefore, was to satisfy the King. 'I have no doubt, sire, that you are referring to an incident a few days ago, when I was compelled to show Prince Panduka that I am not to be trifled with. He was rude to me during a lesson – even threatened me, as well as Prince Gamini, with bodily harm. I but gave him a warning that he could be chastised as any other student. This method I learned from no other than my teacher, the Venerable Rahula, Chief Monk, who physically beat me with his staff on more than one occasion, in order to leave the mark of the *dhamma* on me. Neither the Chief Monk's intention nor his attitude was violent on those occasions. I merely felt the violence of my chastisement.'

The King threw back his head and laughed. It was a wholesome laugh, which Gamini had either inherited or learned from him.

'You must have been incorrigible for one so gentle to take a rod to you,' the Queen broke in, gently chiding.

She was still acting, but too late. 'So incorrigible, sire, that the Venerable Rahula recommended me to become the Prince's tutor,' I reminded the King.

The Queen bit her lip and turned away. She began wielding her bright peacock-feather fan more swiftly, a sure sign of exasperation. Its quiet swish jarred me physically, but I was well pleased mentally.

'Actually, as a matter of fact, Prince Panduka reported to me that you set Prince Gamini up to assault him brutally,' Prince Digha Bahu stammered, his voice high-pitched with anger. 'Do you then deny an assault on that occasion?'

'The position of a tutor is not much different from that of

a monk, in whom people confide their innermost secrets,' I retorted. 'If His Majesty is investigating my conduct, His Majesty must address the Prince, not me. His Majesty will be the first to grant that I must say and do nothing to impair the confidence I have to win from Prince Gamini, if I am to be of any good to him.'

'Bah!' The Prince was shouting now. 'Words, words, words. Actually, as a matter of fact, you're trying to find refuge in words.'

'Enough of this,' the King cut in. 'We find that Prince Rodana has neither preached nor practised violence.' He looked at each of the others in turn. Only Prince Digha Bahu seemed ready to protest.

'I thank you, sire,' I replied, my eyes kindly on the King.

The dark face softened and the fingers of his right hand beat a tattoo on the arm of his couch. He shifted his position, relaxing backwards. 'What we are more anxious to discover is the *cause* of Prince Gamini's conduct. He has been acting strangely of late.' He gestured with a hand. 'Can you throw any light on it?' The King was genuinely puzzled. 'Sit down there.' He indicated a straight-backed ebony chair.

As I moved to sit down, questions began interweaving in my brain, like mat work. How could I use this opportunity to serve the prince I now loved? Should I speak freely? What did I have to say? How much did I really know? What if I remained silent?

'I have known the Prince such a short time, sire,' I addressed the King with an apologetic smile, while looking him full in the face, 'but I sense that his attitude is caused by frustration, created by conflict within him.'

'What conflict?' the King demanded.

'Here is a prince born to a great destiny. The substance of his conception from a warrior turned *samanera*, his royal mother's *dola-dhook* . . .' – I bowed towards the Queen, but she kept her face averted and without expression – 'the

220

prediction of astrologers, even the early preparations of his royal father: all pointed to conquest, to the end of Chola rule, to the establishment of a single Sinhala kingdom.'

While the King digested my words, my gaze shifted to Kirthi Siri. He was a man of merchant origins who had clawed his way to his present position regardless of who came into power. He might influence Prince Digha Bahu, but if he eventually became Prince Gamini's Chief Minister, he would never wield the power, nor have money or influence – not with Gamini. Did he know it?

Finally, I looked at the Queen. She might have been made of Indian marble except for the fan, now working slowly. I could not see through her mystery. I decided that I had to unravel it if I was to help Gamini. The only way I could do so was by talking to her personally, for which I would make the opportunity.

The King was waiting for me to proceed.

'These facts formed the firm ground, the sunlight, the rain, from which the Prince grew during his early years. It was easy for him when he was very young, but as he became older and began understanding the *dhamma*, he found its precepts contradicting the only manner in which he could reach his destiny.'

I glanced at Prince Digha Bahu. I knew then why he was here today, obviously the instigator of the King's inquiry. For the first time since Gamini's birth, he had posed a personal threat to Prince Digha Bahu's aims. This was not the occasion to deflect his fear of Prince Gamini.

'So the Prince started experiencing the tug-of-war between his princely destiny and his *kharmic* destiny,' I proceeded more confidently. 'While the former was the base of his daily routine, he could at least overlook the other, like a tree being trimmed, when it should reach for the sun. But then people – including you, sire – started digging into the base of his day-to-day existence and the conflict surfaced.

The substance in which the Prince's roots were set has become shaken.' A passionate note entered my voice. 'No wonder he resists. He will try instinctively and tenaciously to dig his roots deeper into the familiar soil. He will not be moved.'

King Kakkavan turned the colour of dark-grey ash. 'This cannot be,' he almost whispered.

'I fear it is,' I responded with animation. 'Pray forgive me for speaking thus frankly, but it is too much to expect the Prince, born to a unique destiny, to bow to the destinies of average people – even a great king such as you.'

A smile touched the King's face briefly. I looked pointedly at Prince Digha Bahu and was rewarded with a searing glance.

The King absent-mindedly brushed a speck from his tunic with the back of his long fingers. He finally made up his mind. 'Then the destinies of all must be made to coincide,' he declared. 'And Prince Gamini too must bow before the Doctrine.'

'He certainly must!' Prince Digha Bahu echoed, a note of relief in his voice.

'One way in which we can achieve this is by communication between his parents and me,' I asserted. 'We are all the Prince's teachers. I can appreciate a mother's concern, madam.' I bowed to the Queen and was rewarded by her look of surprise. Having caught her off guard, I drove home the point. 'A mother's love for her child, enhanced by piety and dedication, can surely help determine the direction of his training. I would deeply appreciate the honour of an audience later, with Her Majesty alone, to discuss how the basic principles, that I am now going to suggest should be applied to Prince Gamini's tutoring, can be put to practical use.'

I gave the Queen my most agreeable look. This time I was glad to observe the unclouding of her eyes and the beginning of a responsive smile. 'We can proceed to my quarters after my lord King has terminated this audience,' she stated.

Prince Digha Bahu glanced suspiciously at the Queen, but I was now ready to express the thoughts I had known in Gamini's room yesterday, which I had formulated into a more persuasive form during the night. I must confess to a feeling of power as I sat back, suddenly being elevated to the position of adviser to the King.

'Let me liken what we must do to a holy war,' I said grandly. 'Gamini must be trained to be the combination of the warrior Gotama and the *samanera* that warrior became. It is this combination that constitutes the atom of consciousness in Gamini's seed-germ. We must, however, also take one further step.'

'And that?' the King inquired.

'Gotama was first a warrior, then a monk. Gamini must be trained to retain completely the mind of the *samanera*, while performing the acts of the warrior. We must so inculcate the natural reflexes of the devout in him, into his *prana*, his mind, his brain, that they will remain in Gamini through all his military actions as a prince.'

'Rubbish!' Prince Digha Bahu exploded.

The King clicked his tongue and sternly stopped the interruption with an upraised hand. 'How do you propose that we achieve this?' he demanded.

'All we can do is to ensure that Prince Gamini follows the Noble Eightfold Path as nearly as possible. This is the direction his training must take.'

I did not want to tell them of my fears from watching Gamini beat Panduka. I could not possibly acquaint them with the bloodlust in Gamini. The best I could do today was to ensure that I continued to be his teacher and companion without interference.

It worked.

'You may have the answer,' King Kakkavan conceded

slowly. 'You shall continue as Prince Gamini's tutor. You may confer with us directly on any matter that affects his destiny either as a prince or as a human being. No one else shall interfere with you in this mission. Remember one thing, though. The Prince's destiny is greatness. We would rather he became a great *bhikku* than a brave warrior. Conquest is not for the Ruhuna kingdom. There will be no war against anyone, including the Cholas. We are a people devoted to the true Doctrine.'

I held my peace. Whatever was done would have to be guided by wisdom. For the present it was enough that the Queen and Kirthi Siri too seemed satisfied. Prince Digha Bahu would, of course, always oppose me, but at least I could now continue being Gamini's tutor. Meanwhile, I had to guard against the vanity and ambition that were beginning to simmer within me.

The King retired for his bath and I followed the Queen and two of her elderly ladies-in-waiting to her quarters. Prince Digha Bahu made as if to accompany us, but the Queen put him off with the suggestion that his noon meal awaited him in his own quarters.

I had never been in these quarters of the Queen before. They were not the chambers of the abduction scene. If the anteroom was any indication, she was a person of refined taste, feminine but strong. My eyes were immediately drawn to a striking statue of the Buddha in the lotus pose, carved in white alabaster and placed on an alabaster stand at the far end of the room. It was about eighteen inches tall and was obviously an antique from North India. The expression of peace in the Enlightened One's eyes was so remarkable that it cast a spell over the entire room. My gaze then drifted along the white and green mountain crystal floor to the couches along the wall. They were made of creamy and gold satinwood and had pale green cushions on them. A large rug

224

patterned in deep green, crimson and blue had to be Persian, brought in by Arab traders who sailed across the seas to the annual fair at Devundara for barter. The ornaments on shelves in the room were of gold, bronze or green alabaster.

Noticing my approving glance, the Queen half-smiled her satisfaction. She sat on a couch facing the windows opening to her private garden-court, shady even in that noon hour. She waved me to a separate couch beside her. She had given the ladies-in-waiting permission to retire for their baths, so we were alone.

The Queen half turned to face me. 'We would offer you refreshment, cousin, but today is our day for fasting,' she observed.

My eyebrows lifted. 'I was unaware – ' I began.

'That today was such a day? No, it is not, but we fast once a week. It is good for us.'

'So the Jinas too believe.' I was trying to show off and be understanding at the same time.

'Our beliefs spring from Lord Buddha's doctrine,' she retorted somewhat primly.

I would have liked to ask her what specific doctrines she referred to, except the general one of abstemiousness, but this was not the time for a debate, or for scoring points in a game of verbal *chukgoodoo*. 'Of course,' I agreed with a smile.

This time, the Queen looked me full in the face and smiled back. She caught me unawares. I was immediately captivated by the melting of her black eyes. As for that smile, the small, perfectly formed white teeth beneath even gums of a pale shade of pink, with no dark patches to them, the delicate folding of the skin on either side of the bow-shaped lips, made it irresistible. She knew it, too, for her smile widened and I smiled back like one under a charm.

'You are a good man,' she stated and I was lost.

'I am yours to command, my lady,' I replied gallantly. My fear of her, my doubts, even my hatred of the role she had played in the death of my uncle and my exile in the temple, vanished in that instant.

'Tell us what you plan for our son,' she requested.

'I have outlined the principles. Now it is for us to work out the method,' I rejoined. 'But first, I want you to know that I understand your fears for the Prince. I understand more than you think.' My direct look expressed my desire to convey my knowledge of all her past sorrows.

The Queen stiffened at that look. It was a reflex action. Then a hint of wonder entered her face. 'To what do you refer?' she inquired softly.

'My lady, most people in this world accept us as we are. We occasionally meet someone who, because of human love, sees the unusual tragic experiences that lie beneath the surface.'

'Everyone knows sorrow. After all, Lord Buddha has told us that life is suffering.'

I decided to take the issue farther. 'I refer to what you endured as a child, Your Majesty.'

To my surprise, the Queen did not resist or parlay. Her eyes became moist with unshed tears. I had touched her innermost feelings. 'Fear of the elements is not suffering,' she replied. 'It is nothing compared to the pain of rejection.' The words were slipping out from her in her surprise at my perception. 'Rejection by a father, an entire nation.'

She looked into the distant past as she spoke, probably reliving that dreadful experience twenty-five years ago, when she was cast upon the ocean in storm. Her voice was remote, an echo from the past. A crystal tear welled up on each eyelid. The quiet of her weeping heart was more racking than the roar of those elements whose torments she had endured.

Pulling herself together with an effort, she looked at me again, her smile now wistful. 'There now, you have drawn from us that which we have never spoken of before. You

226

have so much sensitivity, it is power in your possession.'

'And you have the power to move me as never before, madam,' I responded in a low voice. 'I hope you do not regret your sharing.' I had the key to her reactions, but had not quite grasped it as yet. Perhaps I did not want to, because I was too deeply affected.

She looked down. I thought I could not bear it if she denied me. She must have sensed my feelings, because she glanced sideways at me, her eyes bright. 'No!' She shook her head. 'Nor will we ever regret these moments.' She paused, thoughtful. 'And to show you that we mean it, we are going to leave the details of Gamini's education in your hands, without further interference or discussion. We will trust you from now on.'

The Queen rose to leave. I stood up and made deepest obeisance to her. It came not from my princely training, but from my heart.

That same noon, Leela Wathie, dressed in a pale yellow bodice and dark red skirt, returned from her bath with Nona, the elderly chief lady-in-waiting, beside her. A group of talkative ladies-in-waiting and female attendants carrying wet bath-cloths were behind them. Leela and Nona turned into the Queen's quarters. The rest of the group kept walking along the corridor to their respective rooms, to dress for the noon meal in the common dining hall.

Nona, being an old appointee of the Queen with an unassailable position, had no reason to be jealous of Leela. She had begun acting almost as a guardian to the Queen's new fourteen-year-old handmaiden, but when it became more and more obvious that Leela had the Queen's favour, some of the other ladies had started cooling off toward her. Although she was only fourteen, Leela could sense their jealousy.

Leela found her mistress seated on her favourite couch in

the anteroom, obviously thoughtful. Leela spotted the Queen as soon as she opened the door of the anteroom. She liked the Queen so well, a happy laugh escaped her. 'I see you have returned from your audience, my lady.' She ran up to the Queen in her usual spontaneous manner and made obeisance, damp head bowed. 'But you have not yet had your bath. Let me accompany you.'

The Queen's face crinkled into a smile. 'Dear Leela, always bright and smiling.' She rose to her feet. 'You shall be alone with us while we bathe today. Please get our bath things.' Palms together, she graciously acknowledged Nona's obeisance.

Within minutes, Leela and the Queen were quite alone in the bathing enclosure. Above the gentle trickling sound of the artificial stream, a breeze rustled through the green branches of giant *mara* trees and the shorter, thicker-leaved *anodha* bordering the enclosure, then scuffed ripples on the glittering blue waters of the pool. A pair of parakeets chattered at each other somewhere above. Three black-and-white *polkichcha* alighted, whistling and screeching, on a green *rath-mal* bush.

The Queen gazed around. 'Oh! I love the peace of this place when the only chattering is from parakeets!' She changed into a black bath-cloth, her full breasts and hips pushing against it, then stepped lightly into the pool and slowly sank in the jasmine-scented water. Only her milk-white shoulders now showed, and the glorious black hair tied in a knot on top of her head. Her eyes closed in ecstasy and she heaved a sigh of satisfaction, making the water flutter. Leela meanwhile took her place in a lotus pose on the flagstone edge of the pool.

Presently the Queen opened her eyes. They seemed more liquid from catching the reflections of sparkling water and silver sunlight. She stared at Leela awhile. 'We have something to tell you,' she finally declared in a low voice.

Leela merely looked at her mistress in silence. She knew instinctively not to speak.

'Remember some time ago we warned you we might ask you to do something for us?'

Leela nodded. 'Yes, my lady.' She remembered very well and had wondered why the Queen had not given her the task.

'You agreed to do our bidding, but never pressed to discover what it was. You are remarkably wise for your years, Leela. Well, we hesitated, as always before taking important action, and time has proved us right. Events have since taken place which make it best for us to let matters rest for the present.' She paused, raising delicate white fingers to splash water gently on her shoulders..

Leela made no comment, holding her pose gravely, her attention on the Queen.

'We are afraid, as you know, of Prince Gamini's tough ways and impetuous nature,' the Queen continued. 'He will resort to violence some day if he is not curbed. We must protect his younger brother, Prince Tissa.' She hesitated. 'Prince Gamini cannot help being what he is, but . . . we are hoping certain new influences in his life will help restrain him.' A faraway look entered her eyes.

Although flattered at being taken into the Queen's confidence and wanting to be worthy of it, the only words Leela could find seemed hollow. 'People will be what they are, which is what their *kharma* intends them to be,' she remarked thoughtfully. She wished she had as much wisdom as compassion to comfort the Queen.

The Queen's eyes opened wide. 'Yet others can indeed influence our lives.' She uttered the words softly. Except that the breeze dropped and the parakeets stopped their chattering, Leela would not have heard them.

The Queen then sighed once more, causing a tiny ripple. A sigh can move the waters, Leela thought – and even a

229

queen must heave a sigh. 'If our mother had only remained
. . . as she should have been . . .' The Queen was looking a
long way back.

The breeze sprang up again and Leela felt her upper body
sway gently forward with it, so light had she grown with her
own contemplation.

'Prince Rodana will influence our son Prince Gamini
greatly,' the Queen finally volunteered.

'Any influence on Prince Gamini's life will be part of his
kharma, will it not, my lady?'

'Yes, but since Prince Rodana is a good man, his
influence will be to the good.' The Queen turned her head to
look at Leela. Her eyes were misty. 'We intend trusting him.
We shall do nothing to hinder his work.'

It is you Prince Rodana has influence on, my lady, Leela
thought with delight. And why not? He is gentle and refined.
He seems strong and true. She knew a moment of alarm. I
hope a part of your *kharma* is not from your mother's blood.
She took a younger man for a lover and many lives,
including her own, were destroyed.

Chapter 23

King Kakkavan's warriors practised daily in the stadium,
located just outside the Ruhuna palace premises in
Mahagama. Here the people could watch events like
chariot races and sports contests, theatre, military displays
and executions. The stadium was a great circular wooden
structure, with an arena in the centre. It had been built by

King Kakkavan's father and improved by King Kakkavan when he started the military expansion for his son.

By the time I became tutor to Prince Gamini, however, King Kakkavan's interests had changed and his life was centred exclusively on religion. The stadium had lost some of its appeal – that breath of life only a monarch can inject into such places.

A nation takes its cue for pomp and circumstance from its rulers. The gaudy displays of banners and flags, the bright gold, the flaming maroon, the vivid green, the royal purple had turned to white in Ruhuna. The blast of the trumpet, the blare of the war conch, the rattle of the *hewisi* drum, the terrorizing war cries had subsided before the deep throb of temple drums and the bleat of pilgrim cries – '*Sadhu . . . sadhu . . . Saa-a . . .!*' – a pitiful echo of the Sinhala lion's roar.

And what was the king of the lions thinking tonight of his military display, which Gamini had asked for? It was a bold request, following so closely on the heels of the milk-rice incident, but, honouring our discussion the day after the incident, King Kakkavan had consulted me about it. Flattered as well as pleased, I assured him that it was in line with the policy I had advocated. After all, it would only be a display of military skills by the Ten Great Warriors, with the audience confined to other warriors, officers, princes and nobles. Since it was not a civic event, the people need not be infected by the warlike activity. The King approved, but he had that 'I hope you know what you're doing' look on his face. It caused me some anxiety, but this vanished before Gamini's joy at the decision.

The tiered stands were a sea of dark heads when we arrived at the stadium and paused to look down on the scene. Prince Panduka and his father, Prince Digha Bahu, were already seated in the royal enclosure, just above the arena. To my surprise, Prince Tissa, Gamini's younger brother, sat between them. All three were grandly dressed

231

for the occasion. Panduka and his father both wore tunics and pantaloons of red silk and Tissa wore blue.

Gamini was excited at tonight's event, I knew, but appeared outwardly unconcerned. He was a slender, erect figure beside me as we began threading our way down the steps of the aisle toward our seats. He wore only a white *hulwar* and thonged black sandals. His dark chest was bare, because the concluding event was to be a wrestling match between him and another boy. I had some vague information of a challenge issued and accepted, but thought nothing of it because he was in top condition. He showed it in the ebony sheen of his skin, gleaming beneath a light film of sweat. There was a strange manliness to him tonight, too – the confidence of one who knows where he is going.

People moved respectfully aside as we walked down the steps. When we took our places on the wooden bench at the centre of the royal enclosure, Prince Digha Bahu glanced sideways at us. His pale brown eyes seemed dark in the fitful light. There was triumph and a hint of scorn in his expression. Why? I sought the answer urgently, but could not find it. A tremor of apprehension ran through me and that strange feeling of foreboding that I had last experienced so long ago filtered into the pit of my stomach.

Gamini ignored the group. As we settled down, Panduka whispered something to Tissa. The boy looked quickly in our direction. Gamini caught the glance. The brothers looked at each other blankly – just blankly. They might have been looking at stone walls instead of their own flesh and blood. Suddenly, Gamini's eyes hardened. The killer force entered them, terrible enough to see in a man, but appalling in a boy of twelve.

Tissa looked away, shaken. He was a mother's darling, though hardy enough in military training. His keen intelligence would tell him not to cross swords idly with his brother.

Panduka said something to Prince Tissa. He recovered his poise and his scornful laugh rang out.

Gamini snorted grimly. 'Ambition makes strange alliances,' he observed. 'But wait till their ambitions clash!'

'How so?' I inquired.

'Prince Digha Bahu and my brother are allied against me,' he responded soberly. 'But each of them also wants to be king. So does that *musala* wretch, Panduka.'

I was amazed. 'You're not serious?' I questioned.

He was indeed serious. 'Yes, I am . . . and it would be interesting to find out who their respective allies are. As for me, I will have no princely allies. I will be my own man. That way, there will be no friends – only enemies – to try cutting my throat! One is safer with avowed enemies. But we will talk about it later.'

I felt a throb of pleasure at being given his confidence, but said nothing.

I looked around. The stadium was lit by tapers and torches. They sputtered and hissed, revealing a hive of activity and noise. Bare-bodied attendants were raking the sand in the arena. Muscular warriors preened themselves in their separate enclosure. Groups of people chatted in the aisles.

Princes, nobles and officers, who had been standing around, now began filing into their seats. They were all scrubbed clean. The officers in their gold turbans and red-and-gold tunics, swords swinging at the side, looked especially dashing. Everyone seemed delighted at the revival of a military occasion, shouting at friends in the stands, '*Arday*, friend! This is great, is it not?' The air was so warm and sultry it seemed to soak up their voices.

Beyond the areas of light, darkness pressed on the earth. Staccato white glows of lightning revealed lowering clouds, black and grey, before distant thunder rattled. It was a weird pre-monsoon night specially chosen for one of the events.

Men entered the arena from the far side, carrying two cages. They set the cages down. They opened the door of one and dragged out a snarling, snapping jackal. They tied the animal to a stake. It strained at the rope, now yelping pitifully or growling, its white fangs bared.

Gamini looked up at the sky. 'I hope we get through before the rain,' he said. I knew he was thinking of his wrestling match.

Three soldiers of the King's guard marched in. Two of them placed trumpets to their lips and blew a call. A conch shell blared from the lips of the third man. Dozens of bare-bodied attendants, carrying black metal dippers, sprang forward and started extinguishing the lights around the arena, while men within it walked rapidly away. Spectators remaining in the aisles moved swiftly to their seats. Finally, the noise died down to an expectant hush. Save for the jackal, now whining, the arena was empty.

A tall, slender man, carrying a bow three spans taller than him, entered the arena and walked toward its centre. Long arrows protruded from the quiver at his shoulder like a side-head ornament. He paused to lay down his bow, then knelt in salutation to Gamini, clasped hands raised to his forehead. Gamini returned the salutation, seated, elbows at the waist, hands extended horizontally, fingertips touching. I glanced towards Prince Digha Bahu. I could sense his bitter envy at Gamini's role.

The man in the arena rose to his feet. His hatchet face, gleaming momentarily in the final flickering of the tapers, revealed a scar on one dark cheek. He seized his bow and reached quickly back to pluck an arrow from the quiver. He fitted the arrow to his bowstring. The last tapers were extinguished. Darkness swept down on the arena, like floodwaters. Total silence ensued.

Moments passed. Even our breathing was subdued.

The jackal howled. The bow twanged. The arrow's hiss ended in a thwack. A yelp of agony petered out to a moan, Then silence again.

More moments of silence followed, so intense that the striking of a flint was noise. A spark of light burst into flame and astonished murmurs arose.

Men emerged from the gloom. Some tapers were lit. Frantic applause and cries burst loose.

One of the attendants brought the dead jackal to us. He held it up for Gamini's inspection. Phussa Deva's arrow was in its throat.

Gamini nodded and gestured with the back of his hand. The men turned to take the jackal away. Gamini stood up and saluted the solitary figure of the archer standing erect facing him. Phussa Deva bowed low. Gamini sat down. I had heard of such archery, but had never witnessed it.

'Only Phussa can accomplish this feat ten times out of ten,' Gamini informed me. 'To shoot an arrow in the darkness to the source of a single sound and hit it exactly, at one hundred paces. Did you see that? Right through the jackal's throat! He can split a human hair at fifty paces.' A note of pride entered his voice. 'Phussa is one of my Ten Great Warriors.' I noted the 'my' with some amusement. But why not? His father no longer had use for them.

The tapers were extinguished. Darkness settled around us again. I could barely see the figure of Phussa in the arena, but I knew that he waited, with another arrow poised, for the flashes of lightning that would go on intermittently and vividly once they started again.

I looked up at the sky. It was hardly visible. Someone cleared his throat. Others followed. For a few moments, it seemed that the men in the audience were trying to clear away the clouds with their coughing.

Darkness, silence and my thoughts; the clamour of them was suddenly like the roar of seas in torment. Strangely, the torment stemmed from love – and yet, why strangely? Does not all clamour come from love? Even pealing thunder is caused by the conflict of clouds that once merged in sweetness with each other.

Expectant, Gamini was lost in the splendour of these

moments and my loving heart knew fear for him. It was his lack of pity for the helpless jackal that frightened me. As a prince, a king-to-be, should he not, unlike others in the audience, know even a twinge of compassion?

I followed Gamini's gaze. At that very moment, lightning blinked. The hare was loosed. It shot out of its cage, a flash of speeding grey. The great bow sang again. The next flash of lightning snapped in, to reveal the hare lying transfixed, an arrow through its body. A shout of wonder arose as from one single throat, like the roar of a wave, but I only saw that poor, helpless creature, lying pathetically on its side. What right did we have to take its life? Horror gripped me. My throat hurt. I was the odd man here. Was I really fitted to the role of this prince's tutor and companion? What could I do for him? Reduce his strength of purpose by compassion? Turn his manhood to monkishness?

I glanced at Gamini again. He sat as if made of stone. He was lost in the archer's art, entranced. He did not move, even when the tapers were relit to flare defiantly against the dark, wafting their pungent smoke fumes to us in a sudden gust of wind.

He only came to when Phussa Deva saluted him. Gravely, he stood up to return the salute. He seemed oblivious of the cheering audience. He was lost in his thoughts, far away in the future, I knew.

Gamini drew a deep breath. 'Now they will light the tapers and you will see him pierce ten bulls' hides and five sacks of sand. You see, speed and accuracy are not enough. Power is most important. Power!' He savoured the word. The onyx eyes sparkled. 'Whether it be from the thin-shafted arrow, or from a slender body, or from the mind, it is power that finally counts.'

I should have been enjoying the evening, for I had never seen such extraordinary prowess, not even with the best of King Elara's warriors, but my heart was heavy at what all this was doing to Gamini. How could I possibly help him separate his actions from his intentions? He was completely steeped in military strength and skill, physical prowess and violence. More, he seemed to be a part of it all, as if it were the substance from which a statue of him was carved.

After Phussa Deva left, Maha Sona entered. He was a broad-faced, handsome brown giant with rugged features and not an ounce of fat on his body. He squeezed whole coconuts in his great hands, crushing them as if they were eggs. He followed up with a display of acrobatics – spinning, somersaulting in the air, walking on his hands with the grace of a dancer – fantastic for so huge a man. He ended by lifting a great club that two men had carried in, using it as a staff to demolish stones and wooden targets.

Next came the ape-like dwarf, Gotha Imbara, a dark, long-haired man with an enormous hairy chest, great sloping shoulders and legs like tree trunks. He picked up dry soil from the arena and squeezed it so powerfully that moisture dripped from it.

Four holes had been bored in an elephant's tusk and crossed bars had been passed through these holes to form a wedge before the tusk was buried in the ground. Gotha gripped the tip of the barely protruding tusk with his fingers. Through sheer strength and leverage, he slowly pulled the tusk and its wedge out of the cracking earth.

Then Kanja Deva, a lean, brown man with aquiline features, limped into the arena. As he stood silently facing us, a great water buffalo was dragged in by a dozen men, then let loose. The animal was puzzled and angry. Its eyes mean, its head swinging from side to side, it surveyed the scene. Kanja Deva suddenly rushed up to it. He seized the buffalo by its horns, forcing its neck down. A tense struggle ensued between man and beast. The strain became unbearable. Kanja's muscles were taut, his body dripping

237

with sweat. Suddenly he twisted sideways. The buffalo toppled over, its neck broken.

While I was lost in pity for the animal, Nimila, the fleet-footed, entered the arena. He ran so fast around it that charioteers could not keep up with him. His speed matched my whirling thoughts. To demonstrate that he had strength as well as speed, he lay down and bore ten men standing on a plank across his chest.

Bharana followed. He was a man of lean strength who ran almost as fast as Nimila and kicked a boar to death with one blow of his foot. Then came Abhaya, who wielded a great club with a knob three feet around as easily as if it were a battle-axe.

The huge, fair-skinned giant, Nanda Mitta, had once lived in Anu. There he had secretly killed many Cholas, tearing them in two, limb from limb, because their soldiers occasionally desecrated our Buddhist shrines. Nanda Mitta now lifted weights, smashed bricks with single blows of his fist and ended with a display of spear-throwing and wielding the battle-axe.

'He has always been strong,' Gamini whispered to me. 'When he was a child, his mother tied him with a rope to a millstone, so he would not go out of the house while she went next door to chat to a friend. Nanda Mitta crawled out of the house dragging the millstone behind him.' He chuckled. 'Can you imagine the poor mother's amazement when she saw her child crawling down the path, dragging the millstone?' The thought tickled him. He laughed aloud, head thrown back.

Even as Gamini laughed, a godlike creature entered the arena. I had never seen him before, but had heard of his beauty. He was half a span over six feet in height. His curly black hair, cut short, glistened like a woman's when oiled and enhanced the pale golden colour of his skin. His features were perfect. Large, dark eyes framed a straight nose with sensitive nostrils above a strong mouth. He had a dazzling smile, emerging from beautiful white teeth. His body was beautifully proportioned and superbly muscled, with wide shoulders, narrow hips and limbs strangely full for a Sinhala.

What caused my breath to catch was the expression on Gamini's face as he gazed at this beautiful warrior, standing straight and tall in the arena, with flame-light on his body and the cheers of the spectators for his sheer beauty and grace cascading around. I saw the glow of hero-worship in Gamini's eyes and my heart contracted.

Jealousy stabbed me, then began tearing at me. I felt I was being pulled apart while bleeding inside. My mind was sick and my breathing quickened. From deep within me the black of that flame that I had once seen emerge from Gamini came leaping to consume me. I knew I had to extinguish it if I was going to be anything to this Prince.

I prayed silently to my God to help me. My eyes sought Him in the dark skies and inside me, in the essence of my *prana*, which had been created by him.

God answered me. He turned my eyes toward Gamini. I no longer saw a prince gazing at a hero with worshipping eyes, but a boy, helpless and alone.

At that, the love-force came pouring out of me – a great, beautiful fire. Rapidly the flames consumed the black aura of jealousy, until it was gone with a last, licking spurt. I was clear-eyed, clear of mind and heart once more, but I was bathed in sweat, trembling and shivering.

Gamini was gazing anxiously at me. 'Are you all right?' he asked. 'You seem ill as with the shivering sickness. Let us go to the physicians.' He placed his hand gently on my arm.

'It is nothing,' I replied. 'Just that I felt cold suddenly. I shall be all right as soon as the storm breaks.'

I looked up at the heavens and then back at him. He was watching me silently, anxiously. There was a light in his eyes such as I had never seen before and a softening of his features. His love-force emerged at last to meet mine.

We understood each other now. There would be storms, but they could not uproot these foundations if we safeguarded them. It was a tender moment, but with men such moments can only be fleeting. We nodded to each other and looked away.

I know that neither of us saw Vasabha's feats of strength, his incredible prowess as a charioteer and his excellence with sword and spear.

When Vasabha had gone, Velu Sumana gave us a dazzling display of horsemanship. He held the title of the greatest Sinhala horseman. He could not only ride his black Arabi horse with unique control in slow, mincing gaits, making it prance like a dancer, but when he sped around in an ever-decreasing circle, he rode so fast that finally it seemed as if there was only a single horse and man in the shape of a circle. He rode bareback without bit, bridle or reins. He rode with saddle and accoutrements. He rode lying on each side of the horse; he rode standing on its back.

Velu Sumana finished to deafening applause. Strangely, Gamini's response was only perfunctory – negative, I realized with surprise. Why? What did Gamini hold against his Chief Warrior?

Gamini caught my thoughts. I smiled at him. His eyes were cold and bleak. His change of attitude was pain to me. Then I felt his own pain. He was tight as a war drum with it. There was something to do with Velu Sumana which I had to discover, in order to help Gamini.

Gamini must have sensed my preoccupation, for I came out of it to find his dark eyes on me. 'You are puzzled about something connected with me,' he observed shrewdly.

I returned his look, then glanced away.

He laid his hand lightly on my forearm. 'Perhaps we will find the answer later,' he said quietly.

'When?' I inquired.

'I do not know. Perhaps never. For the present, I must go and prepare for the wrestling match.'

'Why must you fight?'

'Because I was challenged. No, provoked to it.'

I snapped alert. 'What on earth do you mean?'

He smiled grimly. 'Just that! I believe Sali was put up to it by Prince Digha Bahu and Panduka the Pig. Perhaps my brother is in it too.'

I could only stutter incoherently in amazement.

'They want Sali to make a fool of me in the ring and maim me if possible. I would make a poor hero with a broken back or leg, would I not?'

For a moment I could not believe him. Then I saw that he was perfectly serious. I felt sick apprehension for him. 'You are not going to fight him,' I asserted.

'Oh yes, I am. I would never live it down if I refused the challenge.' He stood up, slim, dark and tall. 'Time to get rubbed down with olive oil. I will see you after the match.' He strode resolutely away. I half rose to follow him, then sat down again.

So Gamini was in danger. I glanced toward its source. Prince Digha Bahu, Panduka and Tissa seemed to be sharing some private anticipation. It was in the air around their bodies. I was consumed by a cold anger. These terrible people. And that traitor, Tissa, turning against his own brother. I longed to go over and confront them, but that would have accomplished nothing. I had to be wise for Gamini, because he was the tree and I like the soil that wraps itself around the roots to protect, warm and sustain that which is destined to give so much to the world and its people, even if it were but shade. My own enrichment had to come from whatever Gamini accomplished.

I barely saw the chariot race, the displays of shooting with the long and short bows and the duels with chain, battle-axe and war club. The glow and slash of lightning, the growl of thunder were more akin to my thoughts.

Gamini returned to his seat just as the wrestling events commenced. He was clad only in a white loincloth. His body gleamed with oil. In the light of flaming tapers, his skin shone like black silk. Although he was but a boy, he stood out in that crowd of nobles and warriors like a golden *howdah* on an elephant's back. I could sense rather than see the controlled excitement simmering within him, the first hint of heated oil about to boil. Eager for the fray, his mind excluded all else.

The wrestling events moved from the lightweights to the middleweights and the heavies. Finally, the trumpeters sounded their call for silence. The conch shell blared. The master of ceremonies announced the last event. Gamini sprang lightly to his feet, shot me a farewell smile and ran easily down the steps of the aisle, then around the circular approach to the nearest entrance gate of the arena.

The stadium became hushed, except for Panduka and Tissa talking loudly to each other. Their rudeness irritated me.

While Sali and Gamini warmed up in the wings, the master of ceremonies explained the rules of the contest, then called each of the contestants by name.

Sali entered first. I was alarmed to see that he was at least six inches taller and thirty pounds heavier than my prince.

'The Prince is so cocksure, Sali will teach him a lesson he will never forget,' Prince Digha Bahu observed loudly to his son. 'Look at the muscles on the champion.'

'Gamini never could keep his big mouth shut, Father,' Prince Panduka stated, chuckling maliciously, 'so he has fixed himself tonight. The people will see what a fart he is.' A princely choice of words, I thought angrily.

A roar of applause as Gamini stepped from the sandy arena into the glare of the taper-lights gave the lie to Panduka's statement. Gamini stood straight and supple for a moment, then bowed, the palms of his hands together at his waist in salutation, to the accompaniment of thunderous cheering. Cries of *'Appe kumaraya!'* and *'Jayawewa!'* echoed to the heavens. There was no question about Gamini's personal popularity. As the obvious underdog, he also had the sympathy of everyone present, except the princes seated close to me.

The applause died down. The opponents saluted each other with clasped palms. Something stirred in the centre of my fear and hopelessness – something of hope – some words, if only I could grasp them.

The details of what transpired in the arena were later described to me by Gamini.

He had watched Sali wrestle dozens, perhaps hundreds of times, during the past five years. He knew every hold and trick of the champion. Sali, on the other hand, knew nothing about him. Gamini was not yet thirteen and had not participated in championship wrestling. All Sali saw was a much smaller opponent, easily disposed of – except that he had more in mind. His bleak look did not betray the thoughts fleeting through him. Much bigger rewards than winning the contest had been promised him by Prince Digha Bahu, if he took care of this upstart prince for life. There were many ways.

Lightning flashed and thunder crackled, as if to highlight the event.

Sali was light-skinned, heavyset and broad of feature. He looked up at the sky as a few sparse drops of rain fell. He looked back at Gamini, his eyes hard as nuggets.

Gamini crouched on slightly bent knees, hands raised in readiness for the grip. Sali did likewise. They circled each other, flat-footed to maintain balance, looking for the opening. Gamini was watchful as a hawk. At all costs he must avoid submitting himself to a test of strength alone. His hope was in a quick end, because the longer the match took, the greater his exposure.

Sali circled to the right. He reached out to grasp Gamini's hand. Gamini's oiled fingers slipped easily through his grip.

They circled again. Gamini knew that when Sali circled to the right, he generally attacked from the left. Sali was so sure of victory, it was unlikely that he would vary his style. The light smile on his face and the hardness of the eyes showed overconfidence. With this line of attack, Sali's left foot would be off the ground for the kick sweeping inward, his right hand clubbing to complete Gamini's fall.

The merest flicker of Sali's eyes told Gamini when the move was imminent. He leaped to his left as Sali's leg swept in. He dived low for the leg, bending to avoid the chopping right hand. It was a unique move. Wrestlers do not tackle their opponents; they use their feet. Instead, Gamini grasped the leg and swung in the direction of its strike. Sali's very momentum swept him off his feet. He sprawled on the ground. A great shout arose.

Gamini dived to pin Sali's shoulders.

'One . . . two . . .' the crowd roared.

With a convulsive heave of chest and stomach, Sali flung Gamini aside as if he were a leaf.

Gamini fell over, but was up in an instant. Sali was almost on his feet when Gamini shot through the air. Both feet landed on Sali's chest. Sali fell back. Gamini bounced on both feet and jumped on Sali's stomach. The breath was forced from Sali's lungs with the sound of a blacksmith's bellows. He writhed, clutching his sides, lungs clawing for air. Gamini leaped between Sali's legs, grasped his right foot with both hands and twined the leg around his own right thigh. Sali's foot was now between Gamini's knees. It was a unique, deadly hold, such as I had never seen before.

Sali twisted and turned in agony. Each time he tried to rise, Gamini applied pressure. Gamini was like an avenging *deva*, dark eyes bright, white teeth clenched, his look intense, his every sense aware. Each time he applied pressure, Sali fell back, then flapped the ground with the back of both hands to raise his shoulders and avoid the count.

Each time Sali's shoulders touched the ground the delighted crowd screamed, 'One . . . two . . .'

Sali became bathed in sweat. His eyes were contorting with agony. Gamini could smell his fear of defeat.

'Submit!' Gamini demanded through clenched teeth.

'Submit!' the crowd roared.

'No! . . . aagh! . . . no!' Sali insisted.

The voices of the people died down, as if they knew what was coming.

'Submit – or I break your leg!' Gamini gritted in the hush. It was his right. There was no other way.

'Never!'

'Submit – or I break your leg!' Gamini repeated. The fire was in his mind, consuming him. He was panting as much from his exultation as from his efforts.

'Never!'

'For the last time, submit, or I break your leg!'

'Never!'

The crack was sharp, like the breaking of a piece of timber. Sali's cry of pain trailed to a whimper.

Gamini stood over his defeated opponent, panting. The crowd was on its feet, cheering. Even Prince Digha Bahu and his companions had to rise for appearances' sake.

The words I had been reaching for came to me. They were Gamini's, spoken earlier in the evening. 'Whether it be from the thin-shafted arrow, or from a slender body, it is power that counts.' Gamini had known all along that he would win.

I could applaud only perfunctorily. I saw the maimed champion, limp on the ground. I knew the strange

245

exultation at violence and cruelty in Gamini's heart. I felt as if I were completely alone in a world devastated by storm.

Chapter 24

The rain, now beating furiously on the roof, sweeping and receding in great waves, was an echo of the thoughts seething within me. I knew Gamini had no alternative but to break Sali's leg, but was afraid of what this had bred in my pupil – and of what the enmity of Sali might mean.

The closed windows and bright flares in Gamini's study made the room unbearably warm. In spite of this and my fears, it was pleasant to sit with the white-clad prince, sheltered from the monsoon, listening to his gaudy tale.

The smell of roast meat and spices reminded me how hungry I was. The attendants brought in chicken breast, rubbed with saffron and deep-fried in oil, boiled sweet potatoes, a *sambole* of chopped young onions spiced with fresh lime and thin-sliced green chilis, and bowls of fresh fruit. I was pleased when Gamini directed them to place the supper on the table and retire.

Gamini turned to me, laying an eager hand on mine, as soon as we were alone. 'I knew I had to beat him quickly with surprise, brains and power.' His voice was vibrant with excitement. 'Some of it was his own power.' He became thoughtful. The expression on his face could change as swiftly as light and shadow in the jungle. He was tense, though he did not know it. He needed to talk in order to run down, so I let him.

'It's a trick to remember,' Gamini continued animatedly. 'When we go into a battle, we'll use the enemy's own power to dislodge him. Mm!' He contemplated this seriously awhile, then started to bubble again. 'Did you see that first throw? Sali never expected me to get at his knees with my arms. Ha!' The boyish face became flushed with pride. He was still so young, really. 'And the final hold! No one's ever thought of it before. It's something I worked out for myself when I planned the fight.'

'You must show me.'

His eyes sparkled. 'Tomorrow, in the ring,' he promised.

In spite of my elation, I could not overlook my responsibility to Gamini. 'You broke Sali's leg at the thighbone, when you could just as well have broken it at the ankle. Why?'

He paused, the chicken breast between his fingers on the way to his mouth, white against his dark face. 'You knew that?'

'Yes.'

'Are you reproving me?' There was a glint of amusement in his face.

'I am asking you a question.'

'But it sounds like a reproof.'

'Perhaps because you are secretly reproving yourself.'

He flashed then, 'I never reprove myself.'

'And I never reprove you.'

Once again he threw back his head and laughed. 'You're quick and cool. I like you!' The chicken breast was raised to strong white teeth. He bit and started chewing.

'You still have not told me why you broke Sali's thighbone.'

'You do not forget, do you?'

'And you would rather not remember, would you?'

We laughed together then. Finally he grew serious. He set the chicken bone down on his plate, finished munching and wiped the side of his mouth delicately with a napkin. 'Listen

247

to the rain,' he bade me mockingly. 'It is pounding against the roof and splattering on the muddy ground with the force of ten thousand devils.'

'And I am pounding on your head to get the answer to one simple question.'

He was very serious now. 'I broke his thighbone because he had been set up to maim me or take my life. I wanted to break his neck, but I did not dare mix it with him to get close enough to apply this. You know . . .' He whistled, demonstrating the hold where he would be behind his opponent, reach under the arms and grasp his own hands over the man's neck to jerk his hands forward and break it. He nodded. 'Yes, he deserved more than I gave him.'

'How do you know he was set up?' I demanded in surprise.

'My spies told me.'

'You have spies?' I was incredulous now.

'Of course. It is not difficult. People tattle to me all the time. But those who only want to curry favour are never good spy material. I use people of my own choosing to spy. They do not work from loyalty, but for a price – some for immediate reward, others for a future one. There are many ambitious people in a court.' He laughed cynically.

The maturity of this young boy was truly remarkable. He had grown up thoughtful, with no real friends, just like me. Gamini and I were two of a kind – loners who had somehow come together. He had known it before I did!

'I can confirm that you were right,' I responded readily. 'While seated in the enclosure . . .'

'You overheard something that Digha Bahu's group was discussing,' he interrupted.

'Yes. How did you know?'

'I guessed. I believe you are the only one who is truly on my side with no ulterior motives.' He was completely sincere.

'How can you say that? You have your parents.' I nearly

248

added Velu Sumana, but remembered Gamini's lack of reaction to the Chief Warrior's feats earlier in the evening and held back.

A hint of sadness crossed Gamini's face, to be replaced by anger. He stood up abruptly and began to pace the room. I watched him silently until he seemed to make up his mind. 'Are you not on my side then?' he inquired, his eyes sharp on me.

'It's not for me to say it, or confirm it. You must know.'

'I did not ask you.' His voice was gentle, his face soft. 'My question was a statement. Now I'm going to entrust you with a great personal secret, because I think you can help me with advice.' He resumed his seat.

'Me advise you? You don't need advice from anyone.'

'Not as a prince, but as a man.'

I could not believe my ears. 'Go ahead,' I murmured.

'I had a woman,' he volunteered.

'So have millions of other men.'

He flushed at my airy response. 'But this is different. I've never known a woman before and I made a donkey of myself.'

'Then you must have satisfied her!'

He gaped at me for a few moments before comprehending my meaning. He burst out laughing. 'I never expected something like that from you. But listen. The problem is that I didn't, er . . . twice.'

'Tell me all about it.'

He leaned forward, elbows on the table, cheeks cupped in his palms, staring into space. His food was forgotten. In simple terms he told me the story of the maiden's two visits to him in his bedchamber. Sirima had been scornful of his failure the first time, but had shown understanding the next and he was very touched and deeply grateful to her. 'I told her I wanted to keep fit for my wrestling match,' Gamini concluded, 'so she has not visited me for a week now. She insists she is captivated by me and will be visiting me again tonight. But the problem remains.'

Alarm bells had been ringing in my mind as Gamini unfolded his story. My anxiety was increased by the physical forces of warm and humid air, the rattle of the rain and the pungent smell of the flares.

I suddenly remembered my mother. For the first time, a vision of her intercourse with my low-caste father flashed into my consciousness. Never having seen either of them, I had no vision of faces – merely male and female pubic regions – and hips, loins and the sexual organs in movement. I shuddered and blocked the vision from my sight.

As if to compensate, anxiety surged within me, throwing up the answer. A young female court attendant could never slip through the court guards on her own. Her quarters were well patrolled, Gamini's quarters were even better guarded and the corridors in between were frequented by sentries. A lowly attendant would know nothing about the system of guards to be able to slip through. Someone who knew had to be giving her instructions, for good reward.

That was it. Sirima was someone's tool. But whose – and for what object?

Gamini was so full of faith in this maiden that I did not have the heart to disillusion him. Besides, I had to win his confidence, not get his back up with opposition. I decided to change course.

'Do you know that you can cure yourself of your unfortunate . . . er . . . problem?' I inquired.

His eyebrows shot up. 'How so?'

He listened intently as I explained the effect of a fevered mind on the sexual organs.

'Why should my mind be that way?' he finally demanded.

'Because you have intelligence and imagination. Your imagination fires your mind like a kiln, when you experience certain sensations or the prospect of them. The fire accelerates the melting process in you.'

250

'You make sense, but I must think on it. What can I do about it?'

'Remember what I am going to tell you for the rest of your life. A woman is a shrine, meant to be worshipped. Before you can do so, you must offer flowers and your submission to her happiness. Only then can you enter the shrine and know its bliss.'

'Nonsense.' His voice had a rough edge. 'Women are meant to give men delight and bear children.'

'You're wrong, Prince,' I retorted passionately. 'As Lord Buddha teaches us, women are human beings, like us. I have taken a vow to keep away from them, but that was part of the total vow of *brachmachariya*. Women are superior to men in every way, except physically. They are the stuff of creation, while we are merely the accidents that set in motion the forces of life existing in them. They are the earth, we are but the seed. Give them respect, love and tenderness. They will give you life.'

'How can you know this when you do not lie with women, or have anything to do with them?'

'Do you have to feel the sun to know its power?'

He nodded in acknowledgement of my point, his black eyes intent on me, as I went on to explain how he could control his reactions and how he should make love to women, all based on my reading of the Kama Sutra *olas* and an anonymous author's work called Bavalath Gita, a sort of sexual complement to the Bhagavad Gita that is known to few. 'To make absolutely certain of your success tonight, however, I shall give you a balm you can use,' I concluded. 'It will deaden your manhood and enable you to last longer.'

He was so grateful that I felt rather ashamed. The balm would help his mind more than his body.

My own quarters adjoined Gamini's, so I had no difficulty watching from the bushes for her to keep her assignation. She slipped past me as the midnight watch began. It

251

confirmed my theory that someone who knew the guard rotation was behind Sirima.

The period for alternating the guards at either end of the corridor was one hour. She emerged again, shortly after the guard change, a dark figure in a black mantle, and glided back into the bushes in which I was hiding.

I gripped her from behind, one hand around her waist, the other over her mouth. She started to struggle, mouthing into the palm of my hand.

'One tiny squeak from you and I will choke you to death,' I whispered fiercely.

She knew I meant it and relaxed. Holding her firmly, I backed with her into my quarters. She allowed herself to be half dragged without resisting, but I could feel her trembling. Once at the door, I turned her and propelled her through the anteroom and the study into my bedroom. She was trembling now. 'I am going to remove my hand from your mouth,' I said softly. 'If you scream or call out, I will hold you until the guards arrive and tell them you are a thief. You will have some difficulty explaining your presence here at this time of night, won't you?'

She was silent and I shook her. 'Won't you?' I repeated. She nodded vigorously in assent.

'Remember too, it won't look good for the Prince . . . and your master will certainly not be amused!' I paused, then continued. 'I mean you no harm. So stop trembling. All I need is the answers to a few questions.'

I sat her down on my bed and removed my hand from her mouth, scared that she might scream. To my relief she did not, but started crying softly. I let her sob awhile in the darkness.

'Now if we cut this very short you can return to your quarters before your time runs out. Your visits are carefully worked out, are they not?'

She was silent. My window was closed and I could barely catch the gleam of her eyes in the dark.

'Answer me immediately!' I hissed fiercely. 'You will be the one to suffer if you miss the guard change. Remember, it's your whole life. Besides, I have ways of making you talk.' I drew the knife from my waist and placed the point just below her right eye. 'How would you like to have those beautiful eyes carved out, one by one?'

She gasped. Her breath smelled of tears, her runny nose and the rawness of what she had taken from Gamini. 'You wouldn't dare!' she exclaimed.

I laughed evilly in the dark and was rewarded by a shudder. 'Two knife thrusts blindly into an intruder at night? What would I have to explain?'

She began shivering, her sobs juddering quietly in her throat. 'I . . . I . . . I'll speak,' she stammered. 'Y-yes . . . yes . . . it is all timed.'

'You do not love the Prince?'

'N-no.'

'You do not lust for him?'

A slight exclamation of derision escaped her. The insult to Gamini made me furious. I wanted to smack her face, but held back. 'Answer me,' I commanded.

'No! I do not lust for him.'

'One final question.' I paused deliberately. 'Who is giving you orders?'

She started quivering like soft curd then, moving her head from side to side. I felt no pity – only a desire to wrest the truth from her. I pushed gently with the knife. She drew her head back with a little cry.

'I can't tell you,' she moaned. 'He'll destroy me if I tell you.'

'I promise you on my sacred honour as a prince, he will never know that you told me.'

She kept shaking her head. Her motion grew more violent. She was beginning to get hysterical.

I slapped her sharply on the cheek with my left hand to calm her, but with fierce pleasure at having the cause. She gasped, more in surprise than pain, but her trembling stopped.

'The truth is that whoever it is will never know that I am aware of his identity,' I assured her in convincing tones. 'That way you can continue carrying out his instructions, while being on our side. When the Prince becomes king, he will reward you.'

Moments of tense silence followed while she fought the battle between terror and terror. The darkness began to oppress me. The smell of her fear-sweat became intolerable.

I made a mistake then, because of my impatience. 'Is it the Chief Minister, Kirthi Siri?' I inquired.

'Yes,' she whispered.

I gave her instructions before she left. She well understood their significance. There was enough assurance of reward for her at the end to keep her on our side. All I now feared was that she might become pregnant. Bastards did not fare well in palaces. I should know!

We had the exercise room to ourselves at Gamini's command the next morning. He did not want anyone other than me to see how he applied his new hold. The room was large, with a high, boarded ceiling and windows with yellow, red and green grilles of lacquer. Above three tiers of wooden seats, the four walls were painted with frescoes of wrestlers, swordsmen, archers and horsemen in black and white. At the foot of the seats were lockers for storing weapons and accessories. In the centre was a ring with wooden floors covered by *indikola* matting. Doors at the far end led to the changing and massage rooms, complete with oils, scents and unguents and the baths.

Having stripped in separate rooms, we changed into white loin-cloths and proceeded to a massage room. It smelled of a mixture of pungent herbs and sweet spices. We rubbed ourselves down with oil. Gamini was restraining his excitement. He loved any type of sport and his victory over

Sali had made him even more an enthusiast. He looked very much an athlete this morning. The gleam of oil on his skin gave it the depth of polished ebony. His muscles had not yet developed, so the wide shoulders, narrow hips, full buttocks and well-shaped legs combined with the added lustre given his dark eyes by the oil around them to make him look almost girlish.

Gamini had never seen me stripped before. He looked admiringly at my physique. 'I never thought a *bhikku* could have such a beautiful build,' he observed. 'I like a body to have slim, strong lines. A squat, powerful physique is ugly, like a lump of rock.' His eye took in all of me. He sighed. 'I wish I had your golden colour.'

'Any colour is beautiful if it has depth and sheen,' I assured him.

'Not so! Ask any mother. Everyone prefers fair children. We dark ones come to our own only with manhood.'

Rejected because of his colour? True or false, did I have another clue? I was tempted to probe, but Gamini had spoken the words without bitterness, so I judged that my questions had best wait.

'Come along!' I said firmly. 'We are not here to admire each other, but to fight – unless you have turned chicken.'

His eyes flashed until he realized I was joking. 'I shall beat you though you are bigger than me,' he boasted.

'Tell me that after our bout. I shall be more pleased if the victory is yours.'

'How so?'

'What delight is there in defeating a younger, smaller opponent?'

'You won't throw the match away just to please me?'

'I would not do that to you.'

He appraised me suspiciously for a few moments, until he was satisfied. 'Come along then.' He turned and led the way out of the room, down the broad passageway into the exercise room.

We ducked under the ropes and entered the ring. I felt strange as I faced my slim, smaller opponent, for it was the first time in my life I was to wrestle someone in complete solitude. The room was bright-lit from sunlight swarming in through the open windows. The empty tiers of seats contrasted sharply with mixed smells of oil, sweaty leather and the feel of those who regularly exercised here. It was a room for people, but Gamini and I could have been the only people in the world today.

We had agreed on the rules of the bout. It would be decided by one fall, because we were there mainly for Gamini to demonstrate his new hold. If he got me in it, I would submit.

Saluting each other, we took our stances. Knowing a little about Gamini's style and tactics, I had decided to let him take the initiative, avoiding his power, which would include using my own against me, until I was more certain of what to expect.

Gamini's look became one of total concentration and purpose. He reached out a hand to grip mine. I slid it away from his grasp. He began to circle right. I marvelled at his courage. He was taking on someone bigger than him, yet he was preparing to attack. I circled around with him. His left hand flicked out again to grasp my right hand. I let him hold it. He pushed me away from him, instead of pulling, with wrists that were like steel. I gave deliberately. He had known I would. Swift as a striking cobra he pulled me to him, catching my right foot off balance. He kicked my left ankle so powerfully that my foot gave. As I stumbled forward, bending, he got me in a neck lock.

His grip was unbreakable. The blood began rushing to my head. I staggered as if my neck was in the stocks. I would become unconscious if I did not get out of this deadly grip. As he tightened his hold with mad strength, I reached between his legs, heaved with my shoulder and had him in the air. His arm slipped on my neck, but he would not let go.

With a convulsive effort, I reversed and flattened him on his back. I swear I could not have done it if he had been my size. I followed up with a body slam, to lie right on him. The breath left his lungs as if they were punctured drums. I pinned his shoulders. 'One! Two! Three!' I counted him out.

He lay there, his eyes closed, breathing heavily. He was going to have to acknowledge defeat before I moved. His face was very close to mine. He opened his eyes. They were inscrutable. Still holding him pinned with the body and arms, I smiled down at him. 'Do you acknowledge the fall?'

He did not reply. I became alarmed. Was he a bad loser? Would he hate me for my victory, though we had not really had a bout?

As I gazed down at him, his expression slowly changed, until his look became almost one of submission. That did something to me. The fight was over. I was the victor, though against a smaller opponent. I knew the joy of it and in doing so became aware of the smooth slipperiness of the oil, Gamini's young body beneath mine and the love I felt for him. The end of tension from the bout mingled with it all to give me a strange physical thrill. I realized with horror that, despite my rigid self-control over the years, I could still be a prey to sensual delight. Although it was not a sexual urge, it was not right for me, especially with Gamini. But I understood on the instant that men and women who prefer their own kind merely reach for sensations they can enjoy. If a man finds delight in the feel, the composition of another man, this is part of the way he has been created, something of nature's law, and cannot therefore be held unnatural.

I resolved that I would be rock-firm against any intrusion of physical delight from another body against mine, especially when it was Gamini's, for I loved this boy purely and deeply.

'Do you acknowledge the fall?' I demanded again of Gamini.

'Yes!' he replied readily.

I sprang to my feet. As Gamini rose painfully to his, I almost reached out a hand to help him, but held back, knowing he would not want it. In those moments, I knew that the love he and I had for each other was that of two brothers. It could mature or change, but its nature was sexless. At this time, he, alien from his kin, and I, without any, were two fiercely independent people who recognized each other's sincerity and idealism and were able to fulfil each other's needs for kinship, giving without interfering. We were two trees merged by common soil, supporting each other, two islands held together by eternal water.

Chapter 25

King Elara walked along his favourite path in the palace garden with his Chief Minister, Muttu Samy, and Junda on either side of him. The path was brick-paved, shaded by trees and lined with bushes and flower beds. The King sometimes used it to transact affairs of state in a more leisurely manner than from the various official rooms. He now observed that Junda was watching a dragonfly. 'Why do you always watch those creatures?' he inquired with good-natured amusement.

'Because they have the smoothest body-lines,' Junda replied. 'Only the shape of a *dagoba* is more symmetrical.'

The King smiled tolerantly. He had developed more understanding of the dwarf since his son was executed. He had even come to feel that Junda was his only true family in the palace. Yet he sometimes wondered whether the dwarf felt the same about him. What made family was feeling on all sides, a willingness to do special things, self-sacrifice and, yes, love. Could someone like Junda truly love? No matter, he was only a dwarf.

It was peaceful here beneath the shade, in spite of the raucous cawing of crows. Golden sunlight, filigreed through green branches, fell on the King's gaunt figure, the sunlight melting into his tunic and silver hair, the shadows blending with his dark face. He examined his hands and sunspots bounced off them. He heard the crackle of a dry leaf behind the bushes. He paused and glanced sharply in its direction. 'What was that?' he demanded.

'Probably a mouse, or some small animal, lord,' Muttu Samy replied. Some instinct made the King peer closely at the bushes. He could see nothing and the silence reassured him.

Feeling a strange identity with the illusion of light and shade, the King resumed his walk, but something nagged him. He stopped beneath the shade of a giant flame tree spreading over the walkway. The thought of danger always brought to mind the Sinhala. He turned toward Muttu Samy. 'The Ruhuna king has not yet signed the treaty,' he observed. 'On the contrary, this incident of the twelve-year-old prince – what's his name, Gamini – refusing to take an oath of non-violence against us is rather disturbing.'

'I wouldn't take a headstrong boy seriously,' Muttu Samy responded. He was a small man of forty, with sharp features and a swarthy complexion. His thin, compressed lips spoke of a hard character and the struggle to get to the top. His long black hair, gleaming with oil, was tied in a knot on top of his head, which he had a habit of moving sideways like a bird when considering something. 'This prince has been fed a lot of nonsense since birth about being a Sinhala saviour. Even if he were, he will have his own people to deal with. The Sinhala have been content under your noble rule for over twenty-five years now. They have enjoyed prosperity as never before in their history. They are lazy at the best of times, disposed to grow fat and unwilling to be stirred. It would take more than a promised saviour to move them now!'

'But they are the Lion race!'

'Fat old lions, lord – rather drawn in the tooth with *maitriya* and age.'

King Elara noted that Junda was listening with unusual apathy. Ten years earlier, the dwarf would have been outraged by the insult to his people and would have made some acid or ribald remark. The Chief Minister had spoken the truth. Time had made everyone complacent, including himself, the King. He felt a curious sense of pleasure that some of Junda's patriotism had evaporated. It meant that he could expect more personal loyalty from the dwarf. The King was surprised that he should want it.

'Nobler the ageing lion than a bull lacking good taste,' Junda interposed unexpectedly. He never attempted to hide his dislike of Muttu Samy, who always treated him superciliously.

Muttu Samy grunted and turned to stare at Junda. He was newly appointed and not used to the liberties court jesters are permitted. 'Take care you are not smothered by this bull!' he warned.

'Some bull!' the dwarf remarked, scornfully surveying the minister's small size.

Muttu Samy flushed beneath his dark skin. He was sensitive about his height. 'I could easily overpower you, dwarf!'

'Come now, Chief Minister,' King Elara laughed. 'Do not take my jester so seriously.'

Muttu Samy fell into step with the King. 'No, lord, I do not take any jesting fool seriously,' he sneered. 'That would bestow him too much honour.'

'Which politicians know nothing of, anyway,' Junda flung at him.

The Chief Minister ignored him. 'As I was saying when I was interrupted by the noddlehead, sire, you have no cause for alarm.'

'I'm not so sure.' A faraway look entered the King's dark eyes. Some present instinct warned him of danger. 'We fear we have become so complacent that even our security measures have been relaxed. All the events of the Prince's birth were of concern at the time, but their impact has been diminished. It was so long ago. So many things have happened since then.' He sighed heavily, remembering his own son. He lengthened his stride, his figure straight and powerful, his gait soldier-like, a young man of fifty-seven.

Muttu Samy quickened his pace to keep up with the King, while the dwarf started trotting behind.

'We cannot afford to be complacent,' the King asserted. 'The Ruhuna prince is still only a boy; by the time he grows up, we may all be dead. But we owe a duty to our brother, who is our rightful heir, and to our Chola people, who have settled this country in their thousands, and to those who hold office under us. To ensure Chola succession in Lanka is therefore a sacred mission.' He paused suddenly, turning to observe the dwarf's reaction.

'I thought you were no longer interested in a Chola succession, lord,' Junda ventured.

'Only a fool could have thought that,' King Elara responded warmly. 'For all our just and equal rule, we are first a Chola and will always remain so. That is part of our *kharma*. To perpetuate Chola rule remains a dictate of *dharma*!'

The dwarf stared thoughtfully at the King. 'I am indeed a fool, lord,' he replied. 'I ignored what has stared me in the face daily. A total Chola administration governing Lanka, with Sinhala advisers. Many concessions to Sinhala sentiment, but only bones thrown by our Chola masters from their table, as to dogs. And none of us welcome at your board unless we wag our tails to your slightest desire.'

'No, no, dwarf!' the King protested. He regretted his harshness and hastened to make amends. 'You mistake generosity for charity. Besides . . .' Pride forbade him to say anything more. 'No matter!' He noted a faraway expression on Junda's face and a restraint that seemed tinged with regret.

'And what about the apparent heir in Ruhuna, Prince Digha Bahu?' the Chief Minister inquired, turning the subject.

'An ambitious prince with a great deal of cunning, but neither brains nor ability behind him.'

'His brains and ability are certainly in his behind,' Junda intervened, almost absently.

King Elara laughed. He was more at home with the jeering dwarf, or even Junda the philosopher, than with Junda the patriot.

'We can use the prince as a tool, lord,' he heard the Chief Minister declare. 'Such men are easily manipulated.'

'Allow him the Sinhala crown in Ruhuna?'

'Allow him to *think* he'll have the Sinhala crown in Ruhuna. Even allow him to have it for as long as its suits us. Better a jackal on the Ruhuna throne than a young lion.'

'So you fear the young lion?' Junda questioned.

'No, but I fear the jackal less. At least – '

The bushes suddenly crackled. The King swung sideways.

The man burst across the flower bed, a tall, menacing figure, his upraised sword gleaming in the shadows. King Elara flinched and took a step backwards, but his mind was racing. The split-second decision would mean life or death. His muscles tensed for the dive forward to close with the man and escape the sword's swing.

Junda must have sensed the parting of the bushes bordering the walkway before he saw the figure breaking through. He was closer to the man than the King was and slightly to the rear. He dived low between the King and the leaping figure. His head butted the man's thigh with stunning impact.

262

The attacker gave at the knees and buckled sideways. The flashing sword continued its downward swing. It bit deep into Junda's upper arm. He fell to the ground with a groan, clutching at the wound with one hand. The blood erupted from it.

The brief seconds Junda had created were enough for King Elara. His brain sparkling, his right leg shot sideways, kicking the man in the head. The bloodstained sword clattered to the ground. He fell sprawling on the flower bed, like a fallen scarecrow. With the agility of a great cat, the King pounced on the sword. It flashed in the dappled light as he raised it.

The blow would have· split the man's head in two, had it fallen. King Elara stopped it halfway, then deliberately dropped the sword in a slow arc. The attacker lay on his back, a human mass amid crushed flowers, staring up at the descending weapon. He was tall, brown-chested and dressed only in a dark loincloth. Beads of sweat began to glisten on his lean, bearded brown face. His deep-set eyes crossed as the gleaming sword point slowly dropped closer.

All the pent-up anger of the King became drawn into a cold, tight knot within him. His entire being was centred on this one enemy, regardless of how many others might be around. He felt merciless and invincible.

The sword point touched the man's throat and stopped.

'You shall live to tell us your tale,' the King said pleasantly. 'Chief Minister, call the guard. Then see to our beloved jester. He saved our life.' He was exhilarated by the action and his split-second responses. He was also grateful to the dwarf, who might well have saved his life. Junda must really care for him, but he dare not take his eyes off the attacker as yet to look to the dwarf's condition.

The petrified Muttu Samy came to life. 'Ho there, guards!' he screeched, rushing towards Junda.

King and would-be killer stared at each other like characters in a play while the Chief Minister knelt beside

263

Junda. The man's drawn face was now covered with glistening, heavy beads of sweat, dew on grass.

The dwarf rose groggily to his feet, still clutching his right shoulder, from which the blood was streaming. 'It's only a flesh wound,' he muttered. 'I'll be all right as soon as the bleeding stops.'

An enormous relief seized the King at knowing the dwarf was not badly hurt, but he still watched the man at the end of his sword coldly. Nothing could shake his immediate purpose.

Naked swords in hand, two bare-chested guards raced up in alarm. The Chief Minister rose to his feet. He pointed a shaking finger at the attacker. 'Seize that man. He is a Sinhala. We have foiled a Sinhala plot to kill our king.' He looked up at King Elara. 'I was wrong, lord,' he stammered, 'wrong to say the Sinhala have become complacent. They are worse than thieves, they are murderers.'

The King withdrew the sword as the guards roughly seized the fallen man. 'Come now, Chief Minister,' he retorted mildly. 'You draw quick conclusions. A single paddy bird does not mean a harvest. Let us first discover why this man wanted to take our life.' He was feeling elated. Life had been without excitement for too long.

The Chief Minister turned on the attacker, now in the grasp of the two burly guards. 'Who sent you?' he screamed shrilly.

The man's eyes rolled toward Junda. 'Traitor!' he spat out. 'Long live our Sinhala prince!'

'So will you, our friend,' King Elara declared softly, 'unless you tell us who sent you. Until then, you will wish you were dead, we promise you.'

Chapter 26

Not to be outdone, King Elara was answering the military display in Ruhuna with one of his own. He had spent the whole morning and afternoon on the *maidan* fronting the city walls watching military exercises and displays by his warriors, led by the Chief Warrior, Digha Jantu. He was well pleased with his prowess and the state of readiness of his elite troops.

Gaily dressed crowds in a variety of national dress sweated with the heat as they thronged the open ground beyond the improvised arena, the boundaries of which were decorated with Chola flags of green, white and yellow. Bright banners of the Chola regiments, the bull rampant predominating, hung limp in the still air. Vendors touted their wares from open carts – trinkets of gold and silver, copper and brassware, sweetmeats and sweet drinks, fruit and vegetables, even bolts of gaudy-coloured cloth. A *vadai* seller, his face coal-black beneath a shabby white turban, sang a ditty: '*Odi vai, shuda, shuda, masala – vadai!*' His even teeth gleamed whiter than mother-of-pearl. Dancers, snake charmers, drummers, acrobats and medicine men raucously plied their trade. A white-haired *yogi* sent his little brown helper up a rope that stood erect as a pole in the air. Strident laughter streaked above the babble.

Junda had a favourable position in the closely guarded royal enclosure, dead centre on one side of the arena, along with high palace officials. He had recovered from his wound, but still had a *patthu* on his shoulders, covered by a bandage to hold the healing herbs in place. King Elara caught a brief glimpse of him sitting on the edge of his seat before he turned his attention to the task ahead. This was the last event of the day and he had better make it good if he was to strike terror into the hearts of the Sinhala by demonstrating his skill from the back of the State elephant. Opposing him, at the far end of the *maidan*, was the second State elephant, also guided by a *mahout*. But the figure in the *howdah* of that elephant was only an effigy of a man. He signalled his elephant to advance.

First came the crump, then the tread of the great beast's feet. Finally the thudding that broke into galloping sounds. As the pounding became louder, the parched earth began to tremble and shake. The King stood erect in the fortified *howdah*, swaying to the movement of the grey elephant. Goaded by its *mahout* and urged on by the King, the elephant began charging at full speed towards its opponent.

Kicking up brown dust, the pounding and drumming of elephants' feet grew to a frenzy. It seemed as if the earth must fall apart, yet the beasts approached each other without uttering a sound.

King Elara balanced himself more easily now to the sway of the animal beneath him. When the timing was right, he reached with his left hand to seize a short bow. In a flash he had an arrow sped to its mark, hitting the effigy foursquare. On the crowd's cheer, a second arrow sped to quiver beside the first. King Elara flung aside the bow and seized a spear. Still balancing adroitly, he bent backward and flung the spear. Amazingly, it plunged beside the two arrows. The cheering rose above the thunder of the elephants' feet. It filled the King with exhilaration. Another spear followed, unerringly aimed and flung.

The two beasts were almost alongside each other. Darts flew from the King's hand like angry bees, six in quick succession, the last one with a half turn of the thrower's body.

The elephants circled wide and rumbled toward each other again. The King repeated his performance. Circling yet again, the elephants charged a third time before slowing down to return to their starting posts.

The *howdah* of the opposing elephant, with the effigy inside, was removed and carried around for all to see. Six spears and arrows and eighteen darts stuck out of the effigy, making it look like a grotesque porcupine. Thunderous cheers and cries of amazement arose, from Chola and Sinhala alike.

'Our king is a real champion!' Muttu Samy exclaimed. 'He and our Chief Warrior, the mighty Digha Jantu, are a match for the entire Sinhala army!'

King Elara was elated. The display of armed might, the skill of his warriors, the training of the Chola troops, had to be a deterrent to any Sinhala saviour. Those in Ruhuna had demonstrated their powers, but who could match the Cholas? It was the destiny of the Sinhala to be forever dominated by the foreigner.

The King walked up to the royal enclosure, panting slightly, nostrils flaring with each breath. An attendant proffered a white cloth and he mopped his dark brow with it. A burst of cheering from the enclosure greeted him. Cries of '*Haro! Hara!*' seemed to reach the heavens. The King nodded and motioned to his attendants to help him remove his brown leather doublet. They carried it away, leaving him in a grey undervest soaked with sweat. It revealed the dark, rippling muscles of his tall frame. A gold silk tunic was held up to him by an attendant. He began to don it. While getting his arms into the sleeves, he caught sight of the Chief Minister and beckoned to him. Muttu Samy immediately headed toward the King, Junda trotting behind him.

'You are a wanton king!' the dwarf grumbled in his high-pitched voice.

'Why do you say that?' King Elara inquired good-humouredly.

'You wasted so many arrows, spears and darts on a dummy. It takes a king of dummies to attack another dummy so furiously.'

'Beware, dummy. You have just seen the power of this

267

king of dummies. He may turn you into a living porcupine.'

'You know what it takes to attack a dummy clown?'

King Elara threw back his head and laughed. He was in excellent spirits. 'You can offer no more fitting tribute to your king than to bring him laughter!' he declared sincerely. He turned to Muttu Samy. 'Well, Chief Minister, what have you to say?'

'That there is no greater warrior than our king,' Muttu Samy replied proudly, bright eyes flashing with genuine admiration.

'No, no! I mean what news do you have for us. After all,' – King Elara gestured with his hands toward the arena and the royal enclosure – 'this is our counter to the military display of the Sinhala.'

'How would I dare compare your feats, sire, with the gaudy acts of a little boy wrestler. Why, wrestling is not even a sport of kings.'

'You still do not answer us,' King Elara responded, a note of impatience in his voice. 'What of our prisoner? Has he revealed who sent him?'

'I'm afraid not, sire. The prisoner died under questioning early this morning, without giving away any information. A stubborn fellow to the end. All he would mutter occasionally was 'Long live our prince!' We can only conclude that he was sent by a faction supporting Prince Gamini.'

'Then let us make war on that faction and eliminate it.' The voice that intruded was strong, deep and clear. The giant Digha Jantu came up. He made obeisance to the King, then stood up again, looking like a great statue carved out of polished satinwood. His bare body gleamed. The muscles were great, pliant snakes rippling across his massive frame; the sword scar across the right of his chest was a white decoration. His legs were like tree trunks beneath a red loin-cloth. Astride the broad, flat nose curving over the upper lip, his dark eyes glittered with purpose.

'You did well today, Chief Warrior,' King Elara remarked, ignoring the suggestion.

'And you, sire, were the king of champions.'

'Your voice is as powerful as the mighty Mahela's' – King Elara sighed – 'but your words are sweeter.'

'That we should make war?' Digha Jantu inquired eagerly.

'No!' The King smiled. 'You know what we meant.' He turned to Muttu Samy again. 'Have you discovered anything more about the attacker?'

'Yes, sire. He is a Sinhala sweeper, named Pina, who once lived in the palace with his wife, reportedly a beautiful young woman. He was unable to find work because of our policy of . . . er . . . bringing in our own people. His wife supported him by selling flour-cakes and sweetmeats. She was . . . er . . . raped not long ago and blinded before or after the rape, obviously to prevent her from identifying the culprit, who, from the only evidence available, has to be one of our own people.' Muttu Samy paused. Noting the flash of the King's eyes, he added hastily, 'I am sure it could not really have been one of us, sire. There has to have been a deliberate effort to lay a false scent and implicate a Chola. Pina recently sent his wife away. No one knows where, because she had no friends. We can only guess that she was smuggled back to her village in Ruhuna. These damned Sinhala can be tight-lipped when it comes to their compatriots.' He flickered an angry glance towards Junda.

'What do you expect fat old lions to do?' Junda inquired. 'Blab through toothless gums like Chola bulls chewing grass?'

'I'll knock your teeth off and then you too will have toothless gums,' Digha Jantu threatened, taking a step toward the jester.

'You'll do no such thing in front of the King,' Junda smirked self-confidently. 'Besides, only a tooth doctor takes out teeth. Warriors are supposed to extract lives.'

'Your life then . . .'

'Let the jester be,' King Elara directed. 'Go on with your story, Chief Minister.'

'There's not much more to tell, sire, only conjecture. Oh – the one other fact is that Pina was seen drinking *sura* with a stranger in one of the city taverns a few days before his wife vanished. The man had registered as a trader from Matale, but what business would a trader have with a sweeper?'

'Hmm!' The King was thoughtful. He finally nodded. 'You are checking on the trader's identity?'

'Yes, sire! But I doubt he exists as such.' Muttu Samy drew himself more erect, to command attention. His head tilted sideways as he adopted his judicial manner. 'We can conclude that there is a faction that wants you out of the way in order to set up the young prince as king.'

King Elara shook his head. 'We cannot agree with you, Chief Minister. What everyone has ignored is that the Prince is just thirteen. Who would seriously want him to reign now, especially when most of the Sinhala people are happy and contented? If we are killed, our brother would be here with an army in a few months. No! No! There has to be some other explanation.'

The Chief Minister looked down at the parched dust. It was his turn to be thoughtful.

'I understand that the prisoner refused to talk even under severe torture,' Digha Jantu intervened. 'What motive did he have for remaining silent? Loyalty? Patriotism? Even great bitterness? From a poor sweeper?'

The King ignored the questions. 'Mark our words, the woman is in Ruhuna. Get your spies to track her down. It is unlikely that you will find her. Even if you do, she probably knows nothing of importance.' He paused again, this time pleased at his own clear thinking. 'So you see, Chief Minister, this is not an effort to set up the Prince on the throne, but to set him up so we would wreak vengeance on him.'

'Who would benefit from such an act, sire?' Muttu Sàmy inquired incredulously.

King Elara laughed. 'Who but the prince of jackals who is forever making overtures to us to support him in Ruhuna.'

'Prince Digha Bahu.'

'We rather think so. He reacts in fits and starts. All this nonsense from Gamini must gnaw at him. If Gamini were out of the way, he could become King of Ruhuna.'

'We must take vengeance on Prince Digha Bahu then,' Digha Jantu ground out.

'No. He is too useful to us at present.'

'What do we do then, sire?' Muttu Samy inquired.

'Nothing, except maintain vigilance.' He noted Muttu Samy's concern and smiled slowly, white teeth gleaming beneath his dark skin. 'In the palace too, if you like, Chief Minister. But there will be no war, or attempts at blind reprisals. Oh, and one other thing. We want every effort made to find that rapist. He must be dealt with.'

'Your life was nearly taken and you will do nothing, sire?' Digha Jantu stared at the king, disbelieving. 'Why? If it had been my life . . .'

'Your life, Chief Warrior? Remember that a dead king leaves behind more problems than a dead warrior and a live king has more responsibilities than blind vengeance.'

'But, sire, the science of government is punishment,' Digha Jantu persisted.

'And whom shall we punish when the criminal is dead and we do not know who else was responsible for the crime? The empty Sinhala air? And whom should we punish because the criminal's wife was raped and blinded? The suspected Chola people? No, Chief Warrior, the science of government is indeed punishment, but a king must learn the art of punishment to govern effectively.' A note of passion entered King Elara's voice. 'We believe in the concept. We sacrificed our own son and heir in proof.'

His gaze swept toward Junda. 'A Sinhala fool saved our life and in so doing perhaps averted war and bloodshed. We kings must learn equally from wise men and fools. But

271

enough of philosophy. We have had a council of war while the people wait. The display is ended. Sound the conch shells and trumpets. We shall go to the palace to make ready for the entertainment.' He gestured to the attendants, who had been waiting out of earshot. 'Our horses!'

Chapter 27

Gamini's life was obviously in a cycle of crisis at the time of his sexual relationship with the maiden, Sirima. I remember praying to God daily to see Gamini safely through it.

I believe in the power of spoken words. Sight is but a human attribute. Hearing is a sensation from the force of sound upon our ears, and sensation is divine. Even plants have it – for example, the bush that folds its leaves upon touch. I prayed aloud daily, or even more often, for repetition is necessary, because God can miss sounds, as distant temple bells evade the hearing until they finally register on the senses.

Yet praying is useless unless we are prepared to back our pleas with resolve and action, so I kept a specially watchful eye on Gamini after my talk with Sirima. He was becoming more and more open and friendly with me, but there was still an inner reserve that had to be part of his makeup, because of his destiny. He could never be like other people.

Gamini's relationship with Sirima blossomed rapidly. Under her tutelage, he was gradually losing his apprehensions about his manhood. I could not help but marvel at her experience. After all, she was hardly seventeen. She had been chosen by Kirthi Siri with care.

How had he known of her competence? The question bothered me, for it could not have been by reputation, since she was neither a courtesan nor a concubine.

I also feared the influence she could have over Gamini. Although he maintained that all he wanted from her was sex, gratitude could cause him to become dependent on her and too trusting. The strongest men have been known to become like wax in bed. Sirima was young, attractive, beautifully formed. She was an expert at lovemaking. If Gamini was in an evil cycle, she could be a carrier of evil.

We were in Gamini's study one night after dinner in the pre-rain month of Maggasira, discussing the attempt on King Elara's life. The air was so still that I could feel the weight of the silence outside, while the tapers flamed unwavering within the room. Whining mosquitoes pestered us constantly, breaking through the scent of incense and citronella oil meant to repel them. They alighted on our bodies and caused the skin to prickle.

'So you see,' Gamini was saying, 'our friends plotted to start a war and have been advised to remain at peace. King Elara is clever. His principal object is to have peace at any cost, hoping it will outlast his life. But I think this is a foolish hope.'

'Why?'

'He's only fifty-seven. He will be very much alive when I move against him.'

'You intend moving against him?'

'Of course.'

'When?'

'When I'm ready and our army is ready. It is too soon now. That is why I am glad the pig's father attempted this trick. It has given me a few more years to prepare.'

'What if war had broken out now because of the attempted murder?'

'I would then have had no option but to lead our armies into battle.'

I could barely restrain a smile, but he seemed so serious that I made no comment.

'I know what you are thinking,' Gamini broke in. 'You think it is my father who would ride at the head of our armies. I have no faith in his response. Our only other leader is Prince Digha Bahu, but of course you know about him.' He snorted his contempt. 'The people will not follow him anyhow. So it would have to be me. But I am glad it is not yet. I want to be ready when the opportunity arises. I want to attack. I will never fight defensive battles.'

'That makes sense.'

'It is history, as you know. The Chola has won against us so often through the centuries because he has been the invader and always had the initiative.'

'How will you get the army behind you?'

'Now that I have made a start with the military display, I want to proceed with care. Kirthi Siri has promised to help me carry on doing what my father started some years ago and stopped. My father is so preoccupied with religious works that he will not notice my putting the army organization back again into battle readiness. We will not recruit fresh forces as yet, for that would mean increased taxes and levies. What we have is enough to start with. We will concentrate on making it perfect.' His face had come alive, his body was vibrant with excitement.

'I believe you can do it,' I declared, 'and I need hardly tell you that I will help you in every possible way.'

He reached over impulsively and placed a hand on mine. 'One race, one language, one religion,' he declared.

My heart rebelled. My God was a God of all races, languages and religions. 'One race, one language, one religion,' I agreed, hoping that God would understand and comforting myself with the resolve to try to mould Gamini to a more generous philosophy once his crusade was over.

Gamini withdrew his hand, but his eyes still shone.

'Now you must leave me.' His eyes crinkled. 'My lady visitor comes tonight.'

I rose to my feet. 'Enjoy yourself,' I bade him.

'Have no fear. I will. You were right about the need to satisfy a woman. There is a feeling of power in it.' He paused, reflecting. I did not know whether to be glad or sorry that he found only power and not joy in satisfying his partner.

'I believe, though, that Sirima is falling in love with me,' Gamini mused. 'I do not know whether that is a good thing, because I do not love her. All I desire is her body, though I am fond of her and very grateful that she is helping me become a man.'

'I am certainly glad you're not in love with her.'

'Oh! Have no fear of that. When I fall in love, it will be under different circumstances, with someone different.'

I looked at him in astonishment, for his whole expression had become tender. This was a side of him that I had never seen.

'Now you must go,' he urged. 'Tonight is exciting. Sirima is bringing a special drink that will give me more sexual power.'

I bade him good night and retired to my quarters.

Slipping off my tunic, I sat at my desk, under the fitful yellow glare of lighted tapers, to write my *olas*. The dark night air outside was still oppressive, except for the continuous chirp of crickets, which I had not noticed while I was in Gamini's room. When a sound is constant, one can identify it with silence, provided one is accustomed to it and it is not too loud, I thought.

Somewhere at the base of my skull, a pulse was beating. I was experiencing discomfort. Heat and the pressure of clouds frequently did this to me. In primitive times, it may have been a useful warning of the danger of a storm, but now I could do without it.

I toyed with the stylus. The words would not come. I shifted uncomfortably on my stool and wiped the sweat from my face with the back of my hand, then felt ashamed. I would not have done this had I not been alone. In company,

I would have used a cloth for the purpose. It is the attribute of a gentleman to follow his code of elegant conduct at all times, especially when he is alone. *Charlithraya* makes a man civilized, removing him from his barbaric condition.

My mouth was parched. Almost unconsciously, I reached for the clay drinking bowl. It was cool to my touch. I took a few sips of the water. It was cool in my mouth.

I glanced at the sand-clock on my desk. Sirima would be with Gamini by now. My pupil would of course be drinking deeply, I thought, and perhaps of a hot and more fiery liquid. A hot and more fiery liquid! I sat up with a jerk, my mind in convulsions of thought. How in the world would Sirima get such a drink? Kirthi Siri would never have provided her with alcohol or drugs for the young Prince. He would merely have wanted her to win Gamini's confidence. My mind searched feverishly in the recesses of my memory for that night when I had extracted the truth from Sirima. Like some horror emanating from a dark cemetery, the truth slithered in. In my conceit, I had asked her 'Is it Kirthi Siri?' and she had whispered back 'Yes!' I could still hear the tinge of relief in her voice. Anger such as I had never known before surged through me. It had to be Prince Digha Bahu. No one else. Gamini might be dead at this moment!

I pushed away from the desk and sprang to my feet. I had somehow to stop Gamini from taking that drink, whatever it might be, though he would be furious if I intruded.

I sped to my bedroom and snatched up the naked sword from its pegs on the wall. I raced out of my quarters. I skidded in the darkness at the turn to Gamini's room, nearly falling in my haste. Breathing deeply to steady myself, I knocked softly on Gamini's door. No reply.

I knocked again, louder this time.

Still no answer. My heart began to pound. Was Gamini dead already? Should I batter down the door?

I moved back to rush it, then decided to give speech a try.

'Prince, it is I!' My cry was as loud as I dared. 'Please let me in. It is most urgent.'

'Go away!'

I had never heard such beautiful words in my life! Gamini was alive, his voice angry and strong.

'If you do not let me in immediately, I will break down the door,' I threatened. 'You know the consequences. I must see you for just a minute.'

There was silence while Gamini doubtless 'thought on it', then a female voice. I could not make out what she said, but it sounded like pleading.

'You had better have cause,' Gamini finally said.

I heard the sound of feet, followed by the drawing of the door bar. The door opened. Gamini was framed in the light of the tapers, a slim, dark figure, bare-chested and dressed in a sarong, resentment in his glance. At the far end of the study, Sirima stood against the wall. She wore only a bodice and skirt, her midriff bare. She stood slender, tall, shapely, but apprehension showed in her eyes and her delicate features were tense.

I swept the room with a single look. On Gamini's desk stood a small phial and a brown ceramic jug. Beside them was a solitary porcelain drinking bowl. I had arrived in time. The bowl was empty. But it told me the story. The drink was for Gamini alone. Sirima would not share in its frenzy.

Gamini noticed the sword in my hand. The resentment in his dark eyes flickered into anger. 'What is this?' he demanded harshly.

'May I enter, Prince, or must we run the risk of discovery?'

He stood aside and closed the door behind me, then turned to face the room.

I moved slowly and deliberately toward Sirima, my eyes not moving from her. She looked at me transfixed, like a rat before a snake.

'What does this mean?' Gamini demanded again, more loudly.

I ignored him. Now I was close enough to Sirima. Her dark eyes remained on mine. She knew I had discovered the truth. I could see the sickness chilling her heart, feel the terror vibrating through her whole being. She began to tremble.

I circled sideways so Gamini could see her. 'Look at her, Prince,' I directed, 'and know the truth.'

Gamini did as I bade him. I knew without taking my eyes off Sirima. His sudden tensing was physical in the air.

Slowly I raised my sword until the point touched Sirima's slender, creamy throat. 'It's an old Sinhala custom, that the host and guest both partake of refreshments,' I said quietly. 'This custom derives from the time Kuveni, Queen of the Yakkas, unsuccessfully attempted to capture our nation's founder, Prince Vijaya, with a drugged drink.'

I paused to let my words take effect. Sirima never took her eyes off mine.

'You brought the Prince this drink,' I continued. 'As his tutor, I came here to ensure that our customs are followed.' I laughed wickedly and pushed the sword point enough for her to feel its prick. 'Now be the perfect hostess and pour the Prince a drink!' I directed.

Her sob ended in a groan. I pushed a little harder. A hand flew to her face. She backed away along the wall, moving sideways toward the desk. When she reached it, I changed the direction of the sword. Now it was on the side of her neck. 'Pour!' I commanded.

Her hands shook as she removed the stopper from the jug.

'You drop the jug and I will kill you on the spot,' I warned.

She spilled some of the clear liquid on the ebony table as she poured the drink. The stain had a pale froth. She replaced the jug on the desk and stood beside it with head lowered. She had to support herself with her hands on the desk.

I could feel Gamini's watchful silence, but he never moved and I never looked at him.

'As the perfect hostess, you will now drink first,' I said softly.

She looked beseechingly at me. I pricked the sword into her soft skin. 'You may save yourself from the drink, but if you do not take it, I shall make no mistake with my thrust.'

She reached out hesitant hands. She paused before grasping the bowl. It shook as she held it. Suddenly she became resolute. She raised the bowl to her face. She drained its contents. The bowl rattled on the desk when she replaced it. She looked at me defiantly.

As I watched Sirima in the golden light of the tapers, her shadow slowly receded to sweep back over her. The fair skin grew darker. The flesh slowly melted from her face and began to shrivel, like metal in an intense fire. I heard a sizzling noise and smoke arose while droplets of liquid flesh continued to fall from her and vanish soundlessly into the air. Gradually the smoke vanished and her face remained but a skull, with teeth jutting out white as fish bones. Tiny wisps of her hair appeared on the upper and lower jaws. Her eyes alone remained alive and bright, sunken in their sockets, glaring at me in rage. The air between us began to rock and shake.

The vision passed in an instant. I saw her again as she was, but now her eyes were indeed on mine, full of deep hatred such as I had never seen before in a human being or a beast.

My vision told me what lay in store. My mind raced feverishly, then stuck.

'Come here, Prince,' I directed. My voice rang soft and clear in the silence.

'Take this sword and kill her if she moves.'

Obediently he took the sword from me. Young as he was, he was resolute like the iron that must have entered his spirit

279

from Sirima's act of treachery. Sirima avoided his gaze as he held the sword point unwavering against the fair throat he had expected to kiss this night. Remembering that other night thirteen years ago, when I had killed my first man, I shuddered.

I went to the shelf that held Gamini's *ola* and stylus, praying that he would not have to kill Sirima.

I sat at the desk while Gamini and Sirima held their tableau beside me. I wrote out a full confession implicating Prince Digha Bahu in the plot to poison Gamini. Only the scratching of my stylus and the sputtering of the tapers disturbed the silence. When I had finished, I read what I had written aloud, then pushed the *ola* toward Sirima and placed the stylus in her hand. Her fingers were cold and clammy as death.

'Sign your name!' I commanded.

She came forward and slowly signed her name without looking at either of us.

I rolled up the *ola* and placed it in the pocket of my pantaloons, then rose to my feet. 'We have about one hour before the poison takes effect,' I said. 'We shall wait it out. You may sit down, Sirima. Pray to the *devas* that your life be spared.'

In my heart I knew her prayers would be in vain. I was getting the scent of the liquid now and it told me what the jug contained. My studies in the temple had included the properties of medicines, drugs, alcohol and deadly poisons.

The hour that passed was the longest I had ever spent in my life. Total silence, time without end, I had been well accustomed to, in the temple. Tonight the circumstances were ghastly. Gamini sat on an ebony settle by the door, sword in hand, as if keeping guard. He might have been carved in stone, because he barely stirred during that whole time. It reminded me of the way he had lain on his couch after the milk-rice incident. He was not merely lost in thought. He was totally immersed inside the wall he had suddenly built around himself – within which, I knew, was implacable decision. He had allowed someone else to take charge for once and he would go along with whatever I did to the end.

Sirima sat at the ebony desk, chin cupped in her hands, staring into space. Fear emanated from her like a death stench. She was petrified by it, her mind unhinged. An occasional sob or sniff escaped her, but it was a physical thing, not the product of thought or emotion. Remembering the way I had sobbed that last night in my uncle's arms, I felt a stab of pity for her. She was so young and had been misled. But there comes a time in our lives when we have made the mould and have to fit ourselves into it. Sirima had chosen her own fate. Her death was inevitable – and not unjust either. After all, the prince she had sought to murder was five years younger than she was – just a boy, not yet thirteen, though he had the maturity of a man.

I thought of my own part, how beneath all – the training in the temple, the *maitriya*, the *ahimsa*, even the fear of *kharma* – I was a prince, acting as one, not as a *bhikku*.

Sweltering with heat from the closed windows, we played out our roles in the golden light of tapers. It was an unreal scene. I reflected that, but for me, Gamini's dark body would now be coupled with Sirima's, their sweat softening the union. I remembered the day I had wrestled him.

The first sound in the room was a shuddering gasp from Sirima. Her hand flew to her chest. She breathed deeply, then the spasm passed.

In less than a minute, she began to moan. The cramps had begun. Her stool scraped on the floor as she pushed back on it. She doubled up, holding her stomach. Soon her breath came in great, juddering gasps. She began to choke. Her hands clutched her throat as if to free it. Froth appeared on the sides of her mouth. She tried to stand, reeled and fell. Lying on the floor, she twisted and writhed in paroxysms, groaning and gasping for breath. The only sounds from her

281

were her attempts to ease her agonized breathing – pitiful sounds that were really silence.

I looked once at Gamini. The horror of what he had escaped was in his dark eyes, but the rest of him was inflexible, hard. He had no more pity for Sirima than he had for the hare or the jackal that Phussa had transfixed with his arrows. What was more dreadful was some hint of ecstasy at the woman's suffering.

Sirima stretched, doubled up, stretched, doubled up, beat the floor with her hands, clawed at her throat and chest. Animal sounds escaped her. Foam flecked her mouth, mingling with a dribble of blood.

She gave a cry, stretched fully, vibrated like a bowstring and then relaxed.

I looked at Gamini. 'She is unconscious,' I informed him.

He seemed not to have heard, but sat there as if enjoying some secret delight. I stood up. The movement distracted him. He shook himself like a dog coming out of the water.

'You saved my life,' he said.

I made no reply.

'As I watched you, I knew what your uncle, Prince Vipula, must have been like,' he continued, his eyes glowing. 'He would have been proud of you tonight.'

Through the tragedy of that night and all that lay ahead, trumpets sounded in my spirit.

'Thank you, Prince,' I replied. 'My destiny is to help you fulfil your destiny. Now we must act fast, so listen carefully to me.'

He stood up and placed the sword point on the ground. Feet spread, he had the grace of a dancer. 'All right,' he agreed. 'You command tonight.' I caught the hint of 'but never again' in his voice and smiled to myself.

'We should not allow Sirima to die here,' I asserted. 'Your image must be protected at all costs. Besides, if her body is found in your rooms, Prince Digha Bahu will try to destroy you.'

'But her signed confession?'

'Could count for nothing if it is made public. Then a fight would begin, and the consequences would be evil for the palace, the royal family and Ruhuna. Whose word will your father have to take? No, while we hold the confession as a threat, it will make Prince Digha Bahu pause. If we publish it, we will lose its effectiveness in the struggle to prove and disprove.'

'What do you propose?'

'That we use the confession judiciously to keep your cousin at bay. Please leave the handling of it to me.'

He looked sharply at me. I held the look without the flicker of an eyelid, proud in the knowledge of my honesty. It was hard for him to trust even me, with the evidence of his betrayal lying unconscious at his feet, but he finally nodded. 'I trust you,' he said.

'I shall move Sirima's body back to the ladies' quarters, using the timing she had in mind with the guards. I shall leave it there, making it seem as if she had been raped and killed.'

His eyes widened. 'You mean you would enter her unconscious or dead body? Why, you ghoul . . .'

'I thought you were going to trust me, Prince,' I cut in quietly.

Chapter 28

Sirima's body was discovered the next morning. As I had intended, everyone presumed her to be the victim of rape and murder. How I achieved this shall remain unspoken.

Although I would carry the memory of that accursed night forever, suffice it to say that I did not have to perform the grisly act which Gamini had so hastily surmised.

Sirima was accorded a grand funeral. Her murderer could not, of course, be found. After a week of hectic inquiry, the search died down. Prince Digha Bahu alone looked at Gamini in a strained, suspicious manner. Poor man. He could not speak of what he knew without jeopardizing himself!

Meanwhile, I had locked the *ola* in a small metal box, which I buried in the garden just outside my bedroom for security, until I could take it to the Chief Monk for more permanent safekeeping. Not even Gamini knew the hiding place.

Over two weeks went by before I thought it opportune to meet the Venerable Rahula at the Tissa temple. I did not want to draw attention by making a special visit, so I waited for the next *poya* day, when we regularly attended the temple to observe *sil*.

I did not divulge the contents of the box to the Chief Monk, but impressed on him its importance to the future well-being of our prince. For all his loving kindness, the Venerable Rahula was a patriot. He had pinned his hopes for a Sinhala Lanka on Gamini, I knew, so I did not even have to extract a promise of secrecy from him. I merely told him that if anything untoward happened to Gamini or me, he was to open the box, read the *olas* and use his fullest influence, which was considerable, to see that the guilty were brought to justice. With dark, grave eyes on me, the Chief Monk promised.

Two days later I sent a special messenger to Prince Digha Bahu at Dighavapi requesting a meeting the next time he came to the Ruhuna palace, to discuss a private matter of utmost importance. The prince was so excitable that he did not wait for his normal weekly visit to confer with the King, but came especially to see me the very next day.

We met in my study the same evening. The monsoon had broken and rains blanketed the sky. Everything was covered in a sheet of grey, with lashing raindrops, like cascades of silver beads, in the foreground. The drumming on the roofs and the roar on the open ground seemed endless. Great puddles formed in the garden, joined together by muddy rivulets. The earth gave back the smell of wet soil and grass. Only the leaves looked fresh and green, their thirst quenched. Inside, our corridors were soaked. The floors of my room were damp.

I had been sitting at my desk watching the downpour before Prince Digha Bahu arrived, thinking of peasant houses leaking and dangerous to health, of poor people without a dry place on which to sleep – all of them exposed to sickness. The words came out thus on my *ola*:

> 'Who is the poet found music
>   In the gentle patter of raindrops?
> When raindrops patter gently
>   Only on the rich man's window . . .'

Prince Digha Bahu strode in unannounced, his pudgy face damp with rain, his coat dripping. He flung off the coat and handed it to his attendant. He seized a cloth from the man and wiped his face and hands.

'Wait outside!' he curtly directed. 'I have some business with this . . . er . . . prince. We are not to be disturbed. Close the door behind you.'

The attendant made obeisance and departed. The door slid gently shut.

Prince Digha Bahu stood, feet astride, arms akimbo. I rose and made my salutation. He did not return it. His face was tight, the pale brown eyes like washed river stones.

'I am glad you accepted my invitation to a meeting so promptly,' I said, standing evenly on both feet, arms behind my back, fingers locked. 'And particularly gratified that you are so sure of your welcome that you can enter my quarters without knocking.'

'Spare me the cackle and come to the point!' the Prince directed loudly. 'You sent for me. Why?'

I looked at him in mock amusement, then started pacing the room slowly, glancing at him occasionally. Finally, I turned to face him again. 'I wanted to see whether you would come at my command!' I asserted.

The flush started on his neck and spread to his face. He dropped his arms and took a step forward. 'Why, you impertinent bastard . . .' he began.

'Enough, cousin,' I commanded curtly. 'You are in no position to bluster today. You came because you are worried to death – and you have good cause to be. Now sit down and listen to me.'

I looked at his pig eyes and stared him out. He hesitated, then sat gingerly on the red-cushioned couch, one leg tucked beneath it, the other thrust forward.

'Would you like a little refreshment, cousin?' I inquired.

He shook his head.

'A little coconut water perhaps? Or some pomegranate juice? Or perhaps something from a little phial in my possession?'

'No!' Only a twitch of a cheek betrayed his reaction.

'You mean "No, thank you," do you not, cousin? After all, we should observe these little signs of civilization even in the family circle. We do not want to be accused of being gentlefolk only for show. I regret I cannot offer you anything stronger even in this weather. Unlike you, cousin, I only have ready access to . . . shall we say . . . less potent liquors than in that little phial.'

My face was an iron mask in which he read nothing.

The rain intensified as if to crash through the roof. A gust of wind swept its drumming to a crescendo. The drama of the heavens was an apt background for our play. I was surprised at the cold rage within me, possibly the accumulation of twenty-five years of self-control, divested now because of my loyalty to Gamini.

'Yes, cousin, both Gamini and I know of your attempt,' I continued. 'Your agent, the girl Sirima, gave us a signed confession before she died. We have entrusted it to a safe intermediary.'

Prince Digha Bahu struggled to remain impassive. Smothering a tinge of admiration at his self-control, I proceeded coldly. 'If anything happens to Prince Gamini, or me, you will be exposed immediately, regardless of the source of our misfortune. Remember this through the years. You now have a vested interest in our well-being, cousin, which I am sure you will try to protect in future.'

Our glances locked again for long moments.

Finally, he blinked and looked down.

'I am sure you came to the palace on a special visit with good cause,' I then resumed. 'You will wish to go about your business now.'

He rose slowly to his feet. He shot a venomous glance at me, turned and walked to the door.

'One more thing, cousin,' I called.

He paused, his hand on the dark doorknob. He did not look back.

'I expect civility and good manners from you in the future.'

Chapter 29

I awakened that morning in the Mahagama palace to the 'ko-haaa, ko-haaa' of the koel bird resounding through the trees, with the uncanny feeling that a new life cycle was

287

beginning for Gamini and me. Gone would be the comparative peace of the four years following the death of Sirima. I might have known that intrigue and danger lay immediately ahead, but I could not have anticipated the woman who was to enter the life of the Prince, to become part of him until his death.

I stretched and lay back, watching the first glimmer of dawn on a pale grey sky, breathing in a hint of jasmine from the garden above the slumber smell from my warm bedclothes. Was it really intuition I was experiencing? After all, Gamini was now a young man of seventeen and I, still his tutor, thirty. Gamini was at an age when moves for the succession to the Ruhuna throne could be afoot. It was logical that the deeps of my mind should throw up their warning.

I had drawn very close to the Queen in the intervening years. Under other circumstances, it might almost have been a romantic attachment. The Queen's handmaiden, Leela Wathie, and I had become almost like sister and brother in consequence.

Gamini had been cool toward my friendship with his mother, but made no attempt to interfere. 'It may come in useful someday,' was all the comment he would make.

As I reflected on all this, I realized that my feelings this morning went beyond logic. Intuition, while partly deriving from the blessed gift of inner sight, is also a product of our experiences. Some people, especially those born in the month of Citta, undergo these experiences, analyse them, collate them with other experiences and retain them to emerge under the stimulation of circumstances. When the circumstances seem to bear no relation to those past experiences, or cannot be identified with them, we call it intuition. It is like a mango seed planted by a boy, who then moves on to another village and returns years later to find a full-grown tree bearing delicious fruit to appease his hunger, never remembering that it came from the seed he planted, but feeling some familiarity in its taste.

It was still dark outside my window, so those silly cockerels were greeting the false dawn, when the sun lifts a sleepy head to see whether it is time to awaken, then snuggles again under the dark bedcovers of night. Only that faint glow in the sky promised a clear day. A latent chill in the air warned that it would be a hot one.

My need for the privy was a pain. Having used it, washed, changed from my white sarong to brown pantaloons and combed my hair, I stood by the window and prayed aloud to God until I reached my consciousness of Him. Then I hastened to Gamini's rooms, where I found him impatiently pacing his study. His dark chest was bare. He wore deep green pantaloons with black riding thongs beneath and the inevitable gold bands on his upper arms. His face was beginning to take on the manliness of his seventeen years. The ebony skin was tight-drawn, gleaming in the light. The heaviness to come lay more obviously on his wide jaw, his broad cheekbones and the well-formed nose with its full, flaring nostrils. Although he was still a couple of inches below my own six-foot height, his shoulders had grown wider and more solid, while his waist and hips remained slim. The promise of power he had as a boy had become fulfilled. It was most evident now not only in his natural vitality but through the magnetism that vibrated within him like the first notes of war trumpets.

'Ha! The dormouse!' he exclaimed. His voice was deep, but thin as yet from his youth. 'I was about to visit you with a jug of water in case you were still sleeping.'

'Well, now that I'm here, Prince,' I replied, 'if you want to indulge in such childish pranks, let us stay at home instead of going hunting. You know I detest the sport anyway.'

He threw back his head and laughed. It was characteristic of our closeness that we could laugh at our silliest attempts at humour, whereas we looked down our noses at anything but the best wit in others.

'You will always be the *upasakaya*, the holy one,' he responded. 'I believe you would rather kill a man than an insect.'

'I believe you are right.'

He came up and clapped me on the shoulder. 'Come, let us eat and be away.'

It was still dark when we arrived at the courtyard of the audience hall after breaking our fast, but the heightened breathing of approaching dawn pulsed in the air. The godlike Vasabha towered over a group of men gathered around the horses. The animals stamped the earth, ground at their bits, tossed their manes, bared yellow-white teeth and snorted to clear their nostrils of the damp air.

Gamini was to ride a grey Arab named Raja. Unusual for an Arab, Raja measured fully seventeen hands and was trained to jump. He had been brought across the seas by the Arab traders who came regularly each year to the Devundara fair for barter. Devundara is in the Giri district, northwest of Mahagama. The governor of the district was a cousin of King Kakkavan. He had bought the obviously fine-bred horse for a large amount of gold the previous year and sent it as a present to Gamini, requesting Velu Sumana, the king of Sinhala horsemen, to break the horse and train it to jump. Gamini loved the animal the moment he set eyes on it. The horse, too, responded as if acknowledging his future master.

We waited while Gamini mounted before doing so ourselves. We reined our horses sideways and clip-clopped to the palace gates. Vasabha was tall on Gamini's right and I shorter on his left. Phussa the archer rode behind us with lame Kanja Deva beside him. We were followed by a few noblemen, the attendants and Gamini's personal bodyguard.

When we cleared the gates, we broke into a trot, soon increasing our speed to a fast canter. We could push the horses because others, for the hunt, awaited us at the edge of the forest. We do not risk our best horses in the jungle.

Once in the open countryside, we headed south and west toward the Ranna jungle. The orderly pounding of hooves in the first still greyness of dawn was rousing as drumbeats in my ears, the cool air on my face invigorating as scent slapped on a new-shorn face. There is no more pleasant communion than that of men riding in unison, lost in their own thoughts.

Soon the sky to the east began to lighten, slowly turning to rose and fiery red. The crowing of cocks and the cawing of crows sharply pierced the clatter of horses and the creak of leather. As the outlines of the countryside began to take shape, ghostly forms became trees. An occasional mud-and-wattle hut was revealed, with dark-thatched roof and windows pricked by red-gold flames of firelight. Moist green grass on which cattle still lay, grey shrubs, hedgerows, copses and the lighter spread of paddy fields were unbared from the shroud of night.

This is one of the loveliest times of day, when the first heartbeats of awakening life begin to pulse. People in our villages, however, miss it, because they believe that they should not expose themselves to damp humours. Only after the earth is assured of daylight and they can be clothed by the warmth of the sun on their bodies will such folk come out, so not a soul was in sight.

Gamini and I soon outdistanced the others, riding side by side until we came to the first *ambalam*, where the horses were to be given a breather. We were sweating with our exertion.

We dismounted to cool off and water our horses at a small, clear stream that gurgled and rippled over black rocks and red-and-white river stones. We tethered the horses and began pacing the sandy bank of the stream.

'Is it because hunting reminds you of your uncle and his lodge that you do not like it?' Gamini shot the question at me suddenly, his voice somehow jarring at that peaceful moment.

His words found their mark. I had indeed been thinking of

Prince Vipula and the lodge. 'Partly,' I replied.

'What else?'

'You know what else already, Prince. Compassion for hunted animals. Compassion for their poor, beating hearts and laboured lungs. Compassion for their pain and the dreadful knowledge of death.'

'You would kill all my fun if I let you.'

'You asked the question.'

We walked through shadows, silent awhile.

'Have you succeeded in making me like your uncle?' Gamini finally demanded.

I knew then that his silence had been used to digest my words. Now he was really asking me whether his lack of compassion made him any less a prince in my eyes. It was at once an attempt to placate me and a demand for reassurance, for if my answer was 'No', I would admit to my own failure.

I kept my face to the gurgling water. 'I never had to try!' I responded mildly.

'You are cunning as a jackal.'

'No! Cunning as your question.'

'Why do you not look at me when you speak? Why are you so shifty-eyed?'

I knew he was not angry, but merely taking pleasure in goading me. 'I was born cross-eyed,' I replied and now looked at him, deliberately crossing my eyes.

His hearty laugh echoed through the still air. A small flock of birds darted from the trees with angry cries and a flutter of wings. The illusion of a light breeze from their flight stirred up a dank odour of rotting vegetation.

'You have indeed become like my uncle, except in your lack of compassion and your ruthlessness.' I suddenly cut across his laughter to shock him.

'Your uncle hunted often,' he protested, sober now.

'Yes, but there remained an inner compassion in him. He knew to separate what he had to do for his training from the

292

essential elements of him. Your ruthlessness springs from your very *prana.*'

'That is my destiny,' he began hotly, then became thoughtful. 'Your uncle had to be his way to fulfil his destiny,' he finally stated. 'I have to be my way to fulfil mine.' Was there a hint of sadness in his voice? 'Make no mistake. I do not put any of it on, nor do I have to train myself to cruelty, bloodlust and ruthlessness. These things spring from my very being, as you say. I can be no different. Indeed, I often have the feeling that I am being pushed, directed, guided from within by a force that propels me to my destiny.'

'You are the product of God's being and therefore of His will. We are all a part of God. He is life, He is death, but I cannot see wanton killing, such as only man practises, as being a part of God's will.'

Gamini stopped to look earnestly at me. 'Killing is necessary for my existence, for the fulfilment of my goals,' he stated quietly. 'When I have achieved those goals, I shall set aside violence and practise *maitriya* and *ahimsa.*'

'What if it is too late?' I cried. 'What if by then you have developed such callouses around your immortal *prana* that the tender skin of compassion no longer exists?'

'Then I shall balance my *akusala kharma* by doing good works.'

'Balance, Prince, or barter? You cannot alter the effect of evil feelings on your *prana* by doing good works. You cannot bribe the eternal life-force in that manner. Your final thought-moment, which must project you to a better existence upon death, will be conditioned by your nature, which will be what you make of it.'

'Lord Buddha went through it all, but he attained Buddhahood in this life.'

I was aghast. This prince whom I so dearly loved was not only convinced of his destiny as the saviour of Lanka, but even aspired to Buddhahood in this life. The cold hand of

293

dread clutched my stomach. He noticed my reaction and gazed defiantly at me. 'You must show your God to me some time,' he said. He glanced past me and nodded in the direction of galloping hooves. 'But later. The others are coming up – we must rejoin them.'

My destiny was his destiny, even beyond this life. I could only hope that God's nature envelops His every purpose.

We rode on through parklands and reached the dark fringe of the jungle, where men awaited us with fresh horses. The sun shone brightly now from a blue sky, gleaming alike on green leaves, the oiled black hair of the trackers and the bare, sweating bodies of grooms and beaters. The horses that awaited us were small and stocky, a tougher Sinhala crossbreed, better suited for hunting in the jungle.

Before we could remount, Kira, the chief beater, came running up to us. He was a lean, gaunt man with white hair and wrinkled brown skin, yet his step was light and springy as any youth's. He made obeisance to Gamini and rose to announce smugly, 'My men have roused a splendid boar for you, lord. He's a big fellow, fierce-tusked, ugly and mean. An opponent worthy of a prince.' His betel-stained teeth briefly showed in a smile.

Gamini's face lit up. 'Ah!' he exclaimed, raising clenched fists. 'Where is he? Where?'

I could understand Gamini's excitement. This was to be his first test. To be the boar-hunter supreme, he had to execute a kill alone and in the classical manner.

'Over yonder, lord.' Kira jerked his lined face and pointed a gnarled finger in the direction of the jungle some distance away. 'My men have encircled the creature and will drive it to a little glade where we will be waiting. But I warn you – be careful, Prince. This is a king of boars, the most powerful these old eyes have ever beheld.'

Gamini only smiled. 'Wonderful!' he exclaimed. 'The *devas* have sent him. Lead the way.'

We slung our bows and hefted quivers of arrows onto our

shoulders. We donned sword belts, easing the swords to make sure they would draw smoothly. As I stuck a long knife in my waist, I noticed that Gamini only carried a knife in his black belt. He tried several spears, finally selecting the one with the best balance, then hastened to catch up with the chief beater, who was already threading his way through the bushes. Gamini was so completely lost in his mission that he forgot the rest of us, but I followed close behind, with Vasabha and the others beside me. We walked about one hundred cubits before Kira turned into the jungle. Gamini swivelled around and placed a finger to his lips. 'I am going in alone,' he whispered. 'The rest of you stay here.' He was a different person, vibrating within the shell of his purpose, determined to have all the glory.

'I must come with you, Prince,' I insisted quietly. 'You need an independent witness to record the event and speak of the manner in which you executed the thrust.'

His eyes glittered angrily until he understood my seeming purposes. 'All right then, but only you.' He turned on his heel and moved light-footed behind the beater.

I followed Gamini. The jungle closed upon us like a mantle. We were soon in the cavern of a pathway made by elephants into which light barely filtered from above. Dark, thick-leaved branches pressed down on us. Low lantana shrubs scraped our legs. The air became dank and fetid, the rank smell of animal droppings and the silence overpowering.

I suddenly knew fear for Gamini. The wild boar is one of the most fierce and unpredictable of jungle creatures. It has a mean disposition, the ability to stand stock-still and observe, before charging in a trice with the speed of an arrow. It takes its opponent from beneath with compact power, to toss, to tear with its tusks and then to ravage. My vivid imagination conjured a vision of Gamini's young body, barely visible now in the gloom, lying still on the ground, the dark, silken skin torn and bloody before the onslaught of the beast. As I pushed behind Gamini, sweating with the heat, I tried desperately to conquer my fear.

After what seemed like an hour, but was in reality only about twenty minutes, a hint of light shone ahead of us. We made for it and soon stood in pale sunshine at the edge of the glade. It was good to be away from the gloom.

'Stand here, Prince,' Kira quietly bade Gamini. 'The beast was feeding when I left it. On my signal, my men will drive from that direction.' He pointed across the glade.

I stepped beside them and looked apprehensively around the glade. It was so small, just a square patch of clearing with sunlight lying on clumps of matted grass. Tall trees and heavy undergrowth hemmed it in on all sides. The boar could be on Gamini almost without warning. To heighten my fears, the stench of excrement still clung to the intense quietude, like a death smell.

Gamini gave no sign of noticing the poor conditions. He tested his spear for balance and swung it back and forth to bring life to his muscles. Finally, he nodded to the chief beater.

Kira's call broke the stillness more sharply than the cry of a parakeet.

We waited. Gamini was alert but not tense, a slim dark figure blending into light and shadow at the trees' edge. I drew an arrow from my quiver, fitted it to the bowstring and watched across that patch of sunlight, intent on the dark fringe of jungle from which the boar would emerge. I had to be ready to meet any emergency if Gamini failed. The chief beater, knife in hand, clad only in a loincloth, was a timeworn brown statue beside me.

Minutes passed in total silence.

The white-gold air began to blur and shimmer before my eyes with the strain of my concentration. The dry reek of the jungle and a sharp smell of stale animal fur began to smother me. Had I been the hunter I would not have been this tense. My eyes began to burn. I closed and relaxed the lids, allowing my eyeballs blessed darkness for a few moments. I steadied my breathing and unlocked my muscles. My concern for Gamini made me quickly resume my watch.

We waited. The minutes stole by to the beating of my heart. Nothing happened. Gamini had not moved, even to adjust his pose. He stood there, carved in wood, spear poised, as was his gift. I could not help but remember the first time I saw this in him, after the milk-rice incident, when he had lain in bed in the same position at least two hours. I must not let my thoughts wander, I warned myself. My concentration must be as total as that of the hunter.

The first 'Hoo-oo-oo' of beaters reached us. I became alert. Kira's jagged teeth showed in a crooked smile. He nodded slightly. Gamini alone remained still.

I heard the first faint crackle of undergrowth across the glade. It came and went so soon it was almost a non-sound; only the trained hunter could have picked it up.

'Hoo-oo-oo . . .' The cries of the beaters reached us again, closer this time. Birds screeched their alarm. They would be wheeling above the green treetops. The sounds merged into the crackle of undergrowth drawing closer to us, like a slow-moving fire along a line of dry grass. Gamini stepped forward, his sweat-strewn body gleaming. He needed to stand well in the open, to attract the boar's attention and invite its attack. He wiped his face on his upper arm in a swift motion.

The cries of the beaters were constant now, intermingled with their banging on metal plates. The sharp crackling broke through the din. The boar burst into the open. My breath caught. It was the largest I had ever seen, fully three feet to the hump, with big, curving tusks and coarse, prickly grey-brown hair. It paused, snout outthrust, its hot, mean eyes blinking at the sunlight. Angry, frustrated, fearful, this was a boar at its most dangerous. Fear-thrills ran through my body.

'Come!' Gamini quietly invited the beast. Feet slightly

297

apart, evenly balanced, he leaned back for the cast.

The mean eyes flickered to Gamini's lithe figure. Hatred flamed in them. Head down, the boar shot forward across the intervening space like a missile from a catapult.

Gamini waited. He is keeping it too long, I thought feverishly. My mouth ran dry. My breath caught. My heart stopped beating.

The boar was almost on Gamini before he sidestepped. The spear slashed down like a fork of lightning, right on the mark – just behind the ear. The boar screamed. In a flash, Gamini gripped the weapon with both hands. He used the beast's momentum to vault over it, pushing down on the spear as he swept through the air. He swung in flight to land on his feet, facing the boar's rear, still gripping the spear.

Stopped in its charge, screaming and squealing, the boar turned fiercely on Gamini. My hand tightened on the bow and I drew back the string, aiming for the other ear. The boar lunged with its snout, but Gamini had its head transfixed. He started pushing down with all his strength, dark muscles knotted like rope. The spear sank deeper, crunching on bone. Blood and slime gouted from the boar's mouth, excrement from its rear. It writhed powerless, its flanks heaving, screaming its message of hate. It made a last, frantic effort to get at its tormentor, but in vain. The spear had severed its power.

Screeching impotently, the boar slowly collapsed on its side. The spear tore a jagged, bleeding hole down its head. Grey and white matter spewed out. A convulsive heave of hairy sides spilled more blood, vomit and excrement, filthy in the sunlight. The squealing subsided. With a pathetic groan, the boar died. The body continued to tremble and shudder, anguish leaving its seal.

Gamini stood panting lightly, a young *deva* gleaming in the sunlight. He was exhilarated, his dark eyes ecstatic. He was still revelling in the danger and the boar's agony. It was almost physical with him. I remembered the wrestling match years ago and heard the crack of a breaking bone. Fear for Gamini churned inside me, turning my guts so weak that I could have let go like the boar.

'A perfect stroke, lord!' The chief beater stepped forward. His voice was filled with admiration, almost with awe. His brown hand simulated the spear stroke. 'I've never seen it better done – and to a king of boars.'

Gamini came out of his trance. He smiled at the chief beater. Then his eyes sought mine, questioning. He sensed my reaction and the sparkle left them. 'And you, Prince Rodana, what do you think?' His deep voice had a dangerous edge to it.

'You are the coolest, most perfect fighting machine in the kingdom,' I acknowledged, trying to convey to him that my admiration of him was unbounded in spite of my fears, 'but you will surely appreciate and forgive my concern.'

Kira, who was inspecting the dead boar, looked at me quizzically.

Gamini stood undecided for a few moments, then expressed his understanding with a nod. He turned toward the carcass. 'Have it cleaned and bestow it as my gift to the beaters and your village,' he directed Kira.

The murdered prince of pigs – a gift to the people. I shuddered and closed my eyes. In the darkness, I lived the poor creature's terror, hatred and despair. I heard its death screams and was smitten by the vile reek of its discharges.

The shouts of the beaters had turned to an occasional echoing 'Hoo-oo-ooo' in the trees. We could hear them breaking through the jungle now. Soon they would converge on the glade, chattering excitedly and pointing when they saw the boar.

When I opened my eyes again, Kira and Gamini had laid down their weapons and were examining the carcass. Flies were already humming over the dead body, to join the ticks and lice that had fed on it when it was alive. Blood and slime splattered the ground. The reek hung on the air like a cloud.

I stretched, but dared not breathe too deeply, lest I become sick. I had replaced my arrow in its quiver and set down my bow, awaiting the arrival of the beaters.

It was movement rather than an object that I spotted in the shadows across the glade. I jerked to attention. 'Leopard!' I shouted, bending to take up my bow.

Before I could grip it, Gamini came alive. He wheeled on the instant, drawing his long knife. It glittered in his hand as the leopard, sinuous and swift, broke into the open, pausing to blink at the sunlight. Bow in hand now, I reached back for an arrow and fitted it to the string. The leopard saw Gamini. Twin points of light flashed from its eyes. It bounded forward, then sprang in the same motion – a great, silent, tawny streak. I aimed for the neck. Too late.

Gamini leaped to meet the great cat, his motion just as sinuous. At the height of the leopard's spring, he suddenly crouched low. The leopard sailed over him, realized it was going to miss its quarry and struck downward with raking forepaws. Gamini thrust fiercely upward with his knife. The sharp metal tore into the leopard's soft belly. Blood streaked out from twin doors of fur. The leopard faltered. It doubled in agony, then landed flat on its chest.

His knife dripping blood, Gamini turned swiftly. Bloodlust glittered in his eyes. His mouth was half open, his teeth bared in a snarl. He was no longer a prince, but a primitive man in the jungle – a killer. I thought of our ancestor, Sinha Bahu, the lion of Magadha. I stayed my hand on the bow. This, too, had to be Gamini's kill.

He sprang on the back of the roaring, thrashing leopard, rendered helpless by that first knife wound. He plunged his knife into its neck, again and again. Each thrust flashed in the sunlight and ended with a soggy thud. He was an animal let loose and I watched in horror at his primitive instincts.

The struggles of the great beast grew weaker. Its roars changed to growls, then groans. It died with a great, rattling sigh.

Kira's cry diverted my attention. Instinctively I looked across the glade. Another feline shape lurked in the shadows, its eyes like points of fire directed at Gamini. My heart contracted, my stomach clenched with fear. My hands, still clutching the bow and arrow, felt nerveless.

Gamini had his back to the animal. It would pounce before he could turn.

Fear for Gamini restored me. I sprang forward silently, the bow strong again in my grasp. My brain was cool and fluid, sparkling as spring water. I awaited the start of the leopard's leap, timing my arrow for the moment its throat would be exposed. Shoulder to target, I resolutely drew back the bowstring. Its twang was sweet music in my ears.

I dropped the bow just as the arrow left for its mark. There was no time for another shot. None was needed, for I got the leopard right on my target, making it spin sideways. Its roar was strangled as it flipped, trying to dislodge the arrow with great jerks of its neck. It fell awkwardly to the ground.

I had drawn my knife without realizing it. A red mist swam before my eyes. An animal sound escaping me, I bounded forward and tore into the leopard, regardless of its raking paws. Teeth bared, growls emerging from my throat, I plunged my knife into the writhing body again and again. The smell of its fur drove me even wilder. My knife arm continued thrusting, regardless of ribs and bone. Only when the leopard lay still in death did I stop, half-lying on the corpse.

I rose to my feet, panting and gasping, foam on my mouth, blood on my arms and chest from the leopard and the gashes it had inflicted on me.

A dim consciousness of pain from my wounds brought me back to reality. I was suddenly myself again, looking down at a leopard's body, sleek even in death, beautiful in spite of gouting blood, spilled entrails and great red gashes in the matted fur. The enormity of what had happened to me slowly began seeping into me. A desire to protect Gamini had spurred me to action, but once my arrow found its mark, primitive man, the jungle animal, had seized and overpowered me.

Reaching for breath in that sunlit glade, the murmurs of the beaters in my ears, I realized that even I, the prince born and bred, the *bhikku* by training, was no superior being, but a mortal.

Gamini's voice gave me sight again. He was standing before me, bloodstained, dark eyes moist. 'You saved my life,' he said simply. 'We are now two of a kind.'

There in public, he reached for me and held me. At that moment, his blood and my blood, joined by the blood of leopards, mingled.

Chapter 30

On the night following this bloody incident, Gamini and I stood side by side in the Tissa temple, along with thousands of devotees. The Wesak festival fell on the next day and we were preparing for it by taking Ata-sil, the Eight Precepts. The reverent atmosphere around me began seeping into my spirit, calming it.

On the other side of me was a short man with hunched shoulders. Above prominent eyes, his forehead sloped sharply to a bald head. Beneath a beaked nose, his wide mouth receded, almost without a chin, to his neck. In that fitful light, his dark skin seemed green, completing his resemblance to a frog. He was immersed in his devotions. He must find solace in his devotions, I thought, until I noticed the maniacal fervour in his eyes. It jolted me from the peace I was finding.

Before I could recover, a series of sharp shrieks and wails suddenly broke above the murmured chants of the throng. A young girl who could not have been more than seventeen bounded from the crowd. She wore an untidy blue skirt and a loose white bodice. Her long black hair hung, dishevelled, over a contorted brown face. Her teeth were bared with her screaming; her eyes blazed their frenzy. She darted here and there, screeching like a parrot to her gods, chased by her shadow and the flapping skirt. Two plump matrons with anxious faces ran after her, trying vainly to grab her. The crowds politely ignored the poor souls. The demented girl would soon face a devil-dance, to exorcize the evil spirit in her, brought out by the full moon and religious exaltation.

As always, however, the combined fervour of so many people, tangibly vibrating in the air, crept into my being again. The sweet, heady scent of jasmine and temple flowers wafted into the senses while the clanking bell drove into the body and the moon brought madness. The sum total of it all was religious ecstasy. I realized with a shock that God received it all, regardless.

As the eyes of my mind widened to accept this great truth, I knew at last that one need not identify with God to make one's offerings to Him, any more than a blind man has to see a king, or a deaf man to hear him, or a child to know what a king is, in order to acknowledge, make offerings, seek favours. So even those who do not know God and those who will not acknowledge Him give Him the message of their identity with Him by their acts of devotion. If they never perform conscious acts of devotion, they are no less a part of Him, as a leaf is a part of a tree without ever having deliberate consciousness of it, for our every hidden desire reaches God.

As I prepared to move to the *bana* hall, my eyes sought Gamini again – the slim, white-clad figure beside me. His brother, Tissa, was next to him. The King and the Queen had been in the *bana* hall the entire day. All of us princes were merely a part of the crowd of worshippers, with nothing to distinguish us from anyone else.

In all that crowd, I saw her. She was young and tall, her shapely figure in white skirt and bodice. She was wondrously fair. Her pale, pink-gold complexion, the colour venerated by Sinhala poets and bards, glowed even in the fitful light. Dark masses of curly hair framed a delicate face of exquisite proportions. Her soft cheekbones gleamed beneath the large, almond-shaped eyes, dark and mysterious, that were answering my gaze.

The blood pounded in my head. As my eyes remained locked with hers, I forgot where I was. The magnetism of our glances made the air between us shimmer.

A hiss of indrawn breath broke the magic. I glanced sharply toward it. Gamini was staring, spellbound, in the same direction I had been looking. I followed his gaze and a great emptiness seized me. I had been mistaken in thinking that the maiden had been looking at me. She had really been looking past me, at Gamini, who had drawn her attention.

A strange sense of loss, such as I had not known since the night my uncle died, filled my whole being. Why? Why had my ears begun to pound? From my heartbeats? What did this mean? Why should I care for any woman, I who had taken the vow of *brachmachariya*, I who had sworn to dedicate my whole life to Gamini? Why should I know such dismay at the obvious communion between him and this maiden? Was I jealous of him again? With a thud I realized that my jealousy was of her and not him. I did not want this maiden to care more for Gamini than for me.

In a state of shock, I looked deeply at Gamini. There was no lust in his eyes. He seemed taken aback, as if he had suddenly discovered someone he had never seen, but knew he had to meet, someone who cut through his devotions and brought him back from the life of the spirit to that of this existence. The expression on his face was the same one he had worn many years ago, when he spoke of finding true love with a woman.

I looked at the maiden again, my being filled with confusion. Her eyes were wide, still held by Gamini's as in a vice, but not desiring release. She was for him, not for me. My senses and my inner sight told me they had known each other in previous births. What then of my own response to her? Had I, too, known her before? What had I been to her at that time? Somewhere inside me, a seed of knowledge revealed itself and I was caught in the grip of the sorrowful resignation that had once borne it in another lifetime.

God stepped in to show me my lot in this life.

A voice beside me whispered, 'Will you help me?'

Preoccupied with my thoughts, the grieving shadow of a past existence, I barely heard the words.

'I said, will you help me?' The voice was more insistent. The touch of a hand on my arm cut through my feelings. I looked in its direction, but still could see nothing. It was a sad moment for me.

'Did you hear me?' Gamini's grip was like an iron band, suddenly transporting me back to that evening by the hunting lodge when my uncle had gripped my arms to steady my babbling story of Mahela's death. The result was the same. I steadied myself, this time with a sigh.

My eyes had been tightly shut. No wonder I had not seen Gamini. I opened them to find his eager gaze on me. 'What's wrong with you?' He shook my arm for emphasis.

No more than a few seconds had passed, but it had all seemed endless and I was dripping with sweat. Gamini had been so engrossed in the maiden, he had not even noticed.

I shook my head. 'Nothing. I know what you need. I will certainly help you.'

He was stunned. 'But . . . ' he began.

'You wonder how I know?' I demanded quietly. 'Remember, I am an extension of you. My life's purpose is to serve you.' He would never know how much. 'I shall discover who the maiden is.' As I said the words, I felt a sense of release. Do your duty regardless and you are free.

'Remarkable!' Gamini exclaimed quietly. The corners of

305

his eyes softened. I knew what it meant and nodded my acknowledgement of his feelings, though the remnants of a sick ache and some rebellion remained in my heart.

I was about to begin threading through the crowd towards the maiden's group when I heard Prince Tissa observe softly, 'My brother is venerating more than the Doctrine tonight.' His beautiful features were distorted by a mocking smile, the black eyes gleaming maliciously.

Gamini went taut with anger.

I laid a gentle hand on his shoulder. 'Now, Prince, you can afford to ignore the remarks of one who worships other people's business,' I said.

Gamini relaxed into a derisive half-smile while Tissa glared at me. Gamini said something quietly to Tissa and watched him turn red.

Three days later, Leela Wathie, the Queen's handmaiden, now a radiant young woman of eighteen, was attending her mistress in the bedchamber when Prince Tissa was announced. The young prince was fifteen – a tall, slender boy, with his mother's fair complexion, sparkling dark eyes and curly black hair. He had grown more manly looking after the first dark down had begun to appear on his upper lip. He had the right of access to the Queen's quarters at any time, but he always exercised this privilege with consideration, invariably calling, as now, just before the noon watch, when the Queen had finished dressing after her bath and had time to spare before proceeding to the dining hall for the noon meal.

Today, the Queen could relax more than she had done during the time of the Wesak observances, culminating the morning before in the annual great *dana* to one thousand *bhikkus*. Prince Tissa awaited her in the anteroom. He made obeisance as she entered and gave Leela a friendly smile.

The Queen sat on her favourite couch and, as usual, patted the pale green cushion beside her for Prince Tissa to sit on. Prince Tissa knelt before his mother, clasping her knees and placing his head briefly on her lap. In years gone by, he would have remained thus, but since he had grown up he only went through the motions, acting out the sentimental ritual of old. He was soon up and seated beside his mother. Leela remained standing by the doorway, her attention directed momentarily to the alabaster Buddha statue on its slender stand, which she frequently stared at in fascination.

'Well, *putha*, what is your news today?' the Queen inquired.

'I have a little piece of gossip for you, madam.'

'Good, good.' The Queen leaned forward expectantly, her eyes twinkling. 'Gossip is always entertaining, since we never take it seriously.'

'Ah, but you may have to take serious note of *this* bit of news.'

'Really? Why?'

'Because it concerns *aiya*.'

Some of the smile left the Queen's face. 'What has our firstborn been up to?'

'You know I hate your calling him that, lady *Amma*.'

'How sweet. But you are the *bada pissa*, the youngest, our special favourite, are you not? You have no cause for jealousy.'

The Queen and her younger son often had had this exchange, from as far back as Leela could remember. How divine love is, she thought. It can even give sparkle to the dull monotony of repetition. She remembered her father and for the thousandth time missed love's warmth and interchange with him. As always, she shrugged off the pain. Since taking up her duties in the palace, she had only seen her father for two weeks each year, when she was permitted to visit her home. Because she and her father loved each other, it was enough.

'Now give us your piece of gossip.' The Queen's golden voice brought Leela back to the room. 'It had better be good.'

'I think *aiya* has found a girl.'

307

'What do you mean, "found a girl"?' The Queen playfully tapped Prince Tissa on the knee with her closed peacock-feather fan. 'Princes do not just *find* girls in their *petta-gama*.'

'*Aiya* saw this girl in the temple on Wesak night.'

The Queen frowned. 'You mean during our observance of Ata-sil?'

'Just before. She was standing with the crowd in front of the *dagoba*. Quite a pretty little thing, but not really attractive to me.'

'Why not?'

'Because my mother, the Queen, is so beautiful that every other lady looks like a frog to me.'

'Flatterer.' The Queen beamed with pleasure, but soon became thoughtful. 'Are you saying that Prince Gamini displayed interest in an unknown young girl in the temple, when one of the Ata-sil is avoiding such thoughts during its observance?'

'Yes, madam. He kept looking at her and finally sent his tutor to find out who she is.'

'Prince Rodana?' The Queen was immediately up in arms. 'He would not act in any common, ignoble way.'

Prince Tissa squirmed uncomfortably on the cushion. Leela realized that he did so as much because he was jealous of me, her friend, as he was on the defensive about his attempt to speak ill of me.

'Of course not,' Prince Tissa said soothingly. 'It was not Prince Rodana's fault at all. You know how *aiya* is with girls and that is all right. But he should at least restrain himself in the temple, should he not?'

Leela was taken aback. Far from being promiscuous, Prince Gamini avoided girls, though he could, by custom, have taken his pick of concubines.

'Hmm. Then you think this could be something serious?'

'How can one tell with *aiya*?'

308

'True.' The Queen sighed. 'We fear for his *kharma*.'

'The so-called future King of Ruhuna should certainly set a better example.'

Prince Tissa's words obviously stung the Queen. They had to be a reminder of her repeatedly unsuccessful attempts to have the King play down Prince Gamini's right of succession. She opened her fan and began moving it rapidly. 'Well, if you know nothing more, there is nothing we can do,' she commented.

Mother and son carried on a few more minutes of desultory conversation. The Queen remained thoughtful. Finally, Prince Tissa kissed the Queen, made obeisance and left.

The door had barely closed on him when the Queen stood up resolutely. She walked up to Leela and paused, slender, graceful and tall, beside her handmaiden. Leela knew a moment's embarrassment as the Queen surveyed her dispassionately from head to foot. She could have been examining a prize goat. 'You are beautiful!' the Queen finally concluded. 'Shiny black hair, flawless olive skin, magnetic brown eyes flecked with green, a most unusual colouring. You are slim and long-bodied. You have a sparkling personality and enormous charm. The promise of your girlhood has been fulfilled. Now we want to remind you of another promise, one you made to us over four years ago.'

Leela remembered immediately and knew a sudden qualm. She feigned ignorance, however. 'What promise, my lady?' she inquired. 'You know that I would do anything for you.'

The Queen's expression softened. 'Yes, indeed, we know.' She paused. 'You promised that if we so desired, you would cast a spell on someone.'

'Oh yes, I do remember, my lady. And indeed I will.'

'Cast a spell?'

'Yes. If you ask me to.' Leela had no doubt about her ability.

'Just a spell now, using your charm. There must be no involvement.'

The condition told Leela whom she had to influence.

Just before sunset the same evening, I was seated alone in my study, trying to catch the last of the daylight for writing on my *olas*, when a knock sounded on the door of my ante-room.

One can always place knocking on a door. There is the respectful knock of servants, the authoritative rapping of those in power, the gentle tap of ladies and the discreet fingernail ticking of lovers. Instead of calling out 'Enter', I rose to my feet instinctively, because I knew a lady stood outside.

I was surprised to find Leela, dressed in a creamy bodice and dark blue skirt. Her hair, shining with oil, was carefully arranged to frame her forehead and fall in waves around her shapely shoulders. Her eyes were luminous, with black *kohl* on the lids. She had added a touch of colour to her cheeks and the scent of her had to be distilled from queen-of-the-night.

She was exuding something else besides the fragrance of flowers this evening, however. It was as if some part of her, hitherto hidden or held back from our sister-and-brother relationship, was being offered to me. I sensed the difference immediately and wondered about it. Perhaps she was in some deep trouble?

'May I come in?' she inquired before I could speak.

'Certainly!' I stood aside to permit her entrance. I thought of leaving the door open in the interests of propriety, then decided to close it for the same reason. Only the King and Gamini had the right to enter my quarters unannounced. The King would never come and Gamini was in the stadium, coaching some of the younger princes in horseback riding.

Leela walked into my study and stood looking out of the window. Although I liked her enormously, I was somewhat embarrassed by her presence. The last woman to have entered my quarters had been Sirima, whom I had dragged inside.

'I see you have some beautiful mangoes on your trees,' Leela remarked, nodding across the green lawn. 'What kind of mango is that?' She half turned, pointing a slender finger toward one of the trees.

I walked to stand beside her. My gaze followed her pointing finger. 'That is a *girar* mango. The fruit is sweet and has a distinctive flavour. Have you not eaten them?'

'No. The Queen likes only the northern mango.'

'Ah! That is delicious, the very best,' I responded, wondering how this banal conversation justified the Queen's handmaiden being in the quarters of a bachelor prince.

'You have elegant quarters.' Leela sighed. 'And your garden is lovely.'

Indeed it was, with the lengthening shadows of evening casting peace over the green lawn and flowering shrubs. The waters of the fountain splashed silver in the golden air. Three red-breasted *bul-buls* twittered at each other on the branches of a pomegranate tree as they thrust their beaks into a ripe fruit for its honey.

Suddenly the scent of Leela's queen-of-the-night intruded on the peace.

She half turned again to face me, her eyes deep and lustrous. With a blast like the crashing of a giant wave, I knew that her presence in my room, the proximity of a beautiful young woman in that seclusion, had touched the male in me. For moments I stared at her, my thoughts splashing wildly. How could this be? I was the well-controlled *brachmachariya*!

I steadied myself, taking more detached note of Leela now. My conflicting thoughts must have been reflected in a blank gaze that discomfited her. She turned back toward the window. Whatever her reason for being in my room, I felt sorry for her. Under the circumstances, that was not a helpful reaction, for it made me respond to her as a person. As she stared out of the window, I felt a sudden urge to reach out and touch her hair, turn her around and hold her to me.

Why? What did all this mean?

I had warm feelings for the Queen, which went beyond her humanity to her womanhood. I had fallen in love at first sight with the maiden in the temple. Now this, with Leela. Was I no more, then, than the average man, except that I had taken a vow? It could not be. I had never experienced anything of womanhood. Not a mother's love, nor the devotion of a nursery governess, nor any response from a female. My experience of male love had been so brief with my uncle, Prince Vipula, and during the last four years, in a wonderful way, with Gamini. I could not be a normal man. Strangely, for I should have known it earlier, my doubts suddenly receded and in a great moment of calm I realized that there had always been an unidentified, repressed hunger within me for female contact – physical, mental, spiritual.

I was stunned. I thought that life had given me the compensation of immunity because of my deprivation. Now it appeared that I was instead the victim of its insidious affliction, like a man who has been starved for years and learned to live with it, responding to the first smells of exotic cooking.

'The evenings were always the most beautiful time in our home,' Leela said softly. The tiny husk to her voice that I had always found adorable seemed more pronounced. She nodded toward the pomegranate bush where only two of the *bul-buls* remained, their physical hunger satisfied, touching beaks, bowing, caressing to fulfil some other, deeper need. 'Love emerged then to cast its spell on our family.'

My heart went out to her in compassion. At that very moment, she turned. The slanting rays of the sun caught her eyes. They were brimming with tears. She looked so helpless – more beautiful, more a person than I had ever known before.

Her thin, fine nostrils stirred and distended. I reached for her blindly and she came into my arms. I held her close, the fragrance of her youthful body mingling with that queen-of-the-night to sweep through my senses. She was soft and yet pliant, sad and lonely. I kissed her hair gently. With a soft moan, she turned her face up to me. I looked into her eyes and felt myself melting into them. Whatever she had come for, at that instant she loved me and I loved her.

I slowly bent my head to touch her lucent cheek with my lips. In the instant, I felt the warm thrill of her abdomen against me. I paused. Every pore of my skin clamoured for contact with hers. I began to get an erection. She stirred against it and my breath came in gasps.

Some instinct made me turn my head to the sky. It must have been my secret prayer, for suddenly God was there. I remembered that night seventeen years ago, when I had decided that I would do whatever Prince Vipula bade me. I saw his chiselled face, his magnetic eyes in the evening air. 'First honour!' He died for an oath. He died for me. I knew the truth in my heart instantly, even while my flesh clamoured for some argument, any argument, to permit me to plunge into my daze of desire and to fulfil all that for which Leela and I so madly craved. My oath had to be absolute.

How desperately hard. I looked down at Leela. She had sensed my hesitation. Her eyes were on mine, pleading, all her defences cast aside. Her breath was coming short and quick, fragrant from the *valmi* root. Her body was pulsing with desire. Blind longing began sweeping me into that daze again.

'First honour!' The words were a trumpet blast, thundering through my mind, my entire being. I do not know from where they came. Perhaps from one of God's *devas*. Perhaps they were the words on my uncle's lips before he died, sweeping down to me through the years.

I came to with a start, bathed in sweat. My resolve

313

returned. My brain became clear again. My strength flowed as swiftly as it had ebbed. My erection eased.

I gripped Leela by the arms and moved her away from me. She looked at me piteously.

'My life's work is to serve Prince Gamini. I cannot allow anything to turn me away.'

'But we love each other,' she whispered, her head slightly jerking in emphasis.

'Love cannot be a reason for lying together.'

She looked puzzled for a few moments. Then she began sobbing involuntarily and I remembered the anguish that made me sob exactly thus in the mansion at Anu, so long ago.

Suddenly her tears began to flow. My heart became raw with pain for her. I held her to me.

'I c-came . . . for another . . . p-purpose.' Her voice was muffled against my shoulder.

'I know.'

'B-But . . . the rest was . . . because I suddenly realized from . . . being here . . . from knowing you . . . from the . . . feel of the garden, the feel of home, that I love you.'

I laid my cheek against her hair. We stood thus many minutes until she finally stopped weeping. She then drew away from me, smiled wryly and started wiping away the tears with the back of her hands. I went into my bedroom and brought her a cloth. She used it on her face and tidied her hair before my looking glass.

She came up to me. She reached up and kissed my cheek.

'We are family now,' I responded warmly.

She nodded and left as she had come.

I stood by the window. As I looked at the sky, thanking God for my deliverance, I breathed the lingering fragrance of queen-of-the-night and heard the echo of Leela's quiet sobs.

Chapter 31

Whether Gamini's destiny was written at his conception or his character was shaped by his birth and many circumstances, the drama of his mission really began two nights later in the audience chamber of King Kakkavan in the Ruhuna palace. The King, undoubtedly still under the influence of his Wesak observances, summoned Gamini and me to attend the royal presence during the second watch before midnight.

Gamini had been full of questions during the past two days about the maiden he had seen. I had told him that her name was Rajitha, called Raji for short. She was unmarried. Her father was Upa Sena, chief headman of the Kotmale district, which was part of the subkingdom of Malaya, located in the interior mountains bordering Ruhuna. Her family were in the Tissa area to visit relations and participate in the Wesak festival. I pretended that I had no more to tell him, but he could talk of nothing else as we walked along the flare-lit corridors toward the audience chamber. He even proposed visiting Kotmale.

'Be patient,' I counselled. 'You are a prince. You do not go searching out a maiden in her village residence like some yokel.'

But he was impatient to meet Raji and talk to her. 'At least find out where she is staying and take me to her,' he almost begged. 'I am worried that she might already be betrothed.' He gripped my shoulder and stopped me, his expression one of alarm. 'And what if she becomes attracted to someone else?' Gone was the reserve, the restraint, the watchfulness he exercised over all the other aspects of his life. He was a young man in love.

I patted his hand with a smile, removed it from my shoulder and resumed walking. 'Why are you so impatient?' I demanded. 'What do you want of her?'

'I just want to be with her.'

'You can never be married to her. She is not of royal estate.'

'I do not care.'

'She lives many *yojana* away. Would you leave your destiny and go to live there? Planting cabbages in addition to your seed, no doubt?'

'You joke, when I am deadly serious. I cannot stop thinking of her. She must not be allowed to go back.'

'So you would keep her here as your mistress . . . Well, you certainly are of age and no one will fault you for that.'

'Anything. Anything, so long as we are not parted.'

'You have really got a bad attack of whatever it is that you have,' I observed with a smile.

'How could *you* ever know,' he flashed nastily, then immediately became contrite. 'I am sorry. I am so sorry. Please forgive me. You are the only one I can depend on and I say nasty things to you.'

I felt the pain of his words, though. How little he really knew of the ways of love! He could hurt me, yet I would try not to return hurt with hurt.

He looked sharply at me, but kept walking on. There was no contrition in his face. As we continued toward the audience chamber, the Wesak moon was a great copper gong, hanging in a glowing blue sky. A lizard chirped: 'thuk . . . thuk . . . thuk.' The very sound is one of warning, so people believe it to be an ill omen. Was this another warning?

We were announced as soon as we reached the audience chamber. We made obeisance and moved forward to stand before the King. Several others had preceded us.

King Kakkavan looked more crow-like than ever, but now he was ageing, his black hair liberally strewn with grey, the bristles silver on his chin. His white tunic and pantaloons accented the darkness of his wrinkling skin. Age had made the beak-like nose seem to curve more sharply downward and the flaring nostrils go flaccid. He looked tired except for the dark, magnetic eyes with that glaze to them, shining strangely tonight. Sensing him to be moved by religious fervour, I felt disquiet.

Queen Devi, dressed in a beaded blue jacket and skirt, her glorious hair hanging down to her waist, sat upon a carved chair beside the throne. She was as beautiful as ever she had been, her skin still flawless like that of a teenage girl, with never a wrinkle. Only a hint of matronly stodginess at the hips spoke of childbearing and approaching age. I was again struck by Raji's similarity to her in appearance. They could have been sisters.

Prince Tissa, in a white tunic and sarong, stood below the dais, facing the throne. He was slim and tall at fifteen, the image of his mother, with none of his father's features.

Velu Sumana towered on Prince Tissa's right. Like the Queen, he had kept his youth and no one would believe he was forty-four.

On Prince Tissa's left, the tall, craggy Kirthi Siri stood hunched, a bird of prey grown ancient. The few hairs on his bald head were now completely white and his skin was wrinkled like a *kuru pol* – an old, grey coconut.

'We have summoned you to announce a mission of paramount importance,' King Kakkavan declaimed, his deep voice reedy with unwonted pomposity. He leaned forward on the ebony throne. 'We have evolved a plan . . . ' He paused, reflecting. 'It would be more correct to say that, while we observed *sil* in the Tissa temple during Wesak, the blessed gift of the inner sight vouchsafed to us a plan whereby certain prophecies would be fulfilled, sins expiated and the security of our realm established through the Doctrine, for us and our heir, Prince Gamini.'

'Ah! A noble combination indeed,' Kirthi Siri whined

ingratiatingly. 'You are a truly blessed monarch to receive such directives of the blessed inner sight.'

Queen Devi said nothing. Her eyes flickered imperceptibly towards Velu Sumana and then to Prince Tissa before they were lowered again. A danger signal flashed through my brain, but I could not identify it.

'The only obstacle to the unification of Ruhuna these many years,' the King continued, 'has been the presence to our northeast of the subkingdom of Seru, established by King Elara and governed by Siva. As you know, Siva permitted Prince Abhaya of Kelaniya to establish the city of Soma south of Seru, with virtual independence, five years ago, on condition that the Prince swore allegiance to him. This was after our hotheaded elder son, whom we had sent to the Kelaniya temple a few months earlier to improve his studies, foolishly quarrelled with Prince Abhaya over the question of which of our two families, Gamini's Ruhuna father's or his Kelaniya mother's, was in fact the greater. We reproved our son for his lack of judgement and even gave Prince Abhaya our second sister in marriage, but wounds of pride do not easily heal.' He paused with a warning glance at Gamini. 'Still, the people of Soma and Seru are Sinhala and we have a duty to unite them with our people through the *dhamma*.' His expression became intense and unusually grim with resolve.

Gamini began to vibrate beside me. 'Give me leave, lord,' he urged, 'and three of our army corps and I will have Soma and Seru for you in one week. Then we can establish the *dhamma* at will.'

King Kakkavan stared pityingly at Gamini, who wilted. 'Your mind is still full of childish desires, Prince,' the King admonished. 'Even your recent observance of *sil* has failed to mature it.' He gestured with a hand and drew back one leg. 'Military action against the subkingdoms will only create a crisis. King Elara will see it as a threat to his entire rule. Total war would ensue. We will not spread our Doctrine of

318

nonviolence through violence. No! No! That would be
farcical. Our plan is that of the devout. Do you not recall the
prophecy?

> "To Seru that lies o'er the border
> A crow may fly if he dare
> To spread the Doctrine and Order
> Enshrining the Blessed One's hair." '

The King paused for effect, fixing each one of us in turn
with his dark eyes. 'We are the crow. And we dare!' He
leaned back complacently in his chair, as if his words
explained everything.

We still could not comprehend his meaning. How on earth
would he build a *dagoba* in someone else's territory? Even the
Queen half turned to glance curiously at her husband.

Only Kirthi understood. 'I see! I see!' He started a bout of
coughing, which left him gasping. 'Very clever! You will go
on a pilgrimage to build a *dagoba* in Seru. No one will dare
interfere, since the subkingdom is populated mostly by those
of the true faith . . . Ah! . . . I recall that the Chief Monk of
the temple there is also a relation of our noble queen. Hmm!
. . . ' The folds over his eyes, sagging now with age, lifted
momentarily. 'It just might work. It just might work.' He
relapsed into silence.

'How will this help us establish suzerainty over the
subkingdom, lord?' Velu Sumana inquired.

'We have no intention of establishing suzerainty
anywhere,' the King rejoined testily. 'We merely desire to
establish the Doctrine and give the Buddhist people of Seru a
proper place for religious observance. It is our sacred duty.
Our ancestor, King Mahanaga, tried force when he
murdered the ten *kshastriyas* of Kataragama. That bid is
enough for one family.'

'What of your safety, lord?' Prince Tissa inquired.

King Kakkavan looked kindly at him. 'We appreciate
your concern, Prince, but we can have no thought of our

safety on a sacred mission. As for the journey, we will take one army corps with us.'

I could sense Gamini brightening. Was his father really a warrior after all? Would he show himself aggressive, as well as patriotic and devout? Had he waited so long merely until his sons came of age? I saw the questions flashing through Gamini's mind, though, like Kirthi, I already knew the answers.

'But only to give us the safety of numbers and to ensure commencement of work on the foundations of the *dagoba*, and of the *vihare* for the guardian *bhikkus*,' the King added. The eager light left Gamini's eyes. 'The soldiers will go unarmed.' The King's eyes glittered. His arm extended gracefully sideways, pointing. 'Can you not see the scene? An army of pilgrims, dressed in white, sweeping across the green countryside, singing religious chants, carrying *mamoties* and other tools instead of weapons.'

I sensed rather than saw Gamini stiffen. I prayed he would contain his disappointment. The stuff of which conquerors are bred does not take easily to constraint. They can restrain themselves, yes – but cannot be restrained.

To my relief, Gamini said nothing. A curiously blank expression crossed his face. He became remote again.

King Kakkavan turned his attention to Velu Sumana. 'You, Chief Warrior, will be responsible for ensuring that the hosts of masons, carpenters and other artisans we will require for the work are recruited immediately. You, Chief Minister' – Kirthi Siri turned and faced the King – '. . . will have assembled all such building materials as we may not be able to obtain in Seru, all wagons necessary for transportation and all food and other necessities for the journey. Everything must, however, be on the most humble scale. Remember, we are all pilgrims.'

Kirthi nodded. 'It shall be done as you desire, lord. When will you be ready to leave?'

The King's dark eyes became intense again. A little tic

started on his right cheek. He drummed impatiently on the arm of his chair. 'We would leave tonight if possible, but it will take you at least three weeks to be ready. We shall therefore depart with the army corps and surveyors seven days from now. Our astrologers have declared that to be an auspicious day and have indicated the end of the third watch as the correct time for departure. We will proceed to Soma and Seru and establish our mission. Surveyors and astrologers will select the site for the *dagoba* and we will have it prepared for the wagon train of goods and workmen under Velu Sumana, which must leave Mahagama not less than eighteen days from now in order to arrive in time for us to break ground on the Poson, the first full moon after Wesak.'

'What of me, lord?' It was the Queen, her beautiful face turned toward her husband, her dark eyes eager. 'Would it not be wise to take me with you, to temper some of Prince Abhaya's displeasure with your branch of the family? Besides, I would like to acquire the merit from such a pilgrimage.' The glint of religious fervour entered her expression. Here we go again, I thought, joining any caravan of merit for the journey to Nirvana.

A strange look crossed the King's face, but only for a moment. He wiped it out quickly and deliberately. I began to comprehend one of the causes of conflict within this family. The Queen was of Kelaniya stock and proud of her lineage. The Kelaniya capital and temple were highly regarded as seats of learning. Lord Buddha is said to have visited the city. Such disputes between families were frequent at all levels of society and often became bitter.

The King pondered awhile. 'You shall accompany us, not to enhance our safety but to share in the merit of this act of devotion to the Doctrine,' he said.

Velu Sumana started forward. 'If I may say so respectfully, lord,' he suggested, 'there will be much danger on this mission. A whole army corps, even of pilgrims, will be suspect. Our men will be without weapons and completely outnumbered. What guarantees will we have of their safety and that of our king and queen? And what is to prevent King Elara from taking advantage of this situation and sweeping into Ruhuna?'

I looked for Gamini's reaction and saw the strangest expression on his face. For once, I could not even begin to comprehend what he felt except for a boiling anger, as if he had taken affront at Velu Sumana's intervention, but was holding himself back.

The King gave Velu Sumana a pitying glance. 'Nothing whatever,' he retorted, 'except the old reasons. First, you must remember why King Elara never followed up his conquest of Lanka with an invasion of Ruhuna. He feared our mountain fastnesses. The flat plains of the north and east of our island are easy terrain. Ruhuna is different. Secondly, Ruhuna has no Chola colonists and traders to make the foreigner welcome. Instead, it has stouthearted Sinhala, who may accept a neutral peace but would fight to the death for their soil and the *dhamma*. Finally, King Elara no longer has an heir to motivate him. He will only act if and when his personal security is threatened. But what of all that? Our only protection need be the Doctrine.'

His words added rain to the idea that had germinated in my mind a long time ago. When Gamini's time came, we would need to find a cause for the people. The King had just confirmed that they would fight for their soil and the *dhamma*.

'What is my role, sire?' Gamini demanded.

'You will remain in Mahagama as regent.'

I could feel the thrill of pride that shot through Gamini. I shared it with all my being. Gamini's eyes shone, but he gave no other sign of his pleasure.

'And I, sire?' Prince Tissa inquired. There was a hint of petulant jealousy in his voice, a sort of 'me too' in his tone.

'You will take three of our army corps, under the Great Warriors Maha Sona, Abhaya and Bharana, to Dighavapi,

322

to join Prince Digha Bahu's three corps for exercises. The idea is to show a concentration of offensive capability, though at some distance away. Mahaiyangana would be the logical place, but it is too close to the border and the main road to Anu for King Elara's comfort.' The King turned his head toward Velu Sumana. 'The three unassigned corps will remain here with Prince Gamini in a state of readiness.' He smiled dryly. 'The Doctrine surely does not prohibit a friendly display of force to discourage hasty conduct on the part of others.'

Velu Sumana gave a grunt of satisfaction. The King's plan had finally captured his imagination. Gamini was lost in thought. His mind had to be working furiously as to how he could turn the situation to his own ends. Kirthi Siri was gazing out of the wind seemingly absorbed in the silvery moonlight and dark shadows outside.

'Each of you has work to do. Go now and bring us details of your plans, written on *ola*, by this time tomorrow, so we can co-ordinate them. We shall meet here. A move for the Doctrine must be no less smooth than a military operation.'

Gamini's face was a mask. It did not reveal his whirling thoughts, but his stance was that of a champion racehorse awaiting a signal for the race to commence.

'By the way, Prince Rodana will accompany us to act as observer and record the events for posterity. The others may depart, but you shall stay behind, Prince Rodana. We need to converse with you.'

As I watched the others leaving, King Kakkavan's cunning became apparent to me. He was separating Gamini and me. He was splitting the army into three groups. Divide and rule. Removed from Gamini's side, I was to be the King's hostage.

Chapter 32

The King indicated the royal footstool after the others had left. 'Come up and sit here!' he commanded.

I slowly mounted the dais and sat down, wondering what he wanted. We had enjoyed many a discussion throughout the years; these had confirmed my respect for my king as a man and a ruler. He even had a surprising store of knowledge of the history of the region, the Arya code, modes of government and various religions of our time.

Although he was always relaxed with me, I was never able to penetrate his shell, to reach the real person hidden behind the mask of his intellect. We might have been two friendly monks in a temple, close in our purpose, separate as individuals.

The King leaned back on his throne. The dark fingers of his right hand drummed again on its gem-encrusted arm while he was deciding how to begin. I held my peace. One seldom opens a conversation with a monarch, but waits for him to speak. When he finally made up his mind, his dark eyes swept to mine. 'How is Gamini progressing in his studies?'

'Excellently, sire!' I replied with equal banality.

'You have been good for our son.'

I looked sharply at him. There was only sincerity and kindliness in his expression.

'You have faithfully discharged the trust imposed on you by your uncle, Prince Vipula.' A flicker of regret sped across his face. He swallowed. 'You have also justified our faith in you, so we have decided to take you into our confidence. There are things a trusted person must know in the event that we die on this pilgrimage.'

'Death, sire?'

'We do not anticipate ambush or treachery.' The familiar dry note entered his voice. 'The truth is, we cannot expect to live much longer. Indeed, it is strange that we should even have survived this long. Several years ago, we suffered an attack such as our father had known. Severe pain in the upper part of the chest, spreading to the neck and the shoulders, a cold, drenching sweat over the entire body, dizziness and shortage of breath. The heralds of death.'

A chill ran up my spine. 'Two such . . . and the third is fatal?'

'Yes! Time was running out for us, so that first warning made us change all our policies and much of our way of life. Remember, no one must know of this.'

'Of course, sire.'

'Meanwhile, we had much sin to expiate, but more importantly, we had to avoid *akusala* actions. After our ancestor's impious act, he and his progeny after him built five hundred *vihares*. How can one compensate for evil by building *vihares*? Since his *kharma* flowed into his seed before the expiation, we have inherited its consequences. We must do everything in our power to avert them.' His voice was unutterably sad and the feel of him smote my heart.

This poor, lonely man, living all these years under the burden of his ancestor's guilt and the knowledge of impending death.

'We had also to avert the results of having caused the deaths of your uncle and Prince Muthiah, King Elara's son.' His voice was as level as his gaze.

He paused, trying to read my thoughts. I remained impassive, numb before his admission and my memories.

'When we started preparing for our reincarnation, we had to ensure peace for our subjects and a secure reign for our son. The only way we could do this was by confirming the boundaries between the three kingdoms. Yet when we made a peace pact with King Elara and desired our sons to take the oath of nonviolence against the Cholas . . .' – his voice faltered – 'those whom we loved came to regard us as cowards . . .' He cleared his throat again, fighting back unwonted emotion. He resumed after regaining his composure. 'People seldom see that it takes greater courage to dedicate oneself to peace than to war.' He looked earnestly at me, seeking my agreement.

I hesitated. His words were new to me and to our times. They raised conflicting thoughts in my mind. Did he mean that Ruhuna should remain passive before any invasion? Let foreign troops in without opposition and there would be no problems? What of exploitation by the foreigner? What of injustice, prejudice and partiality? And yet, what indeed? If an individual's spirit is free, nothing else should matter. Do not the *yogis* and *sannyasis* live free as the earth? But can a million people and more reach that degree of liberation?

The King was awaiting my response and the only way I could serve him tonight was by seeming to agree with him.

'You have given me food for thought, sire,' I replied truthfully. 'I shall bring these principles to Prince Gamini's notice.' I felt a hypocrite because I could not add that I had already thought about the need to incite our people to give up their placid lives and follow Gamini.

'Good!' But the King's face remained clouded. 'There is one act that we have not revealed to any man but our treasurer, which could be interpreted as cowardice and worse.' He paused, giving me a piercing look, searching for my trustworthiness and proceeding only when he was satisfied. 'What we are about to tell you must be kept secret for the present. We agreed soon after the milk-rice incident to pay personal tribute to the Chola.' He spoke matter-of-factly. 'One thousand pieces of money every year for the preservation of peace. It was the only way in which the Chola could be satisfied and the treaty executed.'

I heard the hiss of my indrawn breath. 'Tribute!' I whispered. 'Then we are not equals, but slaves.'

'Never slaves!' The King's deep voice became harsh. 'We thought you at least would understand.'

I wanted desperately to understand, but I could not. How could committing an entire people to such an act of bondage ever be excused? And, after all, even the King's personal funds came from the people.

Again he sensed my thoughts. 'The money did not come from the people, but from our private treasury,' he said in a defiant tone. 'We entered into personal bondage in order to keep our people free. All else apart, any other course would have made the transaction public. Only two other people knew of it – King Elara and his private treasurer. It is not tribute, but an arrangement between equals, like a dowry in the marriage of two houses. King Elara has a full understanding of its limits.'

Compassion triumphed over reason and patriotism, pride and prejudice. Once more I felt sorry for the King. 'You owe me no explanation, sire,' I responded gently. 'I am but your subject.'

'Spoken like a prince and a human being.' The King nodded gratefully.

I began to feel close to him for the first time, understanding at last how he came to be isolated from his wife and children. He must have misinterpreted my look.

'No pity now,' he directed sharply. 'We have taken you into our confidence only to ensure that you will continue having these payments made from our private treasury in the event of our death. Our treasurer has the necessary instructions. Since Prince Gamini shall succeed us, as is his right by Arya custom, he can decide what to do after he is consecrated.'

My spirit cried out in denial and the words took the shape of that cry. 'Sire, you ask me to do the impossible.'

His eyes flashed, his face suddenly hardening into carved ebony. 'How so?' he demanded coldly.

'I would have to do so secretly. I can keep nothing hidden

327

from Prince Gamini. It would be a betrayal and he would never trust me again.'

'Hmm!' Some of the hardness left his face. His dark fingers beat their tattoo on the arm of the throne again. 'Your point is well taken. Hmm ... well ... You may openly ensure that my instructions to the treasurer are carried out. We would rather be misunderstood by all the people and thought to have been but a *yuvarajah* paying tribute to Chola than have our son lose his faith in you.'

I was stunned. 'Tell the Prince some day,' he commanded. As I looked speechlessly at him, he let me see a glimmer of love for Gamini in his eyes. It was there one moment and he withdrew it the next. 'Also tell him that this holy mission of ours will neutralize the east for him. Although we do not intend preparing the ground for his military actions, we cannot ignore its benefits for his cause. If we are spared, our next mission will be the consecrating of another *dagoba* at Mahaiyangana. Thus our Buddhist people will be linked from east to west along most of our northern border. It cannot do Prince Gamini any harm.' He smiled wryly, sighed and nodded his dismissal.

Chapter 33

Gamini was lying on the massage table, following the early morning's usual strenuous weapons training, when the group was ushered into my quarters by the attendant, as arranged by me. I bade them be seated in my study and hastened to inform Gamini he had visitors.

'Who are they?' he demanded impatiently.

'Those people,' I replied evasively.

'Who are those people?'

'They!'

'They! They! Who the devil are they?' He was becoming irritated.

'Those people!'

'You are stupid!' he exploded. 'What are you playing?'

'The fool! What else could a stupid play?'

'Oh!' He jerked upright. 'I know you when you are in this mood.' He muttered something under his breath. 'You will plague me to death if I do not come along.'

'Certainly! If you are impatient to discover what it is all about, the sooner you get dressed and return to your quarters, the sooner you will find out, won't you?'

He seized a leather cushion to throw at me and I beat a hurried retreat.

I let Gamini get to his reception chamber before I opened the door to ask permission to announce his visitors.

'What are you up to?' he demanded suspiciously. 'Since when have you started announcing visitors like a palace attendant?'

'These are special people. They have come a long way.'

'You are up to something, but go ahead.'

I grinned. 'I would like to present to you a loyal Sinhala.'

Gamini frowned, trying to place the small, fair-skinned man with sharp, pointed features who knelt before him. The chief headman's black hair was drawn straight back, held by a curved tortoiseshell comb and tied in a knot at the nape of his neck. His moustache curled upward almost to the dark eyes with flecks of light brown in them. He was dressed in a white *dhoti* with a white tunic and silver buttons. There was a slightly defensive attitude about him, though he was obviously awed by the situation. Headmen are never permitted entrance to a prince's quarters.

'This is Chandi, wife of the chief headman.' The woman was tall, fair and comely, but running a little to fat. She had long black lashes that gave her large eyes a limpid mystery. She was dressed in a tight blue-beaded jacket and a blue skirt with a blue sapphire necklace, earrings, ornamented hairpin, bracelets and rings to match. She trembled as she knelt beside her husband.

'You may rise,' Gamini commanded graciously. He saluted them with the fingertips of his two hands together, held below the waist.

They stood awkwardly side by side.

Gamini looked at me, perplexed.

'The family have come a long way. They expressed a desire to see you,' I explained.

Avoiding Gamini's angry look, I went to the door again and beckoned. As the maiden walked toward me, I announced, 'And this is their daughter, Rajitha, called Raji.'

As she stood at the entrance to the door, she was stunned to see Gamini. Her eyes widened before she sank to her knees, pale forehead touching the ground, slim hands joined above her head.

Gamini had recognized her on the instant. His jaw dropped and he literally gaped. For once, he was unable to move or speak.

'This is their daughter, Raji,' I repeated.

Gamini recovered. His eyes flickered to me in a brief moment of acknowledgement – reward enough to me for having set aside my own longing. Yet mingling with the peace of self-sacrifice was apprehension as to what Gamini would do. He was of age. He could keep Raji as his concubine. I could see that was what her parents feared and yet desired. Such a cruel decision for them to face, with no power to participate in it. Would it not be better for their only daughter to go back to the village, marry some steady young man of their choice and live the life of a sow in the sty than to be exposed to the short-lived glamour of a

330

concubine's life – one of many whom princes acquired through the years?

'You may rise.' It was Gamini's voice, steady, but deeper than usual.

Raji rose gracefully to her feet. She was almost as tall as Gamini. Dressed in white, she looked virginal. Her fair skin had an ethereal translucence. The large, dark, almond-shaped eyes, flecked with light brown like her father's, glowed luminously. Strangely, they no longer held fear.

During the few minutes of polite conversation that ensued, I kept wondering what Gamini's decision would be. It would reveal his true nature in the one area to which I really never had been exposed. Would he show the integrity of the romantic, or a refined form of lust, or cruel possession? My heart heavy with concern for the maiden whom I had loved at first sight, rather than for Gamini, I wanted to know the worst quickly. 'Now that Raji's parents have been presented to you,' I said, 'I request permission for them to withdraw to your anteroom. I have explained to them that you require conversation with their daughter. It is unusual for a maiden to talk privately with any man, even a prince, but they are willing to risk the slur on their daughter's reputation, provided that I shall remain here as chaperone.' I caught Gamini's angry glance and hastened to add, 'Out of earshot, of course. You will surely understand that this maiden's whole life is at stake.' I looked pointedly at him.

He caught my meaning and relaxed. 'Of course!' he readily agreed.

Upa Sena and his wife made obeisance and withdrew. Chandi shot a glance of apprehension at us before I closed the door of the study behind her.

I walked across the room to the window so that they might have some degree of privacy and stared out, leaving Raji standing by the door. Even before Gamini started to speak, she looked directly at him with glistening eyes. Joy surged within him that she would not lower her glance from him. 'I had thought we might never meet again,' he said softly. 'And yet, a part of me knew we surely would. The same part that recognized you when I first set eyes on you.'

'I too had the same thoughts, lord,' Raji murmured, 'for I did not know who you were when my eyes first found you.'

Gamini was amazed. 'You mean your feelings had nothing to do with my being a prince and heir to the Ruhuna kingdom?'

'No, lord. I did not know who you were until I entered this room. I crave your pardon for having dared raise my eyes to those of a prince.'

'And yet you gaze at me now, while craving my pardon?' Gamini's glad laugh rang free. 'No! No . . . do not look away. If you do, you would wrench my own eyes out.'

She sighed.

A new feeling coursed through Gamini. For the first time in his life, he could truly believe that someone cared for him not as a prince, but as a person. More, it was evident to him that Raji shared his sense of their destiny. He was shaken by a blazing desire to give something to Raji, to make some enormous sacrifice before the shrine at which he felt he was worshipping. Flames of tenderness, the overpowering need to reach out and touch Raji gently, just touch her soft cheek, swept through his whole being. What could he give her? What gesture could he make?

Suddenly he knew. And when he began to speak, the words came out softly, as from some other source. 'When do you return to Kotmale with your parents?'

She was startled by the question, but only for a moment. Then its significance registered. One fair hand flew to her delicate throat to stifle the sob that escaped her. 'My father has duties to perform at the harvest in our village next week, lord,' she replied hoarsely. 'We had intended leaving early tomorrow.'

'You are afraid I would ask you to remain as my

concubine?' Gamini's voice was gentle, but his eyes burned into hers.

She nodded. Tears sprang to her eyes. She made no attempt to wipe them. 'I am afraid that you will, lord – and also afraid that you will not.'

Gamini laughed low. This was a maiden after his own heart.

'In what month were you born?' he inquired.

'In the month of Vesakha,' she replied. 'I was fifteen on my last birthday.'

'Ah! That explains it. The blessed month in which Lord Buddha was born, obtained Enlightenment and reached Nibbhana. You will be lucky for me.'

She blushed. 'I would want to be, with all my heart,' she responded earnestly.

'I must confess that it was my intention, when I sought you out, to have you for my concubine,' Gamini resumed. 'But what I have found in you and what I believe we have found together in these brief moments is too precious for that. I am heir to this kingdom. You can never be consecrated queen, because of your birth, but you shall be my consort and share the destiny of conquest that awaits me. Conquest?' He laughed low. 'The conquest is yours. You will reign in my heart forever. Go now in peace to your home, but before you do, tell me that your heart accepts me.'

'My lord, I cannot give you my heart today, because it is already given.'

'How so?' Gamini's voice almost broke on the words as the earth suddenly turned dark for him.

She smiled gently, her teeth white as coconut kernel. 'I gave my heart to an unknown young man whom I saw in the sacred precincts of the Tissa Maha Ramaya in the light of the Vesak moon,' she replied.

Relief lit Gamini. The sun shone again. He looked at Raji with wondering eyes. She was suddenly, miraculously, making him feel whole again.

'You have been so unselfish,' Raji continued. 'I am ashamed at my own selfishness. I held you my king from the moment I set eyes on you. I was so afraid that I might never see you again. Yet something told me I would. And yet again, I was fearful lest it be only my wishful heart speaking. You have just made me realize that love does not depend on circumstances. It is there. So simple really, lord. Now, I will gladly remain as anything you want me to be, so long as my eyes can behold you even once in a while.'

Gamini was moved as never before. His voice became low and intense. 'There is no world save that born of our love. There is no life save that which you and I will make together, as we have done in every past birth.'

Raji looked like a flower shaken by the monsoon's blast. She gazed at Gamini, merging into him.

A hacking cough from the gardens reached us. One of the gardeners must have the lung disease. It shook the two lovers from their trance, but they had already known in their spirits a consummation more complete than any physical union of limbs locked in coitus.

'The world outside reminds us that it indeed exists,' Gamini observed regretfully. Then, typically of him, 'I must ask the physicians about that man's cough.' He moved forward and took Raji's face in gentle hands. He looked deep into the essence of her being. 'We are now betrothed in our hearts. You are mine and will give yourself to no other.'

She nodded, smiling tearfully. 'Indeed I promise, lord.'

'Go now and may the *devas* guard you. I will come for you when I am ready.'

'May the blessing of the Triple Gem be with you, lord. My body leaves. My heart remains with you.'

Gamini kissed her lightly on both cheeks. Then she was gone.

The door clicked shut and I turned to find him staring after it. The pain of separation would hit him later. For the present he was exalted.

Two days later, King Elara received his Chief Minister

and his Chief Warrior in his study.

The room had been redecorated with tables and couches of tamarind. This wood has a rich, dark-brown grain, with flames of roseate gold running along it, so the white cushions provided an elegant contrast. The floor of white mountain crystal was austere and bare of rugs, but motes dancing on midmorning sunshine streaming through the open windows and a sharp scent of incense from glowing braziers gave the room the feel of life.

The King sat on a high-backed chair at his long writing table to receive the men. He had not changed much through the years, except that the dark skin of his face showed tiny wrinkles and his hair was slightly more grey at the temples. Neither age nor the period of peace had dimmed the alertness of his personality or reduced the magnetic quality of the dark eyes.

He had never ceased to find the diminutive Muttu Samy and the giant Digha Jantu an oddly assorted couple. Today they seemed even more so, because the Chief Minister was dressed in white tunic and pantaloons, of the *khaddar* cotton that important people affected to display simplicity, while the Chief Warrior wore a red *dhoti* of rich silk. The King often wondered how many people wore *khaddar* only to curry favour with him. Shrugging mentally, he opened the conversation with pleasantries. 'You see us without our faithful jester, who is ill with stomach pains,' he finally observed, his eyes glinting mischievously. 'We hope neither of you misses him!'

'I'm prostrated with grief, lord!' Digha Jantu observed.

The Chief Warrior's efforts at humour frequently reminded King Elara of an elephant trying to plough an onion patch. To make the giant feel good, however, he gave a short laugh. 'It always amuses me that a giant should pick on a dwarf. Why do you not find someone your own size?'

'My physical size is dwarfed by the dimensions of your jester's conceit, lord,' Digha Jantu retorted.

The King smiled. 'We **pray** you make your reports

regarding the events in Ruhuna for which you sought special audience,' he commanded. 'Since we have some word of it already, we must, however, warn you that our only method of conquering Ruhuna, unless directly threatened, will be the *manta yuddhaya.*' He raised a hand as Digha Jantu tensed and started forward. 'A moment, Chief Warrior. Remember, the *manta yuddhaya* does not exclude the judicious use of armies.' He high-roofed his fingertips and placed his elbows on the table, leaning forward expectantly. 'Now, your news.'

'Last night my spies from the Ruhuna palace reported an unusual circumstance,' the Chief Minister stated in his prim, high-pitched voice. As usual, he raised a slim forefinger for emphasis. 'Kakkavan Tissa has planned what he calls a pilgrimage to the cities of Soma and Seru.' His small dark eyes gleamed at the King, as if he were a conjurer producing eggs out of thin air.

'What is unusual about that?' King Elara inquired. 'Do we not occasionally go on pilgrimage to foreign territories, such as Muneswaram temple in South India, without exciting their rulers?'

The Chief Minister raised his forefinger again, this time with a tight smile fronting an air of triumph. 'Ah!' he exclaimed knowingly, as if that were answer enough. Finding it was not, he dropped his hand. 'But you do not go to Muneswaram accompanied by one thousand monks and ten thousand warriors of your first corps, lord.'

The King came alert on the instant. This was more than had already been reported to him. He felt his face grow taut and a bleak look enter his eyes. 'You mean that this foolish crow actually intends to invade Soma and Seru?' The incredulity he felt was echoed in his voice. He shook his grizzled head in disbelief. 'Surely there is some mistake, Chief Minister.'

'I must confess that the army corps has instructions to go unarmed and dressed as pilgrims,' the Chief Minister hastened to explain. 'But this has to be merely a blind, to lull Prince Abhaya of Soma, Prince Siva of Seru and you, lord, into a sense of false security. Once they are established in the two subkingdoms, some method will be found of supplying the soldiers with arms. They will then surely be reinforced by Prince Digha Bahu's three Dighavapi corps and three more under Prince Tissa that are scheduled to undertake exercises in the Dighavapi region.'

'Their plan is obvious, lord,' Digha Jantu exclaimed fiercely. 'Give me leave to gather our forces and scatter these Sinhala like dust before the wind.'

'Tch!' the King exclaimed impatiently. He shook his head. 'You are both quick to rush to conclusions – and you, Chief Warrior, are too eager for war. It will require far graver provocation for us to risk conquering the cities of Ruhuna, only to be slowly worn down by attacks in the mountains and jungles, which would constantly endanger our communications and supply lines.' He drew a slow hand across his forehead, remembering. He did not wish to add that the most supreme motive of all for invading Ruhuna had been removed with his son's execution and his expansionist aims had died with Prince Muthiah on a chariot wheel. He sighed.

'Yet our fortunes and those of our ancestors have always depended on taking the initiative, invading, attacking, lord,' Digha Jantu persisted. 'You well know the dangers of being driven into a defensive posture, if the Sinhala do mean to invade.'

The King nodded. 'You are right, but why should we assume that the *yuvarajah* means war after all these years?'

'I beg you to recall the prophecies about his older son, lord,' the Chief Minister suggested smoothly. 'As you know, Prince Gamini is now seventeen. He is said to hunger for invading Lanka.'

'He has done nothing about it all these years. How have circumstances changed today?'

337

The Chief Minister's eyes gleamed. 'A good question, lord,' he pontificated, 'a good question indeed.' He paused dramatically, his head cocked to one side. 'The Prince was held back by his father. Now Kakkavan leaves for Soma and Seru, appointing his son, Gamini, Prince Regent in his absence, giving greater freedom of action. It has to be a deep-laid plot.'

King Elara pondered the news. For a moment he was tempted to give the order to march. Then he remembered his dead wife. She had always counselled caution. What would she suggest today?

As if to reply, Pushpa suddenly appeared in the sunlit room. She stood beside dread Kali, goddess of death, but in the full bloom of youth. Her delicate hands held something he could not make out. Then she held it up for him to see. A grinning skull, the eyeless sockets nonetheless pleading. Death, the prize of war.

'Remember the great Brahma created life to sustain it,' Pushpa said in her golden voice. 'Go to war henceforth only to sustain life.'

As he realized that both Pushpa and Kali, his mother-goddess, counselled patience, the vision vanished. He gazed once more at empty sunlight.

He scratched his chin and leaned back in his chair. The vision had been so real, he was surprised that the others had not shared it more than they did his pain – the pain of remembering and wondering. His first duty . . .

The King straightened his shoulders, rose to his feet and walked to the window. He stood there gazing thoughtfully at the garden outside, eyes sweeping upward at the cawing of two black crows quarrelling from their perch on the branch of a green flamboyant tree. Sound without fury.

The Chief Warrior and the Chief Minister glanced at each other in hopeful silence. King Elara was aware of the look without seeing it. He knew that each of these men wanted war, though for different reasons. The Chief Minister

wanted glory and more power, never guessing that Digha
Jantu dreamed of becoming more than Chief Warrior, for
this was a time when army commanders even assumed
kingship after conquest.

Although he had already made up his mind, the King
turned around with a question. 'You have a plan to meet this
situation?' he asked the Chief Minister.

'Yes, lord,' Muttu Samy piped. 'A two-pronged plan that
would suit your own heart.' He advanced a few steps in
suppressed excitement, his slippered feet clapping against
the smooth floor.

The King listened without comment. When the Chief
Minister finished speaking, the King pondered awhile in
gloomy silence. 'We approve your plan, Chief Minister,' he
finally declared. 'But our army corps will cross the river
border only if there is evidence of aggression by the Sinhala.'

Chapter 34

The convoy was already drawn up by the time Gamini and I
arrived at the audience hall at daybreak. The courtyard was
filled with busy people, their faces showing no colour in the
light mist.

Open wooden foodstuff-containers were being hauled to
the wagons by bare-bodied attendants who called out time to
ease the strain and co-ordinate their movements. Smells of
cinnamon, garlic, onion and other spices mingled faintly in
the air. An occasional 'Make way, please,' broke through
the babble of voices, punctuated by the lowing of bullocks,

the thud of goods being loaded onto carts and the shouted commands.

The six wagons of the royal party and their retainers, drawn by white bullocks, were ghostly silhouettes with the phantom figures of the King's bodyguard, dressed as pilgrims and carrying no weapons, in rows behind them. The rest of the wagons, with open sides and thatched roofs of brown coconut branches bearing a host of saffron-robed monks, were lost in the thicker accumulation of mist beyond. Surveying the scene, I realized that this mission was the inspiration of a shrewd mind that had kept King Kakkavan on the Ruhuna throne for over forty years.

The first beams of dawn, slanting from the east, began to slash through the mist. I could now make out a covey of musicians and drummers loitering by the palace gates, awaiting their signal. Their leader, a proud-looking man with brown skin pulled tight over wide cheekbones and a trim moustache, swaggered up and down, the bells of his anklets chinking softly.

I felt sorry for the drummers. They wore skirts and tight pantaloons and only the traditional strings of coloured beads around their bare brown chests. Their headdresses were impressive. Circular haloes of gold and silver spread around the forehead, topped with a crown of coloured beads and jewels, the whole held in place by bronze earmuffs extending behind the neck. Their heads would be warm, but they must have goose pimples from the chill air.

Dancing is held to be a divine art in our country; no procession would be complete without the professional dancers and the drummers carrying *geta bera*, our cylindrical two-sided drums, strung around their necks.

In the area between the audience chamber and the courtyard, noblemen, courtiers and attendants now bustled to complete last-minute tasks, but everything was beginning to work smoothly as a well-oiled wheel. King Kakkavan had revealed himself to be a master at integrating the plans of his principal staff into a perfect whole.

'What a military strategist my father would have made,' Gamini observed.

'Hardly the subject with which to commence a pilgrimage,' I remarked dryly. 'But I must confess that you start off with greater advantages than your royal father did. Not only do you have his preparation and example, but also a thorough study of the campaigns of the great, such as Sikander, Chandra Gupta, Kyroos and the Yona . . .'

'I will make my own plans,' he interrupted soberly. 'I have learned more from the failures of the great than from their successes!'

'You will not do anything rash while we are gone, will you?' I inquired anxiously.

His slim figure shook with laughter. He had the uncanny ability to change moods like a magician with silken scarves. 'How can I? The King has my only friend as a hostage.' His dark face became alive with mischief, before turning serious in an instant. He laid a hand on my arm. 'I shall miss you.'

A stirring by the palace gates and the first plaintive notes of a trumpet drew our attention. The King must be on his way. In moments, other trumpets blared. The *geta bera* struck a beat, then tattooed and rattled. Finger-cymbals chinked in and flutes began to pipe. I turned around to see King Kakkavan, a small, dark figure dressed in white, at the top of the audience hall steps, with Queen Vihara Maha Devi, in white bodice and skirt, standing stately beside him. Behind them, Prince Tissa was emerging from within the hall.

The King paused. While music began to fill the air, all other activity ceased and we made obeisance. The King returned our salutations gravely and glanced toward the dancers.

I could see them more clearly now, standing in a single row. They wore flared white skirts in layers edged with brown, green and black horizontal stripes, above tight, gauzy white pantaloons. Each dancer had a bare foot poised in the air. The arms were bent and upraised to elbow level, palms pointing downward, thumbs outstretched. They were motionless figures in a graceful tapestry.

The music stopped suddenly, leaving an aching silence. The leader of the dancers pushed his upraised leg forward and started a nasal chant. The drums began a slow beat. The other dancers followed their leader, the bells around their ankles jingling, their voices in perfect unison. The drummers hastened their beat; the instruments flowed back into sober melody. The dancing commenced.

'They will play a different beat one day,' Gamini vowed, 'at this very spot.'

He reached out and embraced me. The feel of him was as beautiful as had been that of my uncle in Anu, the only time he held me. It released the old fear, churning in my stomach, vibrating through my entire body, bringing bitterness in my throat. Was this again the embrace of death?

Gamini released me and moved away. He walked up the steps of the audience hall and knelt before his father. Even at that distance, I observed a kindly light in King Kakkavan's eyes. He stooped and touched Gamini's bowed head. Gamini stood up. Father and son looked at each other briefly. Then Gamini moved to kneel before the Queen. When he rose, he did not meet her eyes, but moved away. Why did he, who always had a direct look, never meet his mother's eyes? He briefly acknowledged Prince Tissa's salutation and stood beside his brother, feet slightly apart, hands clasped behind his back, in his usual relaxed pose.

The King started walking down the steps. I took my place behind him. People hastily moved out of our way, pushing back to clear a path for us. Meanwhile, messengers had already raced ahead to warn the convoy.

When we reached the palace gates, the stream of saffron and white in the brown-topped wagons drawn by white bullocks stirred, like an enormous snake about to commence its slither. In the new light of day, I could identify members of Velu Sumana's white-clad corps, except those in the far distance. The order of march would stretch them out over two miles.

I took my place in the wagon behind the King's and sat on a white cushion between two young princes, leaning back against the side, my legs outstretched. I raised hands together in farewell salutation to Gamini. He was such a lonely figure. He would be lonelier in the years ahead. What had nagged me was a sudden question, something none of us had thought of before. How would Gamini stir the people into war? The question required an urgent answer, because I had the feeling that today's event was bringing Gamini closer to his time.

Armies win battles, but it is people who make armies – and people are not easily moved to war. They must have a cause. The great army of Sikander that marched through arid deserts and rocky mountains, across swollen rivers and vast plains – what had motivated it? Their god-king, the conqueror? No, he was merely the star that led them on. Booty then? Plunder, conquest, a reflected glory? Expectation of gold with which to buy a few *poles* of cultivable land and build a home for retirement? The hope of sitting by a fireside and being able to say, 'I was with Sikander'?

We had to find some answers other than the prophecies.

My thoughts were interrupted as our wheels began to make a different sound and to roll with a smoother motion. We had entered the rock-paved street cutting through the Mahagama township. People had begun to stir. Some emerged, sleepy-eyed but curious, through doorways let into the walls of the clay-brick houses that fronted the street. A bare-bodied *mudalali* with tousled hair scratched his rotund stomach and called to his children to come out and see the procession. Women peeped from behind their menfolk. Three lean little boys in sarongs, their ribs showing, and a pretty little dark-eyed girl minus her front teeth ran out of their doorway shrilling 'Ayubowan!' We returned their greeting with cries of 'Sadhu!'

At dusk on the third night we reached Dighavapi without incident, except for being stiff and sore from the discomfort of being cooped up and shaken in the wagons. We were received by Prince Digha Bahu and his son, Prince Panduka. Prince Digha Bahu was paunchy now. His eighteen yards of white *dhoti*, meant to make even a thin prince or chieftain look worthy, at a time when portliness was associated with wealth and rank – whoever heard of a fat peasant? – merely made him look like a tub. The whites of his pale brown eyes were bloodshot and his face had become flushed, with tiny red veins showing.

Prince Panduka looked as his father had seventeen years earlier, though he was taller and had a mop of shaggy dark hair. His eyes were, however, the identical pale brown pebbles.

I was somewhat disquieted when I saw father and son chatting conspiratorially with Prince Tissa outside the royal tent after greeting us.

King Kakkavan had insisted that we encamp in the suburbs, since we were on a pilgrimage, instead of receiving the hospitality of Prince Digha Bahu's city. It was a cold, crisp night and the moon shone clear on our encampment, an open plain by a river, with a single line of great *kumbuk* trees on its banks. Hundreds of flares and the glow from tent lights were scattered over the vast area of open ground. The wagons were clusters of dark shapes, laid out in orderly groups. People were sleeping in them, or on mats beneath their shelter. The horses and bullocks, tethered separately, disturbed the stillness with their constant neighing and lowing. Toilet arrangements are always a problem on these occasions, so odours of dust, sweat, urine and excrement from temporary latrines lay heavy on the air.

Since the roots of the *kumbuk* tree are known to cleanse and cool the waters flowing beside them, the King's tent had been erected under one of the spreading *kumbuk* trees beside the gurgling river.

After the tent was erected, King Kakkavan and I had barely entered and seated ourselves on settles inside when Velu Sumana, whom we thought to be still in Mahagama, stooped to enter. He was soon followed by the three princes, who unceremoniously brushed past him to take their seats side by side on a long wooden bench. Their movement made the tapers on the table waver and smoke.

The giant Chief Warrior remained standing at the entrance, the usually vacant half-smile belied by grimness around the eyes. 'Forgive my presence, lord, but I deemed it more important to be with you.'

The King nodded approval, but with a question in his eyes.

'I have come to announce messengers from Prince Abhaya,' the Chief Warrior added.

King Kakkavan arched white eyebrows. 'At this time of night? Hardly a civilized hour to call. They must bring urgent news. Have them shown in.'

Velu Sumana turned and beckoned.

Two men entered. They were both tall, dark and stocky. They looked like twins in the fitful light. The great swords at their sides proclaimed them to be soldiers. Having made obeisance, they stood in silence, awaiting the King's permission to speak, but there was no mistaking their air of arrogance.

Dark eyes expressionless, King Kakkavan surveyed his visitors, meanwhile picking his teeth with an ivory toothpick.

Moths fluttered in the constantly changing patterns of taper-light caused by breezes breathing in through the open tent flap. *Kumbuk* branches sighed, ghostly, outside. A mosquito's whine heightened the tension within.

As long moments passed, I became aware that King Kakkavan was using the weapon of silence. The messengers could not know it, however, and they shifted uneasily. Some of their self-confidence began to fade. Soon they were sweating before six pairs of eyes fixed unwaveringly on them.

The King knew what he was doing. When he finally spoke, it was softly, but the way the sound broke the stillness, it might have been the first crackle of thunder. 'Who sent you and what is your mission?'

Relief swept the dust-strewn faces of the messengers. They shifted on their feet and their cheekbones gleamed in the flare-light.

'We come from our lord, Prince Abhaya, Regent of the city of Soma,' the man on the right volunteered. 'He inquires what brings you here?'

The King continued looking at the messengers. He was asserting his own position without words, I knew. Tension began to build up again. Even Prince Digha Bahu shifted uneasily on his settle and Prince Tissa shot a questioning glance at his father.

This time the King broke the tension with a smile. 'Return to your prince, the Regent of Soma, and tell him that we owe him no explanation for our presence in Sinhala Buddhist territory,' he declared quietly. 'For his personal information, however, we have come on a pilgrimage. From here on, only unarmed men will accompany us. We expect to cross the border into Soma territory soon after dawn tomorrow. If your prince so desires, he and our royal sister may join us on the road to Soma City, at our pre-noon halt. They can share in our merit by worshipping the sacred relics of our Master, Lord Buddha, and helping serve the pre-noon *dana* to the Noble Order of Monks. Get some rest and speed back to your master with our message well before we leave.' He waved a dark, imperious hand in dismissal.

The messengers made deep obeisance. Velu Sumana escorted them into the darkness.

'We resume our pilgrimage for the Doctrine tomorrow,'

King Kakkavan directed. His face suddenly looked grey and tired. He nodded to Prince Tissa. 'Instruct your three corps to make permanent camp on this plain against our return.'

Prince Digha Bahu and his son exchanged glances with Prince Tissa. A tremor shot through me. Three army corps under Prince Tissa, whose ambitions I suspected. Three more, plus the border patrols, under Prince Digha Bahu, whom I mistrusted. One corps with the King, but unarmed. Only three corps with Gamini. Suddenly the King's plan seemed foolish. He obviously had no suspicions about his younger son or his brother-in-law. Or was it that he was so lost in the mists of his special need to acquire merit that he had become devoid of common sense?

I made obeisance and withdrew for the night, though I continued to be full of misgivings. My greatest fear was for Gamini's safety and welfare. I paused by the river, gleaming beneath the glow of the night sky, and looked up, seeking guidance, a sign from God the Creator, God who can shape or alter events. I forced my mind to break through to comprehension of Him. He was very real to me, but I had no message from Him. I pleaded, 'Please protect Gamini from harm.' God seemed to ask, 'All these thousands of lives and you pray for one?' I bowed my head in shame and He uplifted me, saying, 'If you pray for one, you pray for all . . . the gift of prayer for others is what matters.' Then my whole being glowed with love, like the sky. I entered my tent, lay on my mat and quickly fell asleep.

I awoke with a start in the cold darkness. What had woken me up? Why was I trembling? Did I have the shaking sickness? I felt fevered, but I was not sick. The cause of my awakening was fear, mushrooming from the pit of my stomach, though I could not identify its source. It was outside me, too, gripping my throat, choking me with the damp hands of a monster without form, except for snarling yellow teeth and red-rimmed eyes larger than platters.

As I lay quaking, something else began emerging from the

347

darkness: a shaft of light, pale and gruesome as an *avatar* in a cemetery, shrinking into a hand with monstrous claws – a murderer's hand. A knife suddenly appeared, suspended. The hand slowly reached out to clutch and turn it downward at Gamini, now lying helpless beneath the gleaming blade pointed at his throat.

I tried to cry out, to warn him, but no words escaped my lips – only a meaningless gibbering.

Oh God, help him! I prayed in unbearable anguish.

How long the vision was with me, how long I prayed so desperately, I do not know, but suddenly it was gone. I lay in the darkness, drenched in sweat, stricken with horror, not knowing whether my experience had been a dream or reality.

Then reason returned, and resolve. I leaped from my bed. Gamini was in danger. I would ride back to Mahagama immediately.

I was reaching for my pantaloons when memory struck. My uncle, Prince Vipula, had stayed at his post regardless, through all those years, battling every desire of his heart. How could I desert my duty tonight?

The air rocked as I fought my battle between love and duty. Finally, duty won and the world steadied. My hands dropped to my sides. The white pantaloons trailed on grey soil. I replaced them on the settle and walked out into the moonlight.

Chapter 35

The duties of a prince regent are not very different to those of a king. While Gamini was elated by his appointment, from the very first he found himself completely enmeshed in the machinery of a monarch's schedule. Wielding power may seem romantic to most people, but it is a fearsome responsibility, especially when one is only a regent. A king is responsible exclusively to his people. As regent, Gamini discovered that he was not only responsible to the people, but also accountable to the King. How he performed his duties could shape his entire future.

Gamini found his schedule was more crowded than that of his father for three major reasons. First, many people came to him who would not have sought audience with the King, whose mind they knew well enough for the answers they needed; some even came to test the newcomer, knowing that they would have received short shrift from his father. Second, being unfamiliar with the ways of government, he could not make quick or instinctive decisions. He needed more care, thought and investigation. Indeed, his very enthusiasm for the work made him study each question more – perhaps too fully. Finally, he knew that, being inexperienced, he was taking on more than he need have.

The end of each day found him taut and frustrated. He wanted to accomplish much, but a day was never enough and there were limits to his powers. He was discovering, too, that the wheels of his father's administration moved ever so slowly. The bullocks had taken over the cart. Everything was organized to safeguard officials and uphold the administration, rather than to cater to the needs of the people and the objectives of their ruler.

Worst of all, Gamini longed for Raji and missed my constant companionship. He did not have anyone to whom he could really talk. Vasabha was his friend and had started devoting more time to him, but the Great Warrior, though a kindly person, did not have a powerful intellect.

On the first two nights after the departure of the convoy, Gamini barely slept. His thoughts raced like spinning fireworks and it was only toward dawn that he fell into heavy slumber, waking up grainy-eyed to his duties. The third night was warm as well, so he tossed and turned restlessly on his couch until midnight. Finding the darkness and confinement of the room overpowering, he slipped out of bed and donned a dark blue sarong. He needed to take a walk.

He felt his way in the dark through his study to the entrance door. The knowledge of flare-lit corridors, challenges from sentries and guards and the obligation to talk to people hit him.

He paused, hand on the doorknob. People were the last thing he needed. All day long ministers, soldiers, warriors, civil servants, spies, attendants, the public pounded at him. He wanted desperately to be alone, completely alone, with nothing but the sky above and silence around him, the silence of the blessed sounds of night.

He turned and made for the window of his study. He opened it and slipped outside. The earth was cool to his bare feet. He felt its power for the first time in his life. We are like plants and trees, he thought – the earth must give us strength. Why do we not call on it more often?

Strength from the earth and peace in the vastness of a clear, moonlit sky. Beauty in the dark silhouettes of trees, joy in the splash of the crystal waters of the fountain. Power from without, stirring up the power within. His tension began to subside. The pressure at his temples eased.

The air was more mellow outside. Somewhere a queen-of-the-night bush, the plant that bursts its blossoming heart with every moon, was in bloom. Its sweet, heady scent, relieving stale smells of earth, dung and manure, somehow reminded him of Raji. For a while, he was lost in silent communion with her; then the problems of the day began to intrude. A proposal had been made to levy a paddy tax for the propagation of the Doctrine. He resented that. People should give freely for religious work, not be taxed for it. The unrelated problem of a complaint against the district chief of

Devundara also remained unsolved. The man had forcibly abducted a *goigama* maiden. That was against custom. Even the royal family could not take such liberties with high-caste people. Chieftains in remoter areas tended to become autocratic. What the man had done was not only against custom, it was unjust. He hated injustice. It was one of the things that could flay his mind and prevent sleep. Whatever its source, it burned, throbbed, nagged frantically inside him, so his mind remained alive and bright, unable to don the blissful mask so essential for dozing away. There were times when he would remain awake, impatient for the morning, so he could start trying to right some wrong.

Stumbling over a root, he immediately became aware of his surroundings. He had walked quite a way and reached a grove beside the ladies' quarters. It was dark here. Threads of cricket-chirping were louder than in the open. Above him was a curtain of shadow from dark branches, with a glowing blue sky across which a fragment of silver moon hurried, revealing itself through tears in thick tresses of white cloud.

He froze at the sound of a cough, then looked around swiftly to locate its source. It was not a man's cough, but a woman's. No woman should be outside at this hour, unless she were a demon. His heart began to beat faster. He feared no man, but demons?

Again that slight cough, more a clearing of the throat this time, as if to attract his attention. He located its direction at the edge of the grove and moved catfooted toward it.

She stood motionless in the moonlight. The dark cloth covering her body was also draped over her head like a hood. Only her pale, gleaming face was visible, black eyes staring steadily toward him. Who but a demon would remain so still? Could she be the demon lady who stands in the moonlight and proffers a baby to unwary men, silently pleading to be relieved of her burden? The man who takes up the baby is immediately struck dead.

His heart began pounding wildly. He broke into a cold sweat. Suddenly he was breathless. Panic-stricken, he turned to flee.

Pride held him back, and some unknown resource within him. He would never fly in fear. He paused in his turning and gathered his courage. With a superhuman effort, he steadied his breathing and restored his heartbeat to normal, as he had been taught. He turned again. In a few short strides, he was on the creature and bore her to the ground. He fell on top of her, reaching for her neck. It was soft, but solid – human. He started to squeeze.

The woman gasped. A cry escaped her, turning to a croak as his grip tightened. Even in the pale light he could not miss the terror flaring from her widened eyes. She began struggling to free herself.

He recognized her for a palace servant. Relief gushed through him! 'What are you doing here?' he demanded harshly, angered that any palace woman should venture out alone at night and furious at the fear she had caused him. She did not reply, but jerked her head silently. His hands were still at her throat. He let go. She gulped air in greedily, sucking it through her mouth, her chest heaving. He let her recover her breath. The soft feel of her chest, rising and falling, began to penetrate his senses. Her breasts moved like rippling waters and her generous nostrils distended with each shuddering breath she took.

'Tell me!' he insisted, his anger waning.

'I sometimes slip out, lord, when my mind is troubled and I cannot sleep,' she whispered between gasps. 'I know I have done wrong. I beg your mercy.' She had recognized him and was terrified now.

He tried to think, but pleasure sensations began taking over. The give of her breasts and abdomen, the caressing softness of her thighs were making thrills run through his entire body. He began to get an erection. 'I can understand that,' he granted, a little breathless himself. 'I feel the same

352

way myself at times.' He was yet too young to know the needs of some women. 'That is why I was here tonight. So I cannot blame you.'

He looked down, noticing that she had tight-drawn golden skin over wide bones. He saw relief sweep the sensual face. Her eyes slowly grew deep and lustrous. As if to ease his weight upon her, she slowly rotated her hips, her lower abdomen pushing against his erection. Instantly his hardness reached bursting point. The memory of the fierce in-and-out of his movement within Sirima screamed its delight from years back. Lust slashed through him.

Suddenly, he realized that the maiden had nothing on beneath her mantle – only naked flesh. He wanted it. Not her – just her flesh smooth and tight around him.

Thoughts of Raji intruded. My love – I must be true to you. His mind reached for the determination to be chaste, but could not find it. He was powerless before his flaming need for the sensation of plunging into the flesh beneath him and moving . . . moving.

The maiden knew she had him. She was responding now with the insistent grind of drumbeats, the feather-soft pubis caressing the hardness of him. The longing to feel her firm, bare flesh gripping his erection consumed him. Lifting himself up on one hand, he tugged open his sarong. He kicked it down and away with one foot. He tore off the maiden's mantle. He gasped at the beauty of pale flesh, ripe breasts and mystic curves in white-gold moonlight. Her waist was tiny, her hips wondrously full. Her gasping breath beneath him had the fragrance of cloves. Her nostrils distended with desire. It drove him wild. The moon became obscured. He lay upon her, kissing her cheeks, blindly seeking entry. It was over soon, because he was smitten by the very power of his passion.

She was not satisfied. She moved gently to coax him to enlarge again. The feel, jarring as a nail scraping brick, jerked him back to reality. A pair of black, almond-shaped

353

eyes appeared before him, then Raji's chaste face.

He saw the moonlight again. The earth beneath his eyes and nostrils no longer held strength. It was vile and he its product. Only three days ago, he had gazed on Raji's beauty with rapture. Now he had been untrue to her.

Oh Raji, my love, what have I done?

A cry of despair escaped him. He sprang to his feet. He seized his sarong and tied it around his waist. He thought wildly of some way of paying the maiden. With one swift wrench, he plucked a gold coin from his arm-bracelet and flung it at her. She half sat, staring fearfully at him. The image burned into his mind: a woman he had taken, sitting naked on the ground, hair dishevelled, pale flesh covered with sweat, the raw smell of his emission emerging. Obscene. He hated it and loathed himself.

The coin glittered on the dark grass like some devil's payment. How could it compensate for what he had done? He turned and stumbled away. Behind him, he heard the dim rustle of leaves and a woman's quiet sobs.

By the time he reached the fountain, he had a burning desire to cleanse himself physically. He stripped and entered the pool. The water was cold. It shocked his body. He shivered, but accepted it gladly as some sort of penance. A fish nibbled gently at his foot. It jarred like those moments after ecstasy. He drew his foot away sharply and kicked to scare away the fish. He reached down for handfuls of white sand to scrub his body. He washed every part of him to erase his guilt.

With the water giving him new life, almost new birth, he lay back, accepting the coldness. Its bite revived him. He watched the silver moon sailing swiftly toward a patch of grey clouds. A dog howled. The sound was ominous. Dogs howled like that at death or destruction. Had he destroyed something?

When he arose, most of the guilt was gone. What was done was done. He would never be unfaithful again, so it had best be forgotten. His resolve cleansed him more than the water. Its strength gave him new life. Everything would be all right. The golden thread binding him to Raji was intact again.

He stepped outside the pool and dried himself with his sarong, then slipped back through the window into his study. The darkness was blinding. He allowed his eyes to get accustomed to it, pausing until he could distinguish the vague outlines of furniture before moving cautiously to his bedroom. He took a fresh sarong from the linen chest and draped it around his waist. He reached for the jar of sandalwood perfume and rubbed it on his body.

He lay on his couch again, exalted now by the clean scent of his body, his love for Raji and his resolve to be true to her. Feeling pure, he found peace and joy. He fell asleep quickly to thoughts of Raji and the future.

He did not know whether it was sound or instinct that startled him awake. Born soldier that he was, he became alert on the instant. He lay tense in the darkness, trying to identify what had aroused him. He heard a soft breath and felt a presence.

A large hand was clapped over his mouth. Sharp metal prickled his throat. 'One croak from you, Prince, and you're dead!' a hoarse voice whispered.

My feeling of intense disquiet had paused by the time we broke camp and resumed our march, well before sunrise the next morning.

Shortly after we crossed the river, the feel of the earth and the silhouettes of trees and scrub began to change. In the first grey light of dawn, the soil showed as pale sand. Frondy coconut palms had changed to circular palmyra. The distant roar of the ocean reached us with every moist, salty breeze. The two young princes with me were showing signs of weariness from the discomfort of our vehicle, now that the feeling of picnic was over. I wondered what the rest of the royal party and the remaining

355

thousands in our convoy were thinking.

Suddenly, I heard a great flapping and sharp bird cries. To the west, a flock of flamingoes had suddenly taken wing, doubtless from their night's rest on one of the great lakes. There were over a thousand of them, sailing across the pale sky in close array. Not one got in another's way. The rising sun, catching the underside of the great wings spread like white sails, tinted them a delicate shade of pink such as I had never seen before. The birds passed over us, keening and flapping, casting their shadows lengthwise on the earth. Their beauty soothed my mind.

'Don't look up with your mouth open,' a tall, spare nobleman walking beside our wagon remarked to his bearded companion. 'You might catch their droppings!'

They both laughed coarsely. At first, I felt sharp anger at the vulgarity of men, especially so-called noblemen. Then I became sad for them. How much they missed.

As we plodded on, the day gradually got warmer. Soldiers removed their tunics, hitched up their *dhotis* to make loin-cloths and marched bare-bodied, their faces and sunburned torsos dripping with sweat. Even the bullocks swung their necks from side to side in the effort of maintaining a trot. The wagoneers frequently clicked their tongues and called 'Chuk-pita-muk' to urge the animals on.

We had almost reached the place selected for our pre-noon halt when we saw the cloud to the north. It rose above a distant green hillock, soon resolving itself into a great company of cavalry riding around a fast wagon drawn by six white horses. They came thundering toward us down the trail.

I could literally feel our ten thousand warriors tense, though they were so far behind us. Only the King, riding in front, and the monks, in the wagons immediately behind, remained calm.

The oncoming troop rode on either side of our ranks like cleaving waters before a swimmer. It came to a grinding halt

356

opposite the royal wagon. The King had reined in his horse and dismounted. He stood waiting beside the wagon, a solitary white-clad figure, very much at ease.

Prince Abhaya of Soma had been riding in front of the wagon. He swung off his horse. Attendants helped his wife, the Princess Soma, down from the wagon. To my relief, both the Prince and his wife were dressed as pilgrims.

Prince Abhaya was a small, dark man, very thin and gaunt, with dull grey hair and a straggly beard. His wife was much younger than he, which was one of the reasons why he had been pleased to accept the marriage King Kakkavan had offered him five years earlier. She was a dusky woman, not unlike her brother, King Kakkavan, in appearance, but of such generous proportions that she seemed to be more round than she was tall. Her hair was long and dark. She seemed more in command than her husband.

The royal relations saluted each other gravely. I noted that neither of the visitors made obeisance to King Kakkavan. Instead of anger, the King's face bore an expression of amused tolerance. He looked at his sister with affection. 'You are more beautiful than ever,' he said. 'Your skin is that of a young girl and look at the way your hair shines!'

You tell a beautiful woman of her beauty and it leaves her unmoved. You compliment an unattractive woman and she will simper. The King lied, but the Princess took him seriously and was disarmed. She glanced at her husband and nodded, as if to reassure him. The King's palpably absurd compliment had paid off.

'We are glad you have come to offer homage to the sacred relics of Lord Buddha,' the King continued. 'You must also help us prepare and serve *dana* to the monks.'

King Kakkavan turned as if this were the most normal event in the world and walked in the direction of the glade where mats would be laid for one thousand saffron-robed monks to sit in the lotus pose for the meal Queen Vihara Devi and the ladies would prepare for them.

Prince Abhaya and his wife had not arrived with an armed escort to worship or to bestow alms. Their dress was merely a concession to form. King Kakkavan simply ignored whatever militant intentions they may have had. Prince Abhaya hesitated but a moment. He glanced once more at his wife. She shrugged her beefy shoulders. They meekly followed the King.

Chapter 36

After the initial panic, Gamini's thinking crystallized. His reasoning returned as he made quick, cold assessments of his situation. A hired murderer would have killed him immediately. Therefore this was not a murderer, but a robber or a kidnapper. Yet a robber need not have woken him up, still less thrust a hand over his mouth and a knife at his throat. Gamini was acutely conscious of the blade of that knife.

So he was dealing with a kidnapper. Who would want to kidnap him? Why tonight? Why not even an attempt during all these years? It had to do with his appointment as Prince Regent. Whom would that disturb?

King Elara, possibly – but would the Chola king have acted so fast? Possibly.

Who else? Kidnappers for a ransom? Possibly.

Any rivals? Prince Digha Bahu?

His lightning thoughts were interrupted by a tightening of the grip over his mouth and a prick of the knife at his throat. 'Sit up, Prince,' the voice directed him, quiet and low. 'But slowly . . . ve-ry slowly! One quick move and you're dead.'

The pressure over Gamini's mouth eased. The point of

the knife moved back a fraction.

Your orders are not to kill me – not here, anyhow. The thought flashed through Gamini's mind. Not unless I force you to it. He slowly placed his palms and elbows on the couch and started to rise. The knife point rose with his movement, as smoothly as the strains of a flute to the player's breath.

'Ve-ry slowly!' the voice cautioned.

Gamini moved even more slowly until he was sitting up. He had begun to sweat, but not from the heat.

'Now move your legs away from the couch . . . ve-ry slowly!'

Palms on the couch, Gamini carefully veered his legs outside the bed. The rug felt soft to his bare feet.

'Rise now, but slowly, slow-ly . . . ' Menace had entered the voice. Gamini could sense the man's increased alertness. He began to distinguish the vague outlines of a form before him.

Cautiously, Gamini stood up, his muscles straining not to move too fast. Anger at his impotence started to mingle with fear. To be caught like this! What the devil were the guards up to? He had known they were slack from years of peace. Why had he not tightened up security once he took over? The thought made him even more furious, this time at himself. Then he was fully erect, trying to breathe easily.

'Move, one step at a time . . . slowly . . . toward the door,' the quiet voice commanded.

The man began to back away, the knife point still at Gamini's throat.

Gamini had taken only three short, shuffling steps when he felt the cold steel beneath his bare left shoulder blade. A slight gasp escaped him, to be echoed by a quiet laugh behind him.

'Yes, Prince, there are two of us,' a slightly lighter voice came from the darkness. 'Now you also have a sword at your back. A prince regent must be well guarded, must he not?'

These were not common people. Their manner of speech indicated their class. Hopelessness seized Gamini. What was worse, although he had sensed that there was more than one kidnapper, he had counted on just one immediate opponent, armed only with a knife. Now there were two and one of them had a sword. A burning desire to survive made him calm again. Think, think. Think clearly and coldly. What is the first information to be sought? Relative strengths . . .

'How brave – ' he began.

The sharp prick of the sword point stopped him.

Pausing a moment, he continued. 'So many armed men against one.'

Again that low laugh from the darkness. 'Not so many, Prince. Just two. Now stop your chatter and move.'

The sword point urged Gamini forward. He walked slowly through the darkness, hope swelling within him. Two opponents – that was better than three or more. He must wait for the right opportunity, meanwhile forcing his mind to be totally clear, his body ready to respond to any command.

They reached the entrance. The man wielding the knife withdrew it. He opened the door and peered cautiously outside. He must have been satisfied, for he opened the door and passed through the gap like a wraith. Standing in the corridor and surveying it, he was revealed to be a giant. He grunted with satisfaction and turned around to signal with a jerk of his head.

A prick of the sword commanded Gamini again. He shuffled out and paused, knowing it was expected of him.

The man in front started walking on tiptoe to the connecting corridor. Gamini's mind tensed. Only the opponent at his back remained. This had to be his moment. He would not get a one-to-one chance again. He waited for the giant's signal from the connecting corridor.

'Move!' the voice behind him commanded.

In a flash Gamini knew that the one split second to catch

his opponent off guard would be the instant when he began to move.

Gamini began to step forward with his left foot. For a fraction of a second, the pressure of the sword point eased. Gamini never completed the step. Instead, he pivoted left, swift as a darting deer, his left arm swinging back to deflect the sword. His opponent lunged in a single motion. The blade streaked past Gamini, searing his skin. He continued his swing, bringing his left leg up viciously, aiming for the genitals. The sharp, forward movement of the man's thrust connected him with Gamini's knee.

A stifled croak escaped the man. His breath left his body. His sword dropped from a nerveless hand and clattered to the ground. He jerked forward in agony, clutching himself, lungs labouring.

Clenched fists together, Gamini chopped brutally down on the nape of the neck. He felt the neck bones crunch beneath his hands. The man collapsed sideways, head lolling like a broken doll's. He was obviously dead. Gamini leaped around for the sword gleaming on the walkway. Before he could pounce on it, the giant loomed ahead of him, the knife now in his left hand, a drawn sword in his right. Gamini knew he could never pick up the sword in time, but hope remained, for it was completely one-to-one now. A strange exhilaration filled him. He would use his brain for this one, too, and his brain was sharp as lightning. He shifted his gaze above the giant's shoulder and laughed quietly. It was an old trick and he did not expect the giant to be caught by it. All he wanted was that one instant when his opponent's attention would waver. Getting it, he jumped off the walkway to land lightly on gravel. He resisted a wild desire to shout for the guards. Pride forbade that.

The giant growled low. He looked downwards at Gamini. 'You have no hope, Prince. Come quietly and save your life.' His words were a blind. Before they were finished, he turned and leaped at Gamini.

Gamini stooped and seized a handful of dust. His hand continued its movement, flinging the dust.

Instinctively the man dropped his sword to clutch at his eyes.

Gamini shot forward like a sling from a shot. His hands chopped desperately on either side of the bull neck. His knee missed the groin, but smashed into the stomach. The giant doubled up, gasping. The knife spun from his hand. Gamini dived for the sword.

The giant recovered immediately, but too late. Gamini's sword point was at his stomach. He stood gasping, rage in his tormented eyes.

Gamini tensed for the thrust, yet some deeper instinct made him hesitate.

'Go on, Princeling,' the big man jeered. 'Are you afraid to kill?'

'Not so,' Gamini retorted, his voice deadly. 'I have executioners for such as you. Meanwhile, I need you alive, to talk.'

It was night outside the city of Soma. Like the *bhikkus*, no one had a night meal. Being on a pilgrimage, King Kakkavan had refused Prince Abhaya's hospitality, so the two cousins and I were seated, chatting in the King's tent.

'Siva is suspicious of your mission, brother,' Prince Abhaya advised frankly. 'And you can hardly blame him, because it could be a prelude to armed invasion. I suppose you are also aware that King Elara has moved at least six army corps to the river border?'

'Yes,' King Kakkavan replied unconcernedly.

Prince Abhaya looked at the King appraisingly. 'You have been very cunning,' he ventured admiringly.

'And you are very mistaken.' The King's voice was gentle as night dews. 'We have not been cunning, but devout.'

Prince Abhaya dropped his gaze before the King's obvious sincerity. 'What if King Elara's army crosses the border?' he inquired.

King Kakkavan remained untroubled. 'We do not blame him for moving his forces. Did we not move six corps to Dighavapi? But have no fear, cousin. Although King Elara will be pressured on all sides, he will never cross the river, unless we give him cause.'

'I fear provocation from Siva, brother. What if Siva attacks us and we are compelled to respond? The Chola would then move his troops east along the north bank of the river, ostensibly to provide protection for Siva, and no one could accuse him of aggression.'

'We have considered it all,' King Kakkavan responded quietly. 'Let the future unfold as it may. We will know soon enough.'

Again, I could not help but feel a flash of resentment at thousands of lives being committed to this single man's desire. I was not afraid to die, but somehow the pilgrimage of atonement and personal satisfaction, at such risk to others, seemed fundamentally wrong to me. Not even the knowledge that the lives of the people have to be governed by the *kharma-vipaka* of their leaders made it right.

. Our discussion petered out into religious banalities, which are more dreadful than common or garden-variety banalities. Prince Abhaya finally retired, fortified by them.

We broke camp before dawn the next morning and headed eastward in the direction of Seru, along the south bank of the river, which forked at Soma. It was at this southern end of his territory that Siva had permitted Prince Abhaya to establish a small subkingdom. We were to proceed east and slightly north, along the south bank of the southern fork of the river, and cross it at the ferry – reportedly close to the ocean – to make our way to Seru.

All day long, we slowly wended our way through an infertile land of grey sand, dry scrub, green cactus and grey-blue palmyra palms, in dry heat that fevered the body. The very stillness of the desolate countryside accented the noise of the convoy. Creaking wagons, straining wheels, an occasional 'chuk-pita!' from one of the drivers and the grunting of tired bullocks became irritating sounds. To make it worse, some of the women started chanting hymns. High-pitched voices, raised in nasal devotion, were hardly soothing under these conditions. I was glad when they gave up, oppressed by the heat.

By the time we reached the ferry, even the animals were drooping. Since it was just before dusk, we gladly made camp. A light breeze from the ocean and the approaching coolness of night were most welcome. Watch fires, golden against the soft darkness of night, the crackle of flames, a dip in the cool river and the quiet voices of people soon eased the discomforts of the day. I knew that everyone, without exception, was now glorying in having endured such discomfort in pursuit of the Doctrine. It increased the merit from the pilgrimage, but by how much, I wondered cynically. And would those who offered such penance be rewarded for their fortitude, or punished for their stupidity?

I was with King Kakkavan and Prince Abhaya in their tent, after dinner, when Velu Sumana was announced.

Even in the dim taper-light it was easy to see that the Chief Warrior was troubled. He made obeisance and came to the point as soon as he had King Kakkavan's permission to speak.

'I regret I have grave news, sire,' he said. 'Our spies report that King Elara's ten corps have taken up position along the northern bank of the river. They are strongest at Mahaiyangana and Manam, obviously for two thrusts, one direct to Mahagama, the other to Dighavapi.'

'That is no more than we thought,' King Kakkavan responded dryly. 'Do you have any unexpected news?'

'Yes, sire. King Siva has gathered his forces and is ready to massacre us on the slightest provocation.' The Chief Warrior was sweating now and his eyes were distinctly troubled. 'I am a warrior, sire. Death is my destiny. But I fear for you and for our queen.'

King Kakkavan looked up inscrutably at the Chief Warrior. 'We do not fear for ourselves either,' he finally stated mildly. 'Our fear is for everyone else. Let us not give Siva any provocation then, or any hint of it.' He turned away in dismissal.

The Chief Warrior seemed about to speak. Years of discipline prevailed, however, and he made obeisance and left.

We struck camp at dawn. On King Kakkavan's orders, the royal party, with the King riding a white horse at its head, now led the procession. 'If there is danger, let us be the first to receive it,' he said, 'and perhaps Siva will be satisfied to capture us alone.'

Behind the King was the State elephant, Kandula, gaily caparisoned, with a golden *howdah* on its back carrying the Buddha relic. Immediately to Kandula's rear, ahead of the royal wagons, I rode my grey.

Knowing a little more about King Kakkavan now, I was certain that he wanted to be in the forefront to deal personally and gently with any threat that Siva might mount.

We forded the ferry and proceeded along low ground toward the foothills less than a half mile away. The saffron stream of monks followed us across the ford, then the white-clad troops of Velu Sumana's corps began their crossing.

The enemy appeared suddenly and unexpectedly ahead of us. One moment the sky above the foothills was blue, the next it was dotted with the stark, menacing figures of bowmen, strings at the ready, with a line of spearmen behind them. Lines of foot soldiers would undoubtedly be supporting the spearmen.

King Kakkavan did not even pause. Instead, he gave his horse a slow, mincing gait.

Suddenly comprehending Siva's plan, I looked back across the river. Having obviously crossed the river higher up by night, Siva's cavalry was galloping in serried ranks towards the rear of our column.

We were encircled. Siva's ambush was complete.

Prince Tissa looked angrily at Prince Digha Bahu across his study. 'You never told me King Elara had joined in your plan.' Tissa's voice shook and his dark eyes were flashing. 'What of the safety of my parents?' He wiped the sweat on his upper lip with the back of a slender hand, rose to his feet and started excitedly toward Digha Bahu, his expression worried.

Prince Digha Bahu held up an appeasing palm. The noonday sunlight, streaming white-gold through high, grilled windows, made the jewelled rings on his pudgy fingers sparkle. 'Your parents will be quite safe,' he replied soothingly. He eased himself on the purple cushions of his carved ebony chair and loudly passed wind. 'Ah! There are few things more satisfying than a thunderous fart after a good meal!' he proclaimed comfortably. 'You should eat more roasted jak seeds. They're excellent for the purpose.' He noticed that Prince Tissa remained fearful. 'Now stop worrying. I have King Elara's word. He knows we need your royal mother for our purpose.'

'How did you receive King Elara's word?' A note of suspicion entered Prince Tissa's voice. 'You have no direct communication with him.'

'As near direct as it takes to make it direct,' Prince Digha Bahu assured him airily. 'Those are the ways of diplomacy. You are ... uh ... too young to know them.'

There was a moment's silence while Prince Tissa strove to assess this somewhat complicated assurance. 'What do you mean by that?' he demanded.

'You see, you do not even comprehend the language of diplomacy and protocol,' Prince Digha Bahu responded. He rose and walked up to place a placatory hand on Prince Tissa's shoulder. 'Leave these details to your elders. A king's job is to rule. He must leave administration to others.'

366

He squeezed Prince Tissa's shoulder. 'Have faith in me. I know what I am doing. Elara is no fool. Neither is Siva. To capture your parents is one thing; to put them to death would be stupid. No! We all have a common purpose – to force your father to abdicate and name you king of Ruhuna, with me as . . . er . . . your chief adviser. This is your one hope of succession, because your father named your brother as successor before he left on this asinine pilgrimage. He is in his dotage. He does not know what he is doing. If Gamini becomes king it will mean instant war for Ruhuna, after all these years of peace. Once you take up residence in Mahagama, your mother will be brought back to you and your father can . . . er . . . retire to a temple.'

There was a foxy gleam in Prince Digha Bahu's pale brown eyes. Prince Tissa caught it only momentarily, being too young to realize that Prince Digha Bahu's real ambition was to become king of Ruhuna himself and even to succeed King Elara when the Chola died. The boy never dreamed that he was merely a pawn in Prince Digha Bahu's game. He sighed. 'I shall certainly love the day when I no longer have to live under the shadow of the *kalu kumaraya*, that black prince!' he exclaimed impulsively. He recognized that he was motivated in part by personal ambition and jealousy of his brother, but he also had genuine concern for the peace and prosperity of the people of Ruhuna. His fears mounting again, he shook off Prince Digha Bahu's hand and began pacing the study, his sandals clip-clopping on the paved brick floor.

Prince Digha Bahu returned to his ebony chair, deliberately relaxed in it and looked at his nephew with a bland expression. 'It is essential to the plan that you co-operate,' he insisted. 'Listen!' He leaned forward, nodding so hard that his double chin bounced. 'It is too late now for you to back out anyhow.'

Pausing in his stride, Prince Tissa turned to face Prince Digha Bahu. 'Not if we act immediately,' he insisted, his youthful voice shrill. 'Your plot to kidnap my brother failed miserably. What assurance do we have of the success of this new plan?'

'It is no longer necessary to kidnap your brother,' Prince Digha Bahu declared. 'The convoy of pilgrims will have been captured by Siva when they crossed the ferry this morning. There is nothing you or I can do anymore. Elara's forces will cross the river in strength tomorrow morning and race for Mahagama, which they will certainly take, capturing your brother in the process. All you have to do is . . . nothing. You and I will remain here with our own forces until we are summoned to Mahagama. You will simply stay on then as – er . . .' He stopped abruptly and stood tense for a few moments, his pale eyes suddenly becoming hard. He then relaxed swiftly. A friendly smile lit his face. 'King Sadha Tissa of Ruhuna! How does that sound to you, sire?' he inquired pleasantly.

Neither skilful interrogation nor torture could make the kidnapper talk. He was stretched on the rack. Lighted tapers were inserted beneath his fingernails. He was locked in the stocks and abandoned to suffer for hours in the sun and rain. He was administered a water-drip treatment on his head. Still he would not talk, except to mutter insistently, 'I am a nobleman. I demand a nobleman's death.'

Gamini slowly came to admire the man for his loyalty to his principles. When he finally realized that he would learn little from him, he summoned Vasabha.

The handsome giant came to Gamini's study the same evening. Gamini invited him to sit on an ebony settle opposite his desk.

'This man's conduct proves him to be noble even if he is not a nobleman by birth,' Gamini declared. 'I command that he be publicly executed tomorrow at the noon hour when the sun will not cast the shadow of his head. You will be personally responsible for the arrangements. You may use the arena. His request to be treated as a nobleman is granted. He will therefore not be hanged, but beheaded. His limbs will not be pinioned, nor will his face be masked. He will have the red hibiscus placed upon the back of his neck, to confirm his nobility. Go now and have the event published by beat of tom-tom. I shall personally attend the execution.'

Vasabha smiled back apologetically. 'Is this wise, lord?' he inquired. 'We have not had public executions these many years. How will your royal father react?'

Gamini straightened in his chair and his jaw jutted out. 'I am Regent, with the power of life and death,' he asserted. 'This man attempted to take my life. If there have been no executions these many years, there have been no attempts against the royal family either. Should my royal father take exception, let him realize that the sin is not his; if he wishes restitution, let him bring the dead back to life.'

'Do not act in anger, lord,' Vasabha begged. 'Your royal father has developed a different attitude toward crime and punishment these many years. He will take it hard that you decreed a public execution while he was on pilgrimage, especially a pilgrimage of atonement for the murders his own father committed.'

Gamini's eyes flashed. 'A son may atone for the impious act of a father, but a father is not to blame for that of his son,' he declared. 'Besides, I do not recall asking for advice, Great Warrior. I gave you an order. Would you have questioned it if it had come from the King?'

'You are right, lord,' Vasabha responded. 'Pray forgive my presumptuousness – it sprang from concern. I would never have questioned any order from the King and I will not question it from you.'

Gamini smiled and rose to his feet. Vasabha rose with him. Gamini strode up to the giant and laid a hand briefly on a muscular shoulder. 'You are not only fair of face, you are fair in every way,' he said softly and paused, nodding. 'Go now and see to it.'

The terraces around the public arena were packed long before noon the next day. Women and children never attended these events, but every adult male in Mahagama and the villages around it had to be present. Many of them were decked in their brightest clothes, as for a country fair. Strangely for a people who believed in the Buddhist doctrines of *ahimsa* and *maitriya*, there was still a latent bloodlust in them. Yet they were an angry crowd, too, for word of the attempt on their young prince's life had got around, and their love and loyalty for the royal family was outraged.

Gamini saw these as good signs. They meant that the people of Ruhuna were devoted to the throne and could be moved to vengeance. Of course, it helped that their prince had, unarmed, vanquished two fully armed attackers. Loyalty feeds on admiration.

There was much conjecture as to who had hired these men. Most were convinced that the Cholas had done so and the event was retailed with suitable embellishments, such as an increase in the number of kidnappers from two to six or more. Bards and storytellers reminded everyone of the prophecies at Gamini's conception and birth. For the first time in years, there was serious talk of a thrust from Ruhuna to free the entire kingdom. None of this displeased Gamini.

Thunderous applause from the crowd greeted Gamini when he took his seat in the King's box, shortly before noon. Everyone stood up and made obeisance. Cries of 'Apé Kumaraya Jayawewa!' – 'May our prince triumph!' – rent the air.

It was a hot afternoon. A fierce sun beat down on the wooden seats from a cloudless blue sky. Its warmth shone directly on the bare torsos of the people while it bounced back at them from the sanded arena in the centre.

The manacled prisoner, clad in white pantaloons and tunic, was led in by armed guards. An angry murmur rose from the crowd. It swelled to a roar as he was moved to the centre of the arena.

The little group halted before the wooden execution block. The prisoner gazed around with a defiant, almost scornful smile. He was a brown-skinned man of middle age, with a short dark beard and long black hair, unadorned by a turban. The broad cast of his features and the flaring nostrils spoke of some Chola blood.

The executioner towered at the right of the block, a grotesque figure, his body stained black, but draped with a white loin-cloth. Sweat prickles made his skin gleam like wet granite. He had a black hood over his face, with slits for the eyes. He held a great double-edged sword in his right hand and, incongruously, a red hibiscus in his left hand.

Drums started rattling through the air, haunted by a discordant wail of pipes. The guards pushed the prisoner closer to the block, facing Gamini. Fierce cries from the crowd slashed above the music: 'Kill him!' . . . 'Tear him limb from limb!' . . . 'Rend him!' . . . 'Have his liver!' Fists were shaken, curses hurled. A doddering old man broke from his seat, tottered down the aisle and spat into the arena. 'You should lie with your own mother!' he quavered. Cheers greeted his act of bravery. He gazed toward Gamini for approval. Gamini ignored him and he returned to his seat, beaming. He doubtless planned on bragging about his exploit until his own death.

For all his distaste at such public reaction, Gamini could not help an inward smile of satisfaction. These were the same people who had worshipped so devoutly at the Tissa Maha Ramaya on Wesak night less than a month ago. They were good material for his Sinhala Buddhist army. His father's religious zeal could never convert them. He stood up and raised his hands to command attention. The pipes petered out, but the rattle of drums increased to signal the crowd. Their roar gradually subsided.

Gamini dropped his hands. The sound of the drums grew fainter and died away, leaving only a throbbing in the air. Finally, there was complete silence except for an occasional cough and the sad cawing of crows.

The sun beat fiercely on Gamini's body. He felt its intense heat and smelled stale sweat from the crowd. Is it better to die in the open sunlight? he wondered. Or is where one dies important? This prisoner, with his loyalty and his devil-may-care smile, was proving that it is how one dies that really matters. He looked at the tall figure standing alone behind the block. He seemed so aloof from the six bare-bodied guards around him, so alone that Gamini could not help but remember the events of the night of the attempted kidnapping. He, too, had been alone that night. One always faces death alone, he thought, and shivered beneath the heat.

Gamini surveyed the prisoner briefly, then glanced at the sword and the red hibiscus in the executioner's hands. He caught the flash of white teeth. Head thrown back, the prisoner was smiling at him.

'I thank you, Prince, for giving me the courtesy of dying as I was born, without a name, but still a nobleman!' the prisoner cried, his voice deep, clear and strong.

Gamini bowed in silence. He recalled what the Buddha had said: We are born alone . . . we die alone. Surely there is no courtesy in the act of being born, or of dying.

As if knowing his cue, the prisoner turned to face the executioner.

The executioner stalked solemnly up. He was much taller than his huge victim. He placed his sword against the side of the block, the red hibiscus upon it. He walked behind the prisoner, seized his black hair and bound it in a knot at the top of the head, exposing the nape of the neck. The prisoner remained motionless and at ease. The executioner moved in front of the prisoner again. He knelt down and begged forgiveness for the death he was about to bestow.

'Of course you are forgiven,' the prisoner declared in clear tones. 'But why should you seek forgiveness when you are about to confirm my nobility and open the door to my immortality?' He smiled again, as if in secret amusement. He raised disdainful eyes at the crowd, turning slowly to bring each of the public stands to his gaze. Fearless and proud, he finally faced Gamini again.

The executioner rose to his feet. He picked up the red hibiscus with his right hand and grasped the sword with his left.

The prisoner raised his head to the sky. His face suddenly became intense. His eyes closed and his whole being seemed to vibrate in the sunlight.

He finished his prayer, opened his eyes and smiled at the executioner. 'Let your blow be swift and sure,' he requested, still smiling.

He stepped up to the block and knelt down. He laid his forehead on the block.

The executioner placed the hibiscus on the exposed back of the condemned man's neck with surprising gentleness. It lay there like a small pool of blood. I have learned what it is like to kill a man, Gamini thought. It had been easy, even thrilling – but that was in the heat of a struggle. What would it be like to kill a man in cold blood – to sever his helpless neck with a single stroke? Does it take more courage, the courage only executioners possess?

Gamini had no time to seek the answers. The executioner was looking to him for the signal, eyes mysterious behind the slits of his hood. Gamini raised his hand and sat down. The seat felt hard and warm.

The executioner stepped back and gripped the hilt of his great sword with both hands. He hefted it for balance, then raised it over his right shoulder. He took a step to the left, shouting 'Dahare!' then a step to the right, shouting 'Dihiri!' He shouted 'Dah!', and the sword swept down. The stroke ended in a soggy thud. It had indeed been swift and sure.

A black head rolled on the grey sand. The crowd rose to its feet as one, screaming with joy. Red blood from the severed neck dripped down the block, then spurted. The unsupported trunk slowly toppled sideways, a solitary inanimate mass.

A breath of wind wafted a fragment of the slashed red hibiscus petals along the grey sand.

There is no dignity in death, Gamini thought, only in the manner of dying.

Chapter 37

Minutes passed while Siva's soldiers held their positions silently in the pale morning and our dismayed convoy slowly ground to a halt. The creaking of wheels subsided. The shouts of the wagoneers petered out. Finally there was absolute silence. Both groups remained stationary, as in a gigantic tableau.

After the first moments of apprehension, the inevitability of our situation made me resigned to it. What could we do? We were powerless, unless we could dig a vast hole in the ground and disappear into it, or drift with the river into the ocean. Neither was a practicable alternative.

I focused my attention on King Kakkavan. He seemed so small and helpless, hunched on his white horse. He had reined in the animal and sat staring at the hills in front of him as if seeking some inspiration. Finally he raised his face to the heavens, as if searching there instead. Never for a moment did he lose his dignity and calm.

He finally seemed to have found his answer, for he half turned to the *mahout* leading the State elephant. 'Follow us!' he quietly commanded, then swung his horse around to face the convoy. 'The rest of you remain behind.' He wheeled his horse again and imperceptibly relaxed his reins. The white steed responded immediately, moving at a slow, deliberate walk.

The *mahout* gave a soft command. Kandula stepped forward, the golden *howdah* swaying on its back. A shaft of sunlight, catching the metal of the *howdah* and the gems on the saddle cloth, made them sparkle. Like a sick reflection, there came the flash of enemy weapons on the hills.

The King continued on his way, almost a pathetic figure, yet crowned with the strange dignity of his courage. One arrow and his life would be ended. One false move and we would all be massacred.

As if totally unconcerned about his opponents, King Kakkavan clip-clopped to the gap in the hills, accompanied by the crump of the elephant's tread. Each step of his horse invested the King with greater dignity. We watched in silence until there was no sound except for the jingle of elephant bells and the hush of our breathing.

The enemy troops continued to hold their ground, doing nothing. It soon became evident that they were perplexed. In this situation, some hothead could act and hell would break loose, for our warriors would fight with bare hands if necessary. The tension in our convoy grew so great that it lay heavy and tangible on the air.

A wind sprang up and whirled circles of sand along the dusty road.

A man on horseback appeared suddenly at the gap in the hills. He was followed by a group of horsemen. This had to be King Siva of Seru and his bodyguard.

I expected King Kakkavan to pause when he reached the group and talk to Siva, but he did not. Instead, he turned around in his saddle and waved to the convoy to move forward.

After the first stunned moments, we came to life.

'Forward!' I said quietly, giving my horse its head.

Like a gigantic snake uncoiling, the entire convoy began to move forward.

One of the *bhikkus* started to chant – an inspiration. Others' voices took it up. The air resounded with sacred chanting, accompanied by the creak of wagons and the squeak of wheels.

'Saa-dhu! . . .Saa-dhu! . . . Saa . . . !'

The roar of the devout rose above the chanting. The King rode proudly on. The elephant and the relic moved proudly on. We all streamed proudly on, ignoring the speechless Siva and his bodyguard.

The soldiers on the hills looked in vain to their master for his orders. What order could he give?

King Kakkavan had scored a *dharma-vijaya* of the highest magnitude. News of it would spread like wildfire throughout Seru and would even reach Lanka. Buddhists and Hindus alike would flock to Seru to have a look at the noble king who had established moral suzerainty over the subkingdom without shedding a drop of blood.

King Kakkavan received King Siva only when the sub-king came unarmed and unattended by armed guards. Swift to assess his position, Siva offered King Kakkavan the hospitality of his rule and every assistance toward selecting and consecrating the land for the temple.

The site for the *dagoba* was selected the very next day. The foundations were dug and the relic chamber prepared.

On the night of the second full moon after Wesak, in the presence of thousands of white-clad people who had gathered to share in the merit of his work, King Kakkavan assisted the Venerable Rahula in the sacred task of enshrining the Buddha relic and its attendant treasures.

When it was done, the King retired to his tent. I accompanied him inside and we sat alone, quietly going over the day's events. Suddenly, he winced and began reaching deep inside for breath.

'What's wrong, sire?' I inquired, leaping to my feet.

'Nothing really! Just passing pain in my neck and shoulders.' He broke into a sweat. Suddenly, he clawed at his chest, his dark eyes glittering with an unspoken torture.

I helped him rise and gently led him to his couch. 'Relax,

sire,' I bade him. I laid him down on the bed. I placed my mouth on his and breathed into him to give him my breath. It was the only way I knew, from my reading and my reasoning, to help him. His body was so wet with sweat that my lips kept slipping on his mouth.

It seemed as if hours passed before his tortured breathing slowly eased. In reality it was only minutes. Finally he lay back, completely worn out, but the sweating had stopped and I could see that the pain was subsiding. During the brief spell of his seizure, what little flesh there was on his normally gaunt face seemed to have shrivelled away, leaving grey skin flaccid over hard bones.

I stood up slowly, exhausted as much from tension and anguish as from my physical efforts.

'We thank you,' the King barely whispered. 'Now listen. We have something to tell you and the time may be short.'

'Please rest now, sire,' I begged him. 'Tomorrow will do, for you will surely live.'

His tired eyes flamed intensely on mine for a moment. I soothed their fire with my gaze.

'Tell no one,' he finally commanded, half raising his head.

'My word on it, sire,' I assured him.

He nodded and lay back. 'We trust you.'

I dismissed the attendants who were waiting outside for the night, saying that the King was tired and did not want to be disturbed. I would keep vigil by his rough bed until dawn, while he slept in total exhaustion.

It was a strange night. The first part of it was filled with conflicting thoughts. Gamini's time was fast approaching. The plan I had devised for stirring the people of Ruhuna had to be perfected, yet I had no stomach for it. I felt like an utter hypocrite, to be considering such plans while looking at the drawn face of King Kakkavan as he lay in the pale, wavering light of the tapers. He was so diminutive, so vulnerable, like a weary child.

Seeing a man, especially a king, laid low in this manner started a completely new trend of thought within me. I had always believed that human beings are the product of a continuing essence. Man-made objects, such as the couch on which the King lay, have a meaning, a use, a content that is established by those who create them and pre-established by those for whom they are created. Humans, trees, animals, the creations of nature simply *are* and their meaning and content change from day to day. If one does not believe in a Creator, a Guide, where does it leave all the living, already existing substances of the world? In essence, is not creation the Creator?

I groped for the answer. Either all things are created, or they are not. If they are created, there must be a Creator, in which case the meaning and content are established by Him. If things are not created, but merely *are*, then we support a new plane of thought, beyond man's experience, but within his perception. This plane includes a state of *is* – a never-ending infinity for matter stretching out into space, a never-ceasing eternity within which matter keeps changing. In the framework of no creation, no destruction, no beginning, no end, change goes on, but only to the extent that it is perceived or experienced. The only true meaning of any entity in any phase of change, including that which takes place every second, would then be only what is relevant to that moment.

This last was a concept fraught with futility. A black depression seized me and I had to direct all my resources of mind control to overcome it. Finding that I could not succeed by myself, I stepped to the entrance of the tent, with the King now sleeping peacefully inside it, shortly after midnight, to commune with God.

All material things consist of *paramanu*, atoms, which can be subdivided into further components, *paramattas*. My own conclusion was that *paramattas* also consist of components and of further components, on and on, until we reach nothing, which we express as zero. True infinity is the beginning without end, the end without beginning. God is that infinity. He is therefore within us. God is also the figure 'one', outside us and able to make something out of nothing, the multiples that go on forever, eternity.

Eternity, infinity are time and space, both the same, for we measure time in terms of the sun in space. Yet the sun is a part of God.

Within the zero of each individual life-force is the seed containing basic life information and the events of each past life of the entity. This product identifies with others of like substance and also unconsciously recognizes them from past births, so death never really separates. Trying to escape from this chain, even to reach Buddhahood, would be attempting to escape from God.

I also discovered during my contemplation that God does not place human beings on the rack of moral order. Cause and effect flow within Him and He has no expectations of us, but permits us to live, as best we can, within the ideals we set up for ourselves. When we fail by these ideals, we suffer the consequences, but they are our own consequences, not God's. If it were not so, what hope is there for trees, insects, animals – or aboriginal peoples?

No entity has an independent existence. Therefore, no entity can have a separate, individual meaning and content, save only the entity. God, Who requires neither. Meaning and content – even responsibility – are all human concepts.

King Kakkavan's death, when it came, would result in whatever volition he gave his immortal *prana*. Although a man could thus influence his rebirth, any volition produced by God would be inevitable.

Whatever the answers and whatever the framework of my own meaning and content, I was a prince, born and bred. Whether from God, or from my own existence, I had been given a role to fulfil by my uncle and I would acquit myself honourably in fulfilling that role. That was the only important answer I received from my God-communion.

379

Even if I was being dictated to by some subtle influence of *dharma*, my path was clear.

I returned to the tent, sat down, and watched over King Kakkavan.

The King opened his eyes to the first crowing of cocks at the false dawn. It was habit with him. He still looked tired, but not as exhausted as when he had fallen asleep. 'You stayed here all night?' he inquired with a faint smile.

'Yes, sire.'

'We might have known you would.' He made as if to rise, then lay back on the cushions, still very weak and tired. 'Before we get up, let us tell you what you need to know.' His voice was half croak, half whisper.

I nodded, unable to speak because my throat had begun to hurt with sorrow for him.

'We have your permission?' A smile curved again on his face.

'Yes, sire.' I barely managed the words before my voice broke.

'Be not sad, Prince. Death comes to everyone. It is merely a change in the physical composition of man. The atom of consciousness, embodying the *prana*, goes on. You, of all people, should know this.'

I nodded dumbly. How could I tell him that the inevitability of events cannot diminish our sorrow at them?

'Listen now,' the King continued. 'We are about to speak of matters involving honour. You must be aware of the rift in our family. Its causes are not important, but they go back many years. Some of them you already know. We and Prince Gamini have become estranged from our queen in consequence. You will find a sort of alliance between the Queen, our Chief Warrior and Prince Tissa.'

Some of the words were coming out slurred and I had to lean forward to catch them. 'We fear that they might even oppose Prince Gamini's succession. He stands alone, with only you to help him. Our Chief Minister, Kirthi Siri, is a loner too. He will pull in the direction of power and influence

380

for himself. Prince Digha Bahu is not to be trusted under any circumstances. He is ambitious and greedy, for himself and for his son, Prince Panduka.' He paused, looking at me with grave eyes. 'But we are sure you are aware of all this, for you are wise beyond your years.'

I nodded again.

A look of intense sadness crossed King Kakkavan's face as he reflected. 'What we are going to tell you now is very difficult,' he finally whispered, his voice hoarse, as if emerging through muslin. 'Very difficult.' He passed a hand wearily over his face. 'The origin of our problem has been our inability to satisfy our queen's every need. We suspect that somehow Prince Gamini has realized this and it has set the seal on his own estrangement from his mother . . . and from us. It is important for you to know this, Prince, if you are to help our son. Help him . . . please.'

A shuddering sigh escaped the King's pale lips while I stared in horror at him.

'Go now!' King Kakkavan commanded. 'The shame is more than we can bear.' He turned his face to the tent wall.

I stumbled into the darkness outside.

Chapter 38

Prince Gamini faced his father almost defiantly, head held high, dark eyes flashing. We were alone with the King in his study at the Mahagama palace the morning after the return of the convoy from the pilgrimage. During all that time, I had not been able to make an opportunity to be alone with the Queen or with Leela, because they were always surrounded by people, but our understanding of each other continued in a look, a glance, the feel of the aura.

King Kakkavan looked more normal today. His face had regained some fullness and its dark colour. His body looked less frail. His attitude had changed subtly since our return from Soma and Seru. I would have said of anyone else that his successes in those two subkingdoms had gone to his head, for he now seemed permeated by an undercurrent of spiritual arrogance.

'Violence has no place in a *Dhamma-dwipaya*, a kingdom dedicated to the Doctrine,' King Kakkavan asserted with a passion rare for him. 'Executions are cruel and inhuman punishment, while public executions can only be called barbaric. We expected that you would rule this kingdom in our absence as we ourselves would have done, not according to your own foolish dictates.'

'I assumed, sire, that you would indeed have meted out our traditional punishment to anyone who attempted to take the life of the ruler,' Gamini replied animatedly. 'How else can we ensure stable government?'

'Your life is that precious?'

'Yes, sire, most definitely.'

'Then you should have venerated the life of this other.'

'He was a kidnapper. My life happened to be that of the ruler of Ruhuna at the time.'

'A ruler must be wise to live, else he is better dead. Wisdom returns good for evil.'

'Good often derives only from fitting punishment.'

'And what have you achieved by your gruesome act? Nothing, except to make others who might wish to harm you take greater care, which will only cause discovery of them to become more difficult. Besides, if you had dealt mercifully with this man, you might have won him over to confide in you and thus discovered the origin of the plot. Then you would not only have the conspirators, but the cause of their dissatisfaction, so you could remedy it.'

'Do you really believe that, sire?' There was incredulity in Gamini's voice.

'Most certainly! And we have given the proof of it these past two months.'

'Neither my uncle, Prince Abhaya, nor King Siva sneaked up on you like a thief in the night, sire.'

'Ha! Not only Siva, but his entire army sneaked up on us. And we bent them all to our way by moral force alone.'

Gamini was about to erupt, but to my amazement he held back. He had indeed learned much these past two months, especially of restraint. His face, however, became set in hard lines. 'Sire, are you seriously stating that we can unify the whole of our island kingdom by moral and religious force?' he inquired quietly.

'Yes. Having brought the entire south and east under our suzerainty through the virtuous actions of the inner sight, we shall proceed to expand these boundaries. You are mistaken to think that the Doctrine can be established by force of arms. Why, such action is abhorrent to its very spirit.'

Gamini shifted and stood evenly on both feet, hands clasped behind his back. I felt for him, but I was also anxious lest he pushed the King too far. 'Sire, I was mistaken in not realizing that you expected me to repay the man who attempted to take the life of your son, the Regent of Ruhuna, with loving kindness,' he replied with surprising gentleness. 'I cannot give this man back his life, but you may have my life in exchange should you desire it.' The last words came out with veiled contempt.

The weeks of ruling had matured Gamini. Although he had been given reason by the King to be hurt and bitter, he remained resolute and dignified. I felt proud of him. I noticed that his face had lost some of its youthful softness, so he looked more rugged now. He had laboured night and day, I knew, to keep the kingdom going in King Kakkavan's absence, and this criticism at his first meeting with the King was a poor reward.

King Kakkavan flushed beneath his dark skin. Pushing back his high chair, he rose to his feet and stood, arms akimbo. 'Taking your life would only splatter more blood on our hands,' he declared. 'You set too much store by life and death, Prince. All things are transient. You should spend more time preparing for a better rebirth.'

'Sire, I have a destiny to fulfil in this life for the Sinhala people. My rebirth must take second place to it.'

'War!' The King's voice was sharp. 'Do you mean to go to war?'

'If need be, sire.' Gamini was deadly quiet. 'I do not believe that we can achieve suzerainty over Lanka by any other means than force of arms. King Elara himself would cut down any group, armed or unarmed, that invaded his kingdom. And why not, sire? For, whatever your method, whether it be the Doctrine, moral force, or physical force, if you entered Lanka you would do so as an aggressor.'

'Silence!' King Kakkavan thundered, moving forwards from behind his desk. His pointing finger trembled. 'We will have no more of this talk, Prince. Never dare to question the basis of our policies. You may do as you see fit after we are gone, but while we reign you will live by our principles.'

Father and son crossed glances more deadly than swords. The King recovered himself abruptly. 'We have decided that you are of an age to have your own establishment,' he declared more quietly. 'You will set it up at our Mahaiyangana fort, from whence you will administer the northern district. You will take over the border there from Prince Digha Bahu, who will continue in charge of our eastern forces. Four of our ten corps – those of Vasabha, Bharana, Phussa and Gotha – will be under your command, but only for defensive action. Remember, we are the commander-in-chief. This is a matter of trust.'

He looked pointedly at Gamini. 'Do we have your word?'

Conflicting thoughts whirling in his mind were for once reflected in Gamini's face. The King had offered him an important post, doubtless in silent tribute to the way he had functioned overall as Prince Regent, yet there were strings attached to the honour. Should he give his promise? His rebellious nature resisted, but prudence dictated that nothing would be lost by giving it. 'I thank you for the honour, sire.' He looked directly at the King. 'And you have my promise.'

The King nodded, obviously pleased, then turned to me. 'Prince Rodana will, of course, accompany you. Prince Tissa will return to Mahagama from Dighavapi.'

I bowed in acknowledgement, but the truth of King Kakkavan's motives hit me. He had told me of his designs on Mahaiyangana. It was said to have been visited by Lord Buddha, but it never had had a temple of any size because it had always been a strategic outpost between the Cholas and Ruhuna. Gamini was not being sent to Mahaiyangana for war, but to ensure that King Kakkavan could acquire the supreme merit of building a *dagoba* there. Once again, Gamini was therefore to be a tool for the fulfilment of his father's *khatma*. Before God, my God, this had to be wrong, for once again people, even the Doctrine, were to be manoeuvred for the spiritual ambition of one man.

After he established the *dagoba* in Mahaiyangana, King Kakkavan would surely cross the border on his mission into Lanka. Either war would result, or the crafty King Elara would let him roam the land unmolested and return to Mahagama with no more suzerainty than when he started.

'You may make arrangements today and leave tomorrow.' The King waved his hand in dismissal.

Gamini and I made obeisance and left. My one thought was that, while I was at Mahaiyangana, I could more easily lay the groundwork for my plan to move the people of Ruhuna to respond to Gamini's battle cry some day.

'My father lives in a dream world,' Gamini said grimly as the study door closed behind us. 'I shall bring reality to it.'

A single knock sounded on Gamini's bedroom window. He blew out the tapers and opened the window. The legs of the maiden showed white as she sat on the sill and swivelled gracefully into the room.

After the night when Gamini had first taken her, he had made discreet contact with her and she frequently visited his room in secret. He could have had her openly, as a concubine, but continuing distaste for this call of the flesh and a desire to protect Raji from the knowledge had made him take the course of secrecy.

She had been gentle and understanding with him, this maiden of lowly estate, and under her care he was learning to give as well as receive, besides acquiring control over his responses.

A part of Gamini lusted for the maiden, but only for the stimulation, the sensations and the physical fulfilment she brought him. He had discovered that sexual intercourse somehow relieved those tensions within him brought by the responsibilities and cares of the day. The rest of him, however, hated her and himself. Each time he lay with her, he bathed in the pool outside his window to cleanse himself of his infidelity to Raji, resolving never to touch the maiden again. Each time, he was fired with exaltation at his resolve. The bath soon became almost a ritual act of purification, enabling him to commit the deed without conscience. He was reaching a stage when even his conscience was becoming numb.

She stood before him momentarily in the darkness, then slipped off her clothes, revealing her pale flesh. He reached for her in silence, his body thrilling, his mind closed to all else.

When it was over, he lay apart from her, repelled as always by her sweat-strewn nakedness and the mingling smells of his manhood and her womanhood.

She knew this revulsion in him and accepted it with gentle submission. Somehow, she always seemed content to give him what he wanted, receiving his lust alone and nothing else. Tonight, perhaps because he faced a new life up north and might never see her again, he realized for the first time that she found quiet joy in the act of giving. Her generosity opened a new dimension of thought to him and made him consider her feelings. She must care for him. The knowledge so touched him that a surge of pity for her swept through him. 'I leave tomorrow for Mahaiyangana, where I shall live for the present,' he murmured. 'This may be our last night together.'

A cry escaped her in the darkness, quickly stifled, but her breathing became heavier. He reached out to touch her face. It was wet with tears. Physical tenderness such as he had never known before engulfed him. 'You may stay here tonight,' he whispered. 'Sleep on my mantle and leave before the false dawn.'

Whether it was his eyes moving sideways in the darkness, or his spirit opening at last to her reactions that told him, he knew that she was almost shattered with gratitude. Suddenly, unusual for him, he was humbled by it. 'You have been good to me,' he continued gruffly. 'Giving everything and asking nothing. Someday I shall reward you.'

'My lord, you have already rewarded me,' she whispered brokenly. 'Giving me, a slave, even the tiniest part of you has made me rich. Now, when I thought I could have no more, you are giving me something beyond measure. I shall wear it on my heart like a precious jewel, all my life. How sorry I am to be barren and unable to bear your child to remind me of you.'

She moved out of the bed. Laying Gamini's mantle on the floor, she curled up on it, covering her body with her own cloth.

Patches of night sky glowed through the open window. The scent of wild jasmine intruded. Somewhere a dog barked and others took up the cry in a distant, frenzied chorus.

Chapter 39

Anger began to seethe within Gamini the very first time he saw Chola troops parading in strength on the opposite riverbank. It began to boil when he visited other Sinhala forts to the east of Mahaiyangana, as ruler of the district and commander of its military forces, and found the same situation all along the border. It was something he had been able to endure while he was at Mahagama and only imagined it. Here, the Chola presence was literally thrust before him all the time. Chola voices, speaking the harsher Chola language, were carried on Sinhala air. The odours of Chola cooking and the sound of Chola singing and music, so foreign to a Sinhala bred in Ruhuna, drifted across the waters of a mighty Sinhala river. Chola soldiers in Chola uniforms carried Chola weapons on Sinhala soil, sacred to him as to no other. The daily reminder was too much. Shame burned deep within him.

Gamini now had firsthand evidence of the combat readiness and support systems of the Ruhuna army. Also, his troops soon came to adore him, giving the impression that they would follow him even to a Hindu hell.

At the end of the third month of our stay in Mahaiyangana, Gamini requested permission from King Kakkavan to cross the river and invade Lanka. The King naturally refused. One month later Gamini requested permission again and received a much firmer denial.

Two weeks later, while awaiting a reply to his third request to the King, we had a formal inspection of our men on the small *maidan* fronting the fort. Across the river, in the golden light of morning, Cholas leaned casually on their spears, watching as they had done once a week for many years.

Suddenly a guttural Chola voice, speaking heavily accented Sinhala, drifted across the broad, muddy waters. 'Hey, puppeteer prince, do you enjoy playing with your toy soldiers?'

These words were just part of the good-humoured badinage exchanged across the border by opposing forces bored with merely facing each other. To Gamini, however, it was a deadly insult. He turned to look at its source, the blood rushing to his face. His fists clenched. In seconds he got hold of himself, yet his controlled rage was more deadly than any outburst. Quietly, steadily, he looked across the river. His face was serene when he finally turned to face his men again. Perhaps he was certain that he would be crossing the river one day, playing with real lives. He continued his inspection without comment, but I could not escape the fleeting thought that cataclysmic events sometimes result from such small incidents.

We were back in Gamini's quarters in the fort that same afternoon when the King's reply arrived.

Gamini dismissed the messenger and quickly opened the *ola* scroll. Giving me a sidelong glance to ensure my attention, he read the King's message aloud:

> 'The Chola army consists of a superb Chief Warrior, twenty Champions and two *lakhs* – two hundred thousand well-trained men. Under no circumstances will you cross the river and attack them. The region to this side of the river is sufficient for our people. Our only unification with the Sinhala of Lanka will be through the Doctrine.'

Gamini flung the *ola* on the ground and began stamping on it in disgust. I had seldom seen him so possessed. As I watched him now, I was suddenly afraid.

Sweat pouring down his bare torso, Gamini left the remnants of the *ola* and started pacing the hard, granite floor

389

of the chamber, muttering under his breath, restless as a caged panther.

To what extent he was moved purely by a selfish desire for glory, conquest and domination, even I will never know. Such motivations are often locked within a man's *prana*. It is part of a secret area, some region unknown even to the individual, that makes it possible for each of us to believe that we are indeed the products of our own idealism.

Upon the first refusal from the King, Gamini had begun to question his father's courage again. The second rejection convinced him that his father was indeed a physical coward. To him, although I did not know it at the time, this was evidence that he could not have sprung from his father's seed. It shamed him, not because the cowardice of King Kakkavan, the person, rubbed off on him, but because it was a reminder of his bastardy.

What Gamini had not grasped was that the army and the people had no cause to go to war. I was judiciously setting the stage for the incidents that could supply this deficiency, but I did not dare tell Gamini of my plans and therefore could not use them as an added argument for my counsel of restraint. His display of anger and frustration at today's third refusal made me thankful that the King's messenger had already been dismissed and I was alone with him.

Suddenly he stopped and faced me. A savage laugh rippled out of him, baring white teeth. He clapped his hand to his thigh in glee. He was about to speak, but restrained himself.

'What is it, Prince?' I inquired anxiously.

The laughter in his eyes compressed to the glint of a smile. 'Nothing that need bother you,' he replied. But he began shaking again, this time with suppressed laughter, and it was not good-humoured.

'I know you too well,' I interposed. 'You are planning some devil's work.'

'On the contrary, I have decided to accept my father's

order with humility. I shall send him a small present in token of my submission.'

'Your newfound humility ill suits you,' I retorted. 'What present are you talking of? Why is a present necessary?'

'Is it not customary to pay tribute to kings?'

'I know you . . .'

'Now you are repeating yourself and you have always told me that repetition, being monotony, is the ultimate sin!' He grinned, came up to me and clapped me on the shoulder. 'You worry too much. To show you my sincerity, I shall have you personally take my tribute to the King. How about that?' He was enjoying my discomfiture. 'Go get yourself an escort and make ready to leave within the hour. Meanwhile, summon attendants to bring me a casket this size' – he indicated a medium-size square with his palms – 'complete with a key and packing materials.'

I looked at him apprehensively. Humility and he were indeed strange companions. He avoided my look. Still in great good humour though, he propelled me to the door.

As I walked toward my quarters, I heard him shout for an attendant and then the peal of his laughter.

King Kakkavan elected to receive me the same night I arrived. Perhaps he thought Gamini's message was important, since I was the messenger. He was seated at his desk in his study when I walked in, followed by an attendant carrying the box. The King motioned to the attendant to leave the box on the desk. The man did so, made obeisance and withdrew. The King glanced triumphantly at Kirthi Siri, the Chief Minister, standing beside him like a moulted parrot. They had obviously been discussing my mission and the box seemed proof of Gamini's submission.

The windows of the study were shut, making the room close and warm. We were all sweating. Knowing that I was smelling especially high from my long ride, I was grateful for the smell of sandalwood incense that hung heavily on the air, yellow with taper-light that wavered on black ebony furniture and danced on the golden statue of the Buddha.

With the King's permission, I proffered Gamini's *ola* to him, right hand extended, left hand on my elbow.

The King smiled, his dark eyes alight with pleasure. 'So our son seeks now to woo us with presents,' he declared, fingering the *ola* and looking at the box before him. 'Well, he is learning civilized habits, thanks to you, Prince Rodana. Do you realize that this is the first gift he has given us?' He chuckled, looking at me. 'You have done your job well. We shall open the box first, then read his message.'

He placed the *ola* on his desk and raised the hasp of the box. He opened the lid and gazed at the contents. A puzzled frown appeared on his forehead. 'What is this – a red silken sarong for us?' He picked up the garment with long, delicate fingers and turned it to the light.

For a moment I did not comprehend what he was holding. Simultaneously with the sharp indrawing of his breath and an exclamation from Kirthi Siri, the horrible truth struck me.

The King's hands shook, making the red silk shimmer in the light. The garment dropped from his hands to the floor. He reached inside the box feverishly. I heard the jingle of metal.

'Ornaments!' King Kakkavan exclaimed, holding them up, then dropping them. 'A woman's skirt and ornaments.' Comprehension dawned in his dark eyes, bringing with it grief and horror.

As a drowning man grasps a floating bamboo, the King accepted the *ola* scroll and opened it. The words Gamini had inscribed came out of him in a hoarse whisper, almost by compulsion:

> 'Three times have I begged you to permit me to lead
> our forces across the river to restore Sinhala
> sovereignty to all Lanka. The first two times your

refusal was based upon the Doctrine. This final time, however, you warn of the strength of the Cholas and declare that our own lands should be sufficient. The entire island belongs to the Sinhala and nothing short of it can satisfy our people. One Sinhala warrior, fighting for his motherland, is the equal of ten Cholas. No Sinhala man need fear their might. I therefore send you clothing more suited to your disposition.'

The scroll dropped from the King's nerveless fingers to the floor. Its flutter disturbed the unreal stillness. Face ashen, eyes wide in their sockets, the King was a stricken man, yet his hard breathing came from fury, grief and shame. I glanced furtively at Kirthi. His eyes were closed. He was carved, immobile, waiting for the outburst to engulf us both.

'Dhusta! Accursed Gamini!' the King hissed. 'To dishonour a parent thus makes you thrice accursed. Dhusta Gamini! So you shall be known forever.'

Then his rage broke loose. His eyes flamed at me. 'You are responsible for this,' he roared. 'You with your stupid philosophies! This is the product of your teaching!' He paused, wiping spittle from the side of his mouth with a cloth. 'Did you know what you bore as the Prince's gift to us?'

His flaming eyes demanded a reply. 'No, sire,' I assured him. I tried outwardly to keep calm, but was recoiling within. I had never known the King to raise his voice before, nor dreamed that such a small man could shout so loudly. I decided to be as silent as possible. Holding my head high, I looked at a point above the King, showing him I was ready to accept any punishment with dignity.

The King paused. Years of experience in leadership and rule came through. His recovery was almost miraculous. 'We decree a fitting punishment for you both,' he said, his smile more chilling than his fury. 'You, Prince Rodana, shall go back to Mahaiyangana as our representative and place this playful Prince Gamini under arrest. You shall bind him in chains and drag him behind your horse from Mahaiyangana to Mahagama, like the pig he is, tied for the slaughter.'

I could think of no more dreadful punishment than that which the furious king decreed. It would hurt me even more than it would Gamini. I could never do such a shameful thing to him, and the King knew it. I mustered what courage I could, though I was hard put to stop shaking. 'You may inflict death, or any punishment you may decree on me, sire,' I replied quietly, 'but I regret I cannot execute your order.'

The King pounded his desk and sprang to his feet. 'You defy us?' He roared the question.

'No, sire! You are aware of my total submission to you as my king and as a person – but the punishment you decree is neither civilized nor worthy.' I nearly added, 'Either of your position as a king or your dignity as a man,' but held back in time, knowing he would take any adverse reference to his manhood poorly tonight.

'Oh-ho!' The King pushed back his chair. Clasping his hands behind his back, he moved from his desk and began to pace the floor, shooting sidelong glances at me from under his eyelids. He finally stopped and looked squarely at me. An evil chuckle escaped him, reminding me of Gamini's not twenty-four hours earlier. 'We shall give you one day to reconsider, Prince Rodana,' he grated. There was no smile on his face now. 'During this period, our Chief Minister shall have fetters fashioned of gold. You shall bear them to the commander of our fort at Mahaiyangana. Meanwhile, we shall have Prince Tissa, Prince Digha Bahu and Prince Panduka attend the fort to bring both you and the noble Prince Gamini back, appropriately manacled with gold instead of iron fetters. . . . Would not gold chains make our punishment more civilized and worthy?'

My stomach quailed at the thought of Gamini being delivered to the hands of his two enemies, his brother and Prince Digha Bahu. I was rooted to the spot, unable even to intercede.

'Go now, both of you!' the King commanded, pointing to the door.

Kirthi Siri and I made obeisance and left. As the attendants closed the door behind us, I thought I heard a strangled sob from the study. I may have been mistaken.

I went to my quarters with my head in a whirl. While I was concerned for Gamini and indeed for my own safety, the worst of my feelings were those of betrayal. Gamini had let me down to suit his own ends. There was no escaping the fact, or the hurt it engendered in me.

I stood before my window. I loved him. I had to support him.

I struggled with myself as seldom before. I called on my uncle's strength to help me. The minutes went by, but I simply could not set aside my selfish hurt.

Suddenly, the scent of sandalwood was wafted to me across the still night air. Where it came from, I do not know. There were no sandalwood trees in the garden outside, and the tiny box of sandalwood scent I once had kept to remind me of Prince Vipula had been emptied before I entered the temple. I knew then that my uncle was indeed with me, trying with his continuing life-force to help me.

'For me!' his deep, strong voice said.

'For you, uncle,' I whispered back and my battle was won. I then knew what to do. I had to ride.

I bathed, dined and walked out of my quarters as if it were the most natural thing in the world. I had a groom bring me a fresh horse.

I kept praying during my ride that the King would not discover my absence before daybreak. Every minute I made might be the means of saving my hothead prince, so I pushed on hard, though my seat was already sore from my ride into the city. Only when I found myself dozing in the saddle, nearly falling off, did I dismount at a deserted *ambalam*. After watering my horse, I slept for two hours before I was off again.

I could barely sit up in the saddle by the time I reached the fort at dusk. Seeing the glow of lights in the window apertures and the dark shadows of sentries patrolling the ramparts revived me somewhat.

For once, I was impatient of the guards' challenges at the entrance. They recognized me immediately, however, and opened the gates to me. I rode into the courtyard, stopped at the open entrance doors of the building and slid off the horse. I patted his heaving flanks and tossed the reins to a groom who raced up. I walked erect to the square of light, propelling my aching legs stiffly, with a great effort. Gamini was alone in his dining room, finishing his dinner. He looked up in surprise as I entered unannounced. His face seemed tight-drawn in the flare-light.

'You back already?' he inquired. He noted the expression on my face, took in my two-day growth of beard and my dusty, dishevelled appearance. His expression softened. He stood up, indicating a seat at the dining table. 'You are bone weary,' he said quietly. 'Sit down and have some food.'

The boiled rice with fish and vegetable curries smelled delicious to me, but I would have exchanged it all for a soft bed. 'Thank you,' I acknowledged and sat down gingerly on the hard settle, the corns and blisters from my ride protesting. 'We must talk alone.'

'After you have eaten,' he insisted firmly.

It was typical of Gamini that he only maintained a flow of casual conversation while I ate.

In spite of my fears, being famished, I ate with gusto. Finally replete, I pushed back my settle and stretched my legs. 'Ah! That's better,' I said, but the blisters hurt.

Gamini waited until the attendants cleared the dinner things and left, closing the doors of the room behind them. 'Now tell me your story,' he directed. He placed his elbows on the table, crossed his hands and leaned expectantly toward me.

I told him, without mincing words. He listened, expressionless save for a tightening of the mouth.

'So I fled before your father placed a guard on me,' I concluded. 'I rode through the night and today to warn you.'

'Hmm. Thank you.' He paused. 'What would you have me to do?' The eyes he turned on me still revealed nothing.

'I thought about that during the ride. You and I must escape to Malaya before your father's men come to seize you.'

'And run for the rest of our lives.' He sat up straight, dark eyes flashing. 'Never!'

The determination in his voice sent a shiver through me.

'What would *you* do?' I inquired passionately.

'Fight.'

I was thunderstruck. 'Fight the King?'

'Yes. You know our troops are solidly behind me.'

'That would be treason. And they may hesitate to support you, though they would follow you to invade Lanka.'

'The King's cowardice is treason.'

'Dear *devas*, are you mad?'

'I have always been sane.'

'Would you seriously consider splitting the people of Ruhuna? Why, that would defeat your own purposes. You would create a divided, bitter nation, ripe for the plucking by King Elara.'

'There will be no civil war,' he asserted confidently. 'The entire army will support me.'

I was too tired to argue. Besides, Gamini could never be convinced by argument. He was riding the wings of his destiny. Nothing could stop him. Suddenly, I felt helpless as a gull swept by a tempest – but only for a moment. From the depths of my despair, inspiration flashed. 'Listen,' I bade. 'I am going to divulge something to you that I have promised not to reveal.'

Gamini's face jerked toward mine. He said nothing, but he suddenly had that intense, watchful look.

'Your father does not have long to live.' I recounted the events of that night in Seru when his father had the attack. 'One more such spell and he is dead. You will then be king without a struggle,' I ended with studied callousness.

'He may live much longer,' Gamini commented with spontaneous callousness.

'Not at the pace he is keeping,' I assured him.

He looked at me intently, trying to probe my very *prana*.

I held his gaze firmly, then slipped the second wedge of my thinking into his mind. 'You and I can leave immediately and ride through the night to Kotmale, where your Raji awaits you.' I had initially considered Kelaniya, but decided to appeal to his heart as well as to his head. 'No one will dream we have gone to Kotmale, and it is so remote in the hill country that word will never filter back to Ruhuna. We will only inform Vasabha, swearing him to secrecy. When the time is right, Vasabha can tell the ministers and they will send for you to be consecrated king.'

Feeling came back into Gamini's eyes like lake water sweeping into channels. His whole being glowed and I knew I had won. 'When can we leave?' he inquired with typical decisiveness.

'Immediately.'

'You are tired. You should rest awhile.'

'I would rather rest on the way than in prison!'

He smiled wryly. 'What excuse can we give for leaving at night?'

Inspiration began spitting in me like salt in a fire. 'We will say that I have ridden with important news from Mahagama about a secret meeting with King Elara's emissaries at the Kasa ferry. You and I are to attend alone. Everyone will see

398

us leave in that direction. We will double back and head toward the hill country, thus throwing pursuers off our tracks as well.'

'Will it not be strange for us to leave without escorts?'

'It is a secret meeting. That is why I, too, arrived without an escort. The Kasa ferry is far enough off for us to take food along with us for the journey.'

'Blankets, too. It gets cold in the hills. Do you know the way?'

'I have never been there, but I have enough information to enable us to find our way until we can get to where it would be safe to ask for directions. I questioned Raji's father very closely for other reasons!'

Gamini looked at me with a strange light in his eyes. He reached out to touch my shoulder. 'I have got you into a mess,' he declared. 'I am sorry. But I cannot say I regret having you as a companion.'

Tired though I was, I warmed to him and placed a hand on his.

I felt no regret at my cunning. I was working for Gamini's good and therefore for that of the whole kingdom. I could not, however, protect Gamini against the consequences of history. Long after his exploits erased his shameful act toward his father, later generations would continue to call him Dhusta Gamini.

Chapter 40

The Great Warrior, Vasabha, listened grimly to our story in Gamini's study. 'Can I not come with you?' he finally inquired.

'No! You must remain behind to bring word to us if we are ever needed,' I replied.

Within the hour, we were riding back south through silvery moon-light along the Ruhuna bank of the Mahaveli River, a flat region of woods and long, tree-sprinkled meadows. We kept our eyes open for the King's men. This was the one part of the journey where we might meet them coming northward to take us. Even though we rode through two villages, however, we reached the ford across the first of the tributaries, south of where the Mahaveli bends westward toward its sources, without meeting a soul. We felt easier after we made the crossing.

We were in the foothills of the mountain ranges now. The way gradually became steeper and more wooded. We proceeded a few miles in silence. Noticing me droop in the saddle, Gamini suggested that we stop in order to allow me some sleep. Exhausted as I was, I refused. We needed to put as much distance as possible between us and the main highway between Mahagama and Mahaiyangana. So, guided by the stars, we kept on angling west. In a way, I was glad to be so tired. It made me incapable of conscious thought and I did not have to face up to the cataclysmic change in Gamini's life and mine.

We forded another tributary of the great river. When I heard the roar of a waterfall, I knew we were on the right route. Soon we could distinguish the silvery cascade. We then skirted up the hill, in the shadow of tall trees, to cross a third tributary at an easy point above the Uma waterfall. We rode down to the valley again and threaded west through moonlit parkland toward the central hills.

The moon was beginning to set and a dark hush settled on the earth. We watered our horses at a gurgling stream and bedded down for the night in an outcrop of rock beneath a giant *beli* tree. We had not passed any habitation, for we had ridden through barren land and jungle on this side of the river. Only idiots like us would travel it at night.

It was too dark for me to see whether the *beli*-tree bore its hard-shelled fruit, a remedy for stomach problems, because its rough pulp binds and the shiny liquid in the seeded pips loosens the bowels. I thought somewhat wryly that Gamini and I needed a more drastic remedy for our present problems!

Although Gamini seemed calm during our ride, I knew he was agonizing over the turn of events. Even at this early age, however, he had the ability to hold steadfastly to a decision and I sensed no diminution of his purpose.

I laid my head on the ground. Gamini was staring thoughtfully at the overcast sky as I pulled the blanket over me to ward off mosquitoes. That was my last conscious moment. I knew nothing more until sunlight hit my face and I woke up to find Gamini, ready to resume our flight, standing above me.

The rest of the journey to Kotmale was uneventful. We kept climbing toward the mountains all the time. We rode slowly by day, making for *ambalams* where we could sleep the night. We were two travellers going on a visit to relatives in the hill country. We met no one who could tell our quality from our fine horses.

The more populated parts of Ruhuna are the vast flat lands along the southeastern, southern and southwestern coast of the island, right up to the *Kalu-ganga*, the black river. The foothills lie to the west and north, inland of the *Mahaveli-ganga*, the great sand river. They rise upward to the central mountain massif. On the other side of these great mountain ranges, many days' journey away, would be Anu to their north and Kelaniya to their west.

We first rode over bare hills, covered with clumps of sharp-scented, blue-green *patana* grass. The wooded ravines and re-entrants were furred by stocky trees, the leaves a dark, shiny green, the dry, grey bark split, the sparse flowers red. Here we only heard the sound of the wind, sweeping the grasses or rustling in the branches. All the villages we passed

401

were in the valleys below our path. Their paddy fields were carpets of light green and generally straddled a silver stream. Grey thatched rooftops, mud walls and dark orchards were patterned up the slopes, ending in the undulating line of the grass, which was scattered with the black, brown or white splotches of peacefully feeding village cattle. The 'hoo-oo-ooo!' of a hill countryman's call, a woman's impatient scolding, the laughter of children would rise on the wings of smoke curling from cottages, cutting through the smells of dry grass and heat-swept earth to bear us back to the world of human beings. We were glad our route passed along the upper reaches of the hills, however, for we wished to avoid people.

'We are only getting a bird's view of the rest of our country,' Gamini complained as we passed a village I knew had to be Udugama.

'I'll settle for that,' I retorted dryly. 'You can visit your people once we have atoned for your sins!'

'Hah!' he exclaimed, glaring at me. 'You are worse than a nagging woman. And spare me your wit.'

'If I did, you would only have the nagging.'

We rode on in silence, but I knew he was muttering to himself, half angry, half amused.

We were in the mountains long before we arrived at Ratna, the region of gems. The entire countryside was now different. Tall trees and pleasant villages abounded, in lush valleys and meadows. The cottages were neat and whitewashed; many of them had roofs of the red, half-round country tile. Elephants would drag timber down from the mountains, to be sawn in open-air mills adjoining great storage areas roofed with thatch. Rafts of timber strapped together were guided down the broad, muddy river by bare-bodied men with dark, leathery skins. The air was cool and often filled with human voices, rasping saws, birdsongs and pounding mortars and pestles. In the afternoon, throbbing sounds of the *rabana* would sometimes reach us, from women

402

sitting around the circular drum, its skin warmed by glowing coals beneath, tapping away with their hands, their heads tilted to one side to hear better. This was their interval of leisure between working in the fields and preparing the evening meal. 'Pith-thala botthang . . . pan paddikkang!' a drum would seem to say. 'Pith-thala botthang . . . pan paddikkang,' a neighbouring drum would reply. There was always competition for increasingly complex rhythms and beats.

In Ratna, we saw for the first time the unexpected sight of gem pits sunk in paddy fields. Somehow both Gamini and I had always imagined that gems came from the earth and the rivers in some romantic manner, like the emerald supposed to emerge from the hood of the cobra, which guards collections of hidden treasures.

We stopped at one of these pits and, to our surprise, found it to be no more than a hole in the ground, with grey mud piled up to disfigure the green stretch of paddy. Brown-skinned men, their muscles lean and hard, clad only in loin-cloths, descended the pits on a rope ladder. Buckets hanging from ropes, supported by pulleys on winches, were dropped to them and sent back up with piles of dirt, gravel and streaming grey mud from the clay soil below, all of which was sifted, then dumped into piles at the sides of the pit.

The expert was a wrinkled old man, bent with age but keen of eye. His name was Rana, he said. 'These treasures come from underground streams,' he explained in a quavery voice. 'They have been formed in the rocks beneath the mountains and are washed down by the streams. We occasionally find garnets in an earth-slip, but all precious gems have to be mined in this way.'

Rana started examining lumps of gravel in one of the piles. We watched for over an hour. He frequently grunted with satisfaction and placed one aside in a pail. It seemed no more than an ordinary stone to us, but he knew the jewel hidden beneath – the red ruby, the blue sapphire, the blue or red star sapphire, maroon garnets or yellow topaz, occasionally a cat's-eye. So must God know the jewel hidden in the heart of man, I thought.

'Ah! This is a superior ruby!' Rana exclaimed, holding up another small lump of rock.

'I would like to buy it,' Gamini rejoined impulsively.

Rana's eyebrows lifted. 'Do you have money?'

'Of course.'

We haggled over the price, in order to retain our guise of countryfolk. Gamini finally parted with two gold coins from the pocket of his tunic, as if they were his last. We did not want to be robbed on the way!

An hour later, after an early meal at Rana's house, we were on our way again. Meanwhile, the gem had been cut and polished and did turn out to be a splendid ruby, a worthy gift from anyone to his love. Indeed, Gamini intended it for Raji.

We reached Kotmale just before noon on the seventh day.

Raji's village nestled on a wooded mountain slope rising from a narrow valley through which a stream cascaded, its waters shining silver or frothing in white foam against black rocks. Cattle grazed on the grassy mountaintop. The bleat of goats and the moo of cattle were music to my ears. Paddy fields, a pale but bright green, rose up its steep slope like giant steps edged with dark brown soil.

The village was a cluster of bamboo wattle-and-daub houses painted white, with straw-thatched roofs beneath jak and breadfruit trees and coconut palms. At its near end, a *dagoba* was poised, the white pinnacle thrusting upward to a blue sky.

The sound of men's voices calling across the valley reached us, then the laughter of children as they emerged from the temple school, their study day ended. They were all clean and neatly dressed in white *dhotis* and overshirts. Seeing strangers, they came giggling and chattering toward us. Their skins were fair and their complexions pink. With the exception of a few with pot-bellies that indicated stomach sickness from worms, they looked the picture of good health. It had to be the mountain air, for Gamini and I were also feeling more alive physically.

We reined in our horses. The children gathered around us, inquisitive as myna birds. The smallest one had managed to get to the front. He had large dark eyes, a runny nose and one finger stuck in a red mouth missing several teeth.

'Can you tell us the way to Upa Sena's house?' I inquired of a tall youth. 'He is your chief headman.'

'Ha! Nilame! Nilame! Where is Nilame?' the children shouted in a chorus, looking around them.

Soon a slim, dark-haired boy, about eight years of age, was thrust forward.

'Here is Nilame!' the children said. 'You want his house.'

'He is Upa Sena's son,' the tall boy volunteered.

I did not have to look twice at Nilame to notice his resemblance to Raji. He had to be her younger brother. He had suddenly acquired great importance in the eyes of his fellows.

Gamini gazed intently at Nilame. I could see he was moved by the boy's resemblance to his sister. 'Where is your home?' he inquired of Nilame. 'We have come a long way to visit you.' The softening of his brow showed that he had forgotten all else before the prospect of being with Raji again.

'I'll show you the way,' Nilame volunteered shyly, reaching up to grasp Raja's rein.

'No! No!' Gamini responded. 'Come here.'

Nilame was puzzled, but moved obediently toward Gamini. His face wreathed into a smile when Gamini reached down, grasped his hand and lifted him up to the saddle.

Raja whinnied and snorted. Nilame looked back and up at Gamini with dark, adoring eyes. We pushed on toward Upa

Sena's house. As the throng of schoolchildren moved out of our way, Nilame glanced at them proudly.

We rode through the village along a dirt road dappled with silver and shadow from sunlight filtering through leaves. The men of the village were obviously in the fields or pastures, but the noise of the dancing and chattering children and a scattering of barking dogs alongside us attracted what must have been the entire female population to their front doors. The sweet scent of a ripe jak, hanging overhead, its prickly, yellowing belly split open, clung to the air. The whole place was genuinely rural and it was heartwarming to see shyly smiling faces and feel the friendliness of the people as they fired inquiries at their children. A dark, middle-aged woman of imposing proportions, her brown midriff bulging between bodice and cloth, stepped onto the road and stopped two of the boys who were racing ahead. '*Kauda boler?* Who are they?' she demanded. They gave her the news eagerly and sped on. The sharp look in her eyes told me she had to be the village gossip. The world is the same everywhere!

We finally came to a brick house with a red-tiled roof, set beneath large, flowering flame trees.

'There! There! That is Upa Sena's house!' the children cried, each trying to be the first to point it out.

The house was built in the traditional Sinhala style. Flame trees and spathodea bloomed in a well-kept garden, the flower beds cascading with colour from marigolds, red salvia, pink begonia and other plants such as I had never seen before. The flowers drooped somewhat in the noonday sun. The rich scent of guava lay sharp on the air from an orchard at the side of the house.

The children stopped at the garden gates. No one enters a chief headman's house except on invitation or for business. We rode alone into the garden.

A large black dog bounded out of the house, barking furiously, as we stopped at the entrance. It skidded to a halt when Raja snorted and showed his teeth, but remained barking in spasms, pretending it was not afraid, while we dismounted. Nilame streaked inside to announce our arrival. We tethered our horses and walked into a cool, stone-flagged veranda, ignoring the dog. We could hear mortar and pestle pounding away at the rear, where rice was obviously being converted to flour.

The house was built around a *meda-midula*, with a veranda running all round it and reception rooms along the front. The ladies' quarters would project back on one side and the men's quarters along the other. The servants' quarters, storerooms and kitchens would be at the rear of the square. I must confess to being pleased at the obvious comfort of the place.

Upa Sena emerged from the rear of the house, squinting against the light to identify us. He had finished his bath and was tying his long, black hair in a knot at the back of his head. His hairy chest was bare. He looked muscular and had an air of authority which had been absent in the palace.

He recognized me first. His jaw dropped, his hair fell back over his shoulders, '*Kumaraya!* O Prince!' he croaked, then cleared his throat. He was about to sink to his knees and make obeisance, but I rushed up to him, gripping his arm and holding him up.

'No!' I commanded, directing a warning look at him. 'I am indeed *kumara*, but I have not come alone, cousin. My brother, Abhaya, has accompanied me from Malaya to visit his betrothed.'

I will say this much for Upa Sena: he was quick on the uptake. He immediately comprehended that I did not want our identity revealed. He cast a puzzled glance in Gamini's direction. A gasp escaped him. I clutched his arm more fiercely. 'You must understand that this is a visit from your relatives,' I said urgently. 'Please forgive us for not sending you warning, but our decision was taken on the spur of the moment. We hope you will extend to us the hospitality of your house.'

'My house is your house,' Upa Sena declared

emphatically. He had recovered himself and seemed to understand the situation. 'Come in! Come in! You must be starved. The noon meal is ready for you, but you will want to bathe . . .'

'My brother and I would like private converse with you first,' I interrupted.

Upa Sena nodded. He turned to Nilame. 'Go to the rear of the house and tell your mother and sister that important relatives have arrived.'

'Yes, *thatha*,' the boy replied and scuttled again to the interior of the house.

With a sigh of relief, I drew Upa Sena to a side of the veranda and rapidly explained the circumstances to him. His dark eyes widened at my story. I could see he was scared.

'You have no need to be afraid,' I assured him. 'Your village is outside King Kakkavan's jurisdiction.'

'That is true.' He was relieved now. 'But what about the young prince here?'

Gamini spoke for the first time. He did so quietly, with certainty. 'You know how I feel about your daughter, Raji,' he asserted. 'I have come here to seek your permission to marry her according to your custom. Since I need to stay in your house, for the present this will be a *binna* marriage. I hope you will not mind that. When it is time for me to return to my heritage, your daughter will accompany me.' He paused, then added, 'You realize she will have to be my legal consort, with no claim to the throne.'

Upa Sena could not believe his good fortune. 'You do me honour beyond measure,' he responded. 'But you do yourself greater dishonour by requesting permission for that which you could have seized. You may marry my daughter whenever you desire, with my blessing and that of her mother. Meanwhile, please enter your future home. Everyone and everything in it is yours to command.'

'Thank you,' Gamini responded warmly. 'But remember at all times to keep up appearances. Now please go in and warn your wife and Raji before we meet them.'

'That was pretty impetuous,' I said.

'The decision was taken long ago.'

I gazed out at the sunlight but did not see it. We had finally arrived at the part of Gamini's life that he could never share with me. I had avoided thinking about it during the entire journey. Now it was upon me and I felt bleak and alone.

I looked up at the sky, seeking God, my God of love, reaching for a tangible sign of His presence, wanting to be assured that I was never alone.

My thoughts were interrupted by the clip-clop of sandaled feet. I turned to see Chandi, Upa Sena's wife, coming up the passageway. Behind her walked a tremulous Raji.

I had only to look at Gamini to know that he found Raji as beautiful as in his dreaming.

King Elara trotted his grey charger along the sodden bund of the Tissa Wewa, followed by his escort of Chola cavalrymen. Gusts of light rain swept silvery across the water, beating on the King's dark face and white riding clothes. He turned his face sideways, inviting the prickles. It took his mind away from the unfailing memory of years ago, when his son raced his last chariot along this very bund. King Elara knew why he continued riding here. It was at once a source of self-discipline and bitter joy.

He swivelled around in his saddle at the sound of a disturbance behind him. The uniformed escort parted to make way for two horsemen. One was the towering Digha Jantu, bare-bodied and firmly astride a great black horse. The other was his diminutive, white-clad Chief Minister, Muttu Samy, bouncing on a chestnut.

King Elara drew rein and halted to enable the men to come on either side of him. 'You must have news to brave the rain, Chief Minister,' he said pleasantly.

'Indeed, sire,' the Chief Minister replied, his teeth

chattering a little from the unaccustomed cold and dampness. 'And it's great news!'

'Well then, let us ride along while you recount it.' The King looked over his shoulder at the greying captain of his escort. 'We have our Chief Warrior here to protect us,' he called loudly. 'You may return to the palace.'

Smiling, the King broke into a slow trot. His horse lightly scattered the grey mud of a puddle as it went thok-thokity-thok through. 'Well, your news now,' he directed Muttu Samy.

The Chief Minister was no horseman and the trot is a bumpy ride. Breathing hard from exertion and his effort to maintain his seat, Muttu Samy poured out the story of Gamini's insult to his father and his resultant self-exile.

They had reached the dark fringe of jungle now and were on the winding route beneath tall trees. In the semi-gloom, only the drip of rain from branches reached them.

'You have indeed brought us good news this rainy morning, Chief Minister,' King Elara declared with satisfaction, when Muttu Samy had finished his report. 'We are not surprised that the young prince allowed his ambition to outrun his discretion. Now he pays the penalty by being a fugitive.' His dark eyes swept briefly toward Digha Jantu, riding easy and tall on his left. 'His gesture would have been comical except for its inherent tragedy. I feel sad for the little king. History will make a joke of him as a man who was adjudged by his son to be fitted only to wear a woman's clothes. He has not deserved it. His rule has been wise and just. Would you not agree, Chief Minister?'

'Indubitably, lord,' Muttu Samy replied, his birdlike head cocked sideways in an unsuccessful attempt at his best judicial manner.

'Would you not grant that our decision to act with restraint all these years has been justified?' King Elara looked pointedly at Digha Jantu this time. The giant had kept his head averted.

410

'I say the time is ripe for us to invade Ruhuna,' Digha Jantu rejoined savagely. He was obviously disappointed at the turn of events. 'The exile of the upstart prince will surely create a split in the ranks of the Sinhala and they will be confused. I pray you, give me leave to advance across the river, lord.'

King Elara urged his mount to a light canter. 'You are right in your basic premise, Chief Warrior, but the timing may not be correct,' he declared, raising his voice against the wind. 'If we invade Ruhuna now, it may reunite the young prince with his father and bring him into favour with the people as a sort of hero who foresaw the event and wished to anticipate it.'

They rode in silence for a while, the King's two companions realizing that he needed silence in which to think.

They had now reached the place where Prince Muthiah had killed the white calf. The King deliberately slowed his horse to a walk and stopped. What better place than this to declare his assessment and decision, he thought without bitterness. After all, whom should he be bitter against? 'Listen then to my view of the situation,' he commanded. 'There will be no war while Kakkavan reigns, so we will not invite war through our actions. If Kakkavan dares to enter Lanka with his *dharma-vijaya* tactics, we will deal with him. Meanwhile, let his people continue practising their faith until their concepts of *maitriya* and *ahimsa* destroy their warlike sprits.' He paused. 'The real problem we face is how to prevent Prince Gamini from succeeding Kakkavan. The only answer is *manta yuddhaya*, diplomatic war, which it is the duty of all civilized monarchs to practise. We will divide and rule.' He paused and a knowing smile crossed his face. 'There are three aspirants to the succession: Gamini, his brother Tissa and the jackal Prince Digha Bahu. We will set the stage for them to fight each other. There will be civil war.

411

It will drain Ruhuna. We need not even invade them, for they will destroy themselves.'

Unusually for him, the King seemed in a foul mood. Hands clasped behind his back, he was pacing his study alone when the Queen and Leela were ushered in. He barely waited for them to make obeisance before turning on the Queen. 'You see what your son has done? You see the kind of child you have bred for us, madam?' he grated. 'As for the tutor you found for him . . .' He lapsed into a choking silence.

The Queen paused. Leela waited, trembling, at the doorway. She was not accustomed to male anger, least of all a king's.

'Why is it, lord, that whenever our sons distinguish themselves, you say they are yours, and when they do something wrong they immediately become mine?' The Queen spoke quietly, but her poise showed that she was not about to take the King's anger lying down.

King Kakkavan stopped in his stride. 'You – you dare speak thus to us? Remember, we are your king! Never forget that!'

'You seldom permit us to, lord. But we never forget that you are our husband either. We have had a report of the incident. Please tell us calmly what transpired.' Then, shrewdly, 'You are the rare human being who recently established suzerainty over two kingdoms through moral force. Now, please permit us humbly to remind you that you are also capable of establishing control over your own mind, your own reactions. Besides, it is not good for your health to give way thus to anger.'

For a moment the King looked as if he would erupt again. Then the Queen's words struck home and he calmed down. 'You are right,' he muttered. He reflected a few moments, nodded, looking down, feet apart, hands still clasped behind him, before quietly pouring out the entire story. Having finished, he lapsed into a moody silence, staring into space.

'What do you propose doing, lord?' the Queen inquired.

'We have sent soldiers to apprehend the two princes, but we doubt they will be found.'

'And if they are?'

'We shall bring them here in chains and publicly punish them.'

'And make equally public the story of our shames, lord?'

The Queen's shaft obviously went home, for the King looked thoughtful.

'We urge restraint and the observance of the Doctrine, lord. As you know, it is forbearance in times of grief that distinguishes noble conduct.'

'What would you have us do?' For once the King was not his usual decisive self. Leela found something pathetic in the question and her heart went out to the dark little figure standing in the centre of the study.

'As we have suggested for years, let it be immediately known that Prince Gamini will not necessarily succeed to the throne. After all, Prince Tissa will make a nobler king. Bring both princes back and forgive them. The reduced status will clear Prince Gamini's mind of all his silly ambitions, for which, frankly, we are in part responsible. Prince Rodana should not be blamed for his pupil's sins either. Let him continue as Prince Gamini's tutor . . .'

I love you, my Queen, so I love even your clever manipulation, Leela decided – but it is an unworthy characteristic, especially for one as pious as you.

The King digested the words in silence. Finally, his white teeth were bared in a cynical smile. 'Your advice is sound, madam. We shall continue our reactions, trading the scorn and pity of our people and . . . and history . . .' His voice broke slightly, but the smile remained fixed. 'History' – the last words came out in a whisper – 'for saintliness.'

'History will judge you by your own actions, lord, not by Prince Gamini's.'

The King passed a hand over his brow, then kept his fingers on his forehead, pondering. 'We must think on it. After all, if we claim to practise *maitriya*, forgiveness should be complete enough to banish punishment.'

The Queen stiffened. You will not easily get your way with this King, Leela thought. He is shrewd, strong and, above all, a good Buddhist.

Chapter 41

Gamini's wedding took place one week later, on the first auspicious day selected by Upa Sena's astrologer.

It is not unusual with hill-country families for a man to be wed in *binna*, which means that he moves in with the woman's family. This is especially useful if the family has too few grown males to look after its land and other interests, so our presence in Upa Sena's house excited few comments in the village. Although people were naturally curious because of the suddenness of it all, they dared not question the Chief Headman, and neither he nor his wife nor Raji volunteered any information.

Due to Upa Sena's position, the wedding was an elaborate affair.

The *poruwa* on which the couple would stand during the ceremony was built in the main hall of Upa Sena's house. A square platform of yellow jak wood was erected on the stone-flagged floor and covered with fine-woven red mats. The *pandal* consisted of slender columns and roof supports of jak wood, but covered with the boles of banana trees, cut in half, the outer skins peeled to reveal the shining, creamy insides, the effect being of an ivory overlay. These columns were festooned with chains of yellow and orange marigolds, red and white temple flowers and blue lotus. The entire roof of the *poruwa* was strung with coloured flowers, while its upper part was hung all around with a curtain of sweet-smelling jasmine strings, shaped to an arch in front. On the entrance steps of the *poruwa* were placed two great lampstands of brass, each glittering with the lighted wicks of its ten tiers of light. Red clay pots, containing pale amber coconut flowers for good luck, were placed around the platform interspersed with clay lamps, their lighted wicks fluttering faintly. The whole effect was that of a flower house of the *devas*.

The wedding invitations were, however, kept to a minimum, in order not to publish the event and run the risk of Gamini's identity being discovered.

The evening before the wedding, Gamini, Nilame and I withdrew with our wedding clothes to the house of Raji's uncle, Banda, who was headman of the village. I was to act for Gamini's parents and Nilame, young though he was, would stand up with Gamini. We were glad to get away from Upa Sena's house, which had been a hive of activity this past week, with carpenters, masons, labourers, cooks, tailors and helpers crowding in to fulfil their appointed tasks, including a feast and entertainment after the ceremony.

The auspicious hour designated by the astrologer was at the end of the second watch after the noon hour. Family members living in the valley began arriving at the house even before noon.

The ritual of the bride was quite elaborate. With much to do until late the previous night, such as greeting guests, having her clothes finally fitted and receiving her beauty treatments, Raji rested late that morning, while her 'court' had their hair combed, oiled and styled. She arose at the selected hour, to be greeted at the door of her room by a white-clad little boy bearing a pitcher of fresh cow's milk, to commence her day with lucky omens. By the time she entered her bath her court was ready and waiting for her in Chandi's room. Having finished her bath, Raji retired to her robing room, where the beauticians commenced their ritual. When they were finished, she was robed by attendants, supervised by her mother. Her underclothes were of fine muslin, her *saree* and jacket of shimmering white silk. Her glossy black hair, braded and caught up on top of her head with long silver hairpins studded with gems, had a circlet of sparkling Matara diamonds with its chain along the centre parting, ending on her pale forehead with the great ruby Gamini had bought for her in Ratna. Her gold chain was the traditional gift from the bridegroom, of fine filigree work, with a heart-shaped pendant at the end, all fashioned from the coins we had brought with us, melted down in a furnace by the best goldsmith of the region. Her gift from her parents was a family heirloom, a throatlet of Matara diamonds. Her heavy bracelets were of silver and her long earrings of diamonds. Her sandals were silver-coloured silk, studded with diamonds. Within all this glitter was the most precious jewel of all, Raji, her large, almond-shaped eyes more luminous than ever within their dark fringes of *kohl*, the long black eyelashes combed out to enshrine their haunting depths.

By the time Raji's robing was done, her six attendant girls and six page boys had arrived, the girls in skirts and bodices of white silk, with garlands of sweet-smelling jasmine around their necks, the boys in white pantaloons and tunics. They all looked very self-conscious in their finery. Upa Sena and his wife were already at the entrance, receiving their guests.

As the guests arrived, they fell naturally into their places by order of the ceremonial and by rank, the women separate from the men, the poorer folk outside. The women were decked in their best, some in bodice and skirt, others in the hill-country *saree*, which is not draped but is held by a belt around the waist, the flap, neatly pleated, lying like a shawl diagonally across the shoulder. They looked such different people in their glamorous makeup, the eyes mysterious with black *kohl* around the edges and on the lashes, light shadow beneath them, the cheeks luminous with light pink makeup. Most of them wore chunky chains of gold or silver, heavy matching bracelets and earrings, hairpins ornamented with rubies, sapphires and topaz. Some wore silver chains around the ankles instead of sandals. The men were less elaborately dressed, but in bright colours of blue, red, green or yellow. When they were finally assembled, the hall presented a glittering scene.

Banda was the first to leave his house. As the bride's uncle, he had a special role to play in the ceremony. He wore his headman's uniform, a *dhoti* and short white waistcoat of linen, with a creamy silk shirt embroidered in front with lace. The *dhoti* consisted of eighteen yards of cloth and made him walk with a swagger. His broad belt was of silver, ornamented with jewels of the *navaratna*. His headdress was the three-cornered stiff turban of white silk. His shoes were covered with silver, a line of gems running along the centre and up the curving points. He looked dashing, his fair skin fresh-scrubbed and glowing with health.

Gamini was simply dressed, in white pantaloons, tunic, turban and sandals. If he could have divulged his identity, his accoutrements would have been of gold. As it was, he declined to indulge in the sham of silver for this occasion. People had concluded long before the event that he was a poor relation, though of headman rank, so it excited no comment. For once, his restless dark eyes held an inner peace, as if he had set aside all else for this day. I had the feeling that he had walked away from the mainstream of his life to a quiet pool in the deeps of which he now floated, his mind closed to all else. When his time in it was over, he would go back to where he belonged and connect himself to the pool with a channel, so it would always be there for him. He was a part of it now. Someday it would be a part of him.

Gamini talked frankly about his future relations with Raji.

He had had no physical contact with her other than that one chaste kiss in the Ruhuna palace. I had sensed a suppressed excitement about him the previous night at the prospect of making love to Raji – a sort of holy lust. He had no worry about his ability to satisfy Raji sexually. He knew he had enough love, tenderness and the desire to please. He was a little afraid of penetrating her virginity and fearful of the blood – this prince who had bloodlust for men and animals within him. He was also worried about inflicting pain on Raji – terribly sensitive about it. On a more practical and selfish level, he wondered what it would be like to make love with, rather than to, an inexperienced virgin. His whole attitude seemed to me to condense his character perfectly.

I was dressed like Gamini. Standing in for his parents, I had already begun to experience what they would have felt. I was losing a part of myself and of my lifetime.

Gamini, Nilame and I, followed by attendants, arrived at Raji's immediately after Banda. We were received by Raji's parents and conducted to two tall chairs placed beside the *poruwa*, in the main hall. We sat down, soon beginning to sweat in the crush, mopping our faces with linen cloths, but unable to wipe our bodies. Gamini remained miraculously calm. Although he had been excited privately the previous night, he had the gift of being able to perform well in public.

Finally, word came that Raji was ready. I escorted Gamini to stand inside the *poruwa*, on its right side, while Upa Sena proceeded to Raji's robing room. Banda and I took up positions facing the *poruwa*.

Shortly after, we heard cries of 'Make way! Make way!'

Upa Sena slowly led Raji into the hall. Banda and I turned to face them. The guests parted like a flock of gaudy-coloured fowl before a white bird-of-paradise. Raji paused for a moment at the entrance, shimmering. I glanced at Gamini. He was spellbound, an extension of that first look he had given Raji at the Tissa temple in the moonlight. This time, the temple bell had to be in his heart, for Raji glowed with that inner beauty radiated by brides regardless of their looks or rank. I closed my eyes momentarily, fighting back the memory of that one precious moment when I had thought she was for me.

I opened my eyes to see the vision of beauty slowly approaching the *poruwa*, her eyes modestly downcast. I felt the pang of my first love for her again and was swept by overwhelming gusts of desolation – yet men brave the worst that fate can bestow on them with dignity. I showed no emotion as Upa Sena led Raji past me and handed her into the *poruwa* on Gamini's left. I did not voice my heart-cry when Raji glanced once at Gamini and he returned her look as if by prior ordination as their spirits merged.

Six uncles of the bride now started reciting *Mahakaruniko natho*, the great stanzas of love and kindness, in a blend of high, deep, dry and mellow voices.

> 'Maha karuniko natho
> Hithaya sabba paninam
> Puretva parami sabba
> Patto sambodhi muttanam
> Etana sacca vajjena
> Hotu me jayamangalam.'

> That Lord of Mighty Compassion
> For the benefit of all living beings
> Fulfilled all perfection
> And attained Supreme Enlightenment
> By the power of these words of truth
> May such joyous victory be mine.

The songs of wisdom that followed carried me to the reality I had established for myself during these many months, especially those during which I had witnessed the closeness of Gamini and Raji to each other and the growing of their love. I had stifled all my own desires and found peace in working for the happiness of these two human beings whom I loved most of all in the world. It was hard though, very hard, and the only way I had achieved it was by not thinking about it.

Silence brought me back. I realized with a start that the chanting was over. With a rustle of cloth, a page boy carried a small roll of white linen up to Banda. Someone coughed. Others cleared their throats. The mingled odours of flowers, the scent worn by women, sweat and the smell of clothes packed away with *kapuru* balls and brought out for this occasion were overpowering.

Taking the roll of cloth in both hands, Banda ascended the *poruwa*. The page boy behind him held the edge of the linen at Gamini's waist. Banda began wrapping it around Gamini, moving to his right and rear, then behind Raji, moving to her left and forward again until the linen encased them both from the waist down. He fastened it at Gamini's side with a silver pin. Thus were the wedded couple symbolically bound to each other in body and mind.

The page boy withdrew, to return with the sacred gold thread, blessed the previous night by the recital of one thousand *pirith*.

As Banda held the gold *pirith nool* in his hands, a woman of Raji's family, acting as Gamini's aunt, began chanting *Jayamangala gatha*, assisted by her daughter and a choir of twenty little girls, dressed in white and decked with purple orchid garlands. Her voice was golden above the silvery peal of the children's chanting. While they sang, Banda tied the right thumbs of the bride and bridegroom with the *pirith nool*. Thus were the wedded couple symbolically bound to each other in spirit.

The sigh that rippled through the hall spun between the strands of the singing and was echoed by my heart. Hot tears sprang unasked to my eyes. I knew not for what I wept, but quickly brushed the tears aside, hoping no one had seen.

The chanting of the *Jayamangala gatha* ended, its final strains hanging over the hall like the last quiet shades of night. Banda slowly unpinned and removed the cloth that bound Gamini and Raji. Facing them, he gravely untied the gold thread.

Neither cloth nor thread had been cut or broken. What bound the two lovers would remain forever.

The chief lady of Raji's court, Kati, a maiden of sixteen, very fair and of delicate features, accompanied by Raji's brother Nilame, came forward carrying gold rings on red silken cushions. The maiden's cushion also carried a gold necklace of exquisite workmanship, another gift from the bridegroom. They ascended the *poruwa*. Gamini took Raji's ring. Raji took Gamini's ring. What long, slender, shapely white fingers she has, I thought – then, with savage loyalty to them both: This will be the last time I think of Raji otherwise than as the wife of the man I was born to serve.

Gamini placed his ring on the middle finger of Raji's left hand. Raji placed her ring on the middle finger of Gamini's right hand. Gamini took up the necklace and gently placed it around Raji's neck. Another sigh, sweeping the hall, rose to the wooden ceiling.

Nilame and Kati withdrew. Banda came forward with a golden tray in his hands. On it was a small golden bowl containing milk-rice. He entered the *poruwa* and proffered the tray to Gamini, who slowly, deliberately took some in his fingers, taking care not to let it spread beyond the first joints, and fed Raji. Banda then proffered the tray to Raji, who in turn fed Gamini. My mind went back many years, to the day Gamini had flung aside the milk-rice offered by his father because he did not want to take an oath. Now, for the first time since then, he was taking an even more binding, though silent oath, committing his whole emotional life to it.

A loud report rent the air. Another sigh, this time of satisfaction, swept the room. The washerwoman had just smashed a husked coconut against a rock, an offering to the gods. It had broken clean and sure on her first fling – another omen of good fortune.

A page boy dressed in pink came shyly up to offer Gamini and Raji in turn a silver bowl containing scented water. They washed, wiping their fingers with a napkin. The page boy moved away. He was very tiny and scared. He stumbled on the stairs. If I had not quickly gripped him, the water would have splashed all over. He dimpled his smile of thanks, grew red with embarrassment and scurried away, helped by his mother, a fussy matron who rushed up to collect her charge.

Banda retired once again, bearing away the tray containing the milk-rice. Upa Sena and Chandi, with me standing in for Gamini's parents on their left, advanced to stand close to the *poruwa*. Nilame and Raji's chief attendant brought brass trays containing green betel leaves, brown areca nut, white *chunam*, cloves, cardamoms and black dried *adathoda* leaves. Raji took her tray first, descended from the *poruwa* and then offered betel to each of her parents and me in turn, kneeling with head bent low to worship each of us. When she was done, it was Gamini's duty. I marvelled at our customs, which made even a prince venerate his parents. Then I recalled the insult Gamini had offered his father and chopped off such thoughts.

Raji's parents and I retired to make way for the uncles and aunts of the bride, who advanced in order of age and were worshipped by the couple.

Gamini, of course, had none of his family present. I was his only family and he mine. Now Raji was of our family, too. It was good that I loved her, for I could only think of making her happy. How close would she be, though, I wondered. I could not tell, because she had had to maintain her distance from us before the wedding.

When these acts denoting respect to elders and the sources of married life were over, the 'courts' of the couple, including the little girls and boys, came forward to receive gifts bought by Gamini and Raji and placed on the *poruwa* the night before: clothes and ornaments for the women, clothes for the men, toys for the children.

Finally it was over. A conch shell sounded. Gamini looked at Raji, his dark eyes alive with a new possessiveness, his whole being vibrant. Lips parted, she melted into his being. In all that crowd, I saw the aura of her emerge from within her white-clad body, trembling, fluttering. It poised before her a moment, then was drawn into Gamini's body until it was totally absorbed. I shivered involuntarily.

The smiling couple began to move into the crush to receive the felicitations and blessings of the visitors. *Magul bera* started beating slow, soon working up to a thunderous throbbing, the nasal voices of the drummers snaking through. Flutes piped in and trumpets blared. The welter of sound would drive evil spirits away and remain vibrating in our bodies forever, so that some deep part of us would never forget this day.

She retired to her room to change her clothes. Gamini waited for her, standing by the open window of his bedroom. The last of the sunlight laid its rosy robe on the mountain across the valley, now darkling in dusk light. A flock of birds flitted, twittering and squeaking, across red-and-gold clouds of a sky in travail. The still-throbbing drums reflected the wild beating of Gamini's heart. The singing and shouting had died down. Within the room was peace and darkness. The flares would not be lit on this nuptial night. Only the faint glow of incense sticks and their pungent scent pricked the stillness.

She came to him in pale beauty, her face white and ethereal, her luminous eyes penetrating the very depths of his being. She paused to stand before him, wide-eyed, trembling, dressed only in a soft, creamy cloth fastened above her white breasts. Her breath was fragrant from *valmi* root and the freshness of her youth.

A great tenderness welled up within him and caught his throat. His hand moved out instinctively to give it

423

expression. He had to steady his hand against its shaking. He gently touched her cheek. She reached up and grasped his hand. Her palms were soft as cotton from a pod.

Moved by an impulse, he half turned her and lifted her in his arms. Her arms went around his neck. She shook visibly, laying her head on his shoulder.

We have both come home, he thought. Even exile was worth it.

He carried her to the bed and laid her on it. She never took her eyes off him as he slowly removed her cloth. His gaze moved over her body, taking in its beauty. The generous breasts, the small waist, the full hips and thighs, the dark patch of hair between them, did not move him to lust as with other maidens, but to a kind of awed ecstasy. Instead of the urge to plunge, he felt the need to be gentle and tender, to caress with body, mind and spirit. He removed his sarong and lay down beside her, every part of his being throbbing to the feel of her silken skin. Each pore of them drew the other as if filling a vacuum, thrilling, vibrating. He could tell she found joy in the pain that took her across the threshold of her virginity. For once in his life he hesitated before another's pain.

When he awoke during the night with his arms about her, he knew a sense of protectiveness and belonging such as he had never dreamed possible. He began merging with her into the womb of timelessness, in which there seemed to be no bodies but a single entity.

Chapter 42

A week after Gamini's wedding, we rode along a sun-dappled road at noon to fetch Raji's brother, Nilame, from the *pirivena*, his temple school. Having readily fallen into the routine of work in the villages, we had been up at dawn and performed our ablutions at the waterspout. We had brushed our teeth with a chewed *kanda* stick instead of burnt paddy husks and salt ground together, because they did not have salt so far away from the ocean.

A hearty breakfast of *appa*, curry and fruit had prepared us for the day. Most of the morning was spent checking repairs to an irrigation channel supplying Upa Sena's fields. We then supervised the bartering of material with families of certain other villages that produced goods appropriate to their castes.

We were already known in the village as Raji's husband and his cousin, so people greeted us with friendly smiles as we clip-clopped along the dirt road. Hamine, the woman of ample proportions whom we had seen the day we arrived, had a special greeting for us. She had indeed turned out to be the village gossip, visiting Chandi that same evening – through the rear entrance of the house, as befitted her lowly rank – with a gift of ripe bananas from her garden, in order to ferret out news in the sly way of her kind. Although she learned only as much as Chandi wished to tell her, it was her social triumph to know more than anyone else in the village at the time.

'What a privilege to see how our village system works at first hand,' Gamini remarked as we ambled along.

'Invaluable training for you.'

'Exactly. I had no idea of the power wielded by the learned *bhikkus*, with their practice of education and medicine.'

'Why not wield some of the power yourself when you become king?'

'How?'

'Just as the Doctrine is maintained in its pristine purity by the annual Assembly of Monks, what about annual assemblies for health and education? They would give you the opportunity to review the systems and effect any necessary improvements.'

My horse snorted, as if in derision, but Gamini seemed enthusiastic, so I proceeded. 'You might even extend the idea to include taxation and *rajakariya* – feudal duties.'

Gamini glanced at me sharply. 'Taxes must remain a royal prerogative.'

'Kings extract the duties of their vassals, but what about the other side of the feudal contract?'

'The elected *gan-sabhas*, the village committees, who look to the life and welfare of each village – '

My eagerness led me to anticipate his statement. 'But they could be dominated by the very individuals against whom the people may have cause for complaint,' I interrupted. 'No, the only way you will hear the voice of the people, discover whether the burdens of *rajakariya* and taxation lie too heavily on them, is to bring them to within hearing distance of you.'

'Hmm. A radical idea. I must think on it.'

We had now reached the *pirivena*. As the white-clad children came pouring out of the gates, I could not help reflecting that a great deal of the future of thousands like them might be affected by our last few minutes of conversation.

Nilame came racing up. Gamini reached down and swung him up on the saddle. The other children crowded around, enviously crying, '*Arday*, Nilay!'

We urged our horses forward to a trot this time, much to Nilame's delight. He giggled with each bounce. The sound of the children's voices gradually receded.

Raji's uncle, Banda, who had officiated at the wedding, was the village headman, the *muladaniya*. He was also a superb horseman, an expert at jumping, and had agreed to teach Gamini.

We made our way to Banda's modest house, a smaller version of Upa Sena's, about a half mile from the temple.

426

We were greeted by the sweet scent of ripe guava. Clusters of banana and papaya trees and bushes of tangerine grew in a garden orchard in front of the house. Birds whistled, though somewhat listlessly, from the dark branches. A sharp camphor tang sliced through the air from flower beds behind the trees. Yellow and orange *kapuru* were interspersed with white jasmine. On one side of the house, vegetable plots revealed an orderly spread of light green onion shoots, red chilis, string beans and a profusion of herbs. On the other side was a large, square lawn, with an exercise ring and hurdles. The stables were beyond.

Banda emerged, smiling, from the house. He was dressed in tight blue pantaloons, his lean, tough chest bare. '*Ayubowan!*' he greeted us traditionally. 'I listened for your approach. I hope you have come for your jumping lesson.'

Gamini nodded, smiling. He lifted Nilame off Raja, then dismounted.

'This is not a Scindi horse,' I heard Banda observe, examining Raja as I swung off my bay. 'It is an Arabi and must have come from the land of eternal sands.' I was glad that Banda had not been curious enough to inspect Raja earlier. 'Arabi horses do not know how to jump. Apparently it is not necessary in their native land.'

'Nor is it in our part of Lanka,' Gamini responded. 'I am afraid you will need to teach both horse and man.'

'Why are you so keen to learn if you will not use the art when you get back home?'

A faraway expression crossed Gamini's face. 'I will need it some day,' he began, then changed direction. 'One never knows when it may come in useful.'

'Have you eaten?'

'Yes, thank you.'

'You, Nilame, did you share *dana* at school?'

'Yes, *bappa.*'

'Very well then, we have a single two-hour watch before I

427

leave for the *gan-sabha* building to try some cases. The worst we have today is cattle theft. May the *devas* keep our people from violent crimes.' He led the way to the green lawn.

A servant brought out a bench for Nilame and me. We sat in the shade of a jak tree to watch.

Banda first made Gamini walk and trot Raja over hurdles just one span off the ground. 'Remember that all animals jump naturally. It is merely an extension of their stride. Do not interfere with the smooth flow of the horse. Your task is to maintain perfect balance with him, so that you both act as one.'

It took Gamini about half an hour to acquire poise in these low jumps. Banda then placed hurdles about one cubit in height around the ring, impressing on Gamini that there must be no undue forward movement of his body when Raja jumped and that his lower legs should be well locked into the saddle, knees pressed firmly on either side.

He watched carefully as Gamini approached the first jump. 'No! No! Go back and start again. Your elbows, wrists and reins must be in a single straight line horizontally and your eyes, knees and the tips of your toes in a vertical line, at all times.'

Banda ran beside Gamini, his bare brown torso now glistening with sweat. 'Move the upper part of your body forward from the knees when Raja begins his jump, maintaining right contact with the reins. Sit on the saddle during the jump, but time the backward movement of your upper body as Raja lands, allowing him complete freedom of movement to resume his normal stride. There . . . there . . . Good, very good! You did it right the first time. You are a born horseman! I shall make you a superb jumper.' Banda's lean face was alight with an unwonted excitement.

At the end of the lesson, both Gamini and Banda were well pleased. Gamini would master the art.

We waited outside for Banda to bathe and change. Gamini gave Nilame a thrill by placing him on Raja's back and allowing him to walk the horse around the ring.

When Banda emerged from the house, he wore his official white clothes, *dhoti* and short waistcoat. A groom brought up his chestnut and we rode to the *gan-sabha*. This was a red-tiled building with half-walls of white-plastered brick, located close to the temple. A crowd of plaintiffs, the accused in manacles and minor headmen awaited Banda. They all greeted us respectfully. We dismounted and handed our horses to attendants. Banda took his place on a high-backed chair at the far end of the hall, to dispense justice, while all of us sat on plain teakwood benches facing him.

It took only about two hours to go through the cases. There were no postponements. The administration of justice was simple and effective. If the law had been broken or someone's rights had been violated, Banda heard the plaintiff and defendant, called for evidence for both sides and gave his verdict. There are no jails in these villages. Sentenced prisoners are kept under guard in stocks in an adjacent building. Civil suitors are awarded remedies, as in the case of the cultivator that afternoon. The man had been a tenant farmer who worked the paddy fields of a wealthy landowner for the usual two-fifth share of the produce. After the last harvest, the landowner had driven him and his family away from their house without paying him, claiming that he had neglected the fields. The landlord never dreamed that the poor tenant would dare to complain. Banda merely established that there was no wrongdoing on the tenant's part and ordered that he be restored to his house and his share paid him.

I could sense Gamini's alert interest throughout the proceedings, though Nilame became bored and asked to be excused to leave and play with his friends.

We were beginning to tire by the time the court session was over. We therefore hurried back home through the golden light of early evening for our bath at the waterspout, which concluded a typical day.

Apart from our daily routine, the life of the village was distinguished by *poya*, full-moon days, which were set aside for religious observance and, in many cases, the taking of *sil*. There were also festival days such as the Sinhala New Year and the Vap, or sowing and harvesting times.

Gamini had confessed to me long before that he found taking *sil* and meditating difficult. Thoughts of waging war, of methods of doing so, and of administering justice and the government of the country kept intruding all the time. He was therefore a little impatient of our nights in the temple, though he never showed it.

We had been in Kotmale more than nine months that *poya* night. Gamini, Raji and I observed *sil* in the temple hall, surrounded by other white-clad devotees, their voices hushed, their murmuring a timeless benediction. The grey flagstone floor on which our mats were placed was cool. The air was golden with flare-light, accented by dark, wavering shadows. The heavy smell of incense wafted the senses to other realms.

We observed the First Watch during the four hours immediately after sunset. This is the time when the Buddha had once expounded the Doctrine to monks and laymen, clearing their doubts and answering their questions. Today, monks fulfilled the Buddha's role.

The next four hours formed the Middle Watch. This was the time when celestial beings had questioned the Buddha about the Doctrine. I prefer to believe that this had really been the time of inner meditation by the Buddha – when God through the Buddha's own wisdom, caused questions in his mind. Having found answers, the Buddha could then expound them in absolute terms. If this sounds like cynicism to those who want to believe in celestial beings and the divinity of Lord Buddha, remember it is not the cynicism of rationality, which I too abhor, but an attitude geared to the reality of consciousness, avoiding the possibly faulty assessments of the mind.

During the Last Watch, until dawn, we alternately walked up and down for physical exercise and mindfully slept. For those of higher development, like saintly *bhikkus*, it would be the time for attaining the fruit of *arahat*-ship or even reaching the bliss of Nibbhana. We spent the last hour of this watch in the Ecstasy of Great Compassion, radiating loving kindness to all the world.

Because of my earlier years of practice, these watches came more naturally to me than to Gamini, so he rose as soon as the Last Watch ended and made humble obeisance to the monks, forehead touching the ground, palms together over the head. He then left the temple with Raji, for a walk, while I lingered behind, moved by I did not know what, except for feeling very close to God.

Gamini and Raji walked down the hillside to stroll along the stream in the valley below. The sun had not yet cleared the line of the mountains, so the pale light of the first dawn tried vainly to pierce the thin grey mist that lies in the mountain hollows of the hill country. The air was chill and damp. Quiet drip-sounds from the branches heightened the solitude.

'There is magic in the ghostliness of red gum trees,' Gamini remarked. He picked a leaf from a low branch and crushed it between his fingers. 'Smell this!' He held the leaf up to Raji.

'Mmm . . . I've always loved its tang,' Raji responded, her delicate nostrils distending to breathe the leaf's scent.

They smiled at each other and walked on. The stream babbled and cascaded over black rock and brown sand to their left. On the right, wild ferns and damp *mana* grass gave back pungent odours upon being trampled. They paused to listen to the sound of the stream, glancing upward at the first cooing of a dove.

'Do you remember . . .?' They both said it together, looked at each other and laughed with joy.

431

Engrossed in their communion, they did not notice the men until they turned to walk on and suddenly found their way barred by a fierce-looking pair, of like build, with black beards and moustaches and shaggy, unkempt hair. Gamini took one look at the hot, mean eyes and the bared white teeth and reached for his knife, but it was not there. He was a devotee, unarmed.

The effects of the *sil* he had observed took over. 'Greetings!' he said pleasantly.

The two men were momentarily taken aback. They were obviously not accustomed to friendly responses.

'Must be the village idiot!' one remarked to the other.

'He's not important,' the other replied, grinning. 'Just take a look at the woman.'

'Juicy morsel!'

The men's eyes were devouring Raji's form, slim and tall in her long white skirt and jacket.

Gamini's blood began to boil. His glance fell to the knives at the men's waists. Some instinct made him look at their ankles. The white, circular scars told of their time in fetters and stocks.

The urge for survival told Gamini he should not react in anger. With a great effort, he controlled himself. 'My brothers,' he said, 'you are obviously not of this village. Nor am I. But you seem to be lost and hungry. Come with us to our home and we will give you food and directions.'

They ignored Gamini's words, their silence more ominous than speech. Raji reached fearfully for Gamini's hand.

The men exchanged glances and a slight nod. The one nearest Raji stepped forward and grabbed her by the arm.

A red light burst through Gamini's brain. He saw the man in its haze. He snatched his hand away from Raji. It shot up across his body and sideways, slashing at the man's neck, the base of his palm striking the jugular with hammer force. The man's jaw dropped. His eyes rolled upward and inward. A strangled croak escaped him. His knees began to give. He

432

crumpled to the ground. As he dropped, Gamini kicked him in the face. The crunch of snapping teeth and breaking bones made him laugh savagely.

With one sweep of his arm, Gamini had Raji behind him. She cried out, but he barely heard her. The other man, caught off guard by the speed and unexpectedness of Gamini's attack, now drew his knife, raising it. He snarled, showing blackened teeth. The long blade, gleaming at his shoulder, had rusted blood on it.

Gamini crouched, his brain ice-cold. Which way would his opponent slash? Downward, straight forward or feinting. The brown face before him had begun to twitch horribly, the nostrils distending, one eye winking out of control.

With a roar, the man flung himself on Gamini, his knife flashing downward. Gamini leaped forward. His left palm, crossed before his face, grasped the knife hand at the wrist, right hand going over the man's bicep to lock on his own left wrist. He gave a swift downward wrench. The sharp cracking of bone ended in a scream of agony while the knife clattered on the rocks.

Gamini's right leg went around and behind his opponent. He lifted the man's hand and levered down on the shoulder with his right elbow. A scream of anguish rent the air as the arm was torn from its socket. The man staggered back, whimpering, his face slack, eyes rolling, saliva drooling out of the side of his mouth. Gamini's leg tripped him. He fell backward, hitting the ground with a thud.

Gamini leaped for the knife. He seized it, swung round and advanced on the fallen man. 'I'm going to have your guts!' he grated. The red mist still swam before his eyes, but within him was a single cold purpose: to feel the savage joy of mutilating this animal who had dared lift eyes to his Raji.

The knowledge of death shone in the man's dark eyes. He was sweating with fear and pain. 'No!' he croaked through drying lips. The left hand grasping his torn shoulder moved upward in supplication.

'My lord!' It was Raji kneeling beside him, clinging to his knife hand. He half turned to look at her, barely saw her, conscious only of the hindering of his knife stroke.

'This is not our way, lord,' Raji implored. 'Deliver him to justice. Do not take his blood on your hands.'

Gamini made to fling her aside. Her face came into focus through the red mist – dark, beseeching, almond-shaped eyes, soft white cheeks strewn with tears. The mist began to clear. This was Raji, his Raji, his wife, his love. What was she saying? Why was she crying? He shook his head violently.

'Do not kill him.' Raji was sobbing now, her hands clasped before her, begging. 'It was but an hour ago that we were exalted by the Doctrine of nonviolence and love.'

'I tried to show them love,' Gamini responded with surprising gentleness, 'but they offered violence instead.' He touched Raji's cheek with his fingers. 'They wanted to rape you.'

Raji nodded acknowledgement. 'Spare them nonetheless, lord.'

Gamini felt an access of love such as he had never known for his wife. His eyes went to the first man. 'It is too late for this one, I am afraid. He is dead.' He turned to the other, now groaning and sweating with pain. 'You will not have long to live either,' he said quietly. 'Get up!'

It transpired that the two men were brothers, notorious brigands named Rana and Suramba. Escaped prisoners, they were already under sentence of death. The whereabouts of a third brother, the worst of the three, named Ravi, was unknown.

Suramba was already dead. Rana was executed by hanging. They were not accorded the dignity of cremation, but were buried in unmarked graves in a far mountain slope across the stream.

Soon after, Raji began looking pale and drawn. One night, she seemed so weary that Gamini questioned her when she came to his room for the night. 'All this trouble about Rana and Suramba has affected you deeply, has it not?'

She stood beside the bed, looking down at him, her face pale in the taper-light. 'Yes, it has,' she whispered. 'I feel in some way responsible.'

'Is that why you have been looking so ill?'

She hesitated and an unaccountable fear swept through him. He raised himself toward her and gripped her arms. 'Are you ill . . . or in pain?' His voice trembled with anxiety.

'I am sick, lord, but not ill.' She looked directly at him now, deep into the depths of him, uncertain, searching.

'What is it? Tell me immediately. Do not keep me in suspense.'

'It is nothing unusual. Nothing to be worried about.' Her whole face softened and a strange light entered her eyes. 'It is just that I am bearing your child.'

Gamini gaped at her. 'My child?' He shook his head as if to clear it. Since he had escaped such consequences from his sexual relations so far, the thought that Raji might have a baby had only remotely crossed Gamini's mind. His first reaction was, How will this affect my destiny? He was surprisingly unmoved at the thought that he had fathered a child, perhaps even a son. He stared at Raji. The large black eyes were moist with tears. To conceal his awkwardness, he took her in his arms. 'Oh, my beloved, now you have given me everything.' Only his mind had responded. The words were hollow, but his love for Raji gave them the ring of sincerity.

Chapter 43

Once again, a long convoy stretched out from the Mahagama palace at grey dawn. I was not there to accompany the royal party, nor was Gamini present to see it depart. Only Prince Tissa, Prince Digha Bahu and his son, Prince Panduka, stood on the steps of the audience hall to say good-bye to the King and the Queen. This time it was Prince Tissa who had been appointed Prince Regent. Strangely, though, he had been ordered to rule from Dighavapi and not from Mahagama.

The appearance of the convoy was the same as before, because its mission was the same: the establishment of a *dagoba* – this time in Nuggala, within the Ruhuna territory. Wagons containing saffron-robed monks and white-clad women, including the Queen and Leela, followed by soldiers without arms, dressed in white, would wind through the green countryside for days. The elephant Kandula was part of the procession, stalking majestically. The Buddha relic to be enshrined in the *dagoba* was in the *howdah* on its back.

'After Nuggala, Mahaiyangana,' King Kakkavan, his black eyes gleaming, had told Kirthi Siri. 'And then . . .' Perhaps he hoped to show Gamini and posterity that the yellow robe was not to be confused with a woman's garments and that it required more manliness to brandish the Doctrine, the power of which was greater than that of the sword. Perhaps the desire to show his son and the world that he was no coward, though he refused to invade Lanka with an army, had secretly become an added spur to his actions. Perhaps the shame of Gamini's insult to him made him want to display a continuity of religious purpose.

Whatever the King's hopes, within six months the two

buildings were completed, through the ceaseless toil of thousands of people. On the night of the first full moon after the *vihare* and relic chamber were completed, twelve thousand monks and many more thousands of laypeople gathered for the ceremonial enshrinement of the relic and the formal gifting of the *vihare* to the Community of Monks.

The plain around the temple was a sea of saffron and white. Cries of 'Saa-dhu . . . saa-dhu . . . saa- . . .' rent the deep blue skies above. Torches flamed and hissed around the work site. The wicks of thousands of little clay lamps fluttered with each breeze. The smell of incense mingled with the rancid odour of human bodies pressed warmly together.

The King walked up the steps leading to the platform beside the relic chamber. The crowd grew still. The King reached the platform and knelt reverently. He held the casket containing the Buddha relic above his head in token of his submission, then placed it within the chamber. A sigh rippled through the vast crowd.

The King made obeisance to the relic, forehead touching the platform. He stripped himself of all his jewelled ornaments – necklaces, armbands, rings – and placed them beneath the relic. He made obeisance once more, then rose and walked backward down the steps, facing the relic all the time.

The Queen, Prince Digha Bahu, Prince Abhaya of Soma and his consort, who had arrived for the ceremony, other members of the royal family and the nobility followed in turn. Each venerated the relic and placed jewelled ornaments in the relic chamber.

Finally, all the offerings were made. The Venerable Rahula, Chief Monk of the Tissa Maha Ramaya, started to chant benedictions on the work. '*Buddang Saranang Kachcha-a-mi . . . !*' Other monks took up the chant. Soon twelve thousand voices were lifted up to the heavens.

When the chanting finally died down, the King escorted

the Chief Monk to the entrance of the graceful granite *vihare*, built to house the *bhikkus*.

Torchlight flickered on the King's drawn face, now gleaming with sweat. His dark eyes shone with religious fervour. 'Our Lord the Chief Monk, other venerable monks, members of the royal family assembled here, honourable Ministers of State and our revered people of Ruhuna, hearken to us,' he commanded. His deep, rasping voice was lost in the vast open space and the mass of humanity.

A hush settled on the crowd. The white-clad queen, ethereally beautiful in the moonlight, walked up to King Kākkavan, holding a golden bowl of scented water in her pale hands. The King took the bowl from her and gently poured the water over the right hand of the Chief Monk.

'We have poured water over the right hand of the Venerable Chief Monk in token of our plea that the sacred Community of Monks should accept this, our humble offering of a *vihare*,' the King proclaimed.

The Chief Monk raised his right hand, water dripping from it in *diamanthi* drops. 'We accept the offering,' he said. 'All is well, O Great King.'

Later that night, when the ceremony was ended, the King retired early to his tent. Weariness drained him. The familiar cramping began in his chest. Soon a cold, damp sweat began to form a thick film over his body. He lay on his couch, relaxing all his muscles, controlling his breathing and reducing the thudding beat of his heart. In that state, he seemed to watch the long minutes drifting by him. Finally, the more intense weariness passed. He began to feel drowsy. He reached over for the bell beside his couch and rang it with a single flick of the wrist.

Bare-bodied attendants, led by their chief, rushed in and made obeisance.

'Have the Ten Great Warriors attend us immediately,' the King commanded.

It did not take long for the warriors to crowd into the tent, curious as to why they had been summoned at that hour. King Kakkavan, still lying on his couch, surveyed them with weary pride.

'We have built a united and prosperous kingdom,' the King said, his voice thin, the words soft, slow and light upon the air. 'Our strength has saved us from aggression – the strength of our armies, which are led by you, the Great Warriors. We fear that on our death, dissension will weaken the kingdom and cause its destruction.' He lifted tired eyes toward the white *dagoba* looming through the open entrance flaps of the tent, gasping for breath from the effort of speaking resolutely.

The Great Warriors stirred, looking at one another, perplexed. Why did the King speak thus? Why was his voice so low? No one could inquire of a king.

King Kakkavan sighed. 'We are greatly concerned lest the two brothers, Abhaya Gamini and Sadha Tissa, take up arms against each other for the succession,' he resumed in that low, tired voice. 'One or the other would then be destroyed and the kingdom might perish.' With an effort, he raised himself on his elbow. He injected command into his voice. 'We desire you, the Ten Great Warriors, to take an oath tonight upon that *dagoba* and the sacred relic it enshrines.' He nodded toward the white *dagoba*. 'Neither you nor any member of your ten corps will take sides with either prince, upon our death, in any armed conflict, until the will of the people has placed one or the other securely on the throne. And you will support that prince and no other thereafter. Speak now to it.'

There was silence in the tent, broken only by the hissing of tapers. Outside, a thousand voices murmured the scriptures. Each of the warriors had his own inner conflict at the King's request. Vasabha loved Gamini. Bharana and Nimila, even the dwarf Gotha and the giant Nanda Mitta, had special loyalties to him. They looked stolidly ahead, unwilling to speak.

Yet a king's request was a command and the Chief Warrior must set the example. Velu Sumana raised his right hand. 'Your request is our command, sire,' he declared. 'It is also full of wisdom, for by this means, the army will remain intact for the true successor and as a warning to any foreign aggressor. I, for one, will take this oath.'

Vasabha stepped forward, flare-light gleaming on his golden body. 'I have a question, sire.'

King Kakkavan knew well enough where Vasabha's heart lay. He hesitated a moment, then decided. 'Speak!' he commanded.

'By Arya custom and tradition, which have the force of law, the eldest son has the right of succession to a kingdom,' Vasabha declared. 'Are we then to ignore the law by taking this oath?' He held the King's glance with level eyes. 'Since when has it been for the people to decide the succession, sire?'

The King studied the handsome face before him. His expression softened for a moment. 'You are right and wrong, warrior,' he stated. 'Any king holds his throne by the will of the people. Even his right to name his successor ultimately stems from the people. May the people not rise and overthrow a king who ignores their will?'

'Yes . . . sire,' Vasabha agreed reluctantly.

'Then you must grant that the Arya laws of custom and tradition flow from the people, must you not?'

Vasabha was a simple, honest warrior. He could not combat the King's subtle argument. 'Yes, sire,' he acknowledged, but his fine dark eyes became clouded with pain and bewilderment.

'Well then, you are bound to take this oath,' the King resumed. He considered awhile. 'Remember, though, that it will not bind your loyalties, or any of your actions other than participating actively in an armed conflict.'

Vasabha's brow cleared. 'I, too, will take the oath, sire,' he conceded.

440

King Kakkavan dismissed the Great Warriors. When they had left the tent, Vasabha drew Velu Sumana to one side. 'I may need to visit my village,' he said. 'I had a message to attend to some urgent family business there, but waited until our mission here was accomplished. Do you think you could keep an eye on my corps for a couple of weeks if I decide to leave?'

Velu Sumana searched Vasabha's face. 'Yes, of course,' he finally agreed. He turned and walked away, leaving Vasabha staring in the direction of the *dagoba*.

In the light of the waning moon, quiet was settling over the great dome. Around its base, *bhikkus* and devotees were settling down for the night and attendants were extinguishing the flares.

Some instinct told Vasabha to remain in the shadow of a tall *suriya* tree. Before long, he heard the King's little bell tinkle. He watched silently as messengers answered the summons. They emerged hastily from the tent and sped away, to return with the Queen, as Vasabha had guessed they would, and Leela, the handmaiden. The Queen entered the tent while Leela remained outside. The attendants closed the tent flaps and took up positions in front to prevent intruders from coming within earshot.

It was almost a half hour before the Queen left the tent. Even in the pale light, Vasabha saw that she had been weeping. Now, controlling herself courageously, she walked slowly and steadily away, followed by Leela.

Vasabha moved from the shadows to the entrance of the tent. 'The king needs me,' he said simply to the attendant guarding it. He brushed past the man and entered the tent.

The King lay on his couch. His normally dark face was grey and drawn, the eyes sunken, the sockets like those of a naked skull. He was gasping for breath, his white clothes soaked with sweat. His eyes rolled sideways and fastened on Vasabha. A croak escaped him. He was trying to say something. Instinctively the giant understood. 'You had Her

441

Majesty leave to spare her the worst, sire,' he stated quietly. 'You are truly noble. Think on all the good you have done, as I will. Think of the peace you have brought this realm at sad cost to yourself, and you will attain *Nibbhana*.'

A flicker of gratitude shone in the King's eyes. Some of the torment left them. Only the physical agony showed when they rolled upward again. He half rose, gasping for breath, his hands clawing at his chest. Vasabha could feel the battering rams hammering at his king's chest as if they attacked his own. He could feel the thudding of the heart, the desperate reaching for the final breath that was not there, but merely rattled in the throat.

So Kakkavan Tissa, the crow, the lonely man, refused the battle with death, and inevitably won.

He died in the peace he had pursued during his later years, in the presence of the gentlest and most beautiful of his Great Warriors.

Chapter 44

Unknowing of the major events that had taken place in Nuggala, Gamini rode Raja to the crest of the mountain. Beyond was the flat, grassy mountaintop, scrubbed with lantana and wild gorse. To his left was the gentle slope up which he had just ridden, broken by the white, black and brown of grazing cattle. To the right was a rocky black cliff, falling sheer, hundreds of feet, to a dark ravine below. On either side, across the dark green valleys threaded by silver streams, were the red rooftops of villages, their smoke slowly curling upward. In the distance were sweeping ranges of blue hills.

The air was crisp up here and not a sound disturbed the

stillness until a click, followed by a crackle, reached Gamini's ears. He identified it as a pebble dislodged and falling into the ravine below. He reined Raja sideways and turned in the direction of the sound.

He tensed at seeing a man standing a few yards away, materializing as if from nowhere. He was a pleasant-faced fellow, with even white teeth showing in a smile beneath a black moustache. His clear brown complexion was disfigured only by a scar running from eye to jawline on the right side. It made his smile lopsided. There was something vaguely familiar about him.

The man walked up to Gamini. 'You are searching for something?' he inquired in a hoarse voice.

'Lost cattle. Have you seen any?'

'Yes, they are in that little copse over there.' He jabbed a stubby brown finger toward a clump of trees further to the right.

'Are you new to this area?' Gamini asked. 'I don't seem to have seen you before, yet somehow your face seems familiar.'

The man threw back his head and laughed. 'Are you new to this area?' he mimicked. 'I've lived in that village down there all my life.' He nodded across the ravine.

Gamini grinned. This fellow has a sense of humour. 'Well, I must go get the cattle,' he said, starting to urge Raja toward the copse.

'You must indeed be new to this area, else you'd know you can't ride that way,' the man interposed. 'There's a break in the path caused by a landslide. Better tether your horse and come with me. I'll help you bring the cattle back. You can then remount and drive them home.'

The man turned on his heel and walked in the direction of the cliff. Gamini dismounted, tethered Raja to a gnarled tree stump and hastened after him.

'We've got to go around that bend beyond the cliff's edge.' The man jerked his head to where the path

443

disappeared into the bulging curve of the mountain.

A gentle breeze sprang up, soon swirling into a strong wind. The man hastened his steps, shifting closer to the mountain. Gamini turned to walk beside him, on the outer side.

They came to the cliff's edge. The man pointed toward the ravine. 'My house is down there,' he said.

Gamini looked down, trying to locate the rooftop. 'Where?' he began.

'There!' the man exclaimed. He grasped Gamini's shoulder as if to point. Instead, he shoved.

Gamini was caught unawares. The sickening knowledge that he had been lured to his death only hit him when he reeled over the cliff, arms flailing empty air, desperately trying to regain his balance.

The man pushed Gamini again.

It was easy this time. Already off balance, Gamini went over the edge. He tried frantically for a foothold. There was none. His feet felt the emptiness. His aching fingers clutched at the void. They struck something solid. He clawed for a hold, terror giving him strength. His fingers locked on a rocky ledge. His arms nearly came out of their sockets as they stopped his fall. His breathing was sick in his throat with the unexpected fear.

He clung, teetered, holding on for dear life. The ledge vibrated. Was it about to give?

It settled and held. Gamini hung in space, breath heaving, the soles of his feet throbbing painfully at the emptiness beneath where death awaited him, hundreds of feet below. He hung there, his body dimpled with sweat and goose bumps. He gazed upward through sweat-blurred eyes at a face now contorted with hatred.

'Tell your gods that Ravi sent you to them,' the man shouted. 'Tell them Ravi avenged the murder of his brothers, Rana and Suramba, whom you buried on this hillside like cattle.'

A bitter groan escaped Gamini at having fallen into the trap of a man crazed, a man without reason or mercy, a mad dog. So much for his destiny, so much for a unified Lanka, so much for Raji and his unborn child.

'Contemplate your death,' Ravi shouted, 'as my brother did before his execution.' He paused, grinning evilly. 'Let me tell you how you are going to die. When your fingers get tired, I'll reach down with my foot and crush your left hand a little. Not to cause you to loosen it, but enough to make you wish that you could. You see what I mean? When your bowels give with fear and you splatter yourself with the stuff of which you are made, you'll beg for mercy.' His voice dropped. He seemed to be speaking to himself. 'Then I'll really crush the right hand that buffeted my brother to death. You know what I mean? . . . No mercy. Hah! No mercy! Only the gods must give you that.'

On the night of King Kakkavan's cremation, the seven Ministers of State maintained vigil beside the funeral pyre. Finally, around midnight, they heard the soft explosion that betokened the cracking of the skull. The brains of the King were now ashes. His rule was indeed over.

The ministers left immediately for their meeting chamber in the Mahagama palace to consider the succession.

Prince Digha Bahu insisted on attending the discussion and bringing Prince Tissa with him. 'We are the only rightful claimants to the succession,' he asserted. 'We must be present at your deliberations.'

Shortly before dawn, the Ministers' Council, red-eyed from lack of sleep, sat around the circular *nadun* wood table in their chamber. Presiding was the Chief Minister, the ancient Kirthi Siri. He was flanked by Prince Digha Bahu and Prince Tissa.

Kirthi Siri represented the sovereign element of the state. The other ministers sitting around the table were those of the Treasury, Justice, the Armed Forces, Land, Fortifications,

445

the People and Religion, which included education. The flares still burned and their light lay upon pale, sweating faces, all drawn with more than tiredness. Kirthi Siri alone looked no different. His face was so tired-looking normally that only death could make a change.

Kirthi Siri opened the meeting. 'We are gathered here, my fellow ministers, on a more tragic occasion than we have ever known. This event can only turn out for the good if we make decisions based on the law, justice and custom.' His normally whining voice was surprisingly firm.

'The sources of our law are *dharma*, sacred precept based on truth, *vyavahara*, agreement, *charlithraya*, custom, and *rajasasana*, royal decree. In the absence of *rajasasana* tonight, we must substitute for it *nyaya*, or what is right, which is the ultimate source of law. For this purpose, we must separate law from justice, because the law is not always just, nor is justice always the law. I must also remind you that we are here merely to express the will of the people, whose one desire, whose only security, is to be governed according to what is right.' He paused to allow his words to sink in, the eye-hoods opening briefly.

'I will now entertain nominations for the succession, based on these principles.' He glanced inquiringly at his colleagues.

The scraping of Prince Digha Bahu's chair on the granite floor broke the silence. He did not rise, however, but merely pushed his chair back to command attention. 'I say there are only two rightful claimants to the succession,' he asserted roughly – 'Prince Sadha Tissa here and I.' His face was flushed. He had obviously found time for a couple of draughts of *sura* since the cremation, so his pale eyes were even more bloodshot than usual. 'It is only necessary that you ministers endorse Prince Tissa and me as the sole claimants. He and I will reach satisfactory agreements as to who will reign and who will govern.'

'You mean that we, the Council of Ministers, should

446

merely state that Prince Sadha Tissa and you are our nominees and you will then decide between yourselves who will reign and who will govern?' The sharp voice was that of Veera Singha, the young Minister for the Armed Forces. His chiselled face was set, his eyes challenging. He seemed to have been named spokesman by his colleagues.

Prince Digha Bahu nodded. 'Right!'

'That implies a difference between ruler and governor?' Veera Singha's eyebrows lifted.

Prince Digha Bahu glared back at the minister. He did not deign to reply this time, merely nodded several times, slowly and emphatically.

The ministers looked at one another. The temperature of the room dropped perceptibly.

Veera Singha turned to Prince Tissa, who lolled, sulky-faced, on his chair. 'Are you in agreement with what Prince Digha Bahu demands?'

'Yes!' Prince Tissa replied, his voice a shade high, his gaze defiant.

Veera Singha's face went hard. 'Is that not an unusual suggestion, Prince, and contrary to *charlithraya*?'

'Any custom is unusual when it is first introduced,' Prince Digha Bahu retorted coldly. 'This one may well become *charlithraya* with the years to come. What is more important today is that Prince Tissa and I are in a position to cause its introduction.'

'How would you do that?' Veera Singha's voice was urbane.

'By force of arms if necessary. We are both duly appointed governors and commanders. Prince Sadha Tissa here is the Regent. All the regular forces of the army are under our command.'

'Governors and commanders are appointed by the King on the recommendation of the Council of Ministers.' Arya Ratna, the plump, middle-aged Minister of Justice, spoke up. His normally jovial face was deadly serious.

447

'Where is the king to whom you would recommend any change?' Prince Digha Bahu demanded triumphantly.

'What of the Arya custom whereby the eldest son must succeed?' Arya Ratna cut in.

'Where is the eldest son?'

'We should search for him first,' Veera Singha retorted. 'Justice demands it.'

'Justice? Faugh! But let us consider right and justice if you will. First, for the Arya custom to take effect, the whereabouts of the oldest son must be known, or he must be present. Second, a cretin, a madman, someone of proven irresponsibility or incapacity obviously cannot succeed, whatever his rights.' The Prince smiled smugly, but his out-thrust face also shone with malignant enjoyment.

'Are you suggesting that there are doubts as to the mental capacity of Prince Abhaya Gamini?' Prema Dasa, the gaunt Minister for Religion, demanded incredulously.

'I am suggesting that the reason for Prince Gamini's absence today is his unfitness to govern. He was not worthy as a son or as a prince. He was over-ambitious and without restraint. He had no respect for anyone. He even insulted his own father and heaped shame on him, then fled the kingdom to escape the King's justice. He is therefore merely a refugee from justice. Seek him out if you will and punish him for his misdeeds. If he desires to demonstrate any capacity to govern, let him first submit himself to the King's justice.'

A shocked murmur ran through the room.

Veera Singha was the first to recover. 'But you have reminded us that there is no king,' he countered gently. 'Consequently, Prince Gamini cannot submit himself to the King's justice. Besides, he fled the kingdom to escape the King's wrath, not the King's justice. If our late revered ruler thought otherwise, he would have set a price on the prince's head and excluded him by decree from the succession.' He paused, his face stern. 'The only question that now remains is this. What will you do if we, the ministers of the realm, decide to name Prince Abhaya Gamini to the succession tonight?' He challenged Prince Digha Bahu with his glance.

The Prince pushed his chair further back. This time he stood up. He drew himself to his full height, with a strange dignity, dominating the room as much by his arrogance as by his portly stature. 'Ministers must only make decisions that can be backed by power,' he declared, his voice hard as rock. 'You gentlemen are well aware that all the army corps are under the command of Prince Tissa and myself. You dare not make a decision unacceptable to us.'

Every face around the table, except Kirthi Siri's, tightened. Prince Digha Bahu glared at each of the ministers in turn. They stared back angrily at him, then looked toward Veera Singha for strength.

It came instead from Kirthi Siri. He had sat hunched on his chair, his face relaxed, eyes closed, looking like a sleeping bird of prey. Now the words emerged as if he were talking in his sleep. 'What happens if we do decide to offer the throne to Prince Abhaya Gamini regardless? Have you brought along a guard to arrest us?'

Prince Digha Bahu fell into the trap. 'No, but your decision could never be implemented!' Too late, he saw the purpose of Kirthi Siri's question. 'And we would have you all arrested anyway within the hour,' he hastened to add.

The ministers cast admiring glances at their chief. They knew that if Prince Digha Bahu had been truly clever, he would have had an armed guard outside that chamber already, to force their decision and prevent them from leaving to reveal the truth to the people. Now, they could make an independent decision and have it promulgated. If Prince Digha Bahu contested it, he would be driven to open confrontation with the ministers, who represented the people.

Veera Singha rapped the table and stood up. He was a tall, broad-shouldered man who held himself very erect. When he spoke it was with the full authority of his person. 'I, for one, say that these two princes have revealed themselves unfit to govern,' he declared contemptuously. 'They have no respect for right and justice, for the will of the people, for the independence of the ministers, or for our *charlithraya*. As ministers, we must do only what is right. I now propose that we name Prince Abhaya Gamini successor to the throne, that we locate him by any means and bring him to Mahagama to be consecrated. We, the Council, will govern until then. If the army moves against us, it will be contrary to directives I shall issue as Minister of the Armed Forces. If the princes use armed force against us, it will be our danger, but let it also be their risk.'

All the ministers emphatically shouted, '*Ahey! Ahey!*'

Kirthi Siri stirred. The folds of his eyelids lifted, revealing the sharp eyes. 'There will be no danger to any of us,' he stated mildly.

Prince Digha Bahu swung around toward him. 'What the devil do you mean?' he demanded. His voice rose to a shout. 'Prince Tissa and I can exterminate you ministers and rule the kingdom with the army.'

'I alone of all of us present know something that you obviously do not know, Prince.' Kirthi Siri's voice now carried an unfamiliar tone of command. He had not been appointed Chief Minister for nothing. He sat up, placing his elbows on the table. He turned his head to stare piercingly at Prince Digha Bahu.

'And what is that?' A tremor had entered the Prince's voice.

'The Ten Great Warriors, who lead the ten corps and command their loyalty, swore to the dying King Kakkavan Tissa, on the Nuggala *dagoba* and the sacred relic it enshrines, that neither they nor any of their troops will take sides in any dispute as to the succession.'

Prince Digha Bahu's cheeks slackened and quivered. 'No!' he said. 'No! That's not true. You're lying . . .' The stern expression on Kirthi Siri's face told him that the Chief

450

Minister spoke the truth. His voice dropped to a whisper. 'That pi-dog . . . that damned accursed little crow . . .' He stared wildly around.

'Perhaps you foiled yourself, Prince,' Kirthi Siri suggested quietly. He drew back and relapsed into his original position on the chair. His eyelids fell slowly over the sharp eyes. He seemed to have fallen asleep again.

Prince Digha Bahu straightened up suddenly. He walked over to Prince Tissa and stood behind the boy. 'This is devil's work,' he hissed fiercely, 'and there will be the devil to pay.' His glare swept the room, landing menacingly upon Veera Singha, then Kirthi Siri. He gripped Prince Tissa by the shoulders. 'Come, Prince,' he said quietly. 'Let us do what we must.'

Gamini knew that in moments the ledge would give. From here on, the cliff sloped sharply inward, with no other ledge or protrusion beneath him. Once his fingers lost their strength, he would hurtle to his death below. Already the fear-sweat of his body was making them slippery. The thought of the drop caused the soles of his feet to prickle.

No! He must live. Somehow, he must live. A savage determination welled up within him, almost flooding his brain. He had to remain cool, to think of a way out. He recalled the abduction attempt in the palace. He had once again to find that split second when the enemy was off guard. An overconfident enemy such as Ravi would surely give him the opening.

Ravi had said he would crush the left hand first. Not too hard. Ah! Gamini relaxed his body and gently eased the grip of his right hand on the ledge. He looked upward. Ravi was lowering himself over the edge of the cliff, resting his weight on his elbows. Imperceptibly, Gamini shifted his hold completely to his left arm, which screamed its agony.

The heel of a bare, horny foot came slowly downwards toward Gamini. Gently it felt for the fingers of his left hand.

451

Gamini let go with his right hand and grabbed the thick ankle. Ravi tried to shake the hand away, but Gamini hung on grimly. Now he had a double grip. His left hand found new strength on the ledge and his right hand had Ravi's ankle.

Ravi kicked madly for Gamini's head with his right foot. Gamini swung his head sideways in time. The kick jarred his shoulder instead. He hung on regardless. This was his last chance. If he went, at least he would take Ravi with him.

Ravi's hold on the lip of the precipice began to slip. He abruptly stopped struggling and concentrated on restoring his grip. Stalemate. Gamini did not know what to do next. How long could they remain like this? How long could he himself hang on? If only he could get a foothold on the ledge to which he clung, he might have a chance.

Gamini began to lever himself upward, bending his knees, trying to get his feet against the cliff. The muscles of his shoulders and arms were on fire, yet he kept pulling grimly upward.

Ravi was motionless, desperately holding on to the top of the cliff now, obviously afraid to make any move lest the two of them hurtle down. Gamini's searching feet found the cliff face. He jabbed his soles flat against it. The feel of solid earth pulsed through his whole body. Ravi's vicious move had given him what he did not have before, a handhold instead of fingerholds. He began using his back muscles to push upwards, his feet flat on the cliff face.

Slowly, torturously, Gamini inched his body upward, using the ledge and Ravi's foot as a rope, pushing flatfooted against the cliff, like a giant spider walking up it.

Finally, he felt the ledge with his right foot. Inch by inch, he slowly raised the foot and edged it onto the ledge. Praying to the *devas* that the ledge would hold, he started to raise his body.

Through the mist of sweat-blinded eyes, he saw the hand reaching down, a familiar hand.

I must be dreaming, he thought. I must have died. This is the hand of a *deva* continuing into death the rescue for which I prayed during my last life-moment.

Gamini blinked rapidly to clear the sweat drops from his eyes. He then focused them again on the hand. It was the hand that had guided his own, to teach him the finer points of writing – the hand of Prince Rodana.

Vasabha, who had a rope around Ravi's neck, ensuring that the brigand did not let go before we got Gamini to safety, unloosed the rope. Ravi struggled to pull himself over the edge. His face was drenched with sweat, the wild eyes pleading now.

Vasabha ground his booted foot on Ravi's face. One tremendous push and Ravi went over. The ravine rang with his screams. A soggy thud ended them, but they continued bouncing off the cliffs before they died down.

Gamini lay panting on the ground, blinking at the sunlight. His face streamed with sweat; his body was drenched with it. He shuddered a few times, shaking his head. Before my eyes, his whole body slowly broke out with prickles. He started to tremble, but controlled himself with a tremendous effort.

He stared into space awhile, then seemed to make up his mind. He sat up and started flexing and unflexing his fingers and shoulders, as if he had only been through manual exercise. 'You saved my life,' he finally announced, his dark eyes moving to Vasabha and then to me.

'You had already saved yourself,' Vasabha declared.

'What are you doing here?' It was typical of Gamini to come directly to the point.

Vasabha, the simple warrior, was equally direct. 'The King, your father, died in my presence at Nuggala five days ago. He had just finished consecrating a great new *dagoba* and *vihare* there. Before I left, I consulted the Chief Minister and also left instructions for my chief captain to catch up with me if you were nominated king. He may well be on his way, because Kirthi Siri clearly told me that he felt the succession was rightfully yours.'

Gamini stood up immediately. The news made him throw off his ordeal as if it had been merely a cloak. He began pacing. The eyes staring out of his dark, sweat-strewn face glowed with a strange new fire.

I intervened to save him the embarrassment of asking what might seem to be heartless questions. 'Your father named no heir. He left it to the Council of Ministers to decide who should succeed him. Since your father's cremation would, by custom, take place today, the ministers will meet before dawn tomorrow to make their decision.'

'What decision is there to be made when I am the only true heir?' Gamini demanded.

'Remember, the army corps are commanded by your brother and Prince Digha Bahu,' I responded. 'Who has the force can have the victory.'

Gamini's eyes flashed. 'You mean the army will turn traitor?'

'Not so, Prince,' Vasabha hastened to reassure him. 'On his deathbed, your father, the King, made us Ten Great Warriors swear on the new *dagoba* and the relic that neither we, nor any of our men, would take sides militarily in any dispute as to the succession.'

Gamini was taken aback at first. Then his anger blazed. 'You swore that oath?' he shouted.

'I did, because it was the only way. It does not bind me to abstain from supporting you. The fact that I immediately left and have ridden these many days to reach you will reveal my loyalty to you.'

Gamini stared at Vasabha. His anger began to evaporate before the sincerity of the Great Warrior. 'You can explain all this to me,' he finally said, his voice more gentle. 'I am sure there is an explanation.'

Vasabha looked puzzled, so I hastened to intervene. 'Let

454

me be the one to give you the explanations, Prince,' I stated. 'Your father was very wise. It would have been stupid for him to name you his successor. Think of what could have happened. In your absence, Prince Digha Bahu and your brother would have assumed control, then had you tracked down and killed. If you had indeed managed to get to Mahagama alive, the army would have been divided, or Prince Digha Bahu and Prince Tissa, having spread word that you were mad, or dead, would already have used the army to seize power. The moment you appeared, you would have been killed. The oath taken by the warriors is therefore to your advantage. Now, let us hasten to Mahagama. The ministers already know from Vasabha's captain that you are alive and well. I am sure they will name you to succeed, so there is no time to be lost.'

Vasabha made to move away and I began to follow him, but Gamini stayed me with a hand on my arm. 'How did you get here in time to save me?' he demanded quietly. His eyes had a look in them that made me melt.

'I had a feeling of intense disquiet shortly after you left on your search for the cattle,' I replied. 'Vasabha arrived just as I rode out of the gates of the house. His news gave me an added reason to find you. Fortunately, soon after we cleared the village, we saw you riding on the crest of the mountain. We followed and found your horse tethered. We dismounted and tracked you from the broken lantana and scrub to the pathway.' I looked at Vasabha. 'The rest was easy.'

'Easy?' Gamini threw back his head. His laugh rang out.

Before its last echoes finished bouncing off the mountains, Gamini sobered. 'We must ride for Mahagama immediately. Raji can follow. She will need a day or two to pack and say her farewells.' His expression was bright, pulsing with excitement.

Vasabha exchanged glances with me. I nodded to him to speak up. 'Lord, it would not be safe for your wife to come to Mahagama until you are firmly established on the throne.'

Gamini flashed into anger. 'What do you mean, "firmly" established?'

'There is a possibility that your brother, or Prince Digha Bahu, or both, might attempt to create problems . . .'

'Then I shall deal with them.'

I intervened. 'Apart from the possibility of danger to Raji, the presence of your future consort might make you more vulnerable.'

Gamini thought on it, quickly this time. The anger slowly faded from his eyes. 'You are right,' he agreed. 'On to Mahagama then.' But his eyes had lost some of their sparkle.

Sunlight bathed the valley below their bedroom windows and cast purple shadows between the dark crags and green plateaus of the mountain. With a fluttering of black and white wings, two *kondaya* magpies poised briefly on the window ledge, then flew away.

'These are all lucky omens,' Gamini said. He glanced sideways at Raji. Her large, dark eyes told him that she knew something was in the offing. He wondered how to put it to her in such a way that she would know the least pain. He turned, reached out for her pale hand and placed the slender, cool fingers against his cheek. 'My father is dead. I am the King. I must go to my duty. But wherever I go, I shall send for you as soon as I can. You know that, do you not?'

Raji's face had a strange, luminous quality even in that bright light. Her *ran-thambili* cheeks seemed almost transparent. The red lips quivered.

What exquisite beauty, he thought. How can I leave her?

'I am but a part of you, lord – spirit of your spirit.'

'Are you afraid of my going?'

'Never, lord. Only afraid for you.'

'Why should you be?'

Her eyelids fluttered. She looked down and was silent.

'Tell me,' he urged.

'There could be danger.' She seemed to make up her

mind. She lifted her head confidently. 'But I know you will survive it all.'

'I do not wish to leave you. With you I am fulfilled.'

Tears came to Raji's eyes. She trembled. He could feel the vibration of her body, though it was not touching his own.

'You are my all, lord. Although you may not take my body with you, you have my entire being, as you have had it since the day we first met in your palace.'

'It would be easier for me to tear off a limb, tear out my heart, than leave you even for a day.'

She reached out suddenly and took his hand. She placed it against her womb. 'Your body is within me now, in our child. See how it greets you.'

He felt a thump against the palm of his hand. She gently removed his hand from her grasp, raising it to her lips. He drew her to his bed, moved by his love for her and by his approaching loneliness.

We rode hard and reached Mahagama after an uneventful journey. The Chief Minister met us at the entrance gates of the palace. He knelt in homage before Gamini and kissed his hand. It was evidence enough. Vasabha and I knelt too, our foreheads to the ground.

'Rise, my friends!' Gamini commanded gruffly.

We rose and looked at each other, joy in our faces and our hearts.

'I regret I have one disturbing item of news,' Kirthi Siri declared gravely. 'Your royal brother, Prince Tissa, has retired to Dighavapi. He took with him the Sceptre of State and Kandula, the State Elephant. Supported by Prince Digha Bahu, he has declared himself King of Ruhuna.'

'What of my mother?' Gamini inquired spontaneously.

'The royal Queen Mother willingly accompanied Prince Tissa to Dighavapi.'

Gamini refused to be consecrated until the entire kingdom was his, with the return of his mother to Mahagama, the yielding up of the State sceptre and elephant and the submission of his brother Tissa. Receiving no reply to a formal demand for these, he decided to march on Dighavapi as quickly as possible, to avoid giving Prince Tissa time to raise an effective army and to prevent the people from becoming resigned to a divided kingdom. Serene in the knowledge of his destiny, he had neither involved his ministers in raising more men, nor wasted time training those men he had.

Our force of some thirty thousand proceeded north, then eastward. Within two days, our scouts had skirmished with the enemy's forward elements. On the third evening, we arrived at the Culan plain, where Gamini decided to give battle.

We encamped on the eastern border of the plain that night. Before nightfall, our scouts had reported light contact with Prince Tissa's main body, but were unable to determine its strength. Campfires dotting the eastern end of the plain after dark told us that our enemies were there in large numbers and that they too had settled down for the night.

We lay under the stars, huddling close to each other for warmth after our own fires flickered low. How many of us prayed, 'May it not be I!' And yet the dread knowledge that a great many must die and many more be wounded hung tangibly in the air. Through the long night, ignorance combined with imagination to produce a hundred devils, whose weapon was the waiting.

We awoke, stiff and cramped, well before dawn. Gamini issued orders for us to put out our campfires and take up our positions. He then called up his commanders and gave them their final orders.

'Our spearmen shall stand in line, with gaps between them, along the edge of the plain, ahead of the bowmen,' he announced. 'Our charioteers shall wait to race through these gaps. The enemy foot soldiers, advancing first, in line, will be met by volleys of our arrows. When they pause, our chariots shall charge them, followed closely by our spearmen and foot soldiers to destroy them. Prince Rodana and I shall remain at the head of our cavalry. We shall attack the enemy cavalry and charioteers when I give the signal. I expect the traitor, Prince Tissa, to be at the head of his cavalry. He is to be spared, so that I can kill him myself.'

As we wheeled our horses and cantered to our positions on the edge of the long copse in which we sheltered, the chill dread at Gamini's desire to kill his own brother went deeper than my fear of the battle.

In the cool, grey dawn, the two armies faced each other across the parched grass and dry scrub of the Culan plain – Sinhala against Sinhala, Ruhuna against Ruhuna. Trapped within the glint of arms and the movement of men, horses and chariots, I became sick at heart. My first battle, and I was about to kill or be killed by my own countrymen.

Dedicated to the Doctrine and to nonviolence in my boyhood, I could not arouse bloodlust within myself even against a Chola. How then had I thought to stir the people of Ruhuna to a patriotic war under Gamini's leadership? Had I been blinded by the ideal of Sinhala rule throughout Lanka? Or had my boyhood promise to my uncle taken over my life, like a bull leading a cart at night while the carter sleeps? What of my love for Gamini and my faith in him? I realized with grim certainty that whatever causes had spurred me, I was led by my own destiny alone. During the past three months and especially since last night, I had fought myself to generate enthusiasm for today's battle. Duty alone goaded me to it. Fight, maim, kill, for the end would justify the means! Not exactly my principle, but it would have to do. I had avoided communing with God about this, but hoped it was part of His plan. My only consolation was that the flower of the Ruhuna army, the ten corps of the Great Warriors, were not involved on this arid plain.

My apprehensions had communicated themselves to the bay I was riding. He kept flicking back his ears nervously and stamping his feet. I glanced at Gamini. He sat firmly on Raja, seemingly at ease. Except for the pulsing of an inner excitement, the strange glow that flamed in his eyes, the set of his jaw, he might have been preparing for a ride through the woods. Any fear he had was totally overshadowed by faith in his destiny, confidence in victory and a curious eagerness for blood and gore, the clash of arms, the stink of sweat and death.

I decided to question his orders that only he should kill Prince Tissa. Perhaps my tensions made me want to carp. 'You never told me that you intended killing your brother,' I remarked.

He smiled, easing himself in the saddle. 'You never asked.'

'But that is fratricide, a mortal *akusala-kharma*.'

He laughed at that. 'Fratricide will not make me any different a person.' He paused and grew serious. 'I have it, I want it, I need it in my heart,' he ground out, smiting his chest with his clenched fist. 'To be a fratricide.'

'What of your oath to your father?'

'What of it?'

'You swore on the sacred milk-rice that you would forever be without enmity toward your brother.'

'I shall kill him without enmity!' he retorted coolly. 'You place too much store on blood ties. The closest relationships of people are with outsiders – wives, lovers, friends.' He grinned impishly at me. 'I am sure you will not contradict

460

that! Besides, it is easier for a brother to be a betrayer.'

He turned away to glance across the plain. Above the treeline, the sky was red-gold with a bursting dawn. Beneath it, we could now distinguish the shapes of a vast array of men.

'I think I have made a mistake,' Gamini muttered.

'What?'

'We are attacking with the sun in our eyes.' His jaw tightened. 'No matter. We shall win, but we must move before the sun comes up.'

Raja stamped the ground nervously. Gamini patted the horse's neck gently. 'Easy there, Raja,' he commanded.

The horse moved its head, trying to look at its master.

Gamini rode forward onto the plain, then turned to face his men. The sun behind him threw the long shadows of horse and man before him. The murmuring of our men and the clank of arms died down.

'Comrades, we are fighting today to establish right and justice,' Gamini cried. He had learned how to pitch his voice so that it carried. 'Those men across the plain are neither Ruhuna nor Sinhala. They are traitors. Yes, traitors to all we cherish. Fight, therefore, with courage and determination never to submit or yield. Today's victory shall begin a new destiny for us all – the destiny of a united Lanka under Sinhala rule. In years to come, your children and your children's children in that free Lanka will say in awe, "He was at the beginning. He was on the Culan plain."' He drew his sword and raised it aloft. 'For right and justice!' he roared.

The men brandished their weapons, now glinting a thousandfold in the sunlight. 'For right and justice!' they roared back.

The sounds travelled across the plain. The enemy gave back an answering roar. Their trumpets blared. Their champions began to advance, screaming insults, getting their men worked up to killer frenzy. Their foot soldiers moved forward in a long, thin line, as Gamini had anticipated, quickly resolving themselves into a wall of tramping men, brandishing their weapons and shouting imprecations. The sound of their advance began to roll toward us.

Gamini waited until the enemy were more than halfway across the plain and within range. 'Bowmen, prepare!' he directed.

The commander of the bowmen relayed his order. 'Prepare to shoot!' they cried.

Two thousand bowmen fitted arrows to bows and drew back the strings, taking aim, each section at a sector of the advancing army.

'Shoot!' Gamini commanded.

'Shoot! ... Shoot! ... Shoot! ... Shoot!' The relayed orders mingled with the twang of bowstrings and the hiss of arrows, like the sounds of a gigantic orchestra. The black hail of arrows seemed to obscure the sky, then reached its mark. Men fell, arrows sticking out of their chests like porcupine quills. Others paused to remove arrows from a neck, an arm, a thigh. They were too far off for the blood to show, but the advancing line began to falter. Screams and groans began reaching us. The commanders rallied their men and urged them on.

'Bowmen ready!' Gamini commanded again. 'Trumpeters sound the advance.'

Trumpets brayed, commanders shouted orders. Horses neighed and weapons clanked in a great welter of sound. The smell of sweat and wet leather assailed my nostrils. I stared at the enemy, trying to work up hate. I could distinguish faces in the mass of humanity now. Fair, dark, bearded, cleanshaven. Young, old. I saw a fair-faced young boy; he could not have been more than seventeen. I was glad I could not see his eyes clearly, for he was no enemy, but a person. Resolutely I thrust the thought aside. These very people would kill me if I did not kill them instead. I remembered my first sword thrust into a man, one of those sent by King Elara to abduct Queen Vihara Devi so many years ago. Suddenly and curiously, I was no longer afraid.

With a mighty creak and clanking, with the slow roll of hooves and wheels, our chariots charged, the warriors lashing their horses and shouting great cries.

'*Hoi!* . . . *hoi!* . . . *hoi!* . . .' Our chariots were soon streaking across the plain, followed by the foot soldiers, the spearmen behind them, a mighty wave stretching unevenly across a half mile.

The blood began to sparkle in my veins. I cried aloud, I knew not what. Gamini heard me. He half turned in his saddle and laughed joyously. Absurdly, I remembered that morning in the glade when we had each savagely killed a leopard. I knew that somehow the same recollection had flashed through Gamini. 'Kill them . . . kill them . . . eat their livers!' he screamed, but still held Raja back. He looked toward the plain. The enemy were already reeling before our second and third volleys of arrows. Our chariots, riding through the gaps in our ranks, crashed into them. Minutes of fierce fighting ensued, then the chariots broke through, leaving death and destruction behind them. The enemy were breaking. Many had fallen. Others were kneeling, some simply standing and staring in shock. Our chariots raced beyond the broken enemy line to regroup, then turned and charged from the rear.

At that precise moment, Prince Tissa's chariots appeared. I gasped, for there were hundreds of them – more than we had ever dreamed. They raced toward our chariots at our weakest moment, when our own chariots were wheeling around. The impact was like thunder. They left our men, horses and vehicles hurtling in their wake. Behind them, a wave of bowmen was revealed.

Gamini was stunned, but only for a moment. 'Prepare to charge!' he directed the cavalry.

'Shall I call up the reserve?' I inquired.

Our reserves had been left beyond the ford, under the orders of Veera Singha, who alone among the ministers was a trained soldier and commander.

'No!' Gamini gritted. 'Not yet!' He gathered up his reins.

'Wait!' I screamed, pointing.

Gamini's head swivelled. Along the northern edge of the plain, a great force of cavalry was streaking westward.

Gamini drew in his breath sharply. He instinctively jerked his head southward. Horrified, we saw an equally large force of enemy cavalry also galloping westward.

'They will make a pincer to cut us off at the rear!' Gamini exclaimed. 'We're heavily outnumbered.'

I knew he was thinking fast and clear, but it was too late. In front of us, our broken chariot force was streaming back, pursued by the enemy. Our foot soldiers began reeling before the combined rush. All was confusion.

'Bowmen, cover with rapid fire!' Gamini shouted.

The twang and hiss of arrows filled the air, but our troops were already in utter confusion. Groups of them were engaging the enemy in hand-to-hand fighting. Others wavered. Most were retreating. Here and there, our men were being trampled or hacked to death by the enemy charioteers. These groups were more difficult marks for our arrows, and the enemy bowmen now began to take their toll as they advanced steadily across the plain.

'Trumpeters, blow the order to withdraw!' Gamini bellowed. His sweat-strewn face was bleak. He kept smiting his thigh with a fist. His horse began backing away from the mêlée.

Our trumpets commenced a dismal blare. Our forces heard, turned and began streaming back, pursued by the enemy. Running men were dropping like tree trunks, enemy arrows sticking from their backs. A brown-skinned giant ran along pulling an arrow from his rump.

Since our own bowmen were under cover of trees, their fire was more effective, especially after the opposing forces

464

separated. Their cool shooting made the enemy slow down. It was too late, however. Our withdrawal had become a rout. In minutes, certainty had turned to defeat.

Gamini's shoulders slumped, but only for a moment. He straightened in the saddle. He swivelled Raja around and signalled the cavalry to follow him. 'Regroup beyond the ford!' he commanded. 'Bowmen, cover the withdrawal.'

Amid the shouts of orders, we raced back toward the ford. The steady aim of our bowmen from the shelter of the treeline stopped the enemy. Their cavalry wheeled and turned around.

By noon all our forces were across the ford, regrouping. Our bowmen and spearmen, who had withdrawn in relays, remained at the water's edge to cover us. We were a sorry remnant of the proud troops of dawn.

King Elara was out on a hunt in the forest north of Anu when word of the battle was brought to him. It had been a successful morning. Single-handed, he had bagged a huge leopard, chasing it on horseback and finishing it off with two spears in its neck. The cured skin would adorn his great canopied bed in the palace. He had returned at noon to the glade where the hunt had first assembled, for the meal that had been prepared. He was hot and sweaty from the hunt. The quiet voices of men, the trill of a bird and the occasional snorting of a horse were soothing to the ears.

Now it was warm in the glade, even in the shade of tall *sal* trees. The smell of curry cooked the Chola way, tangy with lime and powdered coriander, mingling with the smell of sweat, leather and blood, was very heady. He sat on the grass in the shadow of a rock, leaning back, the warmth of the stone soothing to his muscles, and contemplated the scene.

A few noblemen stood inspecting their sweating mounts. Others walked around, drinking water from mugs. Attendants bustled about carrying platters for the meal. At

465

the far edge of the glade, black cauldrons placed on stones sizzled above glowing fires.

This time Digha Jantu was first with the news, having received it from his army sources. He gave his information quietly, then stood towering above the seated king. His body seemed mightier than ever. He was bare-chested as always, his skin shining in the sunlight.

'So the two brothers are at each other's throats already.' King Elara gave a dry chuckle. His eyes twinkled as they met those of his Chief Warrior. 'You see how our plan worked. The Sinhala will destroy each other without a single Chola life being forfeited. The gold we provided the jackal prince to raise forces gave him and Prince Tissa superiority in numbers. Our cavalry advisers provided backbone. Advisers . . . Hah! – a good word for them. Now the entire force of the upstart Gamini will soon be wiped out.' He did not want to break his word to the dead King Kakkavan and reveal the cream of his policy: that the gold provided Prince Digha Bahu had come from King Kakkavan's private treasury each year.

'But we must do more, sire, if we are to retain Prince Digha Bahu's loyalty,' the Chief Warrior maintained, stubborn.

King Elara slapped the ground jovially. 'Oho! You are always pushing for a little more, aren't you?'

'Yes, sire.' Digha Jantu's voice was suddenly fierce, though respectful. 'I am a soldier. My troops and I need action. We have lost our fighting spirit, doing nothing but military exercises these past years. Somewhere in all this political manoeuvring there must be an opportunity for battle. I sense trouble from Prince Gamini down the line. At least provide us with some battle experience as preparation for that event, sire.'

King Elara regarded the giant soberly. A passing cloud threw its shadows on the broad, flat features, making them seem sinister. 'Perhaps you are right,' he conceded. 'We, too, have some unease.' He thought awhile. 'Our forces on the north bank of the river shall move across immediately and seize the Sinhala forts at the Wera, Kasa and Kimbul crossings,' he decided. 'You shall avoid attacking any other forts, especially those fronting Dighavapi.'

The cloud's shadow vanished. Joy spread over Digha Jantu's face, the sunlight silver on it. His splayed-out nostrils distended, making the point seem to droop even more over his upper lip. 'I can scarcely believe what I hear, lord,' he almost whispered. 'After all these years, your yellow leopard can show his claws again.' He expanded his great chest and flexed his muscles. He clapped a large hand to his thigh. 'Neither the promise of gold, nor the blessing of the *devas*, could give me and my men more delight.'

'Do not blaspheme, Chief Warrior,' King Elara reprimanded sharply, his deep, grainy voice taking on a warning edge. 'And remember, you shall advance no farther than the enemy forts. Having taken them, you shall immediately build earthworks to resist assaults from Sinhala territory. They shall serve as bases for our future moves.'

An unusual smile brightened Digha Jantu's face. 'Ah! I have not lived in vain! I shall await Ruhuna's famed ten corps in our new bases?'

'They will not move, provided we do not advance beyond the captured forts,' the King replied confidently. 'The vow the dying king made his Chief Warriors take has divided the kingdom.'

'You are wise beyond measure, lord!' Digha Jantu exclaimed – but the hope of great battles shone in his eyes.

'Let us say that we try to understand people, circumstances and timing,' King Elara responded dryly. 'Our immediate move will give Digha Bahu hope and enable us to infiltrate his forces more easily with our men. It will also provide easier jump-off points than river crossings when we do invade Ruhuna!'

'The *devas* be praised!'

'We shall invade as friends, Chief Warrior, so get all the fighting you can in the next two days. At a future date, our army will advance as the friendly forces of King Elara, invited to be overlord of Ruhuna as well as of Lanka, with a jackal named Digha Bahu on the Mahagama throne.' A note of satisfaction entered King Elara's deep voice. 'It will be a *manta yuddhaya* of the highest magnitude.'

A look of disappointment flashed across the Chief Warrior's face. The wide nostrils flared just once. 'Pray give me leave to depart, lord,' he requested abruptly.

The King turned to the ever-present Junda. 'What do you think of our plan, clown? Would you not like to be the court jester of the Emperor Elara, overlord of the three kingdoms by his wisdom alone, not merely King Elara of Lanka?'

'Jesters are the emperors of their folly.' The dwarf grinned, showing large, discoloured teeth. 'Emperors are the jesters of their wisdom.'

King Elara glanced at Digha Jantu, who shrugged.

King Elara nodded his consent. He watched the retreating figure. You will plot to give provocation to the Sinhala and force them to aggression, he thought, for if a king starts a war, a chief warrior can become a king.

Chapter 46

By noon, all our men were safely across the river, except for the dead and the fallen. Fortunately the ford was long and narrow. Else we would all have been bottled up, Gamini and I included, since we personally supervised the withdrawal and were among the last to cross.

Gamini, Veera Singha and I soon set up a temporary headquarters on a wooded rise close to the riverbank, from which we could direct the disposition of our troops. We observed enemy movement behind the cover of a line of trees beyond the ford. The muddy stream was deep enough farther north and south to present an obstacle, so we did not fear a wide enfilade and assault from the rear. We therefore concentrated our bowmen in the green foliage of the high bank on our side. Having already had a taste of our archery, for a while the enemy made no major move to attack us. Presently, however, random twangs and the hiss of our shafts met feelers they started putting out for a frontal crossing.

Our field kitchens had been set up well in the rear. By early afternoon we were served a meal of cold rice. We were hungry enough by then to eat even the banana leaves on which it was served.

When evening came, Prince Tissa's troops still had not followed up their advantage. We therefore moved our head-quarters to a low, tree-covered hillock overlooking the stream, where we summoned our commanders to discuss the situation. It was cool here, though sunlight still lay hot on the grey, sandy wastes across the stream, where the only shade, as far as the eye could see, was from that narrow copse, the occasional green tree and scattered scrub withered by the sun. At least we had a more comfortable location than the enemy – and I was secretly relieved that the Culan plain itself, on which we had suffered our ignominious defeat, was out of sight. It had to be littered with our dead and wounded.

Apart from Gamini, Veera Singha and me, the commanders of our two infantry corps, our cavalry, our bowmen and the supply units soon assembled. They were grim and tired-looking men, all six of them, dust scouring their sweaty faces and uniforms, but they stood tall.

After some discussion, we agreed that our alternatives were to continue retreating and then regroup closer to

469

Mahagama, or to make a last-ditch stand here, or to defend the stream as a prelude to a more orderly withdrawal.

Gamini preferred the last alternative. 'If we run now, we will never stop,' he declared harshly. 'Over there to the east, the brave lie dead or wounded. My brother's men are not likely to take prisoners. Those who stood for me will be executed summarily on the battlefield by the usurper.' His voice broke fleetingly. His eyes reflected his pain. He paused, fists clenching. 'They must be avenged and it can only be done if we stand here and fight, to prepare for another day.'

'Do you really favour that alternative, sire?' Veera Singha inquired, concern in his dark eyes. 'Would it not be better to make an orderly withdrawal to Mahagama, where we can not only regroup but rally others to our cause?'

'No, Minister! I say we hold this stream for the present, until we have established strong defensive positions across the Kumbuk River, at our rear. When those are ready, we can make an orderly withdrawal. As soon as the enemy has been checked, I shall return to Mahagama and help the ministers raise a new army.' He held Veera Singha's gaze. 'As for today's tragedy, I alone am responsible. Many brave men have died because of my mistakes.'

'Do not judge yourself too harshly,' Veera Singha advised. 'We are all equally to blame.'

Gamini placed a hand on the minister's arm. 'Will your fellow ministers support me in raising a new army in the light of this defeat?' His eyes were grave now.

He was met by a confident smile. 'Have no doubt of it. Most of them advised against a hasty advance for the very reason that they wanted to help you raise such a force. You are the rightful heir, the man of destiny. This is a matter of right and wrong, not of personalities. If the ministers do not support *nyaya* and *charlithraya*, the kingdom will perish.'

Gamini clapped Veera Singha on the shoulder. 'You are well named,' he said quietly. 'Veera. . . Singha. Hero and lion.'

The other commanders readily agreed to Gamini's strategy and we soon worked out a detailed plan as to which units should be assigned the various roles and time-targets for the defence of the ford and the retreat. The commanders left our headquarters bearing themselves even a little taller.

Orders soon began to crackle. Men picked up their weapons for the move to the Kumbuk River, across which they would prepare our new defence line. Others began extending our lines along the stream and digging in. By now enemy troops, having probably delayed on the Culan plain to celebrate their victory, were massing in greater numbers on the opposite bank. Since our side of the bank was high and covered with trees and foliage, our bowmen were able to hold them back behind the copse line.

The sounds of digging and hacking resounded as our men prepared earthworks along the stream, dug trenches on a wide front, or sharpened stakes to be driven into the bed of the ford after nightfall. The catapults creaked and thumped. Our artillery was setting them up and testing for throwing fireballs in the event of a night assault. The dry scrub of the wasteland would catch fire and burn, not only to reveal the attackers, but also to roast some of them nicely. Our remaining chariots and cavalry clattered to reassemble a sufficient distance away from the stream, having established lanes of counterattack through our defensive positions.

Our men appreciated Gamini's choice of the hill for his headquarters as much as they had admired his courage in being one of the last to cross the stream during our withdrawal.

We lived in a time when princes and noblemen, even senior commanders, took luxury to the front. They regarded it not only as their right, but reasoned that the raw earth and poor food were a way of life for their men, while leaders should maintain their higher standards even on marches, claiming that good food and rest were essential for those who provided leadership on the battlefront. Gamini, on the contrary, refused tent, covering, or the bed of vines plaited onto a frame of four low posts and side-poles that could be made in a matter of minutes. 'While even one of my men has to sleep on the bare earth, so shall I,' he declared firmly. His words made my mind go back many years to the day he told me this would be his way. That had been a time of hope. Today?

Gamini and I ate only the rough food prepared for the men's night meal, cold balls of rice and fish flakes. We then lay down to sleep on our cloaks. The ground was hard, but not uncomfortable. The deep blue sky, littered with stars, was totally unconcerned with the mighty events of midget men on the earth. Unconcerned, too, crickets creaked and frogs croaked beneath the sound of men's voices. The smell of human excrement was overpowering. We must get the field latrines better organized, I thought, or disease will add to our misfortunes.

I looked at Gamini, lying still beside me, his head on his cupped hands, staring at the sky. 'We have shared a defeat,' I said quietly. 'We now share the hardships of the men. You must not feel guilt.'

'Battle is survival,' Gamini declared. 'I will make better decisions from a tough body and a mind made lean and strong through living as the Veddahs rather than from comfort.' He stared vacantly at the sky.

I knew what was eating into him and decided that my news might help in a perverse way. 'Do you know who raised several hundred men for your brother and now commands his infantry?'

'No.'

'Sali, whom you maimed in your wrestling match many years ago.'

Surprisingly Gamini did not react. 'Really?' His voice sounded almost lifeless. 'Sali the Lame! All these years and he finally had his revenge.' He continued staring skyward.

I felt great compassion for him. 'It is tough, isn't it?' I

inquired gently. 'Especially since you miss Raji.'

Gamini had hardly spoken of his wife and never of his unborn child during the past months of unremitting toil, when we had worked seven days a week, tumbling into bed exhausted each night. The reminder helped. His eyes became luminous, yet when he finally spoke, it was from that distance to which his spirit had been removed by grief.

'Of course I miss Raji, especially tonight. All my life I have been used to winning. Even when we fled to Kotmale, it was a victory of sorts over my father and over my ambitions. This is my first real defeat. It's . . . it's . . . it's so shameful . . . so humiliating.'

Silently, for Gamini was not yet ready to hear, I gave thanks to God for this shocking lesson in humility, this defeat at the hands of a boy and a drunken uncle.

'My father was right to rename me.' The words came out of Gamini in a hoarse whisper, almost as if he were speaking to himself. 'I am indeed *dhusta* – accursed Gamini.'

Chapter 47

Although he had grown wiry and tall as a man, Prince Tissa was not yet seventeen. Unprepared for victory and without real experience in government, he was more content to rule in the Dighavapi region, where Prince Digha Bahu was strong, rather than to campaign, so he did not press home his victory.

Nor was Prince Digha Bahu ready to proceed. He wanted first to enjoy the fruits of that victory. As was typical of those addicted to *sura*, he preferred talking to action and drinking to resolution.

'Let us consolidate our victory on this side of the ford,' Prince Digha Bahu slurred in conference with Prince Tissa that first afternoon. 'There is time enough to pursue your brother at our leisure.'

He thereupon retired to his tent, which had been erected in a copse alongside Prince Tissa's, and went on a drinking bout with his cronies that lasted through the next morning. He required a whole day to get over it.

Prince Panduka had been left behind at Dighavapi, ostensibly to look after what was now a subkingdom, but in reality to guard the Queen Mother, as well as the State elephant and the sceptre. It was an odd assortment of three entities, with two common attributes – beauty and symbolism.

So Prince Tissa was content to hold fast on the plain, merely sending out patrols to give the appearance of activity and to probe our defences, which were getting stronger by the hour. His men spent their time burying the dead and idling.

Although Prince Tissa now regarded himself as Gamini's superior in intellect and military skill, deep inside him he feared his brother. This fear finally drove him to action.

On the fifth morning, after having tossed and turned on his couch all night, he summoned his courage and called his three commanders to his tent. 'I want you to plan an immediate assault to wipe out the enemy,' he directed.

The commanders were obviously taken aback.

'We cannot attack in strength any longer without risking enormous losses, lord,' Sali, his young infantry commander, protested. 'We have lost momentum and the enemy is well dug in. We should have pressed our advantage on the morning of our victory.' A note of bitterness entered his voice. 'As you know, I recommended it, but was almost accused of pursuing a personal vendetta against your brother, regardless of discretion.' He pushed back his settle and stretched out the leg Gamini had broken, as if to ease it.

'No, no, commander, your motives were never in question,' Prince Tissa assured him. 'Never by me, at any rate.'

Sali shrugged. 'The enemy defences are now too strong,' he continued. 'A river crossing is a complicated action. Were we not taught so at the Sudaliya Academy?' He glanced around, but found the others noncommittal. 'Yet we cannot afford the delay either,' he proceeded. 'Your brother will grow stronger in his part of the kingdom daily and he will never give up. As I see it, there is only one course open to us. We must infiltrate the enemy, lord.'

'How?'

'We must send swimmers out each night. Not at the ford, but farther up and down the stream. These men will be instructed to sabotage the enemy's capability. Their tasks will be co-ordinated. On a pre-arranged night, they will regroup in enemy territory to attack from the rear, while our forces make a three-pronged attack across the stream. Two of these will be well to the north and south, while the third will be a large-scale, diversionary frontal assault . . .'

'My lord, pray forgive this intrusion.'

All eyes turned toward the entrance of the tent. Prince Tissa's chief attendant, Appu, had entered and was making obeisance. He was a lean, wrinkled man, his long white hair tied in a knot at the nape of his neck.

'What is it?' Prince Tissa demanded impatiently.

'The Noble Order are here for alms, lord,' Appu, still on his knees, informed the Prince.

'What Noble Order? What the devil are you talking about? This is a battlefield, not a *dan-sala*.'

Appu remained on his knees, white head bent.

'Speak up, man,' Prince Tissa shouted.

Appu raised his head. 'One hundred *bhikkus*, on a pilgrimage from the Tissa Maha Ramaya to Soma and Seru, crossed the stream much farther south and advanced along the bank this morning. As my lord knows, the main road lies on this side of the stream. They walked through our lines and have paused, with their begging bowls, outside our field kitchen.'

'How do you know they are not spies or saboteurs from the enemy camp?'

'We have recognized several of them, lord.'

'Well, serve them, man, and let them be on their way.'

Appu's forehead jerked down, almost touching the ground. 'Pardon me, gracious lord,' he quavered, 'but it is necessary for you to bestow the alms personally.'

Prince Tissa clucked impatiently. He shook his head. 'Well, I suppose you are right,' he conceded. 'We must create a good impression, must we not?' He glanced at his commanders. 'We will meet here again after the *dana*.' He rose and stalked out of the tent. The silver pre-noon sun pounded down on the plain. Its heat began to burn his skin. He had already decided that he did not like the discomforts of a campaign.

The plain was scattered far and wide with rough tents the men had erected, mostly of branches supported by spears. The troops themselves lolled in their shade, awaiting mealtime, wandered about calling to friends, or chatted loudly in groups. They were burned almost black by the five days on the bare plain. Even those who normally shaved had matted growth on their faces. He would have to do something about the slackness of the men, which was one of the consequences of not having pressed home the victory.

He proceeded to the field kitchen. The smell of rice and a single curry of mixed vegetables reminded him that he, too, was hungry.

One hundred saffron-robed *bhikkus* were already seated imperturbably, in the lotus pose, on the hard, dry ground of the sunlit plain. Although they were shaded by large shell-shaped palmyra-leaf umbrellas, their clean-shaven heads and faces were moist with sweat. Unarmed attendants waited to commence serving *dana*. Men carrying swords, spears, bows

476

and arrows, daggers, battle-axes and knives milled around the apostles of nonviolence. In the far distance, black smoke curled up to a fierce blue sky from the funeral pyres of those who had died the previous night. Prince Tissa shuddered at the whole macabre scene.

He went through the process of the *dana* in a kind of daze. When the *bhikkus* had eaten, they started chanting Pan-sil. The haunting, holy sound emphasized the incongruity of the situation, for it mingled with the clatter of arms, the occasional drumming of hooves and the raucous sounds of the war camp.

Prince Tissa felt discord blaring in his mind. He thought of the impulsion of his desire to triumph over his brother; of those times when the chanting of the Order had been a blessed benediction of peace; of the day when he and his brother had taken the oath, on eating the sacred milk-rice, never to be at enmity with one another. As his thoughts began to scatter, his resolve weakened.

He remembered his mother. She wanted the throne for him as much as he did. She would never forget the shame Gamini had heaped on his father, which had probably hastened the King's death. His mother was a devout lady, but so strong, so very strong. Why did she not practise *ahimsa*? Why had she kept telling him that sentimentality was for strong women and weak men? Whatever he was, these past months of conflict and ambition had brought him no peace. Desire causes clinging, clinging begets suffering, Lord Buddha said. Could desire be at the root of his problem? Was not the life of these *bhikkus*, chanting before him, eyes downcast, more peaceful than that of the prince offering them alms on a hot, arid plain with conquest on his mind?

He suddenly realized that the chanting had ceased. The Chief Monk, the Venerable Siri Suman, a lean, cadaverous *bhikku* with deep-set but penetrating dark eyes, beckoned to him. Expecting to receive the monk's blessing, Prince Tissa strode forward, made obeisance and knelt before him.

'We thank you, Prince, for this *dana*. It accords with the many pious works of your parents and your own upbringing, of which we are aware. It will earn much merit for you and all those who prepared it and all those who helped serve it to the Noble Order. It will also bring merit to those who grew the food and those who distributed it.'

'It is we who must thank you, learned *bhikku*,' Prince Tissa answered, 'for graciously accepting this *dana*, thus enabling us to add good to our *kharma*.'

'There is good *kharma* and bad *kharma* in this world, Prince,' the Chief Monk responded. 'Food can produce good *kharma*, but armies cannot. Pray tell me what you, a devout prince, dedicated to the Doctrine, are doing here with such a large force of men, obviously equipped and ready for battle? Do you not know that battle involves killing, maiming and wounding, the generating of bloodlust and hatred, all *akusala-kharma*?'

The *bhikku* must know the truth, Prince Tissa thought. Why, then, does he ask the questions? Prince Tissa's resolve returned at the implied rebuke. He raised his head and stared defiantly at the Chief Monk. 'We are at war with our brother, Prince Gamini, who would usurp the throne,' he declared. 'He is not worthy of it because of the shame he brought on our parents. Besides, he is not dedicated to peace and the Doctrine, but to a war that will consume this whole *Dhamma-dwipaya*. We seek to forestall him and to preserve the *Dhamma*.'

'We have heard rumours of this war, but we of the Noble Order are only concerned with the war against self – and you, Prince, have set yourself up as the judge of your brother. Is the kingdom of Ruhuna not large enough to contain both sons of the devout King Kakkavan without enmity, as you once swore on a sacred occasion when many of us were present?'

The Chief Monk's final words struck an answering chord

in Prince Tissa. He did not mind what Gamini did at Mahagama. All he really wanted for the present was to rule at Dighavapi, his own little kingdom. Later, perhaps, he would seek to expand it, but for years now he had lived under his brother's shadow. For years, he had been pushed and pounded by his mother, Prince Digha Bahu, Prince Panduka and their cronies. The monk's words gave him an excuse to pause and think. He remained silent, secretly hoping that this *bhikku* would give validity to the excuse, so that he could do what he wanted to without losing face.

'You should not wage war on your older brother,' the Chief Monk admonished him, noting Prince Tissa's silence. 'You should respect your elders. However slight the difference in age, there is some deference due.'

'It is my brother who wages war on me,' Prince Tissa protested, raising his head. 'I was peacefully in Dighavapi when he raised an army and came to do battle with me. I had to defend myself. I defeated him, too, on this very plain.' A note of triumph entered Prince Tissa's voice, as remembrance of his victory struck the chord of his latent jealousy of Gamini. 'The *devas* were on my side.'

The Chief Monk's smile was benign, showing even white teeth, but the eyes had grown steely. 'So now you are ready to cross this river, to defend yourself and the *Dhamma*? You are prepared to pursue your brother, to defend yourself and the *Dhamma*? You are ready to kill, to defend yourself and the *Dhamma*? Think well, Prince. Is this a holy war you wage? Is it truly for country, or *Dhamma*, for the poor, or for justice? Or is it a struggle for yourself? You should fight to overcome self. That war you can win. This other, you will lose, even though you have won the first battle. Remember, the kingdom of Mahagama is strong. It will not welcome you. The *dagoba* at Tissa, the sacred shrine at Kataragama are powerful. They will not welcome you. Your brother is dear to the minds and hearts of everyone in that part of the kingdom. When you have pursued him and lost everything,

including your sacred self, where will you run and hide?'
The words were spoken gently. It had the effect of light rain
upon a parched earth. 'Perhaps your only refuge will then be
the *Dhamma* and the Noble Order.' There was a magnetic
quality about the words. They sounded almost prophetic.
The Chief Monk shook his head slowly. 'Pray look at me,
Prince.'

Moved by instinctive obedience from his earliest days,
Prince Tissa raised his head to look at the Chief Monk.

'The Noble Eightfold Path does not lie in this direction.'
The Chief Monk nodded across the stream. 'Nor even in
that direction.' He glanced toward Dighavapi.

Prince Tissa looked down. His knees were beginning to
get sore from kneeling and his head was aching, but the
sweat dripping down his body was not from the blazing sun
alone. He stared down at the grey soil and crushed leaves on
the plain. He noticed the small size of his noonday shadow.
How small he was, really.

'Covetousness is one of the ten *akusala-kharmas*,' the Chief
Monk concluded. 'It emerges from the mind. That which it
seeks will soon decay, as all material things must decay, like
those leaves at your feet. Its substance will vanish as your
shadow will at night, for like your shadow it is only as tall as
the time of your longing. Kingdoms, as you conceive them,
are material things. They too vanish, like all material things,
upon death, though their substance may remain for some
other foolish one to attempt the grasping. So journey back
with us of the Noble Order to Dighavapi and thence to the
Dhamma, Prince. The blessed inner sight tells us that your
mission will not succeed on this occasion.'

Prince Tissa looked up at the Chief Monk. He met a gaze
that was depthless, the *bhikku*'s eyes seeming to shimmer
more intensely than the glare of the noonday sun. As the
deceit and hypocrisies of his spirit slowly gave way before the
bhikku's knowledge of the truth about him, he faced himself
in truth. Then he was unable to hold the *bhikku*'s gaze. He

480

looked away, troubled, staring through the glare of the plain, past the bodies of kneeling men, toward the goals he desired. A black crow, a *kakka*, flapped across the cloudless blue sky, the only taint upon it besides that black smoke of funeral pyres in the distance. He smelled the stench of rotting bodies again. The sun overhead sent down its pitiless rays, sharpening the smell of curry in the air. He was suddenly consumed by the knowledge that as this food would pass away into dead matter, so would his body some day. His head felt hot, ready to burst. What was the solution?

Finally, the spiritual in him combined with the practical. He had complete faith in those blessed with the gift of the inner sight, and monks did not lie. 'Your mission will not succeed on this occasion,' the Chief Monk had said. While clinging to the implication that there would be other occasions, he was frightened by the warning.

Prince Tissa made up his mind quickly. 'I will follow your advice, learned *bhikku*,' he stated, with as much sincerity as he could summon. 'But only because it is given by a revered member of the Sangha and because the *Dhamma* reigns supreme in my heart. I will be sacrificing a chance of quick victory by doing so, but I trust I will acquire much merit by this act of forbearance.'

The Chief Monk looked at him enigmatically, without replying.

Chapter 48

We stood on our hillock in the first grey light of morning, gazing anxiously across the stream. Our patrols had reported increased activity across the river during the previous afternoon and evening, which had led us to expect an attack during the night, or at daybreak.

The men were spread out before us, some on guard, others farther away washing by the stream, scrubbing their teeth, hawking and spitting on the ground. My gaze drifted farther, across the stream to a plain devoid of soldiers and encampments. The only signs of life were birds wheeling slowly in the lightening sky, looking for scraps of food, and a flock of crows cawing sadly from the line of trees. Smoke rose in the far distance, probably from burning refuse. The scars of enemy earthworks in the forward areas remained. Beyond them lay discarded gear, implements and a great spread of rubbish. An easterly breeze brought across its staleness, mixed with the stench of excrement.

'They have retreated, leaving only their smells behind,' Gamini said, wrinkling his nose. 'This could be a trap.'

I must confess to a lift of my sagging spirits. 'Very inhospitable of them to depart without taking leave of their hosts,' I commented dryly.

'Perhaps so, but it is no trap.'

We turned at the words, to see Veera Singha walking up, accompanied by a group of his men, escorting a youth who was dripping wet. 'We have news that your royal brother has retreated before the Doctrine.'

'How so?'

Veera Singha turned to jerk his head at the young man. 'This is Loku Banda. He was with Prince Tissa's forces, but has deserted to our cause. Let him tell you his strange story in his own words.'

Obviously overawed, the young soldier knelt before Gamini. He was slim, clean-cut and of medium height, with a lean, dark face. Water glistened on his black curls, like dewdrops.

'Stand up and speak,' Gamini commanded.

The young soldier rose to his feet and began telling his

story in a high-pitched monotone, as if he were reciting a *kaviya* poem at school. He had been present at the *dana* to the *bhikkus* the previous day and had heard all that had transpired. True to his word, Prince Tissa had indeed ordered the withdrawal of his army to Dighavapi, over the objections of Prince Digha Bahu. Loku Banda thereupon decided to desert. 'I joined the Prince's army to fight for a cause,' he ended simply. 'When my lord prince withdrew after so splendid a victory, upon hearing the *bhikku*'s words, I felt he could not have a cause, but was fighting for himself.' His gaunt cheeks tightened and he raised himself fully erect, throwing his chest out, the stomach flat and hard. 'Your royal brother could not have been guided by the Doctrine alone. He must fear your resolution and your cause, my lord. So here I am, to offer myself to you, begging your forgiveness for having taken up arms against you. I can guide you in the pursuit of your enemy, if you so desire. They broke camp early last night, to put as much distance as possible between them and your pursuit.'

We looked at Gamini for directions. He first nodded at Loku Banda. 'Thank you for joining us,' he declared. 'You shall be rewarded. Thank you also for your offer to guide us. I shall think on it.' He turned to Veera Singha. 'Attach Loku Banda to your troops for the present, Minister.'

The young man made obeisance and left with Veera Singha.

'We will not pursue the enemy,' Gamini asserted. He ran a thumb and forefinger thoughtfully along the bridge of his nose. 'This may be a trap. Even if it is not, we must avoid another abortive battle against a much larger force. No, we shall follow through with our plan to hold our defence line here until that on the Kumbuk River is ready, after which we shall withdraw to Mahagama.'

I turned to him approvingly. Within the space of three days, defeat had turned him from an impetuous young prince into a budding strategist.

'It is also to the good that you have the support of the Noble Order, all the way from the Tissa Maha Ramaya,' I stated. Then inspiration struck me. 'This is not the season for the pilgrimages to Soma and Seru. I detect the sure hand of the Venerable Rahula behind it. I know him well of old. I am sure he sent those *bhikkus* soon after we advanced from Mahagama, with instructions to intervene if we lost and to bless us if we won!'

Gamini sucked in his breath. 'Are you sure?'

'As sure as I can be.' I grinned. 'Is there any other explanation? And by the way, I have frequently told you not to suck your breath in that way. It is ugly!'

He looked at me in astonishment. 'You pick up something like that when we are considering something far more important?'

'That is just as important,' I retorted. 'Remember, the fully civilized man . . .'

'. . . is the totally aware man!' He completed my favourite saying. 'And remember, too, that monotony is one of the most unforgivable sins,' he quoted.

I smiled tolerantly at him. 'Excusable in a teacher with a difficult pupil,' I remarked.

'Inexcusable before your king!' he flashed.

'Ho, ho, ho! I thought you wanted none of it until you were consecrated.' I paused for effect. 'Besides, you will always be my pupil,' I added loftily.

'So I shall have to endure your dreadful monotonies forever.'

Suddenly lighthearted, we laughed uproariously together.

Gamini sobered first. I could sense his thoughts spinning like a wheel, then coming to a slow stop. 'I welcome the Venerable Rahula as an ally,' he finally declared. 'Every ally will count. The *Dhamma* may end up one of our best weapons.'

'How so?' I inquired sharply, afraid of the cynical way in which his mind seemed to work. 'The *bhikkus* will not

484

actively help you against your brother.'

'You ignore our battle cry,' he retorted. 'One race, one language, one religion!'

We slept soundly that night for the first time in days, but were suddenly awakened around midnight. When you train for war, you develop the faculty of waking to the slightest out-of-the-ordinary sound and coming instantly alert. It can mean the difference between life and death.

Gamini and I were on our feet, swords in hand, almost together. The sky was completely overcast, so we stared through the gloom in the direction of hushed voices on the northwestern side of the hillock.

Gamini uttered my thoughts. 'Could it be a sneak attack?'

As we tried to penetrate the darkness, a torch flared through the dark trees and began moving swiftly in our direction. We heaved sighs of relief, untensed and grinned at each other. 'Hardly a sneak attack unless they first want to make sure we kill them,' I remarked. 'Seems more like messengers to me, but from the wrong direction for Mahagama or Dighavapi.'

Gamini was already moving toward the flare, his sword at the ready. I followed. By now, our eyes had become accustomed to the darkness, so we traced our way down, between bushes and over rough stones, toward the torch. We soon made out the black outlines of figures, slow-trotting up the hill towards us. As we approached each other, they were revealed as a dozen soldiers, led by a grizzled captain, surrounding a tall man.

Gamini recognized him first. 'Nimila!' he exclaimed. 'What are you doing here? You are far away from your troops. You should be up north with them, supporting our border forts.'

It was indeed the Great Warrior who made obeisance to Gamini, but unusually dishevelled. He was dressed in pantaloons. His long hair was loose, his bare brown torso bathed in sweat, his chest heaving. From the smell of him, he had not even stopped to bathe.

Nimila cleared his throat. 'I wish I' was bringing better news.' He paused for breath. The words finally came out slowly, his voice dark and grave. 'It's a woeful time for us. The Chola made sneak attacks across the river the night before last and captured our forts at Wera, Kimbul and Kasa. Many of our men were killed. More were taken prisoner and sent to us under a flag of truce early yesterday morning. The messenger said their attack was purely for defensive purposes, because they fear the civil war in Ruhuna may cause problems to them across the river. They have no intention of advancing farther. He added that they may even go back when we have solved our problems.'

Gamini had been looking grimmer and grimmer as Nimila spoke, his whole body slowly tightening. He shook with a vivid anger such as I had never seen in him since that day many years ago when he had nearly killed Prince Panduka. 'And what have the three corps of Ruhuna done while Sinhala were being slaughtered?' His restraint was more frightening than any outburst.

'We were totally unaware of the attack until it was over, lord.'

'Sinhala forts, on the sacred soil of Ruhuna, occupied by Chola for the first time in history!' Gamini's fists were clenched. Trembling with rage, he took a step forward. The power of him was suddenly so enormous that Nimila flinched. 'What have the soldiers of Ruhuna done before this outrage, this sacrilege?' He was still deadly quiet. He suddenly moved away, as if to contain his wrath. He returned to hand me his sword, placed a balled fist in the palm of his hand, walked a few paces and stared into the night.

'We are awaiting orders, lord.' Nimila finally found his voice.

'Orders? From whom?' Gamini thundered, spinning around to face Nimila. The grizzled captain and his men drew back. I must remember to tell Gamini later never to take any commander to task in the presence of subordinates, I thought.

'From our commander and governor, Prince Digha Bahu. Word is that the Chola have a total of ten corps committed to this action. We will need the three Dighavapi corps to reinforce us if we are to counterattack.'

For a moment I thought Gamini would strike the Great Warrior. He restrained himself with a tremendous effort, letting out a great breath, his nostrils flaring. He turned on his heel and walked away, stopped and began pacing up and down like a caged black panther, breathing hard. His dark face was purple with anger even in the flickering torchlight. He kept darting sidelong glances at Nimila. He reminded me of King Kakkavan the night when he received Gamini's insulting gifts: the same walk, the same glances, the same suppressed fury.

A bullfrog croaked from the stream. A night owl hooted, as if in warning.

'Do you realize that Prince Digha Bahu will never give the order to attack?' I intervened, mainly to allow Gamini the opportunity to recover. 'Some of us believe that he is in league with the Cholas. Surely you and your fellow corps commanders are aware of this?'

'We certainly are. But we all agreed that we should not give the Chola any excuse to advance farther, especially at a time when we are not strong enough to contain them.'

'One Sinhala can take on ten Chola!' Gamini exploded, pausing in his stride.

'Do you really estimate the Chola strength at ten corps?' I cut in, once again to create a diversion.

'They have about six corps plus reserves on their side of the river, besides the troops manning the three captured forts.'

'Have you sent word to Mahagama?'

'Yes. And I came to Prince Gamini personally, because it is with him that our loyalties lie.'

Gamini walked back to face Nimila. 'Oh, indeed!' He stopped, hands on his hips, teeth bared almost in a sneer. 'And where did your loyalties lie when you gave your oath to my father, the late King' – he thrust his dark face forward – 'the oath that has brought Ruhuna to this sorry pass?'

Knowing that Gamini was being unfair to the Great Warrior, I felt sorry for him, but resisted the temptation to intervene. Gamini would come to the realization himself, once his fury had dissipated.

'I am afraid I do not understand, lord.' Nimila had recovered his breath. He was now bewildered.

'If your loyalties had been to *nyaya* and to the kingdom, not to a ruler, you would not have taken your oath, however tragic and compelling the invitation.' Gamini ended his statement waggling a finger at the Great Warrior. He was speaking with restraint now and I admired him for his recovery. He dropped his hand. 'That, however, is a moot point tonight. It would be ungracious of me to take you to task when you have run these many miles to bring me the news personally. Tell me, though, why did you not come on horseback?'

'To arrange relays of horses would have taken more time.'

Oddly, Gamini smiled, white teeth shining in his heavy face. 'I thank you for your effort, but to what end have you come?'

'Vasabha, Gotha and I felt that you might conceive a solution for presenting a united front against the Cholas, lord.'

There was silence at Nimila's words, broken only by the hissing of the torch and the low breathing of men. A light breeze sprang up and bent the flames, wafting the smell of the tar to our nostrils. Knowing Gamini, I realized that Nimila was once again treading dangerous ground, but I had to give the warrior credit for standing up to the young prince.

'Are you saying that you hope Prince Tissa and I will unite?' There was a dangerous edge to Gamini's voice.

'We hoped you would set aside your differences even temporarily in order that we might drive back the enemy from what you have just called our sacred soil.'

'Never!' Gamini roared. 'When a united Ruhuna marches against the foe, it will be with me as its *king*.' He raised a clenched fist, shaking it in the Great Warrior's face with each emphasis. '*That* is my destiny. *That* is the destiny of Ruhuna. *That* is the destiny of Lanka. The Sinhala lion will *never* ally itself with jackals to fight Chola bulls.' Shaking with passion, he paused to control himself. His voice dropped and emerged pitted and hard as granite. 'Any arrangements with Prince Tissa at this stage will only be a semblance of unity. The cancer, the suppuration of wrong-doing, greed and ambition will remain within, making us the weaker and not the stronger to fight a united Chola.'

He stopped abruptly and looked down, wiping his mouth with the back of his hand. As we stared at him, he raised his eyes to Nimila, flashing fire. 'They have dared to attack our fortresses. They have dared to step on our sacred soil. They have dared to kill our soldiers, because Ruhuna is torn by civil war and at its weakest in strength and morality. My brother and his allies did this to the kingdom.' He chopped with the base of his palm. 'For the present I shall seek to pursue right, with what forces I can muster. Let the Cholas advance into our territory, let them seize Mahagama. I shall fight from the jungles and the mountains, at the head of those who acknowledge me as leader and king. I will only lead a united Ruhuna army after my brother is dead, or I am consecrated with his total subjection. Seek you what you need from him, therefore, and from his jackal allies, not from me.'

We listened to Gamini's words in awe, for his life-force had emerged. Young as he was, the aura vibrated around him so strongly that it made the air before us shake. For

489

moments all of us just gazed dumbly at him. Dark, tall, lithe and commanding, he seemed to have been created by the flame of the torch that lit him, to conquer the world.

The Great Warrior knelt before Gamini. 'I shall pray and work for the day when we can all follow you as our king. I want no other choice. I shall return immediately to our troops. The Chola shall advance no farther except over our dead bodies.'

Gamini's aura slowly dissipated. He was real again. He nodded. 'Spoken like a true Sinhala,' he acknowledged. He turned to the captain. 'See that the Great Warrior is fed and quartered as befits his rank. He need not return to his post until tomorrow. Have horses ready for him.' He addressed Nimila. 'Goodnight, Warrior. You have done well in bringing this news to me and I thank you. May the *devas* guard you.'

I was glad I had not remonstrated with Gamini earlier.

We started walking back to our bivouac again, Gamini very thoughtful. The fire he had exuded would have left anyone else exhausted, or at least depressed, but Gamini remained alive and vibrant on the crest of his anger. Reaching our cloaks, we sat on them. I picked a pebble from beneath me and tossed it away.

'Damn! Damn! Damn!' Gamini pounded his head with clenched fists. He thought awhile, then nodded toward the river. 'Look at our defences! Facing the wrong direction – east instead of north, against Sinhala instead of Chola. And we are doing the same at the Kumbuk River. My father really did us in.'

At the mention of his father, the truth suddenly struck me. 'Wait a minute,' I said, holding up my hand. 'Wait a minute.' The picture crystallized before me, as if illuminated by a hundred flares. 'Your father was a very wise man,' I commented slowly. 'I do not think we have given him credit for his wisdom.'

'Wisdom? What wisdom? Why?'

490

'Everything is happening as he planned it. Don't you see? If he had named you king, you would still have been faced with opposition from your brother, your mother and Digha Bahu, but you would have marched off hotheaded to war against the Cholas regardless, leading an army, without the people.

'Now you have the opportunity to prove your mettle and obtain the sympathy and support of the people. Your father knew you could do it, if you were pushed. Through blazing fire alone is the sword produced. The best in you had first to come out.'

I stood up, excited by my own discovery. I began pacing up and down. 'Yes! Yes! Of course.' I turned to look down at Gamini. 'If your father had not forgiven you for insulting him, he would have declared the succession for Prince Tissa, or even Prince Digha Bahu. Having forgiven you, he could not name you directly, because of the pitfalls, but arranged it in such a way that you could better achieve your objective.'

A look of incredulity crossed his face. I dropped my voice. 'It all fits in. Civil war was inevitable on your father's death, and he knew it, wise man. Having held his throne through strength and brains for over thirty years, he knew the result and the outcome. He even guessed what the Chola would do. This civil war will eventually unite the people solidly behind you. Prince, if you act wisely now, it will turn out exactly as he planned.'

Gamini leaped to his feet. 'By the *devas*, you may be right!' he exclaimed. 'And it means that my father forgave me.' He smiled at my amazed look, then grew sad and serious. 'Make no mistake about it, my friend. I have suffered a thousand deaths for that impious deed. Not to reverence parents is an ultimate sin.' He stared at me, his expression unchanging while he spoke. 'I never told you, but it has been a bad *kharma* for me.' He hesitated, as if ready to bring out those deepest secrets that he had never shared. My heart rose. Would I have this from him at last?

491

Moments went by while we stared at each other. Finally, he shook his head like a wet dog. A look of entreaty crossed his face. Forgive me, he seemed to say, but not yet. He gripped my arm with a surprisingly gentle hand. 'I look to you to pull me back when I stray.'

We were facing our darkest hour – defeat from the east, invasion from the north, ignominy, shame, my prince with nothing but a nebulous right of succession to back him – yet my heart sang.

Chapter 49

Queen Vihara Devi was obviously disturbed after Prince Tissa's messenger left. He had brought her news of Prince Tissa's withdrawal from the Culan plain following the advice given by the Venerable Siri Suman. She remained seated on the high-backed ebony chair facing the open window, fanning herself rapidly with her peacock fan. Her face was drawn, showing its fine bones, but even the shadows under her eyes could not diminish her beauty. Indeed, sorrowing seemed to have invested her with a wistfulness that added to it. She was dressed in blue, the colour affected by women bereaved, because Buddhists do not officially mourn, regarding death only as the effect of the cause, birth.

The Dighavapi palace, in which she now resided, was built on the beach, with its living quarters fronting the ocean to catch the eastern breezes. It was a cool morning and the circular branches of the row of palmyra palms along the edge of the white sands looked more grey-blue and fresh than usual from the previous night's rain. Beneath them the ground cover of the island shores spread its green carpet in either direction. A black tortoise waddled slowly along the more russet sand beneath the palace window. A bare-bodied gardener with wrinkled dark skin squatted before a flower bed of yellow marigolds, digging out weeds and collecting snails in a wicker basket. Leela, who stood beside the Queen, knew the snails would not be killed but would be dumped elsewhere.

Since moving here, the Queen's routine, too, had changed. In fact, she had no routine at all, for the first time in more than thirty years. The district almost ran itself under Prince Digha Bahu's supervision, so even Prince Tissa was merely a figurehead.

The Queen had accepted her altered circumstances with dignity. On one of the rare occasions when she had discussed them with Leela, she confided that she would have had to face radical change anyhow upon the death of her husband, King Kakkavan. A new ruler, whoever it might be, would inevitably cause her to be relegated to the position of Queen Mother. Her grief at King Kakkavan's death had been crushing, but she never showed it openly. On a few occasions when Leela was present, the tears flowed. Whatever the relationship between two people living close to each other, Leela thought, there has to be sorrow at the final parting. Besides, to be a queen one day and comparatively nothing the next must leave a person with a different sense of loss, particularly when such a change is as final as the death that caused it.

Leela came to admire the Queen's self-control more than ever during the days following King Kakkavan's death. Her mistress had sat by the bier as if carved in marble. Unlike Hindu queens, Buddhist queens may attend a husband's cremation as spectators, without having to immolate themselves on the pyre. When the final religious observances were over, Prince Digha Bahu and Prince Abhaya, both in the position of nephews of the deceased, who traditionally set fire to the funeral pyre, applied the flaming torches to it. The Queen had stood dry-eyed, motionless, staring at the licking flames until they caught and began to roar. Water for your first tragedy, Fire for your second, Leela reflected, unable to restrain her own weeping. What will your next be? Earth, then Air, to complete the four elements?

When the ceremony was over, the Queen had come to life again, graciously acknowledging the sympathy of those who were entitled to come up and offer it to her.

The one thing that had shocked Leela was the Queen's decision to leave the palace with Prince Tissa, thereby virtually disowning Prince Gamini and denying his claims to the throne. Leela had no knowledge of the legalities of succession, but she had a strong feeling of right and wrong, and the Queen's action offended her sense of justice. Would this move prove to be the Queen's third tragedy, from the earth that made up the kingdom? she wondered, just as the Queen began speaking.

'Why would my son want to leave the scene of his victory? If he desires to be King of Ruhuna, he should press on regardless. Did we not move here to help him to that end?' Her voice trailed off. She patted the ebony settle inlaid with ivory and mother-of-pearl beside her chair.

Leela sat down, adjusting her red skirt.

The Queen gazed deeply into her handmaiden's eyes. 'When Prince Tissa decided to take over the kingdom from Dighavapi, removed from those upstart ministers who rejected him, we were glad to leave because we feared Prince Gamini's remoteness. A palace is impersonal enough, but when there is no love from any member of the family . . .'

Leela fought back the tears. 'But I love you, my lady. I need you. Where you go, I go, with my love ever present.'

The Queen reached over to place a hand on Leela's black curls. 'Of course we know that, *dhoo*.' Leela thrilled at being called daughter by her mistress for the first time. 'We thank the *devas* for sending us a child such as you. And yet, when

494

you have children, you want them to keep needing you, not to reject you.' She paused, a faraway expression on her face. 'There was nothing left for us in Mahagama. Even the spell we asked you to cast was no longer necessary because of our elder son's impious act.'

Leela's eyes misted, but she suddenly felt fearful as well. 'What will happen now, my lady?'

'We do not know.' The Queen stared into space awhile. 'For the first time in years, we fear we do not know.'

In the weeks of feverish activity that followed, Gamini showed energy and forethought that were astonishing in one so young. The energy was his; the wisdom he had to have inherited from his father. In addition to governing the subkingdom from our hillock headquarters, he also planned and prepared for his new campaign and made time for personal combat practice.

As a result of hard work by all our troops, with Gamini and me commuting regularly between the stream and the Kumbuk River, most of our two defence lines were ready in six weeks, with earthworks, overhead protection against flaming arrows, fireballs and stones, sectors for our bowmen to shoot toward possible enemy assembly areas and lines of counterattack for our cavalry and chariots.

'The next time we attack, we can retreat without fear to these defence lines,' I observed with satisfaction to Gamini, as we lay beneath the stars to sleep on the forty-second night after our defeat.

'The next time we attack, it will be from the firm base of these deployments,' Gamini retorted. 'Our men will not be permitted a defeatist mentality. They will fight for glory or death.'

He was deadly serious. His rebuke was justified and I accepted it in silence.

'Let us go to sleep now,' he said. 'We leave early tomorrow for Mahagama.'

When we got back to the palace the next day, we

discovered to our joy that the ministers had indeed been active in Gamini's cause. They had already recruited and equipped a force of ten thousand men, now under training by the Great Warriors, led by the Chief Warrior. This was a strange turnaround for Velu Sumana, who had always seemed to extend his sympathy and affection to Prince Tissa. In spite of his endeavours on Gamini's behalf, Velu Sumana greeted us with cool formality and Gamini responded in like manner.

Additional troops and equipment were also being rapidly gathered. Instead of deserting him at his time of defeat, the people, the nobles and the chiefs had begun rallying eagerly to Gamini's cause. His determination not to accept defeat had aroused feelings for him that would never have been generated if he had merely succeeded his father as king. The people of Ruhuna loved causes. They had not had a cause for a long time. The injured hero, Gamini, was a greater cause than a young king calling them to war.

All this made me more convinced than ever that we were benefiting from King Kakkavan's wisdom. He knew the people of Ruhuna better than anyone else. Perhaps he also knew his son. He had to see to his own afterlife, but he had organized the affairs of the kingdom in such a manner that all ends were achieved. History will surely judge King Kakkavan as a king who sacrificed his own glory for the benefit of Ruhuna and his son.

One would have expected all the encouraging news on our return to draw Gamini closer to Raji and keep him chaste for her. On the contrary, he had a dancing girl sent secretly to his chambers the very first night of our arrival.

I saw the young woman before I bade Gamini goodnight. She was tall and fair in the light of the flares, with a circlet of white jasmine on her shiny black hair and a gold chain around her long slender neck. Her form was slim and pliant, the aureoles of the breasts showing through a light blouse, her hips and thighs pressing against her tight skirt.

When I got to my room, I sat on the settle beside my window and looked out at the night. I realized that I had come to love my quarters and was glad to get back, not just to the musty-smelling rooms, but to the garden outside, rustling quietly in the breeze, the fireflies twinkling in the treetops, and the starry skies.

Feeling a deep peace at being here, I thought about Gamini frolicking in adultery with a woman in the adjoining quarters. I had come to the conclusion that he was incapable of being sexually true to Raji, or anyone for that matter. I knew that he would go through his usual routine after he had finished with this maiden for the night. First would come revulsion at his act, guilt and self-blame. Then he would purify himself by his symbolic bath in the fountain outside his window. Finally, lying in bed afterwards, he would be exalted by the resolve never to repeat this act of infidelity. All this would enable him to surge into mental and spiritual union with Raji, developing a state of euphoria, before falling into a deep sleep made possible by the relaxation achieved through sexual release. Why all the fuss? The man was made polygamous. Why then did he not admit it and get on with the job, instead of playing games with himself? In sex alone he was full of self-deceit – perhaps more because he needed to satisfy the romantic, the idealist in him than from a need for variety in sex. No one but me, not even Raji, was aware of that romantic, and even I had only glimpsed it on a few occasions.

As I sat in the dark thinking of these things, a sudden thought gripped me. Sex was a weakness in Gamini. Nature always extracts a toll from weakness. The memory of Sirima and how his weakness nearly had caused his death at her hands lay cold as a tombstone in the cemetery of my being.

Gamini was given good cause to feel revolted at himself when we sat in the audience chamber the next morning. Kirthi Siri padded in to make obeisance. 'My lord, great news!' he mumbled. 'Your wife delivered a baby boy four

497

days ago weighing seven pounds, on the first day of this very month, Vesakha. She has named the boy Abhaya Sali, as agreed upon by you. Both mother and son are in excellent health. In accordance with your wishes, they will visit you as soon as the mother is fit to travel. The *devas* be praised that the kingdom will have an heir to follow you.'

Strange. Gamini and I looked at each other with the same thought. We had both forgotten the name Gamini had wanted for his child if it was a boy. Now our first reaction to the joyous news Kirthi Siri had relayed was to recall that Prince Tissa's infantry commander, an implacable foe of Gamini, a man who had sworn vengeance against him, was also named Sali. We could read each other's thoughts more clearly than if we had spoken them aloud. Gamini finally smiled at me and shrugged. No matter, his glance seemed to say. Somehow, I could not share his complacency. I wondered at myself and my forebodings. Perhaps the defeat on the Culan plain had made me a gloomier person.

'We will have the court astrologers chart the child's horoscope,' I heard Kirthi Siri declare.

We were in Gamini's study several weeks later when he suddenly fired the question at me. 'Do you believe in people being lucky or unlucky for others?'

'Yes,' I replied readily, having considered this matter often. 'But I do not think it has anything to do with the people themselves being good or bad, lucky or unlucky. Rather it is that different people can motivate others in different ways – to good, to bad, to energy, to lassitude, to play, to work . . .'

I broke off before the amused expression on Gamini's face. 'Now what's so funny about that?' I demanded.

'Nothing is funny about that. *You* are funny.'

'What's so funny about me then?'

'You have not changed in years. I remember the first time I ever asked you a question. It was a very simple one, and I received a learned discourse in reply. You are still the *maha danemutta*, the know-it-all I said you were then.' He was laughing hard. 'Yes or no! Spare me your explanations.'

'Yes.'

He turned serious. 'Do you think that Raji is unlucky for me?' His eyes were sharp in the flare-light, the expression suddenly intent.

The question caught me off guard. Before I spoke, I went back in my mind to the first night Gamini saw Raji and traced events since then. 'I would say that Raji was lucky for you because she afforded you a reason to flee the kingdom instead of trying to fight your father. She gave you sanctuary from your father's wrath and perhaps the most peaceful months of your life.'

Gamini was quick to take me up. 'Then you must admit that women have nobility and are of great value. You should reconsider noninvolvement with them.'

'Nobility is not necessarily a virtue,' I retorted dryly. 'Nor is it a reason for bed. In fact, some of our pillars of female nobility look like public monuments and one would hardly want to take them to bed.'

He grinned. 'You have answered my question,' he said, suddenly sobering. 'I, too, believe that Raji is lucky for me. I feel that my son will also be lucky for me, as the astrologers predict. Being superstitious, Kirthi Siri selected a lucky day for their arrival and sent an escort for Raji and the baby. He did not tell me about it until tonight, the crafty fellow. In case I objected, I suppose. They will both be here tomorrow. I would have liked to ride out to meet them, but our conference with the district chieftains from the west coast in the morning must not be postponed. It would be a slap in their faces, if I were not here when they arrive with news of more levies for our army.'

Shortly before noon the next day, we greeted Raji and the baby Prince Abhaya Sali at the entrance to the audience hall. To allow them privacy, the entire area and the courtyard had been cleared of people save for the guards standing silently at their posts.

As Raji alighted from the wagon, Gamini rushed toward her, regardless of protocol. I saw that she had grown plumper with child-bearing, but her skin looked even fairer, almost transparent. She held the baby prince to Gamini for inspection and my mind went back many years to that night when Queen Vihara Devi presented the baby Abhaya Gamini to King Kakkavan.

This baby was very pink and fair. I looked closely at the ears. The outside edges of the ears were rosy, with no undertone of darkness. My eyes drifted to the wizened little face with its mop of black hair. There was no mistaking Prince Abhaya Sali's resemblance to his mother. I wondered how Queen Vihara Devi, who looked like Raji, would respond to him. Most people feel kinship with those who look like them, even men with women. It is a kind of self-love.

Gamini stared at the baby. He reached out a dark, awkward finger and touched its little face. 'He looks like an old man,' he finally said.

Raji laughed softly. 'All babies look like old men,' she replied. 'Perhaps because they are our older dead reborn.'

'Hmm. I must think on it.'

Gamini made no move to hold the baby. Instead, his eyes sought Raji's with tenderness. 'It has been too long, my love,' he said softly. 'Too, too long ... so much has happened and nothing seems to have gone right. Nothing can ever be right again without you.'

Chapter 50

One month later, on a grey dawn, two Sinhala armies faced each other again across the Culan plain. It was a gloomy day. Dark clouds in the east forced the sun away from the earth; not a breath of wind stirred to challenge their victory. The plain still held some remnant of the smell of baked sand from the previous afternoon's heat. Carrion crows by the hundred cawed above the lonely sounds of a battle about to be joined: the whinny of a horse, the clank of metal and the creak of leather. The watchfulness of the men was a single, all-pervading force, as physical as the oppressiveness of the air.

Gamini had paused on the Mahagama side of the stream for three days before crossing it, sending out flying patrols to probe the enemy. Their reports indicated that the opposing force consisted of about fifty thousand men, today almost identical with our own. King Elara's advance across the river had helped us enormously. The people of Ruhuna were suddenly afraid of Chola domination and began to remember the prophecies about their saviour prince. What was alarming, however, was that our immediate enemies were said to include a large group of highly trained 'advisers' from the Chola's regular cavalry.

Gamini had been determined to settle the score with his brother on the site of his earlier defeat. This time, however, our men were highly trained in weapons and battle tactics, our supplies had been assured and our reserves were well entrenched. I was impressed by the new Gamini who had emerged from the ashes of defeat – and amazed at his flair for military matters. Even his tactics were to be different today.

Firmly astride our restive horses, we awaited the return of

the messengers Gamini had sent across the plain to Prince Tissa at the first light of dawn, bearing a message on *ola*:

> This battle will be more tragic for the people of Ruhuna than the last. While our Sinhala armies are destroying one another, the Chola enemy grows stronger, so victory will be sand in the mouth of the victor. Its fruit, only King Elara will savour.
>
> You are said to be an ally and tool of the Chola. Are you willing to give the lie to this charge before your countrymen and in the pages of Sinhala history? If so, let us resolve our conflict by single combat. Let us two fight alone in the centre of this plain, within sight of our forces, and let the sovereignty of Ruhuna rest with the winner.
>
> If you accept this challenge, our foot soldiers should approach in line within two hundred cubits of each other to watch our battle, pledging themselves not to fight but to concede victory to the victor.

I was fearful lest Prince Tissa accept Gamini's challenge. I was fearful lest he refuse it. The familiar weakness lay in my entrails. I did not stop to reason what I was afraid of, only tried to make my mind a blank, because there was no purpose in guessing what would happen. All I knew, with the morbid satisfaction demanded by my need for courage, was that once battle was joined, the savage would break loose in me. No thought of its effect on my *kharma* could dim the prospect of its release!

I saw the three specks on the plain only after their cloud of dust became visible. I remembered that afternoon, so long ago that it seemed almost another lifetime now, when I had watched Velu Sumana galloping toward my treetop *massa* followed by the mighty Mahela. I shivered from deep within. The drumming of hooves broke into my recollections. While

I was lost in thought, the messengers had galloped halfway across the plain. They headed directly toward us, three bearded men, intent on their mission, leaving dust and flying sand in their horses' wake. They finally ground their foam-flecked bays to a stop in front of us. The horses reared in unison. Grooms ran up to hold the reins. The men dismounted and made obeisance to Gamini.

The leader of the messengers was a young captain with a rakish look. He was panting slightly from the ride, but his white teeth showed in a happy smile. Good soldier that he was, he came straight to the point. 'My lord, your royal brother has accepted your challenge,' he declared. 'He will move to the centre-front of his men as soon as he sees our line of foot soldiers commence advancing. There must be no trumpets, drumming, music or shouting of any kind. Any such and his men have orders to fight. When the two lines have stopped within two hundred cubits of each other, you and he will advance and meet in single combat.'

'Very good,' Gamini responded quietly. He was thoughtful for a while. 'But tell me, did you notice any Cholas with the Prince?'

Appreciation showed in the captain's face. 'Yes, lord. A couple of them tried to dissuade your royal brother from accepting the challenge.'

Gamini smiled grimly and turned in his saddle toward Veera Singha, who had accompanied us. 'This is why I suggested that only foot soldiers advance across the plain to witness the duel. We will honour our pact to the letter. If I fall, my brother shall become king and the *devas* help our kingdom. Since I shall win, we can expect Chola thrusts on our flanks. Have the bowmen cover our cavalry for its countercharges – and have our chariots reinforce the centre.'

A slow breeze started from the east. Our horses took slow, mincing steps. There was silence except for the tiny creak of saddles and the crunch of hooves. Our men extended several

503

thousand feet along our line, slow-marching, shield on shoulder, spear in hand. Their swords were in the scabbard, their knives at the belt. The silence was broken only by the footfalls of men and horses.

Squinting against the eastern glare, I saw the dark line of the enemy advancing. It reminded me forcibly that battles are fought by human beings. I looked down, half expecting to distinguish bloodstains on the dry earth from our last action. I could not rid my mind of the death and carnage, the defeat and shame this soil had witnessed.

I looked up again. The enemy line resolved itself into men in red-and-white uniforms, carrying only spears. Gamini and I both saw the figure at their head at the same time. I almost called out to Gamini. Years of training held me back, but the shock must have hit Gamini as it did me. My whole body felt paralysed. Too late, I realized that Gamini should have specified the method and manner of the duel, for Prince Tissa was entrenched in a swaying *howdah* on the back of a great grey elephant.

Not by a tremor did Gamini betray his feelings, not even when he could see that the elephant was Kandula.

Raja had been trained not to fear the great beasts, but a man on a war-elephant is a man in a fortress. The animal is decked for action with leather coverings against arrows and spears, studded with iron spikes to prevent close contact. The roof and sides of the *howdah*, too, are reinforced for these purposes. With only his sword and shield, a spear fixed to a notch by the right stirrup and a quiver of darts on a saddle cup, the odds were heavily against Gamini.

Gamini had decided to accept having the sun in our eyes once more, to help induce the enemy to use the same battle plan. Now this would be an added disadvantage to him.

I knew that Gamini had no eyes for anything but the elephant ambling forward. He had always regarded Kandula as his brother, born on the day he was born. He would not wish to hurt the animal. Yet how else could he hope to win this duel except by crippling Kandula, since his only advantages were greater speed and mobility and presenting a smaller target?

Our two lines were close to each other now. I could see Prince Tissa in the *howdah*, his face almost white above brown leather armour.

Raja stumbled on a hare hole and Gamini instinctively lifted him with the reins. Raja pulled, wanting his head. Gamini restrained him with firm hands. I swerved slightly to avoid the hole.

Just as a line of men starts with the click of motion, so does it stop. With no commands, merely by common judgement, the two long lines halted two hundred cubits apart. The men glared at each other, or stared at the opposing princes.

The sun had burst through the black clouds. The men in the centre of the enemy line were mostly grizzled veterans. I saw a dark, clean-shaven man, obviously a commander, with the white slash of a scar along one side of his face. A fair-skinned giant stood next to a short, stocky veteran. I had time only to focus on the intensity of dark eyes and long, grey shadows and to smell their animal sweat, carried by that easterly breeze, before Gamini reined in his horse. I paused behind him, slightly to one side. A command from Prince Tissa stopped Kandula.

With both lines halted, a great silence fell on the plain.

Elephants do not have good sight. That is why they sometimes charge at alien sounds and smells that warn of danger. Gamini was watching the elephant. It moved its ears forward, trying to detect sounds in the new silence. Failing to hear anything, it raised its grey trunk to scent the wind, but that light breeze was blowing in the wrong direction.

Prince Tissa gave a sharp command. Kandula started to move forward.

Gamini's one advantage was that an elephant cannot reach the full power of its charge within two hundred cubits of the arena. His brother would have to depend on impregnability and the speed of his own throwing arm, rather than on the manoeuvrability or speed of his mount. Prince Tissa reached for his bow. I watched Gamini intently. What would he do? My heart began to thud against my ribs.

Gamini relaxed in his saddle and Raja automatically began to move forward. Gámini loosened his reins lightly and Raja broke into a trot and then a canter. Gamini dug his heels into the horse's flanks. Head thrust forward, Raja shot forward like an arrow from a bow. Gamini veered right in an arc, then left, to ride in a circle around Kandula.

Prince Tissa loosed an arrow. It twanged harmlessly behind Gamini.

Hanging on to his bow and trying to fit another arrow to the string, Prince Tissa prodded Kandula to move sideways, but it was impossible. A war-elephant cannot swivel in a circle. The *howdah* began to sway more violently, making it difficult for Prince Tissa to retain his balance. Having to hang on to the side of the *howdah* with one hand, he could not get another shot at Gamini with his bow.

Gamini galloped Raja in a wide circle around the elephant, gaining speed with each stride. Prince Tissa dropped his bow. He seized a spear from a full quiver. As Gamini shot across his left front, Tissa flung the spear with astonishing speed. The watchful Gamini raised his shield just in time. The spear thudded against it and glanced off.

'Your spear arm has improved, Prince, but still you are not good enough,' Gamini shouted. His mocking laugh echoed as he sped around the elephant, Raja's hooves drumming an urgent beat.

I knew the sparkle of battle was in Gamini's veins. He was in perfect motion with Raja. The sun was warm on his body, the bloodlust singing within him.

As Raja raced on faster, I was reminded again of Velu Sumana, who had taught Gamini the fast-circle. Gamini was getting the last ounce of speed from Raja, while gradually diminishing the circle.

Prince Tissa stopped trying to swivel Kandula around. Instead, he held the elephant in position facing his troops, but started moving around the *howdah* himself, throwing darts fast and furious whenever Gamini came into his arc of vision. They either fell wide of Gamini or were taken on the shield. Accuracy was impossible, for Raja's speed was so incredible that we could only see the flying shadow of horse and man. Yet, if Gamini did not take the offensive soon, he would surely lose.

Before I could think, Gamini was passing in front of the elephant once more. He seized his spear and flung it with deadly accuracy. Prince Tissa took the spear on his shield, but he was not laughing.

Gamini continued his circuit. When he came from behind the elephant, he brought Raja to a tearing halt. The horse reared on its hind legs. Gamini swivelled it sharply left to face the elephant, then set it for the jump. In a few strides he had Raja with him in perfect balance. Giving Raja his head, Gamini seized a dart in his right hand. Was he mad?

I watched the grey bulk of the elephant looming before Gamini. He was jumping behind the *howdah*. I then knew why. The vulnerable upper groin of the beast could only be pierced from above and it was the area best attacked. I glimpsed Prince Tissa's startled face. Would Raja clear the great back or would horse and man crash to be maimed or killed?

Gamini and Raja were in complete rhythm as they sailed up. I held my breath. Gamini flung the dart with all the power in his arm. It embedded in the soft area between Kandula's left leg-joint and the massive body.

Kandula trumpeted shrilly with pain. Instinctively, he dashed forward. Gamini landed safely on the other side, raising Raja's head to allow the horse continuance of its stride.

The elephant charged blindly forward, screaming. Prince Tissa, obviously terrified, called vainly to the maddened animal. The enemy line scattered before the grey Kandula's pounding charge. The *howdah* began swaying wildly. Prince Tissa hung on grimly. Our men gave a great cheer that reached the heavens. My mouth was too dry for speech. My chest ached because, as always, I had been holding my breath, so only my sigh of relief joined the cheers.

The *howdah* started to give just as the elephant reached the line of men. It teetered briefly with Prince Tissa clinging to its side, then fell to the earth. Freed of its burden, the elephant slowed and finally stopped, its flanks heaving like giant bellows. The *howdah* must have cushioned the Prince's fall. He was up in an instant, running through his troops.

Gamini had brought Raja around. Seeing Prince Tissa fall, he drew his sword and galloped after the Prince, through the enemy and past Kandula. Victory was ours. I screamed my delight.

I saw Gamini slow to a canter, a trot, a walk. I wondered why. He reined Raja in, turned and trotted back toward Kandula. His love for his elephant brother had saved him from slaying his human brother today.

The dart protruding from its rear, legs splayed out, trunk lashing from side to side in fury, Kandula stood blindly searching for an enemy. I urged my horse forward. I was only a short distance away when Gamini slid off his saddle. He threw the reins on Raja's back and turned to approach Kandula. He began to speak the elephant language in a low, soothing voice. 'You are my twin brother. I come to you with love, little brother, to ease the snake's sting.'

Kandula glowered at Gamini with hot, mean little eyes filled with hatred. Fear shot through me. I reached for my spear. The great grey cloaks of the beast's ears came forward. The giant head lowered. In horror and desperation, I raised my spear arm, aiming for the eye. I paused. Gamini seemed unafraid. Was it because he had been made to walk beneath Kandula's great belly as a child? It is said that those who are made to do this overcome fear. Yet what good was

508

courage if it were going to let him be crushed to death like a rag doll beneath those gigantic feet, seized by the powerful trunk, raised aloft and dashed to the ground to be trampled again and again – for that is the way of the berserk elephant.

Miraculously, at that moment the breeze sprang up again. With upraised trunk, Kandula scented Gamini. The soft words reached the tiny brain. In seconds the great ears drooped. The trunk was lowered, then raised again, but this time in salute.

I began to breathe more easily. Like me, Gamini was bathed in sweat, the sweat that had carried its odour to Kandula. He walked calmly up to the great animal and fondled the trunk, then its left ear. Kandula nuzzled him with a trunk suddenly grown gentle. Speaking soft words into the elephant's ear, Gamini moved to its back. He seized the dart and in one swift motion drew it clear. The elephant squealed and stamped; blood welled out from the wound, but the animal knew instinctively that it was being ministered to.

I rode up and stopped. I would not even dismount to help Gamini. This was his triumph.

I could see the wound was only skin deep. Gamini untied his sash and staunched the blood. He moved back to Kandula and quietly gave the command to kneel. The great animal went down on one knee. The grey trunk swirled, seeking Gamini. It encircled him at the waist.

Kandula, the State elephant, raised Gamini in the air, then placed him on its back.

There could have been no greater symbol of victory. Both our men and Prince Tissa's raised a cheer that rent the heavens. They dropped their weapons and approached each other, shouting, whooping, screaming, arms opened to embrace the enemy.

'We are Sinhala! . . . We are brothers . . . We are one!'

The pounding of hooves rose above the cries of greeting. I glanced to my right, then to the left. Through the ranks of

Prince Tissa's foot soldiers, I saw enemy cavalry charging down our flanks. I half turned. Our own cavalry were streaking forward to meet them.

The approaching lines of foot soldiers paused, only yards from each other. Bewildered cries arose.

'What's happening?' one of Prince Tissa's men demanded.

'It is the Chola!' I shouted. 'They have broken the pact. They want war between us.'

The joy of victory and its hope changed to bitter gall within me. I remained helpless for a moment, then blind rage such as I had never known before flamed inside me, so intense that I shook. 'Kill the Chola!' I screamed. 'All you Sinhala, all you brave sons of Ruhuna, unite to kill – kill – kill!'

Friend and foe echoed my words. 'Kill them!' . . . 'They have broken the pact!' Men sought their arms again, then began sweeping toward the real enemy, some north, some south, to where the two forces of cavalry were now engaged in a bitter struggle. Messengers raced to the reserves to urge them into the fray.

The clash of arms, the cries of men, the screams of horses reached us across the plain. Animals staggered and fell, taking their riders with them. Awed at the sight of battle, my anger eased. The blood began flowing smoothly again in my veins. I looked for Gamini. He was riding Kandula toward me, Raja obediently following.

'Haa-a-a! To battle!' he screamed. 'Kill every Chola.' His dark eyes were wild. All thought of pursuing his brother had ended. The bloodthirst had seized him. 'Get some men to take Kandula to the physicians.' His eyes avidly sought the battlefield.

Gamini dismounted. Kandula's *mahouts* rushed up from Prince Tissa's lines to lead the elephant away. By now every Sinhala cavalryman, charioteer, bowman, spearman and foot soldier had turned on the Cholas. The battle on either

510

side of the plain had turned into a massacre.

'There will be a few thousand Chola the less for us to kill when this battle is over,' Gamini shouted. He raced for Raja. He paused, a hand over his eyes. When he looked at me again, it was as if his madness had been erased – a madness I understood at last, for I had just known it too. With a flash of dread, right in the middle of that sunlit battlefield, I saw how this latent force can seize and take over a man's spirit to wreck his whole *kharma*.

'We are not needed here!' Gamini exclaimed, regret in his voice. 'Let the victory belong to all true Sinhala. Have our cavalry regroup on the plain.'

'What is your plan, Prince?'

He looked at me in surprise. 'How can you ask? We must ride on to Dighavapi to seize the upstart princes – all of them – and bring them to the King's justice.' His smile was as fiendish as his choice of words. 'We have the State elephant. We must now seize the State sceptre and the Queen Mother!'

Chapter 51

Too impatient to wait for the regrouping of our entire force, Gamini took off with the household cavalry, after giving orders to Veera Singha to follow with the main body. The outcome of the major encounter on our flanks was already obvious.

We were met in the grove of trees at the far end of the plain by a body of Prince Tissa's foot soldiers. 'Prince Digha

511

Bahu fled on horseback no sooner the victory was yours, lord.' There was disgust in the voice of the clean-shaven young captain who gave us the news. 'And your royal brother snatched one of my men's horses a few minutes ago and galloped away.'

'Which direction did they take?' Gamini demanded.

'Where else would rats go, except to their holes?' the captain asked disgustedly. 'They went to Dighavapi.'

Having won its battle with the clouds, the pre-noon sun beat relentlessly on our bodies. We sped for an hour through dry brown grass and parkland. By noon, we were in dark scrubby jungle where overhanging branches shredded the sunlight. The shade felt good on our bodies. When we cleared the jungle, we were in open country, cultivated with dark green manioc plots. Sweat was pouring down us and our horses' flanks were wet, but we were not tired, only exhilarated. Inside me, however, was a warning voice that kept beating time to our horses' hooves. 'Save Gamini! Save Gamini!' I soon resolved to invite his wrath and become Prince Tissa's executioner, taking the evil *kharma* into my own life-stream, instead of allowing him to become a fratricide.

Now we were riding through green paddy fields. Bare-bodied men, clad only in span-cloths, bent at work, their legs lean and wiry. They stood up to stare after us. Loitering cattle ignored our passage as we drummed past. Before long, a dark grove of jak and breadfruit trees appeared in the distance. Above the treeline, the white spire of a *dagoba*, crystal-topped, thrust upward to the blue skies. As we approached, we could distinguish a village of white wattle-and-daub houses with neatly thatched brown roofs.

'That is the Okkam *vihare*,' I shouted to Gamini.

He nodded without speaking.

We sped through the village. Curious children ran out to the road, staring wide-eyed at our approach. Women, some with little ones at their hips, rushed up to their doorways.

512

The inevitable pi-dogs yapped at our horses' hooves.

At the far end of the village, the wooden gates of the *vihare* came up on our left. We had raced past before Gamini lifted his hand and brought Raja to a stop. I stopped with him and our men halted, too, in perfect column.

Gamini turned, walking Raja back with mincing steps. I followed Gamini. He pointed with his finger. On the dry, sandy road, fresh hoof marks led into the *vihare*.

'He has taken refuge in the temple,' Gamini observed grimly. 'Search it.'

My immediate reaction was one of dissent. A temple is inviolate. I began to protest, but the look on Gamini's face discouraged me. Obediently I dismounted, the men following my example. We tethered our horses outside. At least we would not ride into the temple premises.

Without any need for orders, a group of our men began cordoning off the area. Gamini and I removed our thonged sandals and left them by the gates. We sheathed our weapons. All these acts of habitual reverence, I thought, yet we are entering the sacred precincts with murder in our hearts.

Our men started to search the grounds and buildings. Gamini and I marched past curious saffron-robed monks, directly toward the cell of the Chief Monk. *Dana* being over, he would be there in meditation. We stalked across a neatly swept, sandy courtyard to the line of small rooms that housed the *bhikkus*. We stopped at a closed teakwood door at the far end, which had to be the Chief Monk's chamber. We knocked respectfully on the door. Getting no response, we opened it and entered.

The room was a cell with a flagstone floor. It was devoid of any furniture except for a wooden bed in one corner. The Chief Monk was calmly seated on it. He was an old man with wrinkled skin and a shiny shaven head. His quiet, deep eyes, full of peace, belied the harsh angularity of his features. Seeing us enter, he rose slowly from the bed, adjusting his saffron robe over one shoulder. He stood in front of the bed. At his full height, he was taller than Gamini or me, though slightly stooped.

His look told me that he recognized Gamini. 'I am the Venerable Godagatta Thero, Chief Monk of this *vihare*. What brings you here in such irreverent haste, lord?' The words thumped out quietly through toothless gums with the gentle intonation typical of a *bhikku*.

'We are searching for a traitor,' Gamini replied.

'Would there be such a one here?'

Gamini made an impatient sound. 'Where is my brother, Tissa?' he demanded unceremoniously.

The monk's gaze was tranquil. 'As you can see, he is not on the bed.'

Gamini suspected that Prince Tissa was hiding under the bed. His first instinct must have been to shove the monk aside and look under the bed, but laying hands on a *bhikku* was a grossly impious act. Gamini also knew that if he questioned this monk further he would only be met with the evasive counter-questions at which *bhikkus* excel. Laymen cannot win such battles against learned monks. It was obvious too that this monk would not yield ground and allow him to get closer to the bed, unless he was prepared to commit the ultimate impiety against a member of the Noble Order.

I reached out to touch Gamini's arm. He glanced at me and nodded, understanding my unspoken suggestion. 'You have seen fit to give a traitor refuge,' he quietly told the monk. 'We will leave now, out of deference to the Noble Order, but the traitor will have to remain here until he dies.'

'You set too much store by the span of life and death, Prince,' the monk responded calmly. I was reminded of King Kakkavan's words to Gamini. 'If this *vihare* is a refuge, why would anyone desire to leave it?' He smiled faintly. 'We of the Noble Order, for instance, are content to remain here until we are removed to another *kharma*, in the hope that it

514

might be a better one. It is you who, having searched this refuge with harsh thoughts, seeking to turn it into a place of execution, must seek an escape from your own volitions.'

Gamini's abrupt obeisance reflected his anger. I marvelled at his self-control as we turned and left the chamber, emerging into the warm sunlight.

'Have our men withdraw from the temple premises,' Gamini directed me. 'But post guards around it to ensure that my brother does not leave. He can take the robes or face my justice.' He reflected briefly. 'Have the gates closed too.'

By now the village folk had learned the outcome of the battle from our men. Their headman, who looked exactly like the Chief Monk and turned out to be his younger brother, led a deputation to offer fealty to Gamini. More importantly to us at this time, the headman organized the serving of a good noonday meal of rice and jak curry for our entire band. When our men had been given their orders and quartered, Gamini and I sat down in the shade of a tall banyan tree opposite the temple gates.

'How long are you going to maintain vigil here?' I demanded.

'Forever, if need be.'

'Then you will rule Ruhuna from here?'

'Where better than from the shade of the holy banyan?' he inquired sarcastically, then placed a contrite hand on mine. 'I have a feeling we will see the end of this comedy soon,' he added. 'Let us wait until tomorrow morning. Our main body should arrive by then.'

Backs to the tree, we dozed for about two hours.

We were awakened by a creaking. We shot to our feet. Two acolytes were slowly opening the temple gates. As we gazed curiously, a long line of saffron-robed monks emerged from the temple. Shaven heads shining, eyes downcast, robes clasped in one hand, palmyra fans in the other, they silently approached the gates. At the rear of the column, the Chief Monk walked sedately in front of a canopied bed carried by six young monks. On the bed was a still figure covered by a saffron robe.

'One of the monks must be dead,' a grey veteran volunteered. 'They are taking him to the burial chamber.'

Gamini and I looked at each other suspiciously. Neither a sick nor a dead monk had been reported from the search of the temple.

Three monks in a row, the cortege passed through the gates, turned left and proceeded along the dusty road. When they had all cleared the gates, the Venerable Godagatta walked slowly through, eyes downcast. The monks carrying the bed gravely followed.

Gamini strode up to the Chief Monk. He fell into step with the old man. 'Whom do you have on that bed?' he demanded hotly.

Ignoring him, the Chief Monk calmly proceeded on his way. Having walked a few paces, he started chanting from the Scriptures. The other monks took up the refrain.

For a moment I thought that Gamini would seize the bed and fling it to the ground. Once again he restrained himself. Instead, he held up his hand. 'Please stop the cortege, venerable sir,' he humbly begged the Chief Monk. 'I assure you I will never lay hands on the possessions of the Noble Order. Rather will I multiply them in my time.'

The Chief Monk continued his chant to the end of the stanza, then halted. The other monks knew instinctively that he had paused. The effect rippled up the long saffron line and all the monks slowly came to a stop. Since their eyes remained downcast and they had developed the ability to remain perfectly still, they looked like a collection of statues draped with saffron robes.

'Prince Tissa,' Gamini soberly addressed the figure on the bed, 'I know it is you beneath that robe, feigning the death that you will face by my decree one day. Take your peace while you are under the protection of the Noble Order, from whom we will never seize anything, and remember with

516

gratitude the *bhikkus* who saved you today.'

The figure on the bed did not stir. Gamini made deep obeisance to the Chief Monk. He turned to me. 'To Dighavapi!' he commanded briefly.

The shadows of palmyra palms lay long on the sand when we swept into Dighavapi the next evening. There was no opposition whatever. It is remarkable how quickly a cause can collapse when it is not based upon the fears and needs of the nation. People were going about their routine as if great events were not taking place. We increased our pace when we entered the little township, galloping through it and thundering across the palace gateway, leaving the astonished guards gaping after us. We pulled up opposite the palace entrance, dismounted and rushed to the great teakwood doors.

I drew my sword and rapped on the door with its hilt. 'Open up in the name of the King!' I shouted.

The doors swung open silently. Palace attendants in white sarongs and red turbans made obeisance to us.

'Where is your master, Prince Digha Bahu?' Gamini demanded peremptorily.

'My lord, he has not returned since he left a few days ago.' The voice was that of Appu, Prince Tissa's white-haired chief attendant, who had left the Mahagama palace with his master.

'And Prince Panduka?'

'The Prince left hurriedly with his retainers and the household cavalry this noon, lord.'

Gamini turned to me. 'Bah! He must have had word by a fast messenger. The jackals have all escaped.'

'Your royal mother has not fled. Let us take her and the State sceptre back to Mahagama without delay,' I advised.

'You are right.' Gamini gestured to Appu. 'Inform my royal mother that her son, the King of Ruhuna, requests her presence,' he directed.

Commanding some of our men to remain outside and some in the anteroom, Gamini strode into the reception chamber of the palace with me hard on his heels. I took the opportunity to survey the room. The tapers had been lit, so the floors of mountain crystal glowed with rosy light. Although it was not a large room, it was decorated with good taste. The supporting columns were of light teakwood, ornamented at the base and top. Tapestries done in green, brown, yellow, red and orange adorned the white walls, depicting important events in our history, such as the landing of our nation's founder, Prince Vijaya, and the meeting of Mahinda, the first Buddhist missionary, with King Devanam Piya. The windows were arched, with carved woodwork. Two enormous brass chandeliers, of twenty tiers each, with lighted wicks, stood in front of the dais at the far end. As the doors closed behind us, the wicks flickered, giving off a faint but pungent smell of burnt oil. On the dais were three highly ornamented chairs of creamy satinwood, with red cushions on them. On a low table before the central chair lay the ebony-and-gold Ruhuna Sceptre of State.

I am not generally given to impulse, but seeing the sceptre there in this alien environment outraged me. I strode up the steps of the dais, picked up the sceptre and returned to Gamini. I knelt to make obeisance to him. 'This is rightfully your possession, lord,' I said, still kneeling and offering him the sceptre with both hands.

He received it in grave silence. I looked up. He was suddenly and totally relaxed. His eyes gazed down at mine with the warmest depth to them. Then I smiled at him. 'May it forever remain the symbol of your sacred honour,' I said.

I received the sceptre back from Gamini and rose to my feet, then strode to the entrance door of the chamber and summoned our guards. A young cavalry commander, with tight-drawn brown skin on a lean-boned face, clattered up and saluted. He was followed by six men, who stood to attention.

518

'You know what this is?' I inquired, holding out the sceptre to the commander.

'Yes, Prince.'

'Guard it with your life until we return to Mahagama,' I said, proffering the sceptre to him. 'And thank the *devas* for your happy presence here at this historic moment, for you are indeed chosen of the gods to become the bearer, even for a few days, of this symbol of our kingdom.'

He knelt to accept the sceptre. 'With my life, Prince,' he promised earnestly. He rose, grasping the sceptre in both hands with awe. I returned to the reception chamber and stood slightly behind Gamini.

There were two doors at the rear of the chamber, behind the dais. They would lead into corridors, the one on the left serving the ladies' quarters. Accordingly, our attention was concentrated on the left-hand door. Before long, it opened silently. For a moment we saw nothing but the dark patch of the opening. Then, like a vision on a dark night, Queen Vihara Devi emerged from the shadows and paused in the light.

The Queen stepped gracefully into the chamber. I looked at her closely, hoping she would notice me. The sadness in her eyes stabbed my heart. She had always looked wistful, never sad. Now, there was also an air of uncertainty about her, as if she did not know what to expect. Why? I realized with shock that she was frightened of the consequences of her actions. She had broken a law of custom and exposed herself to the judgement of her son, Gamini. She would know the penalty, for she was aware of Prince Muthiah's fate eighteen years ago at the hands of his own father.

The Queen walked slowly to the centre of the chamber, turned left at the dais, then faced Gamini with wide, staring eyes. I forgot my own thoughts as mother and son looked at each other, almost blankly, for long moments. The silence in the chamber drew as taut as a bowstring.

The Queen was the first to look away. Her eyes slowly

wandered from Gamini's dust-strewn face to his sweaty clothes, returning with a softer look. 'You have grown, *putha*,' she said softly, her voice gentle as honey-dew. 'Many more years than the one since I last saw you. Now you are a man.' She sighed. 'You look tired. You need food and rest.'

Something broke in Gamini then. A stifled groan escaped him. He drew back, then moved forward in a rush to kneel at his mother's feet and make the deep obeisance of a son, clasped hands to forehead.

The Queen's eyes became moist. She began to sob, the tears coursing down her cheeks. 'Poor Gamini!' she whispered. 'My poor firstborn. You have indeed suffered much.'

'No more than you, Mother. I beg you to forgive me the wrong I did you and my father.'

'Your father forgave you. He told me so just before he died.'

Gamini stiffened. His bowed head jerked up sharply. 'Why then did you . . .?' He stopped and rose abruptly to his feet. He looked angrily at the Queen.

I knew the lines of Gamini's thinking. If King Kakkavan had forgiven him, why had the Queen not supported him for the succession? I awaited his outburst with apprehension. Once again, he controlled himself and spoke in a matter-of-fact voice. 'You will undoubtedly be glad to know that Sadha Tissa is still alive,' he said shortly. 'But he will not live long. I shall kill him as soon as I get my hands on him. We depart for Mahagama at the crack of dawn tomorrow. Have your noblewomen and attendants prepare, for you will leave with us.' He raised himself to his full height. His jaw thrust out forcefully. 'I am not the King of Ruhuna today by any right of succession. I am my own man. I have seized power by force of arms. Remember that, madam.'

I did not care for his harsh tone, since I did not know its real cause.

Gamini made obeisance, then turned on his heel and

strode out of the chamber. I followed suit, leaving a grieving Queen. I would have liked to remain to offer her some words of comfort, but it was not my place.

Being a devout Hindu, King Elara began his day by offering *pooja* to Dhurga, the goddess of three forms including Kali, goddess of death, whom he had selected as his family goddess. Being a part of the individual's worship, the ritual of this *pooja* varies from sect to sect. The King first bathed, then meditated in the small shrine room adjoining his bed-chamber. On an altar at the far end of the room was a ceramic statue of the goddess. Before it, a light burned perpetually in a small oil container made of clay. Having meditated, the King bowed to the goddess on bended knees, forehead touching the ground and palms together over his silver hair. He then circumambulated before her, bowing each time he passed the altar. Having thus offered her the submission of his mind and spirit, he adopted yoga positions before her, offering control over his body while training it to higher degrees of perfection.

When his wife and son had been alive, they had all observed Hindu family practices rigidly. These included the rites necessary with each meal, upon receiving household guests and on occasions that perpetuated the family as an entity. It was in the *kovil* that the King would perform his *arete*, which is restricted to one of two gods, Vishnu or Shiva. His god was Vishnu. Although he would not admit it openly for fear of angering the god, he shied away from the *lingam*, which was the symbol of the god Shiva. The *lingam* is the bringer of life, but the King felt that the god Vishnu was its giver.

The *arete* required him, after bathing, meditating and bowing, to offer milk, milk-rice, flowers and fruit to the god Vishnu through the priests. The priests would then chant to the god, pass a light across his face on a painting or statue, invoke his blessing on the offerings and offer them back to the worshippers, so that each received what another had brought. This included feeding them a mouthful of milk-rice and a piece of fruit. The priests would then anoint the worshippers with holy oil on the hair and bestow the mark of holy ash on their foreheads. King and commoner all participated together in the *arete*, for each performed his own. Although the King was considered a deity, he too was there to worship.

Having finished his *pooja* and eaten his breakfast, the King exercised vigorously with spear, sword and darts in his courtyard. When his opponents had left, it was time for his massage. He lay relaxed, face down on his polished granite massage table, his mind soon at peace, his body at ease from the ministrations of his masseur, Pillai, a tall, heavily built Chola, with a hairy black chest and rippling muscles. Pillai had the magic of strong hands and a gentle touch. The King noticed Pillai's skin. It was smooth, though prickled with sweat from the fierce pre-noon sunlight.

The King's eyes drifted lazily down his side. In spite of his age, his body was tight-knit, smooth from physical fitness and the sesame-seed oil used for the massage. Feeling the compactness of his powerful physique, he gave a sigh of satisfaction.

The only other person in the courtyard was the dwarf Junda, clip-clopping around as usual, his great head lolling. He stooped occasionally to smell the sweet-scented jasmine, or looked up at the cooing of doves in the green branches of the trees bordering the courtyard.

A loud knocking on the massive entrance door disturbed King Elara's contemplation. That would be the attendants, bringing in his hot bath. He turned his head slowly sideways to observe them. To his surprise, it was the giant Digha Jantu who entered. The King frowned and raised himself on his elbows. The masseur stopped his manipulation and stepped back a few paces. Junda ambled forward curiously.

'To what do we owe the honour of this unceremonious

intrusion, Chief Warrior?' Elara demanded with chill calm. 'Our orders should place you at the frontier this moment, not in the King's private courtyard.'

Digha Jantu paused abruptly. Realizing that he had overreached himself by entering unannounced, he moved swiftly to the massage table and knelt to make obeisance. His great chest was heaving when he raised his head again, his nostrils distending with each breath. 'Pray forgive me, sire,' he begged, still on his knees. 'Only news of the gravest import would cause me to leave my station and break the rules of ceremony.'

'We have been well aware of that,' the King responded, a hint of mockery in his deep, grave voice. 'It is astonishing the number of times you have had news of the gravest import these past nineteen years. Do give us your present news, however, instead of your excuses.'

The giant's small eyes flamed for a moment at the rebuke, the curling nose seeming to curve even more over the short upper lip. The words came out in a rush. 'The upstart Prince Gamini overthrew his brother in single combat on the Culan plain two days ago. Thereupon both Sinhala camps united to massacre over two thousand of our cavalrymen, who had been acting as advisers. The jackal Prince Digha Bahu promptly fled the scene with his troop of personal bodyguards and crossed the river to find refuge with my forces. His son and the Dighavapi household cavalry have already sought sanctuary in Soma and Seru.'

King Elara took the impact of the story in the pit of his stomach. Single combat was the one thing he had never anticipated. Gamini must have issued the challenge. That fool Tissa had accepted it. To lose a kingdom on an act of bravado!

Showing none of his feelings, the King levered himself up with the palms of his hands and sat on the stone slab, his long, muscular legs dangling. 'You may rise, Chief Warrior,' he bade. 'Where is the jackal prince now?'

'He rode with me and awaits your command in the outer reception chamber, sire. He desires audience with you.'

King Elara was surprised. He pondered awhile. 'His value to us depended entirely on the outcome of our plans in Ruhuna,' he finally stated. 'These must now be altered. It would be a waste of time for us to see him before we know whether and how he will fit into any new plans. Have him suitably quartered.' He felt drained by the bitter news he had received and vicious toward the Sinhala. A sardonic grin crossed his dark face. 'Perhaps in the house the late Prince Vipula once occupied.'

'Very well, sire,' the Chief Warrior rejoined. He looked hotly at the King. 'But what of the enemy? Shall we not invade Ruhuna and teach the Sinhala dogs a lesson? Our men are burning to avenge their fallen comrades!'

'We burn more than any of them to avenge our murdered subjects,' the King ground out. 'But you are impetuous, as usual. You expect that seizing Ruhuna will be an easy campaign for you, in which you will slice through the enemy like a spear through soft clay. Such will not be the case. Here is what will happen. You will be operating in terrain unknown to you, consisting of hills, ravines, rivers and forests, much of it ideal for ambush and hit-and-run tactics. You will meet initial harrying of your flanks by each of the three Ruhuna corps stationed west and east. A joint force of the now united armies of the two princes will then attack your centre. While you are so beset, the enemy will still have four regular corps in reserve at Mahagama, besides all the people of Ruhuna. If it had been otherwise, we would have crossed the frontier long ago. Since the political situation in Ruhuna is unstable for the first time in years, however, we can succeed if our timing is right, our preparation and planning perfect.'

Digha Jantu's muscular shoulders slumped with disappointment. The King felt a stab of pity for him. 'The years have been difficult for you, Chief Warrior,' he granted mildly. 'Anyone of worth and ability must have something to look forward to and you have not had it. Well, here is something for you. When we die, the succession shall pass to our younger brother in India, the great soldier Bhalluka. We shall, however, name you sub-king of Seru. How does that suit you?'

Gratitude flamed in Digha Jantu's face. He knelt and kissed King Elara's hand. 'You are too kind to your humble, obedient servant, sire,' he asserted.

'Look, then, to ensuring that Seru remains inviolate,' King Elara responded. He felt a moment's apprehension, but could not identify its cause. 'Meanwhile, hold your troops in readiness along the frontier, in case the new king of Ruhuna attacks us speedily.' He paused, musing. 'The sooner he attacks, the better, because he will then be less prepared.'

Thoughts of his massacred men finally took the King in thrall. He became sick with it: all those men, their families, their friends. The horrifying thoughts brought on his old determination. 'Begin preparations without delay for the conquest of Ruhuna,' he commanded fiercely. 'The blood of our men must be avenged. Their loved ones must be avenged. The King's justice shall extend throughout this island. You have six months, Chief Warrior. When the year-end rains of Ruhuna are spent, we shall attack.'

PART THREE

Lanka Dwipaya

The State United

Gamini's consecration ceremony began at the Tissa Maha Ramaya, where he spent the entire twenty-four hours preceding the formal ritual living the simple life of the *bhikku* in the temple, meditating and observing Ata-sil. He brought to his religious practice, especially during these twenty-four hours, all the concentration and intensity which he was capable of giving to whatever he was doing.

Being in the Tissa Maha Ramaya was, to me, like returning home from exile. The calm, silver waters of the Tissa Wewa across the bund were mystical after the arid Culan plain. The cool shade of *bodhi* trees, jak, breadfruit and mango gave me rest from the heat of the battlefield. Bird calls and the moo of the cattle, the rustle of wind in the trees, even the barking of the temple pi-dogs were more my *sura* than battle cries and the screams of wounded men. The scent of dry grass and the perfume of jasmine and temple flowers were a relief from the smell of blood and sweat, the stench of rotting corpses. It was indeed a healing, but the grim reminder of the wounds remained.

The hours in the temple were good for Gamini, too. They were meant to help him gather his spiritual resources, see human events from a different perspective, reflect on the duties and responsibilities of kingship and dedicate his mind, body and spirit to the tasks ahead of him.

The Venerable Sri Rahula personally spent much time with Gamini, instructing him in the principles and ethics of government. I was always a shadow in attendance, even when we sat before the Chief Monk in the lotus position and listened to him. I shall never forget the words with which he ended his final discourse. 'In a *janapada*, a people's State, when the king becomes righteous, his ministers and followers become righteous. When the ministers and followers of the king become righteous, the dwellers in the *janapada* become righteous.'

The following morning, we left for the palace at Mahagama, accompanied by the rest of the court, including the Queen Mother, Raji and her baby prince, all of whom had observed *sil*.

Almost overnight, the entire township and palace had been transformed. The streets were lined with white coconut leaves hung from rope and canopied with festoons of white jasmine, yellow and red temple flowers and orange marigolds. At every road junction, giant *pandals* of coconut trunks had been erected, covered with plaited green coconut branches and decked with pink bunches of king coconut. Paintings of Lanka's history and Buddhist events adorned the upper and side panels of each *pandal*. Clay lamps and flares created magic at night. Singers and dancers, mummers, musicians and acrobats plied their trade in the fairgrounds. The noise was deafening, the smells incredible, but the people were happy.

Gamini had decreed that the audience hall, in which the formal consecration was to take place, should not be adorned in any way. The only change in the great hall was that the gold-and-ebony throne, encrusted with jewels, was removed from the audience chamber and placed on a platform at its far end. Above the throne was the tasselled umbrella. On the red-cushioned footstool in front of it were the gem-studded crown, the jewelled sword and scabbard and the gold-and-ebony Sceptre of State.

Gamini had selected me to support him during the ceremony, a role which the young brother of the king-to-be usually fulfils. With Prince Tissa away, whereabouts unknown, this privilege was to be mine. Neither the Queen Mother nor Raji had any official part to play in the proceedings.

I slept fitfully the night before the ceremony, my mind over-eager for daylight. I had finally attained deep slumber when attendants woke me up before dawn with the sound of trumpets. I leaped out of bed to find more attendants already in the anteroom, which they had lit with flares. They assisted me with my ablutions. My barber shaved me and cut my locks. I needed his ministrations badly after the months campaigning. The court tailors had turned out pantaloons of white silk for me, with a tunic of the same material brocaded in gold. My sash and turban were of gold. My shoes were white-gold with pointed ends curling up slightly; the buckles were set with gems. When I surveyed myself in the looking glass, I was startled at my newfound resemblance to my uncle, Prince Vipula, many of whose mannerisms I had cultivated, both deliberately and unconsciously.

It is a proud day, uncle! I have kept my promise to you! I thought, talking to my reflection.

Cocks had begun crowing by the time I was dressed and ready to go to Gamini's rooms. The goat harboured by that confounded prince still bleated its mutton-headed response, but today it was music to my ears.

Gamini and I were using our old quarters for the last time. I did not know whether to be glad at moving to a more luxurious place of honour, adjoining the King's rooms, or to be regretful at leaving my dear, familiar things. The colour, the shape, the size of my rooms, their night sounds and day vibrations, their different scents and odours, and mostly the feel of them, stemming from the varying emotions they had enfolded, had made them home to me.

I had been accustomed to having nothing of my own, whether as a child or during my years in the temple. Yet even the mat I slept on in the temple had become home to me, a refuge as long as I slept on it each night. Not all my training as an apprentice monk could remove this clinging within me and I often wondered whether even the older, saintly *bhikkus*, with their ability to cast aside the clinging that comes from desire, did not secretly cherish this refuge given us by God for those hours when the body, in its semblance with death, finds peace and union with Him.

Gamini's robing was being completed when I walked into his anteroom with the self-consciousness grand new clothes produce. I barely noticed the attendants in their various poses, silently fitting Gamini. He was just over nineteen years old at this time, but he looked majestic. He had acquired the grace of slow motion in social situations. It seemed to come to him naturally. When he turned his head to look at me as I entered, his dark brown eyes alight, I knew that he was indeed a king, though cast in a different mould from my uncle.

Two men whom I loved, both kings among men; whether with joy or some pang of love, my throat constricted at the thought. It tightened more at Gamini's appearance. He stood, proud and erect, to his full six feet of height. Because he was sweating lightly with his exertions, his dark skin shone like polished ebony. His tunic and pantaloons were golden. His belt was of gold, studded all around with the nine gems. His curving-point shoes were covered with gold silk, the buckles gem-encrusted. The elaborate clothes he was wearing for the first time in his life seemed to throw the power of his face more highly into focus. Now that its boyish contours were disappearing, its bone structure showed heavy, with wide jaws, high cheekbones and a generous nose.

He greeted me with a dazzling smile, revealing the perfect white teeth against his dark skin. 'Ha! The dormouse!' I was touched at his remembering the greeting he had invariably given me every morning for years. He studied me approvingly, 'You look fine. You could pass for a prince in those clothes.'

'And you, sire, could pass for a king even without yours!'

He threw back his head and his deep laugh resounded,

causing his attendants to pause in their fussy adjusting of his clothes. 'So witty so early in the day! I would consider making you our court jester, if you had not been so valuable as a friend.'

As soon as Gamini was dressed and the robing·attendants had departed, others brought in our breakfast – sarsaparilla root crushed in goat's milk, followed by milk-rice with curried vegetables and fruit. Although we would need the sustenance for the arduous morning ahead, we could barely eat because of our inner excitement, which of course neither of us openly displayed, though each of us was aware of it in the other.

'I wish Raji were here too,' Gamini muttered as we finished eating. The attendants were bringing in the golden bowls of scented water for us to wash our hands in, and white napkins to wipe them.

I knew a pang. Women do not eat with the men, but could be present to serve them. The King, however, ate alone. Since I had trained my reflexes to accept Gamini's need for Raji, the pang did not last long. I was not surprised that Gamini had not mentioned his son. He had spent little time with the baby. Busy though he was, he could certainly have made some time if he had felt the desire.

When we had finished our meal, we walked to the corridor outside, where palanquins and Gamini's entourage of palace chiefs, attendants and page boys waited to escort us to the audience hall. We stepped into our palanquins and were carried slowly by tight-muscled bearers. The main corridor had been kept clear for our approach, but the entire palace was seething with activity. In the kitchens, staff were preparing for the feast that would follow the consecration ceremony. The princes and nobles would already have taken their places in the great hall.

We turned off along a side corridor toward the courtyard, from which we were to make our entrance to the audience hall. Trumpets started to bray and drums to sound. They became deafening as the musicians broke into a joyous frenzy. The rhythm of the drums pulsed into the bloodstream, the wail of the trumpets crept into the senses. When we got to the courtyard, we saw that it was packed with people in the gayest clothes, extending up to and beyond the palace gates.

Our bearers laid down their burden. I stepped from my palanquin into the morning sunlight and moved quickly to the formality of assisting Gamini from his palanquin.

A mighty chorus arose from the crowd, drowning out the music and drumming. '*Jayawewa! ... Jayawewa! ... Jayawewa!*' The roar arose from thousands of throats. Gamini turned to face the crowd, acknowledging the greeting with palms together. The cries increased. '*Jayawewa! ... Apé Raja Jayawewa ...* May our king triumph!' My whole attention was, however, focused on Gamini, so I did not notice anyone in particular, as I normally would have.

I proffered my arm courteously to Gamini. He took it. We paused briefly on the giant granite half-moon-shaped stone at the entrance to the audience hall, then walked slowly up the broad steps, to the mad cacophony of cheers, drums and music.

The steps were lined by princes of the blood, district governors and chiefs, each on a higher step by order of rank. Behind them, their page boys carried the banners of their houses. Every personage was attired in the colours of his clan. Their clothes were studded with jewels, sparkling in the slanting rays of the eastern sun.

I had never seen such a glittering sight as on those granite steps, worn with use – not even in the Anu court of old. We passed square-faced District Governor Rohan in the red and gold of the Tissa clan, staring squint-eyed, in which direction one could never tell; then my relative Parakrama, in the blue and white of the family. His hatchet face with the slashing harelip looked more stern than ever because of his solemnity. The lean, elegant young Prince Jaya was wearing the purple and gold of the Mahanagas. I observed them, without noticing any detail, as they made obeisance to Gamini.

Palms together, Gamini bowed to right and left, to each man in turn – young men, old men, middle-aged men. I acknowledged none, because recognition had to come from Gamini while I looked straight ahead.

We finally reached the top of the steps. The sounds of drums and trumpets began dying down. Taking their cue, people stopped their cheering. The aged Chief Minister, Kirthi Siri, and the other six ministers, who had been waiting at the top of the steps, advanced to meet us. They were all dressed simply for the occasion, in white pantaloons and *kurthas*. They made obeisance as one and Gamini acknowledged it, bowing deep, palms still together.

Suddenly I found that the whole world had become an abode of silence, the ears of its inhabitants hearkening in reverent awe. An entire people were gazing with sightless eyes toward the expectations of their hearts. To remind us of our mortality, a child's wail streaked through the air, but was quickly quieted.

Kirthi Siri looked at Gamini, his piercing eyes open, bright and clear. 'Our prince has arrived,' he intoned. His voice sounded surprisingly strong.

The people broke their silence, roaring, '*Jayawewa! Jayawewa! Jayawewa!*'

'This prince has been sent by the *devas*,' Kirthi Siri continued. 'He is endowed with all the qualities of birth, education, discipline and character required of a king. He is just in administration, mighty in battle and devoted in his observance of the Doctrine. He loves our people and holds sacred the soil of our kingdom. He shall live for it and if need be, die for it.'

'We have recently lost our great, beloved sovereign, Kakkavan Tissa,' Veera Singha, standing beside Kirthi Siri, joined in. 'We are a people without a leader, a kingdom bereft of a ruler. On behalf of the people of Ruhuna, the Council of Ministers, having deliberated concerning our needs, has decided that we have need of such a one as this prince.'

Now it was the Chief Minister's turn again. 'On behalf of the Council of Ministers, I, Mahage Kirthi Siri Jayatunga, make submission to this prince and beg him to accept sovereignty over the Kingdom of Ruhuna, its lands, its assets and its people and to be the defender of the Doctrine of the Buddha, the Sangha, the temples, shrines and *vihares*, of its laws and moral codes.' His eagle eyes gazed piercingly at Gamini. 'Does this prince accept our humble submission?'

'Sir, I accept your submission,' Gamini replied in ringing tones.

'Enter this august assembly then, for in the presence of the Sangha, the royal family and the representatives of the people, you shall be consecrated to the sovereignty of this realm and its manifold, arduous duties.'

The combined sighs of all who heard these words rippled around us as waters beneath a guiding craft. Kirthi Siri and the ministers moved aside. Gamini entered the audience hall. I followed slightly to his left and behind him. The ministers entered after us into the cool shade of the lofty building. Behind them, the princes and nobles began to move up in order of seniority.

To our left, within the hall, were the heads of departments and other public officials. To our right stood the district chiefs and *gamani*, village headmen, representing the villages, an innovation that Gamini had demanded. When we got closer to the platform at the far end of the hall, the saffron-robed members of the Sangha were to our right. They were the only persons seated in the hall. To our left now were representatives of the people's assemblies, with a vacant space for the princes, the nobles and the Council of Ministers, who had begun trooping in.

Seated on a chair on the platform, unusually grave of countenance, was the saffron-robed figure of the Venerable Sri Rahula, Chief Monk of the Tissa Maha Ramaya. In front of him was a gold stool, containing on it the gold receptacle with oil for the anointing. This oil had been blessed with the chanting of ten *lakhs* of *pirith* over it.

I remained standing at the bottom, while Gamini slowly walked up the platform steps and stood straight and tall facing the Chief Monk, his palms together before his face.

Eyes downcast, palmyra palm fan clutched before him, the Chief Monk began the Ata-sil chant. '*Namo thassa bagavatho, samma san Buddhasa . . .*' Those assembled repeated his words in a mighty chorus. Since the hall was packed to capacity with people, it resounded off the ceiling and through the building, seeking an exit into the country outside its confines. I suddenly wondered whether these sounds would ever cease throughout eternity.

With all my training and discipline, I found it difficult to concentrate at first. I had experienced so many events, so many emotions, since I first entered this audience hall as a boy. At some point, I had stopped thinking about the direction of my life. It had simply followed Gamini's. The events had been diverse, many of them shattering.

Noticing that Gamini was completely wrapped in the ritual, like one under a spell, I made a special effort to focus totally on it again, because the words of the chanting were important for him. It is not merely the effect of hundreds of voices tunnelling through a confined space, but the absolute absorption of everyone in the ceremony that matters.

Then, as before, I was wafted away on the thrumming of devout voices to the extremities of space, finally reaching God within me. He smiled, though without face or physical attributes.

I returned from this beautiful union only when the chanting subsided. As the last echo died away, I moved up the steps, took the Umbrella of State from its holder behind the throne and held it before the Chief Monk for his blessing. He chanted over it, then blessed it.

'Dear *devas*, bless this Umbrella of State. May it always remain a protection for our new sovereign and his people from all elements. May our sovereign likewise remain the protector of the Sangha, the Doctrine, this kingdom and its people.'

A thousand eyes watched, a thousand ears listened, a thousand spirits and more were one with me as I walked back and replaced the umbrella in its holder.

I picked up the Sceptre of State and presented it to the Chief Monk. He chanted over it, then blessed it. 'Dear *devas*, bless this Sceptre of State. May it always remain the symbol and authority of our new sovereign, sustaining and supporting him in his spirit and in all his actions.'

I was in a daze, uplifted, ennobled. I was no longer Prince Rodana, but the embodiment of thousands of expectant spirits, the expression of the deepest aspirations of a nation. I felt humble and rich beyond measure. It was no longer Gamini I served, but the King of Ruhuna. It was not my promise to a patriotic uncle I fulfilled, but the wish of the people, merging into my most sublime desires.

I replaced the sceptre on the stool, picked up the sword and held it before the Chief Monk. He chanted over it, then blessed it.

'Dear *devas*, bless this sword. May it always remain a token of the might and humility of our new sovereign, the hope of our friends and the dismay of our enemies.'

I replaced the sword and waited, trembling, shaken like the earth before an awesome quaking.

Gamini walked slowly in turn to each of two seven-tiered brass lamps on either side of the throne. He picked up the single lighted taper at the base of each lamp and lit all the wicks of the lamps. Each of them took fire instantly. Presently they were all flickering and smoking, the lights dancing yellow-gold with every breath of air.

'May the actions of our gracious new sovereign thus always light the darkness in our kingdom,' the Chief Monk intoned.

Returning to his position in front of the Chief Monk, Gamini stood a moment, intently looking down at the *bhikku*. I watched, breathless, as the monk's eyes slowly began to glisten. Their gaze gradually intensified, so smoothly that there was no break, no push, no added power released. Shining stars appeared in them and suddenly they were hypnotic. The monk was willing everything noble and righteous into the young king. Gamini received it with submission and humility. So the spirits and intentions of the Chief Monk and the King merged into a perfect union, a common all-encompassing purpose for the nation and its people. The work ahead became sanctified by Temple and State.

The communion achieved, its power remained even while its visible effects receded. Gamini sank to his knees and bowed his head. He was now ready for the final act of acceptance.

I picked up the crown. It was unexpectedly heavy, because of its gold and jewels, but I did not feel its weight. I walked to the side of the Chief Monk, knelt down and proffered him the crown. He accepted it with both hands, chanted over it and blessed it. 'Dear *devas*, bless this crown. May it lie lightly upon our beloved new sovereign, but may it always remind him of the weight of his responsibility to the Doctrine, the Sangha and the people of this kingdom of Ruhuna. Dear *devas*, sanctify thy servant, Abhaya Gamini, its wearer, on whose head I now place it as a sign of royal majesty and his kingly virtues.'

He placed the crown upon Gamini's head.

The intense hush gave way as cries of '*Jayawewa! Apé Raja Thumma Jayawewa*' rent the roof. Drums began to throb and pound outside the hall; the wailing of trumpets sizzled like burn wounds through their rhythm. The noise was unbelievable, but so intense and sincere that it tore at the heartstrings. And when its paeans died down and the hush returned, my ears were singing, like my heart.

The crowning ceremony was over; it was time for the benediction. I moved to the gold stool, lifted the golden container of oil and walked up to the Chief Monk. He rose slowly to his feet. I proffered the container to him. He laid his fan on his seat and accepted the container with both hands. He moved in front of Gamini. 'With this oil made sacred by the chanting of ten *lakhs* of *pirith*, I bless and anoint you in the name of the Sangha and the people of Ruhuna. May you ever preserve the holiness, the customs and the traditions that have blessed this oil.'

The Chief Monk tilted the container to pour a few drops of oil on Gamini's dark locks, at the centre of his head. He handed the container back to me and I replaced it on the stool. The Chief Monk gazed down at Gamini's bent head. I was stunned to see that the *bhikku*'s dark eyes were moist. And yet, why not, when my throat was aching with the effort to hold back my own tears?

The Chief Monk backed away and resumed his seat. Gamini remaining kneeling, head bowed.

'By choice of our Council of Ministers, with the approval of the Sangha, our Sovereign, Abhaya Gamini, Lord of Ruhuna, has now been consecrated king,' the Chief Monk declared. 'Do you, the people of Ruhuna, bless him in his duties and responsibilities?'

'*Ahey! Ahey!* We do!' Came the answer of voices thundering through the hall.

Gamini rose slowly, the crown on his head. He stood erect, heels together. I walked up to the footstool, picked up the sword and handed it to the Chief Monk. Holding it in both hands, he delivered it to Gamini. The new king accepted the sword. I helped him buckle it to his belt.

I walked to the footstool, picked up the Sceptre of State and handed it to the Chief Monk. Gravely he received it and presented it to Gamini. The new king accepted it with both hands.

'You now hold the symbols of your office, O King,' the Chief Monk declared. 'All is well. Pray be seated on your throne. Deliver righteousness and good government, justice and mercy from it.'

Holding the sceptre in both hands, Gamini advanced slowly to the throne. He paused, then turned. He held the sceptre with his right hand, adjusted his sword with his left hand and sank gracefully onto the throne. The sceptre remained in his hands, tilted slightly to the right, its base on the floor. Gamini's feet were firmly on the ground, the right knee turned slightly outward. I shall never forget the way he looked at that moment, a shining, godlike figure, sitting erect, head held high. Suddenly his aura emerged. It shone golden around him, shimmering in the lamplight. Soon it spread, ever increasing in size, but keeping his form. It spread through the hall, enveloping me, expanding to embrace everyone in it. Then I knew that it would reach every corner of our land. To my profound joy, there was no black stain within that aura. Instinctively I fell to my knees.

Quivering like a leaf in gentle winds, I remained kneeling, absorbed by the spirit of our king, I knew not for how long. I only came to at Gamini's words. 'We bid you rise, Prince.' I looked at him in wonder. The aura had vanished, but I choked before his majesty. A thrill of joy within me demanded to reveal its source. I searched for it. Ah, yes! My king had used the royal 'we' for the first time!

I blinked back the tears, rose to my feet and moved forward to take my place behind the throne. I turned to face the entrance to the hall. With a rustle of movement, people swung to gaze at a stream of girls, dressed in white with red-and-gold sashes, their faces shining with excitement, filing into the centre aisle. When the girls were all assembled, they burst into Jayamangala Gatha, the Chants of Benediction. Their fresh young voices seemed to cleanse the hall. It had known both good and evil.

Their Gatha ended, the girls departed; walking backward, palms placed together at the forehead in acknowledgement of their king. I moved in front of Gamini and knelt to offer him my fealty. A sob sounded from somewhere in the hall.

When I rose, all those in the hall, except the *bhikkus*, began filing up to the platform to kneel before King Abhaya Gamini and offer him individual fealty.

It took until an hour before noon for the ceremony to be completed. I then accompanied Gamini and the Chief Monk to the entrance of the hall. After the shade inside, the sudden sunlight was so bright that it burned the eyes. The cheering of the crowds started low, then built to a deafening crescendo, rising in great waves of sound to rend the very heavens.

Chapter 53

The palace guard in their ceremonial white uniforms were drawn up once again in the courtyard of the audience hall of the Mahagama palace. Nobles, courtiers and attendants bustled up and down its broad steps as usual, their clothes very white in the sunlight. The smell of incense from joss-sticks and of burnt oil from thousands of clay lamps on the balustrade walls of the great hall tinctured the air. Were these the crows of six years ago, flying lazily overhead, piercing the clear sky with their cawing?

The difference today was that instead of King Kakkavan, Gamini now stood alone at the bottom of the steps to wash the feet of the Chief Monk, at the entrance to the hall where he had once refused to take the oath of nonviolence against the Cholas.

Although it had been announced as an almsgiving, I knew that Gamini really intended it as a charitable offering to bring good fortune to his planned invasion of Lanka. The desire of people to bribe *devas* or the forces of destiny with vows and offerings never fails to upset me. Poor or rich, it makes no difference. A man will give a beggar a bronze coin and one can almost breathe his unctuousness and the hope of reward. A woman will feed seven monks instead of six, believing that the additional *dana* will help heal her ailing child of an incurable disease. People generally call upon life to give them some special favour in return when they bestow charity. I was glad Gamini had much more to help him achieve victory than the offering of an impressive *dana* to his gods.

Presently, the last monk ascended the broad steps and took his place inside the audience hall. It was shady and cool inside after the warm, glittering sunlight outside. The hushed voices of people and the long rows of saffron-clad monks, seated on white-sheeted mats, continued to give the illusion of a great shadow play.

The ladies in their white *sarees*, led by the Queen Mother, emerged through the rear doors, made obeisance to the monks and knelt in groups. I wondered what Vihara Maha Devi was thinking. She had been very withdrawn during our journey back from Dighavapi to Mahagama, as if she had retired into a world of her own. I was present in Gamini's chambers in the Ruhuna palace when Raji and the baby prince were presented to her. She came alive then and, when she took Prince Abhaya Sali into her arms, he obviously entered her heart.

Everyone in the hall squatted, hands raised, palms to forehead. The nasal voice of the Venerable Rahula, somewhat quavery with age, broke the hush to rise in the chant that precedes the administering of the Five Precepts.

'*Namo thassa bagavatho arrahato samma Sambuddhassa . . .*' One thousand other monks took up the chant:

> 'Homage to him, the Blessed One,
> The Exalted One
> The fully Enlightened One . . .'

Once again, I knew that strange wafting of my spirit into the infinite God in this hall.

The chanting finally subsided. Its echo lay vibrant on the air even after all sound slowly echoed into silence. People rose to their feet. The bustle of activity recommenced. Quiet voices issued directions. Bare-chested attendants brought in steaming pots of fragrant-smelling milk-rice and cauldrons of vegetable curries. The scent of cinnamon, coriander, cloves, cardamoms, chili and garlic reminded me that I was really hungry, not having eaten since dinner last night.

Gamini moved forward with his mother to serve the group of Chief Monks of the various temples, who were seated in a separate group. Ever his shadow, I followed to be of service. We moved slowly down the line of saffron-clad *bhikkus* sitting in the lotus pose. Ladling the food into the polished black begging bowls became such a routine that we barely noticed whom we were serving, until we finally reached the last *bhikku*.

Gamini scooped a golden ladleful of milk-rice and raised the ladle. The Chief Monk placed his hand over his black begging bowl, palm downward, in token that he did not wish to be served. I was mildly surprised. It could not be that he disliked milk-rice, because monks refuse nothing on grounds of preference. Perhaps he was unwell.

I glanced down at the *bhikku*'s face. It was vaguely familiar. I noted the wrinkled skin and toothless gums, the dark eyes gravely downcast.

Only when the *bhikku*'s eyes lifted to Gamini with a steady gaze did I recognize him.

Stifling a gasp of surprise, I shot a glance at Gamini. He was stooped, ladle poised in one dark hand, angry recognition on his face. He too had recognized the Venerable Godagatta, Chief Monk of the Okkam temple, where Prince Tissa had found refuge less than five weeks ago.

I tensed, knowing this would be a momentous encounter.

'Why do you refuse to be served, venerable sir?' Gamini inquired in a low voice.

'I cannot permit the hand of one who has murder in his heart to serve me, least of all when that same hand will slay his brother.' The Chief Monk spoke softly, but there was conviction and determination in his tone.

'Why did you then come to this almsgiving?' I noted a dangerous edge to Gamini's voice.

The Chief Monk's eyes became penetrating. 'Surely an almsgiving is an act of the merciful, the charitable, to the Doctrine and the Sangha.'

'Is it noble to refuse alms?' Gamini demanded quietly. 'Can there be charity in the heart of a *bhikku* who refuses even a fratricide the opportunity to give alms in order to acquire merit?'

'Well spoken.' The *bhikku* smiled through toothless gums, but his eyes were steely as once before. 'I will certainly give you the opportunity to acquire such merit. But in order that I, too, might derive the greatest merit from my act of acceptance, let me first permit you to become a fratricide.' The *bhikku* slowly moved his head sideways. He nodded toward a group of temple attendants dressed in white. 'There, lord, is the brother you seek to kill. Kill him now, in the presence of the Sangha. When you have done so, pray return to serve me and I shall accept your *dana*.'

Gamini froze. Then his head swivelled slowly toward the group of attendants. I held my breath. One of the attendants, a tall, slim youth, removed a bandage he had been wearing around his head and neck, to reveal his face. Curly black hair above delicate features now gaunt, dark eyes with black circles around them, a slim build beneath coarse white clothes – it was Prince Tissa.

What a contrast between this fugitive and the proud boy who had last attended this very audience hall as Prince Regent. I had no time for reflection. Gamini's golden ladle fell into the pot with a soggy thud, its handle rattling against the metal edge. The last time this had happened flashed in from my memory. Today it warned of murderous purpose.

Gamini's eyes, fixed on his brother, were ablaze with fury. He looked as he had the morning he nearly killed Prince Panduka. He rose slowly to his feet. Almost unconsciously, his hand reached for the knife at the waist of one of the attendants, intended to cut the monks' food, if required. He slowly drew out the knife. My heart contracted. Chills went through my body.

White-clad, with the steel blade glittering incongruously in his hand, Gamini advanced like a great stalking leopard toward his brother. His silence was more menacing than words.

Gamini was the king. No one dared interfere, even though what he intended doing was so impious that it would scar him and his *kharma* forever. The entire gathering watched in shocked silence.

For several moments I was rooted in horror. Then I came to my senses. I dropped the ladle I was holding with a clatter. Everyone's eyes shot in my direction. I ran swiftly to catch up with Gamini.

Quick as I was, the Queen Mother was quicker. She sped past Gamini to Prince Tissa and turned around, shielding him with her body. Panting slightly with her effort, nostrils distending, beautiful eyes imploring, she begged, 'No, Gamini, our king, my son! You swore in this very hall, before these same venerable *bhikkus*, that you would forever be without enmity to your brother.'

Gamini paused in his stride. 'Lady Mother, we have no

546

more enmity toward this traitor than we have for others who are executed,' he declared. His pleasant tone made his purpose seem more deadly. 'The King's justice is always administered without enmity.'

By now I, too, had reached Gamini. I faced him squarely. 'Lord, when a traitor is executed, the King's justice is effected by an executioner,' I interjected, 'not by the king himself. If you decree immediate execution of your sentence, let me be the one to carry it out.'

Gamini glanced at me. A gleam of secret amusement entered his face and stabbed me. 'You too, our friend,' he said softly.

His mood chilled me more than anger. I knew full well the red mists of rage and hate that must swirl within him, yet I could not let him do it. 'Only to save your immortal spirit, lord, even if I take the evil into my own *kharma*. If you do it, this will not be an execution, but murder.'

Gamini looked at me broodingly for a few moments. His eyes flickered to his mother, considering her without emotion. She seemed to let loose some viciousness in him. A merciless expression crossed his face. His body went taut. He raised the knife.

The Queen spread her arms sideways to protect her younger son. 'Then kill me first and commit the sin of matricide as well!' she panted.

Prince Tissa had been standing unafraid behind his mother, his face strangely calm, almost serene. He now gripped both his mother's arms to move her gently aside. He looked Gamini in the eye, his gaunt face quite beautiful.

'King and brother, I ask you not to kill me with your own hands in the presence of the Noble Order and invite the burden of sin and shame forever,' he said in clear tones. 'I have sinned against you and committed unpardonable crimes of disloyalty against the State for many years now. I have caused the death of innocent people through my ambition. I deserve your death sentence and will gladly

547

accept it. Dying will even be a welcome relief from the guilt I have carried so long.' He shook his head with a strange despair and his shoulders drooped. 'Do not join me in a world of grievous sin.'

The words only made Gamini raise the knife higher in fury. I held my breath, wondering whether to risk everything by jumping in and taking the knife thrust. I would have done so if I thought Gamini would end there. I knew beyond doubt that he would not.

The knife remained poised. Gamini's eyes narrowed. He started to blink. Had the mists of anger begun to dissipate? My only hope was that Prince Tissa would show no fear whatever. It was the one response that could quench the blaze of Gamini's anger.

The knife hand trembled. Suddenly, it steadied, about to slash down. He is going to do it, I thought. Dear God, help him.

'You have duties to perform, Prince.' Gamini observed, almost casually. 'Come help us serve the Noble Order.'

Chapter 54

Gamini's act of generosity in sparing Prince Tissa's life not only helped his *kharma*, it also brought practical rewards. Prince Tissa worked so devotedly that Gamini decided, after discussion with the Council of Ministers, that when he proceeded north against the Chola he would leave his brother as regent in Mahagama.

Gamini continued to treat his mother with cool respect, but his life with Raji and the baby prince was one of supreme happiness, though he only saw them late at night.

The baby slept in his nursery, which had once been Gamini's. It was separate from the royal bed-chamber, so all Gamini had to do was visit his son, play with him a little if he was awake, and return to Raji.

Their love blossomed. Raji was unfailingly kind and understanding. Regarding herself as Gamini's slave, she truly enslaved him and he snatched every possible moment of time to be with her. I sensed that, in part, he was like that creature of the distant desert regions, which stores water in its hump for the long, arid journey ahead.

This was the period when I came to consider Gamini a military genius. His father's foresight had created supply sources for conducting war. Gamini organized its use superbly. He divided production into three departments: war material, including weapons and machines; food and clothing; quartering for men on the field and medical supplies. He also created a separate department of transportation, including chariots, wagons, horses, elephants, baggage trains, rations and field kitchens. He even added to this department a section to establish field latrines, dispose of night soil and prevent disease. He placed all these departments under Veera Singha, whom he named Minister for War.

Gamini assigned Prince Tissa and Kirthi Siri the task of recruiting new forces. He solved the worst problem faced by peasant armies – that of men abandoning the field to return to their villages for sowing, reaping and harvesting – by insisting on alternative arrangements being made in every village. 'We would rather pay our soldiers additionally for these services than hire mercenaries to fight a national war,' he declared.

Velu Sumana, as Chief Warrior, and the other nine Great Warriors were assigned the task of training the troops. Instead of giving each of them a corps, however, for the duration of training, Gamini placed those most skilled in certain arts in charge of that particular body of troops. So Velu Sumana became the cavalry commander, Gotha commanded the chariots, Bharana the spearmen and Phussa Deva the archers. The giant Nanda Mitta took over the foot soldiers and the fleet-footed Nimila the machines of war and communications.

My own role was political, to feel the pulse of the kingdom, to collate intelligence and to create the right mood in the people.

All training in the use of weapons and in battle tactics was carried out under the direct supervision of the Sudaliya and Maravalliya schools of war, but Gamini devised new ground tactics for his army, based on the theory of thrust he had outlined to me on the Culan plain, rather than the customary attack all along the line. The heads of the schools were somewhat apprehensive about these tactics, on the grounds that they broke up the army into segments that could be pincered, but Gamini pointed out that a long, thin line of men could equally well be broken up into segments; also, his tactics called for compact groups, like mobile forts, which could defend their rear.

Gamini also instilled in his commanders an appreciation of the value of reconnaissance and intelligence regarding enemy strength and supplies, of battle plans based upon all available intelligence, including topography, of firm lines of communication and supplies. They were not to pursue a fleeing enemy without adequate reinforcement. They were to advance only as far as support of all kinds permitted. He insisted on consolidation after each successful attack. His directives were based in part on information I gave him of the methods of Kyroos, Sikander and Moriya, but finally his planning came from his own brilliant mind.

'We have four months in which to prepare for our first move,' Gamini told me as we sat one night in his father's study, now his, for our usual talk. It was sultry outside and the tapers flamed straight and tall, making the perfect setting

550

of peace for the golden Buddha statue. 'The Chola does not intend advancing until after the Phussa rains. We shall attack just before the rains, in order to seize the initiative. Ruhuna is poised for war, so our problem will be to keep the Chola's suspicions allayed, but meanwhile you should start creating the incidents necessary to jolt our people and propel them into action.' His face was curiously young and eager in the flare-light, considering the depth of his plans.

I leaned back on my ebony chair. 'There is no need for us to create incidents,' I responded. 'Digha Jantu is making no attempt to restrain his men on either side of the river. They are out for blood, probably trying to provoke us. We have had reports of raids on our villages, plundering, rape and even desecration of our shrines. We are, of course, holding back, but the men are getting restive. Meanwhile, word is being spread to every corner of the kingdom!'

'The time for revenge will come,' he promised grimly.

'Assuredly. The people will find it sweeter for having been restrained.'

'Do you think Digha Jantu has ambitions to overthrow King Elara through military action?' Gamini shot the startling question at me out of the blue, as was his wont.

'I would not be surprised. Remember how Sena and Guttika, the Chola horsetraders, seized Lanka with mercenaries?'

'Do you want to know our plan of action?' Once again Gamini was away in a different direction. Of course I was eager to know.

'We shall make no move until we are ready to take the three Sinhala forts held by the Cholas simultaneously on a single night,' he explained. 'This we shall do before the rains, immediately proceeding northwest along the river as if heading for Soma. This feint should make the Chola divert large bodies of troops to Soma and Seru, splitting up his forces because he will not know our intentions. We shall actually cross the river with our main body above its

551

intersection with the Amban River near Seruwila. The Chola will not anticipate this, because Ambati is one of their strongest forts, located between both rivers with a wide moat joining the rivers to make the third side of a triangle. It is essential that we seize Ambati and cross the river again before the rains make it impassable. We can then sit in the Chola forts until the rainy season is over.'

'Clever! But why do you wish to avoid Soma and Seru?'

'We understand that King Elara has promised them as a subkingdom to Digha Jantu to keep him appeased.' Gamini seemed amused. 'Digha Jantu will obviously send an unnecessarily large body of his troops to safeguard his territory! Why should we confront such a force? Also, why should we not drive as directly as possible to our objective, Anu?' His eyes sparkled with anticipation. 'What a joy it will be to see the Sacred City that you have so often described to me, to live in the palace of the Sinhala kings, to sit on the throne hallowed by the great Devanam Piya.'

He was freely expressing his personal desires now, shorn of patriotism, the pride of the Sinhala and the need of the nation. I should have been elated at having his confidence at last, but I only shivered slightly and stared into space, for suddenly the very name of King Elara's Chief Warrior had laid a cold hand on my heart.

'What's wrong?' Gamini inquired anxiously.

'I am fearful of this Digha Jantu,' I blurted, not knowing why.

Gamini looked closely at me. 'Do you fear him as a formidable warrior?'

I shook my head. 'No, this is personal,' I replied hesitantly. 'I wish I knew what it means.'

Our move to positions surrounding each of the three forts on our side of the river, now occupied by the Chola, was a masterpiece of planning and subterfuge. The defences of each of the forts and their movements of guards and

552

personnel had been well spied upon and analysed. Instead of marching as an army, we first had all our war supplies and equipment assembled in degrees at dispersed locations, as if they were the regular movement of stores. Our men followed in small formations. Gamini's plan was that on the evening of the first day of the month of Phussa the men and vehicles would move to new assembly points close to each of the three forts, from where they would launch attacks simultaneously at midnight.

By organized coincidence, foraging Cholas from each of the forts were able to capture wagonloads of *sura*, our heady alcoholic drink, that very evening. By nightfall, most of the Chola soldiers in the forts had to be drunk!

The location of the forts was important to our plan. Our forts at Wera, Kasa and Kimbul had originally been erected as bases for the protection of the local population from thieves and brigands. They were not located at the fords, but about half a mile further along the riverbank. The Cholas had erected their forts on the other side of the river, but at the fords. Deeming the river opposite our Ruhuna forts impassable at nights, the Chola patrols from their own forts did not even march as far as the riverbank opposite our forts. After the Cholas captured the latter, they merely continued their former routine. Our plan was therefore to recapture our Ruhuna forts secretly in one night, lie hidden in them during the day and take the Chola forts across the river the next night.

Gamini had elected to lead the attack on Wera himself. This was the easternmost of the three forts, located along a bend of the Mahaveli River. It is here that the river alters its easterly course from the central hills to veer sharply north, before proceeding past the ferries and forts at Ambati, Gallaka and Kasa and turning northwest to head for Soma, Seru and the sea. Gamini had selected this fort for his personal leadership because it was here that Chola counterattacks were most likely.

The assembly of our assault forces began shortly after sunset, when the Cholas had retired to their forts for the night. Our guides had thoroughly scouted the staging areas and were soon leading us to them.

Gamini strode ahead of me along the jungle trail in the gathering gloom. He was alert as a leopard on the prowl. We wound our way beneath tall *ehela* and *sal* trees. Only faint cracks of pale night sky showed through their dark, spreading branches. It was a warm, close evening, so the men ahead of us soon left a track of stale sweat behind them. The soft crump of their feet on the soil and the occasional rattle of a weapon were the only sounds until an owl broke from a tree and flapped slowly among the branches, its hooting eerie in that wilderness.

We seemed to wind our way endlessly and I had lost all sense of direction when we came to the open glade. In the night glow I could see our troops spread out, silent, alert. The clouded sky promised total darkness, ideal for our purpose, but the earliest fears of the dark from childhood lingered and I was glad to join the men. I could sense their eagerness for the fray, catching a hint of it in the gleam of dark eyes, the set of a jaw, a quiet smile. Having never tasted battle before, most of them had to find the situation exhilarating.

Our every move had been timed, so we paused in the glade, awaiting the signal for our advance toward the fort – the call of a night bird repeated three times. On receiving it, we would filter in line through the jungle until we reached its fringe, where the fort's field of fire began. There we would await the signal for the final assault.

This wait was different to that on the Culan plain. The ghosts of night emerged, along with weird fears of the dark. My stomach soon began to feel weak. Would that call of the night bird never come? I waited, tense and sweating. The men began to get restless.

Then it came, sweet and clear through the gloom. We

began our advance in line. I was on Gamini's left, the giant Vasabha on his right, the men on either side of us dim figures. Although I had never been in such an engagement before, my courage soon returned. I felt fit and alert from my months of rigorous training, ready for battle.

We were not following a track now, but moved slowly through wooded jungle, feeling the way with our feet. I stubbed my toes against a fallen branch and restrained an exclamation. Vasabha slipped on a spreading root and nearly fell. Gamini, on the other hand, seemed to glide smoothly through the dark. I was thankful when we reached the edge of the jungle and Gamini raised a hand to signal us to stop. Our line and those behind us halted soundlessly.

About two hundred yards across the clearing, the lights of the fort glowed pale red. Most of the flares had been extinguished because it was nearly midnight. My heart began to beat faster. This was the same fort at which I had received my initiation into Ruhuna, nineteen years ago. The flowing sound of the river reached me. Memories swelled, ready to burst forth, but I blocked their recall. This was not a time for reverie, but for total concentration on the task ahead.

It had been reported to us that the defences on the Ruhuna side had been hastily improved by the Cholas immediately after they captured the forts. I could now see the mass of earthworks silhouetted against the night sky. As my eyes adjusted to the light, I distinguished wooden sentry towers, each about sixty yards from the next. With my keen night sight, I even made out the dark outlines of sentries in six of the towers.

Figures emerged from the gloom on either side of us, sank silently down and started crawling toward the fort on their bellies. Twelve of them would have bows slung over their backs; others would be carrying rope ladders with hooks on the ends.

The crawling figures soon became absorbed into the

darkness. Someone stifled a cough. Gamini looked furiously in its direction. Sounds carry at night. His whole body seemed to vibrate, yet he was absolutely still, the same stalking leopard, now ready to pounce. I gathered strength from him.

We watched with bated breath, but our ears gave us the first news. We heard faint twangs across the open ground. The sentry on the tower I was concentrating on seemed to melt into the darkness and vanish. My eyes swept to the other sentry towers. The figures on them, too, had vanished. There was no alarm. Our bowmen had done their work silently and well.

Heart beating faster, I stared eagerly through the gloom. Now the climbers would strike. Minutes passed. Nothing happened. I became sick with anxiety. Something had to have gone wrong.

Stooping figures ran along the earthworks, outlined against the sky. One reached a patrolling sentry from the rear. He rose. The two figures joined in a blob, which narrowed. The single figure stooped and ran on. My heart resumed its beat.

The most critical time of all had arrived. Our men had to open the gates. If they were discovered, a siege lay ahead of us and all our plans would have to be altered.

The tension around me heightened. Gamini was still as a rock. Men gripped their weapons more firmly. We were all holding our breath.

The faintest creak reached our ears, followed by that call of the night bird, sweeter than honey.

We advanced slowly and silently across the clearing – six long lines of grim, determined men. Those in the lead carried ladders. Everyone carried naked spears and swords, but no shields. They are a hindrance in climbing or dealing death swiftly in the passageways of a fort.

That was the longest walk I have ever taken. The alarm could be sounded at any moment and we were completely exposed on that open ground. Flameballs or a hail of arrows could erupt from the dark mass ahead. I heaved a sigh of relief when the pale patch of the open gate loomed before us. Gamini raised his hand. Our ranks rippled to a stop. The rope ladders of our advance party hung like pale grilles against the tall earthworks. Some of our men ran forward and quickly slung more ladders onto the earthworks. The hooks held. The men started climbing, eager to be the first for death or glory. Only when these long lines of men began massing on top did Gamini point forward with his arm.

We wraithed through the gates.

Chola sentries were slumped beside them. Others were scattered in the courtyard, limbs distorted, like great scarecrows. Our lead force emerged from the surrounding shadows. One of them, his face only a brown blur, wiped his knife on a dark loincloth.

Once inside, Gamini waited until several hundred of our men had gathered in the courtyard. He seized a flare from its stand outside the guardhouse and waved it aloft. Others seized torches and lit them. Then, screeching like dervishes, we hurtled inside the fort, fanning out as planned.

Sleepy Cholas rushed out of their quarters in confusion. Gamini threw his flare at them. They backed away. We plunged in. I flung my spear at a slim Chola. It embedded itself in his dark, bare stomach. He dropped his sword and clutched at the spear. I transferred my sword to my right hand and thrust at a giant, exulting as the point sank in. A surprised expression swept his face, then pain. His eyes crossed. I withdrew my sword. He sank to the ground. We swept over dead bodies into the guard quarters. Cholas choked the building in their efforts to make a stand, getting in each other's way. We were a human tide, irresistible. Thrust, withdraw, cut. Withdraw, thrust. We forced them back or killed them.

The fort was ravaged by the clash and din of arms, the screams and groans of the wounded and dying, the fierce cries of men in battle rage. The smell of new blood began tearing at my nostrils. Gamini fought silently, with fierce, concentrated purpose. Others screamed or roared to fuel their fury. Not he. Always I stood with him, alert to protect him. Always Vasabha stood at his right.

Black bodies, brown bodies, fair bodies – muscular, lean, flabby – passed before my eyes. They knew my sword in lightning flashes. Thrust, withdraw, chop backward, chop sideways. My arm began to ache with the weight of my sword.

We cleared the guardhouse, leaving dead and wounded lying in their own blood. We raced back into the narrow street. Half-dressed Cholas ran about in confusion. Groups of men were fighting furiously. We made for the fort commander's quarters and entered the main hall, lit by flares, where I had dined one night as a boy. I had never dreamed how I would pay my next visit.

A Chola appeared through a rear doorway. He was a bearded man, of medium height and massive build, grasping a great sword in both hands. Strangely, he was smiling, his teeth white through the black beard, as he advanced toward us. 'I am the commander of this fort,' he shouted. 'I demand single combat with your leader.' He made for Gamini.

'No!' I screamed back. 'Single combat can only be with one of your rank.'

Vasabha leaped forward, sword in hand, his huge body gleaming golden. I pray it will not be scarred, I thought. The commander came on guard. The two opponents began circling each other. The Chola jumped back, raised his sword aloft with both hands and brought it down with terrific force on Vasabha's head. It would have cleft the warrior in two – only he was not there. He had danced away. It was magical to see him so light on his feet. As if to complete his motion, his sword snaked in, above the Chola's wrists and into the lean stomach. The Chola gave an anguished grunt. His body stiffened. His sword clattered to the ground. He reached to grab Vasabha's sword with both hands. Blood prickled red around the sword blade, then began to spill. The Chola half bent, trying to pull the sword out. His face was suddenly drenched with sweat. He hiccuped. His eyes bulged and rolled upwards. The lids closed in agony. His breath began to come in choking gasps. His eyes opened again, now agonized. With a groan, he slowly slumped sideways to the floor.

Vasabha placed one foot on the Chola's body and withdrew his sword. He glanced up at us. 'This man had no intention of fighting,' he cried hoarsely, indicating the still-twitching figure. 'He only sought an honourable death at the hands of an equal.'

By the end of the first watch after midnight, the entire fort was in our hands. Our men, under quiet orders from officers and section leaders, manned the walls or began tending the wounded and assembling the dead in long rows.

Gamini called a conference in the stone-walled chamber of the fortress commander, once used by Prince Digha Bahu. He sat at the creamy satinwood writing desk, with Veera Singha, Vasabha and me sitting across from him. His eyes gleamed with triumph.

Gamini was bare-chested. He bore no marks of the battle save for a couple of bloody nicks on his chest and the savage gleam that remains in the eyes after battle. 'Do you think the Chola fort across the river suspects anything?' he inquired.

'It's likely,' Vasabha commented. 'We certainly made enough noise.'

'Noise is relative and ours was a comparatively silent operation, I think,' Veera Singha volunteered. 'It is astonishing how earthworks contain sound, which seems to rise up, rather than go sideways. As you know, we had the Chola fort across the river closely watched. It sleeps in the peace of ignorance – no sounds of alarm, no flares being lit. We have accomplished our mission unnoticed.'

'Excellent!' Gamini exclaimed. 'Now we must keep them feeling safe until tomorrow night.'

'As you know, lord, our intelligence reports indicated no normal communication across the river between forts, except daytime patrols greeting each other and the weekly transport of supplies and guard replacements,' I intervened. 'So it is up to us and our men tomorrow . . . or is it today?' I glanced at the sand-clock. Daylight was only four hours away.

Gamini nodded. 'Well, it's time to visit our men. If they are well quartered, we can turn in ourselves for a few hours.' He stifled a yawn. 'It is so warm and close in here, I think I'll sleep in the open.' He rose to leave and we stood up with him. He turned to Vasabha. 'Have you sent messengers to the other two forts informing them of our success?'

'They left almost an hour ago,' Vasabha assured him.

'Wake me when you have their own reports,' Gamini directed. He strode out into the night and I followed him. He had fought hand-to-hand for two hours. His dusky back was covered with sweat and bloodstains, but he was alert and ready to see to his men. As for me, I was bone-weary and sickened by the carnage.

We walked up to the original battlements and paused to look across the river. The sky was overcast with angry clouds, but Lanka lay peacefully under the shroud of night. Dark treetops stretched endlessly into the distance. Behind us were the maimed and the dead. The river gurgled happily beneath, but I did not feel like communing with the river tonight.

'Soon they will not think we play with our toy soldiers, eh?' Gamini inquired softly. His white teeth gleamed in a smile, but his expression was grim.

At first I wondered what he meant. Then I remembered the insult hurled at him from the opposite bank by a Chola soldier. That had been over two years ago and he had not forgotten.

560

Now, for the first time ever, I saw my country, the land, the soil. The air spoke to me from deep within its womb, the magic night air of Lanka, as the earth and the water had done so many years ago, on my first visit to Ruhuna.

When will your fire speak to me from its depths? I wondered and grew sad. I knew the answer.

I gazed at the trees, the hills, the invisible people, all sleeping in the quietude of night, but all sleeping in thrall under the government of foreigners. I could not love it more. For the first time, I became aware of its true shame – my shame.

I heard a quiet laugh echoing across the Sinhala River. It came from the direction of Anu. Startled, I searched for its source. I looked at Gamini. His face was almost serene. He had not heard the laugh.

Then I knew it was Prince Vipula's laugh. His words reached me, borne on winds that suddenly sprang from the Sinhala land. 'You have found yourself at last, Prince. You and I are finally one, for you are now a true Sinhala.'

Chapter 55

The moment I lay down on my couch in the dark, the horror of my actions hit me with stunning force, making my head whirl. I had killed my first man before I was thirteen and been able to live with it, but this was different. In the aftermath of battle, I relived it all. Each time I closed my eyes, faces of men I had killed floated before me, their eyes pleading. My ears resounded with death screams, my nostrils were revolted by the stench of raw blood mixed with sweat and fecal matter. It required all my efforts of mind control to fall asleep.

At midmorning the next day, a messenger brought news that the Kasa fort had been retaken. Two hours later we had word of the Kimbul attack's success.

The scene was set for tonight's assault, provided the Cholas across the river were not given cause for suspicion. In order to keep them happy, all three captured forts already had Sinhala in Chola uniforms at the sentry towers and manning the earthworks. We even had Chola prisoners walking around the open area outside the forts and patrolling our side of the river. Of course they were closely attended by our men, also dressed in Chola uniforms. One cry of alarm would have ruined our plan, but Gamini considered this a worthwhile risk to take.

The daylight hours were therefore full of apprehension, especially just before noon, when a Chola patrol appeared on the opposite bank and hailed their comrades while we held our breath. It soon departed, however, and we breathed easily again.

The afternoon brought relief. All parties withdrew as usual to the forts to avoid the heat, yet that was the longest day of my life. I have never been more glad when dusk fell.

Soon after, our supporting arms moved up from their staging areas in the rear to the edge of the jungle, where we ourselves had awaited the signal to attack only last night. At the same time, an advance party of our strongest swimmers prepared to slip into the dark waters of the river on either side of the fort. They tightly knotted ropes at two levels to tall trees fringing the riverbank. They looped the ropes around one shoulder and carried rope ladders on the other. They had knives in their teeth, in case of attack by crocodiles. Their task was to establish rope bridges, by connecting tall trees on either bank, so our men could slide sideways to the opposite bank, with one rope for the feet and one for the hands. Gamini had made our assault troops practise this for months in the dark, until they could do it swiftly and silently.

Gamini, Vasabha and I took our positions on the river's edge. We were blessed with another gloomy night, the sky overcast as usual in the pre-monsoon month. The *devas* were looking after us, perhaps because we had planned the operations so carefully.

We lay flat in the shelter of trees and low shrub, watching the first group of men with their ropes creep silently down the steep riverbank and vanish below our line of vision. The earth was cool to my stomach, but it smelled unpleasantly of stale animal fur and dung. I guessed wild cattle had pastured here. Hoping they had not dropped ticks or fleas, I felt the inevitable itching commence and resisted the desire to scratch.

Our men really did not have to worry too much about noise here, because the river was narrow and the water flowed deep and fast. Its gurgle, splash and flow would drown any normal sounds. Besides, the Cholas did not expect an invasion or a large-scale attack and had not patrolled the riverbank at night for years. Our waiting troops had practised this kind of assault for three months. Their training held and I felt pride in them, but my attention was now devoted to the two ropes attached to one of the trees. A flip would mean the swimmers had got across. The suspense became intolerable. The ropes began to blur in the dark. Occasionally they seemed to tighten, but when I glanced away and back again, they still hung flaccid. Gamini, on the other hand, lay totally still beside me, very relaxed, his chin propped on the back of his palms. I could feel the warmth of his body and envied him his calm.

The figure of the man on my left stiffened. I looked away, then looked sharply back at the vague outline of the lower rope. Surely it had jerked. The fellow gave a grunt of satisfaction. Another man on our side of the bank signalled back on the rope.

It was easy thereafter. The lower of the twin ropes was tied fast and signals were exchanged for the upper rope to be stretched. By the time Gamini, Vasabha and I leaped to our feet, the upper rope too had been tightened and the signal given.

Gamini was first on the ropes. I followed him. Once I was above the river, suspended in midair, with nothing but a rope between my feet and the black void beneath, I started to tremble. I stopped and looked down, a mistake I had been told to avoid. I saw the dark gleam of water more than ten cubits below. My feet started to prickle, my hand became clammy on the upper rope. One foot slipped on the lower. I hung on grimly and regained my footing. I looked ahead, gritted my teeth and started sliding on.

Gamini let go his left hand and placed it over mine reassuringly. 'Now you can imagine what it felt like on the cliff's edge in Kotmale.'

Finally it was over and we were safely on the other side. We hurried to our assembly point in a dark wood. There we awaited the crossing of our entire force, long lines of shadowy figures blurring into the distance on either side of us as they moved along row upon row of invisible ropes.

We silently endured the whine and needle sting of mosquitoes. Their warning is even more aggravating than the bite when you dare not slap at them.

By midnight, all our men were across the river, in companies of one hundred, at their assembly points some distance from the fort. Signals were exchanged between the various sections, confirming readiness. We moved forward cautiously, in single file, toward the fort. It was pitch dark beneath the trees. Each man had been trained to tread in the footsteps of the man in front of him. With a throb of excitement, I realized that Sinhala troops were treading Lanka soil held by the Cholas for the first time in over thirty-five years.

We reached the edge of the wood in less than half an hour. A cleared area lay before us with the black mass of the Chola fort beyond, pricked here and there with yellow-gold light glow. That fort was the enemy, something impersonal, something Chola. It was different, somehow, to that of last night, which had until recently been Sinhala. I tried not to think of the human beings inside it, as our assault force began crawling on their bellies across the clearing toward the fort.

Our procedure was the same as before, but this time one of the Chola guards croaked an alarm before he died. We charged silently across the clearing then, while some of our men scaled the battlements. Fortunately, our assault force managed to open the gates. As we surged through, Cholas swarmed out of their sleeping quarters in knots, sleepy, bewildered and unprepared. We flung our spears at them, thick as an angry hive of bees, then charged with swords in hand. The killing began with no thought of *kharma*, for we either won or died.

We slashed our way through the main hall to a dim-lit corridor. 'Go for the commander!' Gamini shouted. His sword dripping blood, he ran before we reached him. Vasabha and I flanking him in the narrow space, we fought silently side by side while Chola shouts and screams rang out above the fierce clash of weapons. They could only approach three abreast. As each enemy fell, we trod on their bodies to advance. The granite floors soon became slippery with blood.

A tall Chola swung his sword down at me. I parried, but not swiftly enough. His blade bit into my shoulder. Pain seared through, so intense I felt weak before it; then blessed numbness came. I reversed my sword and slashed my opponent across the neck. His head hung askew. He staggered and fell.

I pushed after Gamini. He was fighting like a demon, cutting, slashing, withdrawing, thrusting. The giant Vasabha was a devil-god on the other side of him. Sword swinging, I plunged beside them. The Cholas began backing before the ferocity of our attack. Soon they turned and fled.

We were at the fortress commander's quarters now. We burst through the door. A lean, handsome Chola of middle age lay sprawled on the white rug. His dark face looked grey in the flare-light. He was half dressed, his chest bare. His head was tilted unnaturally to one side. Blood pulsed from a red gash at his throat, like a half-necklace of rubies. A bearded Sinhala stood beside him, wiping a blood-stained knife against the back of black pantaloons. His sweaty brown body was streaked with blood. Through black moustache and beard, his grin flashed triumphantly.

As we spread word of the commander's death, the fighting died down. The fort was ours, but skirmishes went on here and there until daylight as Cholas were flushed out of hiding places. Several hundred of them had died bravely.

What an event for the Sinhala – we had captured our first Chola fort across the river! Sinhala stood as victors on Sinhala soil at last.

My shoulder wound proved to be a gash easily attended to by the physician. He placed a *patthu* and bandage over it. I felt weak from the loss of blood, but only numbness from the wound.

By noon the next day the entire fort had been cleaned up and Gamini and I occupied the fortress commander's austere quarters, a small room with high windows letting in the light. We had word shortly afterward that the other two Chola forts were also in our hands.

Gamini immediately dispatched messengers to the Kasa and Kimbul forts, commanding them to organize all-round defence, after which the men would have six hours' sleep followed by a forced march through the night to our fort at Wera. He also sped men across the river with orders that all our forces move immediately across the river and assemble at Wera. Other messengers raced to Dighavapi to direct the three corps there to advance north toward Seru, but to halt on our side of the river.

Assembling all our forces at Wera was a shift of plan. What on earth could Gamini be up to? I held my peace until he and I were alone, getting ready at last for some much-needed sleep. We sat across from each other on the plain granite slabs, covered with woven mats, that served for beds. 'Will you now please tell me the meaning of all this, sire?' I demanded. I had begun to call him 'sire' and 'lord', as was proper, after his consecration.

He grinned impishly. 'What do you think the Chola may do when he learns that we have captured his forts and killed several hundred of his men?'

'Try to recapture the forts, of course,' I responded readily.

'Do you really think we can sit tight in these forts and ward off Chola attacks?'

'Well, sire, how else can we consolidate our gains?'

He leaped to his feet and I rose with him, since he was king. I marvelled at his energy. After two nights of intense fighting, while I was bone-weary, his body was lithe and swift, his skin silken as a healthy leopard's.

'We attack!' he cried, brandishing a clenched fist. 'We attack. We attack. We attack.' He shook his fist each time to emphasize the word. 'While we have the advantage, we keep going as far as our lines of communication and supply permit. Or have you forgotten what you told me about the great Sikander's strategy? When the sword starts to bite, let it go to the heart! When your enemy is reeling, beat him down and kill him.' He calmed down suddenly. 'We are now assembling our strongest possible force for a thrust into the enemy heartland. This may also draw his attention away from the forts and permit us to use them as our bases.'

A glimmering of his plan began to dawn on me. 'In which direction will we proceed?' I inquired.

'Against his southern defence, Ambati.'

I blanched. The fort at Ambati was a mighty Chola stronghold, due north of us on the main highway to Anu. I had passed it many years ago on my journey to Ruhuna. It was a strongly held fortress with enough troops to protect the entire region. 'That will mean direct confrontation with the Chola army,' I declared. 'Remember, they have six regular corps not far away from Ambati.'

'Is that not what we seek?' he demanded hotly, then paused, thoughtful. 'But they will avoid confrontation.'

'Why, sire?'

'When they realize that ours is a full-scale invasion, they will depend on their forts to hold us up while they assess our intentions, gauge our strength and capabilities and harness their own. Our planning up to now has been military. While you are a master political analyst, you have not assessed the impact of our present successes on the long-dormant aspirations of the Sinhala people in Lanka, Soma and Malaya. If we ensure that our present successes do not seem like local operations, the people will rally to our cause. Otherwise, the blood of our soldiers will rot in the sun and be washed away by the monsoon rains.' He turned to me, his dark eyes shining. 'The last two days must offer the hope of a new era to our people, compelling them to rise for us everywhere. The old and smug may hesitate until they see which way the wind blows. The young, who have never known a Sinhala army on the move, will rally to us.' He moved restlessly away and began pacing the room. 'The Chola king will know this, but he is an old bull and will not act in haste. If we thrust to Ambati, he will hold back, fearing for his citadel, Anu.'

So this had been Gamini's intention all along. 'Why did you not tell me of your plans, sire?' I inquired, half ready to be hurt. 'And who else, may I inquire, knows of this plan?'

He stood before me, arms akimbo, feet planted firmly on the floor. 'No one,' he declared. 'You dig a hole in the ground in Ruhuna, whisper into it and run a mile to your friend's house if you want to discover the secret. How much worse it would be with the Chola's spies around.' He smiled.

'So you need not worry that we gave others our confidence and excluded you!'

I must have shown my relief, for he gave his deep laugh before resuming briskly. 'The Cholas who escaped from this fort tonight will hurry to Anu, carrying word to King Elara by tomorrow night – so the bulk of our forces in Ruhuna must get across the river with all speed and advance on Ambati before the Chola takes any action. This includes our elephants, cavalry, chariots, machines of war, supplies. Wera can then continue to be supplied from Ruhuna, serving as our main base.'

'What of the six Chola corps near Ambati, sire?'

'They are commanded not to move without orders from their Chief Warrior, who is presently in Seru.'

'In Seru, sire?' I was puzzled. 'What is he doing there?'

'Organizing the defence of the subkingdom, in the expectation that we will thrust westward, following the route our father took on his pilgrimage. As you know, this is the information we fed the Chola's spies. Besides, he has good cause to fear the Sinhala nobles and population in Seru.' He paused, reflecting. 'Since the Chola does not know in which direction we will advance, or whether we will advance at all, his best course is to wait and see what we will do. To this end, he might even pull back the six corps close to Ambati further north, so that he can push them east or south as our own movements demand.' He chuckled. 'For once, King Elara does not have the initiative. Soon he will find a country and its people aflame.' He was so excited by the thought, he started striding up and down the room.

I thought of my uncle, Prince Vipula, who had been the real heir to the Sinhala throne. I thought of the policies of King Elara, who tried to treat Sinhala and Chola, Buddhist and Hindu, alike. Now Gamini would set the whole country aflame. There would be divisiveness, hatred spewing from deep prejudices, loathing of anyone who was different. In spite of my patriotic desires, I was suddenly afraid.

Gamini stopped to look at me. 'One race, one language, one religion.' His voice was quiet, in sharp contrast with the tension of his body and the fire in his eyes.

I had not faced up to the full implications of Gamini's battle cry until now. It had been a series of brave words uttered by a growing boy. Now the boy was a man. He had power in his hands.

Once again Gamini read my thoughts. 'Do you know what caused the degeneracy of the Sinhala people?' he demanded quietly.

I shook my head. 'No, sire,' I almost whispered.

'Misreading the Buddha's doctrine,' he declared. 'People who believe only in loving kindness and acquiring good *kharma* lose their stomach for fighting. They become gentle as deer – easy prey for the leopard. We must get the blood flowing in the veins of our people, to replace the milk of human kindness.'

'And afterward, sire?'

'All of life is tearing down and rebuilding. We are trees that decay only to sprout new shoots. After we have reunited the nation, we shall decree equality for all – but it shall be Sinhala equality, not Chola equality. A nation must be strong, even ruthless. It must never remain the sum total of those individuals who fearfully face life, death, *kharma* alone.'

The Council of Ministers assembled that very night in Anu, to confer with King Elara.

'How did this happen, sire? We have been taken completely unawares. Surely our Chief Warrior is to blame for lack of readiness. I understand he is in distant Seru. We must counterattack immediately, even without him.' The rich, excited voice was that of Maniam, deputy Chief Minister, a portly gentleman of middle age, with a completely bald head and pugnacious features shining in the flare-light.

These ministers, King Elara thought – if they find the news so disastrous, do they not comprehend what their king must feel? They are typical of civilian officials in a military crisis – out of their depth, blaming others, as if that would help. Soon they will try to cover up their panic with brave words. Only Muttu Samy seems calm.

The King's deep eyes filled with a mixture of anger and sadness. 'For thirty-five years we have kept this entire island free of bloodshed. In a few months everything has been changed by a young hothead.' He pushed his high chair back from the long, creamy satinwood conference table and flung out his hands, palms upward. 'The world has gone mad.'

Muttu Samy coughed deprecatingly and leaned forward. 'Forgive me for reminding you, sire,' he said in his prim, judicial fashion, 'but a world cannot be mad. It is people who go mad. This Gamini has been mad since birth. The astrologers, his parents, his people ensured his insanity with all their talk of the prince of destiny. Now he is fulfilling that destiny by acting like a madman. It is for us to be sane. And I say we must act sanely.' He looked challengingly at his fellow ministers.

'How would you advise us to be sane?' There was a sharp edge to the King's deep voice.

'By the exercise of your usual calm judgement in our crisis, sire. It is only if we flash into angry action that we do have a good chance of losing our sanity.' Muttu Samy's glance swept his eight colleagues once more. 'As we ask ourselves, what is madness, let us also inquire, what is war?'

'War is an armed struggle between enemies, generally hereditary,' Armed Forces Minister Raman flashed angrily. 'The Sinhala have been our foes for three hundred years. It is only through the wisdom of our gracious sovereign that we have had such a long period of peace. Now the Sinhala have ended that peace. I say we go to war and destroy them.' He nodded emphatically and leaned back in his chair.

'Well said!' . . . 'He's right!' . . . 'Yes, yes – ' The other ministers obviously agreed with Raman.

'Are you suggesting that we exterminate the entire Sinhala race?' Muttu Samy inquired coldly.

'If necessary!' Raman retorted.

'Let us understand each other.' King Elara intervened, his voice now full of authority. 'You are our ministers, the representatives of our people, vested with a duty to advise your sovereign soberly and wisely. It is obvious to us that you have become so accustomed to peace that you are now too eager for war. None of you has ever fought in a war. You do not know what it means.' He paused and looked around him. 'We can resort to war at any time, so let us now make decisions based on a calm analysis of what has transpired and of our capabilities.'

King Elara's voice became crisp as his gaze came to rest on Muttu Samy. 'You have sent messengers for our Chief Warrior to return immediately from Seru?'

'Yes, sire.'

'And alerted Gopal to hold his six corps in readiness instead of marching to attack the enemy regardless?'

'As you directed, sire.'

'Very well. Let us analyse the situation. The Sinhala of Ruhuna have captured the three forts we wrested from them. Is that a cause for total war, ministers?' The King's eyes swept the room again.

The ministers fidgeted. 'No, sire!' they stated almost in unison, their voices seeming to trip over one another in each speaker's anxiety to agree with the ruler.

'The Sinhala have also captured three forts within our own frontiers. Remembering that war is a total commitment of the entire State, is this cause for total war?'

The ministers expressed their agreement once again in unison.

King Elara felt a surge of contempt for them. They are like goats following their goatherd, he thought. They will stray, only to return at his call or before his stick. 'Let us then consider the alternatives open to the enemy,' he proceeded. 'First, having indulged in an act of bravado, he can remain in his present positions. If he chooses this alternative, he can rot there for all we care. We do not need to dominate the river to ensure the security of our realm. Agreed?'

'Agreed!' the voices repeated in unison.

'Second, the enemy can proceed west toward Soma, which is predominantly Sinhala, and on to Seru. This is the route the late King Kakkavan took on his pilgrimage, though we now realize that his purpose was not entirely religious, for he did succeed in uniting the Sinhala of Soma and Seru with those of Ruhuna in spirit. King Gamini will probably seek to extend that unification through military means. We will crush him in Seru with a concentration of our forces, if he proceeds there.' The King paused. 'If this be his plan, we shall wait for him to reveal it before we move.'

The ministers nodded agreement. One or two of them thumped the table in approval.

'We cannot ignore the possibility of a third alternative, a thrust toward Anu, which could well be his ultimate object. That would be madness, but we all agree that this king is mad! If he moves north, our impregnable forts at Ambati, Vijitapura and all along the route will dissipate his strength, lengthen his lines of communication and deplete his morale. We will strike with our entire army when he is at his weakest and destroy him.' The prospect made him bare strong white teeth. 'The Sinhala soldier is not a professional like ours. He is a peasant offering feudal duties to his overlord. Therefore, he must return home for the sowing, the reaping, the attainment of maidenhood by his female children. So rather than attacking and squashing this upstart king ourselves, we may even allow his troops to destroy him.'

He beckoned to his court jester, Junda, sitting on the floor beside his chair. 'Have the attendants bring refreshments for our guests,' he commanded.

The dwarf levered himself to his small feet and ambled away.

'We do not like waiting any more than you do,' King Elara declared when the door had closed behind the dwarf. 'Soon, however, we will avenge the deaths of our people and the humiliations we are now enduring. We promise you.'

Chapter 56

The drought preceding the monsoon had reduced the Mahaveli River to its lowest levels, so the crossing of our main body proved to be relatively easy, particularly because our capture of the three Chola forts gave us an advance base across the river from which to co-ordinate our troops' movements. We sent strong fighting patrols north, however, to deter any possible advance of the enemy forces. Our cavalry and chariots crossed the river at the three fords, followed by the elephants and wagons in a never-ending line. The cries of the wagoneers and *mahouts*, the creak of wheels, the neighing of horses and an elephant's occasional shrill trumpet went on ceaselessly for three days and nights.

A river crossing is one of the most difficult operations of war, second only to an organized withdrawal. Our crossing had been well planned and was executed in orderly fashion. In the absence of enemy opposition, we accomplished in a few days what might otherwise have taken weeks.

On the fourth afternoon, our forces from the Kasa crossing linked up with us. The same evening the divisions from the Kimbul ford arrived. By the next morning, our total of more than one hundred thousand men, including cavalry and charioteers, artillery with their catapults, flameball throwers and slings, bowmen, spearmen and foot soldiers were all in position in their allotted areas, spread out over many *yojana* in their order of advance, with supporting engineers, service corps and medical regiments at the rear.

Gamini summoned his commanders to a conference in the great hall of the Sinhala fort at Wera that night. When they were all assembled, an attendant called for him and me.

My first impression of the men, as I entered the flare-lit room, was of their size and toughness. Most of them were clean-shaven, with hair cut short. Those with beards had a slightly raffish look about them.

The youthful Veera Singha, who had been appointed Minister of War, sat at the left of the great table, which was spread with maps illuminated by tapers on brass stands. The Ten Great Warriors, led by Velu Sumana, more handsome than ever with his greying hair, sat next to him. On the other side of the table were the corps and division commanders and the commanders of the various arms of the service. Vacant spaces had been reserved for Gamini at the head of the table and for me on his right. Everyone rose and made obeisance to Gamini as we entered.

When we sat down, I could not help remembering that I had occupied that same seat twenty years ago, on my first night in Ruhuna. I had·never imagined what life had in store for me. On that occasion, I had been insulted by Prince Digha Bahu. Now he had plotted himself into exile and I had a seat of honour.

The doors of the hall were locked and armed guards were posted outside. Gamini opened the proceedings without formalities. 'You are undoubtedly surprised at being here tonight under these circumstances,' he said, 'for it represents a change of plan. First, we thank you for your unquestioning obedience of our orders. It is a good sign for the future. You are already fully briefed with the information you require.' He placed his elbows on the table and leaned forward to emphasize his purpose. 'We now come to our intention. We shall invade Lanka and recapture it for the Sinhala people. Our method is simple.' He arose and we all stood up with him, for he was the King. Seizing a bamboo wand, he stabbed at Soma. 'Our three Dighavapi corps are here, with orders to pause on the southern bank of the river, across from Seru.' He pointed to the subkingdom on the map. 'They will provide a diversion to tie up a few enemy corps and will so encourage the Sinhala population that more enemy troops will be needed in the area. Any questions on this aspect of our operations?'

Gamini looked around the room. We all shook our heads.

'With the Chola's forces dispersed, he will hesitate to attack our main body,' Gamini resumed. 'We must therefore retain the initiative and keep up the momentum we have just gained. My aim is to give final battle to the Chola on ground of our choosing.'

'Superb thinking!' Veera Singha exclaimed. 'But, sire, what are your immediate plans?'

Gamini smiled. He jabbed again at the map. 'Ambati!' he exclaimed.

'Ambati! . . . Ambati!' The men looked around at each other in astonishment.

'Yes, Ambati!' Gamini repeated, fiercely this time. 'Our ultimate objective must be Anu, for the war will not be won until our infantrymen stand victorious in the citadel. But there are forty-one more forts before we get there. The principal ones are Ambati, Gallaka, Vijitapura and Girilaka, in that order. We shall therefore move against Ambati at dawn tomorrow in regular battle formation. There are four smaller forts on the way – here! . . . here! . . . here! and here!' He tapped each place on the map with his pointer. 'Our main body will bypass these forts, leaving strong enough forces behind to take them, fire them and rejoin us.'

'Set fire to the forts, sire?' Velu Sumana inquired. 'Would it not be better to capture them intact for our own purposes?'

'Ambati, yes!' Gamini responded. 'But these smaller forts are merely staging posts and centres for maintaining troops for police purposes. We do not need them, and if we keep them our troops may develop a defensive mentality. We demand a total commitment to advance from now on.' His jaw tightened and the dark eyes began smouldering as he fiercely surveyed the group. 'The forts have wooden walls. They will blaze merrily – a call to arms! All Sinhala for many a *yojana* around will respond.'

He paused and drew breath. 'We shall therefore capture Ambati before the monsoon rains. It shall then serve as headquarters and our new advance base. Minister Veera Singha, you shall work out the order of march on Ambati with your fellow commanders immediately. The cavalry, with us at its head, shall form our vanguard, behind the usual scouting patrols and advance guard. You shall also evolve a plan for investing and taking Ambati, based upon available intelligence. Details of the fort's layout are shown on this map.' He indicated the second map with his bamboo wand. 'You already have all the necessary information as to enemy movements and plans, and the disposition of his six corps outside Ambati. Remember, we are dealing with the total enemy capability, which includes twenty champions and two *lakhs* of well-trained troops.' Gamini had deliberately repeated the words his father had written two years earlier, when commanding him not to invade Lanka.

By steady marching that first day we got close enough to Ambati to commence its siege the next day. We camped on open ground that night and were up before dawn. After a quick meal, Gamini and I galloped with our commanders and a strong escort force to a small hill close to the fort that had been selected as our observation point. We rode past the guard that had been placed around the hilltop and dismounted close to the crest of the hill, then proceeded to our lookout in the shelter of tall wood-apple trees. There, hidden by trees and bushes, we silently surveyed the scene.

Dawn had now broken. To the east, above a sea of dark-green tree-tops, a red-and-gold sky flung rosy hues on the silver-grey ribbon of the river journeying north into the distant dawn-haze. Birds, wheeling in the clear air above columns of blue smoke lazily spiralling toward the sky, drew our eyes to the fort. Located where the two streams of the Ambati River met the Mahaveli River, its solid mass lay dark against the pale morning air. It did indeed have natural water defences on two sides. Between them, its granite walls, complete with battlements, the sentry turrets sixty yards apart, seemed to tower and spread forever. Along the third side, forming a triangle of water, was the moat, at least fifty yards wide, naturally served from the waters of the river. Cleared land, extending several hundred yards from the water on each side, provided fields of fire for archers and war machines. If it seemed impregnable at this distance, what would it be like when we were in close assault positions? My hazy recollection of the fort from twenty years ago had not represented its true strength.

Velu Sumana echoed my thoughts. 'By the *devas*, it is worse than I remembered,' he said quietly.

'It will be worse still when the rains come,' Veera Singha observed, a note of gloom in his voice. 'Those cleared areas will become flooded then and it will be like trying to take an island.'

'That is why we shall take it before the rains come,' Gamini declared coolly. 'We shall detail an assault force, including our best swimmers, to move secretly westward today, while our main body openly advances to give the impression of a massive assault on that front. The assault force shall cross the Ambati River along that point.' He jabbed a dark finger toward a ford about one half a *gavuta* westward.

For two hours, we hammered out our plans. By the time we arrived back in camp, I was hot, hungry and a little tired. I wondered at the tiredness, until I realized that my problem

578

was tension from not being entirely convinced of the feasibility of our plan. I felt that some of the corps commanders shared my doubts – yet what choice did we have? That question made the plan a desperate one.

The sixty swimmers had been selected for their experience and daring. They had swum the seas and rivers of the Ruhuna kingdom and had been trained to stay underwater for long periods of time. They wore only black span-cloths. The purple juice of the *bo-vitia*, a berry, had been rubbed on their bodies and faces, to darken the skin and prevent water from gleaming on it. They carried rope ladders with grappling hooks at the ends, and long knives stuck at their waists.

We crouched in low shrub, with men spreading endlessly around us. The fort lay a short distance away. Its massive dark bulk, pricked with the yellow glow of lights, rose forbiddingly against a hazy blue skyline. The splash and gurgle of the Ambati stream seemed peaceful in relation to our mission. The musty smell of dry earth brought to mind that we would soon be engaged in a battle that could send many of us back to the soil.

Nanda Mitta issued his last instructions to the swimmers, a dark blotch of figures punctuated by gleaming eyes. 'Drown before any of you makes a single sound,' he directed them fiercely. 'One sound could mean the death of all. Be especially careful when you have crossed the moat and stand in the water beneath the ramparts. As soon as you hear the barking of a dog – remember, this time it is not the call of a night bird – climb the ramparts and do your work. Go now!'

The men nodded and spread out. They dropped to their bellies and began their long, slow crawl, like great lizards, toward the moat. They were soon swallowed by the dark.

'Are the rafts and ladders ready?' Gamini quietly inquired.

'Yes, sire,' Nanda Mitta replied.

579

Our plan was to have a strong body, including Gamini and me, but led by Nanda Mitta, crawl across the open ground and get as close to the fort as possible. We would wait there for the swimmers to open the gates, then dash across the bridge under cover of flame-tipped arrows and catapults to establish a foothold inside the fort. Meanwhile, the remainder of the assault force would rush to the moat with the rafts and ladders, get across, scale the ramparts and create a diversion for our main body to cross the river at various points and join in finally capturing the fort.

We waited ten minutes. I could have counted the seconds from my heartbeats, so dreadful was the suspense.

Nanda Mitta slowly moved his arm forward. We began our slow crawl, using only elbows and feet. I felt naked when we left the scrub and hit the barren soil. It was cool and dry, but my body had become clammy. What would happen if we were detected? We would be caught in the open, an easy target for enemy arrows and fireballs. We would then have to rise and attack, or run away.

I pushed aside the thoughts and concentrated on the task ahead.

We were within two hundred cubits of the fort when a blaring sound pierced the darkness. I froze, unable to identify it. Even before I recognized it for a conch shell, trumpets screeched and drums thundered out the alarm. My chest tightened and my head started to spin. Gamini had stopped crawling beside me, his face turned upward toward the fort.

Flares lit up the battlements. A great splashing sound reached us. Cascades of what seemed like water were pouring into the moat. What could it be?

A flare arced into the moat like a slow-falling star. Another followed, then another. The moat burst into flames.

'Dear *devas*!' Gamini exclaimed. 'They have poured oil into the moat and set fire to it.' He leaped to his feet. 'Give the order to charge!' he shouted.

Nanda Mitta towered beside him. 'No, sire! That would be fatal – death to so many. Pray give the order to retreat.'

Gamini turned on him. 'Our men out there – ' he began.

'Are dead already.'

Screams and yells arose, then the roar of flames, carried by a sudden wind. Gamini looked in their direction. The entire moat was in flames.

A cloud of grey smoke reached us and I choked on the sharp smell of burnt pitch that reached through my nostrils and into my throat. Desperately I stifled a cough, but the men around me were all hacking away loudly. My eyes began to tear. Through the blur of those tears, I saw the blazing moat. A burning figure emerged from it, shrieking. the sight was forever stamped in my mind, stark as a scene where lightning has just struck. This had to be what hell looks like.

Gamini, choking, made to dash forward. Nanda Mitta held him back with a grip of iron. 'May the *devas* forgive me for laying hands on my sovereign!' he exclaimed. 'Look, sire, as I told you, it is already too late.'

Indeed it was. With one last scream, the flaming figure tottered, then fell back into the moat. Three more burning figures appeared, human torches lit by the awesome source of their flames, but silent this time. They did not even make it to the top. As they slithered back, there was one final death scream, then silence, except for the roaring moat and cheers from the battlements.

'They were dead while they clambered up, sire,' Nanda Mitta quietly urged. 'You could not have saved them.'

Gamini stared wildly toward the fortress. Through the smoke, the reflection of the flames revealed his face, distorted with horror.

I heard the twang of bows and dashed him to the ground. Nanda Mitta dropped beside us. Arrows came hissing overhead. We would all have been dead if we had remained standing.

Gamini pounded the earth with his fists.

'Breathe lightly, sire,' I urged him. 'Remember, this is the price of war.'

Chapter 57

We camped on the southern and western boundaries of Ambati. The eastern boundary, across the river, was Ruhuna territory. We did not wish to cross the river to the northern side because it would split up our forces and invite a losing battle if the Chola decided to attack from the north. Our position permitted the Chola free access to his fort from that side for bringing in supplies. These were hardly needed, however, for such forts carry enough to last them through six months of siege.

We made several assaults on the fort – frontal, flank, daytime, sneak. We were repulsed every time. The defences were impregnable.

Three weeks later, the monsoon rains burst upon us. Now the sky was always heavy with low grey clouds. Cold winds blew from the unsheltered northeast. Lightning forked or flashed, followed by pealing thunder that seemed to rumble across the land. Rain poured down in torrents. The river flooded. The whole earth became wet and soggy.

We withdrew into two holding areas in the shelter of trees, one some distance south of Ambati and the other an equal distance to the west. The makeshift shelters we rigged were never enough against the rain that always found its way through. The air was so damp, we seemed to breathe water. Our men were miserable. Within a few days, colds and coughs became rampant. The demand for our customary remedy, *kottha-malli*, coriander tea laced with ginger and garlic, became so heavy that great cauldrons of it were constantly boiling over glowing wood fires in pits beneath coconut-thatch roofs erected to keep the rain out.

Our army, which had been so full of hope and excitement, would have become discouraged were it not for Gamini. He seemed to be everywhere, cheerful and bright all the time. No one could guess the dark thoughts that consumed him. Almost single-handedly, he kept the morale of our troops high, inspiring his commanders to do likewise, even when he developed a cold, high fever and the shivering sickness.

One of Gamini's first actions, when it seemed unlikely that we would take Ambati before the rains came, had been to arrange for as many men as possible to return to their homes, in rotation, since they could be spared for six weeks, until the worst of the rains ended. He accepted the offer of the Queen Mother, which he had earlier rejected, to bring a corps of women to our baggage train, to act as nurses and cooks. I must admit to hoping that Leela would accompany her mistress.

Huts and latrines were quickly erected for these women, the wives and mothers of our commanders and troops. Several hundred in number, they were to arrive in a wagon train.

Gamini and I were quartered in a valley between two low hills. Although this location gave us protection from the worst of the winds, it exposed us to gales that sometimes swept through the funnel, like steam from a *pittubambuwa*, the bamboo funnel used for steaming flour.

In spite of all the energy Gamini spent visiting his men and seeing that they were properly quartered, he could not sleep at night. He confessed that his thoughts kept whirling toward the death scene in the moat. Flaming corpses would raise imploring hands to him. Their thoughts, their feelings, the agony of burning flesh, their last despair, became living pictures in his mind. When he did drop off to sleep, he had nightmares in which burning bodies pointed accusing fingers at him. He was not normally a fanciful or imaginative sort. While the wounds and deaths of his men affected him, he was able to live with the knowledge and invariably slept peacefully the moment his head hit the pillow. What took place at the moat had been different. He had sent his men on a hastily planned mission and they had been massacred. As his conscience became more and more burdened, he began to lose weight. His face was pale and drawn. I could do nothing except pray to God.

Not being able to comfort or cure Gamini, I merely shared his anguish. I hoped that the arrival of his mother might help somehow. Mothers often have miraculous powers with their children. With the walls between the two of them, though, the hope seemed forlorn.

When the wagons were announced that gloomy afternoon, Gamini and I put on our cloaks and walked down the makeshift path to greet them. He was still suffering with his cold, but the fever had abated. So had the rain, though it still dripped constantly from the branches. The clouds were low. The humid air reeked of mud. To the north, lightning forked, followed by distant thunder.

We trod our way gingerly over brown rivulets of muddy water, avoiding the slippery roots that are always ready to trip the unwary. Plodding around a bend we heard horses' hooves and looked up to see the cavalry escort, the breath of their steeds making steam in the damp air. One of the animals sneezed violently.

The cavalrymen did not recognize us. They trotted past, looking straight ahead, making for their objective, the headquarters hut, with the proud lion flag wrapped wet and tired around its pole.

'Even the horses do not like this weather,' Gamini remarked.

The horse-drawn wagons now appeared. I held up my

hand and stopped the first one. 'Ho there!' I exclaimed. 'In which wagon is the royal Queen Mother? Her son, the King is here.'

The wagoneer stopped immediately. The cavalry escort heard me and reined in. Its leader, a fair-faced young captain, swung his horse around and came cantering back to us. He stopped, slid expertly off the saddle and made obeisance to Gamini. 'Sire, your humble servant has brought your family to you.'

Before the captain could rise, we heard a rustle from the wagon. Our attention focused on the captain, we barely noticed a red-and-white skirt and the woman emerging from the back of the wagon. Our first consciousness of her was when she made deep obeisance.

Gamini turned, then stood gaping. 'Raji!' he finally croaked.

'I simply had to come with your royal mother, sire,' Raji said, still kneeling. 'Pray forgive me if I have erred.'

'Forgive you?' Gamini's laughter rang through the air. 'When you have . . .' He paused, remembering his position. 'But what of the baby?' he demanded. 'Surely you have not brought him in this rain?'

'No, sire. The baby is well looked after in the palace by my parents, who came from Kotmale at my request. Since your royal mother was coming to render nursing service to the Sinhala armies, I felt I should accompany her to nurse my lord.'

Instead of knowing my usual pang of jealousy, I felt a prayer of thankfulness to God. He had sent Gamini the succour which I could not give.

In Anu, sitting on the simple mat placed on the bare boards of his carved four-poster bed, King Elara was amused. He was dressed in his white nightshirt and his tall, dark frame was very relaxed. The dwarf, Junda, quaint in green sarong and overshirt, sat waggling his tiny feet on the

585

little couch below the raised platform on which the King's bed was placed.

'So you see, jester, our plan has worked,' the King remarked. He nodded toward the rain hammering against the closed windows. 'The monsoon has arrived. The King of Ruhuna and his entire army of one hundred thousand sleep in mud, while we are dry and comfortable in our palace. We are told that the rivers encircling Ambati have risen and are impassable.' He felt great good humour for the first time in weeks. 'There are many factors in war that this young king must learn. Among them is using the elements, terrain and the enemy's weaknesses to win – if possible, without battle.'

'Shall our fortresses detain them forever?' the dwarf inquired innocently. 'Forts are men, after all.'

'Aha! You are a clever dwarf. Hmm . . . let us see. First Ambati, where Tittamba is our commander. He is a man of royal birth and the warrior caste, a superb soldier with a distinguished record. Unfortunately, he has a weakness for women and his very nobility of birth has bred in him an overweening ambition. He is sixty-two years of age and capable of some last desperate effort to raise his station in life, but what better can he do? He is governor of the entire district, with the power of life and death and ample opportunity to satisfy his lust!'

Junda grinned back. 'How about Gallaka, Vijitapura and Girilaka?'

The King reflected. 'The commanders of Gallaka and Vijitapura are entirely without weakness,' he finally asserted. 'They are first-class warriors, austere in their conduct and of surpassing integrity. Wait, though . . . Mahela of Girilaka has one weakness. He is greedy for money. Yet, what treasure can the Sinhala offer him? No, dwarf, we can give you no healing balm for the wounds of sympathy you have for your own people, which we have always respected and admired in you. The war is already won.'

'Do you really think it is, sire?'

'With the rains, certainly. We have only to wait until King Gamini starts to withdraw. We shall then advance to crush him. Ruhuna will soon require a new king.' He paused and grinned at the dwarf. 'How would you like to be sub-king of Ruhuna, jester?'

Junda's moving legs stopped momentarily, then started their waggling again. 'You make such a serious jest tonight, O King, that I would accept your offer on one condition.'

King Elara's eyebrows lifted. 'And that?'

'You become my chief jester, sire.'

The King rocked with laughter. 'Good. Very good.' He was so amused he did not notice the pain in the dwarf's face.

Chapter 58

Dinner was served to the three ladies in the room normally reserved for Gamini's daily conference with his commanders. Since Gamini ate and practically lived with the men these days, it fell to me to act as the women's host.

Night fell slowly. Within the room, the glow from the sky seemed a reflection of that from the presence of these three refined ladies. The Queen Mother and Raji were dressed in white, Leela in blue. Their scents of jasmine and temple flowers softened the damp odour of thatch.

'We never dreamed we would have a meal in an army camp,' the Queen Mother remarked. Her eyes roved around the room, taking in the long yellow mango-wood table at which we sat and the floors of mud stiffened with dung. 'You live in greater austerity than you did as an *abithaya* in the temple, Prince Rodana.'

'Soldier and *bhikku* are alike in their living, but what does it make of you, now that you have so gallantly come to share our austerity?'

'May I answer that, madam?' Leela inquired.

'Certainly.'

'Austere.'

'Well put.'

Leela's merry laugh rang out and I warmed to her, noticing that both the Queen Mother and Raji looked at her with kindly eyes.

'Leela can always avoid a trap of words,' Raji observed. 'She has a sharp mind.'

'As sharp as this *sambole*,' the Queen agreed. Our food, at Gamini's insistence, was rough soldiers' fare, but the cook had smuggled in some dry *katta* fish, ground with grated coconut and red chili.

'People may say that Leela has a *miris mollay*, a red-hot chili mind,' Raji put in.

'Better than if they merely say I am a red-hot chili,' Leela remarked. 'Is that not what soldiers call a . . . you know what . . . Prince Rodana?'

I nodded. 'But that is not what I am thinking of. I have always eaten separately in the palace, like other men. Now, suddenly, the mud and rain, the ugliness and disease are transformed by the beauty of ladies in flare-light.'

'Ah! You are ever the poet,' the Queen Mother remarked, but unlike in the past, before she became a widow, it was a statement, not an offering.

As they continued bantering, I wondered which of them most evoked the poet in me. Leela, who had opened herself to me? Raji, who did not? The Queen Mother, who would not?

Of them all, Leela alone was free to receive my words as a woman. She alone had been vulnerable before me, which is the quality of family. Once again, the knowledge that Leela was indeed my family struck me. Looking at her animated face, so perfectly oval, the large, green-brown eyes alight, the lithe body vibrant in tight-fitting bodice and loose skirt, a thrill at her physical presence ran through me.

After the meal, we stepped outside to return to our bedrooms. Only an occasional drip from overhanging thatch told of the lashing we had taken from the monsoon. It was as if the entire earth, following days of storm, was cloaked in innocence. Above the continuing background noise of creaking crickets, the dying night sounds of the encampment reached us: the burst of a *siyupada* chant, an occasional laugh.

It was still light enough for us to see without torchbearers. The Queen Mother and Raji walked ahead up the rugged path, while I followed with Leela.

I nodded toward the red fires from the encampment, glowing through clear, rain-washed air. 'We can dry out for the first time in weeks.'

Leela was silent. I looked sideways at her. She stumbled on a stone. Instinctively I reached out and held her arm. She paused and looked at me. Her eyes had a mysterious depth to them in the half-light. 'You have only to touch me and I remember that evening in your room in the palace,' she whispered.

'I have only to touch you and I forget my *brachmachariya* vows.'

'I have taken them too, so I understand what you are saying.'

At that moment, I knew I loved her as a woman. Our eyes met through the encroaching darkness. I do not know whether we broke our vows, but in those precious seconds we fulfilled our love.

Raji awaited him in his small room. She stood up as soon as he entered. In the light of the single taper placed on a rough wooden table, she was slim and tall, her delicate skin pale pink, fresh from her bath. He felt the start of a cleansing.

He paused at the door. His eyes travelled over the curves of her body, revealed by a white silken nightgown. He took in the gently rounded shoulders, the breasts generous without being gross, the tiny waist swelling to full hips and buttocks, the well-proportioned thighs. Childbearing had only softened her beauty. Needing to identify the person to whom all this belonged, his gaze shifted to her oval face. She was staring, fascinated, at him, her red lips slightly parted. His heart contracted at her love and desire. 'You stand in beauty like the night!' he exclaimed.

His erection grew taut. He felt vibrant with lust, yet held himself back deliberately, because he had something to say to her first. He turned to close the door, then faced her again. 'Did I not tell you that nothing would go right without you?'

Her voice was tremulous. 'And did you not know, lord, that my only world is your world, your grief is my grief? I know you so well that I experienced your tragedy, even as it struck you. You are my whole life. Why else would I have left our baby to come to you?'

He saw her through a mist and fought back the tears that only love could bring to his eyes. 'There is no world save that born of our love,' he began huskily.

She trembled at the words he had uttered that first morning in the Mahagama palace, when he had declared his love to her.

He could contain himself no longer. He forgot what he had thought to tell her that had seemed so important just a few seconds ago. Blindly, he reached for her.

Her yielding breasts cascaded like a slow wave against his bare chest. He had been without a woman for so long. His erection, at bursting point, screamed for the feel of firm, wet flesh around it. He pulled her toward the hard wooden bed and flung her on it. He hastily unbuckled his belt and kicked off his *dhoti*. He reached for her gown to tear it off,

590

but she had already removed it.

He saw the glory of her form, now glowing pink-gold beneath his shadow, the pubis a dark patch that had always enthralled him. He would plunge into it and move and move.

Then he saw her face. Its pure beauty, the delicate bone contours, the *ran-thambili* cheeks, made his breath catch. This was Raji, his wife, not some harlot or concubine before the lust of a common soldier. Dimly, he perceived that only tenderness could provide his escape from the bonds of guilt and grief at the death of his men.

Slowly, he sank to his knees. The need to adore her, to worship at the shrine before entering it, seized his being. He laid a hand on her warm cheek. Her fine nostrils dilated. Her breath quickened. Slowly, smoothly, his eyes unwaveringly on hers, he lay beside her. Wherever her body touched his, tiny drops of rain seemed to sparkle against his fevered skin.

Dawn broke with the early call of the koel bird: 'Ko-haa . . . ko-haa.' He had slept soundly for the first time in three weeks.

She stirred in his arms, smiled at him through slumber-misted eyes. 'I love you, my lord.'

The sleep-coating of her voice, lightly grained, made her sound like a just-awakened child. Tenderness welled forth in him. He reached for her again.

At the end of the fourth week of the rains, in the month of Magha, I received information from one of our spies that Tittamba had heard of King Elara's promise to make Digha Jantu sub-king of Seru someday. Tittamba was visibly upset at the news, not the least because he held Digha Jantu in contempt as merely a professional soldier, while he himself held his present military rank not only as an experienced soldier, but also as a noble member of the royal caste.

591

I brought this report to Gamini's attention immediately and he grew thoughtful. 'We must try to turn this to our advantage,' he declared.

We made no mention of the news when we met our commanders as usual in the headquarters hut that night. When the conference was over, Gamini dismissed everyone else present, except Veera Singha and Velu Sumana.

The rains had abated. Through the open window, I even saw stars glittering in a deep-blue sky. Gamini continued sitting on his rough stool at the head of the makeshift table. 'Tell them about Tittamba,' he directed.

I turned to the two men sitting on a bench at our left. They listened thoughtfully while I gave them my report.

'What you have heard about Tittamba is not only his weakness, but that of the fort,' Gamini observed soberly when I had finished. He drummed the table thoughtfully with dark fingers and gazed at the candle flames illuminating the maps on the rough yellow jak-wood table as if he might be vouchsafed images in them. Like an echo, a sudden squall of rain drummed on the coconut-thatch roof and walls. Its wind made the candles flicker and the pungency of the six flares became more acrid in our nostrils.

'It strikes me that in our present situation, the more important of this man's weaknesses is ambition, sire,' Veera Singha volunteered slowly, his forehead knit and his expression thoughtful. 'If you could make an offer to Tittamba that would place him above Digha Jantu in position, he might be tempted to cross over to our side.'

'How about offering him both Soma and Seru when we win?' Gamini inquired.

'The two hares in their warrens, lord, whereas King Elara has offered Digha Jantu the hare he holds in his hand.'

'You are right. How about Dighavapi, or Devundara? We could declare them subkingdoms.'

'Always subordinate to what the Cholas already regard as the subkingdom of Ruhuna.'

'You are not suggesting that we offer him Ruhuna?'

'Why not, sire?'

We stared at Veera Singha incredulously. He returned our glances with an innocent smile on his handsome face. 'We would not have to fulfil such a promise if it were made, sire,' he now stated.

Gamini straightened up. 'You have something up your sleeve, Minister?'

'Yes, sire. When one makes a promise it must be kept – but I suggest that there is nothing dishonourable in making a promise with the firm intention of keeping it, but with the certain knowledge that the person to whom you make the promise will prevent you from keeping it.'

I saw the light. 'What you are saying is that our king can offer Tittamba the sovereignty of Ruhuna with the certain knowledge that Tittamba, by his subsequent conduct, will forfeit the promise?'

'Exactly.'

I exchanged glances with Veera Singha. Seeing that I understood his meaning, he waited for me to make the suggestion which, being a commoner, he could not make. What he did not know was that it had already been made to me by the person most concerned, but I had rejected it out of hand. Now that Veera Singha felt we could merely use the idea, without any fear of having to fulfil it, I did not find it as obnoxious.

'As I see it, there is one way in which we can give a certain validity to our promise, sire,' I asserted, turning to Gamini. 'I hesitate to propose it, but I do so in the interests of the cause. I suggest that the Queen Mother be offered in wedlock to Tittamba. He is of kingly caste and high rank. Such alliances of royalty are not unusual, as you know.'

I had expected an explosion. To my surprise, there was none. Velu Sumana stiffened in his seat, but Gamini merely nodded. 'The thought had just occurred to us,' he said. 'The problem is how to ensure that Tittamba will prevent us from

593

keeping that promise.'

I spoke excitedly. 'There has to be some way in which we can get Tittamba out of that fort, onto neutral ground, to visit the Queen Mother. Or perhaps we could get into the fort on some pretext and have Tittamba violate the terms of the safe-conduct.'

'We must think on it,' Gamini responded. He stared out of the window, pondering, then quickly shifted his gaze to the silent Velu Sumana. 'It is late now,' he said. 'Let us retire.'

We rose as Gamini stood up. The two men made obeisance. As Gamini and I left, I wondered at Velu Sumana's silence, but did not even guess the truth.

During the night, I worked out details of a plan to use a man's weakness as honourably as possible. When I conveyed it to Gamini in the morning, his eyes lit up. 'It will work,' he stated.

Gamini discussed the plan with his mother. She readily agreed to go along with it, probably pretending that she had not had the idea herself. Her one condition was that she should not be expected to marry anyone. She confessed to Gamini that she would like to become a Buddhist nun after he had united the three kingdoms under his rule and was consecrated king of the entire island. I discovered later that while Gamini believed in the sincerity of her ambition, he suspected that her motive in not wanting marriage to anyone else was her love for Velu Sumana.

No mention was made of these discussions at our regular conference that night, but Gamini was vibrating like a thoroughbred nervous to begin a race and we were all energized by his high spirits. Since the rains had now abated, we worked out plans for the movement of our troops, without mentioning the part to be played by the Queen Mother.

Digha Jantu hastened back to Anu upon receiving King

Elara's summons. Meanwhile, Prince Digha Bahu, joined by his son, Prince Panduka, and Prince Tissa's army commander, the lame Sali, had been fretting in my uncle's former residence. The morning after receiving news of our disaster at Ambati, the King finally summoned Prince Digha Bahu to his audience chamber.

When Prince Digha Bahu was ushered into his presence, the King found him physically different to the descriptions given in earlier reports he had received. Life in the Anu court was austere. Strong drink was forbidden on the palace premises. Because he had been abstaining from liquor, eating simple meals and getting much exercise, Prince Digha Bahu looked very fit. When he was making his obeisance, King Elara noted that he was still stout, but his body was firm, the skin tone excellent.

King Elara could not bring himself to smile at the Prince more than with his mouth, a white smile with the dark eyes brooding. He had never cared for this turncoat, and liked him even less now that he was seeing him for the first time.

'You may be seated, Prince,' King Elara said, indicating one of the teakwood chairs below the platform.

'Thank you, sire,' Prince Digha Bahu responded. He half turned, walked to the chair and sat on it to face the King.

'You have repeatedly sought an audience with us,' the King proceeded. 'Why?' He injected a sharp edge to his normally deep voice. Junda, seated on the floor, playing with his cap, shot a glance at his master. His knowing look told the King that he realized his master was playing a game, though the Prince did not sense it.

Prince Digha Bahu sat up haughtily. 'I am a prince of the royal blood, sire,' he responded. 'It is customary for us to pay our respects to the King whenever we arrive at a capital city.' He paused, reflecting, then decided to take a tough line. 'It is not customary for us to wait so long for an audience, like common peasants.' He stared defiantly at the King.

For the first time, King Elara felt some respect for his guest. He would have given a soft reply, but instinct told him that this man would only appreciate strength. 'In our *dharmista* realm,' he declared, 'the humblest have priority in obtaining audience with the King. Matters of protocol must give way before the needs of the people.'

'So many days have gone by – ' Prince Digha Bahu began.

'Days filled with service to the people, our *only* taskmasters,' King Elara cut in. He placed emphasis on the word 'only' to flash the prince a warning. 'We do not recall inviting you to visit us, or our capital. We understand you are here as a kind of refugee, fleeing from the consequences of your own actions. You can hardly make demands on protocol. If your present visit *is* one of protocol, the audience is over. If it is not, kindly state your business.'

Prince Digha Bahu recoiled before the unexpected steel of the King. 'I meant no offence, sire,' he protested. 'I do indeed have business. It is to remind you of the offers you made me through your emissaries. In return for certain services, which I have rendered during the years, you graciously declared that you would appoint me King of Ruhuna on the death of King Kakkavan. It is through rendering those services to you that my son, Prince Panduka, Sali, our army commander, and our household cavalry are fugitives in Lanka today. I am here to remind you, with utmost respect, of your promises.'

King Elara looked away. The reminder irritated him. He began stroking his chin reflectively. 'How do you expect us to fulfil such promises when we have no suzerainty over Ruhuna?' he inquired.

'Forgive me, sire, but you made promises, when you had no suzerainty, that led me to believe you would establish it.' The pale brown eyes became insolent. 'I would never dream that you made promises without intending to keep them, merely to obtain my services. You are too well known to be a *dharmista* ruler.'

King Elara felt trapped. His finger began to beat a tattoo on the arm of his throne. 'You make a valid point, Prince,' he conceded more gently. 'But our promises were based on the assumption that you would have the support of at least a strong section of your people and that you would be a fit person to govern.' His voice hardened. 'Your actions these past two years have cast some doubts on these assumptions. It is not our way, however, to quibble when a matter of honour is involved. You shall have the opportunity to prove yourself.'

Prince Digha Bahu brightened. His broad features broke into a smile and he looked up expectantly at the King. 'Never fear, sire,' he declared. 'That is all we seek – the opportunity to prove ourselves.'

'Your King Gamini is bogged down outside our fortress at Ambati, as you probably know.'

The Prince nodded.

'The next major fort north of Ambati is Gallaka. We are appointing you commander of that fort, with your son as deputy and your army commander, Sali, as head of the garrison. The Gallaka command also involves government of the district. Your task will not only be to defend the fort, therefore, but to organize infiltration into the Ruhuna forces, sabotage their efforts and rally the Sinhala of the area to our cause. When you have accomplished this mission and created the right climate for an invasion of Ruhuna, we will support you in that attempt, naming you Ruhuna's king. It may even permit you to occupy the throne of Anu someday. In other words, Prince, fulfil your side of our old agreements to the letter and we will fulfil ours.'

Prince Digha Bahu was stunned. 'Majesty! . . . Sire!' he began. 'You are most gracious and wise – so much a king.' His eyes had lost their hard look and were almost moist with gratitude. 'My family and I will revere and serve you forever.'

'Thank you!' the King responded without much

enthusiasm. 'Our staff will be directed to see to all your needs.'

Prince Digha Bahu stood up, made obeisance and backed out. His tall figure vanished through the open doorway. The guards closed the doors at a gesture from the King.

'Now dwarf, do you not think that was a noble gesture and honourable fulfilment of a promise?' The King looked with feigned innocence at his jester.

'You may fool the wise, but not a fool, lord!'

'How so?'

'If King Gamini overthrows Ambati, he will speed to Gallaka. Knowing who is there, he will take Gallaka if he has to tear it down stone by stone. By sending him on a mission assured of failure, you have sentenced this prince to death.'

The King stared out of the open window at the morning sunlight, remembering the son he had once sentenced to death.

Chapter 59

Six days later, on a bright, sunny morning, by arrangement with Tittamba, the Queen Mother was taken across the river to the fort on a Chola ferry. She was carried to the entrance in a jewelled palanquin with blue-and-gold curtains. Leela and other ladies-in-waiting followed in separate palanquins.

Tittamba personally awaited the procession at the entrance to the fort; its massive gates were wide open for the occasion. Gamini had reached an initial agreement with him. He was offered the Queen Mother's hand in marriage and suzerainty over the Ruhuna subkingdom at the appropriate time. Meanwhile, the Queen Mother would call on him at the entrance to the fort. This was a euphemism for an opportunity to inspect her qualifications, which I found odious. Having met his future bride thus briefly and paid his respects to her, Tittamba would send her safely back to our lines, keeping the treasure we had decided to send as added bait and evidence of good faith.

Our entire force had moved into their previous positions during the night, Gamini and I with the assault group directly across from the entrance gates. We were ready to move in the event of treachery.

Well hidden under the cover of trees, we watched the Queen Mother's little procession, escorted by Chola soldiers, halt at the entrance gates, where Tittamba, richly dressed in red pantaloons and a gold tunic, awaited her. Having saluted, he exchanged a few words with her.

He must have been taken by what he saw. His sharp command cracked across the clearing. The Chola soldiers drew their swords and began closing in on the palanquins.

Tittamba was obviously violating the agreement. He probably had no intention of keeping to it in the first place. Lecher that he was, all he probably desired was to use the beautiful Queen Mother.

Our Great Warriors had been disguised as bearers. They burst into action. Seizing weapons concealed in the palanquins, some sprang around and fought back the Chola soldiers while others charged the entrance.

Tittamba was stunned by the turn of events, but, being a soldier, he recovered quickly. His sword flashed in his hand. He leaped toward the Queen Mother's palanquin, obviously intending to take her hostage, perhaps even to kill her.

Velu Sumana had anticipated Tittamba's move. He jumped between Tittamba and the palanquin. With drawn sword, he lunged at the commander.

Tittamba did not take this armed bearer seriously. He paused. With a flick of the wrist, he contemptuously parried

Velu Sumana's thrust, not even bothering to face the Chief Warrior. Velu Sumana's sword was deflected upward. He must have merely tightened his grip for the rotation, because his sword point made a barely perceptible circle around Tittamba's weapon and in the same motion sped smoothly forwards to sink in Tittamba's side. The commander stood still for three seconds, in the casual grace of his parrying position. His sword fell to the ground. He remained standing a moment longer, then slowly sank to his knees before the Queen Mother's palanquin and collapsed in a heap.

'An ignoble end for a royal beast!' Gamini remarked fiercely. 'Now – cha-ar-ge!' He urged Raja forward. We followed with cheers and yells.

The Great Warriors had meanwhile forced the gates. They fought off the enemy until we reached them, under cover of a devastating hail of arrows and catapult bolts from our concealed men.

The fort was ours before nightfall. I was unscathed this time, but Gamini suffered a spear wound on his left shoulder. The Chola who inflicted it died immediately under my sword.

Once we captured the fort, contrary to Gamini's avowed intentions, we did not immolate live Cholas. This time, the delight he felt at drawing blood and killing men reached its high point with victory. Fists clenched, dark, sweaty arms outstretched, he stood on the battlements shuddering with joy, his face lifted to the starry heavens.

Gamini became very quiet the morning two days after we took the Ambati fort, when I gave him news of the appointment of Prince Digha Bahu to command the fort at Gallaka. His reaction was quite different to what I had expected. I had thought he would leap from his sickbed and demand that we move immediately against the fort. Instead, he turned his head to gaze through the high iron window grille, the only source of daylight for the bedroom of the

Ambati commander's quarters, which Raji and he were occupying.

His spear wound had begun turning septic and our physicians had applied medicinal *patthu* on it, so stained bandages covered his shoulder, upper arm and chest. In spite of being sick, he lay on his usual plank bed and mat. On the table beside the bed were the inevitable dark green *cassaya* in a flask and the brown *guli* that would cleanse the blood from within, while the *patthu* drained the wound from outside. I knew that the *cassaya* had to include *puss*, mildew for cleaning the system, but what else there was in these evil-tasting concoctions only the physicians knew. Their secrets of *ayurveda* were handed down from father to son in the Vederala caste and were unknown to outsiders.

Having never seen Gamini physically sick in bed before, except for the various occasions of fever and ailments common to youth, I found him strangely defenceless now, lying there wrapped in all those bandages.

'This is a bait laid by the cunning old jackal in Anu.' I was somehow surprised when Gamini's deep voice broke the silence. 'He wants us to dash along to Gallaka before we are ready.' He smiled grimly. 'We should not allow passion to alter our plans to consolidate. Prince Tissa must be given time to move across the river and establish our base of operations at the three forts. He must then move up to create an advance base here at Ambati. Our men must be given time to recover, our commanders the opportunity to regroup and renew depleted forces. When we move on Gallaka, it will be from strength. We shall then take the fort by storm. No tricks. No deception. We shall seek out the two traitor princes and their lame henchman and kill them with our bare hands.' The deadly words sounded so pleasant, he might have been talking about participating in a sporting event at Gallaka.

He stared dreamily at the blue patch of sky visible through the window grille. His dark, tough face had grown leaner with the campaign and the heavy bones showed. The stained bandages enhanced rather than diminished the power of his frame. Suddenly he was no longer a pathetic figure lying on a sickbed – he was a suave killer of men. I could only pray that his compassion would take over before he committed the murders he contemplated.

On that same morning, King Elara's Chief Warrior, Digha Jantu, quivering with rage, faced the King in his study with news of the capture of Ambati by Gamini. 'Our one hope, lord, is to smash the Sinhala in a single great battle,' he concluded. Although there was pleading in Digha Jantu's voice, his nostrils dilated with his efforts at self-control, making the broad, flat nose droop more grimly over the upper lip.

'You want to stake everything on a single battle?' King Elara deliberately injected a note of incredulity into his voice. 'No, Chief Warrior. There was a time for that . . . Perhaps we should have granted your request to press on to Mahagama after you captured the three Sinhala forts across the river.' He pushed back his chair, stretching his long legs. His chin sank to his chest and he became lost in reflection.

Digha Jantu, standing tall and firm, watched the King impatiently. 'Forgive me, sire, but there is still time to go after this upstart king. He has taken Ambati, which we never thought would fall. Nothing succeeds like victory. The Sinhala of Lanka are rallying to him in hundreds. We Chola will be surrounded by our foes if we do not attack before it is too late.'

The King was normally slow to react to bad news, but today he felt strangely detached. 'Ambati was not impregnable. We agreed on that, did we not, jester?' He glanced sideways at Junda, who was seated on the floor, inevitably playing with his cap.

The dwarf vigorously nodded agreement.

'The Sinhala found its flaw,' the King continued. 'Since

the capture of Ambati has placed them at the peak of their power, it is too late to attack them. When you face a tidal wave, you do not oppose it, but swim until it wears itself out. Now we shall depend on our mighty Vijitapura to protect us and to contain and ruin the Sinhala. Our royal command is that you withdraw the six corps further north, instead of rushing south to give battle.'

The Chief Warrior's small, mean eyes widened. They had developed red rims, the King noticed. With a great effort, Digha Jantu controlled an outburst. 'It will demoralize the garrisons at every one of our remaining forts, lord. We must learn the lessons of history.'

'Kings make history, Chief Warrior,' King Elara retorted sharply. He rose and stood tall, to add strength to his command. 'Our best course, we say, is to let today's wave spend itself. Withdraw our six corps to the plain north of the Vijitapura fort and consolidate there. Those are your orders. Go now and execute them.' He was suddenly tired of the bad news, tired of this giant's continual pushing, tired with something else that lay in his mind and controlled his actions, which he could not identify. His eyes became fierce and compelling from those very frustrations.

Digha Jantu bowed. 'Even as you say, lord,' he muttered, looking down. He made obeisance and started backing away, the King's glance unwaveringly on him. He paused at the door. 'One question, sire, if I may be permitted,' he begged.

'What is it?'

'You spoke of Vijitapura as being impregnable.'

'Yes.'

'What of Gallaka, which stands between that fort and Ambati? Is that not impregnable too?'

The King smiled grimly. 'A good question, Chief Warrior,' he replied, his voice even. 'We shall both know the answer to it soon, shall we not?'

Chapter 60

Three weeks later, in the month of Citta, our entire army was assembled for a conventional assault on the Gallaka fort, which was built at an almost semicircular bend in the river on its northern course. The vast bulk of the fort lay dark brown in the first light of dawn. The gigantic earthworks extended north to south, reaching from one bend of the river to the other. We had approached the fort from the west for a frontal assault over its moat against its one and only gate.

The Queen Mother, Raji, Leela and the ladies had returned to the Mahagama palace.

Gamini and I were at the centre of our army. Veera Singha and the Great Warriors were with us, except for the lame Kanja Deva and Nimila, who were absent, doubtless to their disgust. Nimila was in charge of the three corps that still remained at Mahagama since Gamini had moved one of the original four reserve corps to the river forts. Kanja Deva was in command of the three Dighavapi corps, now garrisoned across from Soma.

We were positioned about six hundred cubits from the fortress gates, once again at the edge of its cleared space. This area had been only four hundred cubits wide, but immediately upon taking command, Prince Digha Bahu had issued orders that a further two hundred cubits should be laid bare. He must have known what Gamini's battle tactics would be.

We assembled quietly enough in the shelter of trees, but soon there was bustle all around us. Messengers rode from point to point on horseback or scurried around on foot. The fighting men were mostly silent and watchful. As always, this was the worst time for us, the time of waiting.

The defenders in the fort knew we were ready. Their figures endlessly dotted the battlements. Their archers would be alert. Grey smoke curling up toward the blue sky warned of boiling oil simmering above glowing fires.

Gamini walked Raja forward and turned the horse around. When he faced us, his eyes were blazing. 'Hear me, men!' he cried.

'Hear the King . . . Hear the King.' The words went around and the sounds of horses and men, weapons and vehicles died down. A sudden stillness seemed to fall on the earth.

'Inside there' – Gamini half turned to point with an outstretched arm – 'are Sinhala traitors. This fort, we seize with our bare hands.' He roared out the words, dropping his reins and raising his hands aloft, the fingers stretched like talons. 'What say you?'

'*Ahey! Ahey! Ahey!*' The men roared back, shaking their fists aloft. A flock of brown paddy birds took off in alarm with a great fluttering of wings and speckled the blue sky.

'One race, one language, one religion!' Gamini thundered.

Thousands of clenched fists rose again in the air. 'One race, one language, one religion.' The mighty cry ascended to the very heavens.

The countless dots on the battlements before us seemed to tense as one. It was a tangible thing – thousands of men alerting in an instant for action because our charge was inevitable after the battle cry.

Gamini was too cunning to give his signal when the enemy was most prepared for it. He turned Raja around to face the fort again and simply waited, staring toward it.

Long minutes passed, stretching out. Gamini sat his horse like a statue. Many of the other horses pawed the ground restlessly or tossed their heads against the reins, but Raja was so well trained he did not move a muscle, only flicked his skin against an occasional fly.

Was this enforced wait good for our men? Would not the suspense demoralize them? No – the more keyed up they became, the wilder they would be in the assault.

A cool breeze sprang up, swirling dust before us. It touched the coldness of my sweat above my warm skin and goose bumps began to prickle all over the exposed parts of my body. I stared at the clearing. The brown earth was scarred with tufts of burnt wood, the remains of trees cut low so as to impede an attacker's progress. The moat would have rows of wooden spikes hidden in the water. Would we ever get to the gates? If we did, whom would I kill today? In the fort were people I did not know, yet they would die by my sword, or I before theirs.

Had we been wise to plan an outright frontal assault?

'Bowmen forward!' Gamini shouted.

My eyes returned to him. He drew his sword and raised it aloft. The swords of the thousands of men on either side of him were drawn and brandished.

'Bowmen forward!' Phussa cried.

'Bowmen forward! . . . Bowmen forward! . . . Bowmen forward!' The voices of commanders took up the order, so that it re-echoed like a single voice repeating itself in a ravine. I remembered the death cries of Ravi on the Kotmale mountains.

A drum struck up a march-time beat. Other drums took up the rhythm. Our grim-faced bowmen started to advance along the whole width of the battlements, in six lines, Phussa at the centre. Silently they broke cover, leaving open spaces in between for the cavalry charge to follow. They marched in orderly fashion to the tap of drums, holding their long bows in their left hands, quivers of arrows at the shoulders.

Tap-tap! . . . Tap-tap! It was the only sound. The silence of the men was menacing. I hoped their training by the champion, Phussa, would allow them to out-range the enemy. That was what Gamini was gambling on.

Tap-tap! . . . Tap-tap! Our men marched on. A gigantic

606

twang as from a single, mighty bow followed, then the rush of wind and a darkening of the earth before us. Hundreds of enemy arrows fell short.

'Halt! . . . Halt! . . . Halt! . . . Halt!' Our men stopped at the commands. The drumbeats ceased. Their echoes hung, painful, on the still air.

Our first line of bowmen reached over their shoulders for arrows and fitted them to their bowstrings. The long line of over a thousand men did it as one.

'Fire!' This time it was a single command. The twang of bows was music, the whizz of arrows like the flapping wings of a great flock of flamingoes.

The enormous flight of arrows arced swiftly into the sky and curved gracefully toward the battlements.

'We can outshoot them!' Gamini exclaimed gleefully. 'The battle is ours!'

A rumbling, like thunder, announced the thudding of our catapult bolts into the fortress. Our fireballs flashed through the air like lightning gone mad on a sunny day. Wooden buildings inside the fort caught fire and began to blaze, their flames licking upward through great mushrooms of dark grey smoke. A rushing wind brought cinders, ash and the sharp smell of burning wood. We were witnessing another Hindu hell. I remembered Ambati and thrust the picture from my mind.

Gamini pointed his long sword, fully outstretched, toward the fort. 'Charge!' he yelled.

We streaked across the open ground on fleet chargers, regardless of arrows and bolts, a compact group of cavalry. Men fell, screaming; horses reared, neighing. The giants Maha Sona and Nanda Mitta were the first to reach the entrances. They dismounted and battered down the gates with great battle-axes. We poured inside.

In a matter of hours we overran that fort by sheer superiority of men and weapons. Only then did Gamini begin his search for the three Sinhala leaders. No thoughts of vengeance had deflected him from his main purpose, the capture of the fort. Now he conducted the search for the two princes and Sali with the same single-mindedness.

We dismounted and fought across the main hall, along the passage to the commander's quarters. We finally burst through, only to find the rooms empty.

Gamini turned, panting. His sword dripped blood. 'There must be an escape route from the fort,' he gasped. 'Find the chief attendant.'

Velu Sumana, Vasabha and I raced along a dark, narrow passage for the servant's quarters. We searched the small cloisters of rooms. We looked under the wooden beds. Not an attendant did we find.

The last room was larger than the rest. An elderly Chola attendant sat shaking on his bed, his dark body bathed in sweat, his mouth trembling beneath frightened brown eyes above which a mop of long, grey hair hung dishevelled. He was probably too old to attempt escape. His sword poised to strike, Vasabha gripped the man by his tunic and lifted him off the bed as if he were a puppet. 'Where is Prince Digha Bahu?' he demanded.

'Pray do not kill me, lord,' the old man quavered. 'Those you seek are in a room at the end of this passage, awaiting single combat.'

Vasabha flung the man back on his bed. We turned on our heels and dashed out of the room, making for the door at the far end of the dark corridor. Gamini, who had rejoined us, got there first. He grasped the door handle. It turned in his hand, but the door was locked. He glanced at Vasabha and jerked his head. The golden-skinned giant understood. Gamini and he backed up.

'Be careful, sire,' I cautioned. 'Do not rush into the room when the door crashes in. They will be waiting for you.'

Gamini and Vasabha flattened themselves on either side of the entrance.

'Have no fear.' Gamini's laugh was brutal. 'We have

come too far for such folly.'

Gamini and Vasabha looked at each other for timing. Gamini nodded. They kicked the door with the flat soles of their feet. It caved in like matchwood. Gamini and Vasabha held back at the entrance.

I looked beyond them into a large room. Bright sunlight streamed through the long-grilled windows to reveal a sight I shall never forget.

The room was bare except for a brown teakwood table. Seated at the far end of the table were the three men we sought. Prince Digha Bahu occupied the chair in the centre. On his right sat the pudgy Prince Panduka. On his left was the lean, saturnine Sali. All three men were fastidiously turned out in blue silk tunics and gold pantaloons, the Digha Bahu colours. They sat very calmly, as if they were merely expecting guests to lunch. On the table in front of them were three naked swords.

Moments passed while we stood at the entrance. In contrast with these cool creatures, we were panting, hot, sticky, dusty, blood-strewn.

Prince Digha Bahu rose. 'Ah! The King of Ruhuna!' he exclaimed. 'How do I greet you? As a king, or a nephew? With obeisance, a laugh, or my sword?'

Gamini said nothing, but his eyes flamed with anger.

'What are you doing here, traitor?' I demanded fiercely. 'Presiding over the fortress of our enemies?'

'No more than the uncle you worship did at King Elara's court for many years,' the Prince retorted urbanely.

I made for him, but was stayed by a back-sweep of Gamini's hand. 'Let the dog bark!' he quietly ordered, his glance urgent on me. 'It shall not be for much longer.' His eyes slid back to Prince Digha Bahu. 'You have a choice between being executed like a common criminal,' he declared, 'or dying in the combat you seem to have avoided today while your men fell like flies.'

Prince Digha Bahu did not seem the least bit put out.

Indeed, in these final moments he appeared to have recovered a long-lost nobility, and I could not restrain a spurt of admiration for him.

'My dear nephew,' Prince Digha Bahu replied, gripping the edge of the table lightly and half bowing, 'when King Elara first offered me this grand appointment, I was elated. It seemed to pave the way to the very heavens. But I soon realized that it was merely a trap, making use of my own ambition to destroy us finally. So why lead these miserable Cholas to our deaths?' He paused. 'Rather a nice turn of phrase that, don't you think?' He looked confidently at us, still holding the stage. 'No matter! My folly was that I did not learn from my dealings with King Kakkavan not to place my trust in kings.' His pale brown eyes became hard as of old. 'You at least need not take affront at my remarks about your father, for such was your own experience!'

I gazed at the man, speechless. He stood there facing violent death and spoke exactly as his relation, my uncle, would have done. Surely there is something in blood. Even Gamini, Velu Sumana and Vasabha were caught off guard. Outside was the vulgar clash and din of battle. Here in this cool, bright room was dignity, nobility, royalty.

Gamini was the first to recover. 'You led our father a miserable dance!' he exclaimed. 'Now prepare for your own dance with death.' He took a step into the room. His sword came on guard.

Prince Digha Bahu's pudgy face creased into a smile. The pale brown eyes were friendly now. 'Your revered father danced miserably to the tune of his own weakness and well you know it!' he countered. 'I was the rightful heir to the Ruhuna throne. Your father should, in all honour, have abdicated when I came of age. Instead, lacking physical force to keep himself on the throne, he used promises and deceit. You are well aware of some of his secret actions. And all of us faced that sickness in his mind, the desire to expiate his ancestors' murder of the Kataragama benefactors.' He

610

straightened to his full height, his presence commanding. 'My son and I have been guilty of perfidy too!' he quietly admitted. 'All men are guilty of it, especially those in high places. Your father, his father before him, King Elara, you, I. Which of us can deny it? Do you wish to judge us for that of which you too are guilty?'

The truth of Prince Digha Bahu's words filled me with horror. They were evil. They could destroy the foundations of our lives, those foundations which to be true must never be the truth, for the truth is not absolute! But philosophy was no comfort to me – not at this time when I had stared death in the face again and again and the blood clots of destruction within me had yet to be dissolved. Those who have the power to corrupt others are evil. Was Prince Digha Bahu evil then? Or was it the truth that was evil?

'Prince Vipula was never guilty of perfidy,' I shot out desperately, needing something to cling to at this moment when nothingness yawned beneath me.

Prince Digha Bahu turned to stare at me as if I were an intruder. Once again that hard, merciless look was in his pale eyes, but now there was a hint of contempt in them as well.

If you deny me this one solace, I shall kill you, I thought.

We glared at each other – he mercilessly, I with horror. Long moments passed as we battled each other with the weapons of our emotions.

Finally, Prince Digha Bahu smiled. 'Even to excuse my conduct, I cannot malign your uncle,' he said gently.

The tears sprang to my eyes. Where mercilessness would have failed, the Prince, my enemy for years, had conquered me with generosity. I could not bring myself to speak. The figures of the three men at the table became blurred images.

'By that one great truth you have saved your life and that of your son and your commander,' I heard Gamini say hoarsely. 'There must still be good in you to acknowledge one such as Prince Vipula.' I had not known how much he revered my uncle.

Gamini's sword point dropped. Large blobs of sweat stood out on his dark face, like sprinkles on lotus leaves. He turned on his heel. The attendant still cowered in the corridor. 'You there!' he addressed the man. 'Come forward without fear and treat these gentlemen according to their rank.'

The old man straightened up and looked Gamini in the face. Some remnant of tattered courage stirred in him. Fear left his eyes, to be replaced by a long, searching look. He nodded in the gloom. 'You are a worthy king, sire!' he exclaimed impulsively, making deep obeisance. 'A saviour, both of your friends and enemies. A boon to all mankind.'

No, attendant, you are wrong, I thought. Gamini is a man born to conquest. He has the power to conquer all things, even himself. But being a man like any of us, that very power will turn, like a sword in his hand. His weaknesses will overshadow his destiny, for his weaknesses too are his destiny. Like any mortal, he was born alone. He will die alone on the sword of his final weakness: bewilderment that his power did not extend to conquering the foe, death.

Chapter 61

After taking the Gallaka fort, Gamini assigned Prince Digha Bahu, Prince Panduka and Sali to assist Prince Tissa in Mahagama with the raising and training of recruits. He no longer needed to fear plots anywhere in Ruhuna, where his exploits had made him a hero and the rule of the Council of Ministers had proved popular – but Mahagama was a safer place, he deemed, for ambitious people!

Three weeks after the capture of the fort, on the heels of

Gamini's birthday and mine, Gamini informed his commanders that our regular evening conference was a special one, which they should make it a point to attend.

Veera Singha, Velu Sumana, Vasabha, Nanda Mitta, Maha Sona, Phussa, Bharana, Abhaya, the dwarf Gotha and our regular cavalry, infantry and support arms commanders sat around the teakwood table of the great assembly hall in Gallaka fort.

Gamini first gave us available information, including his assessment of relative strengths. He then stated his intention clearly and succinctly: 'We shall assault Vijitapura, the mightiest of Chola forts, and take it!'

Gamini then unfolded his plan. When he had finished, he looked at each of the eight Great Warriors. 'You understand how important your objectives are to our goal of taking Vijitapura.'

The warriors nodded.

'You shall move tomorrow with all speed, for a surprise attack sometime during the following week. Having accomplished this objective, you shall cross the Amban River at dawn the next day and arrive at our southeastern staging area near Vijitapura that evening – here!' He used his ebony ebony pointer to indicate the area. 'Abhaya will, however, remain behind with ten companies of his corps at the Great Ford for its defence and will control our three corps below Soma in the east. Prince Tissa has instructions to move six of our ten reserve corps to the northern bank of the Mahaveli, which shall serve as our base. We shall thus maintain a continuous, powerful defence chain along the river, from south going north and from north going east.'

The commanders murmured their approval, looking at each other with sober satisfaction.

Once again, Digha Jantu, having demanded a special morning audience with the King, begged to be allowed to take the offensive. Once again he was denied.

'The enemy force has become too great for you to take on with six corps, Great Warrior,' King Elara concluded soberly. Some of the fire seemed to have left him. 'We could boost your strength with the four corps in the east, but that would expose us to the possibility of a flanking movement from that direction. With the people of Malaya to our west getting restive, it would be an unwise move. Similarly, unleashing our ten corps from Anu would be an almost desperate gamble, which we are unwilling to take at this stage. Let us see what happens to the Sinhala at Vijitapura before we make a final decision. Meanwhile, withdraw your six corps to Anu, but ensure the supply lines to Vijitapura.'

The King did not mention that he had sent messengers secretly to his brother, Bhalluka, in the Chola heartland, to bring ten corps of his mercenaries to supplement his own forces, lest word get around and panic spread. If he had not gone to his brother's rescue nineteen years ago, he might have dealt with the baby Gamini and would not now be facing such a serious situation, with the baby having grown up to challenge his rule. Now his brother would be coming to his rescue.

King Elara noted his jester, Junda, watching Digha Jantu closely before he left the study, as if trying to penetrate the giant's thoughts. He realized that recently Junda had indeed been observing the Chief Warrior closely, while pretending to be unconcerned. He himself had seen that Digha Jantu's skin had acquired a curious pallor and the eyes bore a crazed expression. His face had developed a new feature, a nervous tic that sometimes pulsed on the side of his left eye. There was hatred boiling within the man.

The King felt alone and isolated – not sorry for himself or fearful of the future, but trapped without options for too long. How swiftly the tide had turned! He had to act with complete wisdom and restraint. His troops were superior to the Sinhala; of that he was convinced. His one hope now was to have the Sinhala spread out over half the island, with forces scattered in Mahagama, Dighavapi – the jackal prince had escaped his fate, more the pity! – Soma, Seru, the river border and the captured fortresses. He would then, at the right time, draw the Sinhala into action on ground of his own choosing and win a single, decisive battle. Alternatively, he would hold Anu until Bhalluka arrived with help.

'Fool though I be, sire,' Junda interrupted his thoughts, toddling up to his desk, 'I am tutored and an avid reader of historical *ola*. I believe our Chief Warrior is convinced that you have made the same mistakes that many hero kings throughout history have made, that you are a noble war-horse harnessed too long to the wagon of politics and government.'

'Do you, too, think we are mistaken?' King Elara demanded.

'No, sire, but I believe our Chief Warrior thinks you are.'

'What, then, is the view of our new court strategist?' The moment he said the words, the King regretted the mockery in his voice, for he sensed Junda wincing.

The dwarf's bulbous eyes looked pityingly at the King. 'You are facing one of the inevitable consequences of life. If you had not become the complete political animal, you would have swept to the attack, whatever the odds, the moment King Gamini returned to Mahagama from exile, or at least during the time of the civil strife in Ruhuna. Instead, you played the great political game, *manta yuddhaya*. Ruling made you too civilized, too intellectual. Whoever heard of intellectuals conquering countries or winning wars? That is yet another characteristic of life. People are always wanting to be what they are not, once they achieve something. The rich want social standing, the poor nobleman desires money, the warrior-king to be a political strategist. I alone am content with my lot . . . perhaps because there is no way in which I can improve it. As for King Gamini, he has shown himself to be your superior in strategy.'

'How so?'

'Look at his achievements, sire. He never attacks until he is ready. He ensures adequate supply lines. He lives with his troops and leads them into battle. He never pushes ahead after victory, but consolidates, giving himself firm bases and short lines of communication . . .'

The King looked at Junda in wonder. 'You are indeed a military observer,' he interrupted. 'All these years and we never guessed. Why is it you never told us?'

'You never asked, sire.'

'We always regarded you as a jester, a fool and, of course, our closest friend.'

The dwarf blinked. Once again King Elara regretted his hasty words. What was happening to him? Why was he so insensitive?

'I am honoured, sire!' Junda rejoined without enthusiasm.

'So you, too, think we should attack now?'

The dwarf shook his head. 'It is too late. I have lived with the inevitable consequences of my life since I was born, sire. My appearance ensured that, but it is men, not circumstances, to whom I bowed. Cruel though it was, my mind accepted it. I had no other choice. Now, I have been a clown and jester for years and have never needed to change my act. You, sire, in your position, never had the security of a consistent role. You have had to keep changing. I derived compensation for what life denied me. You have to pay the price for what life gave you. That is life's balance. We each receive the effects of our causes and end up equal in the long run.'

Vijitapura was a dark, sprawling mass, glowing with golden lights. It seemed to spread forever northward into the grey mists of approaching night. In front of the mass, three moats glimmered with the remnants of daylight. Flights of black crows, cawing sadly, winged lazily across a paling blue sky toward the grove from which we watched. As night fell, fireflies emerged to twinkle among the dark branches. The wheels of nature spun lazily while our minds twirled with thoughts of battle.

All land for several hundred yards in front of the fortress moats had been cleared. Within the three moats, the walls and battlements were built of solid grey granite blocks, not wood or earth. The three gates had been revealed to be hardwood and iron. Each gateway had twin towers above it for defenders. Guard towers for bowmen, sixty yards apart, spread along the entire line of the battlements and were sited to allow crossfire. In between each tower were the dark silhouettes of cauldrons, obviously filled with boiling pitch. Looking at the fort dismally, I felt that our one hope lay in the four sabotage teams we had managed to introduce into it, six to a gate.

Only Gamini seemed cheerful. He was whistling softly the marching tune of the Sinhala. I identified it only by the rhythm, because Gamini could never carry a tune in his head. After our contemplation of the fort, we lay down to sleep in the open, beneath dark green leaves that shredded the sky.

Our assault plan for Vijitapura was basically the same as that we had successfully adopted at Gallaka, except for dependence on infiltrators to open the gates and the possible use of elephants in the assault. Gamini planned the attack for ten days later, but he had told no one else. Only I guessed why. He had not received the go-ahead message from our spies.

On the final evening, Gamini, Veera Singha, Velu Sumana, Vasabha, Nanda Mitta and I made a last survey of the fort from the edge of our grove. The dying rays of the setting sun cast a golden glow on the battlements. Between the two dark gate towers we noticed some unusual black objects.

Velu Sumana was the first to identify them. He pointed with a long, shaking finger. 'Look!' he exclaimed hoarsely.

He began cursing softly.

I now identified the objects as six naked bodies, with ropes around their necks, dangling from a girder joining the two towers. They sagged, heads lolling, lifeless, grotesque in death.

'Our infiltrators!' I heard myself stating the obvious.

Gamini stared at the corpses, his body rigid, his face inscrutable. What thoughts were racing through his mind? Did he blame himself for holding back our assault too long? Was he bleeding with compassion for the men he had sent to this grisly death? Was he recalling the tragedy at Ambati? Was he seeing in those six corpses the death of his hopes? Perhaps our men at the other gates were still alive and able to assist us.

Sickened by the dangling bodies, I wondered whether this had been the cause of my premonition.

Before long, we had word from our commanders at the other gates that all our infiltrators had been hanged.

Gamini called off the assault.

Chapter 62

Four months of stalemate followed, during which the strength and competence of our forces grew daily. Vijitapura was actually a small city, containing about three corps of well-trained Cholas, supporting services and civilians. Being strong themselves, the Cholas emerged from the city regularly, often in strength, to harass our forces.

The Chola sorties came to have a definite pattern. Their cavalry would emerge from two gates simultaneously at dawn every other day, followed by chariots and foot soldiers. Since there were three gates, this meant that only one of our three groups was not engaged. We discovered that these unfailing dawn attacks were meant to throw us off balance for the rest of the day. They kept two of our three fronts occupied, the third being insufficient to make an assault on its own. Soon we could even predict which two gates the enemy would emerge from.

Gamini evolved a plan whereby all three of our groups would be in a state of readiness, in formations we practised, the second day after one of the attacks from the fort. When the Cholas emerged from the fort the next day, instead of defending as heretofore, we would unleash a total assault on all three fronts, forcing our way into the fort before the gates could close. If we could just gain entrance, our magnificent fighting men would do the rest. Since we could not ignore the possibility that the Chola sorties might be a preliminary to a more massive attack, Gamini decided that we should not delay too long. We were all glad when he finally told us to prepare to attack the fort the next day.

We were in position by the time the pale light of dawn began filtering through the air. Our mounted cavalry were assembled in columns behind us within the shelter of the trees. Ahead of us, six lines of bowmen stretched endlessly on either side. It was strange to hear the 'ko-haaa . . . ko-haaa' of the koel bird resounding through the air and other birds stirring in their nests, flapping an occasional wing, murmuring querulously, or practising their first whistles on a battlefront redolent with the smells of defecation and unwashed bodies.

Gamini, beside me on Raja, was a still figure carved of black wood. His dark eyes were fixed on the western gate of Vijitapura.

The eastern sky slowly turned to rose, making low clouds shine like cloth of gold. The dark figures dotting the fortress walls became more finely etched.

A faint creak and the grinding of metal drifted across the open ground. The western gates were being opened. The leading elements of enemy cavalry appeared, trotting in columns of six. They crossed the three bridges and fanned out right and left at the outermost moat. Chariots began rattling forward.

The Chola cavalry were still moving into line when Gamini gave the signal.

We charged across the open ground, followed by our chariots, bowmen and foot soldiers. The enemy cavalry paused, undecided, at the thunder of our approach. A hail of arrows from the fort darkened the sky. We took them on our shields at full gallop. Some of our men and horses went down. Undeterred, we sped toward the fort, now beneath the clouds of our own arrows.

We crashed through the leading enemy elements like a battering ram. The speed of our charge carried us across the first bridge, scattering Chola horses and chariots into the moat.

We had to fight our way across the second bridge.

Having lost our momentum by the time we reached the third bridge, we had to rely on ferocity alone. Six of us were abreast in the lead – Gamini, Velu Sumana, Vasabha, Nanda Mitta, Jagat and I. We faced six Chola horsemen at a time. The bridge was not wide enough to hold more.

We angled up to engage them. Dark Cholas on great horses crowded behind the lead rank. I ran a lean Chola through the stomach while his own weapon was still aloft. Giving a great cry, he toppled into the moat, his horse slipping after him with a terrific splash. I urged my horse into the gap, taking on a grim-faced Chola who tried to push through. I swung with my sword. He parried. Sweat shone on his taut cheeks. He slashed back at me with his sword. I took it on my own, reversed and cut. He parried again. We duelled for position.

A shrill trumpeting arose above the din of battle.

'Make way!' someone shouted in Sinhala.

'Make way!' Other Sinhala voices took up the cry.

My opponent glanced past me – a mistake. I ran my sword through his throat. Blood gushed forth as I withdrew my weapon. His horse leaped into the moat with its dying rider.

'By the *devas*, it is Kandula!' Nanda Mitta shouted.

The enemy looked fearfully past us. They turned and tried to flee into the fort. The rattle of chains and a great creaking told us that the defenders were closing the gates, regardless of their men outside. The Cholas between us and the entrance turned and tried frantically to reach safety. A few barely streaked in before the gates closed inexorably. The rest faced us again.

The rumble of the elephant's feet reached our ears. We made way by dashing over the third bridge to the open ground in front of the gates, battling the Cholas trapped there.

Kandula came charging over the bridges, his *mahout* on his back. Chola and Sinhala alike leaped aside. The grey beast thundered past us, making a shambles of the Chola cavalrymen in its path, then hit the gates with an impact that shook the very battlements.

The hinges were loosened, but the gates were held by bars.

Even the enemy on the battlements were awestruck. Kandula dropped to his knees and began pushing mightily at the gates. Bricks and mortar started to give around the hinges, but the gates held firm. Kandula roared with rage at the obstruction. The *mahout* backed him a few paces. He charged again, furiously. The sound was like thunder, but the gates still held.

Kandula backed again, but by now the enemy were coming to their senses. An arrow took the *mahout* in the chest. He clutched it with both hands, trying to pull it out, then fell to the ground. Darts and spears rained on Kandula's back, but the elephant was well protected by the *howdah* and armour.

A black wave cascaded from above the gateway. My blood ran cold as molten pitch rained on Kandula. As the burning liquid went through his leather trappings, Kandula screamed, turned around and dashed away from the gates, still screaming shrilly.

We were caught in the open. Enemy marksmen began directing their fire at us. 'Withdraw!' Gamini shouted. We veered our horses round and raced back, pursued by the enemy.

We began pushing our way over the third bridge, but our own men blocked our path. I felt a vicious blow on my back. I was thrown forward. Searing pain shot through me and I lost my reins. I tried to grip my horse's flanks with my legs, but they had gone numb. As I clung to my horse's neck with my hands, he began floating away from me. I knew I was falling, but could do nothing about it. The pain in my back suddenly exploded into blessed numbness. A black cloud began to engulf me. I must not lose consciousness, I thought desperately. The earth spun in the darkness. I hit the water, heavy as a sack of bricks. Everything stopped.

I swam blindly through pain into reality. I felt intensely weak, then puzzled. Why was I in such pain? Where was I? Why was I lying face down on a wooden bed? I tried to raise my head. A stab of agony flashed through my back. I gasped with it and nearly blacked out.

With a great effort, I kept myself from fainting. When I opened my eyes again, I saw a granite floor. I wondered about that. Then recollection came and I realized that I had not drowned in the moat. Slowly moving my head sideways in the direction of the light, I saw a blue sky through the iron grille of a high window. The noises of battle still resounded in the distance.

With dread, I realized that I could not move my legs. Dear *devas*, was I paralyzed? I wiggled my toes. They moved. Cautiously, I tried to lift my right leg. A sliver of pain went through my back, but the leg rose before thumping down again. Silently, I thanked God.

I was alive and in a fort. I had been rescued. If this was Vijitapura, we had won!

'I am glad to see that you are alive and well, Prince Rodana,' a cultured voice said in the Chola language, 'although I regret to inform you that I must remember to send your king a bill for the damage he is causing.'

He was a cool one, this Chola.

He chuckled and resumed. 'Now that we have finally met, I can leave you. I am Selliah, commander of this fortress. I have a battle to win!' He rose to his feet and left the room.

Why had he waited for me to awaken? The question was lost in a blur as I fainted again.

Chapter 63

Fleeing from the scene of his torment, the giant elephant, Kandula, pounded over the bridges of the moat in the direction of our lines. Our advancing cavalry scattered from his path, men and horses leaping into the moat. Kandula reached the third bridge and veered right along the edge of the moat, still screaming. The elephant slowed his pace, paused and plunged with a great splash into the water, which seethed and bubbled from the hot pitch on the trappings.

Shouting to Vasabha to follow him, Gamini instinctively raced Raja to the elephant's aid, as he had once done on the Culan plain. As he dismounted, six Sinhala cavalrymen took up positions to protect his rear. He began speaking to Kandula.

At first the creature ignored Gamini. After much coaxing, however, he flapped his great ears in Gamini's direction. More words of love and invitation flowed from the warrior-king. The king of the jungle rose to his feet. Water streamed down his pumping sides as he slowly ploughed through the moat and heaved himself onto the bank.

Gamini gave Kandula the command to kneel. When the elephant settled on his great haunches, Gamini mounted. Vasabha and the cavalry escort took up positions around him.

Gamini seized the *mahout*'s prod and gave the signal to advance. The little procession moved toward our lines, slowly at first, then at a canter, while fighting continued to rage around them.

Once they reached the grove of trees, Gamini brought Kandula to a halt. The animal doctor had already been alerted. He had the elephant kneel and started examining his back and sides.

'Where is Prince Rodana?' Gamini demanded of an orderly as he dismounted. He noticed my bay, side by side with Raja, who had been brought back by one of the cavalrymen, snuffling for grass in the worn soil. A thrill of alarm shot through him. He glared at the orderly.

The man stiffened with fear. 'The Prince's horse galloped back alone from the field, sire. We do not know what happened to the Prince.'

Gamini advanced toward the orderly, a strange new feeling of panic surging through him. 'A curse on it, man, did you not think to find out?' Fear for my safety then exploded. 'Get every man available,' he roared. 'Search our lines. Search the battlefield. Forget the fort. I want the Prince found.' He turned on the men hesitating around him and yelled, 'What the devil are you gaping at? Go, find the Prince.'

The full impact of my absence had not yet hit Gamini. At this point he was still acting mechanically, but now he was experiencing something hitherto unknown to him – fear for someone he loved.

'Lord!' Vasabha had to shout to make himself heard above the clamour of battle. 'Our best method of finding the Prince is to capture the fort, not abandon it. Let us first achieve that purpose.'

Gamini stopped dead in his tracks. He half turned, slowly, to face Vasabha. His fists clenched. For long moments he glowered at the warrior as if he would erupt into angry action. As always, Vasabha's coolness calmed him. He finally drew a deep breath, the wide, dark nostrils distending. 'You are right,' he agreed more quietly. 'Search our lines for the Prince anyway.' He turned and walked back to Kandula while Vasabha galloped off.

The doctor, having examined the elephant, directed that the armour and trappings be stripped off Kandula. As he had hoped, the pitch had cooled in the seams of the armour, leaving only superficial burns. He applied a balm made from bay leaves to heal the wounds, with *ganja* to deaden the pain.

'Have thin copper sheaths brought up!' Gamini directed his chief attendant, speaking into the man's ear to avoid shouting. Our army carried copper for a variety of uses, such as sheaths for wagon wheels and buffalo hide for shields and armour. 'And seven buffalo hides. Also have Minister Veera Singha come up with a reserve squadron of cavalry.'

Gamini began pacing impatiently while waiting for his orders to be executed. He was lost in thought. Ten steps up. Ten steps down. Gamini turned to stare at the confusion of men, fighting in the sunlight, only now aware of the curses and cries, the pounding of hooves, the twang of bowstrings from our lines. He heard the ring of metal on metal, the neighing of horses. He saw a huge Chola officer on a great black horse spurring toward a Sinhala foot soldier. The man's back was turned to the Chola. Instinctively Gamini started to cry out a warning. The Sinhala could not have heard, but he turned at the last moment. He was a lean-faced boy with terror in his eyes before he became a headless trunk from the Chola's sword swipe.

The reserve squadron of cavalry trotted up. Gamini turned to Veera Singha, who was at its head. 'Form columns of six facing the fortress gate!' he shouted above the din. The men behind the minister moved smoothly into position.

Attendants jogged up, carrying copper sheaths and buffalo hides. Gamini directed them to tie the hides, then the copper around Kandula, rendering the animal completely immune from any further attack by the defenders of the fort. A groom brought Raja to Gamini and held the horse's stirrup.

Gamini turned to Kandula instead. The elephant was waiting patiently, as if aware of what was going on. Except for an occasional twitch of his leathery skin and the flicking of his ears against flies, he had stood still while the attendants were covering his body.

Gamini stepped up to Kandula's ear. 'Dear twin brother, Kandula,' he whispered, 'the suzerainty of our entire kingdom rests with you. Charge into battle against our enemies and deliver the kingdom to us.'

Turning, Kandula raised his grey trunk aloft to scent the fort, across the medley of men and horses battling in the fierce silver light. The great ears flapped forward like sails. Trumpeting defiance, he lumbered forward.

Gamini leaped onto Raja's back. He drew his sword and raised it aloft, glittering in the sunlight. 'Follow me!' he cried, pointing the sword toward the fortress.

Kandula trotted through the cover of trees. Soon he was in the open at full gallop. As the beast gathered momentum, his giant feet began to pound the hard earth, their rumble like a distant tidal wave. Men and horses scattered from his path like trees swept before that wave. Gamini's cavalry column thundered in Kandula's wake.

Men ran away or jumped into the moats to clear the bridges, which trembled as Kandula thudded over them. Dark molten pitch began to cascade at the entrance, but the elephant never hesitated. Screaming shrilly at the sight and feel of what had tormented him before, the huge animal hit the gates like an avalanche. His great white tusks pierced the thick wooden panels, splintering them like matchwood. The mighty grey shoulders rammed the gates from their hinges. The gates shuddered, gave a long-drawn scream of agony and shattered backward.

Brick and mortar started to fall from the archway overhead. The guard towers trembled. Cholas ran from them in panic. The rain of molten pitch ebbed.

The Great Warriors had joined the cavalry column. With a mighty heave, Nanda Mitta shoved open the gates. Our cavalry swept in. Maha Sona alone dismounted. Seizing one of the gates, he ripped it off its hinges. Nanda Mitta laughed, leaped off his horse and tore out the other gate. 'These are better weapons!' he shouted. Screaming at the top of their lungs, the two warriors plunged into the battle, slamming the Cholas who opposed entry.

His charge ended, Kandula paused. The archway above suddenly shuddered. Mortar started to rain down. The entire battlement had been shaken loose. It would fall on Kandula and crush the noble creature to death.

Nanda Mitta flung aside his gate and charged back to the archway. He placed his palms on the massive granite block overhead, desperately holding it back. His great muscles rippled with the strain. As the weight became too much, Nanda Mitta pushed grimly upward, refusing to let go. Groaning aloud with the effort, he stood his ground, but he was slowly crumpling beneath the weight of solid granite.

Vasabha and Maha Sona leaped to his aid. Together the three Great Warriors held up the archway. Our cavalry streaked past Kandula and the warriors to help Gamini and the men who were already inside. The elephant lumbered forward with them.

The three sweat-strewn warriors exchanged glances, understanding each other. 'Hup!' Nanda Mitta gritted. All three released their holds and leaped into the fort. The granite block tottered and trembled, then crashed to the ground behind them. The entire archway, block upon block, cascaded down in a cloud of dust that obscured the entrance. The remainder of our cavalry scrambled over the debris.

The brave Cholas, heavily outnumbered, put up a stubborn resistance. Fighting went on all day and night, with no quarter asked and none given.

Selliah, the fortress commander, led charge after charge, always seeking Gamini, but never reaching the King. It was Gamini who finally found him in a side passage, after the fortress was taken. Alone, except for his brave dead scattered around him, the commander lay in a dark pool of blood. His uniform was slashed, torn and soaked red, his body cut and bruised. Great gashes ran across his chest. His eyes were closed. Only the straining nostrils in the drawn face and a harsh gasping for breath showed that he was still alive.

Gamini recognized him from his uniform. He knelt beside the man. 'You sought us, Commander!' he said, panting. 'Here we are – too late, we think.'

Selliah's eyelids slowly lifted. His dark eyes were unable to focus. 'I did indeed try to find you, King, but failed. Now you have found me. Funny! Indeed, it is too late. I . . . I cannot even see you! You . . . should have come before! I would have . . . given you . . . a fitting welcome.' One side of his face creased with his effort at a smile. It made him look grotesque, incongruous with his courage and gallantry. A paroxysm of pain seized him. His eyes closed. He gritted his teeth with never a sound. The paroxysm passed. 'So . . . many . . . b-battles. So many comrades.'

Gamini reached out and smoothed back his enemy's hair with surprising gentleness.

A great sigh escaped Selliah. 'For that act of kindness, there is . . . something I shall tell you,' he finally whispered. 'The one . . . whom you seek . . . is on his way . . . to my king in Anu.' He paused to gather his strength. 'He was . . . my prisoner . . .'

628

With an effort, he raised his head slightly. His eyes widened, then focused intently on Gamini. 'In the end, you have to lose in winning, King,' he said in a clear voice. 'I'm sorry!'

His head fell back on the pavement with a thud. Eyes wide, mouth open, he vainly grabbed for breath. He choked. Blood frothed from his throat, dribbled down the side of his face. His body arched and stiffened. It gave one convulsive heave, then he suddenly relaxed and sagged, head lolling sideways, staring eyes blank.

Absently, Gamini reached out with his forefinger and middle finger to draw closed the dead commander's eyelids. He did not know whether to be happy that I was alive or to tear his hair because I was in grave danger.

Chapter 64

The wagon in which I was dispatched reached the south gate of Anu the next morning. My apprehension turned to fear when I heard the guard commander direct that the vehicle be drawn to a side of the courtyard until further orders.

It soon became warm and close inside the wagon, which I shared with Ratnam, Selliah's personal physician, who had been sent to look after me. I could only lie there sweating, staring at the brown wooden boards.

The waiting grew monotonous. I did not know whether to be happy or alarmed at hearing a group of men riding up from within the city and coming to an abrupt stop beside the wagon. Only one person dismounted, with a creak of leather. Footsteps approached the front of the wagon. I recognized the deep, raspy voice even before the rider introduced himself to our escort commander.

'I hear you have a prize. I have come to take it over on behalf of the King.'

'Our orders – ' the escort commander began timidly.

'Are from me henceforth! Report to the chief administrative officer here. His name is Krishnan. But first, you shall have three days' leave. My financial officer here will give you a bag of money. Spend it all as unwisely as you can in the city!'

Suddenly a figure loomed dark against the rear opening of the wagon. 'I am Digha Jantu, Chief Warrior of King Elara,' he announced. 'It has been many years, Prince Rodana!' He paused. 'You and your friend have wrought great evil of late.' His voice had lost its earlier quiet tone. He was snarling now. 'You have much to answer for, but first you will be of immense use to me.'

'To me,' the man said. Even in my weakened state, I could not ignore the significance of the word 'me'. Not to King Elara, not to 'us', but to 'me'.

A prickling, as from a fever, started at the soles of my feet and coursed upward to the top of my head. My hair seemed to vibrate with it. In my mind, a connection was established with self-preservation. I knew why I had once feared this man even more than I had his king.

At that very moment, Gamini sat in conference with his war council in the great chamber of the Vijitapura fort. He had already decided that the one way to save my life was to drive on immediately to Anu. The men seated around him – Veera Singha on his left, Velu Sumana, the other Great Warriors and the field commanders – appeared sceptical of the wisdom of his plan. So was Gamini, but he had rationalized it in his mind. The vacant seat on his right, unoccupied by unspoken agreement as a gesture to me, had become a source of compulsion to hasty action. 'We have a solid advantage militarily and politically,' Gamini declared. 'We should push it through to total victory.'

'You are not suggesting that we move today, sire?' Velu Sumana sounded anxious. 'Our men have fought through an entire day and night and now must prepare the fort as a base. They need rest.'

'If their king can march, so can they!'

'It is easier for those of us on horseback, sire,' Veera Singha volunteered.

'We shall march with the infantry.' That set, stubborn feeling entered Gamini and was reflected in his face, he knew. The humid air outside was devoid of any breeze and the room was close and warm, so his clothes stuck to his body. The wound on his left shoulder had healed, but he had taken a gash on his chest during the fighting for Vijitapura and he could feel blood-ooze commence beneath the *patthu*.

Gamini was not surprised when the golden-bodied Vasabha spoke up. 'Lord! Your whole life, the aspirations of the Sinhala and the destiny of Lanka are at stake today. We will follow you to the gates of the Hindu hell and beyond at your slightest command. We are all ready to do so today. You alone must be sure of the wisdom of your choice.'

Vasabha's brilliant eyes swept the entire conference table. All the tired, grim-faced men seated around it nodded assent. Some cried, *'Ahey! Ahey!'*

The Great Warrior turned to look at Gamini again. His glance had a hint of compassion, but his dark voice was steady. 'Let us act to preserve your destiny and the kingdom, sire, while also asking ourselves what is best for our comrade, Prince Rodana. News of the fall of Vijitapura will have adverse consequences for him in Anu. King Elara may wreak vengeance on him. If we push on forthwith, the King might put him to death. With the deepest humility and respect, I counsel your usual strategy of consolidation and your normal wisdom of restraint.'

Gamini contemplated Vasabha with smouldering eyes. So you are against me once more, golden warrior, he thought. Vasabha returned his gaze, unafraid.

Once again, Gamini was struck by the Great Warrior's complete sincerity. He tried to outstare Vasabha. Not all his power could achieve it, because deep inside him he knew he was wrong. Finally, he dropped his eyes and pushed back his chair. The heels of his sandals scraped as he stretched his legs. His chin fell on his chest. Elbows on the arms of his chair, the backs of his fingers cupping his chin, he thought it out.

'May I, too, urge that we follow your usual plan of consolidation, lord?' Veera Singha quietly intervened. Without moving his face, Gamini lifted his eyes to the War Minister. Veera Singha was a hard man. You could tell that from the cut of his features. His advice would not come from the gentleness of Vasabha. 'That will give the impression that we do not set much store by Prince Rodana's capture. Erroneous, but necessary. Meanwhile, we will find out through our normal channels where the Prince has been taken. Once we have the details, we can organize a rescue. I will personally lead it, I assure you, lord. If any harm is to befall the Prince, it will happen before we fight our way to Anu.' A grim note entered his voice. 'I hate to sound like a prophet of doom, but you know the Chola's methods. We would not want to reach Anu and find the Prince hanging from the battlements.'

The hall was very still as Gamini swung between his love for me and his destiny. Nothing disturbed the silence. The men present seemed to sense that this was his battle and he had to fight it alone. They sat erect, waiting for his decision.

Gamini lifted his chin and sat upright, gripping the arms of his chair. 'It shall be as you advise,' he stated firmly. 'But if we do not have word of Prince Rodana's whereabouts in one week, we advance on Anu.'

I did not know where I was. After Digha Jantu intercepted

us, the wagon carrying me, a wounded prisoner, had rattled for about twenty minutes through the streets of Anu to the clip-clop of hooves moving at a fast trot. My escort from the Vijitapura fortress had left – gleefully, I could tell – to spend the money Digha Jantu had given them. My new escort had to be the Chief Warrior's men. When we finally stopped, I was dragged from my stretcher, despite the protests of the physician, and forced to stand up, blinking in the bright morning sunlight.

I was in some sort of army camp, judging from the half-walls of red brick and the grey coconut-thatch roofs of the barracks buildings, the straight river-sand walkways and the inevitable signposts in the Chola language.

The cavalry escort dismounted and I was marched under an infantry guard of twelve giant Cholas to a solid building which I took to be the camp headquarters. We proceeded through an entrance hall scattered with curious soldiers, some squatting on the ground before low tables, down a passageway and into a dim-lit room. I was pushed inside. The room was long and narrow, with granite floors, brick walls reaching to the roof and no windows. The only light was a single unwavering taper on a wall, its eerie glow falling upon the gloom without being able to dispel it. I could distinguish the paraphernalia of the torture chamber neatly stacked in the far corner of the room: a rack, iron balls and chains, spikes, long tapers and the stocks. The furniture was a bare teakwood table in the centre of the room, with a high-backed wooden chair on one side and two white-cushioned chairs on the other.

The sergeant shoved me onto the high-backed chair. I was so tired and aching that I was glad to be able to sit down, even in these inhospitable surroundings. I practically collapsed on the chair with my arms outstretched, my head on the table.

The guards left the room, leaving me alone with the sergeant. He took up a position immediately behind me and stood there, waiting. The door closed with a bang.

After what seemed like hours the door opened again. The sergeant stiffened. I sensed his salute. I did not have to raise my head to know that Digha Jantu had entered.

The Chief Warrior stalked up to one of the two chairs opposite me. It grated as he pushed it back and sat down. I lifted my head with an effort and opened my eyes. One look at his face connected with my premonitions. The first, I had experienced in King Elara's court as a boy; the next, while waiting at Ambati; the last one, but a day ago.

Digha Jantu stared at me. His eyes were small and beady, incongruous in the face of a man whose massive size dwarfed the table. What shocked me, however, was the feel of incipient madness in him. It made my toes begin to curl.

He came to the point without preliminaries. 'I am Digha Jantu, Chief Warrior of King Elara,' he asserted. 'You are Prince Rodana, friend and constant companion of Gamini, who calls himself King of Ruhuna. You are said to be a *brachmachariya*, so you don't take women, but I suspect your king's affection is for your ass.'

I was stunned. Then anger possessed me. I kept my head up with a great effort and outstared him. 'You are wrong, Chief Warrior,' I said hoarsely. 'My king is married and has a child. He has proven that he has no need for men. You, on the other hand, are neither married, nor a father, nor a *brachmachariya*. Can it be that having no seed, you dare not take a woman? Certainly it is reported that you coerce young soldiers against their will. They must surely have to work hard to give life to your manhood.' I could not hold my head up any longer. It flopped back on my outstretched arms.

I could feel Digha Jantu's venom injected into his silence, but I no longer cared. 'For that, too, you shall pay, bastard prince,' he finally stated very quietly.

The minutes passed. I could not have raised my head even if I had wanted to – nor would it have mattered, for this man would do his worst regardless. Unbelievably, I found myself beginning to doze.

'What are your king's plans?' I heard Digha Jantu demand. There was a hysterical edge to his voice.

I remained silent. He was a fool if he thought I would tell him.

He asked me again, his voice sounding an ominous warning. I still gave him no reply. Something akin to a snore escaped me. 'For the last time, what are your king's plans?' Digha Jantu's normally high voice was pitched low. I could tell from the distending nostrils and reddening tip of his nose that he had reached the end of his normally low level of patience.

I heard a sharp exclamation and the scrape of his chair against the rough floor. His footsteps receded and ceased. There came the rasp of metal and the clack of his quick footsteps returning toward me. His hand fumbled momentarily on my body – I did not know why. He sliced through my bandages with his sword and ripped them off me. A sharp stab of agony began in my wound and scattered all around it. I stiffened.

'So it hurts, does it?' The giant's voice was still low. 'How about this?'

Pain seared in my wound and through me like the blaze of a burning arrow. I closed my eyes tight against it and clenched my teeth. It was a needle-pointed pain, digging deeper and deeper, flashing in all directions. My head jerked up. I stiffened again. A great gasp escaped me. The pain ground inside and all around. My stomach grew weak. My entire back was aflame. He had placed his sword point on the raw wound and was grinding away at it.

The pain became unbearable. The blood rushed to my head. The room started to spin around me.

Suddenly, a flash of light appeared before my closed eyes. It flamed brighter and brighter, spinning toward me, seeming to encompass the whole room. My pain began to ease. Finally, the light stopped spinning. In its centre I saw the face of my uncle, Prince Vipula. His deep voice emerged. 'Courage, Prince! Remember what you learned as a *bhikku*. Remember all this and never, never submit or yield.'

The light started to spin back into the gloom of the chamber. The pain returned, cascading in great waves. I conjured up all my training as a monk. An urgent voice whispered in my brain that it was for this one event that I had received my training and endured so much in my boyhood.

I pushed the pain back to its source, the sword point in my wound. All else was but the response of my mind to that pain, sending signals to my entire body to combat it and receiving back in turn the demands of the body for help. I then withdrew the receiving end of my mind from that source, my wound, isolating it as if it were no part of me. In my weakened condition, it took me shuddering minutes of seesawing between my goal and nature's dictates, minutes of untold agony, but I finally won. Although the excruciating pain was alive, it had ceased to shoot all over me. It was outside the me of my locked mind. My back was, for Digha Jantu's purpose, dead, and my mind looked upon it as a twitching corpse, even if I could not control the stale sweat that oozed from me. He would never get even a gasp from me now.

'So you are brave!' Digha Jantu sneered. 'Let us see how you respond to something different. You are our guest and must experience the infinite variety of our hospitality, Prince.' The way he spat the word 'prince' at me, I knew I was dealing with a maniac who hated royalty. Was it only because King Elara was not of royal blood that Digha Jantu could serve him?

I barely heard him stride to the far end of the room. As he fumbled with the instruments of torture, I wondered which he would select.

Digha Jantu returned and flung something on the table. It

clattered lightly. He came up to me and grabbed my right palm. His rough hand shifted to my thumb. He jabbed violently into it beneath the nail. My mind was unprepared to protect this new part of me. The raw pain streaked through me like fire, almost reaching my heart. My hand jerked back, but he held it with his horny fingers as if it were in a vice. He had stuck a taper in my thumb. He would stick tapers into each of my other fingers and set fire to them, I knew.

I steadied myself as he moved to my forefinger and seized a second taper. My mind was ready as he stuck it in. This time, there was neither sound nor movement from me. I had consigned my entire hand to death from my mind. When he had stuck all the tapers into my fingers, I could feel fierce areas of pain, but they, too, were isolated from me. My only direct consciousness was the warmth of the tapers and the sickly, sour smell of my sweat mingling with the pungent odour of the flare.

'Now tell me your king's plans, or I shall set fire to the tapers!' the giant growled. I noted a hint of discomfort in his voice. He had obviously thought that princes were soft. My unexpected fortitude puzzled him.

Digha Jantu released my hand. It flopped back on the table, sending five ribbons of pain up my arm. I controlled them and kept my silence.

I heard Digha Jantu walk to the single lighted flare in the room and distinguished the soft flaming of another taper, newly lit. He returned slowly to me. The heat of the lighted taper approached my hand. I steeled myself for the new agony. 'Hold him!' he commanded.

The sergeant reached from behind me and held my hands down.

The torture began slowly. As the flame from the five tapers approached my nails, the pain became more intense. Soon my nails began to burn, then the flesh around them was seared. The smell of burning nails and flesh smote me.

The pain became excruciating. My fingers quivered, stuck there, unable to withdraw from the agony. I had steeled my mind to isolate this unbelievable torture, but I was near fainting.

'If you don't want to betray your king's plans, write him an *ola*.' There was a hint of desperation in the Chief Warrior's voice, almost a plea. He did not know what to do in the face of my resistance.

My fingers were beginning to char.

'Tell him to withdraw to Ruhuna and I will return you to him,' the giant declared.

My pride summoned up some last remnants of energy. I strove with might and main to raise my head. But for my pride, I could not have done it. My head was glowing as with molten metal, heavy as an iron ball. I finally lifted it a few inches off the table. Now I had to open my eyelids. They were heavier than sluice gates, but I widened them a fraction. I saw my outstretched hand on the table. The five small tapers were burning steadily on raw and blackened fingers. I gazed at them stupidly, curiously. Surely these were tapers lit before an altar. I wanted to look up at Digha Jantu, but my eyeballs were stuck in their sockets. Only with a superhuman effort of will was I able to roll them up to him.

With detached curiosity, I studied the flat, ugly face, almost yellow in that light. I took in the ugly curve of the tip of the nose over the upper lip, the bestial flare of the nostrils, the high colour of him. I noted the eyes, small but maniacal. You are an obscenity, I decided.

'You are the great writer!' the giant urged. He was almost begging now. 'Only agree to write to your king and you can save your hand from destruction. Think! Otherwise you may may never write again.'

I looked at him, my head shaking and quivering like a puppet's, sweat pouring down my face. My eyes held his with scorn. I tried to speak. Words would not emerge – only harsh croaks from deep in my throat. The sweat began to blind me, but not before I conveyed the message of my eyes: the message of a prince to a barbarian.

My neck went numb. I could not hold myself up any longer. My head dropped onto the table with a thud. The room smelled of vomit. Not mine, but relics of some poor devil who had once sat at the table.

A low growl, almost of anguish, escaped the giant. 'You son of a bitch!' he mouthed. I heard a clatter on the table, a sharp swish through the air, then felt a great smash. Pain tore across my right wrist as if a blazing brand had slashed through it. Excruciating agony shot up my arm and spread toward my heart so that it nearly stopped beating. I reached desperately for breath. My mouth was parched, my lips dry. Fire reached into my mind, blackening it, but stars spun in the darkness. My arm quivered and trembled involuntarily.

Slowly a numbness entered the hand. Blessed relief. Blessed, blessed relief. The blackness began clearing. With a supreme effort, I half opened my eyes. The sword blade shone across my bloody wrist, the point stuck in the table.

My gaze travelled a little further. Five tapers still flamed on my charred fingers, like candles before an altar – but they were farther away from the altar of my hand than before. My family ring winked its great ruby blood-light.

It took me several moments to realize that Digha Jantu had severed my hand at the wrist. My first thought was: Now at least I will not have scarred fingers.

Chapter 65

Music from the dreamy heartstrings of a *sitar* spilled out of the tavern and faded into the dark. Beneath its liquid tinkle, an occasional drumbeat pulsed almost whimsically.

The Sinhala appeared to be casual, but his senses acutely took in the scene. He looked like an average man, but then this was his talent – to pass unnoticed, just anyone in a crowd. He walked boldly into the tavern and threaded his way through the crowd of guests sitting on low stools along the walls, or on cushions behind black wooden tables. Every race was present in the room, listening to the music of Shankar, the great sitar player from Madura, and marvelling at the virtuosity of Anil, the Sinhala drummer, who could even make his two *tablas* sing a scale. Singer and drummer were seated on the floor of a carpeted platform at the far end of the room. Tapers threw fitful light and long shadows on them. Shankar was bent intently over his long-stringed instrument and Anil squatted erect before his *tablas*.

Chola, most of them in uniform, Sinhala, Dasa, Bengali, Arabi, Malayali, Siami, Burma, even a Cheena were crowded into the tavern this night to pay homage to the two masters. Refreshments, including *vadai*, *boosu*, sweet drinks, *nannar*, sherbet and the heady drink, *sura*, were only served between musical renderings. The players were never interrupted.

So engrossed was the audience in the music that no one even glanced at the Sinhala as he moved through the room to a door directly opposite the entrance. He closed the door behind him and walked down the familiar dimly lit passage. He paused at the third door to his left and rapped on the wooden door three times, then three times more, then once again, then listened. The muffled sound of someone's throat being cleared reached him. The door swung silently inward. He slipped into the unlighted room, making no attempt to attune his eyes to the gloom.

'You have something important to report?' A hoarse voice whispered the question.

'Yes,' the Sinhala replied.

'Proceed.'

640

'A prince of the royal blood was taken prisoner at Vijitapura. He had been wounded there and Selliah, the fortress commander, sent him with an escort to King Elara. The escort was stopped at the south gate by the Chief Warrior, Digha Jantu, who took over the prisoner. They did not go to the palace, but to Army Barracks Number One, where Digha Jantu has his headquarters. The prisoner refused, under torture, to give information or sign an *ola* requesting King Gamini to withdraw to Ruhuna. Digha Jantu thereupon chopped off his right hand. He would have died of shock, or later of gangrene, but for the ministrations of a Chola physician named Ratnam, whom Selliah had sent to look after him.'

'When did it happen?'

'This noon.'

'Do you know the name of the prince?'

'Yes, he is Prince Rodana, said to be King Gamini's closest friend.'

Silence betrayed the knowledge of the other man, whom the Sinhala had reported to for more than two decades. The ears in the darkness had received his words; the voice in the darkness had given him orders. Now, for the first time, he sensed emotion in that darkness.

'Do you know where the Prince is presently located?' The voice was more hoarse than before.

'Yes, in the prison hospital at Barracks Number One.'

'Thank you. The news is indeed appalling. You were right to seek an immediate meeting. You have done extremely well and shall be rewarded with extra money in the usual way. Go now. We shall meet again at the appointed date, or earlier if you need to give us special news.'

The Sinhala instinctively made the palms-together greeting in the blackness of the room. He never knew whether or not the gesture was observed, or returned. During all these years, he neither had suspected nor questioned the identity of the man he served.

He slipped out of the room, then made his way along the passage and out of the tavern, this time through the back door. He moved swiftly through the dark toward his home, some distance away at the other end of the city. He did not know that for the first time in more than two decades he was being followed.

On the fifth night following the taking of Vijitapura, Gamini sat with his war council at the long table in the conference chamber for his regular meeting with them. He knew he was showing signs of strain. His looking glass had revealed dark circles around his eyes, making his face seem heavier and darker than usual. He who prided himself on never displaying emotions was revealing their result – the effect of sleepless nights. I was gone and he was not a whole person without his shadow. He was lonely and afraid for my safety. This king who laughed at danger on the battlefield was sick with worry at the peril to the one man he loved.

'You were right to counsel restraint,' Gamini admitted to the men around the table. 'Now we shall turn this to our advantage. Our entire army shall operate from Vijitapura. That shall become our first base, with reserve bases at Ambati, Wera and Kimbul. In addition to being a base, Vijitapura shall also become our citadel. We shall administer the government of Ruhuna and the occupied territories from here. Our next objective, however, shall be the Kahagalla plain.' His dark finger stabbed at the map on the table. 'We shall bypass all the forts in between. At some point in time, the main body of the Chola forces will move against us from Anu, drawing in their reserves from Seru. When we are assured of this, our Dighavapi reserves will move up to Soma and our existing forces in Soma will cross the river and take Seru, aided by Sinhala patriots who are already harrying the Chola forces there in increasing numbers. Having taken Seru, they will immediately sweep farther north, then westward to link up with the forces of our cousin of Malaya, who will simultaneously have crossed the Kelani River and pushed toward the highway north of Anu. By these flanking movements, we will virtually encircle Anu, but it is vital that they take place only after we are assured that the main body of the Chola is indeed moving against us. The strategy of this plan is obvious.'

Gamini turned to Veera Singha and the others with shining eyes. 'The Chola's plan was to wear us down as we jogged from one fort to the next, until we finally stopped, our resources stretched, our momentum lost, our morale sapped. He would then have hit us with everything. Now the reverse has happened. We are not wasting time and men. We will soon be in a position to cut off his supply lines. He will have to come out and fight, or be starved into submission. We shall await him at the Kahagalla plain.'

'Why not push directly for Anu, from Kahagalla, after establishing an advance base there?' Jagat, the grizzled cavalry commander, inquired.

'We desire to beat the enemy in open battle,' Gamini replied quietly. 'This is important both militarily and politically. Our people will only believe that Lanka is finally Sinhala when we have vanquished the Chola army. Besides, if we advance on Anu and surround it, we could be stalemated at the peak of our campaign. It might even turn victory to defeat. No! We shall fight the enemy at Kahagalla, on ground of our own choosing.'

'What if the Chola does not advance from Anu, sire?' the dwarf Gotha inquired.

Gamini smiled. 'Never fear – given enough time, he will. Look at it from his point of view. When he is threatened from three sides, his supply situation near desperation point, his political position that of any army of occupation, he will have to turn and fight, hoping to decide the issue in one great battle.'

'Elara might send to Chola country for aid,' Veera Singha

ventured. 'Bhalluka, the king there, is his brother.'

'Possibly,' Gamini responded. 'But we are counting on a certain group within his ranks to speed things up.'

The eyes of all the men around the table suddenly focused on Gamini.

'And that, sire?' Veera Singha inquired.

'Digha Jantu and the nineteen other Champions,' Gamini answered grimly.

It is said that you dare not utter the name of a devil-god lest he or his emissary appear. At that very moment, the guard commander knocked at the door and entered. 'Sire, pray forgive this intrusion,' he begged from his position of low obeisance, 'but we have Chola messengers under a flag of truce from the Chief Warrior, Digha Jantu.'

Gamini felt a throb of apprehension in his stomach, then reason returned swiftly. Messengers under a flag of truce could only mean a request for the end of hostilities. What were the conditions? He would accept nothing less than unconditional surrender. Let the emissaries come. He would return them with a historic reply! He pushed back his chair, stretching his right leg out in easy relaxation. 'Send the chief messenger in!' he directed.

The guard commander rose and left the room. The men around the table looked at Gamini. The Chola wishes to make peace, they seemed to say. He nodded to confirm that he shared their feelings of triumph. The murmur of voices rose as private discussions began around the table. It died down when the guard commander returned to announce the visitor. 'Warrior General Appa Durai, emissary of Chief Warrior Digha Jantu!'

The man who entered the room was a tall, grey-haired veteran of dark countenance and commanding appearance. His cheeks were almost gaunt; his lean body, in a tight-fitting white tunic, seemed hard as board. Fearlessly he took in the company, his gaze ending with Gamini. He placed a small wooden box on the floor and made obeisance.

A question made Gamini's temples begin to pulse. Why was this man the emissary of the Chief Warrior and not of the King?

Appa Durai picked up his box. Rising to his feet, he awaited Gamini's command to advance.

'You may present your message, Warrior,' Gamini directed.

The warrior strode to Gamini. Bending one knee, he extended both hands, holding up the black ebony box bound in brass.

Puzzled, Gamini accepted the box and placed it before him on the conference table. Something scratched at his memory, but he could not identify it.

Appa Durai felt inside his tunic and produced an *ola*, which he now proffered. Gamini accepted the *ola*, merely staring at it. Appa Durai rose to stand erect before him.

All eyes were turned to Gamini. Silence gripped the room. There had to be drama ahead.

Gamini continued staring at the *ola* for long moments. He did not wish to open it. He was suddenly afraid to read the words it would contain. Finally pride moved him. He unrolled the *ola*, held it up to catch the light of a taper and read aloud:

> 'To Abhaya Gamini, King of Ruhuna, Digha Jantu, Chief Warrior of Lanka, makes salutation. I urge you to retire to Ruhuna and be content with your former territory. Proceeding on your present course can only result in defeat for you and much regret. Your dear friend, Prince Rodana, is a hostage in my hands. Withdraw and we will not pursue you, but will return your friend to you. Advance and he will die. So will you. You cannot win. I send you, with this *ola*, a token of my word.'

'Is your Chief Warrior trying to bribe us?' Gamini flamed at Appa Durai, his eyes on the box.

The warrior smiled sardonically. 'In spite of my rank, I am but a messenger, lord,' he declared.

Gamini flung the *ola* on the table. His chair scraped on the granite floor as he drew it closer. He reached out resolutely for the box, undid the brass clasp and opened the lid. He gazed, uncomprehending, at the contents.

'Your chief must be mad! What kind of token is this?' He half stretched his right hand to the box. A sweet, sickly smell combined with a heady scent was wafted to his nostrils. Resting on a bed of bay leaves, one end packed tight with white cloth, was something mutilated and charred . . . a human hand! The skin on the long, slender fingers was dry and cracked. On the middle finger, a jewelled ring hung loosely, its great ruby winking blood-light.

Gamini recognized the ring immediately as the family ring I always wore, the ring I had inherited from Prince Vipula. 'The fiend!' he choked. 'The unspeakable fiend!'

Gamini's eyes drifted to the box. Now he knew why it seemed familiar. It was in a similar box, only larger, that he had once delivered to his father the present of a woman's clothes and ornaments. Dear *devas*, this is my *kharma*, my punishment, he thought with dread. He shook his head violently, but could not escape the conclusion.

'Dhusta Gamini! . . . Dhusta Gamini!' His father's words echoed out of him like air from a dying man's lungs.

For two days, I lay between life and death. I would have died were it not for the physician, Ratnam.

The last I remembered of the grisly episode when Digha Jantu chopped off my hand was the shining sword blade stuck on the wooden table, partly obscuring the tapers still burning beneath my fingernails and the sight of the great ruby on the jewelled family ring of my uncle, Prince Vipula.

Digha Jantu had given orders for my care. Alive, I was still a valuable hostage. Dead, I was of no use to him. Under his orders, I was removed on a stretcher to a room in the barracks hospital. Ratnam was given orders to ensure that I did not die.

The physician had nowhere else to go, no other patient. He applied powders to stop the bleeding of my wound and *patthus* to prevent gangrene setting in. When I regained consciousness, he told me of the fall of Vijitapura to comfort me. He gave me sedatives to keep me quiet and to bestow on me much-needed sleep, knowing that my mind needed time to adjust to my new condition. During occasional moments of waking, I slowly began to grasp the situation. When I awoke again, I knew I had to face up to the facts of life minus one hand.

As if God himself was merely waiting for some slight act of faith on my part to reveal great truths to me, His force sent my mind spinning back through all the years of my life. In the dark hours of pain, fear, regret and 'if only' that followed, I realized that I had not really suffered at all in the past, in comparison with what I now endured – so what I had regarded as misfortunes before were in fact less dire. But relative to what? To my present misery? No, that did not go far enough. Worse could lie ahead, so it had to be: relative to the worst that my mind could conjure as being painful, anguished or hateful.

So the final arbiter of my degree of suffering – indeed, of whether I suffered at all – was not God, but me. My plight was of my own seeking. So many alternatives to becoming involved in this war had been available to me, but I had chosen to serve a warrior-king.

My mind started to charge forward, then, toward other truths, like a horse whose stable door had been opened. Human beings have freedom of choice, but not free will. We are creatures of reflex. Our responses, our selection from a choice of alternatives, can be no different at the time they are offered, even when that selection seems to be the product of thought and deep consideration. Was my supposed selection then a destiny imposed by God?

From somewhere deep inside me, the products of my thinking, faith and experience arose to guide me. These were products of my own creation, responses to save me from a situation far more dire than the torture I had undergone and the loss of a hand.

I decided calmly to follow the course of honour. I not only believed in God, I knew Him – so I would honour Him by accepting the responsibility for my own actions. God had nothing to do with my being in this war. I, product of His substance, had become Gamini's companion because of the nature I had given my substance during my lifetime. If my body was now maimed in consequence, I alone could save my mind and spirit. I could only do so with God's help, like a child who has erred, seeking a father's counsel and aid. There are those who would say I reasoned thus because, never having had parents, I had a deep-rooted need for them. That need I will not deny, though once I grew up I only experienced it as a regret. But I challenge those who make this accusation to have a hand chopped off and see whether any deep-rooted need will act as solace, rather than a cup of added bitterness.

I became calmer before these truths. I wish I could say that the knowledge solved everything! Far from it. What I had to learn was not just to live with it hour by hour, minute by minute, putting up with the knowledge and the drawbacks, but to absorb it into my *prana*, which was its superior, as blood sometimes absorbs poison and neutralizes it. That would take months, even years, but I possessed a strong will and a good mind for accepting what I could not change. What I *could* change was my reaction – and that I would use all my strength to accomplish.

Now I began to appraise the effects of being maimed.

My first horror was at never being able to write again. All the fine craft of which I was capable, the upright letters, thin at the top and bottom, full on the sides, would be no more! Then came the realization that I could never bear arms again. I did not know whether to be glad or sorry, until I realized that I only wanted and needed those skills to fight beside Gamini and protect him. I suddenly felt the aura of my love for Gamini, like a mantle with which I desired to enfold him. The tears flowed for the first time since I had lain on my bed of pain.

Through these tears of love, I glimpsed the knowledge that God somehow wanted this adversity for me, though I had caused it myself, to save my immortal *prana* from building up any more cruelty. It gave me fierce joy. From the love of God that released it emerged resolve to demonstrate my all-encompassing love, if I ever got back to Gamini, by riding alongside him in battles of whatever sort, even though I could not bear arms.

I thought on through the late hours of darkness until I suddenly became aware of a throbbing, stabbing pain at the back of my head from the wound in my back. Everything is relative! The loss of my hand had made me forget the wound I had suffered at Vijitapura.

In that heightened state of mental and physical awareness, I heard the door of my cell-like room softly open.

Who could it be?

My heart thudded with apprehension. Had Digha Jantu sent assassins to kill me off in the darkness? If so, what should I do – fight a last desperate fight? Try to kill as many of them as possible, with my head, my single hand, my teeth, my feet?

A faint beam of light came from the open door. It widened. The figure of a man became outlined in it.

I decided then that I would not fight. I had just been vouchsafed supreme knowledge. I would not allow my immortal *prana* to be stained by violence just to protect my own life. I would take whatever form of death was meted out to me silently and with dignity. Gamini would be pleased, if he knew. I found myself smiling in the darkness.

Four men filtered into the room.

'Prince!' a voice said softly in that silent darkness. 'Are you awake?'

A thrill ran through my body. The words were spoken in Sinhala. 'Yes,' I replied quietly.

'We are Sinhala. We have come to rescue you.'

'The *devas* be praised. But who are you? How did you get in?'

'It's only how we get out that matters. We must hurry, so listen. You will be taken out on a stretcher, as a corpse. You will travel out of the barracks gates in the funeral wagon for Chola soldiers, we have ... er ... commissioned. Your physician, Ratnam, is co-operating. He has given us the necessary certifying *olas* to get us out of the gates of the city in the hour before dawn set aside for wagons of the dead to leave for the mass burial grounds. He will meet us outside the city and accompany you back to the Sinhala lines.'

'What if we are discovered?'

'Then you will join the corpses, for we cannot risk your remaining a hostage.'

Chapter 66

For long moments, Gamini stared wide-eyed at the dried-up hand. A hushed voice finally emerged from him. 'It is the hand of Prince Rodana! Digha Jantu has sent it to us. He says that if we do not retire to Ruhuna, the body will follow.'

In the shocked silence that gripped the room, he reached out trembling fingers. He touched the hand that had taught him the finer points of writing. It felt hard and dry. Involuntarily his fingers jerked back. With an effort, he reached out and grasped the hand. He raised it gently and held it up for all to see.

Someone gasped. Well may you gasp, Gamini thought. I wish I could end my own anguish with a gasp.

Gently, he replaced the hand on the green leaves inside the box. 'The ring shall remain there until the Prince's return!' he declared, his voice calm. He was to all appearances his normal self again.

'Do you mean that we will withdraw, lord?' Veera Singha inquired in a hushed voice.

Ignoring the question, Gamini turned to Appa Durai. 'We shall need seven days to consider your Chief Warrior's demand,' he said levelly. 'We shall hold our position here until then. Go you back on the morrow, leaving your escort commander behind, and deliver that message to your chief.' He choked slightly. 'In the absence of the foremost writer of the realm, we cannot offer the courtesy of a reply on *ola*.' His voice hardened. 'But say you this also to your master. Regardless of our actions, if any further harm comes to Prince Rodana we shall tear him limb from limb.' His eyes dropped to the ebony box. 'As for this act of barbarism, it shall be avenged.'

Appa Durai blanched before the quiet ferocity of Gamini's face. He made obeisance.

'See that the warrior is quartered according to his rank!' Gamini commanded his cavalry captain.

Barely had the door closed behind the two men when voices broke loose in the hall, all more concerned with the strategy than with me.

'We have come too far to retreat.'

'How shall we account to the thousands who died for our cause, if we abandon it for one life?'

The questions and protests grew to a crescendo, then slowly died down before Gamini's level gaze.

'You do not know us,' Gamini stated flatly when the last murmur had subsided, 'but you will learn.' He stood up and the men rose to their feet. He gathered up the box and clutched it to his chest. Head erect, he stalked out of the room.

The death wagon in which I lay with stiff, cold corpses reached the barracks gates without incident.

'How many today, Pillai?' One of the guards shouted the inquiry. Our men were obviously playing the role of Cholas.

'Only three!' a voice from the front of the wagon responded with a perfect Chola accent. 'At this rate my wife and children will starve.'

'You are a ghoul!' the guard exclaimed with a laugh. 'What a way to live – on the price of burying the dead!'

'Isn't your profession much the same?' the driver demanded insolently. 'You get paid for killing men. We get paid for burying them. Which is worse?'

The guard laughed heartily. 'True! True!' he exclaimed. 'Now show me your pass and get along with you before decent people waken.'

Moments of anxiety followed, during which I heard the rustle of *ola*. I held my breath.

'All in order!' The Chola rapped the yoke of the wagon with a weapon. 'Open the gates!'

The wagon rattled on for about fifteen minutes before slowing down once more. It finally stopped with a creaking and screech of wood and metal.

The silence that followed was ominous. My stomach contracted. We had to have arrived at the north gate of the capital, the last obstacle. Once through these gates, our chances of safety were excellent. I wondered insanely whether the beating of my heart showed against the sheet that lay over my body, atop the pile of stiff corpses.

'How many today?' This time, the guard's voice was almost surly.

'Only three, lord.' The driver sounded servile.

'I have told you before not to "lord" me!' The Chola's

652

voice was angry now. I wondered why the driver had deliberately provoked him. 'I am just a simple Chola soldier.'

'All men are lord to us of the lowest caste, lord,' the driver whined. 'How else shall I address our lords and masters but as lord?'

'You are impertinent in your servility,' the Chola shouted back.

'Each morning you are here, I pray you to forgive me, lord,' the man pleaded. 'I do so again now.'

'Bah! Low-caste dogs! Always whining. One more word from you and I'll clap you in the stocks.'

'And let my corpses rot here, lord? Who else but low-caste men will do this dog's work? Besides' – the driver paused and a crafty note entered his voice – 'there is talk of an epidemic of the black death in this city.'

'You talk too much!' the Chola retorted, but his voice had lost some of its irritation. 'Here's your pass.'

'Thank you! Thank you, lord!' the fellow replied.

'Let me inspect your corpses!'

Fear shot through my guts like a cold steel blade, making them go weak. The clump of footsteps came toward the rear of the wagon. I prepared to sag and hold my breath.

'Yes! Yes, lord, by all means allow me to draw back the curtain and reveal to you the black death!'

'Bah!' the Chola muttered hastily. 'I have no fear of any death, but why inspect corpses in the face of a physician's certificate?' He clumped away and my guts uncoiled.

'Chuk-pita-muk!' We were off again. Soon we were well beyond the gates, trundling merrily along the main highway to the drumbeat of our bullocks' hooves.

Chapter 67

Within four days of the delivery of Digha Jantu's message to
him, Gamini learned of my escape, but he waited until the
seventh day before sending the Chola escort commander
back to King Elara's Chief Warrior with a simple message
on *ola* from his own Chief Warrior, Velu Sumana.

> To Digha Jantu, Chief Warrior, I, Velu
> Sumana, Chief Warrior to King Abhaya Gamini,
> send this message. You are presumptuous to
> address a king except through your own sovereign.

That was all.

Gamini remained in Vijitapura one month. Raji and the
Queen Mother rejoined him there with the other ladies, but
only briefly, for at the end of the month of Jetta, having
organized Vijitapura as a sub-capital, Gamini moved north
toward Anu. As planned, he bypassed all the intervening
Chola forts. Consequently he encountered no resistance on
his route.

He stopped and made camp on the southern end of the
Kahagalla plain. This was a vast stretch of open ground,
tufted by clumps of grass and surrounded by clusters of low,
tree-shaded hills, with marshy ground in the re-entrants of
the hills to the south. Its name was derived from tall groups
of rocks, each with its own peak, all yellow in certain light.

Travelling only on foot, I was disguised, ironically
enough, as a Buddhist monk, complete with shaven head.
Finally I was playing the role for which I once had been
trained. Each time I left Anu, I seemed destined for the
yellow robe! This time, however, I welcomed it, not the least

because I could hide my stump in the folds of the robe. Spies and patrols would definitely be on the lookout for a man missing a right hand.

It took exactly forty days before I reached Gamini's encampment. By then, the stump of my hand had healed into a raw red knob, thanks to the ministrations of the physician, Ratnam, who had accompanied me.

I was so happy and excited I did not recognize the grey-haired veteran who commanded the sentry outpost. Only when he introduced himself to me did I remember the cavalry officer who had escorted me from the border to Mahagama on my first visit to Ruhuna. That had been almost twenty years ago; he had to be over sixty today. 'So your wish was granted!' I exclaimed delightedly.

'Yes, Prince. I have been fortunate and you are kind to remember me. I am Sunil, who escorted you to Mahagama many years ago.'

The officer took me to a tent, where black pantaloons and white tunic had been laid out for my return. My first request, however, was for a bath. Sunil laughed and took me to the well. It was deserted, because the men generally did not like to bathe in the evening and invite the humours of night. What a joy it was to bathe in peace and security. The water cascaded silver from the bucket as I drew it and poured it over my head with my left hand. I was acquiring dexterity with that hand. Sunil observed me, but made no comment.

When I had dried myself and changed into my new clothes, I mounted a horse provided me, bade Sunil farewell and was escorted to Gamini's headquarters.

As we approached, I saw it located on a tree-shaded hill overlooking the stretch of plain, which lay pale amber in the evening light.

Gamini was reported to be at his usual meeting with his commanders. We were led to a large, thatched-roof hut erected to serve as headquarters and conference room. After dismounting, we were ushered in without challenge. My heart leaped at the sight of Gamini sitting dark and erect at the far end of the wooden conference table. How would he greet me?

Everyone stood up when I entered, including Gamini, who rose for no one. The tears sprang to my eyes. The King had risen for me. I made deep obeisance to him, my good hand on my forehead, the stump of the other awkwardly to it.

'Rise, Prince!' Gamini directed gruffly. 'You are most welcome!'

I stood up and looked at his beloved face and solid form. He was leaner and tougher. The broad features had completely shed even muscle. Otherwise he was the person I had ridden with that sunny morning when we attacked Vijitapura, a lifetime ago. In that instant I felt I had come home again. Gamini was my home. He had been my home for many years. In fighting for him, I too had fought for hearth and home, like all his Sinhala soldiers.

'Your chair has been vacant these many weeks, Prince Rodana,' Gamini observed. 'You have neglected your duties!' As he indicated the chair beside him, I realized that it had been kept empty these forty days and more.

Once again my eyes misted. I walked erectly to the chair and waited for Gamini to be seated before taking my seat.

I do not remember what exactly transpired during that conference. I do recall, however, that Gamini treated me as if I had never been away, or as if I had not suffered the loss of a hand. He made no inquiry about it, nor any reference to it. Knowing his concern, I was grateful for such supreme sensitivity. I recognized without conceit that I had helped him toward this end, by inculcating in him the good manners and high standards of my uncle, Prince Vipula, which he had so eagerly learned.

My room in Gamini's hut awaited me after the conference. There, he and I exchanged news in private. Everything was normal again, except that I could not wield weapons. He listened thoughtfully while I told my story, exclaiming only when I told him of all Ratnam, the physician, had done for me.

Dinner was soon announced. It was served in a separate hut intended for the princes of the Ruhuna and Malaya courts, all of whom were now participating in the campaign. Gamini desired me to meet them.

This dining room was a large one, close to the headquarters hut. Sitting on Gamini's right, I could see the dark expanse of the plain before me. Immediately below, the gloom was dotted with the red-gold glow of our campfires spreading endlessly east and west. Above all was a burnished sky of low-hanging clouds. The sounds of our army kept rising through the dark air – a distant singing, some shouting, the shrill neighing of horses. Soon the room was filled with the delicious aromas of fried chicken, boiled rice and the sharper tang of curried jak-fruit, pulses and vegetables. It had been two months since I sat down to such a meal.

Some sixteen princes – all dressed, like us, in uniform black pantaloons and white tunics – were seated around us. At Gamini's left was a son of the King of Malaya, the young Prince Vijaya, who had been sent two weeks earlier to Gamini to learn the arts of war. He was about seventeen, lean, tall and clean-shaven, with dark eyes too closely set across a high-bridged nose. His father was now a useful ally of Gamini, but this could not excuse the Prince's haughty, aloof manner toward everyone save Gamini. I sensed some resentment in him of me from the moment we were introduced to each other, but set it down to youthful jealousy that would evaporate as soon as he understood and accepted Gamini's relationship with me. In any case, I was too happy at being back to allow anything so petty to affect me.

The attendant proffered the bowl of fried chicken to Gamini. He took a leg and placed it on his platter, which was already heaped with white rice, yellow and green curries and the little red chilis he loved for tincturing his meal.

The attendant bowed, moved to my left and proffered the bowl to me. It was the first time since my hand had been severed that I was eating from a communal bowl. Instinctively, I reached out with the stump of my right hand. Self-consciously, I withdrew it and raised my left hand instead.

Before I could even touch the chicken, Prince Vijaya's high voice cut in sharply. 'Just a moment, Prince Rodana!' he exclaimed. 'I pray you do not touch the chicken with your *left* hand. We, too, must partake of it!'

For a moment his words puzzled me; then the emphasis on the word *left* hand hit me with shattering force.

Sinhala and Chola alike are clean races. When we ease ourselves, whether it be of liquid or solid, we wash those parts well with the left hand. The right hand is therefore the only hygienic one for eating.

Shame rose from the pit of my stomach and suffused my face in a burning flush. I withdrew my hand as if it had been stung by a cobra. I stared incredulously at Prince Vijaya. His gaze was scornful. I looked around the table. Each one of the princes averted his eyes. This was the right response, whether they agreed with Prince Vijaya or were embarrassed by his rudeness.

Placing my left hand on the table, I started to rise.

Gamini's hand swept down on my wrist, holding me back with surprising strength. 'We did not give you leave to depart, Prince,' he said. His voice was gentle, but I did not need to look at him to recognize his suppressed fury.

I sat back on my chair, looking at Gamini for directions. His dark eyes were compelling. 'We are very tired tonight, cousin,' he said quietly. His eyes continued to hold mine. 'Will you not therefore please feed us?' He settled back expectantly in his chair.

I hesitated, moved beyond tears. Then I lifted the food to the conqueror's lips.

*   *   *

King Elara's first impulse upon being told that his twenty Great Warriors had assembled in his audience chamber and desired to meet him was to refuse the request. A king did not accept such a summons, least of all before daybreak. If the commanders wished to meet with him, they should have sought audience through the proper palace channels and he would have set a date and time for the meeting.

The message from the Great Warriors, however, had an ominous ring to it. King Elara had enough experience of politics to realize its possible implications. He therefore sent word back through the chief palace attendant that he would see the commanders shortly.

He deliberately kept them waiting almost an hour before he finally proceeded to the assembly chamber. He first finished his bath and the *pooja* ritual in his shrine room before the statue of Dhurga. Which form would she take today – the mother goddess, or Kali, goddess of death?

Birds had begun to sing in the pleasure garden outside his window when he finally left his quarters. In the first grey light of dawn, the palace corridors were deserted, save for sleepy-eyed guards. The King was unattended, by choice. He was accompanied only by the faithful Junda, who trotted at his heels. He felt no apprehension, merely a great calm.

The Great Warriors were in full regalia – red tunics, white pantaloons and swords. They rose and made obeisance. To the King's keen eye, it seemed that the huge Digha Jantu alone, from his place at the right of the gleaming brown-and-yellow tamarind-wood table, gave his greeting perfunctorily.

King Elara gravely returned the obeisance, took his place at the head of the table and bade the men be seated. They did so with a scraping of chairs and the clatter of scabbards. It was still too early for sunlight to stream in through the high windows, so the tapers had been relit by the attendants, who then remained standing outside. The twenty men looked solemn in the yellow light that struggled against the silver of approaching day. Some of them seemed uncomfortable. One cleared his throat noisily; another gave a rasping cough. Digha Jantu, however, was full of suppressed excitement.

'To what do we owe the honour of this meeting?' King Elara inquired when everyone was seated. He ran a hand over his silver hair and turned his deep eyes on Digha Jantu.

'We are in a state of emergency, sire, when normal routines must be set aside,' Digha Jantu responded, almost brusquely.

'It is customary in an emergency for the king to be attended also by his ministers,' the King rejoined. 'Shall we not send for them?'

'They are unavailable, sire!' Digha Jantu retorted.

'Unavailable?' The King raised puzzled eyebrows. 'Surely that is an extraordinary word, Chief Warrior? What has happened to them that they should be unavailable?'

'They are all under house arrest.'

A thrill ran through the King. He did not know whether it was the product of fear or surprise. He remained composed with a tremendous effort. 'And pray by whose orders are my ministers under house arrest?'

'By order of the Great Warriors.' Digha Jantu could not prevent his deep, raspy voice from trembling at his first words of open defiance of his king.

'Oh!' King Elara paused a moment, reflecting, calm eyes on Digha Jantu. Then his gaze swept slowly around the table. Every one of the men avoided his eyes. The King's upper lip curled in scorn. 'Are all of you Great Warriors behind this move?' he demanded.

There was no reply.

Digha Jantu turned a fierce gaze on his colleagues, all of whom avoided his glance too. Finally the small, piglike eyes returned to the King. 'I speak for them all!' Digha Jantu exclaimed angrily. 'If any of them desires to withdraw, now is his chance to do so!' He gave each of the men in turn a challenging look. None of them contradicted him. His face triumphant, he turned to the King once more, nodding as if there was no more to be said.

'Does the arrest of my ministers mean that you have established a military government?' King Elara calmly inquired.

'Yes.' Digha Jantu's chin lifted arrogantly.

'Why did you deem that necessary?'

'A good question, sire. I shall give you the answers. First, our capital city is surrounded for all purposes by Sinhala armies. Second, our Chola citizens in the north and east have been severed from the parent heart which gives them life-blood.'

'You are mistaken, Chief Warrior,' the King replied with an amused smile. 'As always happens when warriors interfere with the political process, you are indeed mistaken in your assessment.'

'With due deference, sire' – the deep new voice was that of Arasu, a veteran commander who had served the King since he first invaded Lanka – 'how can we expect a policy of attrition to benefit us, after it has already taken too heavy a toll?' His voice shook with passion. 'When do we soldiers recover pride and honour, our only possessions?'

King Elara looked at his old comrade-in-arms with sudden ferocity. 'Think you that we have no pride and honour?' he demanded harshly. 'Think you that we do not wait for the day when we can hurl the insolent Sinhala dogs back into the southern sea?'

'But when, lord? When?' Arasu almost implored.

'When our brother, Bhalluka, arrives from India with the twenty corps he is raising on our behalf!'

The room was filled with sudden silence, as after a thunderstorm. The warriors looked at King Elara, stunned. Why had he kept this news a secret?

The King pressed home his advantage. 'We are the sovereign,' he insisted. 'If we made a mistake, we alone must rectify it. We sent word to our royal brother on *ola* over ten weeks ago and received back his assurance of support. It

661

had to be a secret, a total secret, in order to catch the Sinhala. Our brother will sweep in from the northwest, smash the Sinhala there and join us at Anu, from where both armies will drive the Sinhala back to the southern ocean. Your interference has been premature and may have destroyed the entire plan.'

The shocked commanders looked at Digha Jantu for leadership. He was equal to the occasion. He stood up, drawing himself to his full height. 'And when will this army arrive, sire?' he demanded. 'After we have starved to death? Can you give us a precise, or even an approximate date for its arrival?'

King Elara was taken aback. The Chief Warrior pressed home his advantage. 'One month, perhaps? Six months? One year?' He paused to survey his comrades. 'And how does the Sinhala army grow?' He paused again, this time for effect. 'Not monthly, but daily, I say, my friends. This army once consisted of ten corps. Now, in the space of less than a year, it has grown to almost twenty-five corps, with most of Lanka to support it. I tell you, now is the time to give them battle, when we are outnumbered only two to one, for one Chola is the equal of three Sinhala.' His eyes were glaring and a wisp of foam flecked the side of his mouth.

In the stillness of the room, King Elara's sigh was a burden. 'You are clever, Chief Warrior,' he commented sadly. 'You have shown more brains than we credited you with. You compromised these men before you ever entered the room, by inducing them to take the irrevocable step of arresting our ministers. Not one of our commanders dares face up to the consequences of that treasonable act, even if we promise amnesty. No! They can only avoid the consequences of their hasty, lawless decision by remorselessly pursuing the course you have set for them. As for amnesty . . .' – his eyes surveyed the men thoughtfully – 'that will be out of the question. The King's justice will reach out to you all, the moment you relax your hold. So you are fully committed, and we must all pay the price.' His eyes gleamed as the old power surged through him. 'We are prepared.' He paused. 'Are you?'

The King rose to his feet and the generals rose with him. 'We see no reason for prolonging this meeting,' he declared. 'We shall do as you permit us, but only from the freedom of our position as your sovereign and according to the dictates of honour. We suspect that our armies are totally behind you, but our household guard remains loyal. This will at least ensure the integrity of our station. Good-bye. May the *devas* prosper your course of action.'

The King turned to leave, Junda at his heels.

'There is another very important consideration, sire, and it pertains to your very station.' Digha Jantu's deep, raspy voice rent the chamber, this time holding a note of chill warning.

The King paused in his stride. 'What is it, Chief Warrior?' he inquired over his shoulder.

'We recently apprehended a spy.' The Chief Warrior's voice was now like a hacking saw. 'After six weeks of torture we . . . persuaded him to speak.' He paused, obviously hoping to enjoy the effect he was creating. Getting no reaction from the King, he sawed away. 'This spy was part of an elaborate network that has operated from your court for over thirty years. We have seized them all and made an example of them.' He bared white teeth in a hideous grin. 'Now it remains to apprehend the leader.'

'Do you imply he is in our court?' The King's voice was sharp, but he was too proud to turn and face the Chief Warrior.

'Yes, sire.' There was open amusement now in the Chief Warrior's voice. 'The head of the Sinhala spy organization, an intricate and cleverly administered system of reporting everything about you, sire, your plans, the palace, your organization, who enters and leaves the city, is one of your most trusted aides.'

Slowly the King swivelled around to face the Chief Warrior. 'And who may that be, Chief Warrior? You had best have irrefutable evidence before you speak, for our justice is absolute and extends to those who make false charges against others.'

The Chief Warrior guffawed insolently, his great hand thrust forward, the large forefinger pointing. 'It is your court jester, Junda.'

Chapter 68

Years of ruling had trained King Elara to withstand any shock without betraying emotion. His training came through at this moment when he was perhaps more hard-pressed than he ever had been since he put his son to death. Not by the flicker of an eyelid did he lose his poise. He waited until Digha Jantu's laughter had died down before speaking.

'Such uncouth laughter in the presence of your sovereign ill befits anyone, least of all one of your station, Chief Warrior.' The King's reprimand was quiet and low. 'Had it occurred when we exercised power, we would have dealt with you adequately.' His mouth twitched in a grim smile. 'The matter which you report falls within our personal purview, we trust?' His questioning eyes took a poll of the commanders, deliberately excluding Digha Jantu. They all nodded as one. 'Very well, then. Since you say that all members of the spy organization have been seized and punished, it only remains to deal with its head. If the accused admits his crime, he shall suffer the King's justice. If he does not, we shall institute a thorough investigation. Come, chief jester!'

The King turned away and departed, followed by the silent dwarf. When they reached the study, the King closed the door behind them and walked through to enter his bedchamber. Junda hesitated a moment, then followed the King, who strode to the great canopied bed and sat down on it. He then motioned to the dwarf to sit on his little couch.

In the pale morning light of the room where he had bared himself so frequently to the dwarf almost every night these many years since his wife's death, King Elara faced the man who had betrayed him. He was sad and bewildered. His dark, hawklike features were strangely drawn and he could feel his cheeks sagging.

For long moments the King gazed at Junda, searching for a truth that would not hurt him. Whatever justification the dwarf had fortified himself with during the long years did not enable him to face that look. He turned away.

The King waited. The silence grew heavy.

'Sire, just as you are dedicated to the Chola cause, I am first and last a Sinhala.' The words came out of Junda suddenly, in a rush.

'Have I not been *dharmista* – a ruler of principle?'

'Sire, you should never have been ruler here at all. Our people would rather take their chances with a Sinhala tyrant than a *dharmista* foreigner, for then in the fullness of time, even in some future generation, at least they could expect a *dharmista* Sinhala sovereign as successor.'

The King sighed. His gaze wandered past the dwarf, across the length of the room, toward the open windows and the garden beyond, where birdsongs sparkled in the morning sunlight. 'How you must have hated us all these years!' he exclaimed, almost to himself.

'No! No, sire!' the dwarf broke in passionately. 'Never hatred for you as a man. Only love.'

'How can you separate the ruler, the usurper, from the man?'

'I don't know how, but I beg you to understand that I did.'

665

The dwarf stood up to his full height. Despite his grotesque appearance, he had an odd dignity. 'Please hear me out, sire,' he begged. 'I know my fate is sealed. That is no more than I told myself would happen. Some day I had to pay the price for my actions. A pleasant change, really, for life to make me pay for that over which I had some control! But it is important that you hear my explanation.'

King Elara looked at the dwarf, desiring to silence him. Instead he straightened his shoulders and nodded. 'Very well,' he agreed. 'You may speak.'

Junda began slowly, choosing his words with care. 'You never knew my innermost thoughts, my desires.'

The King interrupted him in astonishment. 'We never knew?' he demanded. 'Why, we have known you these – ' He stopped, looked away, reflecting. His eyelids blinked rapidly. He looked back at the dwarf in slow wonder.

Tears sprang to Junda's eyes. He hung his head a moment, then straightened up to look his master squarely in the face. 'Sire, I sometimes think that rulers become so preoccupied in their positions of power that they are incapable of the common touch. I could take the scorn of men, but each time you, whom I loved and do still love, spoke disparagingly of my size and appearance, you sent a flaming arrow through my heart.'

'Thoughtlessly done, jester,' the King broke in vehemently. 'Never intentional!'

'By your own law does that judge you, sire.' A hard note had entered the dwarf's voice.

The King's mind went instantly back to his judgement of his son, the thoughtless Prince Muthiah. A groan escaped him. His face broke up. Tragedy billowed within him in a great wave and engulfed his mind. 'By his court jester is the sovereign judged and sentenced.'

Real pity for his master entered the dwarf for the first time in his life. His immediate reaction was wonder at the reversal of the roles. 'Each time you addressed me insensitively, sire, it hardened my heart. I realized that I was seeking excuses for my own perfidious conduct, but you kept providing them. Your friendly words were frequently more harsh than the taunts of strangers who would mock me, jeer at me. They taught me what it is to be alone.' He paused, looking down at his tiny feet, while the King watched him with haunted eyes.

'There was, however, one role in which no one despised me, in which there was no pain . . . only the respect of those who reported to me, accepted my orders and executed them obediently – the area in which I was king.' A short laugh escaped the dwarf. 'In the darkness I was not a body – only ears, a voice and a brain.' He looked up at King Elara with sad amusement. 'You see, sire, being a king is really an illusion for us all, as you have so sadly discovered today. To you, your position was the reality and I your refuge. To me, you were the reality . . . the position I created, my refuge. All of it is reality . . . and all of it illusion!'

King Elara continued staring at Junda. 'So many years . . . Must we kill everyone we love?'

'I have done no more than hasten an inevitable process. We are all instruments of destiny to each other, because we are constantly providing the causes for the effects of others.' Junda's voice held a pleading note. 'I beg you, therefore, do not think of my actions as betrayal. Know that though your words to me through the years were used for purposes other than you anticipated, they were always received by one who loved you and knew only too well the anguish of wounds such as yours.'

The King smiled faintly then. 'Well spoken, our friend.' He leaned forward, placing an elbow on his knee and cupping his chin in his hand.

Both the dwarf and he knew that Junda's fate hung in the balance. What remained now was to pass sentence on the dwarf. He could decree torture, or torture and execution.

Suddenly King Elara saw a figure materializing outside

667

the window. Why, it was his beloved wife, Pushpa, walking in the garden. She turned, her kind eyes shining in the sunlight, and beckoned to him. He half rose from the bed.

The movement broke the spell. The figure of his wife vanished. Only the sunlight remained to mock him, and the jeering cry of a parakeet from the green branches. What message did Pushpa desire to give him? She had invited him. Where to? Where else but to space, where she dwelt as rain, free, reborn.

'You have spoken the truth and the truth shall set you free.' The King rose to his feet. His voice was grave but steady. 'You have indeed been one of the instruments of our destiny. You shall play your role to the end.' He paused, his giant frame somewhat stooped, to look down at the dwarf. 'We shall release you and have you smuggled back to your king.' His eyes twinkled at the dwarf's amazement. 'You shall tell him all that has transpired, but on your oath, no more. You shall convey to him a single honourable request from one sovereign to another. Will you do that?'

The dwarf nodded, speechless.

'When he stands with his armies outside the walls of Anu, there shall be no more senseless killing of brave men. He shall face me alone in mortal combat for the sovereignty. To this, I pledge my word. I pray that he will pledge his in return.'

He had conquered a whole kingdom. He had ruled it justly, with the power of life and death, for over thirty-five years. He had practised *dharma* to its fullest. Now it had come to this: the final outcome, a physical battle between him and a rival claimant! All he had left after all was a claim to gallantry. He had lived a deity. He would die a deity!

'What of Digha Jantu and the commanders, sire? Will they not seek vengeance on you for letting me escape? Surely you can put me to death and send some other messenger to King Gamini?'

'You have been delivered the King's justice, as he knows

how to administer it at this moment. Have no fear. The warriors still need us as a figurehead. They will not offer us further indignity, or harm.'

It took many minutes of silence for the beauty of the King's decision to reach the dwarf. During those minutes he stared at his sovereign in disbelief, while the King looked down at him, smiling and serene.

The truth entered Junda, penetrating his heart like a final sword thrust ending long-drawn-out torture. For the first time in his life, someone had offered him self-sacrifice. He cried out, 'The laughter and sneering, the mocking and scorn, I know so well, I can take them all – but what you give me now, dear *devas*!'

Chapter 69

It turned out that even as Junda brought us word, Gamini's four months of patience finally bore fruit. Digha Jantu and the Chola army, boosted to twenty corps from the Seru and Malaya commands and the drafting of Chola youths, faced us at the northern end of the Kahagalla plain.

Gamini's reaction to news of the actions of the Chola commanders had been typical of him. 'We shall act as judge and executioner for the Chola king! And of course we shall meet him in mortal combat, as he desires, regardless of the outcome of our battle on the plain.'

The vast enemy army finally arrived and encamped at the far end of the plain. For two days and nights, its patrols probed our forces and the commanders reconnoitred the battleground. Before dawn on the third day, our patrols reported that the enemy were massing for their attack.

Despite Gamini's protests, I intended accompanying him into battle, having learned to manage a horse without hands and to wield a sword with my left hand. Gamini had commanded Velu Sumana, the finest Sinhala horseman and sword-fighter, to teach me.

I also owed a greater gift to Gamini. He started me off on the process of learning to write with my left hand. 'You know the craftsmanship and the rules,' Gamini stated flatly. 'If a child can learn to walk, you can surely master the art, this time using your left hand as the instrument.' He kept after me to ensure that I accomplished this feat.

As the newly awakening eyes of the earth turned to the east, Gamini, his commanders and I sat our horses at the hilltop post and looked down on the plain, coloured pale amber from dried grass. Immediately below us, our men were spread from east to west, mostly in groups, their heads a sea of coloured turbans, their uniforms red and white, their leather armour brown. To the north was the dense array of the Cholas, the individuals blurred by distance.

The grey eastern clouds were soon shot with rose and gold. A cold breeze sprang up and filtered, whispering, through the green branches. Birds were whistling and piping in the treetops, crows cawing sadly overhead, all unaware of the drama unfolding beneath them. The smell of smoke from the wood-fires of night mingled with that of field latrines, which large camps do not seem to be able to avoid. The warmth of the sun had started to dispel a light mist that lay in the hollows.

The beauty of the earth was yet unscarred. What a day in which to live! What a day in which to die.

We had learned before the enemy forces arrived that Digha Jantu had sworn to seek out and slay Gamini, in order to bring the battle and our campaign to a speedy end. Gamini had therefore divided his forces into thirty-two units, each with its own elephants, cavalry, chariots, infantry, bowmen and supporting arms. Each unit also had a giant tusker, closely resembling Kandula, bearing a replica of Gamini's umbrella and royal *howdah*, in which was placed an effigy of Gamini, carefully made by our craftsmen. Gamini chuckled when he finally inspected the elephants. 'Digha Jantu will have a merry dance trying to find us! Meanwhile, we will be leading our main attack group on horseback.'

'When he does find you, for the very reason that he is but a Chief Warrior, you may not fight him sire!' the normally taciturn Nimila stated flatly. 'Kings do personal battle only with kings. I beg you to leave this Chola upstart to your warriors.'

Gamini swivelled his body to look thoughtfully at Nimila. 'Well spoken!' he finally declared, having decided. 'So it shall be, though we would have loved to take on this Digha Jantu.' He faced forward again quickly as the faint beat of drums rolled toward us across the plain.

Soon the peculiar nasal wail of Chola trumpets arose. As we watched in silence, the outlines of the enemy mass formations began to materialize. First came an endless double line of bowmen. These would alternately provide covering fire for the assault troops.

In the centre of the dense array was a throng of elephants and chariots. On either side were the masses of infantry, with cavalry at the distant flanks. Behind these ever-extending waves of advancing men would be adequate reserves.

To the throb of drums, the blare of trumpets and the rattle of chariot wheels, the men slowly advanced, becoming more distinct by the minute. Finally we could distinguish their faces and weapons, and the white and red, white and green, white and orange of their uniforms. Once again I picked out individuals. A towering giant in a white turban brandished his spear from atop a grey elephant. A stout officer, fair for a Chola, rode his chariot expertly. They were approaching us

671

as rapidly as their infantry could advance. Now their shouts, curses and challenges reached our ears, striving to intimidate us and to boost their own morale. The sound grew louder and louder. When we failed to emerge from our positions, the shouting turned to hoots and jeers. 'Termites' . . . 'Sinhala pi-dogs'. . . . 'Whore-sons.' Our troops held fast to their positions on the lower slopes of the hills facing the plain.

When the enemy forces were fully stretched across the plain, the clashing sounds of their approach thunderous, our bowmen commenced their murderous fire. A flight of arrows, thousands in number, arced gracefully through the air, obscuring the ground below us, and fell on the enemy at maximum distance, dropping them like dry leaves in a high wind. Another volley followed, then another.

'Phussa has their range!' Gamini exclaimed delightedly. 'He took his measurements and trained his men well.'

Now we were reaping the benefit of Phussa's planning and practice. Our bowmen could gauge distance, speed and direction to a hair's breadth. The oncoming men were withering before their archery.

The front line of enemy bowmen paused, fitted arrows to their bows and fired under the direction of their commanders, but their volleys were ragged and ineffective. They had not counted on so many different targets. They started advancing again, only to fall into the traps we had prepared: deep holes covered with rushes. The hordes behind, however, pushed on determinedly, avoiding the traps. Soon they were thrusting up the re-entrants between the hills.

Digha Jantu must have sensed the problem. Commands rang out. The front ranks of his bowmen paused, divided into two, folded backward and inward. Hundreds of chariots poured through the gap, avoiding our traps. Disregarding our volleys of arrows, with loud cries and a great lashing of long whips, they formed groups, gained speed and charged down the re-entrants. The infantry sped after them. Their centre hit our men on the hillock to the right of us and the battle started raging.

This was what Gamini had wanted – to break up the enemy flood and direct it into the valleys between the hills. We would then swiftly close up the rear to isolate each enemy group and demolish it piecemeal.

As soon as the Chola onslaught got underway, their cavalry on both our flanks wheeled and converged on us like two raging rivers smashing in. Now both armies were fully engaged all along the front, with our men being slowly beaten back on the flanks by the desperate attacks of the Chola, while their own chariots and infantry were being decimated in the hollows.

It was then that I saw Digha Jantu. He headed the reserve group of cavalry in the centre of his lines. The giant of a man, in black uniform, was riding a black horse and brandishing an enormous sword in his hand.

'That is Digha Jantu!' I exclaimed, pointing.

Gamini nodded. 'One could not mistake him.'

As he slammed into our lines, Digha Jantu must have noticed the first of the elephants, for he began hacking a passage toward it. Nothing could stop him. His horsemanship was superb. His sword cleared the way. He was terrifying. Men fell like rice stalks before his threshing. He reached the elephants in a few seconds. Without warning, he flung a dart as he rode past. It struck the effigy foursquare in the chest. The effigy toppled backward. I shuddered. It could have been Gamini on the elephant. Digha Jantu realized his error. He swerved his horse effortlessly and spurred toward another elephant. We lost sight of him in the crush.

'What a waste!' Gamini observed soberly. 'A leader must never be deflected from his main purpose, which is to win the battle. Digha Jantu is driven by the urge to kill us himself, for personal glory as much as to end the battle swiftly. He is the victim of his own vanity and ambition. All under his command will pay the price.'

'And he too, sire,' Nimila swore grimly.

The battle now broke up into large groups of combatants battling desperately – on the plain, in the hollows and on our flanks. It was hard, sitting my horse, watching our men fight without being able to join them. Men were falling and being trampled underfoot in the savage mêlée. Screams and curses rent the air. Horses neighed shrilly and chariots clanked their protests. With the bulk of the Chola chariots and infantry trapped or engaged, their reserves soon poured into the fray, as Gamini had expected. The clamour of the battle became unbelievable. I kept battling the urge to plunge into action and fight alongside my comrades. I could see that Gamini, too, was having to control himself.

Only when he saw that the enemy forces were all committed did Gamini send a fast messenger on horseback over the hill and behind our lines for our cavalry, which he had hidden in reserve, to gallop along the extreme flanks of the plain and close in on the enemy rear. He then continued sitting Raja calmly, giving our cavalry sufficient time to streak to their attack lines far down the plain. Finally, he stood on his stirrups and saw them wheeling prior to the charge. In a few minutes, they hit the enemy rear with the force of a tidal wave.

The enemy line broke and became confused. Our cavalry pelted through, leaving death behind. Hearing the thunder of their approach, the enemy centre wavered, uncertain which way to go. It was an awesome sight: a great body of massed men in the white sunlight – people, each one a human life – watching destruction sweeping upon them from the rear, powerless to move effectively. The disorder of their minds merged and hung in the air, a single tangible force.

Gamini waved his sword aloft. At the signal, our main body of chariots clattered downhill to the roar of Sinhala voices. It hit the enemy front like a giant battering ram, then spread sideways and charged ahead, scattering dead and wounded like splinters from fortress gates. Gamini pointed his sword, glittering in the sunlight, to the gap torn by our chariots. Yelling and screaming, we charged downhill. Cholas broke and ran before us. We scattered them to the winds.

I guided my bay with my legs. Wielding my sword awkwardly in my left hand, I stuck closer to Gamini than a leech and the thrill of battle became a screaming lust within me.

Our objective was to link up with our cavalry on the plain. We fought our way toward them, yelling and screaming, sweating and panting, cutting at faces, slicing at necks, thrusting through bodies. Gamini was always in the lead, slashing his way through the mass of the enemy like a demon. Suddenly he began veering right. Why was he deflecting from our objective? I quickly glanced sideways and knew the answer. He had spotted Digha Jantu. It was impossible not to recognize the Chola warrior. My guts went weak. I trembled at Digha Jantu's fearsome aspect.

Some link of perception, some awareness, through all the noise and combat, blood and gore, wounded and corpses, made Digha Jantu look across the sea of men towards Gamini at that moment. Their eyes met and sparkled like clashing swords in the sunlight. Digha Jantu knew he had found his opponent at last. With a great roar that rose above the din, he spurred his black horse toward Gamini, cutting his way through friend and foe alike with the ferocity of a wild animal.

'Leave this dog to me, sire!' Nimila cried.

The warrior spurred his grey horse toward Digha Jantu, shouting insults. 'You pariah dog, bred of a Chola whore! You offal from the gutters of Madura! You bowel-wind of a cow!'

We followed Nimila through the crush of battling men, but he had gone berserk and was soon well ahead of us.

Digha Jantu heard the insults. His face distorted in fury.

He swerved toward Nimila, brandishing his mighty sword. 'You shall die before your king, Sinhala pig!' he screamed, setting his horse across Nimila's path. As Nimila reached him, Digha Jantu swerved sharply to face the warrior. His great sword flashed down like a streak of lightning.

It was a terrific stroke. Nimila took it on his shield. The sword bit into the leather as if it were wax. Nimila would have fallen with it, but he deliberately let go the shield, swerving his own horse. The shield dropped. Expecting resistance, Digha Jantu met none. His arm balance was affected. The sword was wrenched from his hand and clattered to the ground.

The two horses crossed each other. All fighting in the immediate vicinity stopped, as if by common accord. Friend and foe watched the battle of the warriors in awe.

Digha Jantu reined in his great black horse. He swung a leg in front of him, over the animal's back, and leaped to the ground with amazing agility, even before the horse stopped. He bounded toward his sword like a speeding leopard.

Nimila too had dismounted. Sword in hand, he ran for Digha Jantu's weapon. The Chola got there first. Seizing it with both hands, he sprang sideways four feet up and swung as he came down. The sword flashed through the air with the sound of rushing wind.

Nimila leaped sharply backward, landing lightly on his feet. The Chola's point swept within inches of his face. The Chola landed from his leap in a crouching position, his sword embedded in the soil from the power of his stroke. He tugged at it with both hands.

Nimila gave a throaty growl. Straightening with incredible speed, he raised his sword high in the air. It flashed down on the Chola's right hand, slicing it clean through at the wrist. 'For Prince Rodana!' Nimila shouted savagely.

I was petrified, remembering.

A grunt of pain escaped Digha Jantu. That was all. He

remained crouching, staring at the bloody stump of his hand in stupefaction. His good hand trembled on the sword hilt; the stump drooped, lifeless. His eyes lifted to Nimila, blazing with hatred. Nimila had his sword aloft again. He paused, shaken by the animal fury of his opponent.

With a great roar, Digha Jantu began rising, the sword clear of the ground, grasped in his left hand. His eyes flamed with madness.

'For the kings whose crowns you would have worn!' Nimila screamed as he brought his sword flashing down.

The blow cleft Digha Jantu's skull clean as an executioner's axe, the sword smashing through brains to jar at the collarbone. The giant was forced to his knees. His face had been cleft in two parts. He was dead before his massive body tottered. Nimila tried in vain to withdraw the sword, then he let it go. Deprived of its support, Digha Jantu's body collapsed in the dust.

A mighty shout of triumph arose from our men. '*Cholay Bungaway! Sinhalay Jayaway!*'

A conch shell blared above the shouting. It was Phussa blowing the victory call.

With a roar that seemed to reach the sunlit skies, our men plunged forward against the stricken Chola. Word of their leader's death spread fast. They lost heart and began to retreat. Soon their rear elements were sweeping back in full flight, only to be caught and massacred by our cavalry.

The battle raged in sectors for hours longer, but it was already ended. The Sinhala had won their first major victory over the Chola since King Asela overthrew the earliest Chola invaders, Sena and Guttika, fifty years earlier.

By afternoon, we were mopping up scattered remnants of the once proud Chola army. Gamini had no need to wreak vengeance on the Chola commanders who had robbed their king of his power. All twenty died in battle that morning. Thousands of Chola were butchered, fighting gallantly or in flight. The pale amber Kahagalla plain was dyed red with blood, mostly that of the Chola.

Among our dead, I found Sunil, the grizzled cavalry commander. He lay smiling in death, as if his life's mission had been accomplished. At the far end of the plain, I discovered the body of the captain who had rescued me from the Chola barracks. He was stretched on his back, his dark uniform covered with the yellow dust of the plain. Blood had dried maroon around a hole in his tunic from a sword thrust through the heart. He looked a little tired. His sightless eyes stared blankly at the sky, but his sweat-streaked face revealed white teeth in a fierce grin.

I was told that he had led his band of men to take the enemy in the rear. Only then did I discover his name – Piya Tissa. He was a prince by birth and a distant cousin of mine.

Chapter 70

With the enemy in full flight and a vanguard of cavalry and chariots to protect us, Gamini sped towards Anu in the warm pre-noon sunlight, directing that the elephants, led by Kandula, be brought along behind us with all speed.

Our main column, row upon row of expectant Sinhala, vibrant with victory, followed, stretching for miles endlessly at our rear, with orders to get to Anu before nightfall and surround the city. Sweat pouring down our bodies to mingle with the blood on our uniforms, we cantered beneath the warm sun. The stench of drying blood and the smell of my horse's sweat soon sickened me, but the taste of victory was sweet.

At every village, men, women and children lined the streets, shouting. 'Jayawewa! . . . Jayawewa!' came from a hundred throats. Even a pink-faced baby in arms was chucked under the chin by its pretty young mother and made to gurgle at us. Young men broke loose from family groups and ran alongside, cheering. Some kept following the column, doubtless hoping to enlist.

I glanced sideways at our young king. As always, he cantered with his seat well in the saddle, waist relaxed, hips moving with the horse, firmly but easily as a boat on light waves. Sunlight beating down on his dark, sweating face made it gleam and glow. There was no expression on it, only a deadly serious intent, yet there was majesty in all of him. My heart filled with joy at his proud posture, then quickened with dread, for he had pledged himself to King Elara's challenge and his final battle lay ahead.

We passed groups of fleeing Cholas. Many of them looked apprehensively over their shoulders, cast their weapons aside and remained stock-still. Others broke and fled across the fields. A few stood defiantly on the roadside, sword in hand, as if carved in black marble. Regardless of their attitude, the once haughty conquerors were pathetic in defeat. We ignored them and swept along the dusty highway.

This was the route I had last ridden twenty years ago. Little had changed. Beggars still sat in front of their temple at the village of beggars. One of them trundled along the side of the road on a plank with four wheels. I suddenly recognized him from my boyhood ride of twenty years earlier. He was no longer young. The black hair had turned grey, the square face had wrinkles, but he was undoubtedly the same person, for he still had that irresistible smile.

I had not yet become skilled at riding with one hand and a stump that frequently throbbed. Seeing this cheerful cripple once again effectively stopped any feeling of pity for myself.

Every village we passed spoke of peace, prosperity, education and the right to worship, which the Chola King

679

Elara had given the Sinhala during his reign. We, the Sinhala, had brought war, death and destruction. The thought jolted the rhythm of my triumph. One race, one language, one religion! Would it be enough? Would we do better than the foreign king? New questions drummed in my brain to the beat of the horses' hooves.

We rode through the Bintenne jungle, past the very tree where it had all begun.

We rode without stopping, without food or drink. We rode through the afternoon, into evening, before we cantered up that steep, green, tree-shaded hill. It seemed strangely familiar and I immediately knew why. Having made good speed from the battlefield, we had reached the hill from which my uncle, Hari, Vira and I had surveyed the city of Anu on that last fateful day so long ago. None of it had changed, but everyone in that group was dead, save I.

I glanced sideways at Gamini and caught his attention. I jerked my head toward the top of the hill. 'You can see Anu from there,' I shouted above the clatter of hooves.

Gamini's white teeth flashed across his face in a smile for the first time that day. His nod made glistening beads of sweat drip down his dark cheeks. 'We shall stop there,' he shouted back, 'and see what you saw!'

At first I believed it was sentiment that prompted Gamini. A feeling of warmth gushed through me. Then I realized that I was being foolish. Gamini never found room for sentiment in situations such as the one we faced. He must have other reasons. 'Why?' I cried at him against the wind.

'We have never seen the great city. Your hill is a good place from which to inspect it while we await Kandula.'

I then knew why he had insisted on the elephants being brought up. He would surround the city this evening and immediately send his challenge to King Elara for single combat in the arena outside the gates the following morning. He was not going to take the chance he had taken with

Prince Tissa, being on a horse while his opponent rode an elephant – least of all this time, when he was not taking on a boy. He had heard of King Elara's deadly skills with dart and spear and knew that he certainly would be safer on an elephant! Respect for a worthy foe would also require rest tonight and a completely fresh body and mind tomorrow.

In little more than a year, the impetuous boy of the first battle on the Culan plain had certainly grown to be a man.

The golden flare-light threw ghostly shadows from Junda's former couch and the ebony furniture inside King Elara's bedroom. A cool breeze rustled in through the open windows and the King, sitting propped up in bed, drew his white short-sleeved nightshirt closer around him. Funny, he mused idly, poor men do not have windows in their bedrooms and rich men keep their windows closed at night. Kings and princes enjoy the luxury of cool night breezes, while commoners say that the damp humours of the dark are unhealthy.

He interrupted his nightly task of writing his own *olas* to glance down again at the one he had just received from Gamini. He turned sideways and held Gamini's *ola* closer to the taper. It was written in a strange, scrawly hand, the script of a beginner. He read the words aloud to himself.

'To Elara, formerly King of Lanka, King Abhaya Gamini sends greetings:
'The flower of your army was destroyed on the Kahagalla plain today. Your Champions are all dead. Our Sinhala forces to the east and west of Anu have linked up along the main northern highway. The city is now surrounded by Sinhala troops. Within it are thousands of loyal Sinhala.
'We do not wish to shed more human blood, or to risk ravaging the Sacred City.

'We therefore challenge you to mortal combat on our respective State elephants. Whoever wins shall have victory in the war.

'If you accept this challenge, appear on your State elephant at the northwestern side of the arena opposite the south gate of the city at the end of the first dawn watch tomorrow. We shall await you.'

All hope was dead unless he could win the single combat tomorrow. *Dharma* demanded that he triumph. But receiving word of the defeat on the Kahagalla plain and news of the deaths of his commanders, just when he was becoming accustomed to the dwarf's absence – to being completely alone each night – was almost overwhelming.

Strangely, he was more afraid of victory than of death, for there was not much left to live for.

The scream of a peacock from his pleasure garden intruded sharply through the window. The King eased himself from the bed and donned his slippers. His shadow stretched dark before him as he clip-clopped toward the sound. He felt a premonition which he was unwilling to identify. Shrugging it off, he gazed out at starry skies and the black contrast of trees below them. He recalled standing there with Junda beside him, looking at the beautiful woman whom he had thought was Queen Vihara Devi. That was twenty years ago, but he still felt a little foolish at having been the victim of a substitution and at the pompous certainty with which he had introduced the lady to Junda.

Tonight, the darkness outside was bleak and the flare-light inside forlorn. Why?

It had been too long ago that he experienced the night before battle. He was so unused to it that it seemed as if he had never experienced it earlier. Young people accept such situations without thought. Older people are more fearful. It is one of the ironies of life that those who have lived long enough to be nearer death frequently desire life more than the young. Well, he was not going to submit to that kind of weakness either. Yet he felt a dry ache in his throat and only his steely determination stifled apprehension about the morrow.

He began thinking of his life instead. It had been a good one, even after he lost his family. A man can live with himself as long as he is certain of rectitude. His daily life, the exercise of his mind and body, both of which were finely honed as a long sword in consequence, gave him great alertness. He had never known a day's serious illness in his life. As for his spirit – meditation, *pooja* and the temple observances had kept him close to his gods ever since the early battles against the Sinhala had been won.

What of the people whom he had ruled so fairly and wisely? Chola or Sinhala, did either love him? He had never cared. Needing to be loved is a characteristic of the weak, a luxury he neither desired nor could afford. He was his own man, sufficient unto himself. Deities do not need to be loved. He did not give his deities love, nor did he expect it from them, or from those who had to worship him as king. Respect. That was what mattered between king and subjects, nation and nation: to command respect and hold it. He had made great sacrifices toward that end. He smiled grimly, recalling many an incident.

Unexpectedly, his body felt cold as cold water. He started to shiver. He clasped his arms across his chest and felt the goose bumps on them. What caused this sudden coldness?

As if to answer him, the branches of a large banyan tree opposite him started to move toward him. It soon became a blackness swirling on the lawn. It began to grow, blotting out the sky and exuding the chill of death. He watched in wonder and terror. The figure slowly took the form of a giant snake with a hood that kept expanding until it filled the earth as far as his eye could see. The peacock screamed again, desperately this time. The ensuing silence was perforated by the familiar chink of a cobra, but so loud it made his ears sing. The sickly smell of crushed green-bug assailed his nostrils and he choked,

683

trembling with fear. The great hood drew closer to him, swaying, a snake without eyes or tongue. This was an *avatar*. What did it want? His body was no longer cold, but fevered.

He backed away from the window. The hood came up to him, slowly swaying from side to side, reducing its size so he could see its entirety at all times. He heard a snake charmer's flute, high, reedy, somehow malignant.

The hood came in through the window. He kept backing away, palms forward to ward off the apparition. He stumbled against something. Panic seized his entrails. Was he being attacked from the rear as well? He half turned to look and saw that he had backed into an ebony settle. He completed his turn and seized the settle. He swung around with it. He would teach this *avatar* a lesson.

It was no longer there. It had vanished whence it came, leaving a cloud of grey dust on the dark grass. Soon the dust was sucked in by the earth.

Shaken, sweating now, the King stood in the golden light for long moments. Had it all been in his mind, the product of fear, overcome by courage? He did not know what to think. What had he been considering before the nightmare experience? Respect. Yes, he had thought a king needed only respect. He recalled his fears. Self-respect was the most important of all.

Ashamed of his weakness, King Elara replaced the settle on the floor. Squaring his broad shoulders, he strode to the window again. The night was quiet except for cricket sounds. 'Come once again, *avatar*, and let us finish this issue,' he challenged aloud.

There was no reply. King Elara laughed into the darkness. 'You do not dare.'

A mocking laugh echoed the King's laughter. 'We shall meet you tomorrow!' a ghostly voice replied from the trees. The King turned in its direction.

'We shall meet you' . . . 'We shall meet you' . . . 'We shall

684

meet you.' The words resounded from every direction in which the King turned.

Defiant, unafraid, the King brandished his fist at the heavens. 'We shall never be vanquished by life or death!' he cried.

He stood there a few minutes, dark eyes blazing, white teeth bared. 'Ha!' he exclaimed contemptuously, exulting at the hard knot of unyielding inside him.

The city lay peacefully before us in the morning sunlight. The white spire of the exquisite Thuparama *dagoba*, built by the great King Devanam Piya, soared gracefully toward a pale blue sky stroked by great white feathers of clouds. Before the parklands on either side of us, accommodating our great host of cavalry, the aged granite fortress walls of the city stretched solid above the shining waters of the moat. Hundreds of dark figures on the battlements told us that the city was heavily defended.

Gamini sat motionless in the *howdah* on Kandula's back. The great grey elephant, scrubbed clean by his *mahout* with coconut husks, seemed to realize the importance of the occasion.

This was the day after our victory on the Kahagalla plain. We had camped on the hillock the previous evening, giving time for our main body, including the elephants, to join us. Immediately after our arrival, Gamini had sent his challenge to King Elara, insisting that I write it in my yet unformed hand.

Gamini's words were indeed true. We had encircled the city, with the loss in action of only one major leader, the King of Malaya, father of Prince Vijaya, who had been rude to me. The King had been the older half-brother of Queen Vihara Devi.

It was now time. Gamini gave Kandula a command. The elephant stalked slowly and majestically toward the southern end of the arena. He halted there and remained still, as if carved of grey stone, his jewelled battle trappings and umbrella and the gold- and gem-encrusted *howdah* glittering incongruously in the sunshine. Gamini was a dark, still, watchful figure, standing erect in the *howdah*. Above him, the tall spire of the *dagoba* soared peacefully to the heavens, as if pointing to a better way.

Before long, the massive gates began to creak. Thousands of eyes flickered to them as they slowly swung open with a loud squealing of metal. The grey State elephant of the Chola, richly caparisoned, emerged in majesty. Advancing slowly, he crossed the bridge over the wide moat. Sunlight caught gold, gems and jewels, making them wink mockingly.

The two elephants faced each other across the arena. King Elara was the first to act, making his mount start to move forward, slowly at first, then gathering momentum.

The dark face of the King, beneath a mane of silver hair, and the powerful upper body, clad in a white tunic, now became visible.

Kandula, too, had started to advance. His speed soon matched that of the Chola elephant. The air reverberated with the mighty tread of elephants' feet. Suddenly Gamini veered right – just in time, for King Elara's spear flashed past the *howdah*, followed by a volley of darts as thick as monsoon rain.

Gamini straightened his course. As the elephants crossed, he leaned back, arm upraised. His spear swept straight and true at King Elara. It thudded harmlessly on the King's shield.

The two elephants made a wide circle and raced towards each other again with a great pounding of the earth. They were within fifty yards of each other when Gamini gave a sharp command.

Kandula turned left across the opponent's path and made toward our lines. Caught by surprise, King Elara had to turn in this new direction. He urged his elephant toward Kandula. The animal responded, swinging right in pursuit.

Gamini now turned Kandula right again, making a half-circle to take the Chola's right flank. He urged Kandula on faster, calling to his twin brother for more speed until Kandula was thundering at full gallop, the *howdah* swaying like a tree in a storm.

King Elara understood Gamini's plan at last. His unique skills with spear and dart were lost to him as he tried desperately to wheel his elephant away from the onrushing monolith.

Trumpeting fiercely, Kandula hit the opposing elephant like a thunderbolt. His great white tusks drove into the unprotected area of the Chola elephant's flank, sinking like stakes into grey mud. The Chola elephant bellowed with pain and rage. The bright, glittering *howdah* on his back was shaken by the impact, like a decorated boat before a churning wave. King Elara clung desperately to the rail with both hands. Gamini flung a dart, straight and true, at King Elara's throat. So fierce was the throw that the point of the dart appeared on the other side.

Head thrown back, the Chola king staggered. His dark eyes widened in agony. One hand flew up to grip the dart. His jaw hung slack. The hand dropped helplessly. He teetered at the rail, crashed through it and fell to the earth, to lie sprawled in the brown dust like a great rag doll dressed in white.

Kandula withdrew his great tusks from his opponent's flank. Black-red blood spilled out in a stream. Roaring and screaming madly in pain, the Chola elephant bounded forward, circled and pounded back to the city.

The cheering of countless Sinhala voices reached the skies. The sun misted before my eyes. Somehow I could not cheer. I was choked with thankfulness for Gamini and pity for the *dharmista* King Elara, lying in the dust. What a tragic end to a mighty ruler's power and glory.

Soberly, I realized that the moment of truth was upon us. We should pray rather than cheer. I turned my spirit silently to God. I hope he understood the jumble of my prayers, for only the future could earn our cheers.

The men looked at me for a command. I signalled to them to ride slowly into the arena. Gamini had dismounted from Kandula. He knelt beside the body of the dead king. As we approached, he rose and turned to face us. He held up his hand, desiring to speak. We stopped, hundreds of us crowding around him in a giant circle.

'Silence!' I shouted. 'The King of Lanka desires to address you.'

Eyes downcast, panting lightly from his exertions, Gamini waited for total silence. Only when he had it did he raise his eyes to us again. 'We have just gained sovereignty of this realm in single combat,' he declared hoarsely, 'but the victory is yours.' He paused as if to allow one and all to understand the significance of his words. 'As your chosen king, consecrated by the blood and suffering of thousands of Sinhala, many of whom have died for this cause, I now command you, for the sake of your immortal *pranas*, to refrain from looting and robbery, rape and murder, or any such crimes within this sacred city, or anywhere upon the sacred soil of Lanka, or upon its waters, or in the air above it. The Ten Great Warriors, who have led you so nobly to this great destiny with their ten corps, shall act as the swords of your righteous conduct.' His fierce eyes swept the crowd. 'Is that understood?'

'*Ahey! Ahey!*' We all shouted in unison.

Gamini held up both hands for silence. The shouting gradually died down. 'King Elara was a just and noble king,' he continued, fighting his emotion. 'By our decree, he shall be cremated at this very spot, with full royal honours, after his body has been embalmed. Every person within walking distance shall file past during one week of mourning, to pay him homage. When his body has finally turned to ashes, we shall build him a monument worthy of his greatness. When men pass that monument, there shall be no music or song, nor shall any person, prince or commoner, go past it otherwise than on foot.'

Gamini's eyes burned into us, revealing his tragedy at this moment of triumph. His last words had been received in silence. I wondered whether our men were disappointed. I soon had the answer. Cheering such as I had never heard before rent the air.

I thought with a great surge of gladness: My king, you have just won a far greater victory than any you achieved in battle.

Epilogue

That was the finest hour of Abhaya Gamini, the greatest Sinhala king, one of the most remarkable men the world will ever know. It was matched only by the time of his death, for he spent the remainder of his life expiating the death and carnage he had caused during the wars, haunted not merely by fear of the *vipaka* that would result from his *akusala-kharma*, but also by the surfacing of a deep-rooted compassion, hidden before and during his campaigns by the overwhelming demands of his destiny. All that he achieved during the years of peace was not merely atonement, therefore, but the fruit of a good man's endeavour. I glimpsed the effects of this *kharma*, at the time of Gamini's death.

True to his word, King Elara's brother, Bhalluka, landed with a force of thirty thousand mercenaries eight weeks later at our northwestern port, Mantota.

We met the enemy on ground of his choosing, the Kolamba plain. We were shocked to the point of humiliation when the beloved Kandula, the State elephant on which Gamini was riding, refused to advance and even backed away from the enemy. The Chola started roaring with laughter. Only when Phussa Deva fired an arrow in the direction of Bhalluka's laugh, piercing his throat, did the invading army waver.

Advancing more cautiously this time, we soon discovered the bog in which Bhalluka had hoped to trap and massacre us and knew that Gamini's twin had saved the day, instead of bringing shame to the Sinhala.

We threaded our way through the bog and pursued the

demoralized enemy to the ocean. Few escaped in the fleet that had brought them to Lanka.

We encamped on the seashore that night. Early the next morning, Gamini was up alone, even before the sun rose. He walked by himself on the deserted beach.

Knowing that the battles were finally over, that no Chola soldier would ever set foot on these sacred sands again in his lifetime, he finally faced up to the *vipaka* of the death and carnage he had brought upon his *prana* and rebirth.

His only hope was to spend the remaining years of his life doing good, but the full force of all he had done suddenly overwhelmed him. What should he do?

He stared with haunted eyes toward the ocean, as if it would unfold a mystery. Long moments passed. He was turning away, beaten, when he saw the silver surface of the ocean begin to turn pink.

It is the approach of dawn, he thought. Then his eyes caught a sudden shimmering of the water and he stopped. As he gazed, spellbound, the vast ocean slowly began to disappear. Finally, there was no water, only a vast cloud of pale pink. His flesh and blood, bone and muscle began to dissolve. A warm breeze sprang up and passed right through him. He was a part of the breeze. It was all of him and a part of everything. Although he no longer had eyes, the cloud of pink remained. On it, as on a great bed, the sacred city, Anu, slowly arose from the earth, rooftops first, then walls, then streets crowded with people in saffron and yellow robes. They were not just monks, but ordinary people – the devout flocking to the city to spend their days close to the sacred *bodhi*-tree, the sacred tooth-relic and the sacred *dagobas*. They came to venerate the sacred Doctrine, to learn of it from the Sangha and to strive for Enlightenment.

Suddenly, within the twenty-five square miles of the Maha Mega gardens, laid out by King Devanam Piya for the Sangha, a dark edifice, surmounted by a roof of brass, began to rise. It stopped when it was ten storeys tall. Supported on a host of granite columns, each storey consisted of one hundred rooms embossed with silver, the window ledges of pink coral. *Bhikkus* gazed out of every window, from rooms where chairs, tables and beds of black ebony, brown-and-gold tamarind and white satinwood, inlaid with mother-of-pearl, gave them honour. Vessels, platters and goblets of gold were there to serve them.

In the centre of this palace he saw a gem pavilion, with a network of pearls around its edge, its pillars encrusted with precious stones. Inside the pavilion was a new ivory throne for the king, adorned with gold and set with the nine gems. Its seat was of mountain crystal and its back fashioned with a sun of gold, a moon of silver and stars of pearls. This throne was surmounted by an umbrella of purest white silk, with foot and handle of pink coral.

'I shall build you and call you the Lohapasada,' Gamini murmured. As he sighed in satisfaction, the edifice slowly sank into the pink cloud, which in turn gradually dissolved. The feel of his body began returning to Gamini. When it was complete, only the vast expanse of the ocean lay before him.

Determination seized Gamini. The *devas* had shown him the way out of the *akusala-kharma* of the carnage he had caused, his bloodlust and blood-letting, the ruthlessness that had entered his spirit, even his sexual lapses, all of which had begun to ravage him after his victory over King Elara. He would take the road to *arahat*-ship by building great works, offering tribute to the Doctrine and acquiring merit. All payment would be from his own coffers. His royal command would be: 'No work may be done on this place without reward from the King.'

Excited by his decision, Gamini turned to leave. As he did so, his eyes caught sight of the sea changing colour. As his body again dissolved in that warm breeze, the city of Anu spread before him on a vast pink cloud once more – but this was a new Anu, the product of his special care. Its streets had been widened. Water had been fed from its great reservoirs to serve the domestic neeeds of the people. New channels and pipes led the means of drinking, washing and bathing to them. The city's sewage was carried away along underground drains, into the northeastern swamps. Great hordes of Cholas were employed in keeping the city clean. These low-caste labourers, who had been induced to come from the barren wastes of South India, lived outside the city in clean huts, looking after its scavenging.

This vision, too, passed. Now Gamini waited, knowing he would have one final revelation.

When it came, the whole island of Lanka lay upon that shimmering pink cloud, plentiful with green paddy fields and farms, poultry and livestock, spinning and weaving. Whitewashed cottages with roofs of dark coconut thatch provided decent houses for a prosperous peasantry. *Vihares* bestowed education, hospitals gave comfort to man and animal alike, temples and *dagobas* supported the Doctrine. He saw houses for orphans and the destitute, *ambalams* for the traveller. No person or animal within the kingdom lacked for care and attention. A beautiful young woman walked its length and breadth alone, carrying all her jewellery, without ever being harmed.

Standing on the very shores that cradled the birth of the Sinhala nation, Gamini knew he would accomplish what he had seen. And he did, during the twenty-two years of his reign.

Gamini proved generous in kingship. I was appointed his Chief Aide; my uncle's properties were bestowed upon me. Gamini rewarded his brother, Tissa, by making him King of Ruhuna. Prince Digha Bahu was made ruler of a new subkingdom consisting of Soma and Seru.

When Gamini rewarded nine Great Warriors by appointing them governors of districts, retaining the magnificent Anu district for his beloved Vasabha, the golden warrior begged to be allowed instead to enter the Noble

Order at a temple in the Kotmale area, far removed from Anu. He wished to atone for the one act of murder he had committed, with anger in his heart: kicking Ravi to his death in the ravine.

Abhaya, too, asked to be excused. He was joining his father as a *bhikku* in the temple on the distant Panjali mountain, in order to continue his work as a Great Warrior, this time against the passions. So two of Gamini's dearest comrades-in-arms left him at the moment of his triumph.

Neither separation was as tragic for Gamini, however, as the revelation he would receive from his mother.

Requesting that Velu Sumana should be appointed sub-king of Kelaniya, she revealed to Gamini that the Chief Warrior was really her half-brother, the son of her mother's union with her princely lover and cousin. Velu Sumana had been spirited away as a baby to avoid the Kelaniya king's wrath and had been brought up by a poor jungle family in Ranna. He discovered his true identity only after he joined King Kakkavan's service as a warrior, through a chance conversation with Queen Vihara Devi, to whom the original secret had been entrusted. The key to his identity was a purple birthmark on his bottom. He had remained the Queen's close friend and confidante.

Gamini made the appointment, but part of the foundation on which he had built his ambition – certainly the entire base of his emotional life as a young boy – was shattered. It was then that he shared with me, for the first time, the story of what he had mistakenly interpreted as the Queen's unfaithfulness. Although I kept urging him that he was not personally responsible – that all the events he had experienced were a part of life's purpose for him – the revelation plagued him to the end of his days.

Soon afterward, Queen Vihara Devi joined the Noble Order of *Bhikkshuni*, becoming a nun. Leela followed the Queen Mother into the Noble Order of *Bhikkshuni*, leaving me bereft of our occasional sweet communion.

Gamini discovered in the palace a gold plate bearing a Sanskrit writing of the prophet Mahinda, who first had brought the Doctrine to Lanka. It prophesied that within two centuries there would arise a ruler of the island kingdom who would re-establish the Doctrine throughout its entire length and breadth, glorifying it with the most splendid buildings of all times. The greatest of these would be a *dagoba* of such size and splendour as to give the King sufficient merit to attain Buddhahood.

Whether moved by knowledge or desire, Gamini decided he was that king.

Eighteen years passed, long years during which Gamini frequently agonized over his *akusala-kharma* and the fate that death could bring him, before he finally began to build the great temple of the Venerable Mahinda's prophecy, on a site adjoining the Thuparama *dagoba* and facing the Brazen Palace. His only hesitation, in light of his revelations on the beach, was at the prospect of taxing people.

There ensued a series of miracles, as if to ensure that Gamini was indeed the king of the prophecy. First, a huntsman miraculously found a vast quantity of bricks and granite blocks in one of the King's forests, probably placed there by a former ruler who had wished to erect a great building, but had fled before one of the Chola invasions.

While Gamini's surveyors were measuring out the foundations of the new *dagoba*, gold nuggets were discovered in one of the King's mines. The largest of these were greater than a hand's span.

Shortly after, in pits which had been barren for over fivescore years, a rich new vein of copper was discovered. Sapphires and rubies were collected in sudden abundance in the village of Sumana. A new lode of silver was struck in a disused mine, pearls and coral were washed ashore on the western beaches and gems were found in a northern cave.

Such treasures had been washed ashore once before, when

Gamini was born. They had helped him fulfil his destiny and become king of all Lanka. He now became convinced that earth and ocean were offering him their abundance once more for a new, greater destiny: the attainment of Enlightenment. He pressed on with the work of the great *dagoba* he had conceived, which he had named Ruwanveli Saya, because its pinnacle would be covered with gold dust.

To form the base of the foundation, crushed stone was first trampled down by elephants and a layer of butter clay poured on it. Over this base were placed layers of brick, followed by rough cement on which copper ore was laid and a network of iron with a sprinkling of sweet-scented *maramba* brought by *samanera* from the Himalayan mountains. Next was strewn mountain crystal and stones overlain with copper sheeting, covered by a final sheet of silver mixed with arsenic dissolved in sesame oil.

The ceremony of laying the foundation stone was held on a full-moon night. When it was over, a great hush filled the air.

Suddenly I realised that this was not the silence of people, but of the very earth – as if man and animal, bird and insect, tree, shrub and flower, the soil itself, had paused in awed silence to listen.

I knew something was wrong even before I heard the first rumblings of the earth's belly. The whole land vibrated beneath us and I trembled. The rumblings increased, juddering. Then the soil fluttered like a flag in the breeze, while the whole world, above and below, throbbed with tremors. The lights around us sparkled and flickered, swaying to and fro before our gaze.

The rumblings rose to a great roar. The earth shook as if it would split open. People fell to their knees in terror. Pride forbade me to follow them, but I would have fallen if I had not spread my feet and balanced evenly on them, rocking to the motions of the earth as if I were on some massive boat.

I glanced at Gamini. He alone of all the people stood firm.

He smiled quietly at me, his teeth very white in his dark, sweating face.

Three times the earth shook in its battle within itself, making my heart quake despite my brave stance. The stomachs and bladders of some opened involuntarily. The whining of terrified animals keened in between like stringed instruments above the earth's drums. Wakened birds screeched, or shrilled in terror.

The rumblings gradually subsided into silence. First came the silence of the earth, then the cessation of movement below its surface. Before human beings realized it, other living things knew that the quaking of the earth was over. They came alive again, as if it were daylight. Now, only the silence of the people remained, as if all were trying to recover their breath and their courage.

'Rise and behold!' Gamini shouted passionately, his deep voice hoarse with emotion. His dark hand pointed at the foundation. 'The *devas* have tested our work and found it good. Not one crack shows. Not one light has been extinguished. We have had our omen. Thus are we assured that this noble work shall be completed.'

Now the completion of the Ruwanveli Saya became an obsession with him because, unknown to us, he had suffered the first of three attacks such as had caused his father's death. He knew that his stupendous energy, the enormous demands of his campaign against the Cholas and of reconstructing the united kingdom thereafter had taken their toll. While accepting these manifestations of cause and effect, he was convinced that he simply had to complete the Ruwanveli Saya before his death in order to expiate his sins and achieve a superior rebirth.

The square foundation platform of the *dagoba*, measuring over five hundred feet each way, was finally erected. Craftsmen had carved one hundred elephants on each side, fitted with tusks and decked with ornamental trappings, so skilfully as to make it appear that the elephants were supporting the structure. The relic chamber of the *dagoba* was walled with cream-coloured river stones that looked like crystal. In the centre of the four arches were giant crystals framed in gold. At each of the four corners of the chamber was a great gem – a ruby, an emerald, a white diamond and a pearl. In the centre of the relic chamber was a throne made entirely of jewels, with a gold image of the Buddha seated upon it. On the night of consecration, sacred relics of the Buddha, which had been brought from India, were placed before this image.

When the ceremony of enshrining the relics was over, work commenced on the building of the *dagoba* over the chamber, rising in the shape of a bell to a height of three hundred feet.

The circular bottom of the *dagoba* was five hundred feet across, with a shrine on each of the four sides, guarded by statues of the Four Guardians of the World. Beside these statues, figures of the thirty-three gods, thirty-two celestial maidens and twenty-eight kings had been carved. Above them all, as if in the air, *devas* raised folded hands, danced, or played instruments of music, beside vases filled with artificial flowers of yellow, white, red and blue. The plaster of the *dagoba* would make it look like polished marble. At its crest, the huge gold-covered pinnacle and silver spire would rise majestically. Above the spire, a great crystal, specially imported from Burma, would thrust toward the heavens, a beacon of the Doctrine. All of it would stand over forty storeys tall.

Gamini knew one of the greatest disappointments of his life when his son, Prince Sali, who had been rigorously trained to become king, refused the succession. The handsome youth married a beautiful maiden of the lowly Chandala caste, to which my father had belonged, and retired to Kotmale. He intended entering the Noble Order some day.

King Tissa of Ruhuna, Gamini's brother, had reluctantly accepted the right to succeed, at Gamini's behest.

In the fullness of time, many who had shared in Gamini's life had died: among them the Queen Mother, Velu Sumana, Kirthi Siri, Prince Digha Bahu, Junda and Raji's parents. So it was King Tissa and me whom Gamini summoned that Wesak morning, twenty-two years after his victory in single combat over King Elara. On this day, Lord Buddha had been born, had died and had attained Nibbhana.

Raji was already in the bed-chamber. We took our places beside the great canopied bed with its white, silken sheets and cushions.

Gamini looked pale and grey in the morning light. His face was drawn and haggard. Wrinkles showed on the dark skin beneath the hollows of his eyes. In contrast, his eyes shone brightly and he was strangely calm. 'We shall die tonight,' he said decisively, as if he were announcing that he was going to a party.

I stared at him through sudden tears, remembering the night my uncle, Prince Vipula, had gone to King Elara's audience chamber forty-five years ago to answer the summons that finally led to his death.

'We desire to die before the Ruwanveli Saya. Even as an unfinished work, it is so mighty that its sight will project our *kharmic* force farther than if we died elsewhere. We beg you three, our loved ones, all others who love us and as many members of the Sangha as possible to be present at our death. We request the revered Sangha assembled there to chant as we pass away, so that our life-force can be wafted to higher realms.' He saw the tears in my eyes and smiled in reproof. 'Now remember, Prince, the noble do not weep openly.'

King Tissa cleared his throat to hide his emotions. 'May I have your leave, my lord, to depart and prepare for this grievous event?' he asked abruptly, his voice breaking.

'Yes.'

Gamini acknowledged his brother's deep obeisance with a half-raised hand, then turned it to summon King Tissa close to him.

As King Tissa drew near, King Gamini opened his arms. King Tissa was shocked. A gasp escaped him. He stood as if turned to stone. Then, with a sob, he embraced Gamini.

My mouth became parched, my throat ached as I thought of what might have been between the two brothers – yet it could have been no different. For it to be otherwise, they would have had to be two different people. Their lives and destinies would have been different, and they never would have shared this moment.

It is enough to know such an instant, I thought – so precious it has no limit of time, but is eternal.

King Tissa released Gamini. Tears streaming down his face, Tissa bowed backward out of the room.

I will not speak of my private farewell to Gamini. Nor do I know what transpired between him and Raji, except that she informed him of her intention to become a Buddhist nun. Her piety and devotion well fitted her for her role, and after being King Gamini's wife, what higher estate was open to her than the Sangha?

It was night and we were before the great *stupa*, Gamini's crowning glory, with the multitude of his people and the *bhikkus* of the Noble Order gathered.

The chanting of the monks gradually subsided. King Tissa approached the couch on which Gamini lay and made deep obeisance. 'My lord king, the great *dagoba* has been completed!'

I felt the imprint of King Tissa's words on Gamini's exhausted mind. First, incomprehension. Then incredulity, followed by dawning wonder. Finally, acceptance in a slow surge of joy.

I quietly took my place beside the bier. A page boy beside

701

me held the Book of Meritorious Deeds in his hands.

King Tissa nodded to me. I moved forward and bent down to help Gamini to a sitting posture. For some moments, the effort was too great for him. He was so weak and tired, my heart cried out in pain.

Then, with a fantastic act of willpower, Gamini opened his eyes suddenly, his gaze clear.

The great *stupa*, his Ruwanveli Saya *dagoba*, was revealed to him in all its majesty. His eyes took in its dark balustrades, terraces and shrines, lit with myriad clay lamps. Slowly, ever so slowly, his steady gaze moved up to the mighty white domelike shape. The tears came, but did not fall.

Slowly his gaze rose to the huge golden pinnacle, the slender, circular silver spire and the giant crystal shining in the moonlight. His eyes kept moving to the starry heavens, where they suddenly lost their focus. His stream of life now was prepared for its cascade.

Gamini was unaware that once his end was near, King Tissa had had workmen labour night and day to cover the unfinished *dagoba* with white cloth that looked like plaster in the moonlight. He had artists paint in the figures and balustrades. He had carpenters construct a wooden pinnacle and cover it with white sheets painted with gold. He had the spire done in silver. Only the giant crystal surmounting the spire and reaching for the heavens was the very stone Gamini had brought from Burma, so if the base of the work was make-believe, it was crowned with truth. The idea was King Tissa's. He had earned Gamini's embrace before he received it this morning.

Rightly or wrongly, Gamini now believed that he had seen his mightiest *dagoba* completed. Whether it was real or not, all his *prana* needed was his belief in it. The only truth is indeed our own reality.

'We wish to be carried around the *dagoba* once.' Gamini's voice was so faint that I had to bend down in order to hear the words.

I had anticipated this request. Eight of his closest kinsmen were standing by the couch. I watched like a lost soul as they knelt before the King, heads on the ground, palms together held above them. They stood up and took their places around the couch.

'*Hoi!*' the leader quietly exclaimed. They lifted the couch in one smooth motion. '*Hoi!*' the leader said again. The procession began a slow march forward.

King Tissa and I followed, Raji remaining behind with the palace ladies. Thousands of eyes, most flowing with tears, watched us. No one even coughed or cleared a throat.

We passed the area reserved for the yellow-robed *bhikkus* and *bhikkshunis*. My eyes were irresistibly drawn to the front row of *bhikkshunis*, to a point that seemed a source of my own grief. In the dim light I saw an olive skinned face, a fine bone structure, a shaven head. Only the eyes were in shadow, so I could not tell whether they observed me. It was Leela. She could not reach for me as a person, but I knew she grieved for my sorrow. I blessed her silently and passed on.

Finally, we completed the circuit. The kinsmen gently replaced the couch on the raw earth and backed away.

The flutter of Gamini's hand attracted me. I peered anxiously at his face. His head was turned toward me on the cushions. His eyes were open, bright with knowledge and purpose. He beckoned with one finger. As I moved close to Gamini and bent over him, the kinsmen backed away, with a rustle of clothes, to their former positions. Gamini's eyes remained intently on me, the old magnetism magically reborn.

Suddenly the most weird sensation shook my being. I started to tremble, knowing what he desired to tell me.

'Fulfil your purpose! It is our command' – he smiled faintly – 'and our plea. You alone can do it truthfully.' He paused to make sure I had understood. 'You shall write about the Winds of Sinhala.'

Stunned, I merely nodded. He who could command me

had made his words a plea. I blinked back hot tears. Gamini's eyelids drooped. I bent down to catch his words.

'You ... and the Great Warriors ... once fought victoriously with us ... through twenty and eight great battles. Together ... we faced death ... and conquered it ... without ever yielding to fear. Now ... when our last battle ... has begun ... only you ... beloved friend, are here. The Great Warriors ... come not to help. ... We think they foresee ...' – his breath rasped harshly – 'defeat!'

'Not so, my lord!' The voice had in it the strength of the warrior, the peace of the mountains and the infinity of the Doctrine. Vasabha stood beside the couch, dressed in the yellow robes of the monk. 'All those Great Warriors who have not yet faced the battle with death are here with you tonight to help you in your final battle.'

Gamini tried to take in the words. What passed through his mind at hearing the voice of his beloved Vasabha, no one will know. What it did was to make him open his eyes in a sudden swift motion toward the direction of the voice. He took in the beautiful warrior's serene face.

Vasabha moved away and the yellow-robed Abhaya advanced to the couch. Each one of the Great Warriors, except for the dead Velu Sumana, passed before Gamini in turn. With some uncanny power, the dying king kept his eyes open. I had summoned them all. I thanked God that they had arrived in time. And who knows that the dead Velu Sumana did not pass before Gamini as well that night.

From Gamini's racked body the words slowly emerged. I bent again to hear and repeat them aloud.

'Formerly, I fought ... with you, the Great Warriors ... by my side. ... Now I have entered alone ... upon the battle ... with Death ... and the foe Death ... I cannot conquer.' For the first time in his life, he was acknowledging defeat.

Vasabha replied in a clear voice that not only reached Gamini, but must surely have carried to God. 'O Great

King, fear not. If the foe Sin be conquered, the foe Death is not unconquerable. Think on all those works of merit accomplished by you unto the present day. Then shall all be well with you at this moment of your death.'

Gamini's eyes closed. 'In single combat too . . . art thou . . . my help!' he whispered.

A fierce joy seized me. I turned to the page boy. Because I had but one hand, he opened the Book of Meritorious Deeds and held it up for me to read. At last I comprehended the meaning of these books, their purpose and their need. How foolish I had been, years ago, when I had thought of them as the hoardings of misers. Now I saw this Book of Meritorious Deeds as the record of my king's spirituality, the bowstring which, when loosened, would send forth the arrow of his belief in himself into a better rebirth. Two other page boys came forward swiftly, bearing flares.

'Ninety-nine *vihares*, *bhikkus*' residences, have been built by our great king,' I commenced, my voice breaking at the first words.

Hearing my voice ringing out through the clear night, the Chief Monk began chanting softly. '*Namo thassa bagavattho* . . . !' Other monks took up the chant, softly too.

I pressed closer to Gamini, so he might hear me above the droning background of the many thousand voices of the monks.

'The splendid Lohapasada. This great Ruwanveli Saya' – I paused and looked at Gamini – 'which will surely waft his immortal *prana* into Buddhahood.'

With a spasm of joy, I saw the dark eyelids flicker in acknowledgement. A trembling finger was raised ever so slightly. I stopped reading and bent low once more to hear him.

'The *devadattas* bring us six cars and six gods,' he said clearly and without pause. 'They invite us to enter into the celestial world. We have bidden them wait as long as we listen to the *Dhamma*.'

'How shall I make known the presence of these celestial cars, my lord?'

'Have those garlands of flowers that lie on the terraces lifted in the air and they will be wound on the poles of the cars as they travel around the *dagoba*.'

The chanting continued without pause. I relayed Gamini's words to his kinsmen standing by. They rushed to the terraces. Attendants brought up long bamboos from the work site. The kinsmen picked up eight garlands and strung each upon a bamboo. One of them raised his bamboo aloft. When the pole was finally erect, the garland twisted and wrenched itself away, to float through the air and finally drop to the ground. The other seven kinsmen raised their bamboos, one following the other, each with the same result.

I looked down at Gamini. His eyelids were drawn. He breathed in low, rattling gasps. His cheeks started to twitch and his face contorted with pain.

Raji wept quietly beside me. The Great Warriors were ranged impassively by the couch. I resumed reading from the Book of Meritorious Deeds. What else could I do?

'In the mountain region called Kotta, at the time of the great famine, many precious gems were given by the King and many a dish of sour-millet gruel provided by him to five *bhikkus* who had overcome the *asavas* desires, offered to them with a believing heart . . .

'When fleeing from the battle on the Culan plain, the Great King, then but a prince, gave up his food bowl to a *bhikku* on the bank of the river that lay between him and safety . . .

'Twenty-four magnificent *dana* have been given to thousands of the Sangha by the Great King during the sacred time of Wesak and many thousand times has he served *dana* to the Sangha and the poor and bestowed gifts upon them . . .

'Five times during the Great King's reign, each time for seven days, did he bestow the rank of ruler of Lanka-

dwipaya, the island of Lanka, upon the Doctrine. And during his entire reign, he had one thousand lamps with oil and white wicks burning perpetually in twelve places, adoring the Blessed One with these offerings . . .

'Constantly, in eighteen places has the Great King bestowed food and medicine for the sick from his private Treasury, while providing over two thousand hospitals for men and over one thousand for animals from the fruit of his people . . .

'In forty-four places has the Great King commanded the perpetual giving of milk-rice prepared with honey and lumps of rice with oil, great *jala* cakes baked in butter and many sweetmeats . . .

'Knowing that preaching to the Sangha affords the highest merit of all, the Great King decided to preach to them, but when he was seated on the preacher's chair, he would not do so because of his reverence for the Sangha . . .'

I paused in my reading and looked at Gamini, my love for him a fountain. He opened his eyes. They were clear. He smiled faintly at me. Whatever the torment of his body, his spirit was finally at peace.

I had one brief look to cling to before he jerked in a spasm. His head came up, the eyes staring. His fingers clutched the white sheets. His lungs clawed vainly for breath. The death rattle emerged from his throat. His head stiffened, then fell back softly.

The monks in their wisdom knew the moment his body dropped away from his *prana*. Their chanting soared to a great crescendo. I continued reading the Book of Meritorious Deeds, determined to finish it before I announced his death and drew the lids over his dead eyes.

It is afternoon. Weeks have passed, during which I have toiled night and day, here in my quarters at the Anu palace, to write these *olas*. I have used my left hand, the precious gift Gamini encouraged me to seek after I lost my right.

I have eaten, drunk and slept only as my body needed to be able to complete my story. I had intended it to be of Gamini alone, but it has turned out to be my story as well. How could it have been otherwise?

Water, earth and air had spoken to me so many years earlier. I had an inkling as to when the fourth element would unbare its spirit, but no certainty. The fire that consumed Gamini's body upon his cremation did indeed commune with the depths of me, to complete the cycle.

King Sadha Tissa sent for me shortly after Gamini's death. Eager to carry on Gamini's policies, he desired me to continue as his own aide. I gave my word that I would perform these duties while I live. I did not promise the new king that I would live forever.

A man needs to be responsible for others in order to exist. Since I have no family, Gamini's death removed my sole responsibility. King Tissa's request would make me responsible again, removing some of the hopelessness.

I must think on it!

Even if I have work, the loneliness will remain.

I was Gamini's shadow, standing with him always, so the shadows were one. In reality, it was our two *prana* that were as one and both of them one with God. This cannot change, so perhaps the part of me that matters is with Gamini; only the useless hulk of a fifty-seven-year-old body, with a stump for one hand, remains chained to this earth.

Men think that when we die our *prana* leave our bodies. It is the other way around. Death is the sloughing away of our bodies from our immortal *prana*. Should I slough away my body then, like the skin of a snake, to emerge shining in the sunlight? Or should I wait for my end, in my loneliness, continuing with Gamini's work, to that extent his shadow?

The evening sunlight is warm and golden in the garden outside. I lay down my stylus on the ebony desk and stand up. I stretch and feel the familiar ache in my back from sitting too long. The sunlight will do it good. For what? To warm my body before it finally lies cold?

I move to the door and pass through the corridor into the garden. I stand on the red-brick-paved walkway, breathing the scent of drying grass. It feels good to my senses. I walk a little way and pause, closing my eyes, trying to root my thoughts in the feeling of life pulsing around me; trying to recall the rhythm of the earth and hear it speak to me as in the beginning, during my first journey to Mahagama; trying to think from that life to death. Am I seeking the fourth element?

I see my uncle, Prince Vipula, standing erect before me, dressed in gold tunic and pantaloons. 'First, honour,' he says.

Beside him is a lady clad in white, who looks very like him, and behind her a muscular, bare-bodied man wearing the white turban of the Chandala. Dear *devas*: the mother and father I have never seen! As my mind starts toward them with fierce joy, they vanish.

Then Gamini appears before the blackness of my closed lids, the boy prince with a wary look. His white teeth flash in a smile.

'You taught me honour.' He too is gone instantly.

What are my dearest ones trying to tell me?

Eyes closed, standing with my back to the sun, I gradually feel its rays soothing my tired muscles. I think, there is always a source of life, even when our eyes are closed.

I open my eyes to the world of green trees lining the walkway, to a mad chorus of birdsongs, to the scent of jasmine in the air, to my shadow lying long before me.

So I do have my own shadow. Then I must have my own body too.

Since Gamini's death, I had forgotten that our bodies are a part of God and must only be cast away in His good time. While I have this body, I must let it remain to fulfil His will as best I can. This is not only the need of my honour as a prince, but also of my destiny as a part of God.

Now, if I remain in the sunlight, my shadow will grow taller before nightfall.

Glossary

The following are the meanings intended for words used in the text.

ABITHAYA   Apprentice monk
ADATHODA   Tobacco plant
AHAIMA NEY THE   Is that not so?
AHEY   Yes
AHIMSA   Forbearance, especially toward enemies
AIYA   Older brother
AKUSALA-KHARMA   Literally, sinful causes; therefore, deeds
AMBALAM   Traveller's rest
AMBALAYA   Large brown ant
AMMA   Mother
ANATTA   Non-soul (From AN-ATMAN. See ATMAN).
ANICCA   Impermanence of all things
ANODHA   Sour-sop, a small tree which bears delicious fruit
APE RAJA THUMMA JAYAWEWA   May our revered king triumph
APPA   A small pancake of rice flour
APPE KUMARAYA   Our prince
ARABI   Arab(s)
ARAHAT   A person who has eliminated all craving, conquered all passions, a holy man, a saint
ARDAY   I say (the figure of speech, not the statement)
ARETE   A ritual performed by Hindus
ARTHA-SHASTRA   The science of government. A book written by Kautilya in the time of the emperor Chandra Gupta Moriya (after the time of Alexander the Great) for the guidance of kings
ARYA   The noble ones; the Aryan race
ASAVA   Desire(s)
ATA-SIL   The soul
ATMAN   The soul
AVATAR   Spectre, ghost
AYUBOWAN   The Sinhala greeting, also farewell
AYURVEDA   Literally, native wisdom; used to designate the practice of medicine

BADA-GINI-VELA   Literally, stomach on fire; used to indicate that one is very hungry

BADA PISSA   Literally, stomach swept clean; therefore, youngest child

BANA   Buddhist sermon

BAPPA   Paternal uncle (MARMA = Maternal uncle)

BAVALATH GITA   Women's songs (The author's invention)

BELI   Slime apple. A tree bearing a hard-shelled fruit, the kernel of which is a remedy for stomach ailments.

BHIKKU   Buddhist monk

BHIKKSHUNI   Buddhist nun

BINNA   A form of marriage in which the husband joins the wife's family

BODHI   Godly blessed. Thus the *pipul* tree, under whom the Bhudda obtained Enlightenment, is called the *bodhi*-tree

BOOSU   A mixture of nuts, spices and pieces of spiced vermicelli fried hard, typically eaten with alcoholic beverages

BO-VITIA   A green bush producing purple berries

BRACHMACHARIYA   Total abstinence from sexual intercourse; therefore, one who has taken such a vow

BRAHMA   The Creator. Supreme God of the Hindus

BUNGAWAY   From BUNGAWEWA. May he or they be utterly destroyed

CADJAN   The thatch of coconut branches

CASSAYA   A (medical) mixture or concoction

CHANDRA GUPTA   The Moriya emperor of that name who took over the territory of Alexander the Great in the area of what is now India and founded a dynasty which included the Emperor Asoka

CHARLITHRAYA   Revered customs and traditions, including good manners

CHUK-GOODOO   A team game in which sticks are used instead of bat and ball

CHUNAM   White lime

CHUNDOO   A small unit of measure

CUBIT   A unit of measurement defined as the distance from the elbow to the tip of the middle finger

CUNJEE   The water in which rice has been cooked until it is soft and mushy; the word is probably derived from the ancient Chinese

DAGOBA   A dome-shaped Buddhist temple, with pinnacle and spire; STUPA and THUPA are also names for such structures

DANA   Alms; includes cooked meals, food, flowers and lights

DAN-SALA   Alms-hall

DASA-SIL   The Ten Precepts; the observance thereof, generally only by *bhikkus*

DEVA   A godlike being, not of this earth

DEVADATTA   Celestial being

DHAL   Pigeon pea

DHAMMA   The (Buddha's) Doctrine

DHARMA   Duty of one's office or station; also the law, justice, righteousness

DHARMA-DWIPAYA   Literally, righteousness island; an island dedicated to righteousness

DHARMA-VIJAYA   A victory for right and justice

DHARMISTA   Righteous

DHIMIYA   A small ant

DHOO   Affectionate form of DHUWA, daughter

DHOTI   A loose cloth worn around the waist and tucked between the legs, trouser fashion

DHUKKA   Sorrow, grief, suffering

DHUN   A tree bearing purple berries that can be used to stain the skin

DHUSTA   Accursed

DIAMANTHI   A kind of diamond

DOLA-DHOOK   Cravings during a woman's pregnancy

DWIPAYA   Island

EHELA   A kind of tree

GAMANI   The word was originally used to mean a king; this probably accounts for the derivation of Abhaya Gamini's name. With increasing Indian influence, the king became the RAJA and Gamini came to be the title of a village head.

GANJA   Hemp, used as a drug

GAN-SABHA   Literally, village societies. The singular form,

GAN-SABHAWA, is also used for the society's building. The word means village council

GATHA   Buddhist psalms

GAVUTA   A unit of measure; 4 GAVUTA equal 1 YOJANA

GETA-BERE   A small drum, generally used to beat time for dancing; plural form, GETA-BERA

GHEE   A sort of lard made from cow's milk, used as cooking fat

GIRAR   Adjectival form of GIRAVA, parrot

GOIGAMA   The farmer caste

GULI   Plural form of GULIYA, a pill

GURU   Teacher

HAMUDURUWO   Priest; venerable sir

HEWISI   A marching drum

HO-GANA-POKUNA   Literally, the HO-sounding pond; a name for the sea.

HOWDAH   A structure placed on an elephant's back. Also HOWRAH

HULWAR   A trouser-like garment; also, a weapon

INDI-KOLA   Indi (a sort of palm) leaf

JAHWEH   Jehovah

JAK   A large tree that bears a large, prickly fruit containing pips with seeds in them; eaten cooked, or raw when ripe

JANAPADA   Literally, people's State

JAYAMANGALA (GATHA)   Literally, joyous event; psalms

JAYAWEWA   May he (she) triumph

JINA   The Jains. An ascetic group established in the time of the emperor Chandra Gupta Moriya, which believes in attaining purity in order to reach God

JUDA   Of the tribe of Judah; the Jewish people

KABOOK   Hard, gravelly soil that can be cut into large blocks

KADIYA   A sharp-stinging ant

KAKKA   Crow; therefore, black as a crow

KALU DODOL   Literally, black (hardened) jelly; a sweetmeat

KALU KUMARAYA   Black prince

714

KAMA SUTRA   Literally, sex art. A well-known book giving directions on the art of lovemaking

KANDA-STICK   A twig from the KANDA tree. Not to be confused with KANDHA (see CUNJEE)

KANDA-UDA RATA   Literally, hilltop land; the hill country, as opposed to PATA RATA, low country

KAPURU   Camphor

KATTA   A kind of fish, especially good when dried

KAVI   Poems; singular form, KAVIYA

KHADDAR   Homespun cotton material

KHARMA   Literally, cause. Therefore, destiny, through cause in effect

KHUMBA   The sign of Aquarius

KIRI-BUTH   Milk-rice. Rice cooked in water and finally boiled in coconut milk. A delicacy, traditionally eaten on auspicious occasions

KITUL   A kind of palm tree from which toddy is tapped; honey is made from the flowers' nectar

KOHL   Mascara (also KHOL)

KONDAYA   A magpie with a tufted crest

KOOMBIYA   A red ant

KOTI   Million

KOTTHA-MALLI   Coriander tea; made with ginger and garlic, it is used as a remedy for colds, coughs and influenza

KOVIL   A Hindu temple or shrine

KSHASTRIYA   The highest noble-military caste

KUMARA(YA)   Prince

KUMBUK   A large tree with spreading branches, generally growing beside streams or rivers

KURTHA   An overshirt

KURUNDU   Cinnamon

KURU POL   Literally, wrinkled coconut. It would contain no water inside and the kernel would be hard and dried up

KYROOS   The emperor Cyrus the Great of Persia

LAKH (LAKSHAYA)   One hundred thousand

LANTANA   A sturdy, flowering bush

LINGAM   Phallic symbol

715

MAGUL-BERA   Wedding drums

MAHA   Great. So MAHARAJA, King of Kings

MAHA-DANEMUTTA   Literally, great knowing grandfather; therefore, a know-it-all

MAHANAYAKE   Literally, the great priest; therefore, the Chief Monk

MAHOUT   Elephant 'driver' (and trainer and groom)

MAIDAN   Parade ground; flat area for assemblies or relaxation

MAITRIYA   Loving kindness

MAMOTY   A digging tool with a long handle

MANA   A tall, spiky grass, the leaves of which exude a menthol scent when crushed

MANTA YUDDHAYA   Diplomatic battle or warfare – an intellectual delight of Aryan kings

MARA   A kind of tree with spreading branches

MARAMBA   A tree with scented leaves

MARSOK   A game played by two teams, each in turn defending squares that the opposing team tries to infiltrate

MASSA   Literally, a mat; used to designate a tree-platform

MEDA MIDULA   Literally, middle or centre garden; atrium

MIRIS   Chili

MIRIS MOLLAY   Literally, chili-brain

MUDALALI   Trader

MULADANIYA   Headman

MUSALA   Wretched; MUSALAYA: Wretch

NADAGAM   Plays; mime

NADUN   A dark brown, fine-grained wood from the tree that bears the same name

NANNAR   A drink made of arrowroot

NARIYA   Jackal

NAVARATNA   Literally, the nine gems; a lucky combination of precious stones

NAYAKE   Custodian; therefore, a Buddhist monk in charge of a temple

NIBBHANA   Nirvana, the ultimate. In the Buddhist conception, Enlightenment or Buddhahood, upon death, removes a being from the otherwise endless cycle of birth and rebirth

NIKKAM   Without reason or cause

NOOL   Thread
NYAYA   The right

OLA   A writing material, such as papyrus, of the kenaf variety, inscribed on with a stylus

PAHLAVA   Persian(s)
PANDAL   An archway built as a decoration
PAN-SIL   The Five Precepts; observance thereof
PARA   Vile, filfthy
PARABALLA   Filthy dog
PARAMANU   Atom(s)
PARAMATTA   Components of the atom
PATANA   Grassy hills
PATTHU   Thick ointment
PETTA-GAMA   Large storage chest
PINI-JAMBU   Mountain apple
PIPUL   The *bodhi*-tree, under which the Buddha obtained Enlightenment
PIRITH   Holy words chanted in blessing
PIRITH NOOL   Thread held in an unbroken chain while PIRITH is chanted, thereby rendering it blessed
PIRIVENA   Buddhist temple-school
PITTUBAMBUWA   A bamboo in which flour mixed with grated coconut, called PITTU, is steamed. PITTU is eaten with coconut milk and curry or honey
POLKICHCHA   Common magpie
POOJA   A religious observance or service
PORUWA   A decorated platform, normally with arches, on which bride and bridegroom stand for their marriage ceremony
POSON   The first full moon after the Wesak full moon, the latter commemorating the dates of birth, Enlightenment and death of the Buddha
POYA   Full-moon day, when Buddhists have special observances
PRANA   The essence of a person's being, deriving from the continuing source of his existence, which is manifested in each birth
PUNKAH   A long overhead fan, moved by means of a rope
PURA   City

PUSS   Mildew, mould (y)
PUTHA   Son

RAJA   King; therefore, royal
RAJAKARIYA   Literally, king's affairs; feudal duties
RAJA PURA   Royal city
RAMA   God
RAMBOUTANG   A small hairy fruit, red when ripe, with a sweet white kernel covering a seed
RAN-THAMBILI   Golden king-coconut. Really a delicate pink in colour and extolled by poets as the colour of a woman's complexion
RATA MAHATMAYA   District chieftain
RATH-MAL   Red flower; pentax
RISHI   Sage of old
ROMA   Roman(s)

SAL   A large tree with spreading branches
SAMANERA   Novice monk
SAMBOL(E)   A pickle-like mixture meant to improve the flavour of food. It can be of various kinds, such as LUNU MIRIS (salt and chili ground together with lime and sometimes dried fish) or LOONU SAMBOLE, which includes onions. (See also SEENI-SAMBOL).
SANGHA   The order of Buddhist Monks; the Noble Order
SANNYASI   A holy mendicant. Also, a stage in the development of the Hindu when he gives up the world and takes to the jungle for meditation
SARA BULATH   Literally, delicious betel. A SARA BULATH VITA includes shredded arecanut, chunam, dried tobacco leaf, cloves and cardamom, wrapped in a green betel leaf (used for chewing only)
SAREE   A cloth, five to six yards in length, worn around the waist to ankle length, the end draped over one shoulder
SEENI-SAMBOL(E)   Sweet sambol(e); the sambol(e) mixture, sweetened and cooked
SHASHTRIYA-NATYA   The classical dance form(s)
SHAYBAH   Sheba

SIKANDER   Alexander (the Great)

SIL   Buddhist Precept(s) (see also PAN-SIL, ATA-SIL and DASA-SIL)

SITAR   A long, stringed musical instrument

SIYUPADA   Folk chants

STUPA   A Buddhist temple structure; a DAGOBA (sometimes called THUPA)

SUL OMAN   (King) Solomon

SURA   An alcoholic drink, probably the equivalent of modern Sinhala arrack

SURIYA   A tall, flowering tree

TABLA   Twin drums played with the hands

TALAM-POTA   Literally, tune folds; finger cymbals to beat time, especially for dancing

THALA   Tune; also, sesame seed

THALA-THELL   Sesame-seed oil

THATHA   Father

THATHPARA   One second (in time)

THELL   Oil

THORA   Seer fish

THORANA   Archway (see also PANDAL)

THUGGEE   A notorious group of Indian professional assassins

THUPA   A Buddhist temple structure; a DAGOBA (sometimes called STUPA)

UPASAKAYA   A holy or religious person

USABHA   A unit of measure; 20 USABHA equal 1 GAVUTA

VADAI   A DHAL savoury, fried hard outside

VALMI   A fragrant root, tasting of liquorice

VANNAM   A chant relating to a dance-tale

VATAKEIYA   Kenaf

VEDA-RALA   Physician

VEDDAH   A tribe said to be the original inhabitants of Lanka

VEENA   A stringed musical instrument

VERTI   A loose loin-cloth of light material

VIHARE   Residence of Buddhist monks

VIPAKA   Effect; the effect of KHARMA (cause)

WEWA   Lake; reservoir

YOJANA   The largest unit of linear measure; as far as can be
determined, a yojana was equal to 12-12½ miles
YONA   Greek(s)
YUVARAJA   A petty king; a sub-king

For the sake of convenience, modern units of measure have been
used in the text occasionally, even though they were not used at the
time.

ANCIENT INDIAN AND SINHALA LUNAR MONTHS OF THE YEAR

Citta	February/March or March/April
Vesakha	March/April or April/May
Jettha	April/May or May/June
Asaha	May/June or June/July
Savana	June/July or July/August
Potthapada	July/August or August/September
Assayuja	August/September or September/October
Kattika	September/October or October/November
Maggasira	October/November or November/December
Phussa	November/December or December/January
Magha	December/January or January/February
Phagguna	January/February or February/March